Praise for *The Woman Who Lost Her Soul*

"Engrossing . . . a soaring literary epic about the forces that have driven us to the 9/11 age. . . . Shacochis darts around the globe over the span of five decades like a sorcerer of world history. . . . always so relentlessly captivating that you don't dare fall behind."

—Ron Charles, *Washington Post*

"A lot of pages here and every one worth reading in this reckless, raucous, brilliant novel in quest of an elusive American heroine."

—Alan Cheuse, NPR

"A love story, a thriller, a family saga, a historical novel, and a political analysis of America's tragic misadventures abroad. The novel yokes the narrative drive of the best Graham Greene and le Carré to the rhetorical force and moral rigor of Faulkner. . . . With a vision at once bitingly realistic and sweepingly romantic, Bob Shacochis has written what may well be the last Great American Novel. What other American writer has put as much heart into his creations, as much drive, as much history?"

—Askold Melnyczuk, *Los Angeles Review of Books*

"This novel amounts to a prequel of sorts to the war on terror, an epic examination of American foreign policy and loss of innocence, a worthy successor to the darkest works of Graham Greene and John le Carré . . . Elegiac . . . a searching and searing meditation on the questions someone might ask a century from now: Who were these Americans? How should history judge them? And us?"

—Jane Ciabattari, *Boston Globe*

"Shacochis has written one of the most morally serious and intellectually substantive novels about the world of intelligence since Norman Mailer's *Harlot's Ghost*."

—Tom Bissell, *Harper's*

"A new masterpiece . . . that will surely stand as the definitive political thriller of those fragile years of relative peace before September 11, 2001 . . .There may be no final drafts of history, but this one will be read and reread for many years to come."

—Dan Zigmond, *San Francisco Chronicle*

"Brilliantly unveils the darker regions of human sexuality, evoked inside a historical buildup of international political deceit."
—Jeffrey Hillard, *Interview*

"*The Woman Who Lost Her Soul,* a showstopper (and doorstopper) of a novel by Bob Shacochis, is an atlas of the ways political violence corrupts both the individual and national consciousness. . . . the prose is never less than lyrical, personal, and intelligent, but the real reason to read is to witness the near superhuman ambition of Shacochis's undertaking. If he were a rower, this would be a circumnavigation of the globe. If he were a sculptor, this would be Mount Rushmore. Lucky for us, he's a writer, and *The Woman Who Lost Her Soul* is a masterpiece."
—Anthony Marra, Salon (Ultimate Book Guide, 2013)

"Heartbreaking and riveting . . . a sweeping, expansive book grounded by details such as epic potholes in Haiti's roads and crowded ferry decks in Turkey. Without veering into conspiracy theories or melodrama, Shacochis builds for both his readers and his characters a sense that something important is being overlooked amid competing agendas . . . an elegant reminder that connections are made one by one—but not everyone is playing the same game."
—Jennifer Kay, *Seattle Times*

"[A] masterful and sumptuous novel . . . deliriously dense . . . No one moves as forcefully through that terrain as Shacochis. He writes tenderly about terrible things. He unearths humanity when the reader most needs to lean against it. . . . This is a memorable book by a great writer."
—Steve Duin, *The Oregonian*

"A compelling and thought-provoking novel . . . it plays a deep game, and it will haunt your dreams . . . [Shacochis] controls a hugely complex plot with great skill and writes set pieces with gripping effect . . . Line for line, his writing is stunning."
—Colette Bancroft, *Tampa Bay Times*

"National Book Award–winning novelist Shacochis makes a long-awaited—indeed, much-anticipated—return to fiction with this stunning novel of love, innocence, and honor lost . . . The wait was worth it . . . Shacochis has delivered a work that belongs alongside Joseph Conrad and Graham Greene . . . it is memorably, smartly written . . . An often depressing, cautionary, and thoroughly excellent tale of the excesses of empire, ambition, and the too easily fragmented human soul."   —*Kirkus* (starred review)

"A big book in every sense of the word . . . Shacochis is a master at the top of his game. . . . In this novel, he gives us real, raw-edged characters and a narrative that grips the reader from the get-go. And he does it with such gleaming word-craft and such a sure hand that the reader's utter engagement never falters. The book is a murder mystery, a tale of political intrigue, a love story and a fraught father-daughter psychological saga. It was ten years in the writing and it is a masterpiece . . . a brilliant, beautiful page-turner . . . luminous writing unfurls across every blood-spattered, sweat-speckled, dust-caked page and makes *The Woman Who Lost Her Soul* a riveting, heartbreaking, and ravishing read. It's a novel of uncommon grace and grit that lodges like shrapnel in the psyche and works its way surely to the reader's heart, without ever losing sight of those 'terrible intimacies.'"   —*Tallahassee Democrat*

"A masterful novel with the power to shake the bones of Graham Greene."   —Bruce Barcott, *Outside Magazine*

"*The Woman Who Lost Her Soul* cannot be put down . . . it never loses its way or its ability to drag you along with it . . . a wild, deadly ride. You won't want to let go."   —Glenn Garvin, *Miami Herald*

"Shacochis thinks big, and his new novel (his first in two decades) is truly magisterial . . . immensely readable, this eye-opener (which could have been titled "Why We Are in the Middle East") is essential reading."
                      —*Library Journal* (starred review)

"A beautifully written, Norman Mailer–like treatise on international politics, secret wars, espionage, and terrorism . . . A brilliant book, likely to win prizes, with echoes of Joseph Conrad, Graham Greene, and John le Carré."   —*Booklist* (starred review)

"A brutal American-style le Carré, Shacochis details how espionage not only reflects a nation's character but can also endanger its soul. Gritty characters find themselves in grueling situations against a moral and physical landscape depicted in rich language as war-torn, resilient, angry, evil, and hopeful."   —*Publishers Weekly* (starred review)

"No one in American literature is better at casting his imagination into the deepest currents of American culture and politics than Bob Shacochis. The long, ardent, admiring wait for his next novel has been worth every moment: *The Woman Who Lost Her Soul* is his masterpiece."
                                                            —Robert Olen Butler

"This big beauty of a book was worth the wait. It's tinglingly ambitious, vast in scope, and magnificently written. I could unerringly pick a Bob Shacochis sentence out of a police lineup of sentences, which is just about the highest praise I can offer to any writer."   —Michael Cunningham

"*The Woman Who Lost Her Soul* will grab you from the first sentence and keep you gasping and laughing and weeping until the end. A murder mystery, a spy thriller, and a daddy-and-daughter story, it is a thrilling gripping lesson in the dynamics that have swept through our world in the twenty-first century. Shacochis writes like an angel, and in this novel of culture, betrayal, and love he has found a perfect subject."
                                                            —Susan Cheever

"Bob Shacochis is the man for all syntheses, confabulating decades of time and volumetric immensities of geography into pitched and vivid dramatic narrative. Long in the making, but longer in the lasting, *The Woman Who Lost Her Soul* is unafraid of its ambitions. Shacochis is, in Glengarry-speak, a 'closer.'"   —Sven Birkerts

THE WOMAN WHO LOST HER SOUL

THE WOMAN WHO LOST HER SOUL

BOB SHACOCHIS

Grove Press
New York

Excerpts from this novel have appeared in Artful Dodger, The Darfur Anthology, Snake Nation Review, Conjunctions, *and* Consequence *magazines.*

The author wishes to thank Florida State University for its grant support in the writing of this book.

Published simultaneously in Canada
Printed in the United States of America

ISBN 978-0-8021-2275-9
eISBN 978-0-8021-9309-4

Grove Press
an imprint of Grove/Atlantic, Inc.
154 West 14th Street
New York, NY 10011

Distributed by Publishers Group West

www.groveatlantic.com

14 15 16 17   10 9 8 7 6 5 4 3 2 1

For Helen   For Liam
—*Meminimus*

I know what it means to beget monsters
And to recognize them in myself . . .
Great was the chase with the hounds for the unattainable
        meaning of the world . . .
Enter my dreams, love.

                                        —*Czeslaw Milosz*

THE WOMAN WHO LOST HER SOUL

Book One

Fuzzing It Up
Haiti 1998, 1996, 1998

It is no secret that souls sometimes die in a person and are replaced by others.

—Fernando Pessoa

In wartime, truth is so precious that she should always be attended by a bodyguard of lies.

—Winston Churchill

During the final days of the occupation, there was an American woman in Haiti, a photojournalist—blonde, young, infuriating—and she became Thomas Harrington's obsession.

Why have you never told me the story of this girl? Harrington's wife asked, dumbfounded but curious. They stood in the kitchen of their gardenia-scented home in South Miami, finishing the vodka cocktails she had mixed to celebrate his reinstallment into her landscaped domain, its calibrated patterns, everything perfectly in its place except her husband. Why have you waited until now? A pained crinkle etched a border of mystification around the brightness of her eyes.

Expecting an answer, she followed him through the house, upstairs to their sun-scoured bedroom where he began unpacking his filthy clothes. Here, he said with a hopeful trace of enthusiasm, this is for you, and he gave her a gift he had brought from Port-au-Prince, a small but moderately expensive painting by Frantz Zephirin.

And what should he tell her? That he had become too involved with a woman, and too involved with the greater infidelities of the world? And would rather say nothing of both?

If he told her everything, he imagined, correctly, she would want to leave him, or she would pray for the salvation of his distant heart, which was the salvation of a man in a time and a place and a country and not the salvation of an immortal self, because when Americans pray, they pray first that history will step aside and leave them alone, they pray for the deafness that comes with a comfortable life. They pray for the soothing blindness of happiness, and why not?

But history walks on all of us, lashed by time, and sometimes we feel its boot on our backs, and sometimes we are oblivious to its passing, the swing of sorrow and triumph through humanity, sorrow, and then, finally, crippling grief fading to obscurity, which is perhaps why Americans want little to do with history, why perhaps they hate it, why prayer comes easier than remembrance, which is how history knots its endless endings and measures the rise and fall of its breath. And when history swirls around you and passes on and you inhale its aftermath, the bitterness of its ashes and the bygone sweetness of time, and excrete history into memory, you never quite believe you had once heard its thunderous God-like whispering, that you had trembled in the face of its terrible intimacies, and you fell silent.

Against this silence, Harrington understood it was possible only to speak to other silences. Why would you choose to expose such ugliness, if not in yourself then in the world?

For two years Tom Harrington did not tell his wife, but now she would hear this story, enough of it anyway, that had so abruptly leaped far, far beyond his ownership, his private collection. And would she know him better afterward? Would she know him as he knew himself? And then what? Would she know him at all?

His own story of this woman in Haiti was a fragment at best, it's important to say, but his silence was not meant to spare his wife from a betrayal, at least not of the sort she suspected, but there are many, many betrayals we visit upon one another, their forms infinite, some beyond comprehension, some no more serious than a quick sting. He had kept the story from her simply because he had gotten nowhere with it in his own mind, and did not understand his role in its events, nor the meaning of its elements, and he suspected that somehow this story would always slip and tumble into the hole of self-indictment. Yet what had he done that was so wrong, what had he done that was not justified by the behavior of others? What was his sin? He could not grasp it, but in the recesses of his soul he knew it was there.

4

There were things you might say, stories you could tell, that would leave you diminished, that might outrage one's sense of conscience or morality with their failings and audacities, their reckless disregard for the well-being of others. Perhaps not in every life, though Tom rejected the very nature of innocence. But yes, some stories diminished the teller, or shamed him in the eyes of honorable people, and often these stories were never told—or only half-told, rife with omissions, as Tom's would be with his wife. They lay quiet yet unpeaceful within the black cave of secrets that was part of anyone's soul, and perhaps their silence was as it should be, the last asylum for propriety, for decency.

It's extraordinary, his wife said, admiring the canvas.

The gallery on Rue Petion had obtained another Zephirin, larger, more fanciful in its circus of cruelties, that he had wanted to buy for her but never had the chance. Why he told her this he couldn't say because it wasn't true, it had simply fallen from his mouth, part of another story he was making up.

She looked at him sideways, measuring what she must have imagined to be the careful implication of his voice. Oh. Do you have to go back? she asked, and he knew that because this was a busy time of the year for her at the office she'd be unhappy if he was leaving again.

I can't. I seem to have been declared persona non grata.

Tom? She was absently pulling clothes from his small canvas bag and tossing them into the laundry hamper and she froze, gasping, her eyes wide and a hand raised to her mouth. Oh, my God, she said. What's on these pants? Is this blood? Her sweet, earnest face, becalmed by the gentle tides of a comfortable life, filled with a look of mortification. Dutiful wife, instinctive mother, she sniffed at a patch of the stains, repulsed. They're covered with blood! There's so much of it. Tom, what happened?

Yes, that. What happened. He would have to tell her something but he did not know where to begin or where to end and he did not know if she should ever, ever know him so well, or how he spent his days when he was away from her.

CHAPTER ONE

He had been home a month, after a month's assignment in the Balkans, and had just begun to reestablish himself in the routines of daily life as husband and father, enjoying the pleasant drudgery of the supermarket, cooking meals for his wife and daughter, exercising the dog at dawn on the beach, afterward the newspaper with coffee in the morning, a novel with cognac at night, videos on the weekend, all of them in the same bed, the dog wedged between like a flatulent pillow, a suburban middle-class tableau repeated endlessly in his life, and endlessly interrupted by his restlessness—the phone rings and Tom Harrington is gone. He and his wife had constructed a life in South Miami that made sense to everyone else but him, though its comforts were undeniable. In fact, they were precious, and at constant risk of going stale, so he had made them exotic novelties, these pleasures, sucked them to near depletion, then ran off to hunt the nearest white whale, that thing we need to do to keep us from our disappointment or lethargy, to jolt ourselves back to feeling. But always, inevitably, he would trudge home, and give himself over to the icing down.

A month away, a month at home, the whiplashed schedule of a humanitarian yo-yo, a perpetual routine of domestic guess who. *Honey? I'm home. Maybe. Hope so. Sorry to have missed the kid's birthday.*

He was sitting on a bench outside the quad of his daughter's small private school nestled within a grove of banyan trees and palms, a cigarette in his mouth, waiting for classes to end. The school offered no bus service or, rather, discontinued it when over-involved parents made the convenience superfluous, and it was Tom's duty to relieve his wife of this chore whenever he was in town. That day he was early; usually he was late. Other parents began arriving.

I never see you, someone said, a woman's voice, behind him, and he swiveled around. This woman lived in the neighborhood but worked in an office downtown for a nationwide private security firm, doing what he could not tell. She was tough and brusque and solid and it was strange to see her in a flowery dress and not in the jeans and motorcycle boots and fringed leather jacket she wore when he would bump into her in the South Beach bars. Her daughter had been the first in seventh grade to wear makeup to class; Tom's wife and daughter were still warring over lip gloss and eye shadow.

She propped her sunglasses into her streaked hair and squinted. Do you know?—and she named a man, Conrad Dolan.

Doors banged open and the children came in streams of ones and twos into the courtyard. No, he said. Was he supposed to?

Without saying why, she explained she had spoken with him a few days back, up in Tampa where he lived. A journalist had been kidnapped last month in Peru. Dolan was the hostage negotiator brought in on the case.

Harrington's interest rose. How does one become a hostage negotiator? he asked.

Twenty-one years with the Feds, fluency in Spanish and Portuguese, she said. He was private sector now, retired from the Bureau of Investigation.

One of your guys?

I wish. He works alone.

Tom had never heard of him. He did not personally know many people like this, although they were always there in the background of his world; their days were different than his, more exclusive, circumscribed by their respective loyalties and institutions. Wherever you encountered them, there was less oxygen in the room for the uninitiated. You see them around, you talk with them when you have to. You stay out of their way—they keep you out of their way.

What happened to the journalist?

Dolan got him out.

Their two daughters marched toward them, pretty faces sullen and pinched as if they had spent the day in court litigating their grievances. His at least knew to mumble a greeting before she slipped past to fling her books into the cab of his truck. The other one narrowed her eyes at them and kept walking toward the parking lot and her mother's car.

What do you suppose that's about?

Being twelve. Being girls.

Jingling her keys, she said she had to run. The sunglasses fell and locked back over her eyes. So look, she said. Can I give Dolan your number? He wants to talk to you.

Their seemingly idle conversation had taken an unexpected turn—Harrington's working days were often spent seeking out authorities or tracking witnesses, knocking on the doors of strangers in search of the texture of lives under pressure or suddenly inflated into crisis, forming ephemeral intimacies with people never quite sure of his identity beyond the fact that he was in their eyes a foreign representative of a monolithic process. *Ah, he has come to find me justice. Ah, he has come to challenge my power. Ah, he has come to help. Ah, he has come to ruin me.*

Why would he want to talk to me? Tom asked.

The answer was at once familiar and tedious and he thought nothing of it. Dolan loved to follow the news, he had seen Harrington's work on establishing a Truth Commission in Haiti, he liked to talk. Tom thought to himself, *What was there left to talk about?* After two hundred years Haiti had remained an infant and still required breast-feeding, but he said, *Sure, give him the number,* and they separated, each to their spoiled child, for a recitation of the day's unforgivable crimes of pubescence.

Three days later Dolan telephoned. Before Tom even had a chance to say hello, the person on the line had announced himself—*Dolan here*—and for a moment Tom paused, unsure of who this was. *I sawr what you said about those bastards in Warshington* . . . It was a voice, a type of nasal tone and run-on pattern of speech, that he associated with the cinema, the urban repertoire of the eastern United States, make-believe cops and make-believe robbers, Irish heroes and Italian villains, an accent resonant of both ivy and whiskey, upward mobility and the working-class neighborhoods of South Boston. It was not a voice he could listen to without smiling and if his wife had been in the room he would have cupped the mouthpiece and held out the phone and said, *Get a load of this.* But the abrupt specificity of his questions made Tom tight and serious: Dolan had connected with the right source. Tom was valuable, Tom had the answers. He knew what Conrad Dolan wanted to know.

Say, what can you tell me about the condition of the Route Nationale One between Port-au-Prince and that town up the coast, what is it? Saint-Marc?

In the earliest days of the invasion, weeks before the American military ventured out onto the road they would instantly name the Highway to Hell, Route Nationale One from Port-au-Prince to its terminus on the north shore was a six-hour-long gauntlet of axle-breaking misery, slamming boredom, heat, and fear. The tarmac had been carpet bombed by neglect, its surface so pocked and corroded that only a sharp-edged webbing of the original asphalt remained, so that the highway resembled a hundred-mile strip of Swiss cheese, many of the holes the size of a child's wading pool. In September of 1994, it was empty except for *macoutes* and bandits, or impromptu checkpoints that provided the opportunity for extortion to gangs of boys with machetes. Regardless of its disrepair, you drove Route Nationale One at top speed to reach your destination by nightfall, for it wasn't a good place to be after the sun went down.

What else do you want to know? he asked Dolan.

The section of the road by the big quarry, across from the swamp, what the hell's the name of it?

Tintayen.

There were stretches of the highway, especially outside of the capital along the coast, where if you focused deep and hard on the game you could rocket up to 120 kilometers per hour for five or ten minutes, slaloming around the hazards, making everybody with you carsick and terrified. Graveyards of wrecks dotted these stretches; pedestrians and livestock were occasionally killed by swerving drivers. About nine months into the occupation, a Haitian company was awarded a contract, funded by foreign aid, to resurface the highway. The requisite embezzlements ensued and a thin scab of rotten asphalt was rolled over the newly graded roadbed. Within a month, though, the pavement had festered and bubbled, the holes began to reappear where they had always been, and if you needed a quick metaphor to sketch the trajectory of American involvement in Haiti, Route Nationale One was there for your consideration.

And this other quarry. There's supposed to be another one, right?

That's right. Up the coast, on the water.

Good place to run and hide?

What do you mean?

If you're in trouble. Trying to get away from somebody.

Not really.

And what about this place on the coast, Moulin Sur Mer? asked Dolan. You ever been there?

Lovely. Clean. Expensive by any standard. Good restaurant. Ruling-class getaway. Well-connected owners. The only reliable R & R between the capital and the north coast. Are you planning a trip? Tom wondered aloud.

This Moulin Sur Mer, Dolan said. Would you say it's a nice place to vacation, you know, take your wife?

The answer was yes, within a certain twisted context of circumstance and impulse. If you had to be in Haiti, the resort was as good as any place to reinvigorate yourself. A qualified yes, if you were the sort of naive, half-cracked traveler drawn to the edge of the abyss, someone whose rum sours were that much more quenching when consumed at the panoramic center of extreme malice and human suffering. Not to be self-righteous about the attraction; Harrington had always found the sours at Moulin Sur Mer to be memorably tart and bracing when he straggled in off the road like a legionnaire from the desert. And yes, he had even taken his wife there on her brief and unpleasant visit to the island.

What else? Tom asked. What are you looking for?

I have a client, Dolan began, and out came the story.

For the third or fourth time in a year, an American couple, husband and wife, were on holidays in Haiti, booked into the Moulin Sur Mer. *That can't be right*, Tom thought. Undoubtedly the man had business in Haiti

11

and for some reason kept inviting his wife along, or she refused to be left behind. Perhaps she was an art collector, or perhaps a nurse, someone with a skill to share, an altruistic streak.

The couple checked out of the resort late on a Saturday afternoon, Dolan continued, put their luggage in the sports utility vehicle they had rented for the week, and began the hour-and-a-half drive to the airport in the capital to board a return flight to Miami and on to Tampa, where they lived. At some point along the road south of the hotel—Conrad Dolan was imprecise about the location although he named the second quarry as a landmark—the man slowed the vehicle to a crawl to maneuver through a series of potholes. By now the sun had set, and although it was dark, very dark, and the road seemed empty, without headlights in either direction, the couple was overtaken from behind by two men on a motorbike who, after blurring past the SUV, swung sharply in front of it, stopped in a blocking position, and hopped off. The husband attempted to steer around them but the shoulder seemed to drop away and somehow he had trouble with the manual transmission and stalled the vehicle. What happened next was unclear, except for the results.

The men had guns. Dolan's client was pulled from the driver's seat and pistol-whipped, and although he never lost consciousness he had the sense knocked out of him and scrambled away into the darkness on the opposite side of the road, finally crashing into a boulder and slipping down to hide, bleeding profusely from a wound in his forehead. A gun had been fired several times, he assumed at him, to prevent his escape. When he regained his senses and came out from behind the rock, the SUV and the motorcycle were gone, and at first he couldn't find his wife but then he stepped on her where she lay on the shoulder of the road, faceup, shot to death.

Disoriented, the man stumbled around until finally a car came up the road from the direction of Port-au-Prince and he flagged it down. As luck would have it, the driver turned out to be a staffer from the American embassy who used his cell phone to dial the local emergency number and the response was unexpectedly quick; before long a pickup truck carrying uniformed officers from the police station in Saint-Marc arrived on the scene. The police spent a few minutes glancing around with flashlights, asked the man some basic questions using the embassy staffer as translator, and then put the body in the bed of the pickup truck and drove off, telling him to wait there because someone else was coming to ask more questions. Some time later, another car arrived from the direction of Port-au-Prince, driven by a detective from the National Police Headquarters.

Conrad Dolan paused in his narrative and Tom took advantage of the moment to ask him the obvious question: Why was this unfortunate man, clearly the victim of assault and robbery, his client?

I'm closing in on that, said Dolan. Assault, yes. Robbery, no. Would you say, he asked, that such incidents are commonplace in Haiti?

Aid workers, missionaries, the rare tourist—the ambushes weren't everyday occurrences by any means, but they happened. The roads were dangerous. You stayed alert, practiced prudence, of course, and hoped you were lucky.

Okay, said Dolan, and continued. The detective from Port-au-Prince was fairly vexed that the body had been spirited away to the Saint-Marc station before he could survey the crime scene, an examination he performed hastily because there was nothing left to see other than a blot of jellied blood in the dirt by the side of the road.

Although the detective only spoke Kreyol, the embassy staffer, who was headed north with his wife to spend their Sunday on the beach at Moulin Sur Mer, expressed his sympathy to the client, gave him his card, and left. The husband's skull was pounding, he felt numb, dazed, and when the detective opened the passenger door for him he climbed in and slumped into the seat, never saying a word during the ride south to Port-au-Prince, never hearing a word he could understand. The detective took him to a police station near the airport, sat him down at a table in a room, and left him there alone. A while later another detective came in, a guy who had lived in Brooklyn and spoke English. He gave the husband a wet rag to wipe his face, water to drink, and talked to him for about ten minutes—standard procedure, predictable questions—but the man was distraught, his head was not clear, and his answers were not helpful. The detective asked if he wanted to see a physician. The man said no. Okay, the detective said, I'm sending you to the Hotel Montana for the night but I want you to return in the morning to make a full report.

The manager of the hotel and her staff were shocked by the man's condition and saddened to learn the fate of his wife, and they treated him with exceptional kindness, summoning a doctor to stitch up the gash above his right eye, finding him clean clothes and toiletries for the night, sending a meal to his room. In the morning the manager called the room to say that a car was waiting for him downstairs to take him back to the police station and that she had asked the hotel's accountant to accompany him, to serve as his interpreter.

At the police station, he was met by the same detective who'd driven him back to the city the night before and was informed that his rental car had been found abandoned on the edge of Tintayen and impounded in a lot behind the building. He was also told that he and his wife's possessions—their luggage, jewelry, laptop computer, cell phone, camera—had also been recovered from the car but could not be released back to him until he had signed the statement he had made the previous night in the station. The client said he couldn't remember what he had said last night but okay, give it to him to sign, but the detective said no, not yet possible, it was still being translated from English into Kreyol and French.

In the meantime the detective asked that he come along to the impoundment lot, where he was shown the SUV and told to get back in the car and drive it to the crime scene for a reenactment of the event. The SUV had a bullet hole through the passenger's window, its seats were splashed with blood, and the client refused, offering to drive any other car than this one, stinking with the smell of his wife's death, back north on Route Nationale One. They returned to the station and the accountant, who had been translating the conversation, was told by the detective to leave.

The man was taken to the same room as the night before and told to wait. Hours passed until, eventually, the detective returned, sat down across from him, and pushed a document and a ball-point pen across the table. The handwritten statement was seventeen pages long but the client didn't have a clue what it said because it was not in English, so naturally he wasn't going to put his name on it. The detective, out of patience, got up and left the room. Moments later the door banged open, a pair of cops

14

came in, grabbed him by the arms, and led him out and when he realized they intended to put him in a holding cell he began struggling. Three more uniforms joined the fray and the five of them succeeded in muscling the man into the cell.

He didn't understand what had just happened to him, didn't speak Kreyol, spoke but a few words of French, and nobody would speak to him in English. He wanted to call the embassy, call a lawyer, the manager of the hotel, call anybody, but nothing was getting across. The sun went down, nobody comes. A little later someone brought him a carton of warm orange juice and a plate of beans and rice, and then that's it, they left him there alone throughout the night.

So you're my client, said Dolan. How do you think you're feeling right now?

Jesus, Tom said. In shock, enraged.

Something like that, said Dolan. So listen to this.

The next day, they took him out to the street where a black Chevy Blazer with smoked windows was parked at the curb and they put him in the backseat between a security officer from the embassy and an investigator from the National Police. In the front seat was a civilian from the consulate, who handed the client's passport back to him with a plane ticket and explained that the Haitian police would not release his luggage and personal effects because he had refused to sign his state-ment. The consul also told him not to despair, that his wife's body had already been shipped back to her family in Washington, DC. Despite the client's repeated questions, the answer is always the same—he's being deported—which sounds pretty good to him about this time, right? Just get me the fuck out of here, he's thinking.

They drove to the airport, through the security fence, and onto the tarmac, right to the boarding stairs on the American Airlines flight to the States. The client was the last passenger, the attendants closed the door behind him and showed him to his seat in the first-class section where, with his first sip of complimentary scotch, the man of course began to feel that he was waking up from a very bad dream.

But now listen to this, said Dolan. My client steps off the plane in Miami and two marshals take him into custody. Next thing he knows he's downtown at the federal courthouse being arraigned before a judge.

On what charges?

Dolan rattled off some numbers identifying the statutes. Murder of an American citizen on foreign soil. Conspiracy to kill an American citizen on foreign soil.

Your guy staged a hit on his wife? asked Tom, who frowned at the sound of this, for he had grown accustomed to the presence of death in his life, cold-blooded senseless slaughter, murder on so vast a scale he sometimes felt like the impresario of his own necropolis, and these gangster words sounded ridiculous and puny.

Christ. Maybe. Who knows? said Dolan. My client is not an upstanding citizen. He'd taken out some insurance policies on her, which is not a troublesome fact until the Haitian police notify the embassy that an American has been murdered and they have her husband and he's being, in their words, uncooperative.

Given the going rate for assassins on the island and the incompetence of its police force, if you wanted to make your wife disappear into oblivion, Haiti was an accommodating country. And yet if Dolan's client were innocent, Tom thought, how would you begin to measure such injustice, the horrific multiplication of wrongs?

The Bureau sent a team down there to poke around, said Conrad Dolan, but it was a dry fuck.

Business as usual.

Well, it puzzles me.

I would guess then that you've never been to Haiti.

There you have it, said Dolan, finally able to make his point. So, look, I've got to go down there for a couple of days and piece this thing together and I need somebody who knows his way around, right? You came to mind.

I'm going to have to think about it, Tom said.

Murder? his wife said later that evening, intrigued, her dry amusement peppered with irony, while they prepared for bed, as if Tom had only now discovered the novelty of America's greatest form of entertainment, as if what he had been looking for out beyond the horizon was flourishing in his own backyard. I thought this isn't the sort of thing you care about, she said, unless a government is pulling the trigger. What was it about a straightforward domestic homicide, she wondered, that now appealed to him?

It's Dolan, he said. And of course it was not a simple homicide, because it was Haiti.

Like an object snatched from the top of a junk pile, Haiti had been collected by the genteel world, the world of infinite possibility, turned over in its manicured hands, sniffed and shaken, and discarded back on the heap. With the arrival of the Americans in 1994, Tom could not quite fathom the magnitude of their power or the grandness of its orchestration and was struck, like everyone else on the ground, by a naked sense of wonder, the beautiful bay that mocked the seaside slums floating an armada of enormous warships, glittering at night like waterborne villages on oceanic prairies, the dark waves of Black Hawk helicopters fluttering insectlike against the orange screen of sunset. Tanks on the garbage-piled streets. Marines huddled in igloos of sandbags. Grenades exploding in crowds, crowds exploding in joy. A blubbering *macoute* lynched from a signpost on Martin Luther King Boulevard, piss cascading off the dusty toes of his bare feet. A dead schoolgirl in a frilly pink dress lying in the street with her face burnt off to a matching pinkness. The Special Forces injected like antivenin into the hinterlands, liberating the villages. The peasants lining the road to cheer *America! America! America!* The soldiers hammering the roofs back on schools, digging wells, feeding children, handing out democracy like sweets.

And then the idea behind the thing became unclear and atrophied and no matter who made it, a white man or a black man, every promise was a type of fantasy, if not an earnest lie, each hope an illusion, every sacrifice an act of unrequited love. Once again in Haiti there was no glory and too little honor and too much of God's indifferent truth. The army arrived in thunder and left in a foul haze of smoke, having performed a magnificent pantomime of redemption, and throughout it all Harrington carried on with his work, the many, many graves he was obliged to locate, some as fresh as his morning's breakfast but others grassed over and as big as swimming pools, his pursuit of the dead undeterred by futility until the day arrived when he, too, turned to walk away from it all.

It seems to me that your world and Dolan's are much the same, his wife said.

He had watched his wife undress, disappointed because he seemed to merit the teasing reward of the colorful silks of new lingerie only on the nights of his homecomings, when she yielded to their lovemaking with varying degrees of eagerness; then the ritual was discarded for drab synthetics and stained sports bras and the familiar inertia of fifteen years of marriage. He believed in people trying to comfort one another but the comfort he found with her came from the life they had made together more than what she might or could provide by herself alone, the attention she afforded him no longer the precious commodity of their youth, and in the previous year when he had confessed in the heat of an argument that she no longer excited him, she set her eyes upon him in a fury and hissed, *Haven't you had enough excitement, Tom? Haven't you had more than your share?*

Dolan has a different perspective.

And I thought you'd gotten beyond your death wish, she said, her way of being droll, sliding into bed beside him and picking up her book from the nightstand.

I have. I'm staying away from the working girls at the Oloffson.

These unsubtle banterings between husband and wife were the gloss on so much tension and unspoken dread, a glib pattern that contorted into foolish promises to not do anything stupid and cold pragmatic decisions like medical evacuation plans and life insurance policies. Dolan's client had one on his wife, Tom's wife had one on him.

I thought you were done with Haiti. Diddled out.

Don't try to shame me, either.

Like everyone else who had swarmed to Haiti during the intervention— the soldiers, the journos, the diplomats, the spooks, the analysts and lawmakers and civil servants, the aid workers, the deal makers, the pimps of the spectacle—Tom Harrington had abandoned the country to its fog of misery. Everyone had left, with or without regrets, with or without bitterness, letting the island drift away from consciousness on a raft of indifference, the more cynical among them muttering that the country was too fucked even to throw a good war.

His wife knew very well that he nourished an investment in Haiti, not of money or blood but of inexplicable hope, and she knew he could navigate the streets of its capital better than those of Dade County, and that he had adapted to the rhythms of its futility to the extent that he saw, perhaps wrongly, the people's lives in Haiti as extraordinarily difficult but ordinary nevertheless, and not exempt from grace. Tom admitted he even liked the island, though it made him afraid—the idea of it, the dark myth, his anticipation of its treachery—but almost never when he was there on the ground, slogging about through its landscape of ruination.

And a simple murder, yes. He couldn't explain that compulsion more than he'd tried. Without a single expectation he felt drawn to Conrad Dolan, Dolan's unnamed client, and his case. A domestic homicide, a violence between a husband and a wife, had become worthy of Tom's time—surely no more than forty-eight hours; it had become a vaguely vulgar but compelling opportunity. The sensation was embarrassingly odd, but somehow the transition, the funneling down from the carnage he had witnessed in many of the world's most violent places to the events surrounding the fate of two individuals struck him as inevitable, a predetermined sequence in the ongoing education that would lead him home, once and for all, having learned whatever lesson still eluded him. And what lesson might that possibly be that had yet to take hold? Love thy neighbor, or exterminate the brutes?

Several mornings later he met the unimposing Dolan at their gate in the Miami airport, dressed in the clothes he had described to Tom on the phone—khaki pants, a collegial blue button-down cotton shirt, a navy blazer, and tasseled loafers—the uniform of Florida's retired power brokers. Dolan had described himself as looking like a debauched Irishman who had taken a wrong turn coming out of Fenway Park but actually he reminded

Tom of the old parish priest whom he had once served as altar boy at his grandparents' church in the cold streets of Burlington, Vermont. Dolan was considerably shorter than Tom, round-bellied, and older than Tom had surmised from his voice. His white hair was balding on both sides of what Tom supposed he could call a widow's peak, and he wore wire-rim glasses, the thick lenses cut in an aviator's style. Some people who choose to carry a badge can't hide the fact of their profession merely by dressing out in street clothes; there's no day off for their aura of authority, their congenital need to scrutinize. Tom had observed them from the periphery in Haiti, an ensemble of high-end cops, the exotica of law enforcement, special agents and security officers and God knows what in blue jeans and business suits, bureaucrats with shoulder holsters, stiff with prosecutorial self-confidence, much like Harrington's classmates at Yale law school, arrogant and dismissive in their brilliance but dull outside the clubhouse, of no apparent use to Haiti beyond their ability to spend money and scare people with their profound whiteness.

But Dolan could have been anybody; he was different, not because he blended in—he didn't—but because, Tom quickly learned, he shared Harrington's preference to look at the world through the eyes of a foot soldier or a cop on the beat, from the ground up. Most of all he loved to talk, his head an archive of stakeouts and busts running back to the glory days of J. Edgar Hoover, and he was enamored by the mystery of personality enough to preserve it from his obligation to rip and dilute and defeat that mystery into paperwork. On the island Dolan would tell Harrington the most difficult type of suspect to interrogate is a raconteur: you ask him his name and never get in a follow-up question. You hear a lot but you never really find out anything. And Tom had thought ungenerously, *Dolan is talking about Dolan.*

When I was supervisor of the Bureau's office in San Juan, Dolan said as they checked in for their flight, the only whites in a queue of Haitians, we had a saying, it was like our motto: There are only two types of Americans in the Caribbean, those who are *wanted* . . .

Yeah?

. . . and those who are *not* wanted.

20

As they walked down the ramp and stood in a second queue waiting to board, Dolan leaned in to Tom to tell a story. The hotel in this airport, I made my last collar here before I retired from the Bureau, he began, lowering his voice. The guy was huge, six foot six, a serial killer, twenty-three victims. A tip came in about two o'clock in the morning that he was staying here, I got a backup from the Miami police force, and we came on over, took the elevator to the fifth floor, and there he is, in the hall with this little white guy. I identified myself and said, You're under arrest, and he goes like this—Dolan's right hand reached for his left side. He was wearing a sport coat and I said to myself, *Just show me a peek of that gun and I'll blow you away, you son of a bitch,* but he didn't have a gun on him, it was all reflex, muscle memory, he was drunk and acted instinctively. So we handcuffed the two of them and walked them outside and put them in the car and I told this Miami cop, Fuck, that guy's lucky, I almost shot him, and the cop says, I was waiting for you to whack him and I was going to take out the witness. The little guy, we find out, is just some good samaritan cabdriver helping a drunk customer to his room.

Dolan's snapshots from the everyday battle of good and evil were entertaining, but Harrington didn't know what to say. You married, Mr. Dolan?

Connie.

Connie?

Yeah. Married twenty-nine years. Three kids, all grown. You?

Yes. A daughter in middle school.

Their seats were not together on the plane. At one point during the flight Connie Dolan unbuckled himself and Tom watched him move down the aisle toward him, not light on his feet but energetic and savvy, nodding gregariously at passengers who met his avuncular blue-eyed smile, pausing to exchange words with an older woman dressed in her Sunday finery, not uncomfortable to be a white man in a world turned suddenly black and, by any account except Haiti's, exceedingly foreign. Even the African American community in Miami looked upon the Haitians as indecipherable hicks. Stopping at Tom's row, Dolan combusted once more into storytelling, a Cold War tale of a morning spent in farcical surveillance of a Soviet sleeper cell in West Virginia, two agents lost on the highway, missing their exit, turning around, missing it again. Then Dolan asked about the byzantine power struggles on the island and Tom could sense tension in the men beside him, his two seatmates in the row, and although his reply was polite it was not illuminating. This was a matter not to be discussed in front of strangers, and Tom was wearied by the subject. Each time he left the island he would tell himself the situation there couldn't possibly get worse. Each time he returned, things were worse. Haiti was postfunctional, a free-range concentration camp, and Tom had abandoned faith in the country's ability to save itself. Haiti couldn't find its bottom.

Dolan wanted Tom to teach him how to greet a person in Kreyol.

Como yé? How are you, how's it going? They'll answer, *Na'p boulé.* We're boiling, we're on fire.

On the ground, inundated by the mundane details of arrival, Tom felt grateful for Dolan's composure, his affable patience with inefficient procedure, and saw for himself that Dolan was a man who glided easily into the muddle. They shouldered their bags through customs and, outside in the steam bath, pressed themselves into the scrum of need that surrounded the terminal, a thick ring of suffocating humanity that began to percuss with Harrington's name. *TumTumTum.*

Yes, he had been gone too long. Yes, I remember you and you but just as before I am not your savior. No, he had not brought this one shoes, that one a visa.

The sooner you relinquished yourself to somebody, the sooner you could reclaim control, and in the thicket of grabbing hands he selected two boys with familiar faces to carry their luggage across the street to the bare cinder-block building that housed the car rental agencies. The two became four became six and followed behind in a quarrelsome knot, each boy tugging at the bags, each loud boy demanding payment at the door through which they could not enter, each boy merrily given a crisp dollar bill by Dolan.

I see you speak the universal language of shakedown, Tom said wryly, nodding at Dolan's gold-plated money clip before it disappeared back into his pocket, and Dolan smiled at the illusion of his largesse, a good-natured

22

businessman taking care of his staff. For the first time Tom wondered if he should consider himself Dolan's employee; he hadn't thought about it beyond their gentleman's agreement—Dolan would pay expenses, the ticket, food and lodging, but beyond that there was no arrangement and Harrington supposed he could stay or go as he wished. They did seem to be in agreement about which rental company to use.

Sir, we thought you had forgotten us, the lugubrious counter agent said with wounded dignity, putting his slack hand in Tom's, as though the white man were another disappointment to his day.

I did, he confessed.

We have not forgotten you.

No, I wouldn't think so. Tom had managed to return one of his agency's vehicles in very bad condition and another with bullet holes through a door panel. How are things? he asked.

We are enjoying the freedom you give us, the agent said, to go to hell. This democracy you give Haiti is killing us.

Tom handed the agent his driver's license and Dolan's credit card and a minute later Dolan looked up from the form he was signing and Harrington watched his methodical style come into focus, the script of investigative habits that he understood existed between them as both fraternal bond and ground for competition, brotherly or not. Tell me something, said Dolan, setting his briefcase on the counter, flipping the latches without opening it, and Tom listened to his conversation with the rental agent, whose expression hardened warily as he realized the white man in front of him was a type of policeman. The briefcase opened. *Oui,* said the agent, examining Dolan's copy of an invoice; he was the one who had rented the SUV to the American couple several weeks ago. True, the woman was murdered, the vehicle stolen and left a short distance off the road near the swamps of Tintayen. Everyone knew these things, *monsieur.*

And the man and the woman, said Dolan. Tell me your impression of them.

I had no impression.

Happy, sad, irritated, friendly?

Normal.

Dolan reached back into his briefcase and extracted a brown envelope containing a photograph of the client with his wife, the two of them side by side, lovers in bathing suits, his arm clasped around her suntanned shoulder, posed in front of a giant concrete reproduction of a conch shell that Harrington recalled having seen among the garden of landscaping kitsch at Moulin Sur Mer. Let me see that, Tom said, and took the photograph from Dolan as he pushed it across the counter toward the agent.

Harrington released an involuntary gasp. What's the problem? asked Dolan, and he gave Tom a hard look, studying his reaction. You okay?

I'm fine, he said, trying to stand straight and breathe normally. I know this woman. Jackie. Jacqueline Scott. A blade of grief twisted into Harrington and through him and then, replaced by arid pity, out, perhaps the only honest emotion he had ever felt for her besides lust and anger, perhaps the only two responses a woman like Jackie could expect from a man once she had his undivided attention.

That's not her name, said Dolan.

All right, he said, steadying himself. Her hair's cut different, and it's been dyed, but I know her. She was freelancing here during the occupation.

I was hoping you'd say that, said Dolan.

You knew? Harrington's along-for-the-ride equanimity drained into a chilling emptiness and he felt entrapped, his world contracting into Dolan's, and for a moment on the edge of his consciousness he was aware of a doubling into a second self, his first self receding into the psychic numbing he knew so very well from his years of graveside interviews but had never, not even at the unearthing of a stadium filled with bones, experienced at a depth where everything, all the madness and pain, is meant to disappear. He was sick in the revolting airless heat of the room, on the threshold of a lifelong haunting.

No, I didn't know, Dolan said. I knew it was a possibility.

Well, shit, he said, his mouth watering, and a foulness at the top of his throat as if he might vomit; he spit on the floor to try to stop the sensation. Back in Miami, Tom had not been clever in his appraisal of the retired special agent, imagining that Dolan, always talking, one anecdote after another, a stream of true-crime monologues, wanted Tom along just to have someone to attend his stories, drive the car, pick the restaurants, make everything easy.

I was thinking, Tom said, the next time somebody invites me along on a trip, I might ask for more particulars.

I'm sorry. I didn't think you'd come if I spelled it out up front.

You were right.

When Tom Harrington calmed down, he allowed that if Dolan's client did not kill his wife, whatever her name was, then perhaps there was a small chance that maybe he knew who did, and Connie Dolan was expecting Tom to say that, too.

CHAPTER TWO

In the final days of the occupation, a Hollywood director came to Port-au-Prince as a special guest of the National Palace to celebrate the great success of democracy and the inauguration of the new president, swept into office by an election free and fair in which no one felt inspired to actually vote. The director, whose work had earned him an Academy Award, had loaned his celebrity to Haiti's cause; he had championed the refugees washing ashore in Florida, lobbied Congress, raised funds, advised the president-in-exile, spoken out at rallies in Boston and New York and Miami and, with his documentaries, had shown the world the reason for his outrage and his broken heart—the brutalities of the tyrants, the blood of the innocents. His crusade had been noble and for that he was welcomed and loved in the wasteland, and Tom Harrington himself had admired him, and still did.

The director was part of the scene and, to a less public degree, so was Tom and Tom wasn't entirely surprised, the afternoon before the inauguration, to receive a message at the desk of the Hotel Oloffson where he kept a small apartment, inviting him that evening to dinner with the director and his group. After a shower and a change of clothes he descended to the bar to listen to the day's scrapings from the correspondents who regularly gathered there to decompress—most would be leaving the country by week's end—and at the appointed hour drove himself up the darkening mountain, following its sluggish river of traffic and black exhaust, to the once luxurious suburb of Petionville and the gingerbread coziness of the Kinam Hotel.

The entourage—several producers and assistants, a screenwriter and her husband from Santa Monica, a local driver who tripled as an interpreter and bodyguard—had already taken seats around a long table on the patio, cocktails in hand, robust and mirthful, cosmopolitan, the men in their black jeans and linen shirts, the women in flowery sundresses. Had they gathered in the Seychelles or Saint-Tropez, they would have appeared no different, and perhaps to Harrington's discredit it had long since ceased to offend him that even the worst places on earth somehow managed to cater to the appetites of the well-heeled. He was offered the flattery of the one remaining chair at the head of the table, lowering himself on a cushion of exchanged compliments, the director to his right, a balding impish producer to his left.

Tell me, the director said, about Jacques Lecoeur.

Where the rutted track stopped at the bank of an aquamarine river flowing out from the rugged and still timbered mountains of the northwest lived Jacques Lecoeur—without meaning to, Tom made it sound quite like a fable. Lecoeur, a cocoa farmer and labor organizer turned, in reputation at least, guerilla chieftain, provided the tyrants with their only form of resistance in the years after the coup d'état. The generals had sent their army marching day and night up the valley where Lecoeur's people— peasants, cultivators—resided, burning houses and schools, shooting whoever proved too slow to flee. Lecoeur and his men and their families retreated into the refuge of the high mountains, living in caves, scavenging for roots, lost to the world in the most paradisiacal landscape Tom had ever seen anywhere in the tropics. Certainly this much was true: the tyrants' obsession with hunting down Lecoeur; and after the invasion, the Special Forces's obsession with outtricking Lecoeur, which they were never able to accomplish in Lecoeur's endless game of hide-and-seek. In this way, Lecoeur had become an enigmatic celebrity, perhaps the only one Haiti had to offer the world. Because the U.S. military's intelligence units listened without discrimination to any voice that would whisper a confidence into their many ears, their profile on Lecoeur was confounding, fragmented, and contradictory: one week Lecoeur was a freedom fighter, the next a bandit and a murderer; he was a warrior messiah, or maybe a gang leader; he and his men were weaponless save for Lacoeur's own pistol and a few M1s they had lifted from the Haitian army; on the contrary, a Special Forces intel officer once told Harrington, the Cubans were shipping them arms.

In the course of his mission, four times Harrington had hiked up through that burnt-out valley and into the mountains to document the former regime's crimes in the region, twice unsuccessfully with American commandos, twice with various journalists who were also Tom's friends. When Lecoeur finally allowed himself to be found, appearing wraithlike out of the jungle to sit with them in a clearing and endure their questions, Tom didn't know what to think about this unassuming man. He was shy, well-educated, articulate without being dogmatic—Tom theorized he was perhaps nothing more than a modern-day maroon, a runaway, a man who had refined the feral art of saving his own skin. No hard evidence suggested otherwise but, even now, months later, the bloody reports crackled down from the northwest mountains: overrun outposts, attacks on garrisons, summary executions and assassinations and torchings, each incident of vengeance attributed to the wily, bearded Lecoeur, Haiti's Che Guevara, her Robin Hood. Personally, Tom believed none of it, but the appeal of the myth was not lost on him. Lecoeur had what moviegoers would recognize as star power.

The director was intrigued, engaged by these accounts of a true son of the land, a reincarnation of the slave chieftains who had defeated, two hundred years earlier, the slave owners, Napoleon, and the French.

I want to meet this guy, said the director. He wanted Harrington to take them up there.

Who? Tom asked, mildly alarmed. All of you? Around the table, their optimistic faces bobbed excitement. It was possible, Harrington said, but the request made him uneasy. He had a mental image of leading the sweaty troupe on a ghost chase around and around the mountains, doused by squalls and roasted by the sun, their energy never flagging, surrounded by a mosquito-cloud of ragged, mesmerized children. These were not timid or naive people who readily balked at obstacles, yet when Tom explained the expedition would take a day or two to arrange and two more to accomplish, with, of course, no guarantee of safety or success, that was the end of the scheme, there was not enough time to squeeze in the adventure. The entourage groaned their disappointment and picked up their forgotten menus; the director turned to the screenwriter and began a separate conversation; the waiter came and the table ordered and the director followed him back to the kitchen to say something to the chef.

Sighing, the producer leaned toward Tom and laid his chin in the palm of his hand. We've touched a nerve here, said the producer. Oliver Stone's been to Chiapas, you see, to meet Subcommandante Marcos.

Harrington did not think more or less of the director for this explanation; famous people, powerful people, were drawn to each other, compelled to sniff out the scent of their peers and judge them equal or inferior, look into the mirror of their own importance, and he did not feel the compulsion was necessarily shallow or gratuitous or insincere, only inevitable. There was no glory left in Haiti that wasn't hollow anyway; the grand campaigns, the highest principles, had all decayed or would soon fail, but all of them were still pretending that their swords remained sharp, that their crusades held meaning. It was simply the way you had to be in Haiti until the day arrived when you could not be that way ever again.

And then there was a blast outside the Kinam, the concussion sending the faintest kiss of air across the cheeks of the diners, who collectively tensed and caught their breath. Excuse me, Harrington told the producer and slid back his chair. Someone nearby out in the darkness had fired a gun and Tom had been conditioned by Haiti and its predecessors to appreciate the coincidence of right time, wrong place. Now it was pure curiosity; before that, in El Salvador, pure paralyzing fear. The driver stood up with Tom and Harrington could see the butt of his pistol like a broken hip bone jutting out from his waistband. Everyone else stayed in their seats. If there was a story, they could hear it later.

But there was no story to bring back to them with their meals. The hotel manager and the director were already on the sidewalk by the time the driver and Tom came out to peer into the darkness of Petionville's decrepit plaza, empty but for a few hardened shadows passing underneath the vault of trees, a lone cook fire near the corner where the tap-taps stopped for the hordes of passengers during the day. They listened carefully for any further trouble but the streets were almost serene with the emptiness of their secrets. A few police milled about on the apron of the station across the block at the top of the square and it was there, the manager guessed, the shot had been fired. Sometimes, he said, these fools even shoot themselves accidentally, playing with their weapons.

The four men returned to the patio in an expansive mood, the director asking the solicitous manager for a bottle of Barbancourt Special Reserve to be delivered to the table. Their food was served in a steamy cloud of garlic and chili vinegar and grilled fish and the talk turned to the year Tom Harrington had spent on the island investigating its massacres. Had he seen much of the American commandos who controlled the countryside? What did Tom think about the various pundits who were saluting or decrying America's *rehabilitation of the warrior culture*? And then—Tom shouldn't have been surprised but he was—the discussion turned to moviemaking. The people at the table were planning to make a soldier movie set in Haiti.

This will be different, he overheard the director say to the screenwriter. We're not doing this for our Haitian friends, he said and she smiled knowingly and nodded once that she understood. Let's think patriotism, romance. A Green Beret and an aid worker? A Green Beret and a Haitian woman?

Think *The Sand Pebbles* meets *M.A.S.H.*, said the producer.

What does that mean? Tom asked.

I don't know, said the producer, except they're both great movies. You'll help us out on this, won't you?

The waiter replaced their dishes with slices of lime pie and glass chalices containing smooth globes of mango sorbet. The director refilled Tom's empty brandy snifter with Barbancourt, which he compared to the finest cognac.

Tom smiled politely and sat back in his chair, not meaning to ponder the invitation but he looked to be doing just that. The proposition seemed so offhand and uncalculated that it struck him as cavalier, as if he were being gathered up to go to a party—come on, hop in—and although he had no idea what he might possibly contribute to such a novel enterprise as the making of a movie, of course, and perhaps naively, he agreed to the unlikely project.

Haiti was the director's true cause, his central passion—but Tom couldn't say why, and never dwelled on it. Harrington saw him twice more: the next day at the inauguration, dressed in a business suit and seated among the dignitaries in the grandstand erected in front of the National Palace, and then a final time coming out of Galerie Issa with his entourage, stacks of paintings cradled in their arms. No one mentioned the movie to Tom again, and it was never made.

On the periphery of the conversation, while they finished their pie and sorbet, Tom had noticed the screenwriter get up from the table and disappear back around the corner of the wall that separated the patio from the interior bar, presumably to find the toilet. Now she returned light on her feet, a gust of excitement, her face flushed with serendipity.

There is the most perfect, lovely girl around the corner, she announced breathlessly to the table, and named a pixieish Hollywood actress who starred in romantic comedies as the perfect, lovely girl's identical twin. The screenwriter imagined the wolf in her male friends' expressions because she playfully admonished, You men stay away from her, with a theatrical drawl.

The table trafficked in ingenues, though, and had no interest in her. On the other hand, the actress who had been compared to the girl around the corner was one of Harrington's favorites, the standard-bearer for every Sally-next-door heartthrob fantasy the studios could confect, and he found the temptation to have a quick look irresistible.

Excuse me, he said, popping up, a boyish grin on his face. I'll be right back.

For once in Haiti, he was having an unqualified good time. The evening had made him dizzy and unselfconsciously energized, drunk from the unaccustomed attention of well-known people, and Tom Harrington felt he had rare gifts to hand out to any audience: charm or knowledge or, god knows, some cause for happiness.

He walked toward the soft-lit pool at the rear of the hotel, turning where the patio elbowed to the right along a stuccoed arcade, each of its arches providing a discreet shelter for diners seeking privacy. She was in the third alcove, her back to him, having dinner with a correspondent from the *Guardian* who had returned to London several months ago after the elections. The correspondent glanced up from his conversation with the girl and, smiling broadly, his eyes met Tom's and he called him over. Suddenly embarrassed by his game, Tom lurched forward to the side of their table, trying to remember the fellow's name, and took the journalist's hand with unnatural exuberance, saying loudly, *Good to see you,* and *When did you get back?*

Yesterday, he said. It's too fucking quiet, isn't it.

Tom shifted his eyes expectantly toward the girl but her head was tilted down at her plate, only the golden crown of her head visible, the cut of her neck-length hair shielding her face—a remote angel—and she made no effort to acknowledge Tom's presence, and so he returned his attention to her companion and they spoke for a few minutes about mutual friends, Tom's eyes darting back and forth between the fellow and the girl until finally his *Guardian* friend felt prompted to introduce him.

Do you know Jacqueline?

When she raised her blue eyes to grant him an insincere smile, Tom was indeed astonished by her resemblance to the famous actress, and instantly inflamed by her cover-girl wholesomeness, the appearance of it at least. She had a nervous body, clapping knees and restless arms, but was not timid under the scan of yet another pair of fixated eyes, and regarded Tom with an utter absence of interest. Instead of dazzling, her beauty seemed to be the source of profound comfort and unending satisfaction, the American ideal, the girl every boy dreamed of courting and winning, the girl who made every one of them crazy in high school and wretched in college, their universal torture queen, blithe collector of tormented young hearts, the first and last girl to occupy their beautiful self-told lies of perfect love, perfect companionship, the one they could never stop needing and never stop hating and never get out of their minds. Hers would be a slavish cult of eager youth and wicked men, and Tom could only be thankful that, given the manifold distances between them—she in her midtwenties, he entering his forties; a mathematical separation not quite tainted by the dread of imaginary fatherhood—any intimacy they might impossibly stumble into would be short and bitter, rather than what it would have been otherwise: prolonged and destructive. Still, she was a cookie, a forbidden treat you may or may not be allowed, and although he had nothing to say to her and nothing came to mind, he could not take his eyes off her.

Jackie's a photographer, said the fellow from the *Guardian*, and Tom tried to see her more clearly through the perspective of her profession but she was too green, too studied in her wrinkled clothes: baggy, many-pocketed khaki pants and an immaculate V-neck T-shirt the color of a lemon. No jewelry, not even a wristwatch, except for small gold studs in her ears—not a total naïf, then; at least she knew not to bait herself for a mugging.

Who do you work for? Tom asked.

Nobody. She shrugged and examined her unpainted fingernails. Tom looked to the *Guardian* for an explanation but he cocked an eyebrow and shrugged as well. *Weird chick,* said his face, and Tom thought, *Does she not understand where she is?*

Good luck, he said and retreated to his table.

Later he would always think how peculiar it was, the way he met her—hardly a meeting at all. A comic impulse to mock the implication in the screenwriter's half-serious warning to stay away from her. Tom had only wanted a look. It was nothing really, a sixty-second charade of voyeurism and desire.

A quick look, and then he could tell himself that he knew her story, but it was the other way around, somehow she knew his, and it would be a while before he began to believe she had meant to be at the Kinam that night, sitting with an acquaintance of Tom's, and only the details of how he came to her table could be called coincidence.

Well? prompted the screenwriter, giddy with anticipation. Did you see her? What did I tell you? She's fabulous, right?

We're engaged, Tom said, and everybody snickered. But he was afraid that somehow she embodied a cycle in his life, a bad old season blowing in, and already he hoped to see her again.

CHAPTER THREE

As they were leaving the airport, his anger with Connie Dolan receded toward the fact of the matter; the girl was dead—murdered—and he could not escape the guilty notion that he owed her this if nothing else, the decency of caring. Despite Dolan's manipulations, he would consent to the intent of their partnership, without making much of an effort to explain to himself why.

Tom merged with the traffic headed into the city, four lanes on a two-lane road and everybody doing as he pleased. Over on the right, that big compound is the LIC, he said. The Americans headquartered there, once they secured the airport.

Yeah, yeah, fuck, said Dolan, paling, his attention fixed nervously on the road. You're driving too fast.

I should probably tell you about Eville, said Tom.

On his final visit to the LIC, Harrington was overwhelmed by its stark atmosphere of pathos and impending abandonment, and it struck him as a pitiful thing when a great army decamps quietly at the end of an ambiguous campaign, neither victorious nor defeated but simply done, a giant suddenly weary of his own strength and the raw lack of circumstances to use it properly, the world rendered arbitrary by a vacuum of purpose. What was once a paranoid protocol of security checkpoints, identity confirmations, pat downs and wandings and assigned escorts from the Public Affairs office had dwindled to a lone guard waving Tom through the gates and past the outdoor souvenir market, an on-base convenience for the eternally busy Americans, the vendors staring out from their ramshackle kiosks like people resigned to the perpetuity of their thirst. They were there to sell to the soldiers, but the soldiers were gone. Well, very near gone.

It was late in the afternoon the day of the inauguration and Tom had just come from the ceremony at the palace, where he had stood sweating on the lawn in front of the portico, straining to make out the portentous words of the new president, wearing for the first time the tricolored sash of his office, as he addressed his nation. He was tall and gaunt, bearded and handsome, impeccably dressed in a black suit—a former baker converted to the religion of politics by an ex-priest ascended through the politics of religion, but he mumbled into the thicket of microphones on the podium, and Tom couldn't understand him.

What's he saying? Tom asked a stick-thin Haitian journalist pressed against him in the crowd.

I don't know, either, said the Haitian. He's drunk.

Did he just say, Fuck America?

Non, monsieur, the journalist smiled with sly eyes, enjoying the question. The president cannot say that today. The president said, *Beaucoup. Merci beaucoup, America.* Tomorrow he can say this other thing.

A dwindling afternoon of sepia-tinted air and smoky, dark palm silhouettes in the gauze of light. In a grove of hardwood trees next to the cavernous metal building where the military had established its command and control center, Harrington saw what he mistook for a barbecue, merry soldiers in running shorts and olive T-shirts attending burn cans topped by a blue whip of flames. Out the open door at the side of the building—a former warehouse for the boatloads of cheap bras and dime-store undies manufactured at the LIC before the embargo crushed what passed for an economy in Haiti—another soldier appeared with another carton of documents to tilt into the burn, the attendants stirring the heavy sheaves of files with iron rods, a self-cleaning military, emptying the infinite bureaucracy of its mind of petty obsessions, institutional whisperings, the myriad little secrets of the occupation. If you wanted to know what happened here, he thought, learn to read the ashes.

Anybody seen Eville? Tom had asked.

Who?

Master Sergeant Eville Burnette, Third Group Special Forces.

Their shaved heads nodded him through the door and his boots echoed the length of the concrete, through a space he had last seen veined with cables and wires and branchings of line, everywhere hookups and uplinks and patch-ins into the mad electric flow of information, wall to wall with cubicles and folding cots, gear everywhere, coffee urns and water coolers, uniforms bull-penned in a cacophony of briefings and debriefings, the human heat and stifling wet air shoved back and forth by industrial fans. Troops sacked out, officers on the phone, on the computer, talking to satellites, officers giving stand-up interviews to the networks, troops watching themselves on CNN, and if you asked anybody inside the LIC what was going on, the only true and enduring answer you could never get was, *Nothing,* or simply, *Behold—we exist.*

Tom loved coming here, the odd sense of visiting a very efficient factory that produced essentially useless things.

The Special Forces hated it at the LIC. Coming out of the countryside to Port-au-Prince, coming to headquarters, was the worst sort of punishment they could handle without dropping their legendary composure and going berserk. Here, in the LIC, generals weaned on the Cold War screamed about their mustaches, about the sleeves of their battle-dress blouses tucked in a jungle roll, told them to put their helmets on, take their sunglasses off. Stand straight, put on your seat belt, get a haircut *now,* I want to hear you sons of bitches speaking English. *Yessir,* sir. When they left their outposts in the hinterlands and walked into the LIC to deal with the conventional army, the SF pretended they were among foreigners, in another country altogether where they may or may not be the enemy.

Eville and his team had been up north in Saint-Marc, the last Special Forces unit to be pulled back to the capital and now the last operational detachment left in Haiti, assigned the delicate honor of training a palace guard, the president's own private army, its predecessor known worldwide and to history as the Ton Ton Macoutes, a synonym for paramilitary terror. They were the debutantes of the inauguration, the new guard, their presence heralding the official end to the American intervention in Haiti, and since the palace guard had gotten through the day without launching a coup d'état, and had further established its professionalism by restraining its natural urge to shoot, beat, or club the citizens, Harrington imagined Eville and his guys would be congratulating themselves for this memorable afternoon spent in the maternity ward of democracy, handing out cigars.

But inside the LIC that day instead of celebration he found only gloom and disgust, its mighty enterprise humbled into the far corner of the vast warehouse that was a constantly shrinking warren of plywood stalls, bare walls without ceilings, blankets and rain ponchos draped for doors. Before calling Eville's name, Tom stood on the threshold of the colony and listened: the springy patter of a keyboard, faraway rock and roll leaking out from someone's headphones, a tubalike fart greeted by a groan.

In here, said Eville, and his voice led Tom through the maze to the sergeant's kennel.

Eville sat on the edge of his cot, hunched over, elbows on his knees, the son and grandson and great-grandson of a Montana ranching family, staring at his massive steer-roping hands as if they had been painted with disgrace. Tom lowered himself down on a footlocker facing him and sat quietly for a while, waiting for Eville to speak but he could not stitch together words and Tom was bewildered and saddened by the sight because the master sergeant was a strong man in every way, open and true even in his unmilitary emotions, and now Tom was seeing him made weak.

Say, Ev, you all right, man?

His team had been shipped out in the middle of the night. No warning, said Eville, nothing, just, *Listen up, girls, there's a C-130 waiting for you at the airport and I want you on it in one hour because you are outta here.* Eville raised his head, his eyes red with the sting of betrayal. They left me and Stew and Brooks to sweep up, we have a couple more pallets to pack and then that's the ball game, back to Bragg by the end of the week, *Hey baby, I'm home, let's pick up the pieces of our sorry-ass lives.* He paused and shook his head like a boxer after a roundhouse punch, his flat, plain face contorted by anguish, and said softly—Eville was always soft-voiced, you could look at him and guess that about him—Man, we should have been there today. We were screwed by our chain, man.

Command—not Special Operations but the dinosaurs, the fossils, the holdbacks in the regular army, the ones still fighting communists and Vietnam—had forbidden Master Sergeant Eville Burnette and his captain and warrant officer and the nine other commandos on their A-team to go anywhere near the National Palace during the inauguration, and it didn't matter that the team had a right to be there in the background, taking pride in the moment with the men they had trained, and it no longer mattered that for eighteen months, while the Green Berets had been living hard and working like sled dogs, the politicians in Washington couldn't decide who the enemy was. Were the good guys the bad guys or were the ones they had come here to kill—the *macoutes* and the vampires and the tyrants—the bad guys, and after a while it seemed the answer was, well, everybody's a bad guy but work with them anyway. But now here was a fresh new answer, definitive and irreversible, the bad guys were the Special Forces, a magnet for negative press, straggling back in from their little kingdoms with weapons missing and vehicles unaccounted for, guilty of the twin heresies of self-reliance and self-importance, and no one stepped forward to protect them from the outrage of the generals.

It always fucking ends this way, said Eville, and Tom couldn't help but feel sorry for him, his congenital optimism replaced by this devastation of malaise, the insinuation that he had not done the job he had been asked to do, that he had somehow performed shoddily, dishonorably. Harrington, who had seen them, watched them—Eville and his men and other Special Forces teams salted throughout Haiti—knew that the truth burned brightly at the other end of the spectrum. They came and left with a deep faith that they could fix things, but they couldn't fix Haiti, and now in their failure they had begun to hate the island in order to keep from doubting themselves.

Eville Burnette waved off Tom's attempt to commiserate; he didn't need an apologist and he didn't want a cheerleader and they would have this mandatory silence between them on the subject of failure. Instead Harrington invited him to dinner the following night though he wasn't sure if anyone was actually free to leave the base.

Bring some friends if you want.

I have friends? Eville asked, but he was smiling.

The sergeant warmed to the idea of stepping out, stepping away, the one thing you could almost never do on a deployment but who was left to tell him no. His mood swung up and the smile expanded into his eyes. Hey, he said. It's okay. I did what I came to do, the people of this country are free again, we only lost one of our own, and I didn't have to kill anyone.

But Harrington found himself thinking darkly that maybe we'd all be better off if you had.

Harrington and Dolan came to a stop in an infernal tangle of traffic, opposing lanes suddenly head-to-head, drivers standing in the road engaged in the popular theater of shouting matches.

Connie Dolan said with a mischievous lilt that he had no idea humanitarian do-gooders like Tom were inclined to be so kissy with the military and then laughed when he saw the spark in Harrington's eyes. No, come on, he said. What's the deal with Eville?

This is an easy one, Tom said, his voice deliberately tight. What did you say you used to do? Special agent for what?

Okay, I got it, said Dolan, bemused. Everybody gets a kick out of playing wiseass with cops, right? You want me to guess. He knew the girl.

Right, but Tom didn't know how the sergeant knew her, only that he had the uncomfortable feeling they knew each other from somewhere else besides Haiti. There was something about them together I couldn't see, couldn't understand, said Tom. Something about their relationship was really off. Or really on. Maybe that was it.

You're saying they had a thing together.

I doubt any man could have a thing with Jackie.

You say that because?

She was insane.

Dolan seemed to consider this. And you're familiar with the insane, he said. That's not a question.

That goddamn girl, Tom said, talking to himself, a gravelly release of breath. She had managed to make him less of a man than he thought he was and he had done everything he could to forget her, to will her nonexistent, but there was no reprieve from a succubus and for the two years since he had last seen her Jackie had found her way into his dreams, waiting there for him on the street corner of his libido like a neighborhood whore, and now here out of the blue was Dolan, delivering her volatile presence back into Tom's life and in that respect it hardly mattered if she were dead or not.

What do you mean, *That's not a question*? he said, snapping at Dolan. What the fuck is that supposed to mean, *I'm familiar with the insane*?

It's a joke.

Give me a heads-up the next time you plan on being funny.

Drivers slammed horns, threw up their arms, got out, yelled, and Tom thought, being summoned as an expert witness to pronounce over the dark adventure of Jackie's life was the last thing he ever wanted to be doing with his own and yet once again he was trapped by his unhealthy curiosity for her. Unhealthy to the point of diseased, he'd say—he had caught something from her, some decay transmitted from soul to soul, but then he recollected contemptuously that by her own admittance she lacked a soul.

At the intersection ahead they could see a scarecrow of a man urging a dump truck to back up to allow a group of men to push a battered pickup, its bed loaded with passengers who refused to get out, off the road where a row of grimy makeshift garages strewn with iron carnage awaited it. Across the street, a dealership's lot was filled and gleaming with row after row of Japanese-made SUVs. A few minutes later a pair of men dressed only in soiled pants, a ruffle of sweat at each man's waistband, came weaving through the clot of traffic with a casket balanced on their heads, six brass handles to a side and upholstered in velvet the color of a green lollipop. Good God, Dolan observed drily, they's burying James Brown, and they inched forward toward the sooty crucible of the city.

What do you think? Tom asked Dolan, nodding out the windshield as they began to enter the ramshackle neighborhoods and Dolan said he'd seen worse, the slums of Rio, San Juan, Bogotá. But he hadn't seen anything yet.

Where the road gullied at the next intersection a traffic cop stepped out of nowhere and whistled for Tom to stay put and when Tom tried to go around the policeman skipped in front of him and banged his fist on the hood. All right, Tom said, smiling coldly back at the man's glare. No problem.

And as they sat watching the cross traffic pour through he told Dolan of the night a month after the invasion when he was stopped in this exact spot, everything pitch-black except the double and sometimes triple row of taillights of the cars in front of him snaking up the hill toward the choke point at Delmas, bumper-to-bumper and no one moving, no one coming down, either, because the people trying to go up had blocked the lanes. A storm that had been up on the mountains had slid down on them and it rained catastrophically for twenty minutes like it was coming out of a fire hose, a constant artillery of thunderclaps. In the white flash of lightning he saw a roaring avalanche of broken, brilliant glass crashing down, and then it stopped for a minute and Tom rolled down his window to get some air. Everything was quiet, people had turned off their headlights and everything was dark. Then he began to hear a deep, approaching rumble and as the wall of water came down the gully Tom could hear the screams of the pas-sengers inside one of the cars in front of him as it surged up and rolled and tumbled in the flood down toward the sea. Lightning flashed again and he could see people, families, children, swept out of their shacks, their arms flailing, the water rising until he could feel it tugging at his front wheels and he got out shaking and went down the line of cars behind him trying to get people to back up but they were paralyzed. Tom could see the glowing terror of their eyes as he came out of the darkness to their windows, the white ball of his face bobbing around, adding to the horror, but the flash flood wasn't the worst of it.

He went back to his car and the water hadn't come up any more but it started raining again, not heavy this time but steady and unpleasantly cold, and as he looked across the new gorge of the flooded intersection at the line of cars on the other side, four cars up he saw a cracking sprinkle of lights, like flashbulbs popping out little tongues of hot color, then a huge boom detonated off over the harbor and the sky was illuminated just long enough for him to see a guy move from the fourth car up to the third car up and then it was black again and then he saw another pop of yellow-red lights

41

and then the form of this man moving to the next car and *bzzrt*, he had a machine pistol or an Uzi and was going from car to car spraying people as they sat cowering from the storm and Tom thought, *Shit, there's only one car left and the water's going down and what's he going to do, wade across and keep going down the line?* but when the killer walked up to the driver's window of the last car and bent over to look in, a blue-edged cone of white light took his head right off. Finally, cars behind Tom were backing up, their tires spinning on the wet tar, and he got his own car turned around and got out of there, going the opposite direction from where he wanted to be, and he wasn't thinking clearly because he thought he'd go to the airport and get a plane out in the morning but of course there weren't any flights because the airport had been closed for months and he thought, *Okay, I'll still go to the airport because the 10th Mountain Division is there,* thinking they can do something, they can help, so he drove up to the main gate into a sudden blinding sun of kleig lights and voices yelling at him to get the fuck out of his vehicle and lie on the ground and he's lying in the mud screaming, *I'm an American for God's sake,* and they shout back, *Are you in trouble?*

Not me, Tom tried to explain, but there's people—

The soldiers he can't see behind the lights shout back, *Then get the fuck out of here, man. What's wrong with you, you crazy asshole?*

So he got up out of the mud and gave the finger to the 10th Mountain Division and drove across the road to the LIC, which was still abandoned and full of squatters and refugees and he parked next to the night watchman's kiosk and crawled into the backseat and smoked a pack of cigarettes and then pretended to himself, *I'm sleeping.* The sky began to turn light and Tom wanted a shower and his bed back at the Oloffson and he wanted a drink, he wanted ten drinks, so he got behind the wheel and went back the way he was trying to go the night before and the road was empty. The intersection was ripped up, a gouge in the earth stinking strongly of death and sewage, the cross streets above it and below it torn apart, houses sheared in half, awful-smelling red mud and soggy household trash everywhere but no cars, nothing, empty. Nobody and nothing on the road but Tom. Nothing in Haiti ever gets cleaned up, so what was he supposed to think? He climbed down into the debris-strewn channel of the intersection and followed the raging path of the water down to the sea, where he stood staring at the unspeakably contaminated shallows. Nothing. He couldn't go to the police—the police had been disbanded—and the American military was too obsessed with protecting itself from God knows what to be bothered. For days he queried everybody he thought might know something, he knocked on doors of the houses that had survived the deluge, he went to the Haitian radio stations, but no one had heard of a car being washed away or a gunman going from car to car assassinating people and then getting shot himself and Tom thought, *What am I supposed to do with this?* And it dawned on him, if he wrote it into a report, it happened; otherwise, it never happened.

So what'd you do? asked Dolan.

I haven't really thought about it, he said, until that cop brought his fist down on the hood, and Dolan told him, You know, Tom, you can't go bearing witness to every fucking terrible thing.

CHAPTER FOUR

In the final days of the occupation the photographers owned the veranda at the Hotel Oloffson. From midmorning until lunch you'd find them here in their bulging vests stirring coffee and passing around a pack of cigarettes, their cameras in pieces on the tables, a glossy-black clutter of expensive metals and indestructible alloys, canisters of film scattered about like unchambered rounds of ammunition, telescopic lenses like mortar tubes, their vernacular as esoteric as the military's, distilled with acronyms, equipment referenced by numbers alone. But most of the time, and this, too, like the soldiers, the photographers were waiting, slumped on the cool veranda in wicker chairs, passengers on an old riverboat trapped in the stagnant eddy of Port-au-Prince, saying little, the light gone, the light coming, the light something nobody has time to stop and think about, the story over, the story just beginning, the world being created here and the world in agony and dying.

On that Thursday morning, on a day as dull as all the others in the aftermath of the elections, the photographers gathered as usual for a late breakfast—nothing planned, exactly; a farewell meal but they didn't bother to call it that. Like the correspondents, they were always forming and dissolving, bumping into each other in New York and London, in Berlin and Paris and Rome, Tokyo, Mexico City, regrouping as a tribe in every god-lonely place in the world where hatred gushed through the streets in order to supply the citizens back home with the images of the endlessly playing movie called Other People's Problems. The ones who had gotten up early to find something to shoot were trudging back in from their prowl across the festering city; the ones who had closed down the bars straggled red-eyed to the veranda from their rooms in flip-flops, shirttails out, hair still wet, camera bags slung over their shoulders. Tables were dragged together. Joseph, the waiter, brought glasses of watery orange juice and omelets.

Tom Harrington sat by himself at the table to the left of the diamond of steps leading to the flowered grounds, doodling in the margins of his running list of phone numbers. He waited for a callback granting him an audience with the recently installed Minister of Justice or a few minutes of conversation with somebody, anybody—the incoming president, the outgoing president, the chief of the National Police, the family pets of the children of any member of the high court—but the new government and its followers were no longer immune to the international press and its toxicity, no one was talking, and for the immediate future, it seemed, that phobia had splashed over onto the NGO community as well and Harrington's painstakingly arranged schedule of meetings had stalled in a limbo of post-ponements. Give us time, the nouveau politicians had assured him, to get accustomed to the idea that we are actually running the country, since we've never even run so much as a gas station in our ass-whipped lives. Even Gerard, his fixer, had become bored after their breakfast together and had gone down to the gates of the compound to sit with the other drivers and translators playing cards in the shade of the coconut palms.

Eventually latecomers began to sit at Tom's table—a tall, freckled, red-haired lunatic from Colorado whom Tom had once seen photograph over the shoulder of a *macoute* gunman as the gunman emptied his pistol into a teenage boy; a shy photographer from Japan with an upturned bowl of shiny black hair and a permanent smile who had begun his career by snap-ping soft-porn shots of high school girls in Osaka; a blonde-haired, deeply tanned woman from the *Washington Post,* all arms and legs in trekking shorts and tank top who had cataloged the most grisly human rights abuses after the coup d'état, hundreds of photos she had shared with Tom, the entire trove copied, cataloged, and stored in his Miami law office in boxes marked Evidence. She was headed home to Washington, the Japanese fellow had booked a thirty-six-hour flight to East Timor, and the lunatic was off to Chechnya to disappear, Tom later heard, into the bloody storm of Russia's unforgiving little war, and if you love the zone too much that's what happened—one way or another you became your own vanishing act. A friend of Tom's, Daniel, an AP photographer, took the last empty chair, unclipping a walkie-talkie from his belt and setting it on the table; he wasn't going anywhere because Haiti was his home. It was a fact few outsiders readily appreciated because it made no fucking sense to most of them and to many Haitians as well, that Haiti was a world you might freely choose to live in—You *live here*! For God's sake, why?

The story was dead, the Haitian people were becoming invisible again, imaginary creatures, right before the magnifying eyes of the international press and there was nothing the *pep* could do about it—their success would not bring the journalists back, their failure would no longer earn the dubious privilege of the media's attention. The woman from the *Post* mentioned she had gone to Cité Soleil yesterday morning, to document the inauguration from the perspective of the gangrenous slums, but had left after twenty minutes, unnerved by the hostility and threats. Journos had always been welcomed in the slums as protectors, their presence evidence that somebody in the world had taken notice of the people at the bottom but an unscalable fence of acrimony had been erected, kids with guns were taking over the infested grid, forming gangs, against all *blans* because everybody was leaving and nothing had changed and in fact nobody cared. In the past she would have persisted but now even persistence felt like part of the larger betrayal of these youth who had paid in blood for the fraud of democracy.

Freedom has made them feral, said the red-haired lunatic.

None of the whites at the table wanted to talk about these things.

It was at this moment, sitting on the veranda of the Oloffson with the photographers, that Tom Harrington saw Jacqueline Scott for a second time. She took one step out of the shadow of the lobby onto the veranda and paused to glance around and she seemed dulled in some way and uncertain, common traits of someone freshly arrived in the muddle, but still her beauty rifled through him and he wanted very much just to be able to look at her quietly and dream, as he might at the movies. A mere glimpse of her energized Tom in the doldrums of the morning.

Do you know this girl behind you? he asked the *Post* photographer, who turned to look as Jacqueline Scott stepped back into the hush of the lobby, all dark wood and rattan furniture and ceiling fans.

I think that was Jackie, she said. Right. I took her along yesterday to Cité Soleil.

You know her then? She's a photographer?

She's new. She asked to go. She needs someone to help her out. We all did, didn't we?

She looks like that actress, said Daniel.

She looks like Joan of Arc, said their future emissary to Chechnya.

I can't quite picture her in Cité Soleil, Tom said.

Don't you guys sell her short, said the woman from the *Post*. She doesn't back off. She handled herself well.

Who's she work for?

No one just yet. She has some names, contacts. So that's it, the *Post* photographer sighed and stood up. Good luck, everyone. I have a plane to catch.

Without a word, the red-haired photographer from Colorado stood up as well, lifted his bag over his shoulder and descended the steps to the parking lot and into oblivion. The large group at the pushed-together tables began to break up; accounts were settled, embraces exchanged, drivers summoned. The gear, piles of it, humped away. The Japanese photographer finished cleaning his lenses and replaced them in a foam-lined case with the care and delicacy of explosive charges.

Daniel said that he and his wife were hosting a dinner that evening for stay-arounds, but Tom told him sorry, he had made other arrangements and couldn't make it. Then Jackie was there at the table, asking to buy black-and-white film, if anyone had extra. She looked ready for the streets—a tan cotton vest over her T-shirt, olive-green slacks, hiking boots, camera bag, a huge Nikon strapped around her elegant neck, her expression unnecessarily grave, a slight urgency in her voice. It struck Tom, as it had that night at the

Kinam, that she was without charm, and perhaps that was her intention, a way of muting or dampening the blaze of her physical appeal.

He offered her a seat but she didn't acknowledge the invitation. The Japanese photographer rummaged through his bag and found six rolls of Tri-X and she made no objection when he gave her the film and wouldn't take anything for it but karmic goodwill.

So what's happening today? she asked with her eyes darting along a line somewhere above their heads.

Zed, zero, zip. Everybody's pulling out, said Daniel, but no sooner had he spoken than the walkie-talkie began to fizz, and they listened to the crackled report of his colleague checking in. A roadblock, a protest, tires burning on the highway in front of Cité Soleil, a commonplace excitement but Daniel was the last man chained to the story and his presence was required. Anybody want to come along? he asked and Tom expected Jackie to jump at the chance but she said no.

What do you *want* to happen today? he asked her. She was beautiful and he didn't know her and it would be a game, he thought, to get to know her.

Can I sit and have a cup of coffee with you guys? she asked as she pulled out a chair and sat. Impossible that anyone had ever told her no.

The conversation did not flow. She talked haltingly for a few minutes with the Japanese photographer about editors and magazines and syndicates and then he, too, joined the exodus to the airport. Her coffee arrived and she sat stirring sugar into it, clearly uncomfortable, and so he stopped watching her and asked the simplest question—about her home, where she came from. She jerked her posture straight from her intense, nervous hunch and met his eyes and Tom didn't think she had even heard what he said but instead asked a question of her own.

Are you busy today?

Impossibly, he joked, hoping she would suggest a common adventure, an enterprise through which he might invent some small usefulness to Jackie, a mutual purpose that would legitimize his interest in her. Something in him—not his heart—reached toward her; he was neither a fool nor a lecher but certainly a man intrigued by the myriad possibilities that, at least on the surface, her youth and beauty and intrepidness implied. In fact, he explained, since she didn't seem to pick up on his sarcasm, I have a thousand things to do but nobody in the government seems to want to work today.

I don't want to get in your way, she said, and the hint of adolescent whine in her tone annoyed him, as if now, after cracking a window to the possibility of their companionship, she felt compelled by fickleness to close it without delay, the come-here-get-away dance of teenage girls, woefully familiar to teenage boys and a glum memory for their older selves.

You in my way actually sounds pretty good, he flirted, without an effect on her expression, and he began to wonder if she ever retreated far enough from the constant tension of her self-control to smile. Then Tom himself became more serious and wanted her to tell him why she was here, just arriving when everyone else couldn't jump ship fast enough.

The UN isn't leaving, she said. The Haitians aren't leaving.

Point taken, Tom said, for what it's worth. Then he couldn't help himself and he lapsed into a grand soliloquy, like every other horse's ass who had ever sat too long on the veranda of the Oloffson. And for what it's worth, he continued, the pictures of ordinary people, the ones mired in pathos, bearing the weight of it all, right? Rather than the sensational images or the images that disseminate information, it's those pictures that explain the most, or have the deepest impact, but first somebody must care, and you know exactly what I mean, care deeply and honestly, and right now people are very, very weary of caring about Haiti, so best of luck because I think you're going to need it. He pontificated, his lawyer's mouth running away from him. Personally, Tom said, I can no longer believe in that which demands we see things anew. I think that perspective is fundamentally dishonest, I think it's a fucking lie. How about, instead, images and words that make us finally see what we've been staring at blind and dumb for most of our daydreaming lives. *To see things anew* makes it sound like insight awaits those who can't make sense out of seeing things *as they are,* as if our innocence and inexperience were actually virtues. What do you think? You think in pictures, don't you?

But she did not want to philosophize about photography or altruism or ways of seeing and his own impulse toward abstractions seemed suddenly not passionate but tedious and didactic.

Can I ask you something? she said. Do you know about voodoo?

Know what about *vodou*? he repeated skeptically but thought, *aha*. With her question, the brooding enigma of Jacqueline Scott seemed to deflate into the banal. He guessed she wanted to hear the drums, sweat in the pagan heat and immerse herself in Haiti's timeless theater of light and darkness. If you could not explain what you were doing in a place like Haiti, here was a genuine reason that required no attachment of war or revolution or screaming horror or saintly crusade. You were, you could tell yourself, a tourist of the spirit. You were drawn by the mysteries, such as they were.

Is it a real thing? she asked, and Tom found it somewhat disconcerting, the repellent pained transparency of need in the way she asked the question.

I'm not sure what you mean.

I mean, it's a religion, right?

A religion, yes, I suppose. Another way of looking at the universe, a way to try to understand what's in God's mind. If you choose to see it that way.

How do you choose to see it? she said.

With due respect. A way of looking at, and trying to understand, power. Spiritual power, political power—they're inseparable anyway, aren't they?

Which was not to say *vodou*, much like Catholicism, had not burdened many of its practitioners with superstition and fear, he explained. The potions and powders, some of them anyway, were real; zombies, however rare, were real; spirit possession, he could assure her, was no joke, unless you were a species of white fraud hoping to bluff your way into the melodrama of it. And yet still, in its daily manifestations, *vodou* was a strong, good thing, he told her—it was Haiti's only strong, good thing, the expression of the abiding spirit of the people, the expression of survival. Whatever it was beyond that expression, or beneath it, was not for Tom or any *blan* to say, and existed if at all as a curiosity for educated men and women, the theater of the African genesis, at best an anthropological pursuit. Or, shamelessly, a type of neoprimitive entertainment, a game of the occult that whites played with blacks, perhaps to scare themselves, to flirt with the macabre, perhaps to feel liberated and unrestrained in their contempt for the answers their own world had provided, or failed to provide.

To see herself anew—and what was the American dream if not this?—was that what Jacqueline Scott wanted? Or to find herself in mankind's ancient past, and see herself clearly, as she always was and would be? Transcend, or descend, or howl at the magic of the freaking moon? Tom had no idea. Americans were not built to take these matters seriously until their faces were rubbed in the awfulness they sometimes made when they were seized by the exalted passion to remake the world.

Her request, her original request, was predictable, what any tourist might crave in Haiti if Haiti had tourists—she wanted to meet priests, the *houngans*. Of course he readily agreed and she accepted his proposition of a daylong excursion out to the countryside, where she had never been, rather than spend their time gagging in Port-au-Prince's traffic, crawling over the frying-pan heat of the road to Carrefour to visit Max Beauvoir—a cyberliterate *houngan* who spent more time on the Internet than in his peristyle—or patrolling the stack of Bel Air's sinister maze of neighborhoods, cousin by cousin, trying to track down Abujah, the video cameraman, a stringer for the networks, who had become the heir apparent to *vodou*'s throne. Instead Tom suggested a short trip via Route Nationale One to Saint-Marc, a port an hour and a half up the coast on Gonave Bay, where, on the town's outskirts, a temple, padlocked and shuttered during the occupation, had, he noticed on his last expedition into the northern mountains, raised its flags and repainted its exterior murals and presumably was back in service, come one come all.

The only tricky detail was they had to leave that minute to be back by dinnertime but Jackie said, *Let's go!* Good girl, Tom replied, relieved to have finally inspired her spontaneity. Everything about her so far, especially her callow questions about *vodou*—he thought she could have read a book, for Christ's sake, before she got on the plane—had impressed him as naive and untested, though for the first time she offered him her smile. Not warmly, though, it was as if mocking his approval of her readiness, her implicit availability, his little pat on the back.

They hoisted their shoulder bags and moved into the assault of sunlight and he was already sweating out his half-dozen cups of coffee by the time they descended the Oloffson's steps to the car park and his rental. At the end of the driveway Tom pulled over and collected Gerard from beneath the coconut palms, the happiness draining from his face when he realized he had been demoted to passenger. He slid stiff-limbed into the backseat, not his regular place and certainly not his preferred, but he was intuitive enough to decline when Jackie, who showed no interest in him otherwise, offered to switch.

By the time Tom had navigated through the wretched chicken coop of a city to its leafy outskirts and the open road, he had begun to feel joy, the most appropriate response to escaping Port-au-Prince.

Jackie did not say much, and Tom considered her silence a virtue. He was perfectly at ease driving for hours without sharing a thought with whoever his companions might be, and he generally found talkative passengers distracting from the manifold hazards of the road. Nor did he talk about Jackie to himself—he was not willing anything to happen between them, but letting things happen as they may. He was little more than a harmless parasite on her beauty, which seemed so dismayingly separate from her other traits—a paradox but an irrelevance as well and not so troubling as the wide margin for error we grant those among us who are beautiful and nothing else.

They drove out into the glare of the barren coast, the mangrove swamps and copses of thorn acacia of Tintayen sloped uninvitingly toward the bright sea, along the alluvial plain of a valley funneling upward to the mountains of the interior. She rummaged with increasing frustration in her camera bag for sunglasses and Tom was glad she could not find them because already her eyes were inscrutable. Instead she settled for lemon drops, turning in her seat to pass the bag to Gerard and then pausing for a short conversation with him that seemed more curt than polite. Did he have a family? Yes, a wife and two children. Did his wife work? No. How old were the children? Were the schools satisfactory? Where did he learn English? Tom waited for her to plumb the angry shadows of Gerard's feelings, but she did not ask him anything that would not appear on an application for a visa or a bank loan.

Nor did she offer any comment on the ever more rugged spectacle of the countryside or the hapless peasants trudging the rut of footpaths following the road, and Tom wondered if she was overwhelmed by the strangeness of Haiti, or even stunned by its unexpected though ravaged magnificence. Whatever preoccupied her, she would allow almost nothing to penetrate its envelope, which made her a rather ideal traveling companion, accepting without complaint or censure the heat, the roughness of the road, his hell-bent driving, the fate of the Haitians. Still, she exerted a slight but constant counterweight against Tom's own happiness, a humorless neurotic, no more carefree than a penitent, which he supposed she was, and the trip seemed less and less like a lark than a task or mission, which was exactly what he had hoped to avoid this day in Haiti, the outsider's relentless sense of obligation.

Are you enjoying this? he finally asked, and again it was as if she would not hear him but seemed to grow more unrelaxed and tense in her seat, fidgeting her body but staring straight out the windshield at the miles flying before them. They were hurtling through an arid, corroded landscape, the foothills brambled with cactus and thorny scrub and above them a tremendous wall of emaciated mountainsides and bone-white peaks once crowned by forests, mountains like a queue of cancer patients. He thought in her agitation she might be carsick but she flatly dismissed Tom's suggestion that they stop for a moment and stretch their legs.

A few minutes later Tom sensed her attention on him and glanced over to see her studying his face, her lips pursed but her expression otherwise blank. He looked back at the road and then back at her and she was still intent on trying to see him, the unflinching scrutiny of a woman who wants to know if she can trust a man, but if that was the case he wasn't pleased she was taking so long to make up her mind.

What is it with you? he said.

I have to ask you something, she said, but as soon as the words left her mouth she averted her eyes and shook her head, regretting her decision, or perhaps not, perhaps she intended to be cajoled.

He knew not to say anything and waited but then he gave in and said, Go ahead. Ask.

She was looking at her knees, her head bowed, her hair streaming back from the breeze of their open windows, her pained face in exquisite profile and just then he slammed into a pothole that made her grab the dashboard and jerk herself upright, wearing a new look of determination.

You can't think I'm silly, Jackie said, not a plea but a cool demand. I don't want you to laugh. If you laugh I'm getting out of the car.

What was she going to do—hail a cab? Tom glanced over his shoulder at Gerard to check his reaction to such a threat coming from such a person in such a place, which was itself reason to laugh, and they lifted their eyebrows at one another in stone-faced amusement.

I won't laugh, Tom promised and instantly her words rushed out into a question that was a type of falling or jumping, although he did not immediately recognize its nature because he had never met a woman anywhere in the world who was so defiantly literal and without irony. Tom wanted her to be cute, a ditz, a sexy ideologue, a glib bitch, a camera junkie, a news hound, a crusader, anything but this—literal and seemingly unschooled and tormented and wrapped as tight as you get before you explode.

Do you think it's possible, she began, and with the drop in her voice Tom leaned over to hear her better, for someone to lose their soul?

He made a token effort to ponder the question. Sure. What do you think, Gerard?

I don't know, said Gerard. It's possible, maybe.

You're lying. What kind of a Haitian are you? Tom said, grinning into the rearview mirror and then looking over at Jackie. If there's anybody in this car who believes you can lose your soul, it's the Haitian, not the Americans.

You're not taking this seriously, she said.

He thought it would only make things infinitely worse between them if he explained that right now everybody in Haiti was taking this outlandish question quite seriously indeed—the Green Berets, the *houngans,* the Baptist missionaries, the Catholic priests. Any villager in the hinterlands would eventually tell you the village's number-one problem was loup-garous— werewolves—coming to their huts at night and stealing their babies' souls, gobbling them up like werewolf vitamins, and then in the morning of course the baby would be dead and cemented into the statistical afterlife of Haiti's horrific infant mortality rate.

Just forget it, said Jackie.

Too late, said Tom. He had suspected she was being frivolous and theatrical about matters that did not fare well in casual conversation. He thought she was asking about *vodou* again, teasing herself with the undercurrent of its *diabolique*, but again he had misunderstood her. Let's start over, he said, if you actually want to have a real conversation. Do I believe in God? I could believe in God in Latin, or in any other language incomprehensible to me, but I cannot believe in God in English. English exposed everything wrong about our approach toward a supreme being, the core platitudes of the institutions behind the ritual, and I'm not even going to tell you what I think about the politics of religion. So I suppose you might say I believe in the mystery of God and I don't appreciate anybody fucking with that mystery or trying to grease it for me if I'm having trouble swallowing. Do you want me to go on?

He missed her nod and finally she said quietly, Okay.

Do I believe in the soul? Yes. What is it? I don't know and neither do you. An eternal essence within us? Sure, why not? The life force that appears from darkness and reenters darkness or, here's the happier scenario, appears from light and reenters light, and is not flesh and is our single connection to what some of us call the divine or the infinite or the force behind it all. Do I believe that something like that is in me? Yes, I choose to believe that. Do I believe I can lose it? I don't know. If I lose my shoes at the beach I can go back the next day and find them or just go buy another pair, but if I'm at the beach and lose my arm to a shark, that arm's not coming back, is it? When we say someone has lost his soul, what are we saying? That somehow that person has been emptied, that a light has been extinguished at the center of his being. He sold his soul to the devil, we say. What happens to people who lose their souls? They seem to die and be reborn in order to breed horror and misery in the world. Whether they are full of hatred or not, they seem to be without love, loveless, emptied of all love, the enemies of love. Where do those souls go, and are they coming back? Maybe you can buy a new one, but where, and with what currency? Penance? A life dedicated to good acts?

Am I being serious enough for you, Jackie? And then he sighed loudly with his own frustration, unhappy with his release of words, unhappy that he had even bothered to say them, shadows cast by shadows.

She did not shrink from his unfriendly monologue but instead seemed emboldened. It's me, she declared. I've lost my soul.

Now how in the fuck did you lose your soul? Tom said. This confession was absurd and bewildering and he did not want to hear it and he did not know what she expected of him and as far as he was concerned she was in every sense too young and too affluent to be having a genuine spiritual crisis, something that would pass out of her system like a kidney stone, naturally although not painlessly, in another year or two, and even then she would not be thirty.

I don't want to talk about it.

How could you have possibly lost your soul?

I am not going to talk about it.

Look, metaphorically, everybody experiences—

Fuck. Metaphors. Fuck. Metaphors. Her words brittle and sharp and clipped. I'm not talking about my imagination. This is not about the imagination.

What she said he didn't understand, yet when he tried again—We all have our demons—he sounded fatuous even to himself.

That's not what I'm talking about, she insisted.

What in the hell *are* you talking about then? What is this all about?

Believe what you want.

All right, Tom said. Look, I believe you.

I don't care, she blurted childishly, her hands fluttering upward, and Tom thought, *Oh, brother, ain't this entertaining!* and concentrated on the unimpeachable reality of the road.

There were trees now shading the highway, generous and lovely, and two-room clapboard houses side by side by side in the coolness beneath their canopy. The dusty shoulders thronged with pedestrians, bicyclists, children in school uniforms, wandering goats. Occasionally a boy would lean out toward the car, dangling a line strung colorful with reef fish or gripping a brace of spiny lobster by their antennae. Jackie did not remark upon this sudden oasis of life surrounding them and they rode through the village in the new silence of the contorted intimacy of her secret. They now knew each other less by knowing each other more—at least Tom felt so. The allure had drained from the tantalizing shell of her perfection, the robust clichés of her youth and unblemished femaleness, and he felt pointlessly manipulated. Their conversation had not been engaging, it had only been weird and dumb, and Jackie's alleged loss of soul and the evasiveness that followed, her refusal to yield as much as a particle of explanation to appease Tom's incredulity, seemed a variation on cock teasing, and he thought again, cruelly, glibly, *How many years are required of us on this earth before you can plunge yourself into serious moral complications and actually have a soul worth losing, or do we arrive afflicted by the original sin of our births?* His brain idled on such thoughts, the abandoned catechism of a Roman Catholic upbringing, as they accelerated away from the village and Jackie, to his astonishment, continued her inquiry.

Do you think he can help me? she said.

Who? Help you what?

This voodoo person. Help me get my soul back.

I don't know. Ask Gerard.

I am a Christian, Gerard protested from the backseat, and Tom doubted whether he had heard such nonsense between *blans* in his entire life.

But he's a priest, right? she persisted. A type of priest.

Yes, a *houngan*, Tom said again. The best ones were keepers of an encyclopedic knowledge of folk medicine, they were repositories of the history of their people, they single-mindedly preserved the songs and rituals that shaped the Haitian psyche, they practiced healing and they battled against darkness, as any truly religious person does. The worst ones trafficked in nightmares, when they weren't trafficking narcotics. I don't know if this *houngan* in Saint-Marc is a good one or a bad one, he said, and if she was determined to see a priest, why not start on more familiar ground and go speak to a Catholic priest, someone with whom she might at least share a culture and common language of faith.

They don't know anything, she said matter-of-factly. They're part of the whole fucked-up problem.

You've talked with them then? he asked, and received, in the peripheral frame of his glance, a thin-lipped frown and an angry toss of her head in reply. No answer. No comment. My spokesperson will have a statement for you in the morning. Jackie was beginning to rattle him. Lost your soul, eh? Tell me about it. Lost your soul? Listen, who cares? He tried to stop caring, that occupational habit, but for Tom caring was a need, however deformed, and he couldn't make it go away, he could only be a smart aleck about it.

They crested a bald hill at a speed that caused a moment's sensation of levitation inside the car, the threat of being sent airborne, and Tom swerved wildly to avoid a broken-down tap-tap parked half in the road, throwing Jackie into his side, their first touch, neither of them wearing seat belts. The lurching awoke Gerard out of his doze and Tom heard him clear his throat and spit out the window—the money was a godsend but Tom was fully aware that this day so far was beneath Gerard's dignity, chauffeured around like some missionary boy—and Jackie, straightening up in her seat, seemed utterly unconcerned with both Gerard's presence and Tom's recklessness. Below them, the white sand of a crescent, palm-lined beach beckoned like a postcard, and they descended to where the road hugged the coast between sheer mountains and turquoise sea, such an inviting sea, the moist brine of its air a balm to the senses.

Several more miles up the road they flew by the entrance to the Moulin Sur Mer and went on to Saint-Marc and through the decaying hive of its center to the northern outskirts, in search of the metaphysically puzzling spark of whateverness the young and beautiful and immensely troubled Jacqueline Scott had declared as her soul.

That air of unfathomability that intelligent young women cultivated—what was that about, that calculated? that subconscious? that natural? turn in the self toward the art of deception? I am more than you see, and what you see is flesh? Duality (body and soul) begets duplicity (self and self and self and self, and who could dare say which one was real)? In any case, Jackie's soul was gone.

Don't laugh, she said, and Tom didn't, but neither did he mourn or suffer, as one might, somewhere in one's own soul, at the loss of another.

CHAPTER FIVE

Above the city, high enough to give everything below its balconies the distance required to establish an appreciation for the disfigured beauty of Port-au-Prince, the Hotel Montana, flush from the windfall of the occupation, had renovated its terraces since Tom Harrington's last visit, adding brooklike fountains and goldfish ponds, an oval poolside bar, a marble-tiled dining area open to sweet mountain breezes. Bougainvillea cascaded over the ledges into the clouds that passed above another less generous world. The elevation was not simply a physical fact of the hotel but a bracing state of mind as well, a reassuring sensibility, suggesting that the Montana was a fortress and sanctuary, evidenced most bluntly by the shotgun-carrying guard manning its steel gate, a secure oasis of calm luxury and competent service, a symbolic outpost for the globalization that Americans and Europeans, in their smiling overconfidence, were convinced would be tomorrow's remedy for what ailed poor Haiti. The United Nations ran its office out of a ground-floor apartment; corporate businessmen met superbly dressed government ministers on the patio for lunch. Dignitaries stayed here, foreign-aid impresarios, mainstream correspondents intolerant of local color and unreliable phone lines, and now men like Conrad Dolan, private detectives on open-ended expense accounts. Scruffs lodged downtown at the infamous Oloffson, which Tom preferred, falling asleep to the disturbing lullaby of gunfire beyond the compound's walls, although more often than he would have liked the nature of his business had made him a guest at the Montana, where his status as a professional would inflate in proportion to the surroundings. At least at the Oloffson, Tom reasoned, you knew you were in Haiti, not hovering above it with all the answers.

He left his bags and passport with Dolan, who lingered at the front desk, waiting for an introduction to the manager, and took a stool at the small bar off the lobby, the only customer and a greedy one, silently imploring the bartender to hurry with his rum sour, then drinking it down in gulps and ordering another, his thoughts clotted with the once living Jackie. He wanted to feel more for her—the anguish of her mortality and the terrible fullness of grief—but it wasn't there; wasn't, at least, available, and what he did not want to feel was what he seemed most in danger of, an ugly spreading stain of guilty relief that she was as far out of his life as the dead could be. But she was dead and he could not tell himself he was glad about it.

In a trance of return and memory, he gazed out toward the lobby as Connie Dolan stepped into it, paying a bellboy to carry the luggage to their rooms and Dolan then removed his blazer, hooking it over a shoulder with two fingers, turning and planting his feet to the expanse of the room, fixing himself into place with a predatory scan but there was nothing, nobody to merit his attention—two middle-aged white women on a bamboo-print couch sharing a pot of tea—until through the archway of the bar he spotted Tom, who regarded his approach for the first time with a healthy measure of suspicion.

Dolan eased himself down on an adjacent stool and wanted to know what Tom was drinking and they had an end-of-a-long-day contretemps, a testy little argument about whether Barbancourt or Havana Club, Flor de Caña or some swill Dolan had tasted in Bogotá, was the best rum in the world, and then as if to spite Tom, he ordered a vodka tonic and offered the gratuitous opinion that rum was an inferior liquor regardless of where it was manufactured or by whom. They shared a minute of petulance, nothing to say to each other while they finished their round and then backed up and began a fresh start with another, watching mindlessly the vivid green limes in the bartender's black fingers, sliced and squeezed.

What was her name anyway?

Who? Dolan cocked his head just far enough to acknowledge Tom's drink, Tom's hand on his drink, if not Tom himself.

Dolan's cooling into dyspeptic impersonality, both puzzling and a growing irritation, seemed to serve final notice that their relationship would not enjoy the harmony Tom had expected, that far from being Dolan's guide and counsel, he felt himself being drawn into some vaguely macho competition, Dolan willing to challenge every trait of Tom's, every insignificant decision and idle preference, on the base scorecard of who's winning and therefore who's not. Tom told himself to try not to make too much of it, that Connie Dolan was a cop and he was just being a cop, a big nasty dog, hard-nosed, mistrustful, and untrustworthy, not his sudden best friend or any friend at all. Jackie's real name, Tom said with more sincerity. Back at the airport you said Jacqueline Scott was not her name.

Dolan shook his head and grinned, easing the tension between them. Dorothy Kovacevic.

You can't expect me to believe that.

Born and christened Dorothy Kovacevic.

Oh, Christ, that's awful, said Tom. That's like a brand name for old women in Chicago. Dorothys wore shapeless blue wool coats. Babushkas tied under hairy chins. Breath rank with stewed cabbage.

I guess she felt that way, too. Her family and friends called her Dottie. Mother was from the Midwest—Kansas, Missouri, one of those . . . that might explain Dorothy. Her father was Croatian, immigrated after the war, ended up in the diplomatic corps. But Dorothy Kovacevic isn't her real name, either. When she was still a toddler, the father legally changed the family name to Chambers. Has a nice all-American ring to it, I guess was the point.

Dottie fits. So, why Jacqueline Scott?

Why Renee Gardner? said Dolan, not looking to Tom for the answer, but explaining that Renee Gardner was the name she had used on her marriage license to his client.

Tom was flummoxed by what seemed to be a private and complicated joke—the surplus of names, this strange proliferation of make-believe. Dottie, Jackie, Renee . . . Get it?

61

No.

He knew more than one person who had cried *Time's up!* on whoever they happened to be at some stage in their lives, the season of their happiness shifting underneath them. A salesman who wanted to be a doctor, a mother who no longer wanted to be a mother, Tom himself a journalist who walked off the beat and out of the newsroom and went to law school, but none of them changed their names every time they changed their minds about who they were. Yet there was in him a general sense of women in constant passage from one identity to the next, starting with their own biology. Could a woman even recall a self without breasts and hips, or remember loving the firmness of those breasts and hips after the trial of childbirth or the malfunctioning furnace of menopause. Every woman he had ever known who woke up one day sick and tired of *something* in her life by lunchtime had lopped off her hair for the superficial relief of becoming someone else. The daily cosmetic painting and repainting of identity seemed to create a psychic disconnect between who a woman was and who she needed to be in her dissatisfaction with herself, and how, in the midst of all this flux and fabrication, the redirection and repackaging and metamorphosis, was a man supposed to hold a clear idea of who any woman, even the one closest to him, was? And yet to know a woman too well . . . was that a greater or lesser option? There were good answers, Tom knew, and answers that were very, very bad.

Who does that? he wanted Connie Dolan to tell him. Who needs so many aliases?

Dolan peered at him not unkindly and told Tom he had been around the block enough to know the answer—criminals, cons, crazy people. Actors, spies, strippers. Runaways. Refugees.

Harrington's first reaction was to resist these categories but he sighed and said, So which was she?

You tell me.

Maybe none of the above.

Maybe all of the above.

Come on, Tom snorted. A stripper?

I'm serious, my friend.

She was a lost soul.

What the fuck's a lost soul? That's everybody and nobody. We're all lost souls, are we not? Let me ask you this—do you believe in original sin?

No. What kind of question is that?

You'd be better off if you did. Because then the governing principle in your life would be the rising up, not the falling down. Repair and improvement. You see what I'm saying?

But Tom ignored Connie Dolan's barstool theology except to say that Jackie—he could not think of her as other than Jackie—traveled with an entourage of demons and so maybe, said Tom, taking quite a leap, her death was a mercy killing, an exorcism, maybe she welcomed her death, the fucked-up bitch—anyway, that was Tom's theory on his third round of rum sours and Dolan stared at Tom with a derisive smile bunched to one side of his mouth and said, What a load of shit, and went to his room to shower before dinner. Harrington moved to the poolside bar and watched the darkness seep down the mountain into the city and the lights, one by one, make it lovely.

I usually don't drink so much, Tom said, coming late to breakfast on the sunny terrace where Dolan, more casually dressed than the day before— polo shirt, blue jeans, running shoes; the meringue of his hair damply flattened—stabbed sections of papaya from a bowl of fruit salad.

I usually do, said Connie Dolan.

Monsieur, Harrington called to a waiter walking past. *Café, s'il vous plaît. Omelette avec jambon et fromage.* Turning back toward Dolan he asked, What's the plan?

They had not talked about a plan at dinner but instead Tom had pushed his *griot* around on his plate in a fog of rum and occasionally listened to Dolan's tales of his eight years with the Bureau in Puerto Rico, locking up miscreants and vermin, until Tom had abruptly held up his hand for him to stop and said he wanted to know how Dolan had discovered that he had an association with Jacqueline Scott. Dolan said he had read it in a report, and Tom, of course, did not take this information well—he could vaguely recollect shouting; oh, Christ, he wasn't shouting, was he?—at

Dolan, who made no attempt to calm him down but said sympathetically that there wasn't much there. Just two or three lines alleging that, in 1996, Thomas Harrington, a human rights lawyer under a UN-funded contract to the Haitian government, and the deceased (Dorothy, Jackie, Renee) had traveled together to the northwestern cantonment of Limbé and, in the vicinity of the village of Bois Caïman, had been involved in an altercation of unclear nature with followers of the alleged gang leader, Jacques Lecoeur. Tom was speechless and finally croaked, That's it? feeling a bolt of panic and then another bolt of paranoia shoot through the rum, and Dolan had eyed him curiously and said, That's it.

There was nothing mysterious or out of the ordinary about the existence of the report itself, which had been copied at the American embassy in Port-au-Prince and passed to Dolan by an old friend of his in the Miami office of the Bureau—PIs were dead in the water if they couldn't rely on old friends in law enforcement or the clerks of the court. The parties involved in the murder were American citizens and, after interviewing his client in Florida, the Bureau had sent a team of agents to Haiti to figure things out, but they botched it, said Dolan, they were dumber than pet rabbits, they didn't talk to the coroner, they didn't talk to the cops who took her body away that night, they never bothered to take a look at the car, and they resurfaced in Miami forty-eight hours later with much the same information with which they had started.

At that moment, though, Tom Harrington had no interest in who had killed Jackie or why. All he wanted to know was who was the source of this report and how had he ended up in it. Dolan said it wasn't anything to worry about. When the agent had interviewed his client in the federal lockup in Miami, his client had suggested that his wife had an enemy or two in Haiti, and that the Bureau should talk to a driver named Gerard Hurbon, and although the Feds did track down Gerard, who subsequently named Tom Harrington and mentioned Tom's trip up north with the girl, they never pursued the lead, according to Dolan, because they already had fallen in love with the scenario of least resistance to their limited capacity to operate in a place like Haiti. Here was a guy who had arranged a contract killing of his wife for what else but the money, and chosen Haiti as the venue for the crime because who was ever getting to the bottom of anything in Haiti.

The problem was, said Dolan, his client was adamant that the life insurance policy was *her* idea; maybe he was lying but how do you prove the assignation of an idea. So after all this, Dolan wanted to know from Tom if the girl had any enemies in Haiti, and Tom had sucked the dregs off the ice from his last of too many drinks and said, yeah, I guess she did, and went straight to bed, his mind not spinning but pickled in astonishment, trying to understand how Eville Burnette had escaped mention in this report, or if for some unimaginable reason Connie Dolan was keeping that card facedown on the table.

So here's what we'll do, said Dolan as Tom revived himself with bitter coffee. First and easiest, talk to the accountant, already arranged by Dolan, and on cue the Montana's obese accountant, Monsieur Frantz, walked duck-footed across the terrace, his white dress shirt like a broad sail on a barge of hips, the knot of a pink tie loosened around his enormous neck. *That's possibly the biggest man in Haiti,* Tom thought, marveling at not a drop of sweat on all that flesh while Tom himself had, by the simple act of eating, already soaked his collar and underarms, but the mystery ended when the two Americans stood to shake Monsieur Frantz's hand, which was as wet as a dishwasher's, and Tom absorbed this greater marvel, a fat man whose sweat glands seemed to reside solely in his palms. The accountant dragged a chair out several feet from the table and slowly lowered himself into it, closing his eyes for a moment and bowing his head in reverence, his face a dark moon of regret, and declared without prompting, Oh, poor Mr. Smith, Mr. Smith was a very nice man.

Who's Mr. Smith? said Tom.

Mr. Smith was the client.

Hold on, said Tom, under the impression that the client's name was Gardner.

Connie Dolan explained that Gardner was Renee's surname, not the client's.

Cute, said Tom, and asked if the client's name was really Mr. Smith.

No, said Dolan. His name is John Doe.

This is really very aggravating, said Tom. What's his name?

Don't ask, said Dolan. The Feds have a gag order on his name. They arraigned him under John Doe.

Why?

Ask them.

Is that legal?

You're the lawyer, my friend.

Tom leaned back from the table in exasperation and swung his head toward Monsieur Frantz, who had removed a cheap fountain pen from his shirt pocket to doodle tiny precise daisies on the paper placemat in front of him, the side of his hand leaving a crescent-shaped blotch of moisture behind. You must have seen his passport, Tom said. What was the name on his passport?

Monsieur Frantz stopped his pen and his eyes seemed to swell with mirth. Mr. Smith, he said and then proceeded to laugh good-naturedly in response to every question Connie Dolan asked him. In five minutes it was over and the accountant set sail back to the ledgers in his office behind the front desk, followed by Dolan, who intended to exchange dollars for gourdes, ignoring Tom's suggestion that they could get a better rate on the black market. Lingering over his fourth cup of coffee, Tom watched the two men go and thought, *What a waste of time*—Fed or retired Fed, what's the difference? Even if you stopped working for the government you didn't stop thinking like the government. He stood up from the table and bent down for the shoulder bag that went with him everywhere and happened to notice an addition to the garland of Monsieur Frantz's flowery doodles, two names emerging from the petals, Mr. Smith and Mr. Doe, overlaid with a bar of Xs, and a third name, Mr. Parmentier, underscored by a row of daisies given improbable happy faces. Tom walked out toward the car park weighted down by an all too familiar angst, crossing a line that he could feel strongly but failed to see, struggling to come to terms with what he was doing here in Haiti with Conrad Dolan, why he wasn't at this minute in a taxi on his way to the airport and home.

The truth was, Tom Harrington had no business in Haiti anymore—the graves of the massacred had been exhumed, the remains—some of them—identified. Tom himself had deposed scores of witnesses and relatives, the Ministry of Justice was a toddler seesawing between tantrums and nap time, and the Truth Commission had decayed on the vine of his idealism. The sly Mr. Dolan's ability to establish a close association between Jackie and Tom was pointless and poisonous. He had no answers for Dolan; there was nothing about his relationship with the girl he wanted to explain, nothing that needed to be explained for Dolan's purposes.

But it was not a mystery, after all, was it, he admitted to himself on his way through the foyer and back into the smash of light and the tightness in his brow of an approaching headache. He was staying because of the girl, because of the disease he had contracted, which was the girl, the only woman he had ever truly hated without first having truly loved. Even in her death he was without a cure for her, and he began to imagine that he might have always been this way.

CHAPTER SIX

Voodoo, *vodou*, the ancient religion of Guinée, was transported from Western Africa in the hearts of slaves to the New World, a rational theocratic view as theocratic views go, despite the ignorance with which it is commonly judged. *Vodou* is a pair of eyes that sees the divine in everything—trees, oceans, crossroads, rivers, mountains—and honors that divinity while striving to manipulate it as well. It assigns every force—love, hate, lust, death, health, success, failure—its guardian spirit, its *lwa,* saints by any other name, only unlike the saints the *lwas* could be summoned to take possession of mortal beings, to borrow for a few minutes or a few hours the flesh and the voice of a dancer or petitioner or priest, although the exact point or purpose of these earthly visitations was lost on Thomas Harrington. Every force begets a counterforce, and in that sense *vodou* was little different than the other religions of man, and like other men Haitians lived with the fears bred in and of darkness, and Haiti's darkness was the darkness of another, lost world that its people were not yet ready to let fall away, even as they diluted it with the powdered milk of Christianity.

Tom admired Haitian *vodou* because he admired Haitian culture, the drumming especially and splashy colors, the exuberant aggression of its rhythms, the beguiling cartoonishness of its imagination, the bawdy good nature and earthy metaphors of the language and, more seriously, the strict ethics and commonsense codes of the village, and he saw how the people found courage and a last reservoir of hope in *vodou*'s animistic rituals, but beyond this benevolence, he did not actually know much about it, nor did he much care to, given his fundamental indifference toward all religions and the swaddle of their illusions. A disciple of anything but the law he was not. He enjoyed *vodou*'s spectacle and creativity and had seen the naked pilgrims in the waterfalls of Eau Claire, had witnessed the sacrifice of an enormous bull, beheaded with several mighty swipes of a ceremonial sword, had watched women young and old ridden by the *lwas,* and had been the invited guest of Haiti's most famous *houngan,* the emperor of the Bizango Society, one of *vodou*'s five secret sects, at a celebration deep in the countryside, three neighborly days of drinking and tireless dancing and feasting and had come away with the impression that the event had much in common with the Knights of Columbus holiday weekends his parents had taken him to as a child.

Don't expect Hollywood, he told the girl, Jackie, as they parked in the dust alongside a bend in the road north of Saint-Marc. It's not like that.

But she either did not hear him or did not care and started up the footpath that traversed a dirt bank, her camera bag slung over her shoulder and the Nikon with the big lens in her left hand. Gerard, in a rare mood, said he preferred to remain with the car but Tom coaxed him to come along by promising to switch seats with him on the way back, and the two men climbed the bank after the girl, who had disappeared over the top. Flags tied to hand-cut poles stirred in the breeze above them. Tom asked Gerard the word for soul and Gerard said it was, *ang*—angel.

Why are you here with this business? Gerard grumbled.

When have I heard you complain about any business? Tom asked.

Houngan business is different.

The temple compound was modest, built of mud and wattle in the bare packed dirt on the small plateau above the bank, its three adjoining sections forming an open courtyard where Jackie stood, surveying without reaction the fabulous murals painted on the *hounfour*'s walls: St. George slaying a dragon from atop his white horse; the braided serpents of Dumballah, creator of the universe; the three-horned Bosou, the *lwa* of crops and fecundity; and the skull-faced Lord Baron in top hat and tails, the master of the graveyard and the implicit mascot of Tom and the various teams of forensic anthropologists he had brought to the island and supervised during the occupation. The paintings, at least those with human figures, were strikingly Byzantine, and Tom had expected he and Gerard would have to wait while Jackie photographed the images but she never raised her camera, not once all day had she raised it, and he had begun to wonder about her lack of motivation. He could not remember having met a photographer for whom Haiti had been anything but an endless unwrapping of violent and beautiful gifts. Yet as he came up next to her he realized she wasn't looking but listening and when he stopped walking he heard it as well, the chanting of a single voice, deep and sonorous but subdued and not close by, coming from somewhere inside the compound.

Where do we go in? said Jackie.

Each of the three rectangular wings of the *hounfour* had its own wooden door but only the central entrance was not chained and Tom opened it and looked into the darkness beyond at the chamber's barrenness and its smoke-blackened beams, Jackie peering over his shoulder, the sudden current of her breath in his ear. On the center post a leather bullwhip hung from a nail and in the dimness along the far wall there were several large ax-hewn drums. She wanted to know what this space was and he told her it was the main ceremonial peristyle, although it seemed no more suited for ceremony than a livestock pen. The walls muted the chanting, its source was elsewhere, and they backed away from the door.

Gerard stepped out from around the corner at the front of the courtyard and called for them to come his way and they circled behind the building toward the chanting, following him to what appeared at first to be a narrow wattle cook shed attached along its length to the rear of the compound, its outer walls like coarse cloth woven from thin branches, its roof a single section of rusted tin, a crooked door frame hung with a soiled curtain of moss-green satin.

He is here, said Gerard, pointing toward the curtain, and Harrington knew on this occasion he could depend on Gerard for little more than that.

Bonjour, Tom said, pulling the curtain aside, his vision glancing off the bright daffodil yellow of a woman's skirt and across a dark row of faces, adjusting to the dappled shadows. Something burned sweetly in the air, an incense of cedar and perhaps herbs. He was prepared for the awkwardness of his interruption but the people crowded inside the little shed—five, on old metal folding chairs along the inner wall and, at the far end facing the doorway, a sixth; the chanting *houngan* on his humble throne, a wooden chair elevated on dusty planks in front of an altar of burning candles and votives and trashy fetishes—hardly took notice of him. The priest acknowledged him with an accepting nod and after a moment gestured with his left hand toward the chair nearest him and the man who occupied it stood up and wedged himself into the remaining space in the corner.

This generosity could not be refused and Tom left Gerard and the girl behind him in the doorway, easing forward from the curtain, stepping around a calabash bowl on the ground with something filthy in it to the seat, which was missing its back support. He sat quietly with a bow toward the priest and the man he had displaced. Then, without a word, Jackie handed her bag and camera to Gerard and stunned Tom by slipping forward onto his lap, the bones of her pelvis rolling into his thighs. His body tightened with the shock of her weight and the fruity scent of her hair in his face and he tilted his chest away from her until his back was glued against the cracked mud wall and he could feel himself sweating into it. Not knowing what to do with his arms he let them hang down toward the dirt floor and struggled to regain his senses.

He settled into the cadence of the *houngan*'s low voice, a stream of spoken music that began to cohere as Tom concentrated on the words, his mind slowing into Kreyol, and he and Jackie stared freely at the man, Tom rapt, the girl curious but unimpressed. Here in the countryside there was nothing remarkable about the *houngan*'s appearance: he wore chestnut-brown field pants tied at the waist by a length of hemp rope, the toes of his wide bare feet as gnarled as roots; a clean white short-sleeved shirt with the tails neatly tucked, and a gold-banded wristwatch, the one overt symbol of his success in life. His face was the face of an ordinary man, certainly not brutish; his sweaty cheekbones and brow glinting and striped with blades of sunlight stabbed through the weave of the walls. He sat erect and looked straight ahead with clear eyes—no boogeyman droop or blear to them at all—that concentrated on a phantom presence somewhere in the air before him. Without meeting Tom's eyes, Jackie leaned her head back and turned her face as though she might kiss him and he unconsciously held his breath while she brought her mouth to his ear. Her movement disrupted the balance of their two bodies perched together and he put a hand on her shoulder to steady her.

What's this guy doing? she whispered and turned again so her own ear was at his mouth, his lips accidentally brushing its soft fold, but Tom drew back and could not speak. He was trying to understand all the words and to hold very still because the friction of every infinitesimal shift of her hips was having its effect on him and the language was difficult to comprehend without Gerard's assistance.

As he listened, though, he understood enough to become amazed— they had walked in on an exorcism. The priest was addressing a *djab*, demanding that the demon leave but leave what or whom Tom couldn't make out, and for this sacred task the *houngan* had summoned a *lwa* for assistance, Erzulie Mary, but apparently she had not yet chosen to attend or was for some reason resisting his entreaty. The *houngan* seemed to grow impatient with the spirit, his invocation more insistent and coaxing. His arm dropped to the floor beside his throne and he raised a bottle of *clairin* in the air and spilled an offering into the dirt below his platform and then for the first time paused in his chanting to take a gulp from the bottle himself and then the chanting resumed with greater passion. Jackie wiggled in his lap and Tom, who had all but forgotten the others in the shed, was startled into a broader awareness as people began to moan like souls in purgatory.

He bobbed his head around Jackie's and looked to his left, to the four throwaway chairs and their human cargo. There was furtiveness in the heavy-lidded eyes of the first three—an old farmer in his straw hat and a middle-aged woman and a younger one—but it was the woman in the fourth chair, the chair nearest the doorway, that transfixed him. She wore a housedress with its top half pulled down to her waist and there she sat, her emaciated torso naked and streaming glittering feverish rivulets of sweat across the washboard of her ribs, her bare breasts haggish and surreal, withered to triangular flaps and repulsive, and yet even the agony of her face could not mask the youth that refused to leave it—Tom guessed thirty, which might well mean twenty; it was impossible to tell anyone's age in Haiti—and her hair was pulled into girlish braids on each side of her head. Clearly the woman was ill and, unlike her companions who occasionally emitted piteous cries, she herself was seized by panting and her eyes seemed to float unanchored in the pooled expanse of their sockets.

Yet even as he registered the overwhelming nature of the woman's suffering he turned away and again forgot her, his attention reclaimed by the heels of the *houngan's* pink palms now booming on the goatskin head of a large drum clasped between his knees, the chant rising to such a pitch of fervor that his eyes bulged and flecks of spittle clung to his lips. In this squall of primal rhythm that sought to wake up the gods, the drum made Jackie squirm, the squirm's inevitable creation a mad pulse between his legs, and as he hardened beneath her and the drum roared its challenge to the spirits the squirm modulated into a subtle bounce, a straining thrust downward and release upward in the tense muscles of her buttocks. There was a scolding voice in his head —*Hey. Please. Stop this*—but he felt his resistance weakening, felt the need to reach around and cup her breasts with each hand, felt his mind draining toward blankness and his flesh jolted into trembling reflex and he felt himself succumb to the deliciously stuporous possibility of just shoving himself straight up into the center of her where he would explode.

Her waist twisted again and she readjusted her hips atop his left thigh but still exerted the faint invisible clutch of press and release that was like a vibrational echo from the drums into his aching groin, her head rotating her profile into his line of vision, on her face the look of cool dispassionate attention she directed at the priest, the entirely credible deception of that gaze, the alert observer, revealing not the slightest clue of sensuality or the unbearable desire of the man throbbing beneath her. He looked away down the row at the other faces, compressed and disfigured by the effort of propitiation, until at the end of the line he looked again at the woman in the daffodil dress, her lips pulled and turned so tight by disease or hunger that despite her terror she was already grinning like a dessicated corpse.

Curiosity had gotten the better of Gerard, or perhaps he understood that the ceremony was about to end, for he came to stand in the chapel's doorway, half-draped by the curtain and scowling. And then the drumming stopped and soon the chanting as well, their urgency replaced by torpid silence, and Jackie relaxed. In only seconds, though, a new tension swept in and flared along the connection between the ill woman and the *houngan*, who stared at her naked swaying torso with doleful resignation until the other women in the chapel began to softly weep and the farmer and the man standing in the corner choked back sobs. The *houngan* lifted the drum from between the vise of his legs and set it aside with a thud of finality, done, finished, his abandonment of the woman in the daffodil dress as sharply deliberate as cracking a stick over his knee, and he turned with studied cordiality to the next order of business, looking past Jackie to Tom.

You have come to see me? he asked in Kreyol.

Oui.

You are welcome here. Please tell me what you want.

Jesus Christ! Tom yelped.

Without a sound the sick woman had come hurling out of her chair and pitched facedown in the dirt at their feet, vomiting a cloudy ocher liquid that splashed across the toes of his boots and the cuffs of his pants but missed Jackie, who jerked her legs up just in time. His instinct to somehow help was immediate but just as quickly blunted by the confusing response of everyone else, the *houngan* calm and unconcerned, not looking down at the woman but still at Tom, chin up and expectant, waiting to hear his response. One by one the other Haitians snapped out of their gloom to collect themselves and glide, noiseless and wraithlike, through the curtain, their communal obligation to the prostrate woman apparently terminated. Just as puzzling was Jackie, who scooted off Tom's lap onto an empty chair, crossed her legs impatiently, and leaned forward, oblivious to the woman on the ground, her crisis a slight annoyance at best, looking back and forth between Tom and the *houngan*, anxious for them to get on with it.

Tom's eyes were fastened on the woman's back, her shoulder blades like embryonic wings ready to burst through her black skin. He was going to reach down and check her pulse when the *houngan* repeated his question and Tom asked, without thinking, *What is a soul?* and the priest answered this and every question without hesitation.

That in you which belongs to God.

Can you lose your soul?

No, *monsieur*. It can be stolen by the devil.

It can only be stolen?

Oui, monsieur.

You can't misplace it?

Oui, monsieur, you can misplace it.

How?

What followed was an elaborate but often cryptic explanation about big and little angels—*gros bon ang* and *ti bon ang*—celestial checks and balances, the cosmic vulnerability of humans when they fall asleep, and an unintelligible caveat about bad deeds—literally, the mistakes of man—in a jumble of Kreyol. He was relieved to find Gerard still there, posted like a sentry in the doorway, but his translation was even less coherent than Tom's own grasp of what was spilling out of the *houngan*.

What are you guys talking about? said Jackie. She seemed peevish and edgy.

Hold on, Tom said to her, turning back to the priest to make clear the nature of the problem. This woman says she lost her soul. She wants to know if you can help her get it back.

The *houngan* looked away from the white man and considered Jackie for the first time with more than courtesy, examining her from head to toe while she stared back at him impassively. He kept his searching eyes on her even as he asked Tom how she had misplaced her soul, and Tom, eager for the answer himself, relayed the question to Jackie but she shook her head with an almost imperceptible flash of defiance and said it wasn't important. Looking at her, trying his best to comprehend her, Tom realized that should he ever mention it, she would never acknowledge what had just happened between them, the secret conversation of their flesh; she would cluck her tongue and say he had quite a horny little imagination, didn't he?

Can he help me or not? she insisted, her eyes locked with the *houngan*'s, who did not wait for the English to be translated but answered, *Oui*, and Tom found himself brokering an unreal negotiation. For ten dollars, the *houngan* said, he would pray to the gods for her protection.

What will that do? Jackie asked, and the *houngan* admitted, Not much. To do more, he said, would require an offering to the *lwas* to merit their full attention. Tom asked for further specifics before he translated and the *houngan* allowed that he could perform a small offering for fifty dollars and a bigger offering for much more. How much more? Tom asked him. A goat for a hundred dollars, a bull for five hundred dollars. If he sacrificed a bull for the woman, the priest said, the *lwas* would be very happy and certainly he could persuade one of them to go locate the woman's soul and return it to her. When Tom turned half-around and began to explain this to Jackie, he was taken aback by the smirk on her face and her unlikely self-assurance.

Look, he's not being unreasonable, Tom said, exasperated. The animals cost money. This is how he makes his living. This is the only way he knows how to help you. And, after a sullen pause, This is what you wanted.

Jackie guffawed. Fifty dollars to kill a chicken! That's bullshit.

He had, at Jackie's bidding and despite his common sense, taken her seriously up to this point and for a moment he thought the issue making her balk might not be the bargaining price as much as her own poverty and he foolishly offered to lend her the money.

I'm not giving this man fifty dollars. Don't be ridiculous.

Suit yourself, he said indifferently although he struggled to contain his anger and ignore her arch tone, the juvenile play of contempt across her lips. Suddenly she seemed to him traitorous and venal and crass and he felt duped by this woman, her frivolous seduction of his inclination to be sincere and useful. But there was a ceiling to his ability to care, wasn't there? A ceiling to anyone's ability to care, unless you were deranged. It's your soul, he told her. I would think that it's worth at least fifty dollars.

I have news for you, she said. It's not.

All right, then it's time to end this game.

It's not a game.

Tell me what you want to call it then, he said to her back as she jumped to her feet and ducked past Gerard through the curtain. And honestly, what was he supposed to think about her grinding her lovely ass into his cock like that? How excruciatingly intolerable to think she might one day tell this story at a dinner party back in the States and set the table howling with laughter.

Don't laugh, she had pleaded with Tom in the car, and he had no doubt now that to laugh would be impossible. He felt at a loss to even imagine what her motive might have been for soliciting his help to come here. Her bratty fickleness, skating from one impulse to another, preempted any thought of motives—motives seemed simply beyond her. But what's a soul worth after all? Not a goddamn cent, not one gourde, and if you're in hell kicking around with a hapless lot of humanitarians and do-gooders, even less.

The sheer farce of it all.

He felt a rash of guilt heat his face as he glanced at the woman on the ground, shocked by his inability to see her as anything but an inanimate object, and then he refocused on the *houngan* to be done with the protocol of their visit, offering an awkward explanation of his friend's wish to think things over before she made a decision. Perhaps he would return with her another day, he lied, and the *houngan* said *Bon,* but send word so the animal could be purchased and made ready. Tom extended his hand and the *houngan* shook it with limp goodwill.

What is your name, monsieur?

Bòkò St. Jean.

Harrington came to his feet in a slow rise, absently patting his pocket to give the priest a few dollars for his time but as he stood he felt himself pushing up through a heavy cloud of dread and he understood what he knew he should have realized earlier, that, distracted by Jackie posting in his lap, something was terribly wrong, that the exorcism had not been a success, that the woman half-stripped of her dress hadn't simply lost consciousness from the strain of the ritual. Wearily, he bent his knees and lowered himself next to her body, wrapping his fingers under the wrist of her flattened hand, a hand unadorned by the priceless rings of friendship or love, unable to find a pulse. Her face was smashed straight down in the dirt, her mouth opened as if she were eating it, and beyond her head the bowl he did not want to look into but did, the calabash shell filled with liquid as black and viscous as crankcase oil, floating with blackened sprigs of herbs and ghostly tissues of flesh and grayish globs of unidentifiable organs, unspeakably detestable and lurid as death itself.

He stood up and was going to say something useless about an ambulance or a doctor but the *houngan* waved a hand to tell him not to worry.

She is ours, said Bòkò St. Jean. We will attend to her, and Tom gave him money so that the woman might have the otherwise unattainable dignity of a pinewood coffin.

He walked blinking back into the sunlight, past Gerard and Jackie who followed him around to the front of the compound, across the shadeless scorch of the courtyard, down the steep bank to the road and the roasting car. He opened all the doors to let the heat out and handed the keys to Gerard and after a minute they climbed in and Gerard made a U-turn and they drove south.

I could use something cold to drink, said Jackie.

Tom sighed heavily in the backseat and announced that the woman in the daffodil dress had died. Jackie looked over her shoulder at him, inscrutable, without any visible emotion or conciliatory gesture, not the faintest suggestion of either regret or compassion, as if she had lived a life already overpopulated by dying women under her feet.

What did she have? AIDS?

I don't know.

He became fixated, though, on the intense color of her irises, robin's egg blue, and she returned his gaze, holding it until it seemed to Tom they both knew and understood each other much too well and had formed a shameless bond that he couldn't conceive as being anything other than dark and fiery and heartless. She turned away to look ahead out the windshield and he bowed his head in thoughtless reverie, noticing for the first time the dried oval patch on his olive-drab pants, the left leg, mid-thigh, where she had melted into him, the stain mocking the pretense of his altruism. He ran his fingernail along it, exploring the slightly starched texture of the patch, and rode to Saint-Marc in a glassy state of distress, confounded by the outrage and exhilaration of her audacity. *She's dangerous,* he thought, which was not a particularly differentiating trait in Haiti, nor an isolating condition, and he knew it was not unthinkable or wholly impossible that he might find himself, in more appropriate surroundings, enjoying this woman's brand of trouble.

Gerard slowed down as they entered the ruined streets of Saint-Marc and Jackie, sweet-voiced, reminded him that she was dying of thirst.

CHAPTER SEVEN

He speaks English, Tom Harrington said. You won't need me.

Harrington would not go into the morgue with Dolan but waited outside near the rental car, ignoring a promise to his wife by smoking a cigarette. Of all the vile horrors to which he had willingly exposed himself, the morgue in downtown Port-au-Prince was in some respects the most ghastly, the one that produced in him the most unbalanced existential sense of spiraling vertigo, and he had no wish to have his shoes defiled by the fulsome ooze channeling its concrete floor, or stare in cold despair at the boxcar-sized room where the bloated corpses of infants and children were stacked like cordwood, waiting for the loan of a dump truck from Public Works to be hauled to the swamps of Tintayen.

He knew the coroner, Monsieur Laurent, well, knew he was at heart a good man, educated and courtly and gentle, but Laurent had been over-supplied by his country's harvest of death, with no resources to manage his vocation with competence or delicacy, the excess rotting out of sight until its eventual disposal. Cause of death? Why ask, why bother? To understand what? To satisfy whom? Does God ask such questions of the dead? What most disturbed Tom was the violation of the principle, his conviction that death presented an obligation to the living to restore value to lives without overt value, to declare at last to the society that which the society never seemed able to acknowledge—here is a human being, let us show respect.

Dignity first and then, perhaps, justice, but here at the morgue both were rebuffed by crude practicalities.

He watched a swarm of skinny, bare-chested boys weaving through traffic kicking a scuffed soccer ball, a gift from the American soldiers who had tossed out hundreds from their passing convoys in the final months of the occupation. By the time his interest had turned to a pair of toiling stevedores up from the wharves, enslaved to a wooden pushcart stacked overhead with bags of cement, Conrad Dolan was emerging from the stinking depths of the morgue, his face red and splotchy and his eyes hardened, wiping his mouth with a bandanna pulled from the hip pocket of his jeans. He walked past Tom to the SUV and got in and waited for Tom to start it up and crawl back into traffic, headed for the American Embassy, farther downtown toward the port.

A few blocks on, Dolan, straightening the slump of his back and shoulders, released a long groaning sigh and blew his nose into the bandanna with enough force to clear his senses. Son of a bitch, Dolan rasped. If anything happens to me down here, burn my body in the friggin' streets before you let anybody put me in there.

Tom asked if Monsieur Laurent had been able to tell him anything new about Jackie's death and Dolan said, *Yeah, yeah,* as if whatever he had learned inside the morgue amounted to a vast annoyance. This guy, this coroner, never properly examined the body, said Dolan. Laurent's name was on the death certificate under the inexact description of the cause—*gunshot to right side of head*—with no reference to forensic particulars, powder burns or caliber or exit wound or time of death. When asked to explain himself, Dr. Laurent had told Dolan that he had done no more and no less than what had been required of him by the laws of Haiti and by the Americans. When the coroner had arrived at the morgue that morning several weeks ago, a dark blue embassy van was parked by the door; apparently it had retrieved the body of the woman during the night and brought her down from the police station in Saint-Marc's.

As the doctor had approached the van, its front doors opened and two white men dressed in coats and ties stepped out to meet Laurent, waving embassy identification badges and handing him four copies of the Republic of Haiti's Certificate of Death, each form completed except for his signature. The men had apologized for being in a hurry—a military flight was waiting at the airport to receive the body and deliver the remains of Renee Gardner back to the States. If you don't mind just signing each copy, one of the men said, and Laurent had replied, *Mais, oui,* Of course, but if the gentlemen didn't mind, he preferred not to sign without first viewing the deceased, it was his duty, and the men seemed to expect this request and slid open the side door to the van and there inside was a squared aluminum casket. One of the men unbuckled the clasps to its lid; the other man held the woman's passport in Laurent's face, open to her picture. The first man raised the lid of the coffin to a forty-five-degree angle and the coroner stepped forward. *Bon,* he said after a minute, and signed the papers.

Dolan had asked the coroner if he had noticed anything unusual about the body, something he might remember of its condition. Laurent had said no. Anything make an impression on you, Dolan asked. No . . . , said Laurent elliptically, and then, after thinking about it, said, Yes. Poor child, no one had troubled to wash the blood from her, she was a terrible mess. And I remember I was filled with shame, Laurent continued, because she was a *blan* and her feet were bare, someone must have stolen her shoes. Unfortunately, this is not so unusual. We take from the fallen, like soldiers on a battlefield.

The traffic unclogged and slowly began to move again and he put the car in gear and drove toward the embassy, Tom's thoughts looping back toward a single bit of information he was unsure how to interpret. Jackie's body had been returned to the States on a military flight and he wondered why, and if such an arrangement was common. Apparently Dolan was thinking the same thing.

That kid got special treatment, said Dolan.

The military flight. The dispatch of a van. As a special agent working out of the Bureau's office in San Juan, Connie Dolan had become familiar with standard procedure for dealing with American citizens murdered throughout the Caribbean. A consulate would notify the victim's family, help them make the necessary arrangements with a local funeral home, shepherd the paperwork through the bureaucracies, provide flight schedules for whatever U.S. carriers serviced the island, and, if no family member showed up to accompany the body home, be there at the airport to oversee the transfer of the coffin from hearse to cargo hold and sign off on the documentation. The process took days or weeks, depending on whether the crime was a political asset, a liability, or a wash for an existing regime and its opposition—and every government saw opportunity in even the accidental death of an American on its soil, ransoming the body back to the bereaved family for many thousands of dollars.

What would you like to bet, said Dolan, that your lady friend was pulling a paycheck from the U.S. government?

Harrington had half-expected to hear this about Jackie because no other explanation of her behavior made much sense. She was working for the Feds then? That's what you're saying? he said neutrally. Dolan clicked his tongue in exasperation and Tom, with a sidelong glance, felt the reproach of his flinty look.

Feds who? said Dolan, caustic, bristly. I can't say yes and I can't say no. Sometimes you can be in it and not be in it at the same time, if you get my drift, or you can be in a part of it that's at war with another part and go missing in action. The goddamn thing only looks monolithic from the outside. Inside, it's all tribes in the jungle, my friend.

At the fortresslike entrance to the embassy, they slid their passports through the slot in the bulletproof glass to the marine on duty and endured the menace of his scrutiny. Dolan repeated the name of the deputy chief of mission, the hour of their appointment, then watched as the guard phoned upstairs and wrote their names in the log and finally buzzed them through the doors into the relief of the air-conditioned building. They were greeted by the garish red smile of a birdlike woman in heels, blouse, and a pencil skirt whose silent mistrust was reciprocal and reminded Tom of why he disliked coming here, crossing the street of a sovereign nation to enter a parallel universe of power to which you always came a beggar, bowing to its vanity. Without bothering to identify herself, she invited Dolan to have a seat in the reception area and, before Dolan could protest, whisked Tom down the hall and up a set of stairs to the DCM's office, past a formidable-looking secretary, knocked on the door of the inner sanctum as she swung it open and chirped as she retreated, There you are.

The deputy chief of mission, tall without appearing athletic, his narrow face beaming with the pride of reason, rose from behind his desk to shake Tom Harrington's hand and congratulate the human rights advocate on his work, Harrington's tenacious efforts to achieve what the DCM's predecessor had done everything in his power to prevent him from achieving. Tom nodded cautiously, recalling the erstwhile DCM's shrewd joviality and aversion to eye contact. The predecessor, an African-American with the unfortunate name of Lynch, a former basketball star and student activist at a midwestern state university, had, during the early days of the occupation promised Harrington, in the name of the ambassador and the president, all aid and assistance at his disposal in support of the establishment of a Commission of Truth and Justice for the newly democratic republic. And instead, in the passing months, the embassy seemed more inclined to act as pimps for the ancien régime, good at providing the ringleaders with golden parachutes, silk lifejackets, Washington's attitude—let's just forget it and move on—surely not conducive to righting wrongs but to burying them. His final meeting with Lynch had taken place two days after his disastrous trip up north with Jackie Scott and was attended by the embassy's general counsel, Haiti's interim Minister of Justice, a senile and imperious member of the high court retired by the tyrants, and a staff member from the National Security Council.

Harrington had listened to the counsel's bland tone informing him of the embassy's position on the Commission and why it was never likely to be seated: not in the interest of the common good, no absolute necessity, the road to the future must not detour into the past, and so on. After a sentence of flowery boilerplate praise for Tom's service to the republic, the minister consented to this betrayal and doddered from the room. Lynch, who had seemed indifferent to the proceeding, his pensive gaze directed out the office window toward the glare of the late morning, had turned toward Tom with an insipid half-smile and said this democracy thing was still playing out down here and let's not be so hasty as to give anyone an advantage. The general counsel nodded glumly and declared we don't like the old guys, but we don't much like the new guys, either. Who do you like? Tom had asked. We're constantly working that, said Lynch. Still in diapers, said the general counsel. The unborn are looking pretty good too. The staff member from the NSC, a black, not from Arkansas like Lynch but from Massachusetts, educated at Haverford and Georgetown, tipped forward in his chair and confided in Harrington, *You can't get around the fact that they're crazy niggers.* Everyone stunned into silence. The general counsel frowned. Lynch chuckled through a grimace and threw out his hands as if to say, There you have it. *Face it,* Tom had said, bellicose, standing up, *you're a fucking disgrace.*

We appreciate all you've done, said Lynch, rising to his feet as well to walk Tom to the door. It's had a great impact on our ability to scout the players, keep score, leverage out some of the bad guys who should never be given the ball.

Lynch had opened the door for him and followed Tom out of the office, lowering his voice to say he had heard about Tom's adventure up north and was pleased to learn that Tom—good old Tom, the Great American Tom Harrington—knew how to take care of himself. Lynch had extended his hand, smiling, exaggerating the whispered enunciation of his words, as if he were a singing messenger.

Unless you really dig it down here in the pit, bro, pack your bags and go home.

Sleeves rolled up, tie loosened, flanked by the Stars and Stripes, the new deputy chief of mission sat at his desk beneath a row of framed photographs—autographed portraits of the president of the United States and the secretary of state, an unsigned portrait of the president of Haiti, pictures of the DCM shaking hands with Nelson Mandela, eyeball to eyeball with Fidel Castro, sharing a joke with Slobodan Milosevic, a much younger, mustachioed DCM among a trio of envoys meeting the Shah of Iran. Tom saw in him the perfected embodiment of the diplomatic caste: an attentive, inquisitive smile, intellectually fit, at least for the fluid conversation of receptions and dinner parties, among people cozy within their own ranks but otherwise aloof, supernaturally calm and thus naturally and perhaps even unconsciously brave, displeased by confrontation, self-assured in the blithe arrogance of their optimism, prepared to push their mothers off a cliff for the sake of almighty policy.

I love Miami, said the DCM, and they pretended to relax into a chatty dialogue about favorite restaurants in South Beach and Coral Gables. But as Tom began to feel courted by the official, his own half of the conversation became more guarded and at the first lull he broke the pretense of their ease.

Why am I here?

Sorry? said the DCM, ostentatious in his puzzlement. You made an appointment.

A private investigator by the name of Conrad Dolan made the appointment and you have him on ice down in the lobby.

Ah, Connie Dolan, said the DCM. His eyes brightened and he raised his arms and leaned back into the cushion of his chair, locking his fingers behind his head.

You know him? asked Harrington, trying not to show his surprise. Without quite answering, the DCM lifted his eyebrows in coy encouragement. Then you probably also know he's working a case, a homicide. An American, a woman.

Yes, he is, isn't he? the DCM said with strange enthusiasm and sat forward again, folding his large hands together on the desk. Which returns us to the interesting question you yourself asked—Why are *you* here? Your legal and investigative skills are better applied to noble projects. Causes, crusades. You're quite a legend here in this building, an inspiration. The march you led with the bishop of Gonaïves—my God, Tom, you're lucky to be alive. And I want you to know that we are doing everything within the limits of our power to restore the rule of law here, and when that day comes, the work you've done will serve as the foundation to round up all the people guilty of gross human rights violations and other such crimes and prosecute them in a credible manner. The day is coming. You have my word on that, Tom. But my point is this—What does the tragic murder of this woman have to do with you?

Nothing, said Harrington, which was as true as if he had answered, *everything*. Dolan asked if I could help him out.

And you said yes. That's very interesting, said the DCM absently, looking at his wristwatch and then pressing a button on his intercom to tell his secretary if so-and-so had arrived, send him in, and in he came, immediately recognizable to Harrington as an abstract ideal packaged in human form and erected in a moral landscape of bold silhouettes. Charcoal business suit, silver necktie, shoes like gleaming cubes of obsidian. The fraternal Ivy League thuggishness of his sharply handsome face. Clean-shaven, youthful despite graying temples, well-tended, and in his goading eyes the steel of fierce discipline— Tom could imagine him in a Dartmouth sweatshirt, jogging during his lunch hour on the mall in Washington. When a person was so dramatically successful at inhabiting his own stereotype, it seemed to Tom that that person was in fact endowed by a pure exoticism, an individuality like a Bengal tiger.

Let me guess, said Tom, rising to offer his hand. Department of Justice.

Albert Neff, he said, introducing himself with the thin smile of hubris and an unexpectedly flaccid grip, as if he found such things as manners and etiquette to be a delay of game. I have colleagues who speak well of you, Neff said as he lowered himself onto a leather couch to the side of the DCM's desk, the accordion file he had carried in with him resting on his knees. Harrington acknowledged the compliment and recited the names of several people he had coordinated with at Justice until Neff interrupted him. And I have colleagues who think you're a sanctimonious prick.

Fair enough, said Harrington, his face reddening, and sat back down warmed by the splash of animosity into his veins. Men like Neff didn't just represent the system to him, they were the system, and in their proximity he could feel the inescapable gravity of the state tugging at his viscera, and he instinctively tugged back. For your own verification, Tom said, his riposte delivered with a frozen smile, would you like to have a little suck? Just to be sure? You're familiar with the taste of sanctimony, I take it. We're talking pricks here, right?

Fellas, said the DCM, uselessly.

Have you known Mr. Dolan very long, counselor? Albert Neff asked.

I want to know why you're asking me that.

Neff retrieved a black-and-white photograph from the file and passed it to Harrington. Do you know these two men?

Dolan, said Tom, looking at an image of the grandfatherly Irishman bellied up to a bar, a bartender pouring a martini from a shaker. Who's the other guy?

Mr. Dolan's client.

Parmentier?

No comment, counselor.

All right, gentlemen, said Harrington. If it hasn't yet dawned on you that I have nothing to give you, it's just become clear to me that the same would not be true for you.

In confidence, said the DCM. Mr. Dolan has some very interesting friends.

Mr. Dolan's client murdered his wife, said Neff.

Maybe so, said Tom, but how do you know that?

Mr. Dolan's client killed his wife, Neff emphasized. What complicates that fact, and troubles us, is that Mr. Dolan's client was also Special Agent Dolan's informant during a sting operation the Bureau ran in Tampa before Dolan retired.

I see, said Harrington calmly, but then couldn't stop himself from blurting out, No shit?

No shit, counselor. Under the protection of Special Agent Dolan, Mr. Dolan's client was implicated in an extravagant variety of crimes, including homicide, for which he was arrested but never indicted.

Tom Harrington tried to keep his head clear from the cloud he felt pressing in. What's Dolan doing in Haiti?

The same old, same old—trying to save his ass. Once you start protecting a fuckhead like his client, you're married for life.

And what was his client doing in Haiti?

The DCM chose to answer. Selling forged passports to some very interesting people. That's what interested us most, but he was also involved in a number of business deals that the US government, unlike our Haitian friends, did not look upon with favor.

Okay, said Tom. Got it. And what about the girl, Renee Gardner?

Not her real name. Cokehead, bimbo, gold digger, said Albert Neff.

Are you telling me she wasn't working for the government?

Are you suggesting she was? Neff asked, and he exchanged a sidelong glance with the DCM, who returned his questioning look without a hint of evasion and shrugged.

Not to my knowledge, said the DCM, and Mr. Neff removed a notepad and fountain pen from the inside pocket of his suit jacket and jotted a few words. Uh, hold on, the DCM thought for a moment. I seem to recall someone mentioning she was on the DEA's rat list. He paused, looked down at the surface of his desk, looked up, less sure of himself. No, actually, I think I'm confusing her with someone else.

If that's true, said Harrington, why was her body shipped out within less than twelve hours of her death, on a military flight? And why an embassy van to retrieve the corpse?

Right, said the DCM, looking nonplussed, these details are unusual, but the flight was on the up-and-up, nothing irregular there, and the ambassador accepts responsibility for any embarrassment that might possibly result from these details.

I'm not clear about what you're saying.

Favoritism, taxpayer expense, that sort of thing.

I still don't get it, said Harrington.

You wouldn't, unless you knew who the victim's father was, said the DCM. One of our own at State, an undersecretary. A *gwos neg*, so to speak, he smiled, using the Kreyol phrase for Big Man.

Not exactly a family background that produces coked-out bimbos.

You know better than that, counselor, said Neff.

We cabled him the night of the murder, the DCM continued. He insisted her body be returned to him ASAP, even if it meant we had to charter a plane. The army flight was a happy coincidence, a scheduled exfiltration of troops.

What troops? The marine guard here at the embassy? I thought the Pentagon had cleared out.

Advisors, trainers, small SF contingents—it's not a secret, said the DCM. But the point is, the father was distraught, the strings he pulled were readily available to a man of his position. And just between you and me, he was furious that his daughter had married this criminal, and he wanted him brought to justice.

Well, that's a pretty irony, said Harrington.

I'm not following, said the DCM.

You spring him out of jail and put him on a plane to Miami before there was any chance you might lose him here in the tar pit.

The alternative was extremely messy, as you well know.

A pretty irony, this justice.

Am I finished here? Neff, impatient with the conversation, asked the DCM.

I have a question, said Harrington. If you're certain Dolan's client arranged for the murder of his wife, the motive is what? Dolan mentioned an insurance policy but that seems rather tawdry for your suspect, who, from what you've implied, seems to operate at a more artful level and I'd guess for much higher stakes.

Men like him, girls like her, said Neff with condescending distaste. You never go wrong handicapping their colossal stupidity. My guess is she attempted to extort her husband. Marital problems among crooks are often resolved with a double cross and bloodshed. She had filed for a divorce. That might explain it.

Does Connie Dolan know that? asked Harrington.

I don't know what Dolan knows, Tom, said Albert Neff. That's why we're talking. But I can tell you this. Dolan's days of protecting this dirtbag are over. That's why you're here. In this room.

Well, that's only partially true, added the DCM. Keeping you out of trouble strikes me as a worthy goal.

Anything else you can tell us? asked Neff.

I knew her, you know. Back during the occupation. She was using a different name.

Yes, we know, said Neff. I'm told you had an adventure together up north.

Right. That's what people here like to say. An adventure up north.

Anything to that?

No. I don't know.

I've heard a bit of the story, offered the DCM. Sounds harrowing.

You want my opinion, said Neff, face-to-face with Harrington. What happened up north in those mountains with you and this little bitch has nothing to do with this case. Dolan's boy murdered her and the only issue unresolved in my mind is what it's going to take to get retired Special Agent Conrad Dolan to back off. He's complicating a very straightforward affair. In my book, that's called obstruction. Tell him to step away.

I don't know about Dolan, said Tom, but I think you're right about the north.

Then let's leave it at that, Tom, the DCM said magnanimously. No sense dragging yourself up there to stir up old grievances. Am I right?

So you're aware of what happened up there?

The unpleasantness, yes. We heard some things.

The girl made enemies.

As did you, correct? But those enemies vanished into thin air, is what I understand. You can't connect dots that don't exist.

You just said you didn't want me stirring up old grievances. What's going on in Cap?

I'm simply trying to save you from a very strenuous, risky journey that would be a complete waste of your time. You've already agreed with us. The north is not part of this investigation. We're certain of it. Believe me, we know what happened up there.

The hell you do, thought Tom, and yet he didn't understand why he was pushing back against them when they were intent on giving him a pass, giving him what he most wanted, a reason, any reason, to stay out of the mountainous north.

And we're confident we know what happened down here. The two events aren't related, unless there's something you're not telling us.

Harrington shook his head without saying anything, feeling the blood drain from his face. On the intercom, the DCM told his secretary to call downstairs for Mr. Dolan to come up. Neff collected the photograph from Tom and slid it back into his file and, without their original animus, they rose to their feet and shook hands again.

Tell me this if you can—why did she use so many aliases? That bothers me.

She was a nutcase, said Albert Neff. According to her father. Lived in a world of fantasy. You knew her, you know the type. Am I wrong? He turned to leave the room but then turned back, feigning afterthought, a business card in his fingers. I have another theory, he said. It's probably way off base, but if it ever starts to make you tingle, get in touch.

Yeah?

Maybe she was working for Dolan. You know, keeping tabs on Dolan's boy. Wild, huh?

Suppose that were true?

You've already made the point yourself. Dolan's boy didn't kill anybody for insurance money, counselor. I can tell you that.

See you around, said Tom, but the man from Justice grabbed his elbow as he moved toward the door.

I want this prick, Harrington. He's been running loose way past his expiration date. The problem is what the problem was—I have to go through Dolan to get him.

Yeah? Well, good luck.

And when I do that, counselor, I need you to do one thing for me.

Let me guess. Step out of the way.

That's right, step out of the way.

The thing is, I'm not in your way.

Best news I've heard all day, he said, tugging at his sleeve to check the time. I have a plane to catch back to Miami. Are you on the flight?

No.

You should be on the flight.

Neff disappeared and the DCM's secretary marched Tom out of the office and down the hall to an elevator, its door opened and held by a muscular man dressed almost identically to Tom in chinos and a polo shirt and running shoes, smiling warmly at Harrington as if they were old friends. Got a minute? he asked, and Tom looked at him blankly and said, Just tell me what's going on so I can get out of here.

Here's what you need to know, said the guy. Parmentier did not kill his wife.

Why do you say that?

I know Jack Parmentier. He's solid.

Solid?

He was doing important work down here. You know what I'm saying.

You're saying he was an agency asset.

I don't believe I said all that.

Excuse me, you said that he was so devoted to his lovely wife that under no circumstance would he cause her harm.

I'm saying under no circumstance would he ever jeopardize the project he was working on.

The project?

The project.

So then, who killed her? And why?

Maybe you might have some idea about that.

What the fuck is this? Everybody seems to think I've been appointed independent counsel on the Jackie Scott case.

I've heard you're the kind of man who can't stand the thought of a killer going free.

Just about every killer I've ever met in Haiti is dancing around in the streets, having a good laugh. Some of them even happen to be your assets.

The elevator opened on the ground floor and Tom's fellow passenger caught the closing door as Harrington stepped out into the hall. I know you're the type of man who can't look the other way, he said with a wink. You know what I'm saying.

Harrington began to walk toward the chairs in the waiting area. He took a seat, nodding at the receptionist behind her desk, who picked up a ringing phone and nodded back at him and said, Excuse me, are you Mr. Harrington? holding out the receiver. It's for you.

Mr. Harrington, said the voice in the phone, this is Special Agent Woodrow Singer. I'd like to buy you a cup of coffee. Alone, if you don't mind.

Let me get back to you on that, said Harrington, returning the receiver to the receptionist. When he turned around, there was a black man occupying his former chair, sphinxlike, his eyes obscured behind a wrap of sunglasses, a chain of fat gold links around his neck, oversized rings on his long fingers, pink scar on the side of his chin. Haitian, Harrington had to believe, and of course thug, except for the fact he wore a lanyard around his neck from which hung an embassy security badge. Harrington sat down, keeping an empty seat between them, and grimaced. The black man shifted in his chair toward him as if he might speak, but didn't. Harrington, staring back at him, finally did.

You want to tell me something, right?

He spoke with a Brooklyn accent in flawless and customarily vague Kreyol. His business was narcotics. *Production or distribution?* asked Harrington, but the joke went unappreciated. In this business, the fellow said in a low voice, he had been watching certain people, a man and a woman and another man, you know who I am talking about, he said, and these people were doing this thing, and it was his business to stop these people from doing this thing, but each time he tried to stop them, other people stopped him from stopping them. Do you understand, *mon ami?*

Yeah, said Harrington, these people you were watching had very big friends.

Exactement, monsieur.

And you are saying that this man who I came here with today knew this woman, this dead woman.

Exactement.

But this man has never been to Haiti.

Haiti is not the only place to know this woman.

Okay, thanks, said Harrington, switching to English, and if you see Dolan tell him I said to go fuck himself, and then he felt himself detach from it all, sleepwalking through the turbulence, and he went out from the embassy and drove straight to Petionville, left the SUV that Dolan had rented in the car park of the Hotel Montana with the key in the ignition, checked out of his room, and then telephoned the airlines only to learn there were no seats available to Miami until the following day. He booked the next day's afternoon flight and then took a taxi to the Oloffson, checked in for the night, and ate his lunch on the veranda, ignoring familiar faces, remaining at his table until twilight, speaking off and on with Monsieur Richard, the hotel's owner, who came intermittently to sit with him—Have you seen Gerard? No. If you see him tell him I want to talk to him—and then retired to the bar. Conrad Dolan found him there later that evening, and threw himself down next to Harrington and said, seething through clenched teeth, So how many scoops of bullshit were those assholes able to pile on your cone, Tommy Boy?

You knew the girl, you bastard.

Yeah, I did, and what of it? said Dolan. You killed a guy.

Did I? said Harrington, quick and churlish. Then his stomach tightened and seized and his voice weakened. You don't know what you're talking about.

Oh, you wouldn't know, would you? You never stopped to check it out.

Is that in the report too?

Yeah, said Dolan, waving for the bartender's attention. I seem to remember something like that.

CHAPTER EIGHT

You could see it as Tom's punishment for her, a token administration of penance, his instructions to Gerard to keep going through Saint-Marc. He wanted to stop instead at one of the hotels along the Cote des Arcadins where they could sit at a bar in perfumed shade, immune from the everyday frenzy and crush of a town like Saint-Marc, the monotonous wearying attention paid to their whiteness. He wanted none of that tax on his energy this afternoon, but then why did he speak to Gerard in Kreyol if not to prevent Jackie from understanding the conversation, and of course she was going to understand it soon enough, pointing out one shop and then a second that looked like it might sell bottled water or soft drinks, only to be ignored by Gerard while Tom played dumb. Gerard threaded his way methodically through the rubble of the town's central market, the channel of vendors and peasants and animals and trucks and tap-taps and cyclists opening and closing in front of him, cresting and ebbing against the sides of the SUV, streaking its dust with their sweat. Finally she snarled at Gerard. Tom explained what they were doing. Frustrated, she plundered her camera bag for a lemon drop and sucked on it angrily and loudly for a few seconds. Tom expected her to stay sulky like the spoiled child he was tempted to believe she was but then she surprised him and resigned herself to her status as obedient passenger, proceeding without complaint, stoic and immobile for the next half hour to the coast.

When he saw the sign marking the long entrance to Moulin Sur Mer, Gerard downshifted but Tom told him keep going, today for some reason he wanted to bypass this preferred and dependable watering hole in favor of exploring one of the lesser known hotels farther south, by far more ordinary and modest resorts that he had always wondered about—who stayed there? Was the service adequate? Were the rooms clean?—but always flew past on his trips between Port-au-Prince and the north. Visible from the road, the most modern-looking was a two-storied building of whitewashed stucco and clay-tiled roof with what he could pretend was Mediterranean appeal; eight or ten units a floor, he guessed, and imagined small balconies overlooking a poolside bar and a private strand of beach and the beautiful water. If it had a name, he couldn't remember, but as the hotel came into view in a grove of palms and mango trees, Tom told Gerard to turn in.

The car park was empty, its normal condition, Tom figured, except on weekends. The glass double doors leading inside were unlocked but the lobby was empty too—deserted, its check-in counter coated with a layer of grime and the puddled wax of candles, the splayed wires of a phone line dangling from a wall. But the obvious was never the final word in Haiti. Somewhere on the premises would be a caretaker married to a shotgun; otherwise the building would have been cannibalized, antlike, down to its skeleton, its doors and windows carried away, the frames themselves ripped from their rough-outs, even the floor tiles pried up, painstakingly cleaned, resold. Jackie wandered seaward through the breezeway, looking for a bathroom. Tom and Gerard remained in the lobby, calling out *Bonjour,* expecting someone to come but no one did.

Let's have a look around, said Tom.

Beyond the breezeway was a concrete patio, its surface webbed with cracks, poured to accommodate a swimming pool that although emptied remained mysteriously clean, free of rainwater or leaves or windblown trash. Seaward, behind the pool, the patio ended in a waist-high block wall, its top row composed of airy arabesques, with a passageway and railing implying a cliffside stairway down to the beach. The sweep of the view toward the horizon—the sparkling expanse of the Gonave Bay, the misty whale-backed hump of the island in its middle—was sublime, a tropic dreamscape, begging you to imagine the romance meant to unfold on the dilapidated patio: cocktails, dinner straight from the reefs, dancing with the soothing winds of the sea ruffling your partner's hair, an ideal venue for slow, salty, languorous love most anywhere in the world but Haiti, where love was synonymous with impotence, powerless to keep any of its dazzling promises, a perverse magnet for wholesale grief, and maybe, Tom thought, whoever owned this little slice of treacherous paradise had been right to run away and not look back, if that was the story.

He heard Gerard calling to him and turned, cheered to see him standing behind an outside bar in a shallow service area recessed below the balconies jutting from a pair of second-floor rooms. Tom joined him behind the counter and (Gerard was too timorous for this impropriety) began flipping back the tops along a row of refrigerated aluminum coolers, but the electricity was off and the bins were empty.

Where'd Jackie go? Tom said.

He called her name with no result and Gerard thought maybe she had gone down the steps to the *plage.* Together they walked across the patio to the wall and peered over the side without saying anything, just standing there watching, eyes glued to Jackie, until finally Gerard snickered and said, *Oo la la.* Tom, you will fuck this woman, eh? I think she would be a good one to fuck.

I don't think that's the case at all, he said, surprised by his tone, meaning to express dismissive amusement but instead he had only sounded offended.

In all fairness to Gerard, Jackie was providing him with every reason to behave otherwise, but it was unlike the circumspect Gerard to be vulgar about women, especially white women, because the ones he saw and met in Haiti he most often admired for their courage and selflessness, their disdain for privilege, and sex was a topic Tom and he almost never discussed, not in regard to their personal lives, and even those nights on the road, stuck in Cap-Haïtien or Jacmel or Les Cayes, Tom never said a word when Gerard would disappear into the darkness in search of an old girlfriend or new girlfriend or, Tom suspected, anyone at all he could find to take the edge off the all-consuming substance of death that shaped their days, returning to the hotel at breakfast hungover and grinning in a most unmarital manner.

On one such occasion, Gerard had stirred his coffee and asked con-spiratorially, Tom, you never look for woman? and Tom had answered grudgingly that Haitian women were beautiful but AIDS was a problem, wasn't it? And besides, he was married. To his credit, Gerard didn't scoff. But marriage had little to do with Tom's celibacy. Although he had not slept with anyone during his time in Haiti he had, in fact, hoped it might happen not once but twice, the first with the stupendously sexy bartender at the Oloffson, a girl with the perfectly angled and proportionate features of an Ethiopian princess and the attitude of a Motown diva, the second at one of the notoriously raunchy television network parties in an apart-ment at the Montana, his temporary partner a sleek battle-hardened senior correspondent from one of the news weeklies intent on cutting loose and having herself a memorably wicked evening. She was wearing heels and a short black cocktail dress and invited him to dance by stepping out of her panties and throwing them merrily in his face. But the bartender wanted a relationship and a visa, not a lover who would spend more time on airplanes than in her arms, and by the time he escorted the woman from the magazine back to her room and, in the midst of a slack embrace, they toppled onto her bed, she was beyond the moment, so cross-eyed, slurry drunk that she lost consciousness midkiss and, like any gentleman, he withdrew and took himself home and masturbated.

Despite his desire to the contrary, he never ran into her again. On the other hand he had no time for this sort of play. Month after month of tracking down witnesses and survivors, taking depositions, organizing the bone diggers, providing logistical support for the teams of forensic anthro-pologists to exhume and catalog the sites, writing reports for the Haitian government (the palace, the Ministry of Justice), for the UN Human Rights Commission and the human rights entities of the Organization of American States, writing reports that he could only pray would find their way into the hands of legislators and prosecutors, massaging the perpetual crisis of his preposterous budget, waiting and waiting with a phone to his ear for operators and secretaries to connect him, to put him through to anybody with a voice, until his neck went stiff and his arm went numb, and by the end of each unending day it was all he could do to unknot his bootlaces, brush his teeth and spit and fall, every cell humming with fatigue, into bed for a few hours—who had time for chasing skirts, for God's sake?

But now the pace and fire and crusading purpose of those days were dead-ending and here was Jackie, down below in the water, breathtakingly naked below the waist, boots and socks, pants and lilac panties, scattered behind her on the sand, the heavenly slope of her ass agleam from the lick of the sea . . . and the temptation was mighty, the torment exquisite.

Yet he had never considered his desire, how he acted on that desire or didn't, as anybody's business but his own, certainly not a topic to be bantered about in testosterone-heated bonhomie. There was no one—no buddy, no tennis partner, no colleague or old friend, and definitely not Gerard, an employee—that he wanted to have that conversation with, one sportsman to another, tallying scores. Years ago, he remembered reading somewhere that boys talked and men didn't, and that insight seemed to divide the world of male sexuality correctly. More to the point, perhaps, the sudden sense of transparency Tom experienced hearing Gerard's crude declaration made him wince; he felt caught, exposed, not necessarily ashamed but chastened, standing there looking down on Jackie not actually thinking he would sleep with her but beginning to roll out the spool of justification that might allow for it, tasting the hope of it on the tongue of his lust, and how many times a day, in an office or on the street or in a restaurant glancing up from his plate or gazing over the rim of his glass in a bar did he look at women, all variety of women, and feel just that, and then feel the hunger for what one cannot have, the eros of everyday life with its miles of locked doors, its unquenchable desire.

He was a good enough husband and, when he was in place, a better father and did not like to think of himself as unconscionably adulterous, but he did in fact have a mistress in South Beach, an erstwhile college girlfriend from Gainesville who had had her fill of commitment—two marriages, two divorces—and now professed to be satisfied simply by no-strings sex, safe, amiable, unattached, the passion between them neither obsessive nor dulled by overuse. The arrangement seemed only right and fair to Tom. Necessary, like checkups at the family physician. A matter of health and balance and, not to be dwelled on, abundance. A release of endangering amorphous pressure, in his life much more than his body, that could not otherwise be released. Was that wrong? Yes. No. Perhaps. It was difficult to care about the wrongness of it when the rightness seemed so compelling.

His perfectly lovely, increasingly predictable, sometimes resentful and frustrated wife, had a waistline expanding at a rate commensurate with her material vision of what a good life in Miami was intended to encompass and absorb, regardless of how many times she jogged in slow motion around the neighborhood. Somehow letting it slip her mind that, Oh, Tom isn't that type of lawyer, is he? Not the kind whose job description translates as *raking it in*. But why wasn't he? Oh, yes, she had momentarily forgotten, he's trying to save the fucking world. Bravo, Tom. In my heart I approve but here's the bill for the wind damage on the roof, and please phone the plumber because that asshole seems incapable of returning my calls.

He didn't object to being middle class, not as a measure of his financial status, but he was disappointed that her values seemed anchored there, without the raw ingenuity of the low or the expansive imagination of the high. Tom could be depended upon to meet all her conventional needs, to support the orthodoxy of her sensible desires. Having things her way—the quiet neighborhood, the kid's school, the Swedish cars in the driveway, the guest list for her overly prepared dinner parties—was a given, what with his many and prolonged absences, his fidelity to the unnamed dead. Her domestic will exerted a potent force that he often acquiesced to with only a gesture of resistance, knowing it would be worse to fight it out, his eventual defeat by definition hers as well, in possession of a husband who had taken up the habit of being pounded into submission.

Her needs—he found them impossible to engage with any strong sense of empathy. If her weekends had a theme, a mission statement, it was, *What do we need right now, this instant, that can no longer be delayed?* Pretty things and comfort and pride and the ever elusive confidence of self-esteem. But what did it mean, Tom sometimes found himself worrying, if all the abstract dread he felt about his marriage of fifteen years could be peeled down to its core and there in the hiss and steam all that remained was sex and its imperatives?

Impossible to know—should he feel horrified or thankful?—but something, hormones or entropy or both, had diluted the high concentration of erotic Sicilian energy she had inherited in her blood. Increasingly over the years he had an inconclusive sense of his wife's passion for the bedroom. These days, did she ever experience sexual need? Yes, but. When they had first started living together and before their daughter's birth, she would sometimes suggest role-playing games that secretly embarrassed and intimidated him—he wasn't her gynecologist and he wasn't her assailant. At some point he had missed altogether, oral sex began to disgust her, or maybe it had all along and she had only resigned herself to the earlier packaging of their lusts. Fellatio was nothing and everything, depending on his mood, but he resented the scope of their intimacy being reduced in any of its interlocking parts. And although he could never keep his thoughts quiet about these things, neither did he want to talk about them, feared talking about them, feared ever being able to explain himself, feared most of all the idea that here was the one part of himself that was better off misunderstood than known and fully understood.

Yet no matter what was pitching through his mind, he believed the living quarters of his heart were only filled by his wife, and then again by his daughter. Gazing down at the inflammatory taunt of Jackie's ass, he knew that to be true, and still he had to tell himself, *watch out for Jackie,* stay away from her or she was going to get him into some rare kind of trouble, and he didn't want that, did he? He was more sensible than that, wasn't he?

Jackie had to know the two of them were there at the wall, watching her, but she turned back to the beach without looking up at them, perhaps not caring what they saw. What is she? Tom wondered as he looked at the sleek corded muscles in her neck and arms, the smooth sculpted pack of muscles in her calves and thighs, and remembered the rock-hard clench of her body in his lap. A marathoner? A gymnast? She stepped back into her clothes but left her feet bare, bending to collect her socks and boots and when she straightened up she raised her head and looked at them, her eyes steady on Tom for an instant but her face unreadable, and he smiled back involuntarily even though at the moment he wanted to scorn her and thought, not coherently, Don't be silly; trouble, whatever, she's just a girl, he could handle it.

Their eyes followed her progress up the stairs.

Strangely, in the car again she was yet a different person, a new spirit behind her words and gestures. She seemed to become the person Tom actually wanted her to be, witty and logical and open, talking naturally with her two companions, and so he didn't challenge her for the outrageous way she had behaved with the *houngan*. He didn't want to quarrel with this improved Jackie, this pleasant, smiling, and sometimes coy Jackie, and throw away what he began to imagine with increasing focus was the chance to have her, to make her want him as a lover, a desire that needed no further explanation if she was now intent on just being normal, being rational, because when she was this way, she was, like any woman, a suggestion of what was irresistible in life. Perhaps it was the ocean, he thought. Stepping into its surge of cleansing reality had transformed her, brought her back from whatever dark spell had befallen her, somewhere that she wasn't meant to be.

He had expected an apology and he wanted her to apologize, but she said nothing to that effect, and so Tom let it go, deciding there was little chance she could explain her behavior with Bòkò St. Jean. It was, he decided, an anomaly and too bizarre to ever make sense. Given the new-found lightness between them, when they arrived back at the Oloffson and she casually asked what he was doing tonight, he told her about his friend in the Special Forces. Why don't you join us? he said and she said, That would be cool.

Jackie went on to her room. He stopped at the desk for messages—three phone calls from a lawyer he vaguely knew and did not respect, who represented one of Haiti's oligarchical families—and was already at the table he had reserved for the evening at the far end of the veranda when he saw her again, immersing herself in the burgeoning crowd. He watched as she searched for him, her extraordinary beauty amplified by how she had chosen to present herself for the occasion in a low-cut peasant blouse and gauzy white skirt, her hair gleaming from the shower, her blue eyes enlarged and emboldened with makeup, an unsubtle metamorphosis from hard-bitten tomboy photojournalist (if indeed she would ever shoot a roll of film) to glowing ingenue and playmate. She saw him finally and the timid smile of her acknowledgment pleased him immensely, more than it should have, given the fact that he knew already not to trust her.

Is there something going on here tonight? she asked happily, reaching the table. She wanted to know where all the people had come from and he explained these gatherings were a weekly affair.

The Oloffson's Thursday night fetes—a lavish buffet and a live band for dancing—were legendary for the clientele they customarily attracted, a volatile mix of the city's opposing factions who were drawn to a night's saturnalia in the demilitarized zone of the hotel. Terrorists and sunny-faced do-gooders, spies and the politicians they spied upon, the MREs—morally repugnant elites—and the foreign journalists who had christened them with the pejorative acronym, chic American-educated ruling-class girls with Ecstasy and pistols in their handbags and skeletal downtown whores dressed hopelessly in third-hand clothes, embassy technocrats, narco-traffickers and clueless missionary pukes—all bound together every Thursday night inside a Noah-like ark of decadent compatibility. Except some nights, not. Some nights the orgiastic bubble broke and gunfire erupted, which explained why two very big men were now stationed at the top of the stairs, disarming customers as they arrived and issuing claim checks for the handguns—Glocks and .357s and 9s—piling up in the footlocker at their feet.

Touching his shoulder affectionately, Jackie sat down next to Tom and he finally caught Joseph's attention and ordered rum sours from the bar and turned to admire her, as any man would, and although she returned his gaze, when he made a lighthearted tease—I hope you don't think I'm trying to put a curse on you—about the jewelry she had chosen for the occasion, a bracelet and a talismanic pendant made from the sea-blue glass of evil-shielding eyes—the subject seemed to interfere with her mood, made her less warm, and she responded drily. They were gifts from an old friend, she said.

Egyptian?

Turkish. He gave them to me in Istanbul. My seventeenth birthday. Then pointedly, nodding at the gold wedding band on his left hand, mischief in the way she raised one eyebrow. Tom, we don't really want to talk about our jewelry, do we?

I want to talk about you.

With a little prodding he learned more. Her father worked in the foreign service, she had attended grade school in Hong Kong and Kenya, middle school in Rome, high school in Turkey and Virginia, college in New England, graduate school in Boston. Actually, Cambridge.

Really! he replied to her vita without thinking. But you seem so—
What?
I don't know.

She looked at him as if she knew exactly what he thought, as if his response was a familiar one, and she had gotten used to it.

I've learned to be resilient. I adapt well.

Why Haiti? People don't generally adapt well to Haiti.

It seemed a good place to start.

Because nobody else wants it.

But I want it. That's all that's required, isn't it.

She asked about his work and how he came to do it and he told her that in the eighties he had been a journalist, a foreign correspondent in Central America for one of the Florida papers, and then someone told him about a program at the Yale law school for reporters like him.

What kind of reporters are those?

You keep filing the same story, year after year, war after war, and the only thing that changes is the dateline.

You wanted to do more.

I wanted to believe I could make a difference.

I want to believe that too.

He was about to ask her why she so rarely seemed inspired to use her camera but their drinks arrived at the same moment a hush spread across the veranda and everyone's attention swung in unison toward the unprecedented sight of American commandos materializing like phantasma in the dim globe of light at the top of the stairs, the diners silenced by the provocative surge of tension the warriors seemed to generate. The Special Forces had operated primarily in the hinterlands and kept a low profile in the capital, where they were prohibited by their command from visiting bars and restaurants, but here they were, mythic and exalted, savages commissioned by a superpower, and instantly engaged in a standoff with the two house guards collecting weapons. There were three of them, Master Sergeant Eville Burnette and two companions and they wore camouflage uniforms, holstered pistols and green berets and, from the looks of it, had spent the day in a fight.

Don't they look like you just better not fuck with them, said Jackie.

Sliding out of his chair to intervene, Tom reached the confrontation a few steps ahead of the Oloffson's owner, coming from the kitchen, alerted by his staff. The commandos were stone-faced yet unconcerned, mocking themselves over the mound of guns in the footlocker—There's a few we missed in the buyback, I feel so much better now that we disarmed the population. Within a minute everything was smoothed over and Tom paid the prix fixe for the soldiers, who were allowed to keep their weapons after all, although it became immediately evident that the three men had been more in their element facing down the house goons than walking the length of the veranda, weaving through the tables, self-conscious in a milieu where the only challenge was to enjoy yourself.

Introductions were exchanged as Jackie stared wide-eyed at the men with an appreciation that jolted Harrington with unexpected envy. They removed their berets and nodded politely at her as they sat down, stiff and uncertain except for Eville Burnette, leaning over to play the gallant. He pecked each of her cheeks and said in French that she was a sight for sore eyes, a flattery that she did not ask to be translated but smirked back at him as if to imply he had gone too far, her eyes rising to the nasty lump on his forehead, the split in the skin closed with a pair of butterfly stitches. His companions had gotten more of the same. The soldier Tom did not recognize, a warrant officer named Brooks, had a black eye, and it was obvious that Captain Stewart Butler, the short, charismatic SF officer the Haitians called Tet Rouge (because of his shaved and sunburned skull) had had the side of his face raked by someone's fingernails.

Oh, come on, tell us, Jackie coaxed with an exaggerated pout, responding to the nonchalant shrugs they used to dismiss Tom when he asked what happened. You can't sit there like that and not say anything. That's not fair.

Joseph approached the table and Tom asked the soldiers if he could stand them a round of beers.

Can't, said Warrant Officer Brooks.

Tet Rouge's thin lips formed a flat, wolflike grin. I have a signed note from my mother says I can.

We're on the road to hell, said Eville and ordered three bottles of Presidente.

Somebody kicked your ass, Jackie taunted. That's why you won't tell us.

It was a reckless comment, Tom thought, noticing the twitch in the warrant officer's face—Brooks was all varsity, all business, laconic, uncomplicated, his firm mouth quickly entertaining and discarding a sneer—but Jackie's brazenness animated Brooks's comrades, their eyes flashed and brightened, their faces broadened into smiles; the woman had thrown just the right bait to lure the story out of them, a typically screwy account of unconventional operations amid widespread anarchy.

One month ago, when Eville Burnette's team had exfiltrated from Saint-Marc to the capital, the *gwos neg* who had reigned over the port city during the bloody years of the de facto regime, Jean Petreau, had slithered out of hiding and reestablished himself overnight, at least down at the harbor, where he fell back into the habit of extortion—collecting astronomical dockage fees and on-the-spot tariffs from legitimate shipping while allowing vessels of dubious registry and unknown cargoes to be off-loaded surreptitiously under cover of darkness. Big deal, same old funny business, who cares, not my problem, right? said Burnette, his mouth wide and elastic, his lips stretched euphorically or pursed with thoughtfulness or at other times what seemed to be remorse. But then what happened next, he told them, sent alarm bells ringing across the hemisphere.

A freighter comes in to Saint-Marc from Martinique, ties up at the wharf, Burnette said. Jean Petreau and his band of goons pay a call, the Surinamese captain—a white Dutchman—tells Jean Petreau to go to hell. Petreau and his men take the captain hostage, the captain's wife and first mate barricade themselves in the communications room on the ship's bridge, the wife radios Surinam and Martinique, someone in Martinique radios the owner in Miami, the owner telephones his congressman, the congressman calls the Pentagon, the Pentagon calls the UN, the UN notifies the National Palace, the palace wakes up the guy in charge of Saint-Marc's new, American-made police force and tells him to get his men together and rescue the hostage, the cops go to grab the hostage but take a burst of automatic weapons fire, and, lo and behold, they freak, and before you know it rounds are flying everywhere, into houses, into cars, it's rock and roll in Saint-Marc.

Act two, said Burnette. The police chief gets on the emergency frequency and dials up the UN troops—Nepalese chaps—at their base ten klicks down the road and they send an entire company of bootless conscripts to the scene, all of whom are immediately surrounded by thousands of good citizens issuing demands—food, water, electricity, road repair, et cetera, and something stickier but more doable, at least under the auspices of a few good men: they want the UN troops to arrest the entire police force for corruption and widespread abuse of power. Petreau's only been shaking down foreigners, so Petreau is not an issue to the people of Saint-Marc. But then the mob begins to argue with itself and splits into factions and starts to riot, so the unfortunate and nonplussed Nepalese boys—not Gurkha mind you; Kathmandu does not rent out Gurkha to the UN—have their hands full with this collateral situation and, meanwhile, the hostage crisis is unresolved.

Act three. We get the 911 call at the LIC, said Eville Burnette, and within minutes a chopper comes to pick us up. Next, you'll love this, Brooks here was on the original ODA that liberated Saint-Marc during the invasion and he knows Jean Petreau because he saved the shithead's life the day the team infilled into town, pulled Petreau out of a crowd of very excited townsfolk who were about to give Petreau the fashionable necklace treatment for *malfacteurs*. We arrest him but within forty-eight hours we were told to push Petreau back onto the street with a promise of good behavior, whereupon he proved his intelligence by finding himself a hole to crawl into for the next eighteen months.

And this was how he thanked you for saving his life? Jackie asked Warrant Officer Brooks. By giving you a black eye?

No, ma'am, answered Brooks.

That's right, said Tet Rouge, sputtering with laughter. A lady stamped him with that shiner.

Not a lady, Brooks said, slapping his hand on the table. Just a cunt.

Excuse him, ma'am, Eville said to Jackie.

Oh, give me a break, said Jackie. Women, cunts, bitches, whatever. What happened?

What happened, said Eville Burnette, is what happens when people aren't more careful about who they choose to disrespect. Up to a point, Jean Petreau understood this basic code of survival, and when the three soldiers approached the door of the house where Petreau held his hostage, and Warrant Officer Brooks called out, *Jean Petreau, goddamn it, I'm really busy today and I don't have time to save your life a second time,* Petreau himself opened the door to offer an effusive welcome to his old friend, explaining that the Dutchman was not a hostage but a criminal, and Petreau had no choice but to arrest him because the police would not, *but here,* says Petreau, *Here's the guy, you can have him, I'm sick of him, to tell you the truth,* so they go in the house and there's the ship's captain trussed up in duct tape.

So we take him, said Burnette, but we take Petreau as well, drag them both to the police station to sort this thing out. Finally the soldiers begin to understand the heart of the matter: that the ship is loaded with contraband; that the owner had prepaid the police but the ship's captain had not been authorized to bribe both parties, Petreau (the ancien régime) and the police (the nouveau régime).

Brooks, Burnette, and Tet Rouge head down to the harbor: they want to know what's on the ship, and they want to talk to the captain's wife and determine what her role is in all of this. Down on the quay, Petreau has parked a pair of thugs with little spray guns to guard the ship but they are gracious enough to take flight at the sight of American soldiers marching toward them, preceded by their reputation, but perhaps Petreau has other men aboard the ship who might be more inclined to resist. They trudge up the long, hot gangplank to midships, recon the deck, calling out words of peace and comfort but no one's responding and the vibe gets spooky. They trudge up to the bridge, turn the corner around a wall, and here's a fellow pointing a shotgun at them and, compelled to raise their own M4s, they persuade him to lower the barrel and put down his weapon. *Who are you?* they ask. *Where's Madame?* They have boarded a ship owned by an American citizen and want to know if she needs assistance. He's the first mate from Martinique, and Madame is in the communications room, down the passageway, next to the wheelhouse.

They try the handle; it's locked. They knock on the door; no one answers, but they can hear the woman inside on the ship-to-shore radio, shrieking in Spanish. Brooks starts to kick down the door but on the third try the woman flings the door open at the same moment Brooks's boot would have made contact and his momentum propels him off balance through the opening, where she's waiting for him, the telephone-like receiver from the radio clutched in her hand. She swings at him, and connects, pow, right in the eye, and Brooks is looking at stars. Tet Rouge leaps ahead and she swings at him, too, he grabs her wrist but she claws his face with her free hand and he staggers back from this wildcat. Burnette is right behind Tet Rouge, shouting for the woman to back away and calm down, but she gets him too, ripping the phone off its cord with the force of her blow. Brooks comes to his senses and steps forward, rifle up and aimed, but she commits a cardinal sin, seizing the muzzle of his M4 with both hands and now here we have a real problem, said Eville. She and Brooks are engaged in a tug of war over his rifle and he's never going to let go and it seems neither is she. The gun is pointed straight at her chest and suddenly she begins screaming in English, *Shoot me, you cocksucking American pig, shoot me, you yanqui motherfucker, shoot me, shoot me,* which doesn't sound like a bad idea but the safety's on and Brooks isn't going to shoot anyone, is he? But you can't overstate the seriousness of the situation, an out of control woman with her hands on your gun, and so Burnette unholsters his pistol and brings the butt down on her skull, which, sorry to say, does not do the job. There's blood pouring down her face but she has kept a death grip on the rifle and she's still screaming, *Shoot me, shoot me.*

So what are my options? said Eville. I swing again and really crack her one with the pistol butt and down she goes and it looks as if I killed her.

Man doesn't know his own strength, said Tet Rouge.

I feel terrible about it, said Eville.

I feel good about it, said Brooks. I wish I had done it myself.

Jesus, said Tom Harrington. He was having fun with the story and now he would have rather not heard any of it. Is she all right?

All that blood, man, said Brooks. The bitch probably gave us AIDS.

Don't know, said Eville. We took her to the hospital. She's in a coma. Skull fracture. The owner's threatening to sue the US government.

We're the perps, said Tet Rouge. That's how the story ends. We're the bad guys.

So what was the whole thing about anyway? Jackie asked.

Just one of those crazy things, said Eville.

It was about a coke whore, man, said Warrant Officer Brooks. That's all you need to know. Not worth the bullet in my fucking rifle.

God, you're quite the misogynist, aren't you? said Jackie sarcastically, taunting the soldier again, and Harrington glared at her.

No, ma'am, he's not, said Tet Rouge. He just doesn't like to argue with women.

Jackie seemed to think this answer was hilarious.

CHAPTER NINE

All Thomas Harrington knew, sitting with Conrad Dolan at the bar of the Hotel Oloffson, his mouth sealed tight with anger while he waited to return to Miami for fund-raising and grant applications, then off to a job interview in The Hague and the customary slog toward survival and relevance, *amen,* was that he had suddenly been elevated to the role of love object among the pack of intelligence hounds set upon the mission that was Haiti. Tethered out from the acronymic spawn of agencies and departments and service branches that generated a veritable Babylon of institutional incompatibilities, a classic orgy of interagency perspectives were unable to agree on the answers to a set of elusively simple questions: Who was Jackie Scott? Why was she no longer among the living? Why are we bothering to care?

Among the troupe of players at the embassy, everyone—and that meant Connie Dolan too—seemed to believe Tom had in some way volunteered to attend this event as its guest of honor. No, thanks, gentlemen, he told himself, I am remitting myself to the one place I most belong and that is home, to love my wife and raise my daughter and prepare my briefs and white papers and be otherwise unavailable to the muddle.

Instead of trying to talk him out of it, Dolan turned the round chin of his priestly face toward Harrington and said, *Listen, Tom,* and lowered his voice and his head and spoke about the girl with a damp expression not unlike earnestness. Connie Dolan wanted to offer Harrington a few naked minutes within his own reality.

* * *

He had met her less than a year ago, one Saturday afternoon aboard Parmentier's sailboat *Payday* in Tampa Bay. Parmentier, yearning to show off the trophy that was his new bride, had asked Dolan out to the boat three or four weekends in a row and finally Dolan went, though not with any eagerness for the occasion, because Parmentier was an ugly and often pointless complication in his life, and so although he could not be ignored the less Dolan saw of him the better. The fact is, said Dolan, Parmentier had helped him out on a major case. He ran Parmentier as his inside man on a scheme that lured selected racketeers and mobsters from up north to cavort in the Florida sun, which was only possible because Parmentier had a colorful résumé himself. This is what guys like Dolan did, this is what guys like Parmentier did, and once they helped you, no matter how much they misbehaved in the past or might transgress in the future, you protected them, you were stuck with the precedents and the antecedents of protection, even though you hoped they slipped in the bathtub and broke their necks. It was a serious act, a dangerous and self-defeating act of irresponsibility and ultimately dishonor, to cut loose informants and witnesses and sources, to reward them for their trust by turning them into suckers and dupes and fools, and if that was old-school then so be it, Connie Dolan was old-school. But there was always a limit on what you might do for them, and you never knew where the edge might drop off into the blue until one day you found yourself there and had no choice except to shove them over and walk away, before they were inspired in their perpetual cleverness to do the same to you. With Parmentier, maybe that day was fast approaching. Maybe not.

Despite the continuing necessity of his unpleasant relationship with Parmentier, Dolan had balked at the social implications of meeting his informant's wife, and couldn't begin to imagine the destructive stupidity of a woman who would marry or date or even handle the cock of a man like Parmentier. Someone who must know herself only as dirt. Someone wrapped up in the pernicious appeal of walking though life as a victim, victimhood being the potter's clay of martyrdom, martyrdom being the last resort of love.

That wasn't Jackie, Tom interrupted.

Right, said Dolan, that wasn't your gal Jackie. That was Renee.

Dolan found a parking space in the palmy shade at the marina and headed for Parmentier's slip out on the docks, a familiar clandestine rendezvous for both of them although he had never known Parmentier to actually weigh anchor. Parmentier was in the open cockpit with an ice chest and martini shaker and a bottle of vodka, wraparound sunglasses obscuring his chestnut eyes and a Buccaneers cap pulled down over his shaggy black hair, relaxing under a canvas awning, legs up on the cushions, his Cajun good looks and the cheerful swagger of his pose suggesting the Errol Flynn version of a yachtsman, while Renee, a sleek bronze goddess in a red-and-white striped thong bikini, glided around the deck of the sloop, untying sails and clipping their points to the halyards, methodically running down the checklist for casting off. *Honey*, Parmentier said, *stop dicking around for a minute and come here and meet Special Agent Connie Dolan of the F for fuck you, every time, B as in bullshit, I.*

He was not undercover, he was no longer even an active agent, but Dolan did not care for this tiresome introduction. Wives were entitled to know one thing only about your business, wherever it took you when you left the house in the morning: that you worked very, very hard to secure their happiness. Beyond that you were creating the potential for fatal indiscretions. And if your wife was a tramp, even, as he first suspected of Renee, a crafty, high-end working girl, the exclusive spread of her legs limited to satin-covered mattresses in five-star hotels, she came from a culture shaped and burdened by the daily enforcements of the law and survival dictated a pragmatic formula: a cop was a cop was a cop, never a friend; or, as a type of friend, then a type of possession, a servant indentured by his own venality and cravenness, and this type of friend could be found all the way up through the chain of command.

But if Renee was only now finding out who Dolan was in the world, discovering her husband had managed to cultivate some unusual friendships, the news had no impact on her preoccupation with the boat. From the bow she stretched on the balls of her bare feet to wave hello to the men in the stern and called back for Parmentier to start the small diesel engine belowdecks while she uncleated the ropes that moored the *Payday* to her slip. Then Renee—Jackie—was pressed between them in the cockpit, smelling of coconut oil, the gleam of her marvelous body causing Dolan to take a full swallow from the can of beer pressed into his hand by Parmentier. She stood at the wheel, its apex nearly as tall as she, geared the engine into reverse, and throttled up just enough to nudge the sailboat backward out into the channel, then geared forward and gently swung the bow toward the cut leading to the bay. She might have been a showgirl onstage at a strip club the way the two men watched her, without words, intent only on the supreme mystery suggested by the agility of her flesh, the most ordinary thing and yet extraordinary.

Great ass on this girl, eh, Connie? said Parmentier, gesturing with his martini. As if this were her cue to perform, Renee naughtily wiggled the tanned globes of her exposed backside.

Dolan was not at all comfortable with the newlyweds' lack of inhibition. Where did you two kids find one another, if I may ask?

Sunday school, she said.

Crazier than that, man. An art gallery. Renee had a show.

When she turned to look over her shoulder at Dolan and shook the bangs out of her face he was intrigued by the clarity of her expression, not obliging her husband but mocking him, and Dolan thought to himself, Jesus Christ, Parmentier can start counting the days until she moves on and up the line of credit. She turned the opposite direction toward Parmentier and said, smiling without sweetness, make yourself useful now—he had to stand up and take the wheel. Then Dolan watched the sinewy muscles in her arms and legs bulge as she hauled and trimmed the mainsheet and the sailboat heeled into the breeze with the awakening groan of an enormous beast. Parmentier, who had purchased the boat primarily as an enchantment to use to procure women from the lounges and raw bars and air-conditioned steak houses of the bay area, was euphoric, the captain of beautiful moments made possible only by the labor and skill of others.

Parmentier's answer teased out Dolan's natural skepticism. What were you doing at a gallery? Since when do you like art?

Come on, man. I've always liked art, I just don't like to talk about it. You ever heard anybody talk about it who made sense? But hey, I went to see Renee's work. She was having a show. Photographs of Haiti. Voodoo niggers, devil worship. Unbelievable shit.

Yeah? What the fuck do you care about Haiti?

Hey, now, that's another story.

Renee told Parmentier to cut the engine and he did, the noisy silence of the elements now at the heart of a sudden exhilaration, thrumming wind and hissing water, the boat singing its music of speed under sail. Point her up while I raise the jib, she ordered Parmentier, but he didn't understand the command and began to fall off the wind, spilling the jib out in front of the boat and Renee shouted, *Turn the wheel to port, to port, to the left, damn it,* and Dolan sat back on the cushions of the cockpit chuckling at Parmentier, the sailing hoodlum from New Orleans, a French Quarter party boy dopehead who had quickly figured out dealing was the cheapest way of doing, the former pimp elevated to narcotrafficker without the nautical acumen to know port from starboard, left from right, right from wrong.

When Renee resumed the helm, Dolan asked where she had learned to sail.

The Sea of Marmara.

Pardon my French, Mrs. Parmentier, but where in the fuck is the Sea of Marmara?

That's what I said, said Parmentier.

The Sea of Marmara, the Dardanelles, the Bosphorus Strait.

Turkey? As they talked, Dolan's attention wandered to her left hand where it gripped the wheel, the unexpected impoverishment of a modest gold wedding band on her ring finger.

She only offered that her family had lived in Turkey for a few years and then she noticed him staring at her hand and volunteered that she had never cared for the spectacle of a diamond.

Get this, Connie, said Parmentier. She speaks Turkish. Arabic. French. Hey, what else, honey? Some African crap.

You didn't want a diamond? said Dolan, incredulous.

Parmentier had given her one, something overlarge and beyond expensive, custom-made to match a gaudy ring he displayed on his pinkie, like something athletes receive for winning championships, but she had tried to explain to him that she disliked ostentatious jewelry and refused to accept it. They argued about the ring and its implications for weeks. Finally Parmentier made a concession: his family and friends were not to be given the opportunity to paint him as a cheap son of a bitch, therefore . . . if she would wear the diamond when they exchanged vows in front of a priest, during the reception and dinner afterward and throughout their honeymoon, that would suffice for his ego and reputation. But she would have none of it—no diamond, no priest, no family and friends, no reception, none of the adornments or pieties of the matrimonial sacrament, just the two of them in the Tampa courthouse, signing papers, a blasphemy in Parmentier's tribal world of approval through attainment by any means, every transgression forgiven except disloyalty, and what could be a more incomprehensible and personal betrayal than to deny your pals and blood relatives the bash of the century—a zydeco band, tubs of oysters and crawfish and blue crabs, étouffé and gumbo coming out your ears, an open bar stocked with the best call brands in endless supply, an ounce of coke for his mates—on the day of your first and only wedding to a woman everyone could see was too good to be true and better than you and no one thought you deserved. And still he agreed to everything she wanted.

Chicks, said Parmentier, rolling his head with the pitch of the boat. Vodka splashed his khaki pants as he refilled his martini glass. It's what you can't do for them that really gets their attention. Am I right, Connie?

Really? said Renee. What is it you can't do for me?

Hey, what did I tell you. From where he sat he blew a kiss toward the back of her head. For you I can do everything, baby. Everything. That's the deal.

I like that deal, she said.

She asked Dolan to man the winch on the mainsheet and he put all his strength into it, struggling without effect, until she leaned over behind him and added her weight to his effort, a leg braced for leverage against the top of the cockpit. The winch clicked its teeth, the sail droned with an

116

extra degree of tautness, the starboard gunnel dipped closer toward the foaming water, and the race was on, the *Payday* inching ahead of another, bigger sailboat off their port headed for the last channel markers before the open bay.

Five hundred dollars says she beats that cracker to the buoy, said Parmentier. You in, Connie?

What, do I look nuts?

But the skipper of the second boat, a wood-hulled ketch, saw what the *Payday* had in mind and appeared determined to assert the right of way of his own more downwind tack, sending one of his crew up front to add a jib to the sails, and trimming the main for more power. As they approached open water, the wind and swells increased and the boats tossed combs of spray into the air, surging forward like thoroughbred horses, funneled toward the gate by a narrowing channel through banana-colored shoals. By now they could see the angry skipper of the ketch trying to wave Renee off her westerly tack and out of his lane but Renee had planted her feet and set her jaw and seemed intent on maintaining her course. It soon became clear that to avoid a collision, one boat, the winner, would have to cut across the bow of the other, yet neither boat seemed capable of outdistancing the other by a full length before it reached the markers. Parmentier had hopped unsteadily to his feet, cheering his bride onward against the ketch, which was near enough now for them to hear its bearded skipper screaming at Renee to fall off, and Dolan himself, though he wasn't going to tell her what to do, had begun pleading with her under his breath, in a minute or so he was sure the *Payday* would ram the ketch at midships and as he debated with himself whether to knock her off the wheel and take the helm himself and end this senseless competition a curl of black exhaust shot into the air over the ketch's stern as her engine fired up and she added speed.

But was it enough? As he watched the ketch's brilliant white sails strain forward and fill his vision, Dolan thought no, it was not enough, yet as he prepared himself for the inevitable impact, it was just enough. The two boats, crisscrossing, slid past each other with no room to spare, the *Payday*'s bowsprit scoring a jagged line through the paint of the ketch's transom, the two captains hurling insults at each other, Renee full of contempt for her rival, a coward and cheater. *You fucking pussy,* she hollered across the widening gap between the boats. Parmentier threw his martini glass and it shattered at the feet of the ketch's skipper. Then the drama was over, the sailboats bucking away from one another into the sparkling dance of light across the bay.

Real cute, said Dolan, glaring at Renee. He understood he had made a mistake, agreeing to anything outside the boundaries he had established over the years with Parmentier, but against his better judgment he was fascinated by the girl.

You don't approve of the way I sail? she asked, and even her sunglasses couldn't mask her amusement at his displeasure.

I don't approve of losing, he said. If you do whatever it takes to win, you better fucking win.

Whatever was driving the aggression of her mood that morning broke with laughter and the fight lifted from her shoulders and she told Dolan she couldn't agree with him more. Next time, she said, you're going to want to bet on me.

Parmentier wanted advice and the two men left Renee at the helm and went below to sit at the small fold-down table in the galley and talk. This Haiti thing, said Parmentier, you know about it? I don't know about any Haiti thing, said Dolan. What Haiti thing are you talking about? Two things, really, said Parmentier. His people had asked him to go down there and analyze the business climate, opportunities created by the political situation, find out who was quietly advertising for partners, who needed to be capitalized. After the American military pulled out, Haiti was an attractive prospect for Parmentier's associates, all action, no risk, because who's going to fuck with you, and everybody, I mean top to bottom, crying to jump in your pocket for pennies on the dollar. So, said Parmentier, I help my people get going down there.

And that would be doing what? said Dolan. Fixing the sewers?

Well, you know, Connie. Business. Finance. Trade. Men making the world go 'round. So my thing's up and running and it's sweet. I'm not making enemies, I'm making friends. We're shipping high-quality product in

118

and out with zero interference and the team is happy and then one of your guys finds me and he wants to step on me, but guess what, he doesn't want to shut me down, he wants to add on, he wants to expand the action, bump the value, join the party.

Hold up, said Dolan. What guy are we talking about here?

One of your guys from Miami. He knew all about me, all about you. Fed named Rice, Reece. One of yours.

Dolan grunted ambiguously with no intention of telling Parmentier he had never heard of an agent from the Miami bureau named Rice or Reece, and Dolan was certain no one would ever think of looping Parmentier into another federal operation—offshore, no less—without consulting him first.

Okay, said Parmentier, so maybe I'm a misty-eyed idealist, but I wasn't expecting this, Connie. My understanding was, the day you closed the Tampa shop was the day I walked back into my own thing, no strings attached, no recalls; shred the files and burn the house down and keep your buddies off my ass because I have served my country and I'm a mother-fucking patriot. I'm not saying I make the world a better place, but we balanced the books, right? We zeroed out.

Dolan said, What's Reece asking you to do?

Nothing I can't do but that's not the point. If the Feds can gin up an illegal casino in Tampa, I guess they can do whatever the fuck they want, right?

Dolan said, What are you asking *me* to do?

Fuck, Connie, I don't know. Tell me I don't have to do this.

You don't have to do this.

What I wanted to hear.

But if you were smart, Dolan said, you'd think about it. You know what I'm saying.

I know what you're saying.

One more thing, said Dolan, and he nodded his head aft, Renee above them at the wheel framed from the waist up by the open hatch.

She's straight, man, said Parmentier. She'll blow a line of coke every once in a while but that's it. Beginning, middle, end of story.

Tell me a girl that smart doesn't have your number.

I'm a businessman, I do some work for the government here and there—what's to know? She knows I make a lot of money and when she asks a question I tell her something and she doesn't ask again. She does her thing, I do mine. And hey, bro, she loves me.

Why?

Don't go hurting my feelings, Connie.

Conrad Dolan spent the following week on the phone, trying to pin down the operation but could only establish that agent Reece's bona fides were in order, that the operation wasn't Miami-based but had originated up the food chain in Washington, and that the field officer assigned to Parmentier in Port-au-Prince was none other than an erstwhile colleague, Woodrow Singer, in Dolan's opinion the embodiment of a worthless breed of special agent infesting the ranks throughout the decade like termites chewing into the Bureau's wood—midwestern evangelicals and razor-cut Mormons and born-again millenarians dedicated to spreading the word of Christ from behind their desks, more inclined to ask a source to pray with them than pass on information important to a case. In the convolutions of their moral universe, hell on earth was being ordered by a supervisor to stake out a brothel, consume an alcoholic beverage with satanic rock and roll pounding in their ears, look at tits, and talk to a bad guy who had no regard for Jesus. The Prissies, Dolan called them, this new half-breed of hygienic agents. In Dolan's experience, too much religion, like too much bureaucracy, watered down a nation's ability to remain strong; he could feel it happening in the Bureau, he could feel it happening in America, and when he learned that Woodrow Singer had been assigned to Parmentier to develop an operation in Haiti, the nature of which no one in Dolan's network of contacts seemed to know, his heart sank because he understood Singer would never be able to exert control over a con man like Parmentier, that, sensing Woodrow Singer's weakness, eventually Parmentier would work the setup to his own advantage, a prospect that unsettled Dolan because the benefits and immunities accorded Parmentier for his participation in the Tampa sting were already beyond the pale.

Soon after that day on the sailboat Parmentier and his wife disappeared south, back to Haiti, Dolan had his own business to attend to in Latin America and it was another month before they were all back in Florida and Parmentier finally answered his cell phone and Dolan said, *Como sa va*, fuckhead, and Parmentier said the reception on his phone was lousy and how did tomorrow morning at nine sound. Dolan said fine, bring a gun to shoot yourself with.

They met, as was their habit, on the boat. Dolan said let's ring some bells and then said the name of Woodrow Singer. He wanted to know why Parmentier had solicited his advice on a decision that had already been made, an operation that was already up and running and assigned a handler. Parmentier swore he hadn't been misleading Dolan when he asked for advice, although he admitted he hadn't explained himself well or completely. He had only spoken to Reece in Miami and had only promised Reece he would think about it, take the project under consideration, then, on his next trip to Haiti, there was Woodrow Singer—the Deacon, Renee called him, God this and the Bible that, Haiti is Beezlebub's workshop, you too are a sinner boy and I can help you come back to Jesus—and Parmentier knew he had to close the door on this jackass but, Connie, said Parmentier, things got complicated like they always do. I got word from one of my associates that the big dogs wanted me inside the operation.

One of your guys? asked Dolan, astounded. How come you're not dead yet, letting it be known you work with the Feds? You're out of your everfucking mind, my friend.

Hey, no, it's cool, Connie, I'm covered, said Parmentier. He said he had a board of directors, and one of them took him aside and said in confidence he had someone on the payroll inside the Miami bureau and this guy told him about the Haiti project the Feds were starting up and mentioned Parmentier's name and the big dog fell in love with the project and thought it would fit in well with some other things they were wanting to do and he said, hey, just between you and me, let's do it. So I've been doing it but honest to God, Connie, this guy Singer is like a god-robot, he doesn't understand how to work with a businessman, he's got no sense of humor, he thinks all Haitians are maggots—which, you know, causes its own set of problems—and I wasn't shitting you when I asked back then if I had to do this.

Let me assure you, said Dolan, your organization has no one on its payroll inside the Miami bureau.

Don't be too sure about that, Connie.

Your associate found out about this project from some other source.

Whatever, said Parmentier. Water under the bridge, all right?

Dolan thought he had heard Parmentier say he was withdrawing from his role in the operation but that wasn't the case. Parmentier's enthusiasm for the project had only grown, as had his belief that Singer, however irritating, would become less of a problem over time.

What's so great about this project anyway, said Dolan. What are we talking about here?

It's one of those things, said Parmentier. I can't say. This has been made very clear to me.

What? That you can't tell me? They said my name?

No, that I can't tell anybody. Even, like, my wife, although she knows some of the pieces because she's useful, right. There's only four guys in the loop. Actually five. Me, the dog, Reece, Singer, a local guy in Port-au-Prince.

Make it six, said Dolan.

Aw, Connie, come on, you know how this stuff works.

You bet I do, you little prick, said Dolan, his voice spilling out the wrath. Whatever you're doing, when it goes wrong, I better not see any blowback headed in my direction. Anybody comes after you, you ask that motherfucking Holy Roller Woodrow Singer to take care of it.

Aw, Connie, come on, don't be that way. It's just a little backroom paperwork. Passports, visas. You know what I'm saying.

Dolan, though, hadn't expected this, the government slipping clients across the border with forged documents. Who are they bringing in? he asked.

I don't know, said Parmentier. Some guys they said who helped them in the Gulf War and other places who couldn't stay where they were and when they tried to come here I guess got fucked by the system. Sand niggers, towel heads. You know the kind of people I'm talking about.

Helped who? asked Dolan, mystified. I'm trying to understand this. Are we friends with these people anymore?

They don't sketch it out for me, Connie. I just assumed the military. Like those mountain people helped our guys in Vietnam against the communists. We put them in Kansas or Minnesota or some shit hole, right?

I don't get it, said Dolan.

Sure you do, Connie, said Parmentier. It's like me and you, right? You make me a promise and you keep your promise. Hey, when the trooper pulled me over on the turnpike, right? He didn't know he was wasting his time? Same thing, right? This guy over there makes you a promise, this guy over here doesn't know or care about the promise, the guy who made the promise has to fix the problem. It's his duty, right?

That was the last Dolan saw or heard from Parmentier until he phoned from the Miami courthouse where he was being arraigned for murder. But he ran into Renee one more time.

By now Tom Harrington had felt his anger devolve to a familiar lethargy— the same sense that he disappeared into during every narrative told to him in Haiti, like a theatergoer dragged onstage and swallowed into the ensemble, and he broke his silence with the well-rehearsed lines of his frustration, the refrain that he couldn't make go away.

Are you a good guy or a bad guy? he asked Dolan.

All Dolan said was that he thought lawyers weren't supposed to ask questions to which they didn't want to know the answers. Harrington's rage seemed to jerk him up by the collar of his shirt and send him out of the bar and up the Oloffson's creaky wooden staircase to his shabby dormitory room in a wing of the hotel that had once been a hospital ward earlier in the century. In the stifling darkness of the room a scythe of panic cut him at the knees and he tumbled into the lumpy heat of his bed, choking back sobs of self-pity. He had seen all the dead but had never seen the dying. There was a dog once, his dog, when he was fourteen years old. Rubbernecking accidents on Interstate 95. Breathing fast and hard he made himself light-headed, staring blindly at the slow rotation of the ceiling fan. Sometime in the middle of the night gunfire erupted down the hill toward the palace, the echo of the unseen violence carrying him safely past the dread and grief and torment to a terrible calm.

What Dolan said. He had killed a man, hadn't he?

Maybe. Probably. Yes, most likely he had. Add it to the list. Most likely he was damned, a condition remarkable only for the lack of difficulty or regret with which he accepted it before he fell asleep.

CHAPTER TEN

In the serving line the three soldiers heaped their plates with stewed beef and grilled fish and varieties of salad but barely touched the food back at the table, their appetites lost or perhaps they just didn't trust the cooking or had become so accustomed to eating pouches of ready-made rations they were unable to stomach anything better. Tom saw the melancholic weight of this, their final night in Haiti, upon them, their shoulders hunched forward and spirits sagging and Jackie cocked her head to show concern and asked what was going on, guys, why so gloomy? They were going home and leaving the job hanging in the air and there were no follow-ons and no Plan Bs and no satisfaction and they were without glory. The arc of their narrative in Haiti had begun with the roads lined ten deep with teary-eyed wretches screaming *thank you* and had climaxed with the curtain closing on a loud chorus of *fuck you*s, a coda of resentment. They were going home to pick up the pieces of their lives or going home to an empty house or irate wives and children they hardly knew and after forty-five days they would ship out to Bosnia or Chad or Colombia or some other land of the eternally cursed and forsaken where everyone was at each other's throats and you had every reason to expect your neighbors were coming after you during the night.

Eville Burnette apologized to Tom and Jackie. We're here but we're not here.

We're gone but we're not gone, Tet Rouge agreed, a weak smile in the corner of his mouth.

Inside the hotel's lobby the house band began to tune their instruments and Warrant Officer Brooks looked at his wristwatch and pushed back his chair and said, No, we're just gone, but Eville Burnette said if it was all right with them and all right with Tom and Jackie, he would stay and listen to the music for a while and get a taxi back to the LIC or maybe Tom would give him a ride. The soldiers had a two-man rule and Tom could see that the warrant officer did not like this idea of splitting up and was surprised when he heard the officers defer to the noncom and Brooks say, Plane's at oh-six-hundred. See you there. They stood up together like boys accused of trespassing, Brooks and Captain Butler, fixed the berets on their heads and said sorry for being bad company and left.

Burnette and Jackie let Tom buy a round of rum sours and when Joseph returned with the drinks the waiter told Tom there was a man who had asked to see him and then the voodoo drummers sent a thunderclap of rhythm into the night. Jackie looked at him knowingly, her eyes suggesting their common secret, and the drums were like a call to arms to Harrington's obsession.

In the story Tom told his wife, Jacqueline Scott had been displaced from his lap to sit properly at his side, a realignment necessary to create an official version of the story. Because what was he going to say otherwise, even though for Harrington the truest part of what happened in the *houngan's* private chapel, the part that would always cause him to lie, was Jackie there atop him, pressing herself into Tom's lap every day for the rest of his life, his mind sown with the indelible desire that seemed to invade him so suddenly when the space between the two of them widened, as if these small distances—she below him on the beach or crossing a room toward him or Tom watching her now above him in the veranda's aquarium of happy light, drinking with Master Sergeant Eville Burnette—were somehow aphrodisiacal, the atmosphere between them swirling with the fumes of attraction that seemed easy to ignore only if he were at her side, close enough to measure her afflictions, reacting to the imperfect details of a person and not a white-hot, fever-dream blaze of yearning.

Sitting poolside on the lower terrace with François Colon, the Haitian lawyer who had left messages throughout the day and had now begged

Harrington away from his dinner guests for a few minutes, Tom couldn't take his eyes from her. He decided he didn't like it very much when Jackie leaned in to Burnette to confide her thoughts, or touched his arm when she laughed, and Colon, increasingly perturbed, received only the residue of Tom's attention.

But then François Colon ended a sentence Tom did not quite hear with a phrase that jarred him. The spell snapped and he made himself focus on the light-skinned lawyer, the last scion of a family annihilated by the dictator Papa Doc while Colon was away at university in Paris. He was an elegant, green-eyed mulatto with the fluffy manners of a Creole aristocrat who had made a fortune protecting other people's fortunes from the internecine cupidity of the ruling class, and Harrington did not care for his smug superiority or his list of clients.

Sorry, he said. What was that?

I said, Don't you?

Don't I what?

Believe in mass graves for the right people.

You don't know what you're saying, François, Tom responded, and by the time Colon explained his point, Harrington found himself buried under the edifice of the principles that had defined him, first as a correspondent and now as a lawyer and activist, not vague notions but once-clear ideas battered into merciless diffusion by Haiti.

He had come to understand that we choose the lies in which we participate and, in choosing, define ourselves and our actions for a very long time, perhaps forever—Haiti invited such participation, Haiti was a feeding trough for the manifest appetites of egos and illusions and simple schemes of rescue, Haiti offered its players a culture of impunity not just for the atrocities that devoured body and soul, but for the self-deceptions best described as crimes of enlightenment. Tom Harrington understood this, understood that the notions of civilization he had devoted himself to were mostly myths meant to replenish one's inventory of motivations, and if power could be used for moral purposes, he had seen very little of it in the world. Justice was the blood sport of kings, human rights were the toilet that powerful men shit in. Am I wrong or right? demanded François Colon.

127

BOB SHACOCHIS

The rights of man—was that the benediction he recited as he stood over the freshly opened pits, counting the bones?

Somewhere along the line, standing over the graves watching the bones boil up to the surface, Harrington had lost a firm sense of the value of life and, knowing that was the case, fought for its value with more ferocity but less inner faith in the battle and in himself, a humanitarian wandering around hell in a stupor. Now it seemed he would be tested again.

For some months the bourgeoisie in the north, the big landowners in the mountains west of Cap-Haïtien, had begun to return quietly from exile in Miami and New York and the Dominican Republic to live in the democracy created by the Americans. Colon himself had encouraged them, assured them—your fields are fallow, your coffee beans unpicked, your workers unpaid, your prayers unanswered: be patriots, rebuild your homeland, restore its dignity and beauty. Yes, there were troubles between the families and the peasants in the past; yes, there was oppression; yes, there was exploitation; yes, bloodshed; but Haitians were one people sharing one destiny and would, perforce, accept the new order. And, monsieur, how do you suppose it has been for them since they have returned to their country? asked Colon. What in their birthplace did they find to lift their spirits? *Merde.* Shit. Instead of democracy, anarchy. Instead of police, bandits. Instead of new friends, old enemies. Instead of harmony, revenge. Instead of human beings, animals. Instead of peace, death.

François Colon asked Tom to remember back to the second week of the invasion when American marines had occupied Cap-Haïtien. You know, of course, of the massacre by Jacques Lecoeur and his men in the countryside during that time, said Colon. The houses of the *chefs du sections* razed to the ground, the men and their families nowhere to be found, two FAHD caserns attacked and overrun by Lecoeur's gang, the soldiers unaccounted for.

You investigated these massacres yourself, monsieur, I recall.

I heard the rumors, yes.

Rumors!

You're right, I did investigate. No bodies, no graves, no witnesses. And yes, the *chefs du section*'s houses were burned, but these men were *macoutes*—

128

Ah, monsieur, I'm happy you make this point, because it answers my original question: You believe in mass graves for the right people . . . the so-called bad people, yes?

That's not at all what I'm saying, Harrington protested. I mean they were men hated by their communities, by the people, and they abandoned their houses and abandoned their posts and ran away.

Perhaps we must think of it as justice, when bad people are killed by vigilantes, said Colon, offending Harrington, because advocates like François Colon, men of his position, men with no apparent use for the inconveniences of process and transparency, were the ones who had maneuvered adamantly behind the scenes to thwart the Commission for Truth and Reconciliation.

Yes, I admit as much, said Colon, but now I am here to help.

But it's over, Harrington wanted to say. Talk to me about it, he said instead.

On a page he removed from a yellow legal pad, Colon gave Harrington the names and last known location of six men and one woman—all members of families notorious for plundering Haiti generation after generation—and Tom read the names and stared at the piece of paper. Where are these people? asked Colon. He wanted Tom to find them. You know how to do this, he said. Arrangements had been made. Find their bodies or find their killers, he said, and doors that are closed shall open.

But it's over, Harrington again wanted to say but knew he couldn't, and his vacant gaze drifted up to the veranda and settled on Jackie, the gabled and spired backdrop of the hotel like a haunted house in the moonlight, and the longer he looked at her the more he felt a stranger to himself, sensing she would stalk the periphery of his life if he did not know her.

His return to the table interrupted a debate about the wisdom of disbanding the collection of brutes and idiots formerly known as the Haitian army, Jackie wagging her fork at Eville to make a point Tom imagined she had picked up from the newspapers. The conversation stopped, the two of them studying the change in Tom as he sat back down. There's a situation, he said, his brow furrowing. Something's come up. It wasn't his nature to be evasive and his reluctance to explain himself, acting as though he had something to hide, made him uncomfortable. He looked at Jackie, her eyes quizzical, her expression waiting for him to speak, and could not resist the impulse to tell her everything. Neither she nor Burnette seemed to understand or care about the moral ambiguity of his mission to the north.

What's this Lecoeur like? Burnette wondered, impressed that Tom had hiked into the mountains and tracked down the guerilla leader, a goal that had eluded the Special Forces.

I doubt very much that he's a killer.

He's a warlord.

Bad intel, said Tom. He's a freedom fighter.

How can you be a so-called freedom fighter and not a killer? said Master Sergeant Burnette. Explain that one to me.

Can I go with you? Jackie said to Tom and though he hesitated and said he wanted to think about it and Eville thought it was a bad idea to take her up into the wild heart of the mountains, again it was not possible for Tom to tell her no.

Eville said thanks for the night out and wished them luck and Tom walked him down to the car park and there was Gerard still hanging about with his crowd of fixers, playing dominoes. He gave Gerard the keys to drive the sergeant back to his base and told him he could take the car home for the night but be back early to go to the airport. Gerard asked if he was leaving for Miami and Tom said, no, Le Cap. Gerard wanted to know if he should pack an overnight bag but Tom told him he was flying up with the UN and Gerard knew what that meant, no Haitians except *gros negs* and murderers. If you're ever in Fayettenam, said Eville Burnette. They shook hands and Tom felt they had both come a long way in the past year toward respecting each other's place in the world but doubted they would ever see one another again.

Jackie had left the veranda—Tom could see that as he walked back toward the wall of sound coming from the Oloffson, the air fragrant with potential, anxious to be alone with her again. Maybe someone had asked her to dance he thought and pushed his way into the bar and searched the cramp of dancers out on the floor but there were only two white women there among the heave of black bodies and she wasn't one of them. He waited by the line to the WC until a man came out and then he went to the front desk and asked to be connected on the house phone to her room but the line was busy and still busy when he tried again after squeezing back through to the bar for a cognac, then back again for another as the band unplugged and the place began to empty down to Tom and the bartender and a lost pair of unlucky whores, one with four or five strands of billy-goat hair on her chin. He phoned one last time and she picked up with a sharp, *Yes?* He said, You just disappeared, and Jackie said in a bothered tone *that it really been a long day* and she'd see him in the morning. When he went back to the bar to sign his bill he heard pistol shots outside the high walls but that was normal and he went to bed.

Of all the things he might have said to her he said the worst, telling her she looked pretty as she thumped across the floorboards of the veranda toward him the next morning shortly after dawn. Her face was open and fresh and painfully young, without makeup except the slightest bit to enlarge her eyes. What she could pull back of her hair was banded in a ponytail, what she couldn't pull back hung to the sides like a dog's floppy ears, a black baseball cap on her head sans logo or lettering, her tan photographer's vest over a white V-neck T-shirt, the same baggy many-pocketed pants he had seen her in before, hiking boots, camera bag, the straps of a nylon day pack pushing her breasts together into a pronounced greeting. Her sleepy expression hardened as she lowered her bag and removed her pack and sat across from Tom at the table bringing a whiff of talcum and skin lotion to his nose. She looked right through him and he could see she was this other woman again, severe and bilious and bitchy, the one he knew first and still most expected.

Is that why you're taking me? Because I'm pretty?

Forget it, he said, shaking his head. He had been at the Oloffson long enough to enjoy early morning kitchen rights, permission to make coffee before the staff arrived. Would you like some? he asked, holding the pot over an empty cup and she nodded.

131

No, really, she said, unwilling to not challenge him. That's the reason, isn't it?

You sure run hot and cold, don't you?

What do you mean? she said archly.

He drank his coffee because he wasn't going to say any more. Yesterday he had put aside his identity to be with her but today he had folded himself back into the resolve of his profession and could not let himself be distracted by a neurotic woman. They sat for several minutes without speaking, listening to the flute of birdsong below in the gardens, Jackie's head bowed, the purse of her lips inches from the rim of her cup. Finally she sighed and raised her eyes and looked at him, her mouth gradually forming a half-smile of contrition.

Sorry. Okay?

What we have to do is very difficult. You have to trust me. We have to get along. It will be a serious mistake if you go and you don't trust me and we don't get along.

I know, Jackie said, reaching across the table to take his hand and squeeze it with reassurance. We will. Just don't underestimate me because I'm a female. That would be a mistake too. That's all I meant to say.

Our friends in the Special Forces will appreciate that.

Oh, my God, that woman beat the shit out of those guys, didn't she, and they both laughed and Tom felt more at ease.

Gerard arrived and they drove to the airport and then to the opposite perimeter of the compound where the UN had established its headquarters and Gerard waited while Tom and Jackie went inside to add her name to the flight manifest but immediately there was a problem. No matter how many times Tom waved his documentation in the face of the flight operations manager and insisted that the photojournalist be allowed to accompany him on his official mission to the north, the ops manager repeated mechanically that Jacqueline Scott had not been properly accredited and was ineligible for free rides on military helicopters. The argument brought the public affairs officer—a friend of Tom's who tried to help—out from his cubicle but when Jackie couldn't produce any ID affiliating her with a media outlet or NGO, there was nothing he could do but smile cockeyed at Tom and his little friend.

Walking back to the SUV Tom asked her how bad she wanted to go and she said how bad do you think and he hated to see her crestfallen and felt a sudden strong need not to disappoint her. Okay, he said, let's talk to Gerard and see if he's up for a trip, but Gerard took him aside and confessed he did not want to drive all day alone with this *foo* white woman who had lost her soul and he didn't understand why Tom wanted her along when he already had a taste of what a problem she could be.

She's a photographer, this could be an important story. She wants to work, and you want to work. True?

I don't know. I don't trust this woman, but Gerard nevertheless agreed to take her north.

Jackie thanked Tom but Tom said thank Gerard. He promised they would all ride back together in the SUV in two or three days. They drove out on the tarmac to the Chinook helicopter the UN leased from the Americans and Tom walked around under the tail of the bird and handed his rucksack to the cargo chief who checked his name on the manifest and handed him earplugs. Tom looked at the clipboard and up the ramp of the Chinook into the tubular cave of its interior, its center deck loaded with palettes of supplies and the seats along both sides of the fuselage unoccupied but for a squad of Caricom policemen and three civilians he assumed were contract employees. He turned back to the cargo chief and said not many passengers.

We pick them up in Gonaïves.

Tom nodded toward the SUV where Jackie and Gerard were still standing. See that girl over there?

Yes, sir.

Let's take her along.

No can do. Bird's full after Gonaïves.

She'll sit in your lap, man, he said.

I wouldn't make it through the flight, sir.

He walked back to tell her he had tried and that he would reserve rooms for both of them at the Hotel Christophe and see them there at cocktail hour. Out of the habit of Haitian manners, he leaned forward to peck Jackie on the cheek farewell but she jerked her head away and down so that the kiss fell awkwardly where her baseball cap met her ear. In his seat at the rear of the helicopter he buckled into his safety harness and the rotors began to whine but he couldn't get the image of her unnecessary rejection out of his mind, and as they lifted into the air he told himself of course it was out of her control and slowly he forgave her.

On the flight across the Bay of Gonave the Chinook speared through the top of a squall, bumping in and out of the storm's cluster of cells, purple whirlwinds of rain opening into brilliant white celestial amphitheaters of billowing cumulus, then slamming back into the tempest, the rain shearing off into calm blue fields scrubbed with sunlight, then shearing back into a dark whip of chaos, and when it was over Tom felt spiritually alive and filled with gratitude. Then they descended to the infested wasteland that was Gonaïves.

The three *blan* civilians disembarked, as did the police, and Tom walked across a soccer field sown with broken glass and garbage to a line of vendors behind a chain-link fence. He bought a Coca-Cola from an old woman squatting next to a filthy plastic bucket of melting ice and a banana fritter from another woman just like her and stood with them in the blistering sun and listened to the merchants' scrape-bottom litany of proverbs and misery and jokes while he waited for the ground crew to offload a palette of bottled water and another of canned food and vegetable oil and meals ready to eat. A pair of white pickup trucks arrived at the landing pad, their beds lined ten each with Pakistani troops crammed together on wooden benches, and Tom watched them file onto the ramp of the Chinook with their heavy rucksacks and their rifles, thinking they seemed more geared up and professional than the typical Central Asian cannon fodder. Finally the cargo chief waved him back and Tom strapped himself in and they waited for the better part of an hour without any explanation and then took off.

At the airstrip in Cap-Haïtien, he was met by a Pakistani aide-de-camp who drove him a few hundred yards to the UN bivouac where he sat down in the officers mess for an early lunch of dahl and rice, fried cauliflower, and chicken with Colonel Khan, the base commander for the northern district. The colonel's briefing took Tom by surprise. Now that the Americans had left, said Colonel Khan, he had been successful in his attempt to coax Jacques Lecoeur out of the mountains for a negotiation. To negotiate what? asked Tom.

What else is there to negotiate? said Khan. To lay down their arms and join the political process, inshallah, said the colonel.

When was this? asked Tom.

One month ago.

And?

Mister Lecoeur agreed. But he has not turned in his weapons. He has not come out of the wilderness.

Tom asked the colonel about the reports of people missing from the big families.

It's difficult to know, said the colonel. Some are gang members, very slippery characters. Some might have returned to the States or gone to the capital without telling anybody. But you are here to solve the mystery, I am told. You are the expert, the one people will talk to.

Not everyone.

You promise them what you can't give them and they come to you like children.

What do I promise?

Justice.

What do *you* promise?

The wrath of God. The divine right of kings. And failing that, then order. Have you ever been to Pakistan? the colonel asked.

No.

These people who can't control themselves. In Pakistan, we know what to do with them.

I've heard that's true. Such an orderly nation, Pakistan.

Good luck in the mountains, said the colonel, his gaze circling around the tent. Sorry, where is your bodyguard? You're not alone, are you? You should not go up there alone.

Tom explained that he never traveled with security personnel and the colonel said he had been told that Tom had been assigned a bodyguard.

I don't know who told you that, said Tom, but it's wrong. I have a photographer and a driver coming, that's all.

Then the aide-de-camp took him into town and dropped him at the Christophe, where he learned from Henri, the proprietor, that the hotel had been occupied for weeks by international police monitors and UN consultants. Two rooms remained available for tonight, but Henri would only guarantee one for tomorrow. Harrington told him brightly, *We'll make do*. He checked in and stowed his bag in the room with the larger bed and hired a driver to take him to a neighborhood on the southern outskirts of the city where he met with Père Dominique, a leftist French priest who had gone underground to escape assassination during the de facto regime and had served as a contact for Jacques Lecoeur after the Americans came ashore. Dominique made arrangements for Tom to meet a pair of Lecoeur's men where the road into the mountains ended, at the hamlet of Bois Caïman, and these men would guide him to Lecoeur. In the midafternoon, he instructed the driver to take him farther south into the countryside, to a sugar mill where he met with a representative of the old families, who presented Tom with a computer disc that contained a file on the missing persons. Then it was back to the Christophe for a much-anticipated cocktail with Jackie but when he walked into the bar and saw her wave from a table he could not even begin to comprehend why Gerard wasn't by her side instead of Eville Burnette, out of uniform, all smiles, saluting Tom with a bottle of beer.

CHAPTER ELEVEN

In the morning he stripped off the rank clothes he had slept in and stepped into the bathroom. The hot water was no hotter than the air and he chose the better option and showered cold, trying to rethink Jacqueline Scott's ambiguous relationship with her camera, of no more substance than a hip ornament or stylish prop, he was sure, until they were up in the mountains and had rendezvoused with a party of Lecoeur's men and everything went to hell. But any doubts he had back then about Jackie as a photographer had been dispelled by something Conrad Dolan had revealed during last night's bar-stool confessions. Her interest in *vodou* had been genuine; she had documented the *houngans* and their ceremonies; her work had been good enough (or sensational enough) to merit a gallery show in Tampa.

What, if anything, did this foretell, and did it at least mean she had mingled with the *lwas* with enough sufficiency to have her soul restored? When Tom Harrington asked himself that question, he was not serious. Jackie Scott, he thought, never had a soul to lose, or had long ago lost sight of it, and she had drawn him into this dark vacancy of hers with the irresistible skill of a succubus.

Refreshed and clearheaded, he toweled off and shaved, careful not to nick himself and go home with hepatitis, then dressed in chinos and a T-shirt and went barefoot down to breakfast, Joseph so happy to see him on the veranda that he threw his arms around the American lawyer. Tom stiffened in the embrace as he looked beyond the waiter's shoulder at the

137

table where a rumpled and chagrined Connie Dolan sat with Gerard, who, from the conflicted look of shock and pleasure on his face, had not yet been told Tom was in town.

I tell myself you will never come back, Gerard said in Kreyol, rising to his feet as Joseph released Tom and Tom pressed Gerard to him briefly and stepped back and Gerard lowered his voice to a mumble. The *foo* woman is dead, Tom.

They continued speaking in Kreyol. Yes, I know.

You have come back because of the woman, yes?

It is not my business, said Tom, his eyes avoiding Dolan's, adding that he was, in fact, leaving the island that afternoon, and inquired if Gerard was free to give him a lift to the airport.

From the pained expression on Gerard's rough face he understood the answer was no, his services already procured by Dolan for a trip up the coast to the police station in Saint-Marc. Dolan interrupted to ask Harrington to sit and have breakfast with them but Tom ignored the invitation and Gerard told him that, like this white man now at the table, Americans had come from Miami to speak with Gerard about the woman.

Yes, I know, said Tom. You told them that she and I went up into the mountains.

Yes, said Gerard. The Americans wanted to know about the north but I told them I was in Port-au-Prince and could only say what I know from what the people say.

Bon, said Tom. Gerard, tell me. What *didn't* you tell the Americans?

Come on, Harrington, Dolan tried again. Let's get past last night.

Slyly, Gerard smiled. He liked this question of Tom's. Three things, he said. The woman and man make a business with all the bad people, and the foreign people too.

That is what I'm finding out, said Tom.

Dolan no longer seemed interested in placating Tom. Stop acting like a jackass and speak English and sit down, he said, which provoked an outburst from Tom, who spun on his feet and took a hard step toward the table, teeth and fists clenched.

I want you to know something, Connie. This person I'm supposed to have killed. Damn it, it was an accident.

It wasn't an accident, my friend. It was nothing other than self-defense, said Dolan, surrendering the irritation in his voice. You ran an ambush. I would have done the same. He pulled a chair out from the table as a peace offering. Give me the chance to tell you the rest of what you don't know and then you can catch a flight out of here, if that's what you want. Gerard, you too, sit. Just speak English, for fuck's sake.

Joseph brought a fresh pot of coffee and took their orders and Tom listened to Dolan's encore performance, the bewildering and ultimately outlandish tale of what had happened when he saw Jackie for the second time, months after his last encounter with Parmentier and only several weeks before she was murdered. Dolan said he was at a steak house in Ybor City with a prospective client, a local woman who had requested a meeting over drinks and dinner. Her dime, so why not? A young woman dining alone in a booth along the wall smiled boldly at him and fluttered her fingers hello. She was audacious but beautiful and he thought here's a paycheck to paycheck gal, après-office-secretary overexerting herself when the rent's due, because he didn't recognize her, but she was persistent and finally he stared at her long enough to realize it was Parmentier's wife, Renee Gardner—Jackie, although he never knew her as Jackie. Her hair was dyed auburn and cut in a bob that revealed a dangle of sparkling earrings. She had put on lipstick and her nails were painted candy-apple red and she wore a black cocktail dress and high heels and flagged over a waiter to take a note she quickly scribbled on a napkin. A minute later the note was in Dolan's hands along with a fresh scotch on the rocks courtesy of the lady. *Nice to see you again, Special Agent Dolan.* The woman who wanted to engage his services to discover how much her husband was really worth took one bite of the pasta on her plate and stood up, saying she'd call him, and left with an abruptness that you would be tempted to call premeditated. Dolan rattled the ice in his glass, deliberating his cue to take the drink over to Jackie's table but she was already sliding into the chair across from him.

The lovely Mrs. Parmentier, he said. Why not just pick up the phone?

She looked demure and said she wasn't good on the phone and surprise parties were fun, weren't they, less inhibiting anyway, and he tried to overlook the element of flirtation in her voice and manner by being brusque and skeptical. In her present incarnation, less salty voluptuousness and more the perfumed glamour of sophistication and class, he had to keep reminding himself—it was like a commercial jingle looping around in his skull—*This chick married a fuckhead.* Anything multiplied by zero equals zero.

How's Jack?

Jack was on a business trip down south, she said, and after a long pause, waiting for Dolan to say something, she told him she was worried about her husband.

Why, because he's the light of your life?

That's rude, she said but he could see the actress behind the pout, that she wasn't really insulted.

Dolan apologized, almost guilty for his instincts toward her. How's the photography going? he asked, but she didn't want to change the subject and said that Parmentier was in over his head down there and didn't seem to know it, or didn't seem to care, and she suspected it was all going to end badly if something wasn't done. It was not a lament but a report, a briefing so shorn of tones of distress as to be almost scripted.

Down where? asked Dolan.

Okay, Special Agent Dolan. You're going to bullshit me, right?

Retired, said Dolan. Call me Connie.

Well, Connie, Jack's fucking over your people at the Bureau, did you know that?

How would I know that?

Parmentier liked to boast to her about the Tampa operation but she hadn't believed the stories until they went to Haiti together and there waiting for them was an emissary from God and country, an absurdly pious disciple named Woodrow Singer, who would meet them for Saturday lunch on the beach up the coast at a place called Moulin Sur Mer. If Jack worked with the Bureau in Tampa, she told herself, then she shouldn't be surprised or alarmed that he was doing it in Haiti as well. Perhaps she should have been proud of him, a private citizen and businessman answering the call of his government. Even in the heat of the tropics Singer wore a coat and tie and linen shirts with a small gold crucifix monogrammed on each cuff, never removed his aviator sunglasses, always ordered boiled lobster and meticulously picked its shell, cleaned his hands with packaged wipes before and after eating, always drank bottled water he had personally imported from his home state of Utah, and inevitably made enthusiastic reference to the earthly benefits of salvation by a higher power. Jackie would roll her eyes. Parmentier would smile and nod agreeably and burp, *amen*, blasted on rum sours. At the end of these lunches it was understood she would go for a swim and Singer would deliver to Parmentier a list of names, usually Near and Middle Easterners, and the following week Parmentier would go to an art gallery in Port-au-Prince owned by a Syrian and the Syrian would have photographs and basic information about the men on the list and he and Parmentier would put together passports and visas for the men and Singer probably expected that only the names on the list were given new identities and documents.

The problem is, said Jackie, Jack's been double-dipping on the paperwork, forging documents for people who aren't on the list, or forging an extra set with different identities for some of the men who *are* on the list.

Huh, said Dolan, trying to understand why she was telling him these things.

That's it? *Huh?*

From the sound of things, Dolan suggested, she seemed rather involved in it all.

Honestly, no, she said. She kept her distance, she claimed, consumed by her own projects. But sometimes he needed her to translate documents from Arabic, she said, so I know more than I want to about what's going on.

Arabic? He had forgotten Parmentier bragging about her proficiency with languages. Why do you know Arabic?

Because I do.

And just what is it that's going on? asked Dolan.

That's why I'm talking to you. What's going on, Connie?

The one thing I don't understand, he said. You're smart, beautiful, talented.

Blah blah blah.

What are you doing with a criminal like Jack Parmentier?

A criminal? she scoffed. He's not so different than you. Why don't you ask yourself that question?

Dolan couldn't bring her into focus. What's your angle here, Renee? Money? Drugs? Outlaw thrills? Sympathy for the devil? Was she one of those otherwise straightlaced girls who sought out rogues as an avenue of rebellion against their demanding fathers?

I don't care about drugs, she said dismissively, and he said, then that would explain why it doesn't bother you that your husband is a narcotrafficker. She smirked and said if the government didn't mind, why should she? And, anyway, how could she explain herself or her motives let alone the unlikely passions of her heart to a mind as unimaginative as Dolan's. You are the product of a system, she told Dolan, and I am the product of a vision.

Well, you're right, honey, I ain't Dostoyevsky, said Dolan, but I ain't wrong, either. You either have a predictable, and predictably dirty, reason for marrying this lowlife, or you should think about visiting your mental health care provider because you're certifiably nuts.

Let's stop, she said, fixing her eyes on Dolan. She needed him to be her friend and ally, she needed his help. I want you to tell Parmentier to stop doing what he's doing. I mean with the Arabs.

You have a thing with Arabs?

Trust me, she said. Make Jack stop before he gets himself killed.

Really? said Dolan. Who's going to kill him?

Who knows, she said dispassionately. People are lining up. Could be *moi*, she said with a flippant toss of her hair.

Dolan thought, with my blessings, sweetheart. He knew better than to guffaw, having learned long ago the cold truth good citizens spent their lives denying, that the right context could rip away every boundary of self-restraint from the most virtuous person, but his eyes reflected bluff and she did not react well to his assessment of her threat. Slipping off a shoe under the table, she suddenly jabbed him hard with her stockinged heel, the quick stab of pain taking away the breath he had meant to use to ask her—Why? But did it really matter why, because he knew if she was being straight with him she was doomed, tomorrow, next month, next year, condemned already and sentenced to death.

You're taking me for granted, Agent Dolan.

Goddamn, he hissed. Don't you think just leaving him is the better option here?

I'm serious, she said. And you fucking know it.

Conrad Dolan hadn't been kicked square in the balls by a female since grade school. He was furious and, inexplicably and ridiculously, smitten by the fantasy of roughhouse sex with Parmentier's overreaching wife. I'll talk to him, he promised, but Renee Gardner was dying on the side of a road in Haiti before he even thought about trying.

Tom Harrington had made himself into a listener, the most reliable asset of his personality, there at the center of the self he believed in. Listening, he had come to understand, was his vocation, his gift. Even as a child, raised like so many other children by an unedited mother with too much to say and a father who practiced the mental golf swings of inattention, Harrington determined that although not everybody felt the need to talk, most people did, compelled to spill out their stories and opinions to any audience within range but very few found value in the art of listening, least of all to themselves, or found virtue in the discipline of concentrated silence. Harrington, though, had successfully adapted, perhaps helped to create, the persona of a new genus of roving therapist, a global receptor, circuit rider for the world's unattended pain, patient and respectful, habitually sincere, gently prompting yet diligent in his questioning. The difference between his previous life as a correspondent and his life as an activist began where the listening stopped.

Even so, concerning all things Jackie, he found himself frequently lapsing into a form of preoccupation that seemed without shape or content, unalert and dull, distracted by the inability of his own mind to cease its rummaging with no purpose through a bin of images that the woman had left behind in his life, sucking him inward like a dark force. Conrad Dolan had stopped talking and Tom, not listening, knew he had just been told something earth-shattering but he could not yet summon the mental energy to align the pieces into a logical whole. I don't have a stellar intellect, he often reminded himself as a way of taking his bearings, I simply have one well-calibrated to manage an endless assault of practicalities, so let's get to work. But what was before him now seemed beyond him, this gathering of shifting shapes, foremost his own, inspired, if that was the word, by Jackie. He felt dreamy and stupid and wasn't going to embarrass himself by asking Dolan to repeat the story and so he cracked and peeled the shells off his soft-boiled eggs and sprinkled their tops with pepper and unconsciously gagged himself, an entire egg stuffed in his mouth.

Counselor? said Dolan.

Tom nodded and kept nodding, his mouth full, not chewing for some reason that made him feel childish and queer. Without regard to Conrad Dolan, Gerard broke the silence, speaking again in Kreyol. The second thing, Gerard told him, was that he had never said anything to the Americans about the day they all went to Saint-Marc, when the woman called herself Jackie. And Tom, the third thing is this: I took the woman myself to Bòkò St. Jean's, not once but many times. Tom nodded, his eyes widening with curiosity, still unable or unwilling to chew or swallow. He raised an imaginary camera and clicked a picture. Gerard shook his head and said maybe but he didn't know, he would stay in the car or sometimes leave her there and spend the night in Saint-Marc and return for her in the morning.

Harrington, said Dolan. What the fuck are you doing?

His eyes bulging, Tom nodded energetically at Dolan, then across to Gerard and back to Dolan again, never having known himself to behave like this, the egg sealed behind his lips like a concealed bomb, and rising from his stomach to block its descent a dread telegraphed the obvious, that whatever happened next would trigger his dissembling. He needed to be away from Haiti to have this discussion, he needed to be in his office in his own friendly chair at his own desk with a notepad on the blotter and pen in hand, glancing in front of him at the framed photographs of his family and Dolan across from him in another chair, the air-conditioning cooling down their imaginations, the walls lined with the books of his ideals and his assistant bringing them coffee, and files and the safe and familiar vista of downtown Miami and its circling buzzards out the window. They needed neckties and briefcases to get through this. They needed talking points and an agenda and a realizable goal. He should be able to pick up the phone and say to Dolan, *Sorry, I have to take this call.*

But here they were, Tom nodding with less and less composure, Dolan opening his mouth to speak again but closing it prudently when Tom expelled the egg into his hand and sat there wild-eyed and breathing like a runner, massaging the egg until it began to fissure and ooze orange yolk, saying nothing but feeling that there seemed to be no limit to his capacity for aggression because it had become clear to him that the only possible thing to do with the egg was smash it into Dolan's face. Yes, he was listening despite himself; yes, he had heard. Dolan had made a crack about fucking the girl. Dolan had just explained that Parmentier had killed Jackie Scott—didn't he say that he was protecting a client whom he knew beyond reasonable doubt to be a murderer? Hadn't he heard Dolan confess he knew his client would murder the girl and had spent no effort to stop it. They were frozen, baleful eyes staring into each other's regret, until Dolan said, Hey, are you all right? Drink some water or something, and carefully removed the egg from his hand and replaced it with a napkin and Gerard took Tom's arm to get his attention and said the last time he had taken the woman to visit Bòkò St. Jean, the man came from the north to meet her and when Tom heard this he slammed back into himself.

Her husband?

No, said Gerard. This man was the army man.

A soldier? An American?

The same one, confirmed Gerard. The one who took the woman to you in the north.

Special Agent Woodrow Singer arrived for an appointment that Tom Harrington could not remember making, appearing like a seraphic messenger at the top of the staircase to proclaim Jack Parmentier's innocence, a tall but heavyset sandy-haired American whose arid western voice clucked with feigned disappointment. Oh, how the mighty have fallen, he said, extending his hand to his erstwhile supervisor, lowering it and the chummy grin on his face a moment later when Dolan said, Kiss my ass.

145

Connie doesn't understand that I'm on his side, said Singer, pulling an extra chair next to Tom.

What side is that? said Tom.

Singer removed his sunglasses and looked across the table at Gerard with penetrating, unfriendly gray eyes. Who is this man?

What brings you around, Woodrow? asked Dolan. I thought you didn't like to be seen with me. To Tom he said, I embarrass him.

He's my driver, said Tom. What's the problem?

Ask him to leave.

He's eating his breakfast, said Connie. He's not going anywhere.

I'd like to speak with Mr. Harrington in private.

That's up to Tom, said Dolan. I'm eating my breakfast too.

What side? Tom asked again and Singer nudged his chair closer to Tom's and said Parmentier was an innocent man.

Tom glared at Dolan, who was intent on eating, and said, Innocent? You arrested him.

Point of fact, said Woodrow Singer, speaking under his breath to explain that Justice took Parmentier into custody, not the Bureau. You can describe this as an interagency misunderstanding. A young and ambitious prosecutor who has not paid attention to how things work. There is some zealotry involved. These misunderstandings will straighten themselves out, and it's my opinion, Mr. Harrington, that you have a role to play in that process.

No. Not me.

You're bringing fresh eyes to the game.

Connie thinks Parmentier's guilty, said Tom.

I never said that, said Dolan without looking up from his plate.

You fucking well did, said Tom loudly.

I'm confident that Jack's in the clear on this one, said Woodrow Singer, rapping his knuckles on the table, his eyes requiring consensus.

Dolan raised his head to beam contempt. Let's all get down on our knees and pray for Jack's deliverance.

Jack loved his wife, said Singer. He would never harm her.

Gerard sat poised, clutching his fork and knife in opposite hands, keeping his eyes down to protect his dignity as he muttered in Kreyol. *Tom, this man just told you a lie.* When Gerard continued muttering about the time he drove the newly married couple to Jacmel, Singer became perturbed and demanded to know what was being said.

He says you're a liar, said Tom, watching the agent's face blanch.

Son of a bitch.

Okay, Tom persisted, Parmentier's innocent. Who are we talking about then? Drug lords? Arabs? He paused to think for a moment. What's the deal with the Arabs?

Singer pointed at Gerard with his sunglasses. Get this bastard out of here.

Can you tell? Tom said to Gerard. Guy loves Haitians.

Dolan fished in his pocket for keys and asked Gerard to fuel up the rental for the drive to Saint-Marc. Singer's unforgiving eyes followed him across the veranda and down the stairs and then he angrily scraped his chair away from Tom's and said, I think this would go much better if we could speak in private.

What's Parmentier have on Connie? Tom asked Woodrow Singer.

Nothing, snarled Dolan. Himself. His existence. Nothing but the fact of himself, that I was protecting him. Now I guess that would be Woody's job.

I want to say something to you both, said Tom. Here's the picture I'm getting. Let's imagine it's better for both of you if Jack Parmentier never comes within a mile of a plea bargaining situation.

I think you have a very clear idea about that, Mr. Harrington, said Woodrow Singer. And I also think you have a clear idea about who murdered Jack's wife, and why.

He looked from one man to the other, their identical blank expressions, unable to see them as anything but fabulists and conspirators. Am I supposed to guess?

Let's all guess, Dolan said derisively. I guess the *cocaleros*.

Connie, Singer warned, stay in the box.

Who am I supposed to guess? said Tom. Lecoeur's people?

Not them, said Woodrow Singer. Not possible.

Why not them? asked Tom.

Those people were gone. Disappeared. Vanished. Singer had told the team sent down from Miami the same thing but they were fixed on a motive of revenge.

How can that be? Gone where?

Bad things happen to bad people, said Woodrow Singer. Connie didn't tell you? It was all in the report. I thought you knew.

I'm fairly sick of hearing about this report. Somebody tell me who wrote this report?

It was a standard military sit-rep, said Singer. Author's name redacted.

Wait, said Harrington, this wasn't a Bureau report? and Singer told him there was one of those too.

That leaves us with the Arabs, said Dolan. What kind of a mess have you got yourself into with the Arabs, Woody?

That is not a Bureau project, said Special Agent Woodrow Singer.

Horseshit.

We are facilitating. That's all I can say.

What about this gallery owner? wondered Tom. Did you speak to him yesterday, Connie? but Dolan stared past Woodrow Singer with undisguised loathing and wouldn't answer yes or no.

Tom shrugged and assented when Singer asked one more time for the opportunity to talk in private. His head tipped, Singer spoke under his breath even though they were alone on the far side of the veranda, saying to Tom that Jack Parmentier was not so fallen a sinner that he was not deeply disturbed by what he saw here in Haiti. If you're a Christian, said Singer, you understand what I'm saying.

I haven't a fucking clue what you're saying.

And I told Jack that this was no place to bring a woman in Renee's condition.

What condition? asked Tom.

Look, Singer whispered, Connie's a good man but without the faith that would allow him to recognize root causes. He sees bad apples. He never thinks: bad tree.

What condition?

She was in crisis, whispered Singer as if in prayer. Spiritual crisis. Jack adored Renee, and only wished she would bring the Lord into her heart.

Tom looked at Singer, the agent's hands clasped below his jowly chin and his lids quivering over closed eyes, the unpleasant tip of his tongue sliding at intervals across the purple swell of his upper lip, and he felt a perverse expansion of sanity, hearing Jackie's own insanity confirmed by this modern Shakespearean madman assigned to speak the truth.

She told me she had lost her soul, Tom said to Singer. You're a man who would believe that, aren't you?

Singer's voice strengthened as he proclaimed that was indeed her undoing, that any righteous man could not fail to see she had been possessed by demons.

Demons? said Tom, and Singer nodded grimly. Why do I have this bad feeling you know who killed her.

The devil.

Exorcists, proselytizers, crusaders wearing suits and shoulder holsters, lobbyists for the blood of Christ, data analysts of the apocalypse—who else was the government hiring these days? thought Tom, unable to respond with anything but an expression of mockery, but Special Agent Woodrow Singer was not to be deterred from his revelation.

The devil and his worshippers, Mr. Harrington. Now you understand what I'm saying. If it were in my power I would destroy in the name of God the entire blasphemous cesspool of this island.

Without another word, Tom Harrington walked off the veranda and went back to his room knowing he could not ignore the marvel of this convergence, Woodrow Singer and Gerard, unknown to each other, dialing in the same coordinates. He stretched out on the single bed with his hands behind his head, watching the ceiling fan and its lethargic rotation, surprised that he was not surprised to learn Jackie had threatened her husband, because there was something vicious in her, a terrifying unstoppable wildness, and he had seen it, and he had suffered from its consequence. But the distance between *vodou*—Singer's devil worshippers—and whatever went wrong—Arabs. Arabs?—in the misbegotten relationship between Jackie and Parmentier was inhabited by a fog bank of government skullduggery and infighting and cynical misdirection that made his brain twitch when he stared into its mists, looking for the connections.

I'm not going back down, he told himself, a right and reasonable decision that lasted all of ten minutes.

Someone knocked on his door and he barked back, *Go away, go to hell,* but it was Gerard, not Dolan, asking to be let in. Tom assumed Connie had sent him but Gerard denied it, the white men didn't know he had returned to the hotel, and they sat on the bed together in the stifling musk of the room while Tom pulled on his socks and leather boots, obliged once more to listen but for once to someone he knew to trust, a Haitian and a friend and an honest man.

The day Gerard took the woman to Bòkò St. Jean's *hounfour* on the outskirts of Saint-Marc it was understood that he would drop her off and come back in the morning but Jackie—she had a new name, said Gerard. Renee—was unusually happy and excited this day, said Gerard, and she encouraged him to stay to observe the ceremony, already in progress from the day before. They're killing bulls, she told him with a broad smile.

Tom, this ceremony was very big, very grand, said Gerard. Many people came from far away, hundreds of people.

What was this ceremony for? What was going on?

I think it was for the woman, said Gerard. Who is rich enough to afford two bulls?

Gerard, she didn't even want to pay the *houngan* five dollars for . . . what? I don't even know what to call it. A consultation.

This day Bòkò St. Jean was a big man with two bulls to sacrifice to the *lwas*. Two, Tom. Not one, two. Only the whites have this money to waste. One bull would be enough for the Haitian bourgeoisie.

Gerard did not see the bulls sacrificed later that day. He drank a little *clairin* and ate some food and watched people dance to the drums and left by midafternoon to visit friends in Saint-Marc. But when he returned after dark to drive the woman back to Port-au-Prince, Eville Burnette was there, and Gerard heard people talking about something happening, something that he would remember when he heard that the woman had been killed. One of the guests at the ceremony was another *bokor,* a powerful *macoute* during the time of the dictators, named Honore Vincent, from the northeastern mountains, who ruled as the emperor of one of the secret *vodou* societies in Haiti. Honore Vincent was very drunk with *clairin* and jealous of Bòkò St. Jean's good fortune. When he saw the two whites among the people, he went to them, said Gerard, and acted stupid.

Tom groaned, afraid to hear what had happened next. What kind of stupid? Aggressive?

Yes, that.

Did he lay his hands on her?

Yes.

Did she go after him?

The people tell me yes.

And the soldier was there? asked Tom. Was he wearing his uniform?

No. The same as we.

Eville Burnette had stepped between the woman and Honore Vincent and pushed him away hard and he stumbled to the ground and Bòkò St. Jean and his followers cautioned Vincent and warned him to behave properly or be expelled from the ceremony and then somebody took him away. In the weeks ahead the incident was responsible for many rumors and Gerard heard what the people were saying, but of course they were not all saying the same thing. Some people believe she is one woman with two names. Here was the second *gros neg* who had been defeated by the white woman, who could not then be a mere woman but a *mambo,* a *blan* sorceress, and that she had been possessed by a *lwa* during her battle with Honore Vincent, that only Erzulie Mary could fight a *bokor* as powerful as Vincent, and that this was not a fight that took place on earth but in the spirit world. Others said no, she was an army woman, she knew military fighting, she knew how to kick and fly like a Chinaman in the movies. And other people said no, they were there, the woman was very drunk and falling down but they never saw her fight with the *boko.* And eventually Gerard heard second- and third-hand accounts of Honore Vincent's fate, that Bòkò St. Jean had weakened him with a spell, and strengthened her with a potion, and that

Bòkò St. Jean had done the same thing for her when she went after Jacques Lecoeur's man up north because both men were nationalists and strong leaders who resisted the occupation. What is going on here is plain to see, Honore Vincent had been heard to say: She is an American spy, and Bòkò St. Jean is an American spy, and I will take care of them both. You know Haiti, said Gerard. You know how the people talk. You know how the stories grow from small to big.

The last thing, Tom, said Gerard. The day after the woman is killed, the American soldier comes to me in Port-au-Prince.

Why?

To drive to the north. And in Le Cap I hear people say someone kill the *boko*.

St. Jean? he asked and Gerard said no, the other one, Vincent.

All right, said Tom Harrington. Let's go to Saint-Marc.

CHAPTER TWELVE

From the moment they had arrived at the clearing on the banks of an emerald-green river in a valley deep in the roadless mountains, everything had escalated at a rate that left the exact chain of events a hallucinatory smear in Tom's mind. A dozen or so men—unarmed, as far as he knew, though several carried machetes—had materialized out of the jungle where the land steepened above the clearing. Jackie began taking pictures, a lot of pictures, the long lens of her camera sweeping from one glowering face to another. Dashing forward from the group, a man began yelling in Kreyol for Jackie to put the camera down yet she ignored both Tom's translation of the command and his own emphatic effort to underscore it. The men came closer, Jackie continued shooting. Eville Burnette, to Tom's relief, moved back and out of the way where he would not contribute to the growing tension. Tom recognized the yelling man, Lecoeur's second in command, from a previous expedition in these mountains, many months before. He was not a large or tall man but strapped and banded with muscles, whom Tom remembered as being a hothead, speaking always in bursts of rage. Attention, tell her to put the camera down now, Lecoeur's man said, focusing on Tom, declaring her as Tom's responsibility, and Tom stepped in front of Jackie to block her view.

What the fuck are you doing?

What's it look like I'm doing? she said. Come on, you're in my way.

An elbow banged against his right ear as the guerilla fighter reached across Tom's shoulder to seize the camera and he was knocked aside, his attention lost for the fleeting span of seconds it took Lecoeur's man and Jackie to become violently entangled, each with a hand on the camera, the man's other hand grabbing for her hair but finding the neck of her shirt, which tore away, and his hand fell down her chest to place a twisting grip on the middle strap of her bra. In the struggle the white globe of a breast emerged and Jackie's other hand whipped out of her vest pocket with a can of spray. She aimed for his eyes and when he howled in pain she lunged at him and they tumbled together to the ground, she on top of him, the nozzle of the can shoved into his mouth, blood flowing from where his teeth broke the skin on her fingers.

Everyone rushed forward to intervene but in the same instant jumped back, choking from the sear of fumes. Jackie rolled onto the grass, coughing and spitting, her face afire and eyes a fountain of tears. Then Eville was kneeling beside the man, his own tears streaking down his cheeks, his open knapsack on the ground, a radio or transponder clearly visible within as he searched its contents, his hand stopping on an unseen object. A calm issue of instructions wheezed from Eville's mouth and Tom obeyed—Explain to these men that this man will suffocate without an emergency operation, explain the procedure, explain not to be alarmed by the procedure, explain that the procedure will save the man's life. When Tom finished these explanations, no one said anything, and out came the knife from Eville's knapsack and then came a pistol from the waistband of one of the guerillas, pointed at the American but uncocked.

Now tell them this, said Eville, as he made an incision below the man's larynx. Tell them this man is gravely injured and must go to a hospital. Tell them a helicopter is coming to take him to the hospital.

You planned this out, didn't you? Tom said, his ears already tuning to the faint sound of a machine, its premature arrival suggesting it had been in the air and shadowing them all along.

You're wrong, said Eville.

You think these guys are pissed now, wait and see how unhappy they are when a helicopter shows up.

Tell them the UN wouldn't allow this mission to proceed without security.

This is not a UN mission. I am not under UN jurisdiction.

Whatever you say. Tell them I tricked you.

When the bird was above them in the valley, Lecoeur's men became more agitated, hollering accusations, air whistled in and out of the lungs of the man on the ground, and Jackie, red-eyed and disheveled, was back on her feet, clutching her vest closed and shrieking for her camera.

Get this crazy bitch to back off, Eville said to Tom, and then he yelled at Jackie not with anger but as if she were on the other side of the river, to stand still and accept what he was asking Tom to do.

Don't fake it. Smack her a couple of times.

I can't do that, said Harrington.

Our friends here need some satisfaction.

That's not who I am.

Kneel down then and keep this guy breathing, said Burnette, and he jumped up in a fury Tom had never before seen him express and with the back of his hand slapped Jackie hard enough to snap her head around and then he hit her again with enough force to send her spinning to her hands and knees.

How do you say stupid cunt in Kreyol?

I don't know.

Then the medevac was down and they had to wrestle her aboard. Her camera had disappeared and she brayed for it relentlessly, refusing to get on the helicopter with Eville Burnette and the man she had almost killed, who was strapped down to a canvas stretcher and lifted by his angry comrades and passed through the hatch to the waiting hands of Pakistani soldiers, his face strained and bloated over and smeared with mucous, the tube from Harrington's ballpoint pen implanted in his windpipe. There was a fair chance it might go bad for Tom if he did not get on the helicopter himself.

Harrington told Eville he still had a job to do and was confident the situation remained manageable as long as Jackie did not stay behind as she insisted, her own eyes swollen half-closed and cascading tears, a madwoman in a tempest screaming over the roar of the propellers that she wanted her camera and that Tom needed her. But she and Burnette were the last people on earth he needed now and the only thought in his mind was to separate himself from them. Eville was in the hatchway yelling for her to get aboard, Tom was behind Jackie pushing against her manic resistance, which suddenly turned Amazonian and he found himself flipped sideways onto the ground, looking up as Burnette hopped out and wrapped her thrashing and kicking into his powerful arms to heave her inside the fuselage and then Burnette bellied inside himself as the helicopter began to rise and veer away, leaving in its wake a hurricane's eye of silence.

When the shouting and protestation began anew he sat up and slowly stood, dispirited but resolute, repeating to the guerillas that they must honor their promise and take him to Lecoeur. But Lecoeur was there already, had mingled among the band of his men who had come out of the forest but had not stepped forward to identify himself and Harrington had not recognized him. His bushy hair and Che beard were clipped off, his clean-shaven face revealing a weak jaw, the vocabulary of his clothes—a tracksuit, cheap running shoes, and a sports jersey, as if he had just come from a soccer match—separating him from the insurgent peasants and their idiom of torn and muddy trousers and straw hats. His bitter questions were to be expected, and Tom, without answers, first told the lie that Eville Burnette had suggested and confessed he was as dismayed and outraged by the behavior of the girl as they were, and could not explain it. But Lecoeur and his men had suspected from the beginning that the man was an American soldier and were now convinced the woman was a spy and Tom thought wearily, *Well, we're all spies, aren't we.* It seemed to be a preexisting condition, like whiteness.

She's a journalist, said Tom. She didn't come with the soldier, she came with me. Then, feeling the unease of his former lie, he said the soldier had tricked him and immediately regretted this declaration of naïveté. Lecoeur asked what the soldier had hoped to gain by coming into the mountains but Tom again had no answer except to say that Eville Burnette had assured him that it wasn't his idea. But the *blans* had compromised the security of Lecoeur's stronghold in the mountains and Harrington said he was sorry. I cannot explain any of it.

I believe you are our friend, said Lecoeur. But is it true you have come to investigate me? You have come to examine our hands for innocent blood?

It's true that I have come to talk to you about the bourgeoisie who are missing. Maybe you know what happened to them. Maybe you know where I can find them.

Monsieur Tom, here in the mountains, the *macoutes* have not stopped their war with the people.

Yes.

What do the Americans want in Haiti? They said they came to throw out the *macoutes,* but the *macoutes* are still here.

Yes.

If you ask me if I still must fight for freedom, the answer is yes. If you ask me if I still must fight to protect the people from the *macoute,* the answer is yes. If you ask me is there freedom without justice, the answer is no.

Lecoeur's hand signaled toward someone behind him and a skeletal youth stepped forward from the circle of men who had listened solemnly to the conversation. Monsieur Tom, this boy will take you back to the village. Lecoeur called another man's name and the camera reappeared, the unspooled celluloid curled on the ground like a molted snakeskin. Tom put the camera in his day pack and turned to leave but Lecoeur placed light fingertips on the white man's arm and steered him aside.

In the night, no one is in control, Lecoeur said. Walk fast.

They moved swiftly along the narrow trail through the steam and scratch of the jungle, fast enough to reach the village of Bois Caïman before twilight. By the time they arrived the muscles in Tom Harrington's legs were a persistent ache, his shirt transparent with sweat, pants wet to midthigh and boots soggy from the last river it had been necessary to ford. A helicopter passed unseen, somewhere overhead, headed up-country, and he began to feel the vibes, something wrong in the air, when none of the village's children ran out to greet them, and then his guide pulled up and, pointing ahead, uttered the words, *Armée Rouge.* Tom looked toward where he had left his SUV on a vacant lot at the edge of town. Two white Toyota Hilux pickup trucks were now parked next to it and heavily armed men were milling about.

Who is the Red Army? Tom asked the boy.

Macoutes.

What are they doing here? he asked, but the boy reversed down the path back toward the safety of the bush and Tom braced himself for trouble and walked on, crossing a footbridge over the cool invitation of the rushing river that separated the village from the wilderness.

They were from the elite families and not hostile and in fact greeted him with a pretense of camaraderie that he did not bother to reciprocate. He was surprised, though, to see that he knew the man who presented himself as their leader, Emil Gaillard, a slightly obsequious mulatto educated by Jesuits in New Orleans and said to be the bastard black sheep of the family of Gaillard landowners. During the first weeks of the invasion his ambiguous loyalties tipped toward the peasants when he joined a mob in the town his family had controlled for centuries to uproot the Haitian army's casern and afterward had handed over captured weapons to the Special Forces. Not long thereafter, Harrington had interviewed him briefly about a massacre during the time of the de facto regime, and Gaillard had introduced him to a tenant farmer, a survivor of the atrocity. We are here, Gaillard explained, to protect you from the *chimères,* but Harrington was unfamiliar with this word.

The phantoms, they come from the mountains to do us harm.

This recurring irony of protection merited only Harrington's ingratitude. Obviously Emil Gaillard and his gang were using his presence in Bois Caïman as an excuse for a show of force. But Gaillard reminded him the northwest district was notorious for its Balkanized mentalities, the unpaved road back to Route National One winding through partisan villages in perennial conflict with one another, daylight being the only condition for safe passage. Now the sun was setting and Gaillard offered an escort to the highway.

You call yourself Red Army, said Tom. Is the Red Army on the side of the people?

But there were no sides beyond the blood of one's own. The *chimères* attack our families, Gaillard said, his nervous eyes and the timidity of his English creating a supreme impression of untrustworthiness, and please don't say we have no right to defend ourselves.

Bon, said Tom. Where are the bodies and the graves? Give me evidence, eyewitnesses, police reports, something to work with beside rumors and, receiving no reply, told Gaillard, Look, I don't think I can unravel this on my own.

The sun is down. Please, for your safety, accept the escort.

That would send the wrong message. No one in Haiti is my enemy.

Perhaps the wrong message is the only one you have brought, said Emil Gaillard, and in another minute the paramilitaries of the *Armée Rouge* had shouldered themselves together in the cabs and beds of the two trucks and driven away into the darkness with headlights off. Looking at his wristwatch, Harrington gave them a five-minute lead before driving slowly down the dusty lane through the center of Bois Caïman, glancing at the shacks on either side, their interiors a warm glow of candlelight crossed by cautious shadows, then accelerating at the edge of town onto the rough road through the countryside.

He did not slow his approach to the next village a few miles farther on, unable to recall if it was a good village or a bad village, but sped through without incident, nearly hitting a dog that ran barking toward his tires. Intermittently along the shoulder of the road, pedestrians loomed out from the void and flashed away, silhouettes of blackness absorbed by blackness, their unseen faces turned from the glare of his lights. Neither could he remember the affiliation of the next village, or the third, so that by the time he saw the firefly radiance of a single lantern in the middle of the road at the entrance to the fourth village and then the rocks lined up behind it, he could not be sure which faction might be manning the roadblock, friend or foe, or even assure himself that anyone was his friend, this night in the mountains, but he had been waved through countless roadblocks during his time in Haiti, more often than not by swaggering kids extorting a toll of a few gourdes, and was not automatically concerned.

He downshifted to cut his speed, and peered ahead at the boundary where his lights met the darkness but saw no one and tried to determine if he could leave the roadbed and go around or if he would have to stop to clear the rocks when, in front of him, the illuminated road suddenly filled with wild shapes and he kicked the brakes to avoid slamming into their midst.

Before he could roll down his window to speak with someone, a large rock shattered the windshield, a boy ran forward with a club, and the driver's-side window caved in like a cup of stinging ice thrown at his face. Hands thundered on the roof and a man tried to open the door to pull Tom out at the same time Tom released the clutch so abruptly that the vehicle nearly stalled before squealing forward, bodies diving away, bodies flying back, the sound of hands thumping the side panels, a clatter of stones bouncing off the hood, the underframe grinding against the rocks piled across the road. He could smell the tires spinning and a man rushed forward waving a machete. The front end of the SUV reared up and seemed to jump the obstruction and race ahead and Tom swerved just in time, he thought, to miss the man but the left headlight went dead at the precise moment the man somersaulted into the night and vanished, a laceless shoe sailing through the broken windshield like a wingless bird to land in the passenger seat. He had been holding his breath without realizing it and let out a gasp and began hyperventilating as he navigated the seamless, sinister pulse of emptiness that was the road. The night had not produced the first flood of terror he had experienced during his time in Haiti, but the first that seemed shockingly personal, the first that seemed to be only about him.

The moon began to float above the eastern mountains, silvering the road, the light in the trees ghostly. Finally his hands stopped shaking on the wheel and his breathing returned to normal. Not far from where the route rejoined the highway, when he ran straight over a dog rocketing into his path without slowing down or stopping, Tom Harrington cursed Jackie Scott and Eville Burnette and then cursed himself for the harm he had done and drove on in despair.

The lateness of the hour had softened the edges of Cap-Haïtien's ubiquitous decay, the city's unfortunate residents shuttered behind a self-imposed curfew, abandoning the filth-strewn streets to the scurry of rats and garbage-fed dogs and the otherwise peaceful slink of the nocturnally homicidal. The Hotel Christophe had switched off its generator for the night and he left the SUV in the car park without summoning the courage to inspect the damage to its front end. He went through the darkened lobby toward the

160

bar, knowing it would be closed but hoping the bartender had forgotten, as he sometimes did, to lock its cabinets. But his luck continued downward and when he couldn't locate the night watchman he went back out to the street to roam for a drink, walking toward the smell of the sea and glancing up each decrepit avenue for any sign of life, though even the buildings appeared dead and rotting. Finally he saw tiny tongues of flame flickering on the pavement a few blocks up one of the side alleys, like votive candles placed at a shrine, and as he came closer he saw the shadows under a balcony assemble into a chiaroscuro tableau of women tending homemade oil lamps in front of an open doorway dusted with light so weak and granular it seemed to Tom you could wipe it away with a rag. A man's overexcited voice argued from inside the shop. They were vendors, these women, their hope for a sale unchecked by the dread of midnight, and he glanced at their small piles of wares spread out on scraps of cloth—individual cigarettes from a crumpled pack of Comme Il Fauts, Chiclets, a meager pyramid of oranges, matchsticks, lumps of charcoal, a tiny container of Vicks VapoRub. He saw in their saucer eyes Christ risen with money in his pocket and he bought the cigarettes and nodded sympathetically at the pleas from the other women and stepped into the shop and back out a minute later with a Coke bottle tapped with *clairin,* the smell of the homemade rum like fruity kerosene and the taste like molten tinfoil in his dehydrated mouth. By the time he found himself ascending the Christophe's stairway to his second-floor room, he had sucked up half the bottle and his head seemed to dance, free of weight or substance, and his feet were made of stone. He keyed open the door and stepped in and stepped halfway back into the hallway, speechless.

There you are, said Jackie, her face brightening in a way that struck him as shameless and bizarre, considering the tenor of the day and the unexpected shock and seizure of her nakedness, a spasm of unwanted lust suffocating Tom like a knot binding his diaphragm, her body and its litheness a searing memory of something powerful he had once owned but had misplaced or forfeited or left behind. She was lying atop the bedsheet, reading what he could see was a Kreyol language primer by candlelight, and she calmly placed the book in the cradle between the scoop of her pelvic

bones and folded her arms over her breasts and looked at him now with
an uncertain smile.

That very morning he had woken up in a dreamy state of arousal, fantasizing about their night together but, quarreling with Eville Burnette at
breakfast, he had forgotten to mention the arrangement, the shortage of
rooms and beds, and the whole idea of being with her had been spoiled
by the turmoil of events.

You're bleeding, she said, her absence of great concern equal to the
numb indifference he felt at this hour for his own well-being.

He could not find words in his mouth for anything but the obvious.
Where are your clothes? he said stupidly.

It's hot, she said, unapologetic. Her hair, stringy and unbrushed, made
her appear less guarded. Perspiration trickled down her face as it did his.
Why are you bleeding? I was getting worried about you. How did it go?

Where am I bleeding? His hand rose instinctively to his face and he
tried to focus on her eyes and not the untimely puerile thrill of her body,
the moist flush of her skin.

Your cheek, she said, studying him, directing. The left side. Higher.

His fingertips found the dried edge of the cut and the almost imperceptible ooze and he looked at the blood on his fingertips and looked at
her and asked in a daze of puzzlement, Why are you here?

On the nightstand next to the candle was a glass of water and as she
reached for it and sipped he stared blindly at her breasts, seeing but not
seeing, and then averted his eyes when she turned back to lean toward
him on an elbow with a look of guileless concentration. I actually don't
understand your question, she said, her appraisal of him matter-of-fact.
Where else would I be?

Why aren't you with Eville?

Why would I be with Eville? she said, making a sound of exasperation.
Tom, close the door. Or just stand out there all night, but either way you're
stuck with me, she said, the press of her lips making a coquette's quick pout
and he noticed the caterpillar of discoloration above her jaw where she had
been tattooed by Eville Burnette's knuckles. You could have told me there
was only one bed.

Okay, okay, he said, shutting the door behind him, conceding his day pack to the floor yet still unable to step forward into the room. Look, this isn't going to work, is it? Not after today. Not like this.

Not like what? she said.

You know what I'm talking about, you lying there. This is how women change the subject, isn't it? He rediscovered the bottle of rum in his hand and took a nasty swallow. It's too much.

Is that what I'm doing, changing the subject?

This isn't our goddamn honeymoon, is it? You need to put something on and we need to talk.

But it's so fucking hot. Honestly, aren't you hot?

Unchastened, she had made him think about it and he felt the swampy airlessness of the room and suddenly he was sweating through his shirt and he could feel the rivulets dripping down his forehead and his feet were stewing mercilessly in their boots. Yeah, he admitted, it's hot.

The room came equipped with a ceiling fan, and a leaky air conditioning unit in the window but the electricity had been off since nine o'clock. The water too, she said. I can't even shower.

She wanted to negotiate and he grudgingly allowed it, letting her convince him that in another minute he would be as miserable in the heat as she was if he didn't come into the room and relax and at least get into a pair of shorts if he had them, and while she talked she put her book on the nightstand to get up from the bed and with her back turned toward him she squatted by her pack and he found himself electrified by this perspective of her nakedness, the angularity of her ass and the swell of her vulva from behind and its pale haze of pubic hair, thinking he needed to get out of there. She stepped into navy blue panties and went back to the bed and he said thanks, what about a T-shirt too, and she said with an edge to her voice, *Oh, just get used to it.* Upright against the headboard and cross-legged, she watched Tom as he undressed down to his boxers, which he exchanged for a pair of gym shorts in the privacy of the bathroom and then dipped water from the bucket on the floor and washed his face at the sink and felt not refreshed but refocused and went back into the room, determined to have it out with Jackie.

163

I'm sorry to be so immodest, she said. Like, I'm not trying to offend you or anything, right? But it's too fucking hot in here for me to pretend I'm in high school and the world will end if a guy sees my tits. Feel better?

Yes. Thanks, he said and looked at her warily but he still did not know what to do with his eyes and he could feel the restlessness forming beneath his skin and a current of tension seeping into his groin. He took another swig from the Coke bottle and put it back on the floor but then picked it up for another swallow. Look, he said, I'm enormously stressed, and told her he was craving a cigarette. Do you mind?

Oh, perfect, she said. I have ganj.

He lit a Comme Il Faut and inhaled deeply and began to cough with such violence that for a second he thought he might throw up but he waved away her sudden mask of concern and composed himself and she lit the joint she took from her makeup bag and lay back down and exhaled a lavish cone of blue smoke into the heavy air.

I'm pretty mad at you, Jackie, he said evenly, shifting in his chair. I'm very upset.

I know, she said, subdued at last, with the regret he hoped to hear in her voice. She got up from the bed and crossed the room and bent over him, her breasts ballooning again into his vision. Want some? she asked, holding out the joint, and he saw the greasy sheen where she had salved the bite marks on her right hand but his eyes were drawn back to her breasts and he struggled with the possibility that leaning forward a few inches would allow him to circle the lovely pink aureoles of her nipples with the tip of his tongue, knowing that to do so would make him nothing more at this point than a bigger fool than she had already proven him to be.

Maybe a taste, he said without thinking about why, because the cannabis on the island had an insane potency and he did not enjoy it. As soon as he inhaled he felt a dissolving swirl pass through his shoulders and lift his head from his body, and he anchored his eyes to the set of gashes on her fingers. How's your hand? he asked.

It's nothing, she said, retreating to the bed and positioning herself with a stubborn look that let him know she was ready for his questions.

How's Lecoeur's man?

Tom, okay, listen. I'm sorry. I freak out when somebody grabs me. It's bad, I know.

Bad. Stupid.

I know.

You could have killed him.

I suppose. The Pakis seemed to know what to do with him. It's pretty simple, really, and he could hear the dope loop its strange energy into her speech as she explained in detail the antihistaminic recession of the inflamed tissue and the suturing of the tracheotomy.

I want you to tell me why you were taking pictures? I never see you shoot a frame and then all of a sudden, *wham*. Tons of pictures.

That's my thing. Why else even invite me along? she said coolly and met his eyes with a hardening defiance and propped herself with pillows against the headboard of the bed.

He stared at her without kindness and a craven thought ranged into his head that he could not accept, that what was most troubling about this situation, this moment, was her beauty. If it were not for her beauty, he never would have had anything to do with her. He would have known better, given her a wide berth, after the game she played in Saint-Marc.

I told you to stop, he reminded her. You have to talk with these guys. You have to ask permission. Some will say yes, some no. It's delicate. You don't just walk up and fire away.

But come on. Don't you think their faces were so amazing, said Jackie, her desultory words coming at a rate he found increasingly hard to follow. So fierce, and the lines of their expressions making this web of pathos and hope and belligerence and I just went with the moment, you know. Like you're not even conscious of anything but getting the shot, which is not a cliché, man, it's a crazy state of grace. You've got to get it no matter what and I know you probably think I'm not much of a photographer but, you know, photojournalism is like, Oh, look, get out of my way, there's somebody killing somebody else, snap snap, or the herd heads off into the slums but where is the substance to poverty, poverty has no substance, that's the definition of poverty, the context is inert, nothing's happening to raise it beyond what it is, it's like a form of paralysis. Do you see what I'm saying?

No.

What I'm into is making portraits, vernacular photography, visual anthropology, right, I want to paint figures, I want someone looking at the picture to say, who is this person? I don't want to document, I want to interpret, and it's important for me to find a subject, guerilla fighters is a classic, it's modern, it's timeless, it's us, it's not us. Think of Mao and his fighters in 1946, think of the French Resistance or Fidel and Che in the Sierra Maestra. Incredible, right? And to find a core theme, something transformative and magical in the spirit—like, where the fuck did this come from? You know? Don't you think so? Then more harshly, Look, I said I was sorry, okay.

What's going on with you and Sergeant Burnette? he asked impatiently.

What do you mean what's going on? I've been here for what, a week? I've known him for like twenty-four hours. What are you trying to say? That we cooked up a scheme to ruin your day? Wow, that's a fucked-up question. Fuck you, Tom.

You weren't taking pictures for him for some reason?

Fuck you, Tom. She sang it like the chorus to a jolly song. Fuck you, Tom.

He felt himself on the brink of shouting at her, making clear the damage she and Burnette had done, interfering with serious matters, and their actions had placed him in the unthinkable position of being the driver of a car that had hit a man and sped away. But he did not want to tell Jackie this last piece of information, he did not want to hear himself say it out loud. The rum and the wing-tip brush of ganja had dizzied him and the dizziness lay spread like oil on the greater pool of his fatigue and the heat had begun to feel like a fever. His confusion about Jackie made him oddly fragile and not altogether rational and he did not want to spend this night in such close quarters with her chaperoned by his anger. Because she appeared to be telling the truth he wanted to comfort her but the impulse felt too close to desire and unmanageable and so he rewarded her instead.

I have your camera, he said, reaching down for his day pack.

Oh, my God! she said. Oh, my God! She came flying off the bed and in her excitement said I love you and kissed him not passionately but a

166

moment longer than she might have, her eyes searching for his reaction as she pulled back, glancing down at his lap and quickly back up. Sorry, she laughed, taking the camera. Thank you, thank you, how the fuck did you get it, I thought I'd never see it again. Her happy steps bounced back to the bed where she plopped on her back with her arms out wide, the camera in one hand, as if in a swoon to the sudden wonderfulness of life. Here we are, she half-sang in a familiar melody he failed to identify, and ever shall be in our memories.

Tom slumped, dumbstruck, in his chair.

Fuck fuck fuck! She examined the frame counter and popped open the back of the Nikon. They took the film.

Right, Tom said woodenly. They yanked it.

No! she wailed again like a child. We have to go back for another shoot. You've lost your mind.

No, really, stop kidding. Let's go back tomorrow. Are you going back? I'm never going back.

No, no, no, Tom. Bad Tom. She left the camera on the bed and crossed the room, humming the tune he could not name, placing a hand on each arm of the chair to capture him, leaning over, her nose inches from his and her eyes puffy and blinking, unable to sustain their focus. Bad Tom, she whispered, and repeated it silently to make him read her lips.

You are so stoned, he said. Way out there.

He did not try to stop her from climbing into the chair, sitting crossways on his lap, her long bare legs draped over the armrest and her right hand sliding up the sensitive nape of his neck into his hair, the gentle kneading switching on and off to a rough caress, a clumsy attempt at sensuality. Her mouth was slack, her lips parted too much, and he held the drift of her gaze long enough to see that her eyes were empty of desire, and he did not know what he was seeing except the parody of a vixen and the suggestion of a shared knowledge that might allow them to slip effortlessly forward into the role of lovers or send them simultaneously blazing off in opposite directions.

Bad Tom, she said again. Let's go back. Please, please, and she squeezed a fistful of his hair to punctuate herself.

167

He told himself she was out of her mind and now so was he, Jackie there again in his lap, the stick of skin against skin, her crotch atop his, the boundaries that seduction took such exquisite art in dismantling cast aside from the moment he had opened the door. He dropped his eyes to her breasts and she allowed this, her fingers curling along his scalp, and Tom became acutely aware of his hands and what he might do with them— unless he raised them in the air there was nowhere for them to go but on her body—the right hand in a tentative pause on her closest knee, the left hand clasped on her rib cage below her left breast, and he stopped looking at her breasts and watched his right hand turn so that the shelf of his fingers was snug between her closed knees, her own hand in his hair, squeezing harder, her nails pressing painfully into his scalp as his hand took its time traveling from her knees up her slick thighs and stopped without touching her panties. He moved his hand then infinitesimally closer yet not all the way and she gasped and in the sublime and terrible tension of the moment he looked into her eyes and saw them become empty and although she did not stop him he knew something had changed and something was wrong and he stopped himself, withdrawing his hand.

Jackie, I need you to get up, he said, and she got up awkwardly and stood before him with skittish eyes in a confusing posture of submissiveness, telegraphing both a strange challenge and imminent surrender. I need to use the bathroom, he explained, getting up himself.

He stayed in the darkness of the bathroom a long time, too long, a deep dull ache in his balls, wondering what to do, and when he started to fall asleep perched on the toilet he went back out. The candle was sputtering in a puddle of wax on the nightstand and she lay on the top sheet, naked again, on one side of the bed with her eyes closed and her hands cupped protectively at the top of her legs. He would not get into the bed with her and returned to the upholstered chair and slouched onto its cushion, finding its comfort incomplete, his body unappeased. When he looked back at her again her eyes were open, lambent, watching.

Why are you over there? she asked.

I'm not sure.

He made himself stop thinking about it and came to the empty side of the bed and lay down and wrapped his arms over his head, careful not to touch her but disabled by the citric smell of her sweaty body. She asked if he wanted her to blow out the candle and he did and then they were in darkness. Listening to her breathing he could barely draw a breath himself.

After a while she said, What were you doing in there so long? and her voice was strained and reedy and not beckoning, she was not being playful or teasing but mocking the desire she must know he could not silence forever.

Nothing. Sitting.

Were you thinking of me?

He turned on his side facing her, the dense but indistinct shape of her, and wondered if he was imagining this, the impression that she was touching herself while she talked with him. I'm too tired to think.

You were thinking about fucking me, weren't you?

The crassness of her mood jarred him but still he replied as if she were joking, wanting her to stop being weird.

Maybe. You got a problem with that? he asked, trying to sound lighthearted, but she didn't answer.

For several minutes they lay quietly in the rippling hush of the darkness, Tom trying to determine if her breath actually quickened as he imagined it, trying to decide if it would be all right if he reached over to put his hand on her shoulder or pet her cheek. He was telling himself how could it not be all right when she spoke again.

What's your daughter's name?

How do you know I have a daughter?

You told me, she said, but he could not remember ever mentioning such a thing.

Her name is Allison. Why are we talking about her?

How old is she?

Eleven. Let's stop there.

She made a thoughtful sound and whispered, That's the age, isn't it?

Age for what?

169

When they become luscious. When they start resisting.

Resisting what?

You.

Yeah, he said, misunderstanding her implication, she's getting around to that.

How old was she when you first finger fucked her?

What the hell are you talking about? He bolted upright. That's fucking sick.

The bedsprings creaked again as she changed positions, turning on her stomach, her answer muffled by the pillow.

What? Tom said, leaning closer.

Have you ever fucked her?

What?

You've wanted to fuck her, right?

What galaxy are you from?

You've thought about it, haven't you? Is your dick hard?

What do you think? You're getting off on this, aren't you?

Then in the darkness her hand reached over to his face and then his mouth, clutching, pushing, the pissy scent of her fingertips flooding his nostrils and he moved and straddled her and unbuttoned his shorts and underneath him felt the power contained by her body and its exquisite summoning as he pressed himself between her legs where her other hand, underneath her, blocked his entrance. He pressed harder, tried to pry an opening with his cock but she filled herself with her fingers and he heard her say something and Tom said *What?* unsure if she had said *Don't. Stop.* or *Don't stop,* and so went higher, pressing himself beyond the halo of tightness into her anus and he heard the sharp intake of her breath and the root of a sound she made behind the grit of her teeth. When he blinked his eyes stung with his sweat and after several thrusts she said to the pillow, *Get off,* or maybe, *Get off me,* and after an uncertain pause and then several more strokes he was shuddering and done and off her, gulping the air like water and as he fell to his side of the bed for an instant he no longer knew who he was and the day had become a death that crushed him under its weight and left him, for seconds or minutes or an eternity, in an insensate afterlife, his body so heavy it hurtled away through black space and all that remained was the disconnected awareness of a world from which he had been evicted.

In the morning he woke to a sour residue of grimness in the room and saw that she was gone. *Thanks for the lecture on permission,* Jackie had scrawled on a page in the notebook she had removed from his day pack. *Now you know what kind of a man you are.*

CHAPTER THIRTEEN

Cui bono?—the question he was peppered with by his professors at law school. *Who benefits?* The line of inquiry would, on occasion, arc and plunge away from the perpetrator of an act and burrow itself into a labyrinth of concealed interests, which may or may not deliver up the wizard, the ultimate and unexpected source. Was Conrad Dolan the wizard, Tom Harrington asked himself, or was he simply a man in the difficult position of having to save himself by letting go of the rope he had thrown to save another? Or was the rope itself a subterfuge?

No matter how he looked at his increasingly unsavory relationship with Dolan, he could find no like-mindedness and thus no common purpose between the lies he told himself and the falsehoods and manipulations manufactured by Dolan, a man who circumambulated the truth like a Buddhist monk speaking in riddles and koans. Stories truly told are true, except when they are not. Harrington felt duped and duped again, and this journey north to Saint-Marc must, he told himself, be the end of the game, forfeit as acceptable an outcome as any other.

Silent and brooding, he sat in the back of the SUV with his face in the wind to avoid the church-lady odor of Connie's aftershave and chain-smoked from a pack of Comme Il Fauts and looked out the open window at the slums between the road and the harbor, the rubble-spread of shantytowns resembling landfills or refuse dumps inhabited by bent-over crews of scavengers, pigs rooting through the sulfurous heaps of garbage. What

172

had Jackie said when they had driven past these abominations?—*You'd never see that in a Muslim country.* Pigs in the streets. *It would cause a riot.* In the front seat, Conrad Dolan scowled out the window at the city passing by in a haze of filth and the increasingly open violence of its population and waited for Harrington to tell him what Woodrow Singer had said to change his mind. Then they were well beyond the congestion of the capital, on Route Nationale One, and encouraged by the change of season evident in the countryside, the oven-hot air suffused with an aromatic elixir wafting from the flowering trees that lined the road and the vendors camped in their shade, selling watermelons and tomatoes. Tom felt the nostalgic sense of freedom he had always experienced, escaping Port-au-Prince. Now it seemed his thoughts were organized, questions clipped together like rounds of ammunition in a magazine. He poked Dolan on the shoulder to make him turn around.

Why am I here?

You tell me. I thought you had a plane to catch.

No. Why did you bring me with you to Haiti?

I'm not going to bullshit you, said Dolan. I was hoping you could bulletproof me. Tom knew the place, he knew the girl, he had investigative chops. If Harrington could not prove Jack Parmentier had murdered his wife, chances were nobody could. But you've already worked this out, Tom, Connie said. I'm not telling you what you don't know.

Who's Albert Neff?

You know that son of a bitch? Jesus Christ.

He was at the embassy yesterday. He didn't talk with you?

The only place Mr. Neff wants to converse with me is in front of a grand jury, under oath. The unfortunate thing about family quarrels, Dolan explained, was their unintended consequence, another type of collateral damage, tripping over deceptions and secrets that no one ever intended to expose and all parties suffering from a distinct feeling of ambush and collision. While the Bureau wanted Parmentier to just go away, Justice was determined to use him as a broom to sweep out the dirt of a disorderly house. You're a smart man, Tom. Nobody but Albert Neff wants to see Parmentier plea-bargain his way out of the hole he dug himself.

Tell me what you believe.

Dolan glanced over at Gerard behind the wheel as if to measure the importance of his existence. There would be a precedent, he finally said. My guy has some history.

That would be what Parmentier has on you.

Between you and me and the mermaids in the sea, said Dolan. You know who my hero was, the guy I hoped to emulate, the guy I wanted to be? Bobby Kennedy. The way he went after the mob. But during the Tampa operation, Dolan had received a call late one night from Parmentier, who said he was down on his boat and had a problem. You can guess this problem. This problem doesn't take a genius.

Someone figured out what Parmentier was up to.

And that was that.

That was that. Jack invites this guy down to the boat to talk things over and ends up beating him to death. If you ask me, said Dolan, he did the world a favor, but that would be a technicality. Two wrongs can, in fact, make a right but that's worth one complimentary glass of iced tea in hell, right? So the dumb shit calls me and wants me to come down there and help him dump the body in the bay because he doesn't know how to drive his own fucking boat! *Are you out of your fucking mind,* Dolan said, and hung up.

But the pattern Connie expected him to see was not visible to Tom— Parmentier had let Jackie in, he let her come close, he let her see everything. Then she goes to you complaining about Arabs. I don't get that.

Yeah, I don't know, said Dolan.

Who did you talk to at the embassy yesterday? The DCM?

Yeah. I said I don't know why you want to make my job hard but just make this one thing easy, will you? Let me talk to the staffer who showed up at the scene the night of the murder. No can do, says the DCM. The man's been reassigned. Fine, I say, tell me his name, position, place of reassignment. Brussels, military liaison, but I'm not going to be the one who tells you his name, says the DCM. Turns out the woman he was escorting to Moulin Sur Mer for the weekend was not his wife, and the DCM promised to keep his name out of the investigation. Let me talk to her then, I say. He says he can't do that, either, because the woman is the wife of some other person on the staff who thought she was away feeding the poor or something like that. I've talked to her myself, says the DCM, she never got out of the car that night. All right, I say, I want to see the report this guy wrote up when he got back to town. Have it right here, says the DCM. The bastard wasn't going to give it to me unless I asked.

And?

And nothing. I could have written it myself.

What did you do yesterday afternoon?

Listen, it's not in my interest for Woodrow Singer to know my business, said Dolan. He went to a downtown gallery to see the Syrian, an entrepreneur with a curious disregard for his property, a colonial-era warehouse with puddles of water on the untiled concrete floor, mold on the flaking walls, canvases stacked everywhere in disarray. He sold me a painting, said Dolan. You can have it, take it home for your wife. I don't want that crap in my house.

The Syrian did not bother to forget the friendly American who came to the gallery often to use the copying machine. Oh, yeah? Dolan said. What the fuck did he have to copy so much? The Syrian says business documents. Dolan said, Yeah? Did these documents look like US drivers' licenses for guys named Mohammed and Ali Baba and he smiled and told Dolan a long story about how his people had fled the Levant in the twenties and came to Haiti and lived happily ever after among the blacks, who produced a more amenable class of dictator than the Arabs. He wanted Dolan to know how much he loved Americans too. Working with the Americans was a family tradition. He said his father and uncles used to sell pot pies and lemonade or something to the marines who were down here shoveling out the muck in the thirties.

You're saying he gave you nothing.

He inclined his head toward Tom and smiled indulgently. Maybe if I put a gun to his head.

But at the Oloffson, after Tom had slipped off to his room, Woodrow Singer had come back to the table to soft-sell Dolan on the Arabs. He said it was, quote, an OGA operation with a little fraternal boost from some people at Defense.

I don't know OGA, said Tom Harrington. What's OGA?

Other Government Agency. You ready to puke yet? A Washington euphemism beloved among the intelligence community. It almost always means shut up, don't ask. You can take it from there.

Dolan continued with Singer's explanation of the operation, people taking care of a diaspora of indebtedness, promises made but not kept, loyalties never repaid—abandoned cadres left behind in northern Iraq during the Gulf war, exiles from the Taliban, opium smugglers, mujahideen manques. The imperium's tribal proxies morphed into a culled and select clientele, resurrected and reinvented on the basis of a nefarious range of criteria. Singer had told Dolan the Bureau's involvement amounted to a courtesy, much like running an off-the-books witness protection program for people whom various agencies couldn't seem to expedite through the system.

Kurds and Afghanis are not Arabs, said Harrington. You said Jackie was translating paperwork from Arabic.

Dolan said that he had to assume that Arabs were in the mix but that something had gone awry with the operational process. That's the sense I get, he said, and that's what Renee Gardner went out of her way to tell me. It had become apparent to Conrad Dolan that Parmentier and the Syrian were both assets, but whose? That they doubled up on the forgeries meant a trap door had been installed into the protocol, but why? What it all added up to, Dolan wasn't prepared to say. But my instinct tells me we should be looking elsewhere, said Connie, and that's why I want to talk with these cops up there in Saint-Marc. They were on the scene. Nobody else I can find was on the scene. So here we are, or rather here I am. Are you going to tell me now why you changed your mind?

You're saying Parmentier was—? He stopped himself because he always felt like an idiot mouthing the acronym, and his glancing experience with the men and women of the Agency left him with the impression of their incapacity to express themselves beyond the raw vernacular of cowboytalk or the chant of dataspeak or the glassy-eyed prophecy of Christian millennialism. In his experience, they were anti-intellectuals—civilization's drones. He had seen them—handlers or case officers or field agents, whatever they were called—at their hangout, what was commonly known among the expatriates as the spook bar in Petionville. They were never furtive or discreet or genteel; they were, instead, simply smug, mundane personalities attached to a grand adventure or perhaps only a tawdry escapade, and ultimately self-important and tiresome.

Working with, for, under, alongside—fuck, I don't know, said Dolan. Singer claims him, that's what I know. But so does the DEA. Our Jack was busy. Jack was much in demand, given his expertise. Jack was industrious. From what I gather, the DEA set him up as a drug lord so he could squeal on the other drug lords. The margin for error there is as wide as the River Nile. Look, Harrington, Jack was running a hatchery for enemies down here, not to mention the old ones back in the States with long memories. My guess is the contract was meant for him. They missed him, got her. If my best guess is wrong, then Jack is where he belongs, behind bars in Miami, and my own day of reckoning is on the horizon. How much farther is this fucking place?

On their left, between the road and the Bay of Gonave, lay the thorny wasteland of Tintayen, a bone field for the ancien régime, and three years before Harrington had spent a nauseating week scouring its desecrated ground with an Argentinian forensics team, cataloging the bleached remains, corpses devoured by land crabs and swamp rats and feral dogs. Somewhere in a box he kept in his Miami office there was a file.

On the inland side they began to pass a ramble of blistered foothills, and visible ahead an eroding stack of parched mountains seemed to nose into the sea. Tom Harrington told Dolan they were coming up to the quarry and asked if he wanted to stop and Connie said sure and they slammed along through the potholes until Gerard pulled over.

They stepped out into the swelter of an amphitheater cut into the mountain's flank, the dusty mineral scent of crushed rock and the blood-iron pungency of the opened earth. The sun like a dentist's lamp in their eyes. More than anything, the living weight of silence bracketed up and down the road by greasy waves of mirage.

These were the boulders Parmentier would have hidden behind, they guessed, staring into the quarry, and then they walked across the baked surface of the road to the drop of the opposite shoulder and stared down at the coarse earth and its shrivel of weeds and brush and turned a circle to let their eyes sweep the pavement and then looked out at the shimmer of the distant sea. Dolan squatted down to pluck a diamond of broken glass from the pimpled tar and turned it over in his fingers before throwing it away.

Why here? Dolan squinted up and down the empty highway and looked at Tom. You know the road. What do you think?

I haven't thought about it before. Standing here now, it's obvious, isn't it?

Yeah. I guess so. Sorry to say.

The land behind was wide open all the way back to the outskirts of Port-au-Prince. About a mile or two farther north the ecology changed and there was a stretch of villages up the coast to Moulin Sur Mer. Between the villages and the capital, said Tom, there's no place like this.

You can run to the quarry and take cover.

Or walk to the quarry and wait.

Yeah. Let's go.

Something in the rigidity of Conrad Dolan's face and movement as he turned back to the car made Harrington pause and he gazed down at the various patches of stain on the surface of the road—incredible to think that what was in you would one day burst out and evaporate or sink—darkened blots of oil or maybe an indelible residue of old sun-broiled blood or maybe nothing, waiting to feel the one thing he had felt most strongly in Haiti, what he had trained himself to feel, the faint or intense but always unmistakable presence of death, but there was nothing there for him, only his cold heart stalled on a precipice of feeling, but then as he surveyed the unloving desolation of the landscape that had absorbed the last moments of her life his stomach wrenched against a bloom of nausea and, for the first time since learning of Jackie's murder, he experienced the stabbing power of loss. Death had made him ravenous for life—it was imperative he keep moving, seeing things, feeling things—and into that hunger had walked Jackie and she had enraged him and inflamed him with the fullness of living even as she imperiled his soul.

He stared up the road, imagining the journey beyond Saint-Marc, out ahead into the Artibonite, where mud men walked with hoes over their shoulders, imagining their sucking steps across the rice paddies, then the eternally disquiet city of Gonaïves and the massacre that had once occupied so much of his time and all of his passion, farther north into the Savane Desolee and farther still into the *marronage* of the mountains, the bare-breasted women gathered along the blue-green rivers with their wash baskets, and then the end of the road, Le Cap, where he had been reintroduced to his lizard brain. Up there something essential had shifted in his moral universe and the girl was not the cause of it but the invidious effect.

He looked up at the sky, at the towering clouds, and saw their magnificence.

Gerard asked if they wanted to stop at Moulin Sur Mer and Tom said he didn't care and Connie said, *On the way back.* Tom revisited his inventory of questions.

This report you enjoy holding over my head. Who wrote that report? Was it a military sit-rep? Something about the people I had gone up there to investigate? A person named Jacques Lecoeur?

Yes and no, said Dolan. A situation report on file in the defense attaché's office at the embassy.

Who wrote it? Sergeant Burnette?

The name was redacted.

Eville Burnette brought Jackie to me up north. Gerard was supposed to do it but Burnette did it. Did you know that?

No.

I didn't want him along, but he came with us up into the mountains to contact Lecoeur. Did you know that?

I didn't know it was him.

Tell me what was in the sit-rep. No dicking around.

The first half was you and the girl. The last half was about a UN operation to clean out this warlord Lecoeur and his gang. I take it they sent in a team of Pakistani commandos after you left.

I was still there.

Mission accomplished, from what I gathered. There was an addendum. Some raid or takedown of the cops up there last month, about the time of the girl's death.

With American soldiers? That couldn't be true. Gerard, is this true?

People say this is true, said Gerard.

My God. There's another wad of good intentions you can shove right up my ass.

But they were thugs, right? Criminals. Bad guys.

Who? Which ones? Jesus, I don't even know anymore. Goddamn it.

Used and abused. Go ahead and have a good cry.

What's it say about the girl? Was she in on it?

It doesn't say. Did you do the trach? It wasn't you, was it?

No, it was Burnette, Tom said.

And then they medevac out of there leaving you to the wolves and that's what I've never understood.

Yeah, what?

Why you didn't get on the chopper. Why you stayed behind.

I don't know myself anymore.

Well it sounds like quite a party.

You don't know the half of it, thought Tom. I'm rethinking everything about the north, said Tom. That it's very possible—*very* possible—that whoever survived this massive motherfucking betrayal that I seem to be responsible for tracked her down when they discovered she was back on the island. The only thing that seems to work in Haiti is retribution.

Good hunch, slim chance, said Dolan. From what I understand, they're all dead or long gone over the border. Number two, all that time afterward when she was running around snapping pictures of witch doctors, why didn't they take care of it then? And when she came back she didn't come back as Jackie, she came as Renee, new look, new identity.

Someone could have found her out.

Tom, said Gerard. They are not all dead. I think you will be very surprised.

What do you mean?

180

The man who fought with the woman. His name is Ti Phillipe.

He's alive?

Now? Maybe. He was the commander of the police in Cap-Haïtien but he ran away.

Explain that to me. How could that have happened?

The palace was very angry with the foreign soldiers for going into the mountains to kill Jacques Lecoeur and the palace make the soldiers give back Ti Phillipe and make Ti Phillipe *chef* of Le Cap.

Then, as Gerard explained it, the story became incontrovertibly Haitian. Ti Phillipe quarreled with the United Nations mission in Cap-Haïtien, the men on his force shot and wounded several Pakistani blue caps on patrol, the incident was repeated a few days later with deadly force returned against the police, order was not only restored but reinvented when Colonel Kahn called a truce and advised Ti Phillipe to find other, more profitable ways to make trouble than shooting it up with his conscripts. Before long, Ti Phillipe, with a newfound gusto for corruption and illegal activity, was quarreling not with Colonel Khan but with the palace, which did not appreciate the unlawful expansion of Ti Phillipe's authority or the equally unlawful increase of his wealth. The United Nations mission was dismantled on schedule and the president's quarrel with Ti Phillipe escalated into the bitter irreconcilable realm of the ideological, the result being an unlikely poisonous alliance between the erstwhile guerilla, the bourgeoisie, and the *Armée Rouge*.

Okay, said Connie Dolan. My supposition is our man here was too busy with his manifest disloyalties to waste time whacking the girl. And from what I gather from the addendum on that report, the palace took him down.

Tom asked Gerard if he knew of any business Parmentier and the girl had conducted up north and Gerard said he didn't know but it was possible. Something else is going on here but I don't know how it connects with Jackie, said Tom.

You mean the Arabs? asked Dolan.

No, said Tom. I mean the US military.

Tom, said Gerard. The people say the Americans train Ti Phillipe how to make coup d'état.

All of the wisdom he could muster about the relationship between the United States and Haiti, and countries destroyed enough to be anything like Haiti, told him this rumor would prove out, this information was true. And indispensable to the truth of it, inseparable from the truth of it, in Harrington's mind anyway, would be one man, the elite and unanticipated common denominator, the connective tissue, Master Sergeant Eville Burnette, the Special Forces commando who didn't go away when he was supposed to go away. *Why didn't you get on the C-130 back to Bragg, Ev? Why aren't you sitting in some titty bar in Fayetteville drinking off the unnecessary failures and calculated shortfalls of the mission? What are you doing here with us in Le Cap? This is deeply, badly fucked and I don't need a babysitter and you need to disappear.* But Burnette had told Harrington to get used to the idea of his company because he wasn't going anywhere, his command had pulled him off the plane at the last second and ordered him into civvies and took him across the airfield to the UN HQ and hooked him up with the girl. *You're doing something that people seem to think is very interesting,* he told Tom, who wanted to know what people, and Eville said, *Above my pay grade, man.* The UN requested the temporary loan of his sad ass from JSOC, and here he was. *Bullshit,* said Tom, *this is a fucking vanity mission. You SF hotshots have spent a year and a half trying to track down Lecoeur and all you've come up with are the banana leaves he used to wipe his ass. I don't want you along,* but Burnette suggested that Harrington had little choice in the matter.

Of course I have the choice. What I'm doing is not in any way your concern.

The only choice you have is to not go into the mountains. Is that your choice?

They're going to know who you are. It'll take Lecoeur five seconds to figure you out.

I'm a reporter from AMI, he said, flashing UN-issued press credentials. *It isn't your decision and it isn't mine. You either take me, or you don't take me and I follow you in another vehicle, or you stay here and we get drunk and tell stories and you don't go.*

Why is this such a big deal? Jackie had asked Tom and he told her, *Just shut up,* and she left the table in the Christophe's dining area and went to her room and Eville Burnette walked off into the night but he was back in the morning for breakfast, leaning against the SUV in the car park at sunrise in his lightweight boots and acid-wash jeans and beige journo's vest and Oakley sunglasses and he didn't quite look like a soldier and he didn't much look like a correspondent but he surely did resemble some ranch-hand version of muscle-bound sneaky-Pete spook and there was nothing Tom could do about it and he had already forgotten why he had agreed to such a worthless and foolish affair, a waste of time and, finally, a waste of life.

He watched Gerard eat up the miles to Saint-Marc and rolled Eville Burnette's name around in his mind, the slide and tick of the syllables like an incomplete access code to a vast encryption, guessing that Eville was probably up there in the mountains now, counting jumping jacks with Ti Phillipe and his rogue police force, and maybe he had been in-country when Jackie was killed, and maybe that would be no coincidence, and maybe this, and maybe that, and maybe nothing, but Eville Burnette had been with Jackie at Bòkò St. Jean's for some ceremony of no little importance the day before she died. Eville Burnette, Eville Burnette. Eville and Jackie . . . sitting in a tree? Was that the code? Doing what, for Christ's sake? Sacrificing bulls? Bobbing for wayward souls? Come on, man.

They were deep in the muddle of the center of the city now and Dolan had rolled up his window to shield himself from the *marchands* running up to the vehicle and Gerard began to turn right to connect with the street that would, in a few blocks, lead them to the station but Tom told him in Kreyol to keep straight and take them to the *hounfour* on the outskirts of town.

We'll come back, Tom explained to Connie.

From where? asked Dolan.

Why do you think Woodrow Singer wanted to speak to me in private?

Unless he wanted you to kneel and pray with him, I don't have a clue.

Mr. Singer knows more than you give him credit for. For instance, he seems to know that I brought Jackie up here to Saint-Marc. For instance, he told me who he thinks killed the girl. What I want to know is why he didn't check it out himself.

Everybody but Parmentier killed the girl—that would be Woody's point of view. Who does he think killed the girl?

The devil.

That's fucking great. The devil.

He was serious.

If he's serious, then you know why he didn't check it out. In the House of Hoover, he is what we call not field-oriented. Woodrow Singer wouldn't be caught dead sitting next to a bar whore in Okinawa or taking a statement from a Hindu. Woodrow Singer loves his desk and his computer and loves Jesus and hates dirty people and dirty foreign countries and hates sinners and loves the unborn and the twice born. He puts on latex gloves just to take out the trash. Singer is a sidestepper and a buck-passer. Now why don't you tell me what you're talking about? Who's the Devil of the Month? Why are you in this car instead of on a plane back to the States?

I don't know who killed Jackie or why, but I think now I know who does.

Good. Let's have it.

We're going to pay a visit to a voodoo priest, said Tom.

Oh, brother, said Connie Dolan. This ought to be good.

Clambering up the chalky bankside from the road, Harrington began to think of Conrad Dolan as neither colleague nor rival nor the man in charge but as a nuisance, in the way and out of tune, his role reversed and reduced to that of a spectator in this encore performance of the Tom and Jackie show, his vision of the truth bent cross-eyed by an excess of motives and dubious intentions.

Then they were atop the plateau wiping the sweat trickling down their brows and staring back into the frightened eyes of the Haitian peasant who had popped up from his seat, a rusty metal folding chair in the shade of an avocado tree to the side of the *hounfour*, the rifle at his waist trained on them, not an effective way to aim a gun unless it was a shotgun, which it was, and double-barreled; there's yours, here's mine. Dolan instinctively stepped sideways so they could not both be taken down with one blast and the Kreyol rushed forth in a stumble out of Tom's mouth and the tilt of the guard's head seemed to imply no matter what he was hearing he could not understand it and when he didn't respond and didn't lower the gun Tom called back down to the road for Gerard to come quick, and Gerard came right up and went unsmiling to the peasant with his arm extended and made the man shake his hand, saying *What is the problem, these men are friends of Bòkò St. Jean and wish to say hello.*

Big problems, said the peasant with the shotgun. His voice was soft and high and sweet, like a girl's, and despite the gun he seemed otherwise docile and unintimidating.

Gerard, said Dolan, tell this gentleman to stop pointing his weapon at me or I'm going to take it from him and insert it backward up his ass.

Big, big problems, said the peasant. *Please, go away.*

Let's move back and let Gerard talk to him, said Tom. Gerard, what does this man have to tell us?

The _____ is not welcome here, he heard the peasant tell Gerard.

The what? said Tom. Who's not welcome? I couldn't understand the word.

The bishop, said Gerard. The bishop is not welcome.

Tell him we don't have any association with the bishop and just want to give the *houngan* some money and make an offering to the *lwas.*

What is the nature of the problem here? said Dolan. What's he saying?

He wants to know if you are Baptists, said Gerard.

Tell him I said fuck the Baptists.

Gerard and the peasant spoke and Gerard turned around and told the two white men, He says okay. The *houngan* is inside the temple. You can speak with him and then we must go. Tom, this man is very nervous about *blans.* I'm trying to understand why.

They walked across the packed earth of the courtyard toward the center of the compound, Connie Dolan giving the murals on the whitewashed mud walls his imperious scrutiny. Look at this shit, he said and Tom ignored him, tugging open the heavy door, and they dipped their heads under the timbered lintel and went in and paused, letting their eyes adjust to the dimness, the honeyed light splintering down through the roof thatch and the crude ribbing of hand-hewn beams. There on the ground between two wooden pillars on a slatted pallet spread with burlap sacking was a boy, a young man, his nappy head pillowed with rags, asleep or dozing or perhaps only lying there with his eyes closed and his mouth open, grubby hands spidered on his bare chest as if he were keying an accordion, his slender torso sprinkled with the cracked shells of pumpkin seeds he had eaten, big pink-soled feet poking from grimy trousers with legs too short to reach his shanks. Who's this? asked Dolan and Tom said not who we're looking for and they withdrew out the door.

A gaggle of shirtless children had appeared outside the compound, toeing the dirt with an air of expectancy, as if some wonderful form of entertainment would soon be forthcoming. Gerard had found a bucket to sit on and he and the peasant had retreated to the shade of the avocado tree. The guard sat with the shotgun across his knees and tracked the two white men with watchful suspicion as they approached. Tom, there is a problem, said Gerard, this man is still very worried you have come from the bishop because he thinks *blans* only come to the *hounfours* when the bishop sends them to make *dechoukaj*.

Ah, said Tom, so that's what this is about. Dolan asked for a translation and Tom said this word he used means uproot. *Dechouke*—to tear out by the roots.

The island was experiencing the revival of an internecine conflict that had most recently surfaced back in 1986, during the ensuing chaos Duvalier *fils* left in his wake when forced to flee the palace for a gilded exile in France. At that time there had erupted across the countryside what the international press reported as a voodoo war, the delirium of blood revenge, a spontaneous cleansing of the old Duvalierist *houngans* who had assisted first Papa and then Baby in their vile romance with darkness. Whether the spiritual inquisition had piggybacked on the political vendetta Tom could not quite remember and most probably both were too entwined to be anything but different sides of the same coin, the wallows of faith being identical in their superstitions if not their blasphemies. In any event the Catholic church found itself split as well, into separate camps, each faction equally troubling to Rome, the *ti ilgis* of the liberation theologists and the conservative patriarchs who served the dictatorship's status quo. The liberation theologists had a score to settle with the *houngans* serving the Duvaliers, and the hierarchy saw the opportunity to obliterate their competition from the voodooists. Several notorious

Duvalierist bishops found common cause with the grassroots priests of the *ti iglis* and stirred up their parishioners. In the spirit of ecumenical bloodlust, the Baptist and Protestant missions joined the fray and soon mobs of Christians armed with machetes and shovels had bludgeoned and hacked up and beheaded any voodooist in their sight, on one horrifically memorable occasion pitching a dozen *mambos* and *houngans* into a pit and burying them alive in concrete. Once the worst collaborators had been *dechouked,* and the passions dispensed, the conflict waned to an uneasy calm, and the surviving *houngans* formed an ethnographic society and established international alliances with universities and folklorists to protect themselves, but no one could realistically expect such a fundamental struggle for Haiti's identity to ever be fully or permanently resolved, the Haitians battling in effect over control of the graveyard, the top-hatted Baron Samedi squared off against the robed and white-bearded Holy Ghost, both religions adept in their capacities to comfort and terrify and provide temporary refuge from the agonies of the fallen world, yet even in their combined force they redeemed little for the Haitian.

Their presence here was a cause for genuine concern—Tom could see the mistrust unabated in the peasant's nervous eyes—and he became solicitous and took the man's hand in both of his and held it sympathetically and asked him his name.

Marville.

Marville, my friend, is there fighting again between the Christians and the *houngans?*

Oui.

Marville, we are not part of this problem. We only want to speak with the *houngan.* He is my friend. Where is he?

Marville pulled his hand away and replaced it on the stock of the gun and pointed with the barrel toward the temple that formed the center of the U-shaped compound.

Inside.

There's no one there but a boy, said Tom. Where is the *houngan?*

He is the *houngan,* said Marville.

Bòkò St. Jean is the *houngan,* said Tom.

He is not here.

Marville, like most peasants being questioned by a white man, was not generous with his answers and Tom persisted.

When did he go? he asked the peasant and was told *After the harvest,* and Tom said, My friend, when was that?

Two weeks ago, maybe.

Was that the time the white woman was killed near Tintayen?

I don't know.

Did Marville know the white woman? Marville said he did not.

You don't know the white woman who came with a white man and made a sacrifice of two bulls?

Yes, I remember her.

She was killed on the road two weeks ago.

Yes, I remember.

The night she was killed, was that the night Bòkò St. Jean went away?

Yes, said Marville, it's possible.

Was Bòkò St. Jean *dechouked*?

It's possible, monsieur.

Why else would he go away?

I don't know.

Is he dead?

I don't know.

Is he coming back?

I don't know.

Do you know who killed the white woman?

No.

Why do you say the *houngan* is inside?

The boy, according to Marville, was the new *houngan,* a nephew of Bòkò St. Jean who had been trained by his uncle and now replaced him.

Bòkò St. Jean knew he was going away? asked Tom. Is that why he trained the boy?

I don't know.

What is the new *houngan*'s name?

Toussaint.

We want to go back inside and make an offering to the *lwas*. Is this okay, my friend? Do you trust me?

Yes, said Marville, but Tom saw no trust in his eyes and did not expect it.

Fill me in, said Conrad Dolan.

It's nothing, said Tom. Let's go back and wake up that kid.

What for?

Did you ever see Jackie's exhibit at the gallery in Tampa?

No, said Dolan, I never did, and Tom explained that in all likelihood the boy's uncle had been one of Jackie's favored subjects.

The relevance would be what? asked Dolan.

Tom swung open the door to the *hounfour* and paused before going in, turning back to Dolan. And when Woodrow Singer talks about the devil, he said, devil worshippers, evil, his implication is clear.

Not to me it isn't, said Dolan.

The point is this. The voodoo priest we came to see, this guy's uncle, disappeared the night the girl was killed.

What about Parmentier? said Dolan. Was he hanging around here too with the boogeyman?

I don't know, said Tom, stepping into the darkness. You probably want to ask him.

The youth had not moved from his sprawl on the pallet and Tom stooped and tapped his shoulder, calling his name, staring into his soft face until Toussaint's crabbed fingers flattened on his chest and he awoke, bleared eyes swimming in and out of focus, puffed lips rolling across his teeth, and Harrington guessed the young man had spent the morning drinking although his breath did not smell of rum and when he swung his legs in front of him and sat up off balance and looked at them as if they were walruses, Tom began to feel there was something wrong with the boy more serious than a hangover. Narcotics? Perhaps the youth was mildly retarded. Whatever it was, Toussaint seemed glazed with slowness, and he intermittently jerked his head as if trying to shake it clear from a blow.

Tom asked him where is the *houngan,* and Toussaint said I am the *houngan,* with ludicrous self-importance. Tom said I mean your uncle,

Bòkò St. Jean, and Toussaint said, *C'est moi,* it's me. To every question Tom asked about his uncle or the girl, Toussaint insisted he must ask the *lwas.*

You can summon the *lwas*? asked Tom.

Mais oui. I am the *houngan.*

Ask him who owns a red motorcycle, said Dolan, restless with skepticism. Did you ask him that?

Will the *lwas* tell me about your uncle and the white woman?

How should I know? said Toussaint, surprising Tom with his sudden surliness. You must make an offering and find out.

How much? said Tom and when Toussaint named an absurdly high price Tom said that's too much and they settled on one hundred gourdes. Tom told Dolan the *houngan* had agreed to perform a ceremony in Dolan's honor and Dolan grimaced and said what a crock of shit.

Bon, come, said Toussaint and stood up, no taller than Conrad Dolan and, in his slenderness, only half the detective's size. He led them to a lightless place in the room, a back corner sloppily partitioned from the central area by a few lengths of planking to make an alcove for an altar, which they could begin to see as Toussaint, on his hands and knees, struck matches to light the candle stubs plugging the necks of green wine bottles or stuck to the floor, a rough concrete pad where, in the strange dance of ghoulish shadows, Tom saw a drum and footstool set before the shrine itself and more dusty bottles, some empty and dribbled with wax, some surfaced with beads or half filled, he surmised, with herbal potions, an array of tawdry fetishes and talismans, no suggestion of sacred mystery in their seemingly arbitrary and whimsical selection, pink baby-doll heads and a surplus human skull, creepy only in its banality, after the scores of skulls he had witnessed unearthed in Haiti, and a femur looking like the bone a child might draw. A flag pinned to the wall with the geometric heart and *veve* of Erzulie Mary. Toussaint lowered himself onto the stool, the gleam of candlelight on his oily black skin, playing across his high nostrils and prominent eyes, and positioned the drum between his knees and Tom sat cross-legged before him and Connie Dolan stood back and blessed himself, muttering in a mock-weary voice that if the nuns of his childhood could see him now, holy mother of God.

The ceremony began and almost immediately Tom determined that the young *houngan* was a fraud. Toussaint's stammering invocation of the *lwas* amounted to little more than singsong nonsense, and his inept hands slapped the goatskin head of the drum with random spurts of coherence, the rhythm faltering and re-forming, the boy lacking the skill or experience to both drum and chant simultaneously. The charade went on for several interminable minutes until Toussaint seemed suddenly to have been hit with a cattle prod, an electric charge convulsing his arms, the drum knocked from between his flailing legs, his spine arching and his eyes rolling back in his swaying head and spittle flying from his lips.

You enjoying this, Connie, Tom whispered, and Dolan said, You can't be serious, let's get out of here, and Tom said, No, wait.

Perhaps the youth realized he was in danger of losing his audience, or grew bored with his exertions; at any rate, as abruptly as the convulsions began they now ceased and here before them was a new Toussaint, composed and effeminate, pantomiming sensuality, speaking in a high raspy voice of her desire for Tom.

Who is here? asked Tom, and the voice said Erzulie Mary, and Tom asked her about Bòkò St. Jean and the voice said, he is with me, and refused to elaborate.

I want to know about the white woman who came to Bòkò St. Jean because she lost her soul, said Tom, beginning to believe, like Dolan, they were wasting their time.

What do you want to know about this woman? said Toussaint, acting out the voice of the *lwa*.

I want to know if she found it, said Tom. Did she find her soul?

Toussaint's reaction had, for a few moments, a flash of authenticity that unsettled Tom, almost convincing him he had been wrong about this masquerade of possession. The youth's head shook violently, the veins at his temples throbbed, his hands jittered in the air, and an alarming stream of alien language gushed from his mouth. But the spell broke when Toussaint looked directly at Tom and said in his own voice and in English, *I am sorry for you.*

Is that so? said Tom, also in English. And why would you be sorry for me?

191

I am sorry for you, Toussaint repeated, and appeared to lapse into a trance.

What the hell, said Dolan. He speaks English.

He's faking it, said Tom. I think it's time we left.

Did you ask him about the red motorcycle? Wake him up, said Dolan, and ask him about the red motorcycle.

In a burst of sinister laughter, Toussaint's eyes flew open and he reached into the shadows toward the altar, shuffling bottles, looking for a particular one, finding it, raising it to his lips and guzzling, the alcove stinking with the fumes of the *clairin* he then poured on the floor for the *lwas,* and Tom's eyes remained fixed on the rearrangement of bottles. Connie, he finally said, Jackie had a bracelet that a friend gave her. It's there on the neck of one of the bottles.

Dolan asked if he was sure it was hers and Tom said, no question about it. What do you want to do?

Ask the kid how he got it, said Dolan. Maybe she gave it to this guy or his uncle.

I don't think so.

When she was taking pictures. She took a lot of pictures here, right? Maybe it was a gift.

No, said Tom, standing up. It was a birthday present from her old boy-friend who she told me died. You don't give something like that away.

Tom stepped over to the shrine and took the blue-glass bracelet off its dusty bottle and turned toward Toussaint, the strands of blue and white eyes dangling from his fingers, but with a cowed look Toussaint had no answer for Tom's questions other than *Se pa fot mwen,* which he repeated several times in an injured voice.

He's saying it's not his fault, Tom explained to Dolan, but he won't say what it is that's not his fault. He asked Dolan what he thought they should do and Dolan said Let's take him with us down to the police in Saint-Marc. The boy would not move, and when Tom took Toussaint's arm to make him stand up he bolted from the stool and tried to run but Conrad Dolan, defying his age and weight, moved into his path with an agile ferocity, wrapping Toussaint in a bear hug, chest to chest, Dolan's back toward the door and Toussaint wailing for Marville and Marville came.

The first explosion stunned Tom, filling the *hounfour* with white light and a painful bolt of sound that deafened him. Where the shot had been directed he couldn't say. Without letting go of the boy, Dolan spun around so that Toussaint's body shielded him from the second blast, tearing into the youth's upper thighs and buttocks, a few of the pellets striking Dolan's legs as well. Together still, they tumbled to the ground and Marville, in a panic, threw down his rifle and fled. They sent Gerard to Saint-Marc for help and the police arrived and soon an ambulance. Toussaint was taken to the clinic in Saint-Marc and the next day transferred to the hospital in Port-au-Prince. When he had recovered from his wounds, Tom eventually learned, Toussaint was delivered to court and sentenced to prison, the verdict not the result of any confession but based on the evidence provided by the police of Saint-Marc, who, upon further investigation, had discovered what had always been there, parked out of sight along the network of paths behind the *hounfour*, a small and inexpensive Japanese motorcycle, its original color only partially concealed beneath a fresh but badly applied coat of white house paint.

He would remember himself and a bandaged Dolan escorted by the police to the airport in the ripening twilight, an apologetic Woodrow Singer the only one there to see them off, telling them this wasn't his idea, the order for their deportation came from Washington and not Port-au-Prince and I swear to you, Connie, I don't know any of the particulars. He would remember his astonishment to find that there, in the sweltering police station of Saint-Marc's, amid the crush of personnel brandishing their new M16s and the grinning fat-boy chief who conducted their interrogation, the composed and calming presence of a white American standing off to the side with an amused air of authority, his military bearing not particularly well disguised by civilian clothes. When the chance came for them to speak Tom said, *Who are you?*

The American said, *The trainer,* and Tom said, *Army?* And the guy said *maybe,* and Tom said, *Special Forces?* and the fellow said, *You never know* and Tom felt a light turn on and asked, *Where's Eville?* And the trainer said, *Busy,* and winked and then they were told it was time to go.

Back in the States, Eville Burnette stayed on his mind and, a few days after his return, when he read an archived *Herald* story reporting the uprooting of the renegade police chief of Cap-Haïtien by a special unit of the palace guard, Tom contacted Daniel, the AP photographer who had been on the scene, and asked to see his shots from that day and downloaded them onto his computer. In the scroll of images there was Eville, at the side of the black uniformed squad of paramilitaries from Port-au-Prince and Tom could make no sense of it, believing all along that Burnette had been orchestrating a coup, not preventing one. For several months he made an effort to contact Eville through channels in Fayetteville but nothing ever came of it and when, on a hunch, he petitioned the Air Force for the flight manifest of the C-130 that flew Renee Gardner's body out of Haiti he was told the manifest was classified and even when he filed a Freedom of Information Act request for the manifest nothing ever came of that, either.

He remembered on the flight back to Miami Dolan's supreme relief, despite the pain of the superficial wounds to his legs, that Parmentier was not responsible for the girl's death and then the next day Connie had phoned him from Tampa to say Parmentier had been released from the federal penitentiary and he didn't know where he was and good riddance and that was the last that Tom Harrington ever expected to hear from Conrad Dolan.

Several months later, Harrington, recently back from a month in The Hague, walked out of his office in downtown Miami and hailed a cab to Little Haiti, where he often liked to have his lunch and catch up on the latest news and rumors from the island, and as he sat down that day at a tiny wooden table and studied the menu scrawled in Kreyol on a blackboard behind the restaurant's counter, a man looking very much like a storefront minister stepped up to the cashier to pay his bill and Tom jumped out of his chair, certain that he was seeing Bòkò St. Jean risen from the dead, even more certain when he approached him and looked into his eyes, but the man said No, monsieur, you are mistaken, and then in English, Have a nice day.

Tom Harrington managed, as well as anybody, the half-formed truths of love with an acceptable amount of grace and honor. He did not neglect his daughter, and sometimes he was happiest with the dog, walking the shoreline of Virginia Key, and sometimes he was most gratified helping Allison with her homework or reading to her at bedtime. Aware of her looming sexuality, Allison in her skimpy bikini at the beach, Allison in the kitchen at night wearing only a T-shirt and panties, the presence forming in her that a father had no choice but to resist, and from this struggle he felt for the first time an erotic apathy that puzzled both his wife and his lover in South Beach. Sometimes he felt that, except for his daughter, he could not name one thing about love that was unconditional, and though he loved his wife he was aware with an indifference he did not understand that he did not love her enough, that they were not the match he had hoped they would be, and when they fought their predictable and futile battles over money or the time he spent away from them, a moral crusader without the benefit in his private life of a moral center, an unimpeachable core, if there was such a thing in a human being, an attainable infallibility of virtue, he sometimes thought about leaving her and perhaps he would when their daughter had grown and was away, as she must be, on her own.

Occasionally in the lonely hotel rooms he spent much of his life in around the globe he thought as he fell asleep about ape souls, something that bothered him, the six-million-year split from a common ancestry. What was in an ape's soul? Was it very much different than what was in his? In our own ability to see and confirm ourselves, had our rise as a species been propelled by one simple skill, the slick repackaging of our brutish heritage into an alliance with the divine? Thus, men have souls. Thus, apes are without. Thus the ordination of violence. And this—When a nation lost its soul, where did that soul even come from to begin with? What was the genesis of a nation's soul? The answer seemed only to be war.

He had told her the story now and she wanted to hear it once more. I need to understand this, his wife had said, but he couldn't remember precisely what he had said, where the lies mixed with the truth, where the truth diverged from his imagination, the correct order of fact and fabrication, and he knew he could not tell it in the same way again.

Book Two

How Peace Begins
Croatia 1944, 1945

If only there were evil people somewhere insidiously
committing evil deeds and it were necessary only to separate
them from the rest of us and destroy them. But the line
dividing good and evil cuts through the heart of every human
being. And who is willing to destroy a piece of his own heart?
—Alexandr Solzhenitsyn

CHAPTER FOURTEEN

During the final days of the German occupation of Croatia, there was an eight-year-old boy in Dubrovnik, Stjepan Kovacevic, who would be introduced in the most indelible fashion to his destiny, the spiritual map that guides each person finally to the door of the cage that contains his soul, and in his hand a key that will turn the lock, or the wrong key, or no key at all.

In Stjepan's case, the map was drawn by an act of retribution: the brutal death of his father, beheaded before his eyes. One apostate held the boy with a forearm clamped across his throat, the canvas sleeve of his uniform reeking of paraffin; two men escorted his mother upstairs for interrogation, three more forced his father to prostrate himself before the hearth in the kitchen, then side-kicked his severed head into the fire like a soccer ball, the boy crying as much from shame as terror because for months now, as the war turned against his people, he had been ravaged by hunger, and the smell of his father's sizzling flesh made his mouth water pitilessly and his stomach foam.

The Serb who held him said, And this one?

The Bosnian partisan who had wielded the crude saber stepped away from the headless corpse, muttering introspectively. Who is the beast? Is it me? I am a slayer of beasts. Who kills children? I do not kill children, even fascist brats with fathers who kill children, he said and came and stooped before the boy, taking his measure, a child of Europe in the hands of the barbarians.

Stjepan, who would not look at him, remembered little more than the stink of black tobacco steaming from his mustache, the splatter of paternal blood on his greasy trousers, the winter mud streaked on his boots.

My name is Kresimir *mrtvac,* he told the son of the former Ustashe vice commander who had orchestrated the pogroms in central Bosnia. Kresimir *mrtvac,* Kresimir the corpse. He was one of Tito's Partisans, Serbs and Bosnians, Communists and Muslims, men who shit on God and men Stjepan would spend the rest of his life calling, as all Slavic Christians, Roman and Orthodox, called such men who bowed to Mecca, the Turks. Their actual origin hardly mattered.

When you are a man, Kresimir said, come find me, okay, and I will kill you then. He lifted the boy's quivering chin with blood-slick fingers. Yes? Promise? But Stjepan kept his eyes downcast and finally the Bosnian chuckled drily and patted him on the cheek as if he were his own.

Good, he said. Don't forget.

The partisans left to continue their orgiastic purge of Dubrovnik and Stjepan stood in place, exactly where he had been released from the grip of the man who had held him, the satin pool of his father's blood inching toward his shoes. Over the crack and stutter of gunfire in the nearby rialto he strained to hear any sound from the floor above to tell him his mother was alive, not knowing then that she listened, too, lying in catatonic stillness where the men had left her in her child's urine-smelling bed, commending to the Almighty the souls of her husband and the boy, convinced they were both lost to her on this earth but absorbed by eternity as martyrs of God and saints of the fatherland, their names already on the lips of unborn avengers. To have such a prayer to pray was a sacred honor, and lifelong.

Outside the house the old city shrieked and whistled and banged but inside endless minutes passed in catastrophic silence until she heard the boy retching and bolted down the stairs into the kitchen in time to see him drop his father's charred skull, which he had managed to recover from the flames with cast-iron tongs, into a pail of dishwater. She wiped the vomit from his slack mouth with a rag, the bloody smudge of handprint from his cheek, pulled his soiled sweater over his head and replaced it with two clean ones, made him put on his overcoat and gloves, scarf, and felt hat as she ran back upstairs for their documents and cache of banknotes—what was there to buy anymore with all this money? Then she packed toothbrushes and her hairbrush, a bar of homemade soap and hand towels, extra underwear and a sewing kit, jewelry with sentimental value, saints' reliquaries and an ivory-beaded rosary blessed by the Pope, a Confirmation gift from her parents, and the few family photographs she cherished, rushed belatedly to the toilet to cleanse herself and clear her thoughts of the rape, no time for that now, buttoned a cashmere sweater on over her housedress and a stylish fuchsia wool jacket over the sweater and hurried back downstairs to where the boy stood in the ruins of his world, his face ashen and immobile, a tiny mannequin fattened by winter clothes staring eyeless into space. She made the sign of the cross over her dead husband and fished his billfold from his pocket and his gold crucifix and its chain from a pudding of blood.

We're leaving now, she said, looking back at her headless husband as she pushed her son out the door, away once again from the city of her birth into the peril of a future known only by its past.

They fled the walled city to its outermost quays and were packed aboard the fishing boats filled with other panicked refugees that would take them that night and the next day north to Split, Ustashe-controlled and two weeks in front of the partisans' advance, where Dido Kvaternik's men secured passage for them on a convoy to Zagreb, the city rising from the plain in a dome of sulphurous fog, arriving two days before Christmas, 1944. In Zagreb, they shared a bedroom in his Aunt Mara's lugubrious apartment, like a private chapel infused with grief, on the northwestern corner of Jelacic Square—Mara, his mother's sister, widowed herself by Chetniks earlier in the war. For months it seemed they did little more than huddle together in its sunless freezing rooms, insensate, bewitched by the fizzing radio and its diabolic spew of contradictory reports, waiting for the end, leaving the apartment's sanctuary only to plod uphill to Dolac and its barren stalls, scavenging for bread and turnips and coal, or to attend mass at the cathedral, over which his father's cousin reigned as archbishop, spiritual leader of the land described in 1519 by Pope Leo X as *Antemurale Christianitatis,* the outermost ramparts of Christendom, a belated and feeble acknowledgment of a reality superior to geography—Asia meets Europe not where the seas divide the continents but here, deep in the savage wilderness of the Balkans, where empires and religions grate against each other to produce a limitless supply of bloody slush flowing east and west into the gutters of civilization.

In February the Bolsheviks captured Mostar, the same month his mother fell ill drinking an herbal remedy, a traditional midwife's abortifacient meant to trigger miscarriage, and afterward lay curled into herself like a sick cat, mewling in bed throughout Lent. In April, Srijem, Vukovar, and Valpovo followed Mostar into Stalinist hell. As May approached and the partisans moved inexorably westward toward Zagreb, Stjepan and the two specterlike widows joined the city's exodus—hundreds of thousands of soldiers and civilians—on a Boschian trek toward the Austrian frontier, the army and home guard choosing to surrender to the Allies and not the Reds.

But at the River Drava the national troops of the Independent State of Croatia were disarmed by the unsympathetic and ideologically ambivalent British, shuttled aboard overcrowded trains, and transported straight back to Yugoslavia, into the hands of the Communists, massacred as they filed out from the boxcars like the eighty thousand Jews they had dutifully shipped to Poland throughout the war. Stjepan and his exhausted mother and increasingly demented aunt had already turned back from the border, deterred by partisan raids on the tail of the column where they trudged like stock animals in a desperate herd of hollow-eyed disheveled women and bawling children, reaching the deserted streets of the city only hours before Zagreb fell to Tito on the eighth of May, the same day Germany surrendered.

They stayed indoors, the heavy brocade curtains drawn across the apartment's bay windows, fearing every sound as they dreaded every silence, phantom shapes in flickering candlelight, saying the Rosary together in hushed voices or lying like invalids numb in their beds. Occasionally the boy took a book from the shelves of his uncle's library to stare with zero reaction at pictures of farm machinery or let his mind fall into a sentence and wander aimlessly through the shadowy canyon of its words. On Sunday mornings they ventured out for mass, scurrying like frightened mice along the damp pavement uphill toward the beckoning spires of the cathedral. It had been in this same cathedral, two years earlier on the feast day of Christ the King, that the boy and his parents had heard the archbishop's sermon condemning religious and racial intolerance—*All men and all races are the children of God . . . one cannot exterminate Gypsies or Jews because one considers them of an inferior race*—although the boy had forgotten everything about the service but the heroic and rare presence of his father sitting next to him. His harried, preoccupied father, his beautiful uniform smelling of saddle soap and rain and peppery gunpowder, had been ordered back to the capital from the Bosnian front for consultations, his wife and son joining him from Dubrovnik for a holiday in the Esplanade, the grand hotel across from the train station. *What's a Jew?* he remembered asking, too loudly, and he remembered his father lightly pinching the side of his bony thigh and whispering, *Someone preferable to a Turk, now shh,* the expression in his father's friendly gray eyes fixed on something far away, and not friendly, not forgiving.

After church they walked hand in hand in hand to a café, the parents sometimes swinging the child between them like a bell of joy; Stjepan ate ice cream with berry preserves, his parents laughed and drank beer with the Waffen-SS, and even the obliging waiters seemed like emissaries of happiness, that lost Sunday afternoon in the middle of war.

The archbishop, released from partisan custody the first week in June, distributed flour and the comfort of absolution to his burgeoning congregation of refugees. Stjepan, who had only known compassion from women, fell in love with the priest, the dark crescents of mercy like bruises beneath the archbishop's eyes, the pure hand of tenderness resting on the boy's shoulder, kneading the back of his rigid neck or warming the top of his shaven head, the compressed grace of his beatific smile in a city where smiles were as unlikely as roasted chickens and laughter had been consigned for safekeeping to the insane. The Sunday when Stjepan announced to the archbishop that at the moment he received the Eucharist and felt the buttery melt of the consecrated host on his tongue, he had heard God's voice instructing him to join the priesthood, the archbishop, deeply touched by the child's faith, studied Stjepan with sad resignation.

My son, he told the boy, I am reluctant to encourage you, it is a difficult time to want to be a priest in Croatia. Partisans were hunting down and executing Catholic clergy throughout the parishes, intent on decapitating the Church with as forceful a blow as they had lopped off the heads of the Ustashe puppets; the archbishop himself accused of inspiring, if not advocating, war crimes. Nevertheless he admitted Stjepan to the ranks of altar boys serving the cathedral. In this role, and the starched, incense-fragrant security of its ritual, Stjepan began to reawaken from his family's coma of defeat. His excitement was uncontainable when, in July, the new regime, for the first and last time, granted permission to the archbishop to hold the city's annual procession to the shrine of Marija Bistrica, north of Zagreb, and he was selected to lead the file of priests in scarlet cassocks and white lace mantles, swinging a brass censer, intoxicated by the puffs of frankincense he created. Behind, in the flock of forty thousand pilgrims, walked the two sisters—his mother and aunt. Tito's soldiers, many still dressed like forest partisans but others wearing the new uniforms of the Yugoslav army, lined the route, inflamed by the audacity of so large a crowd, the impertinent bereavement of the families of the Ustashe collaborators, the husbands and sons and fathers who had been annihilated while trying to surrender at the frontier. No shots were fired but the verbal abuse escalated, sporadic, convulsive, to sudden and unpredictable acts of violence. Somewhere along the route of the procession, a bull-faced partisan thrust himself into the flow of pilgrims to block the path of the widows.

Do you recognize me? he demanded of the boy's Aunt Mara. I am from Siroki Brijeg—her husband's village.

Yes, she said, get out of my way.

I am from Siroki Brijeg, he repeated like an imbecile, bellowing.

Yes, his Aunt Mara said, I often saw the drunken slut they called your mother fucking Turks in the alley.

For her insolence she received a rifle butt to the head, the stock turned sideways, striking cheekbone to cheekbone, her aquiline nose crushed backward into her sinus cavities. After the benediction at the shrine, the boy, yearning for praise, looked for the women and was disappointed but not overly surprised when he failed to locate them among the vast expanse of the devout, who had pressed onward in their pilgrimage despite the harassment. Meanwhile, his aunt and mother had been taken back to the city by a white-haired peasant with his horse-drawn wagon, first to a clinic where his once glamorous aunt was hastily diagnosed as unfixable, the weary doctor injecting her with a syringe of precious morphine after settling on the amount of his bribe, then back to the apartment, where his mother stood on the street pleading with passersby to help carry the half-conscious woman up the steps, her pale blonde hair gelled with black blood, eyes like tomatoes, swollen closed, purple face bloated beyond recognition. When the boy returned at sundown, he found the women in the musty parlor, his tall scarecrow aunt laid out on the sofa, his mother kneeling by her head with a washbasin of cold water and a mound of bloody tea towels, the sound of his mother's prayers entwined with the gurgle of agony coming from his slowly suffocating aunt.

Go to bed, Stjepan, his mother said when she realized he had returned home. Get some rest. If she dies, we are leaving tomorrow.

His mother's side of their bed remained an empty blue glow that night, her absence a bottomless pool daring him to come close and swim away. In the morning he found the two sisters together still, his aunt in a royal shroud of velvet curtains patterned with silvery fleur-de-lis, his mother asleep on her suffering knees, her head cradled atop her sister's unused womb, her right hand cupping the dead woman's left hand, its cold whiteness stuck out from the folds of the shroud as if to catch at life's shreds, the parlor bathed in what the boy experienced as an angelic aura of radiance from the columns of previously banished sunshine entering the apartment. He knelt beside his mother, praying mindlessly, until she cracked open her eyes.

She was just like your father, his mother murmured. If you want a Dalmatian to shut his trap, what can you do but kill him. She opened her reddened eyes fully, looking at Stjepan without expression or feeling. Get dressed and pack your valise, she said.

Where are we going? he asked, and an edge of rebelliousness in his tone made her raise her head from the corpse of her older sister and straighten her back to look down gravely on the boy.

We are going away, she said.

Where?

God willing, we are going to the coast to find a boat.

To go where?

Be careful how you speak to me, she warned.

I won't leave, he said, uncustomarily stubborn.

Stjepan, we cannot live with the Communists, she explained impatiently. And we cannot live without God. You are old enough to understand these things.

His anger reared up and he told her he had decided to live with the others—the fugitives—at the archbishop's palace.

Soon Tito will come for the archbishop too, she said. He will die alone a martyr in Lepoglava. Get dressed now. Not another word.

No, he said, his face bright red, shrieking. I must stay. He confessed he had made a deal that prevented him from leaving and she thought he meant the bargain he had struck with God to join the clergy and tried to hug him, perhaps to mitigate his piety with the touch of her flesh, but he flapped away from her arms like a bird. Stjepan, she said, they don't want priests here anymore. You can study to be a priest in Italy.

No, he screamed, eyes spurting a fury of tears. I promised.

Stop this, she said. You promised what? To whom? To God?

A heart-piercing wail—Yes, God.

Quiet. Calm down. Promised what, darling?

To kill the men who killed my father, he said.

Ah, I see, she said. You and I will talk about this.

CHAPTER FIFTEEN

To protest openly would reveal the sin of his thoughts—worse, expose the sin's appeal— and so he kept quiet and watched with sullen resentment, later that morning in the sacristy of the national cathedral, as his mother bartered with one of the priests, trading a bundle of currency wrapped in newspaper and tied with butcher's string for the promise that the church would attend to the remains of his Aunt Mara.

Why are we bothering with her? Stjepan thought bitterly. What makes her so special? And then, unwittingly, he found himself back across the bridge in his mind to where he had abandoned his father in the fog on the other side. Who buried Father? Was his head soaking still in the kitchen bucket? If they buried him, did they place the head with the body? Wasn't that more evil than even killing, to put his head over here and his body over there? Shouldn't he and his mother return immediately to Dubrovnik to make sure these unspeakably important matters were properly addressed? Why didn't she care? She didn't care.

They called at the archbishop's private residence at the massive neo-Gothic palace behind the cathedral, his mother desperate for any assistance her husband's cousin might find in his heart to offer for the difficult journey ahead into exile—their second exile together, although the boy had no knowledge of the first. She was determined to make contact with the Americans but remained terrified of the Allied forces, foremost the treacherous British, the venomous sting of their centuries-old contempt for the Croats, who controlled the border crossings along the northern frontier and continued their unconscionable wartime alliance with Moscow and the partisans. Italy, which she had spent much of her life admonishing—in fluent Italian, no less—seemed for the second time in her life the only reasonable destination. To her relief, the archbishop, inviting the woman and the boy into his sitting room for the forgotten luxury of coffee and biscuits, counseled her to go to the Italians and pray for the best. There is a ship, he told her, that would arrive soon in Zadar to pick up refugees and take them across the Adriatic to Ancona. On this ship, he said, he hoped to place an envoy, who would report to the Vatican on the relentless persecution of the Church. She and her son should consider accompanying the envoy to the coast, where passage might also be arranged for them on the ship.

Should, she repeated to herself. *Might.*

Marija, before you say yes, the archbishop said solemnly, there is one complication you must know about—the boat has been leased by Zionists, the refugees they will collect are Jews. Are you guilty of anti-Semitism? the archbishop asked his mother.

No, she said, let the Jews live in peace, but they will throw us overboard and who could blame them, Father. In Bosnia, my husband had orders to send them all to the camps.

Yes, everyone obeyed, some more than others, said the archbishop, reciting the platitudes that could be thrown like a golden cape over the shoulders of atrocity. Your husband never drew a breath nor, I am certain, extinguished another's that he did not commend to the glory of God. To be honest, I don't think he cared much about the Jews one way or another. The Jews were never a genuine problem in this country—not like the Masons, for instance. Why bother with these poor souls when the devil himself is at the door? In any case, trust in God these Jews on the boat will not put you in the water.

Surreptitiously, the boy ate the last biscuit; the archbishop stood to extend his hand. Mother and son lowered themselves side by side to their knees to press their lips to the papal ring and receive his blessings. Without warning, Stjepan became inconsolable and the archbishop finally had to pry the sobbing child's fingers away from his own.

*   *   *

They spent the night with other refugees housed in the overcrowded fetid recesses of the archbishop's palace, the boy forbidden by his mother to speak to anyone of their plans; spies were the reason she gave him but secretly she feared the jealousy of the others should they learn of their privilege, beneficiaries of the archbishop's personal intervention. In the morning they walked with their belongings to the cathedral to attend a mass for the dead, his Aunt Mara occupying one of the seven pine-board coffins arrayed between the nave and the left side of the altar, the pews filled with anonymous mourners, the air weighted by the humidity of their bereavement and the gloom-heavy fumes of beeswax. The grave diggers were days behind in their labor and to remain in the city for her burial was out of the question. After mass, his mother led him down the aisle to the forbidding row of coffins.

Which one is Aunt Mara's? he asked. I don't know, she said, kiss them all.

They returned to the pews where the boy stretched out and fell asleep to the anguished sussuration of his mother's rosary and she did not have the heart to wake him when the archbishop's driver arrived but scooped him into her arms and carried him to the car.

She folded the boy onto the front seat while the driver, a large elderly man with white cropped hair and the piercing amber eyes of a falcon, tied their bags to the roof and then she sat in back, sharing the seat with a pugnacious-looking man dressed in a brown worsted suit, unsuitable for summer weather, red, meaty hands resting on his knees, his brush-cut black hair and steel eyeglasses amplifying the severe virility of his face. The driver too, despite his age, seemed intimidating. He had the rolling, flat-footed gait of a brawler, one of those men who would rather fight than explain themselves, his bulky face sculpted by pugilism, she thought, and engraved with a vestigial sharpness she vaguely associated with criminals—perhaps the war had done this, branded him with its harshness, or perhaps he was a redeemed thug come home to serve the Church. Both men, she realized, made her uneasy. The driver slid behind the wheel, bringing with him a lemony trace of hair tonic, and as they drove west through the maze of Zagreb's colorless streets she waited in vain for her fellow passenger to present himself, say anything, the small courtesy of a greeting, an acknowledgment of their common humanity, a gesture of fellowship based on the danger they now faced together, but the man offered nothing beyond the arrogant profile of a glare directed out the windscreen.

Where is the archbishop's envoy? she finally found the courage to ask.

I am the envoy, he said staring ahead.

Yes? she said. I thought you would be a priest.

I am a priest, he replied with a trill of strange glee. He crossed his arms over his chest and tilted his head in her direction, as if to share a confidence. Today, however, he said, lowering his voice, and tomorrow, and until we are on the boat, I am your husband—and now he looked at her with frost-blue eyes and a patronizing smile. With your permission, he said. In name only, of course—and he shifted his body to glare again at the streets.

What is your name? she asked dully, resigning herself to this unexpected ruse.

Our name is Bauer, he said. I am Slavko.

I see, she said. And what is our business in Zadar?

Your business, madam, is to be my wife.

At first she was concerned but then overwhelmingly gratified that her son, as if he'd been drugged senseless, would not wake up, his surrender so deep that he slept through two checkpoints, the first on the outskirts of the city and the second a few kilometers beyond. The driver proved himself to be well-versed in the protocols of danger, exceedingly calm, cautiously gregarious, his deflections a humble art she had not imagined he possessed, exiting the car in his dark suit and yellowing dress shirt unbuttoned at the collar and his eyes shining with camaraderie to smoke with the partisans, packs of contraband cigarettes handed around, opening the trunk for a bottle of plum brandy, telling barnyard jokes and mumbling lies, the passengers overlooked and soon forgotten. Those interminable minutes at the checkpoints she thought she would faint from terror, anticipating the boy surfacing back to reality, confused and innocent, unable to recognize the peril they were in and not understanding that truth was a poison they would not survive. The privilege of the archbishop's assistance, she now realized, came at a price she had not been clever enough to foresee.

210

The road was in poor condition, cratered and rutted, trafficked by oxcarts and an occasional jeep, its soggy ditches littered with curious wreckage and the torn remains of animals, women distant in the fields scything barley hay, chimneys rising above the ruins of the countryside, infrequent reminders that nothing was settled—a crossroads where she saw a gouged and severed head mounted on a stake, a turn in the road that slowly revealed a tidy row of executed men, naked, facedown in wildflowers, their bound hands crossed palms-up atop the pumpkinlike swelling of their buttocks. There were no more checkpoints that afternoon until twilight, at the entrance to Karlovac, and at the same moment she noticed the barrier across the road the boy began to rouse and sit up. Listen to me, she screamed, diving halfway into the front seat, shaking the boy by the shoulders while he stared at her, dumbstruck with horror by his mother's assault. Talk to nobody, she said frantically, if you talk they will kill us. But she had frightened him needlessly, her heart thundering as the soldiers inexplicably raised the wooden bar across the road and waved them onward into the city.

In an alley behind the central square, the envoy disappeared into the rectory of Holy Trinity Church and they passed the night in the house-keeper's apartment where, as they prepared themselves for bed, she had tried to explain to the boy how important it was, should they be stopped by the rebels, to keep his mouth zipped, but he seemed increasingly with-drawn and restless, and she sensed her control over him slipping away. I don't know who this priest is, she said, who cannot travel as a priest under the flag of the archbishop. Maybe he is just afraid, like the rest of us, she told her unresponsive son, yet he wants us to pretend we are his family. So if I say he is my husband, you say yes, if I say he is your father, you say yes, but if I don't say these things, you will not say these things. Do you understand? You must understand, Stjepan. You must agree.

In the morning there was leftover ratatouille laded with paprika, reheated and served for breakfast. Outside, the car in the alley was just as they had left it, and there was the envoy in the backseat, unchanged in every respect except for his breath, which carried the slightly decrepit scent of vinegar, she noticed, as she eased in beside him, as if he'd been eating rotten apples or drinking bad wine. Good morning, she said, and because he offered no other response than an aloof nod she did not ask him if he had slept well or poorly or not at all, to hell with him.

She had slept fitfully, dreading what lay ahead of them, and that morning she did not have to wait for her fear to manifest itself because it sprang, iron-jawed, upon them instantly, the car turning a corner out of the alley into the central square, suddenly occupied by soldiers. They jumped down from the flatbeds of two battered trucks, an officer sprinting forward, signaling to the archbishop's driver. *Halt!* his voice punctured the air. *Out!*

To the driver—*Step away!* To the woman and boy—*Stand by him!*— the officer gesturing toward the envoy. She clasped the boy protectively to her legs and stared into the air at pigeons taking flight until her vision spiraled with black confetti. The soldiers formed a horseshoe and they waited, for what she didn't know, no one speaking, the sun too bright in her eyes and the world itself blurred to an abstraction.

Then, in the unnatural stillness, the painful vividness of everything ebbed back into her consciousness as the faint rhythmic purr of engines somewhere nearby in the otherwise silent city approached the square. The mushy rip of tires on the cobblestones preceded the dreamlike appearance of a pair of familiar black sedans, German-made and previously favored by the gestapo. The envoy tried to grasp her elbow but she shrugged away his hand.

Two men in ordinary street clothes with holstered pistols strapped on military belts got out of the second sedan and spoke briefly with the officer. Then they were standing in front of her and the boy was pulled from her arms, the man turning Stjepan around so that she could observe his reaction, but the man could not see what she could see on her son's face, only how it shocked her, how his expression broke her spell and cast her into a clearheaded state of alertness, seeing for the first time in the eyes of the boy his intractable disregard for authority, the impudent but desolate fearlessness he now assumed in the face of danger, some unbreakable defiance in his character that had not been there yesterday and made her immediately afraid the boy was determined to cause great trouble.

Who is this man? the second of the two asked in a voice so disarming it confused her with its veneer of pleasantness.

Which man? she said, struggling to comprehend the obvious.

Him, said the man, smiling, pointing with his stubbled chin at her companion, who stood exposed and rigid as a fencepost, sunlit face drained by the pallor of his fallibility.

I don't know, she said, ignoring the shameless *tsk* of irritation from the tongue of the priest in the brown suit.

You don't know? the partisan said. His smile collapsed into something flat and ominous. Her denial seemed to cue both men to unbuckle the flaps of their holsters; the one who held Stjepan rapped him on the head with the barrel of his gun in the checked way someone would strike the shell of a boiled egg with the edge of a spoon. Stjepan's expression contorted with indignation, a small gash bloomed brightly atop his shaven skull, out crawled worms of blood, and she marveled at his refusal to acknowledge the pain of the blow that had stabbed her own heart.

I don't know, his mother whimpered. She heard the pistol's hammer being cocked and watched its barrel nuzzled obscenely in her child's ear and saw the boy breathing fire.

The archbishop's envoy, she screamed out. As God is my witness, I don't know his name.

But you are the archbishop's envoy, the partisan said to her. Step over here with me.

What? she answered weakly. I don't understand.

Step away from that miserable bastard.

Flinging the boy aside, the man pounced forward and she closed her eyes. The blast was so forceful it seemed to lift her off her feet and beyond the deafness ringing in her head the shot repeated itself, echoing in the stony chamber of the square. When she opened her eyes the priest in the brown worsted suit had crumpled to the paving bricks, life bubbling from his forehead and nose, his executioner sweeping the air with the pistol. Go, he said to her with a crazed look of happiness. He brandished the pistol carelessly at the driver. Go, old man.

Wait, said his partner, and she instinctively shielded the boy with her body. Wait, said the man, there is someone in the first car who asks for your courtesy.

My courtesy? she said to herself, stunned, and the word itself seemed to rob her, as nothing else had, of her strength. Whatever had held her nerves together for so long she felt disintegrating; her legs would not move, crippled by the black weight of violence in her stomach, nor could she find her breath. The boy and the old man supported her arms and she shuffled between them through the cordon of statue-faced soldiers to the black sedan and its hallucinatory summoning.

My God, I don't believe it, she said, bending to the open window, straining cronelike to squint in dismay at the broad forehead and narrow chin of a ghost.

Marija, the passenger in the front seat answered in a quiet voice. My apologies.

The boy would always remember his mother's transformation at the moment she recognized the man, her backbone snapping erect and hands flying upward, brazenly reanimated and self-assured, contempt flowing through her like a return to health.

Your apologies, she scoffed, unwilling to use his name, to allow the intimacy of old friends. Quisling. Murderer. God forgive you.

Marija, he said, untouched by her insults, think strategically. I fight the same battle, now from the inside, at the next stage. You can see the necessity. You can understand.

How could you ever become a Red? she asked, incredulous and then cold, then vicious. Ethnic trash is what Karl Marx called us, unfit to drink from the piss pot of his lofty schemes. Tell me, how could you forget this? Ah, wait, it's a question of brains, she sneered, happy to see the crimson stain that flowered on his neck when his literacy was challenged. You can't remember what you can't read, is that it?

Marija, we survived. Now we must win.

God take you straight to hell, she said, rediscovering her son as she turned away, then whipping back around. Why must you hurt the boy, you pig? she raged, dabbing tendrils of blood from Stjepan's face with the hem of her skirt. Damn you, give me your handkerchief, she demanded, but he had no handkerchief to give.

Marija, I regret this very much, he said, and she noticed he had difficulty turning his head to look at her directly. It happened because it happened. Are you all right, boy? he asked. You stood bold, like your father. You have guts.

You knew my father? asked the boy.

I knew your father, Stjepan.

Fuck yourself, his mother said.

His face blanched. Don't speak like a whore, he admonished her, and the boy came through the window, his fist striking snakelike, breaking the skin on the right side of the man's upper lip. He swung again without effect, his mother yanking him back by the collar of his shirt, and the man laughed with stiff appreciation, waving away the two pistol men who came sprinting toward the car.

He's a little wolf. This pleases me, Marija, he said, wiping his bloody mouth with the back of his hand. When he rotated his entire body to look the boy in the eye, she put her own hand to her mouth, gasping, able to see his injuries for the first time, the gruesome scarring, the curled hand flopping from the lifeless left sleeve of his summer jacket, the partially missing ear and its ugly hole. It's okay, boy, he grinned. You are a Croat. Against all enemies, defend your mother, defend your motherland.

Defend the Lord Our Savior, Jesus Christ, Marija said but wavered in her bitterness, moved by his act of forgiveness, the mutilation of his youthful, athletic body. Who was he anyway, this priest who asked that I be his wife? she asked.

A transgressor, a criminal, said the man in the car, whose name was Davor Starcevica, her husband's erstwhile comrade, a peasant from Slavonia who had wandered from the land to the slums to find his purpose in life, which was, as with so many others at the time, insurrection. Some priests, he said, will do all the things that other men must hang for.

This priest was the archbishop's envoy, she said, knowing the distinction now made little difference.

This priest was a Franciscan who baptized Serb infants and Turk children and afterward wrapped their heads in towels, Marija. Why the towels?

To dry the holy water? No. To prevent his robes from being sprayed with gore when he took a mallet and smashed their skulls.

What do you want me to say? Heaven welcome their souls, she said. Was my husband part of this?

Six years of war, Marija. Everybody was part of everything. We created a democracy of madness.

And the archbishop?

It's complicated, he sighed. The archbishop understood we would eliminate this butcher if we caught him.

And you caught him, she said. Too easily, I think.

Perhaps, Marija. Everyone played the game well.

What game is this, when an archbishop sends his envoy to his death?

The archbishop's envoy has a laissez-passer. Immunity to the coast.

The envoy has a bullet in his head.

You are mistaken, Marija, he said. Despite her distress at the moment, the archbishop's envoy seems in fair health.

What nonsense are you saying? Stop hurting my head with this nonsense.

He reached across the seat to pick up a small packet, sealed with red wax impressed with a star and addressed to His Holiness. Please, take it, he said but when she reached for the envelope he did not give it up. Stay with me, he said. Don't abandon your country. It's coming now, it will bring us a good life, the future we dreamed together.

Do you know Kresimir? Stjepan interrupted.

I know many Kresimirs, said the man in the car.

You know which one the boy means, said his mother, recomposed by anger, tugging at the packet until he released it, the invitation of his fingers emptied into the air.

Yes, I know him, the man admitted. He escaped from Jesenovac by being dead.

Tell me, Davor, she said, finally using the power of his name to condemn him. If you destroy the churches, what church will we be married in? What priest will marry us, if you kill them all? Who will baptize our children? Tito? Stalin? Taking her son's hand, she began to step backward

216

away from the sedan, trembling with fury. Stay with you! she mocked. The future we dreamed together! I must be confused, Davor. Did we dream of a future of Croats betraying Croats? Did we dream of a future of fratricide? Did we dream of licking the boots of the Serbs, of our children becoming communist slaves? Did we dream of a future where we tear down Christ from the cross to bury him in an unmarked grave beneath a mosque? Did we dream of a future where the Turk who beheads my husband becomes the Turk who is now your brother? Was this our dream, Davor, when they exiled all of us to Italy? I don't remember. How could I forget our dream!

If you don't release the hate, Marija, he said ruefully, I fear for your soul.

This hate is my blessing! she spit and heard her voice become hysterical but wouldn't stop. This hate is my gift to Christ Our Lord, she shouted like a madwoman. This hate is sacred. May God take this hate and use it to vanquish His enemies. She grabbed the boy by the shoulders, bent her knees until they were face-to-face, her chest heaving, mother and child each searching the fierce activity in the other's eyes. When you come back as a man to liberate Croatia from these devils, Stjepan, she said, promise me you will kill this one as well.

Who is he? asked the boy, nodding his loyalty to her, stern-faced in agreement to the pact that would consume the last faint shades of his innocence.

Tell him, screamed his mother.

I am your godfather, Stjepan, said the man in the car.

CHAPTER SIXTEEN

Leaving the square, the boy thrust his head out the open window, looking back to see where the soldiers had hung the priest from a lamppost, his corpse stripped and inverted, a crucifix carved into his fish-white flesh now upside down as well, pointed hellward, its crossbar dripping scarlet flames. Stjepan, don't look at these beasts, said his mother from her seat behind, blessing herself, but then she changed her mind and told her son, Forget what I said—*Look. Remember.* When he sat back, she pressed a washcloth to the top of his head, heedless of his protest.

Minutes later, a short distance beyond the edge of the city, the driver slowed at the sight of a checkpoint ahead, if that's what it was, though its strangeness in this season of anarchy seemed less strange than worrisome. An object of manor house stateliness, an antique banquet table with sinuous legs made of dark wood had been placed lengthwise across the road, barricading the single lane south across the plain to the upland pastures of Kordun and Lika, a seating and service for ten occupied by as many stubble-bearded partisans who seemed, even from this distance, out of sorts.

As the car approached they leaped up in their grimy underclothes, nervous as startled crows, reaching for their weapons but then sinking back unconcerned. An eleventh soldier, obviously fatigued, paced mechanically around a nearby cook fire, feeding its black clouds with the aftermath of war—busted furniture and rain-swollen books—the thick smoke belched into the leafy branches of an oak tree, an upright piano hauled under the dismal shade of its canopy, a dead or drunk or sleeping man in the scatter of rubbish in the dirt next to the piano's vacant bench. Farther down the road was a burning farmhouse, its bouquet of orange flames shimmering above the fields.

For fuck's sake, said the driver under his breath. What now?

He braked and stopped a prudent distance from the barricade and went to greet the rebels with the false air of a man who never met an enemy, his confidence buoyed by the envelope in the pocket of his suit coat and the black art of survival he had mastered long ago. In the dark symmetry of his own life he knew these fellows, a motley group of schoolboys and farmhands, juvenile delinquents and tenured cutthroats, and he recognized where he was, where he had spent much of his life, the warp of time and sensibility that twisted into the small raw spaces created by the ending of wars that resolved nothing—the First Balkan War, the Second Balkan War, the Great War, this war—lawless dead zones where armies factionalized and territorial obsessions defied ideologies and generals begat warlords and warriors begat gangsters. He knew what it was like to stand in the yard of a farmhouse, the family huddled somewhere inside, and give the order, not only absent of regret but with the extreme satisfaction of nihilistic acquiescence—*Burn it down!* How do you explain this? If you believed in the clarity of violence, explanations were redundant.

The expanse of the table's surface held a clutter of inharmonious worlds—grenades and soup pots, rifles and lovely blue bowls, bayonets and butter knives, bottles of wine and brandy and tubes of medicines, crystal goblets and brass handfuls of ammunition. He saw immediately that the men around it were possessed by unwholesome decaying energy, ruddy-faced but sickly with apprehension, their countenances governed by the permanent jolt of paranoia in their bloodshot eyes. By all appearances they were an ill-disciplined and unpredictable band who seemed exasperated by peace and indifferent to the nature of their victory or their role as victors. Like wary dogs, their eyes tracked his movement while they continued shoveling gray porridge into sour-looking mouths, munching links of burned sausage, their weathered skin boasting an array of new scars and old scabs and dusted with grit and soot.

219

Ah, Bogdanov, you're too old for this, he groused to himself, bowing toward the rebels. Gentlemen, he said out loud, comrades. Good morning.

Stjepan's mother lifted the washcloth to examine the boy's wound and overcame her reluctance to add to her son's pain. I'm going to sew you up, she said.

But I'm fine, Mother, Stjepan insisted, slouched under her attention. It doesn't hurt.

It's deep, this cut. It won't stop bleeding, she insisted. I can see the bone. Flies will lay eggs in your brain.

She got out of the car and stood on its running board to grope through the luggage strapped to the roof, locating her sewing kit and a perfume bottle she'd had the forethought to refill with antiseptic. Cross your arms and lean on the door and put your head down, she instructed, standing outside his window to do her work. Doesn't it hurt?

No.

It must hurt a lot, she said, gently sponging at the ooze.

I don't care.

That's good, she said, then you won't care when I do this, and swabbed the wound with alcohol. He flinched and exhaled, hissing between clenched teeth, but was as silent as a mystic, squeezing his face smaller with each prick of the needle. *That bastard Davor was right,* she thought, her deft fingers tugging the heavy black thread through his scalp, closing the pucker with four tight stitches. *You are a little wolf, my little wolf.* God and the war had made her son strong or else made him crazy, but strong and crazy meant you were born normal, more or less, for a southern Slav. Now he had suffered far too much, seeing and knowing what he shouldn't, to ever be anything but a Croat—first to throw off the Byzantines, first to stop the Turks, and now, God willing, the first to slay the pagan onslaught that was Communism.

A streak of high-pitched noise made her lift her head in time to see the flash of a motorcycle and its empty sidecar as it passed, a young soldier racing back into the city, and she was given a memory to brush away, of her husband's passion for these machines. Finished, she announced, compelled to skip aside as the door flew open and Stjepan vomited eggplant at her feet and she brought him what she could—pity, water, and the solace of her pride.

The archbishop's driver returned, looking like a man who could not sell an egg to an infertile goose. She had never asked him his name—beyond the formalities of class and stature, if you lost a war it was a bad time to know people's names or stories—but last night she had heard the housekeeper address him playfully—*Bogdanov, you're not getting younger; Bogdanov, where are you running off to with this frisky mare*—and it cheered her secretly to hear the old man incriminate himself with foul language, disobeying the archbishop's strict draconian ban on cursing, a ban that she herself had adhered to effortlessly, unthinkingly, a natural extension of her upbringing and education, the once-clear division between good behavior and the indecency of what was unacceptable in thought or action. But this morning . . . ! The nasty words had erupted from her tongue, ready-made for her collision with the man she would have loved if she had not first loved another. My God, the deplorable hypocrisy: clean mouths, dirty hands. *Don't talk like a prostitute, Marija—Pardon me, who is the prostitute!?* The driver's beer-hall vulgarities, which she knew were not meant for her ears, had begun to appeal to her remaining sense of humanity, making him seem oddly but authentically trustworthy and natural in a world that was itself inauthentic and profane, and, criminal or not, she had decided, *Sir* was insufficient for a person so entangled with her fate.

Bogdanov, she said, coming around to the front of the car to meet him, her hands fidgeting with the cloth belt of the dress she had worn since leaving the apartment in the capital.

Madam?

Oh, God, she said, blinking back a surge of tears, the facade of her emotions shattered unexpectedly by his deference and grandfatherly disposition—the tendered bow, a grateful smile, a sudden kindness in hawkish eyes—the small things that exposed large hearts or offered, at least, their illusion. Bogdanov, she said again, unable to continue, leaning her weight against the grille of the car.

Marija? If I may.

Bogdanov, she tried again, sniffling. I can't cry. Now is not the time.

No, you're right, he said, patting her hand, apologetic and consoling. Perhaps now is not the best time. Excuse me, I must ask. Can you play a piano?

But what was the old fool talking about! A stampede of feelings overwhelmed her and her voice sank plaintively to a wretched sob—Yes! I can— then trampolined upward into a strangled squeak—No, I can't—her fists hammering the grille while she wrestled herself under control. I'm sorry, she said between shuddering deep breaths, it's possible I'm losing my mind.

No, missus, Bogdanov reassured her, but I'm afraid I must introduce you to a man who has.

She instructed the boy to stay in the car and went with the archbishop's driver down the road to the men, her steps slowing when the soldiers sprang to attention, their eyes settling on her, instinctively homicidal, then reassembled with lust. Her feet stopped and her own eyes skipped quizzically from Bogdanov to the men and back again to see the uncertainty molding the driver's face as he began, too late, to register his mistake and she thought, *Mother of God, have mercy, I am the black lamb taken to the altar.*

Bogdanov, she said, light-headed. A whisper of despair—What have you done to me?

Turn, he said. Walk. We're going back.

But the officer in charge had come forward, bare-chested, clumping toward the pair in his unlaced boots, his head tilted like a mockingbird and displeasure reflected in his sun-creased eyes. One moment, he said. A moment, please.

Bogdanov, she said, how could you have been so blind! You see what they want.

Chauffeur, what's the problem? asked the captain. Can she play?

No, said the driver, but the captain shoved him backward and ordered him to leave.

Bogdanov, dear Jesus, no, don't leave, she pleaded. Help me, you must, she said, but the captain shoved him again and slapped his head—Get out of here, old fuck—and she panicked seeing the quick cold glint of malevolence in the driver's eyes and told him yes, go, it's better, and he left without another word. *Even big as he is, what could the old man do anyway,* she told herself, except witness her humiliation.

He had, he would report to Marija at their camp that night in the forest, respectfully produced the laissez-passer, dated and signed by the hand of Colonel Davor Starcevica, regional commander of intelligence for the new regime. Let me see, the corporal had said, a middle-aged man with receding hair, whose eyes resembled boiled plums. He grabbed the document away, glancing at its content, handing it down the table, each man examining the page with the darting intensity of a monkey, until it reached the shirtless captain of the platoon. A man of Napoleonic height with unruly hair and a flattened nose, his shoulders and chest sculpted with furls of muscle, he wore only boots without laces and army pants with an unbuttoned fly and spoke with a Bosnian accent in a loud incoherent croak, his liver-colored eyes dilated and twitching beneath the jet-black hedge of his brow.

There is a crisis, said the captain, his violent expression fluid with whimsy. He brushed away an insect the driver could not see. Do you think I'm joking?

No, sir, said Bogdanov, I would not think that. May I ask the captain, is the pass not acceptable?

One of the pimple-faced teenage soldiers had stood up sneering, making accusing jabs with the spoon gripped loosely in his bandaged hand. I know you, he threatened. What village are you from, Ustashe? Globs of porridge rained down on the soldier sitting to his left. *Ass breath!* his comrade shouted and popped up with a backhand swing of his forearm, catching the scrawny youth in the jaw and knocking him off his feet.

He doesn't know me, the old man said to the table, although no one seemed to care. My family is from Zagreb.

I know him, said the kid on the ground, dusting himself off and returning to his breakfast, grinning and unaffected. He used to suck the cocks of every priest in Mostar.

That was your sister, said another soldier to barks of laughter, and food sailed across the table until the captain promised to shoot the next man who interrupted the train of his disturbed thoughts.

The captain, it soon became apparent to Bogdanov, was a drunken, overstimulated lunatic in charge of men liberated by his delusions, and doubtless they would never be more free in their lifetimes than here under the captain's command. The pass was confirmed valid, the checkpoint had received previous instructions to provide an escort for the driver and his passengers, but the order, the captain said cryptically, was under review. He would be looking into it shortly, he would make a decision and devise a plan—but first, the crisis.

In their rampage through Karlovac, the soldiers had plundered the apothecary, carrying off a trove of medications, some, asserted the captain, with unusual magical powers. It's very dangerous here, said the captain. My wife and four children are fucking dead, he announced. Our village was torched to the fucking ground. We were attacked. It never stops. But you can see for yourself we are vigilant, we are tireless. You can't go south, not yet, and never after sunset, so don't be impatient. The road is filled with bandits, terrorists, blood drinkers, evil the likes of which few men have the strength to overcome. I can tell you, there are land mines, crazy people, farmers with axes and swords, Gypsies stealing children, priests with bombs. We need petrol and then we go. In a few minutes, you'll see. Ah, but the jeep. These imbeciles wrecked the jeep.

So now, here's how it is—we want to go to sleep. We can't sleep. Go on, ask the boys. You Ustashe shouldn't have kept this secret to yourselves. Pills that turn men into eagles—what else are you hiding from us? We hear the snipers crawling through the fields like rabbits. In the dark we know everything. Now we just need to lie down and catch our breath. Slavko is a musician, very clever, always with good ideas. In the old days he had an orchestra, did you know that? Yes, in Sarajevo. So the piano, you can see how it makes sense. You know about music—it helps to relax. It's restful, it's soothing, it reminds us of nice things. Bring me a piano, says Slavko. Okay, good idea. The men deserve it, don't you agree? We can close our eyes and see our mothers, our homes. But please look, who is that over there on the ground? Slavko. What's the problem? You can clearly see the bastard is asleep. And we are not. What did he take? He took something and did not tell us. How can he tell us his solution if he's asleep?

224

So look, the captain had said fervently, taking the driver aside, the old man repelled by the zoo-like stench of the officer's body. We'll scratch each other's backs, eh? That's the way among countrymen. You see what I'm saying? Take it or leave it. Indulge us for a few minutes. Bring the wife of Kovacevic. She'll know what to do.

And like an old fool I came to get you, Bogdanov said, pouring her a brandy. Like a stupid old fool.

His chest thrust out like a Prussian, the captain mimed chivalric grace; perhaps in his former life he had imagined himself something of a courtier. He offered her the crook of his naked arm and, gagging from his smell, she averted her eyes from the frightening, crazed earnestness of his stare. She took his elbow, disconcerted by its tremble, which she found contagious, and by its feverish heat, which felt lascivious and seemed to scorch her stomach. To her chagrin, he strolled like a former intimate reuniting after a quarrel, the captain feigning solicitousness, trying to impress and appease, scuffling in his loose boots like a novice skater, a ridiculous guide, pivoting on his heels, his free arm presenting the sights—here are the men, this is the table, there is our camp, there is our pillage, here is the road, and, over here, the roadside—not far or long but enough for her to feel keenly the closing trap of her position, a female on display before a gathering of men capable of anything—deranged, battle-poisoned brutes. Her cheeks flushed, her blood began to chill with numb acceptance. He flattered the blonde waves of her hair, the modesty of her high-collared dress, steering her ineluctably toward the fire and through its smoky curtains into the theater of the oak tree. Ah! he said, delighted, as if he were seeing the piano for the first time. The piano! What do you think? Okay? Yet she found it impossible to accept that this was what he wanted from her.

She looked back, momentarily relieved to see the other men had remained stationed on the road, their eyes nevertheless boring into her. *Bogdanov will save me,* she told herself but knew the hope was irrational and that saving the boy was all that mattered anyway. When she asked, respectfully, if the captain had a request, his unshaven cheeks inflated like a blowfish but he said nothing, studying her with mute inscrutability, overfocused like the madmen you sometimes saw on the streets. She heard herself stupidly encouraging him—Something happy?—moving the bench away from the buzz of flies feasting on the dead man on the ground.

She sat down, her palms damp, and watched her hands, poised above the keys, shaking.

The Internationale! yelled out one of the soldiers.

Silence! Shut up!

She felt his feral presence behind her, the hot current of his obsession, a terrible counterweight to the terrible feeling of absence she found occupied by her husband. The captain's voice tapered from snarl to purr. Please, just play, he said reasonably, and she commanded her bitten fingers to open and spread themselves above the keys and fall like a shattering release of sorrow.

No, no, no, said the captain, his hands digging painfully into her shoulders.

What then? she gasped, frozen by his touch, the roughness melting to the nauseating softness of a caress. Just tell me.

Not that. He leaned closer, cooing into her ear. Your Blessed Virgin must wait her turn.

My God, my God, why hast thou forsaken me? she thought, shivering with disgust, and prayed for hate to overtake her fear. Strike this monster dead.

Opera, said the captain with an inflection of triumph, his hands lifting off her body.

She asked which one and he answered, Why not something beautiful? and with surrendering bitterness she said, Of course.

She summoned forth Pamina, the abducted daughter of the Queen of the Night, her sister Mara emerging with the notes, Mara's artistic pretensions invigorated in the cosmopolitan bliss she experienced studying theater in Vienna. *Oh, this Ibsen, he understands families! Brecht, he's better off in Hollywood!* Marija had joined her on a weeklong visit only months before the start of the war, the two of them attending a Saturday matinee of *The Magic Flute* at the opulent Freihaus. How typically melodramatic, Marija thought, when the lovesick soprano moved Mara to tears, quaking with emotions she found difficult to conceal, refusing and then accepting a monogrammed handkerchief from the man seated next to her, blowing her nose like a duck. Marija herself could only gape at the elite spectacle of Viennese society, the highest of highs, the swallow-tailed coats and top hats and Chanel gowns and elbow-length gloves, the diamond brooches and jeweled crucifixes, Parisian shoes and Italian wraps and German wristwatches, tuxedos and cravats and imperial officers' dress and swastika armbands of an audience captivated by the romance of its ambitions for the world, by the excitement of the war everyone knew was coming like a long-awaited correction—the robust glory of Hapsburg aristocracy, underwriting their cupidity with culture, the self-affirming superiority of empires that conquer in the name of civilization. War, the answered prayer, the only realistic remedy to the unfinished business of the previous war, what a disaster.

The captain replaced his fingertips on her shoulders and her own fingers stiffened and her existence shrank to a single anguish, the unrelenting pressure to protect her son, the music perhaps an unlikely safeguard, a charm against wickedness. Don't stop, he warned gently. It's beautiful. Mozart. Yes, beautiful. You think I don't know.

But her mind faltered from the path of the chords and she stopped and within an instant the captain's hands had locked around her throat. It is forbidden to stop, he said, and she continued, choking. Then his hands relaxed back to her shoulders, massaging her flesh, and traveled down the sides of her rib cage, rising and falling from her waist to her armpits, smoothing the green cotton fabric of her dress. Don't stop, he said again and his hands rounded her body and found her breasts. Don't stop, he said, leaning over her, his breath a hot circle on the back of her skull, it's beautiful, and she could feel the lump of his penis enlarging against her spine, directly below the last button of her dress, which the fingers of his right hand proceeded to unfasten. She considered shitting herself in defense but feared they would simply beat her to death for such a filthy trick. Beautiful, beautiful, he said, don't stop, and his fingers spidered to the next button. When she tried to stand up his fist came smashing against her temple and white roses of pain exploded behind her eyes and her dress was being ripped from her shoulders. In a moment she regained her senses and her fingers searched for E-flat major, bells of hatred ringing through the aria of her submission.

A motorcycle pulled alongside the car, gliding to a stop, and Bogdanov, his head bent under the yawning lid of the trunk, looked over to see the goggled moon-face of a young partisan, shouting to him above the clatter. Okay, he's coming, said the soldier, tossing the sweep of his golden hair back toward the city, and they studied each other for a moment, the youth's expression obliquely curious and reassuring. Bogdanov, preoccupied, was uninterested in the implicit offer of an elucidation. *Was death coming? Yes, probably so.* He glanced politely over his shoulder at the empty road behind him, the hint of a distracted smile on his lips, and then returned his attention to the contents of the trunk. The soldier revved his engine and went ahead.

He unlocked a portmanteau and opened it like a sacred book to a text composed of Swiss francs and American dollars, stuffing the front pockets of his coat with banded packets of hundreds of dollars. Even drug-addled hooligans like these peasant soldiers knew a dollar was a dollar in every language, and in any hand money was strength, money lubricated intransigence and clouded moral choices and, like a pointed gun, invited men to rethink everything. He folded and relocked the portmanteau and, from its concealment under a throw rug, removed the shotgun and closed the trunk and went to the front of the car and spoke with the boy. Out, he said, close the door, stand right here, take the gun. You know how to use it, don't you? You've seen men do it. Hold it like this, at your waist. These are the triggers, two of them. Pull one, then find your next target and pull the second one. Don't aim, point. Stand right here and wait for your mother to return. If she doesn't come and soldiers come you let them get close and then step out from behind the car and let them have it. You can do that? Yes? Good. Then run like hell into the fields.

Where's my mother? Stjepan asked. What's happened to her?

Nothing has happened, said Bogdanov, encouraged that the boy was not frightened but peevish. I'm going to get her now.

He searched in the car for the short iron bar cut to the length of his forearm and the loaded Luger pistol he kept beneath the seat, their cold familiar weight like a consensus between thought and action. The bar went up the left sleeve of his shirt, its lower tip secured in the leather band of his wristwatch; the Luger was hidden under his coattail between his belt and the small of his back, its muzzle playing coldly between the broad cheeks of his ass.

Wait here, he told the boy again, and marched back to the checkpoint, each resolute step multiplying the lethal potency of his raging sense of honor, which he knew to contain until the exact moment it would prove itself most effective against unthinkable odds—bad odds merely an inspiration to the quick-witted, and no quality found in a man's character better defined the distance between winning and losing than self-control. *Who's coming?* he chanted to himself. *I'll tell you who's coming, Turk. The old fuck is coming. Boys, the lion is old and sleeping, but go ahead, kick him awake, see what happens. He will shit in your mother's milk.*

The last time he had killed a man he had broken his neck, but he did not intend to break the Bosnian captain's neck. Good news, he called out, striding back toward the soldiers, who could not be bothered to peel their spellbound eyes away from the depraved spectacle of the captain and the woman, his groaning mouth nested in her hair, his red elastic cock bouncing from the fly of his pants, her dress torn open to her waist and her bra drooped into her lap, the captain with one hand fondling her left breast and the other fondling himself, half-erect, trying to jerk off.

Comrades, good news. New instructions from the colonel. I am to give you money. American dollars. How much do you want?

The three soldiers nearest to Bogdanov each found himself holding a two-inch stack of green currency, a magnetic wedge of good fortune driven into the wood of voyeurism, their uncomprehending expressions lighting up with generous increments of greed as they understood what was happening. Dollars, said Bogdanov. One hundreds. American. Go on, divide them up, and he spun away from the ensuing scramble and hurried with bloodthirsty enthusiasm toward the oak tree, waving the three remaining packets above his head—Captain, for you, American dollars. How much do you want?—and then the last few steps between them he came like a charging bear from the forest of his deception, unseen, single-minded, berserk.

Almighty Christ, he wanted to wring the life out of this Bosnian scum, who was not to be interrupted at any cost from his formidable depravity. You fucking animal, he panted, incredulous, trying to subdue the captain. Even in the vise of a choke hold, the iron bar in Bogdanov's sleeve strapped fast against the captain's windpipe, he would not quit masturbating. At the same instant the boy's mother felt the weight of the driver added to the captain, who sank his unclipped fingernails into her breast and she screamed in pain, biting his knuckles, her hands prying at his as he strangled above her, his body bucking still and more rabidly against her. Bogdanov used his thumb to gouge an eye, applying every ounce of his strength to the bar, cutting off the man's air and the captain, writhing in the throes of his perversion, spasmed warm pelts of his ejaculation down the pallid knobs of the woman's backbone. For a moment his body rippled with the aftershock of its crime and then he slackened in the clutch of Bogdanov's murderous rage, expiring in ecstasy.

When Bogdanov eased the pressure on his throat a blast from the captain's elbow struck the pit of the old man's stomach and suddenly they were off her, stumbling backward toward the fire, the captain's head slinging froth and drool, pop-eyed, rearing and thrashing like a man with electrodes clipped to his balls. Gurgling, he clawed at the forearm crushing his windpipe, boots kicked off and legs swimming in the air, Bogdanov unable to free his right hand from the contest but then he did and out came the Luger from his belt and he began pistol-whipping the captain senseless in front of his men, an audience jaded beyond Bogdanov's most optimistic expectation. Perhaps not surprisingly the captain's men displayed a reservoir of tolerance for violent antics, counting money with a cynical lack of both urgency and loyalty, looking over occasionally to check the progress of the beating, in no hurry to rescue anyone.

Unnoticed coming toward them was the boy with the shotgun who stopped and stood transfixed by the sight of his mother seated at the piano, radiant in her nakedness. His memory would hold her in this pose, a vision that over the years his imagination would enshrine and render beatific, this image of his mother and her persecution and its torturous gift, a permanent and consuming secret excitement, hidden in the darkness of his soul.

She watched teardrops of blood weep from her breast onto the ivory keys, mesmerized, listening to a girlish voice in her head fretting about her performance, her inadequate interpretation of Pamina's acquisition of strength, wanting to shame her for clumsy sequencing and phrasings not to mention forgetting the notes, her fingers convulsing with inchoate Mozart, three chords of one thing and three chords of another and somehow a trickle from Strauss's *Salome,* growing perplexed by her inability to fit them together, unable to find the place in her mind where she kept the music that was the repertoire, precocious and virginal, of her adolescence, there at the headwaters of her self, now a turbulent cascade flowing nowhere. *What's happened?* she asked herself, her fingers printing a gibberish of blood across the keys.

Marija, stop, Bogadnov said, breathing hard from his strenuous work. Get up, cover yourself. He supported the half-conscious captain with his forearm still clamped under his chin, the gun in Bogdanov's right hand flat against his jaw. This man is my hostage, he yelled out.

Old man, we don't give a shit, said a soldier. You're both crazy bastards.

We're Serbs and Croats, said another soldier. We're sick of this Turk.

Go ahead, take the Sultan with you, said the first soldier. Give us the rest of the money and get out of here. The corporal picked up a rifle and raised it tentatively at the pair but took the advice of the soldier who had ridden the motorcycle now warning him that the colonel was coming, don't get involved. The soldiers argued shares and Bogdanov helpfully reminded them of the packets he had dropped near the piano, extending the advantage he knew not to trust more than another few minutes.

Marija, please, hurry, said Bogdanov, his strength drained and the captain senseless in his arms. Pull up your dress and come. Boy, he ordered, get back to the car.

Horrified, she returned to life, looking around to find her son staring at her. Stjepan there with the soldiers, armed with a gun he could barely hold steady, watching her with a similar intensity as if he too found her to be an object of his nascent desire. She rehooked her bra and held the flap of her torn dress against her chest and rose from the bench shaking, furious at the child for being there, watching, fixated, absorbing her abasement, a little mascot to the men's depravity. Go to the car! She made a beeline for him, screeching, as if the child were to blame for this nightmare. Goddamn you, I told you to stay in the car! and then she had him by the back of the neck, pushing him roughly back down the road, and he did not understand his mother's anger and was terrified by its tornadic shift to hysteria.

At the car, she made him put down the shotgun and get the blood-stained washcloth she had held to his head. A filthy crow did his mess on me, she told the boy, scurrying to appease the shrillness in his mother's voice. Take the rag and clean it off. And now, scrubbing his mother's skin to a fiery pink, he understood the problem—somehow his mother had torn her dress and a bird had crapped on her back. Is it off? she said, her body beginning to heave with sobs. Is it off? she demanded, and he scrubbed harder and the two sedans came down the road from the city. Then he heard his godfather talking with the archbishop's driver and shouting orders at the soldiers and walking back toward the two of them and Stjepan picked up the shotgun.

Boy, do you know how to use that? said the colonel, challenging Stjepan with a look of amused skepticism and then ignoring him to remove his linen jacket, Stjepan staring at the shoulder holster at the top of his withered left arm. He held the coat out to his mother, who seemed to slip into a trance and let her dress fall open and pulled down the blood-patched cup of her bra to make him see her breast's crescent of throbbing welts. The colonel pinched his eyes closed, stroking the furrows of his forehead, and then opened them again. With his good arm and the stick of the other, he tried to help her, creating a strange, dipping minuet between the two of them, and like a child she let him guide her palsied arms into the sleeves and, fumbling one-handed, button up its front.

Marija, he said, I will give you back your dignity.

My dignity? she said, wagging her head ruefully. Your honor! Give that back to yourself.

He told the boy to come with him and her mind blinked off and she let them get halfway down the road toward the soldiers before she grasped his intention and ran to catch up and stop this madness, arguing frantically, Davor, he's eight years old, he's a child, dear God look at him he's a baby, you cannot do this, I won't allow it, Stjepan go back to the car, but the boy gave her a look that he wasn't going to listen and with spite in his voice Davor replied that an hour ago she herself had sworn her son to vengeance against his own godfather. He stopped and shook his finger in her face and the boy continued walking. You want to raise the child as an assassin? he asked. Good. Let's begin.

Davor, let him be, she implored. I forgive you.

With weary fatalism, Bogdanov hugged the captain from behind, uncertain of the changing circumstances. The stern-faced agents who had executed the priest in Karlovac had drawn their pistols but kept them lowered, waiting, and the soldiers stood penitent off in loose formation, also waiting, all eyes on the boy's advance, wondering what this was about. Then the boy's mother rushed forward to take the shotgun from him but he would not readily give it up and the colonel took it out of their hands and turned his scalding attention to the archbishop's driver.

Bagman, you are standing on your grave. I suggest you move.

Bogdanov released the captain and stepped away and offered to surrender his pistol to one of the agents but the agent did not want it. The bloodied captain swayed on his feet, his head lolling but his eyes upraised with a slippery focus on the colonel, a lithe but plain-faced man who, before the war had bitten into him, would not have attracted much attention on metropolitan streets thronged with office workers and bureaucrats. Who is second-in-command? Starcevica asked. The question seemed innocuous enough. Here, said the churlish corporal, stepping out of the ranks, and the colonel ordered him arrested. The rest of you, he said, let me remind you that you are Tito's men, and let me advise you of my disappointment in that fact.

Comrade Colonel, interrupted the captain.

This man is guilty of criminal dereliction, said Colonel Starcevica. Which of you will speak in his defense?

Comrade Colonel, said the captain, it's like this. Allah and his prophet will not be joining us in the new Yugoslavia.

Comrade Captain, the colonel said thoughtfully, as though he found the pertinence of the captain's observation worth considering. What business would Allah and his prophet have with the likes of you?

This is a mistake, said the captain sadly. Unacceptable.

Anyone? asked the colonel, addressing the platoon.

She is a Ustashe whore, said the captain with a disgusted laugh, pointing at Marija as she came up the road to stand behind Stjepan. Why all this trouble about a Ustashe whore?

The colonel told the boy that the Bosnian had dishonored his mother and must be punished and when he offered the child the gun Marija snatched it away, the driver obeying her shrill command to take her son back to the car. She took one step toward the captain, raising the shotgun to her shoulder, afraid to breathe.

One moment, please, said the captain, his arms bent at his side, palms up, to request the satisfaction of a final intimacy. He wanted to know the name of the wife of Kovacevic, her Christian name, but she could not answer and he asked the colonel—Comrade, may I know her name?— and finally he shrugged and resigned himself to the impenetrable silence of their judgment upon him.

Madame Kovacevic, thank you, he said, how beautiful the music, and she fired into his chest, the kickback from the double blast cracking her collarbone and throwing her to the ground.

Did I hit him? she asked, and Davor, looming over her, nodded with a worried look, helping her to her feet. When he began to lead her away she said Let me go, and went to examine her work and felt her hate transcendent, looking into the captain's dying eyes, and she thanked God for granting a woman, a Croatian widow, this rare and exhilarating satisfaction of justice.

CHAPTER SEVENTEEN

The grassy smells of midsummer, ashy shadows of carnage, pale sun. Hayricks, linden trees, a revival of orchards beyond the bone-jarring road. Bands of drunken but garrulous soldiers, drifting from one reprisal killing to another like holiday revelers. The solemn trudge of refugees into purgatory.

Fifty kilometers south of Karlovac, below the hilltop village of Slunj, the motorcycle stopped at an abandoned settlement of water millers. The self-important young partisan riding in its sidecar hopped out to tell Bogdanov he and his comrade were hungry and were going into town to find something to eat. Rest here by the river, he said with callow officiousness, until we return. Bogdanov parked in the overgrown yard of an old stone-walled mill and the boy got out to explore. Because the afternoon was warm and because he had spent his childhood jumping off the quays of Dubrovnik into the emerald Adriatic with all the other boys too young for war, Stjepan soon had his clothes off and was swimming in a pool between a foaming set of rapids, calling for the grown-ups to join him.

Bogdanov removed his suit coat and sat on the riverbank, watching the boy swim and listening to the sound of his carefree splash and laughter. How life skipped so quickly past death to seize small pleasures, and it seemed only yesterday, no matter the season or weather, he had watched his sons frolic in the Sava River, practicing their father's daily custom to exercise in water, the Sava or, when he made his rounds for the archbishop throughout the country, whatever nearby lake or river he could find. He had trained for the Olympics before the army put him in the trenches in 1914. He had taught his sons the sport of boxing, had taken them climbing in the Italian Alps. Even during the war he had hunted wild boar in the mountains, bringing the dressed carcasses out of the forest on his back. Never assume failure, Bogdanov had schooled his own boys, never accept the incompetence that festers from a weak, complacent will. Now his eldest son lay in a mass grave at Novi Sad, the second son assassinated by the mafia, and the youngest missing in action in the Ukraine, his daughter emigrated to Argentina and his grandchildren dead or among the rebels and his remaining loyalty parceled out to the ones left to save, the viscera of the Croatian phoenix, he had no doubt, to be reassembled by the future.

Marija remained in the car as she was, disheveled, remorseless, her body aching, spread out on the backseat with a fresh towel folded over her eyes and another under her head. When Davor Starcevica had walked her back to the car she recoiled from the excitement and awe in the boy's eyes, the thrill of approval—*Momma, did you kill the bastard!*—and for the only time in her life she slapped him, hard and unrepentant. The colonel took care of him and that's all there is to know, she told the boy. I never want to hear another word about it, and with nothing more to say to anyone she changed into the last dress she owned and lay down on the seat and covered her eyes and heard Bogdanov and Starcevica behind the car—You, old man, are going to give me something right now—and eventually Bogdanov got back in, striking a match to light a cigarette, and they left.

She inhaled the willow and stone scents of the river wafting through the open windows and said to the water, *Carry us far away,* and in the long but always broken conversation she kept with her dead husband she experienced a surge of insolence and told him they were leaving now, she was taking their son to the place of his birth, and get used to it, if he comes back he comes back, and she would not guarantee her own return, nor venture any promise to the dead except memory.

The teenage boy-soldiers returned from their forage, the moon-faced driver with a carrot stuck cigarlike between his grinning lips and the one in the sidecar with a goat kid squirming in his arms. Stjepan came shivering out of the water to admire their riches and the partisans shared their lunch with Bogdanov and the child, cheese and bread with slices of salty *prsut* and a paper cone of greasy *burek,* his mother unresponsive to their offers and everyone seemed to know to leave her be. Clouds gathered and the light collected into burnished lumps and the afternoon became more humid and when Stjepan jumped into the river again the young soldiers followed along, their undressed bodies like the boy's, colorless and bony and mal-nourished, and all three played a game of tag, which became a game of tossing the boy into the air between them, and his mother listened to the yips of their exuberance and could not stand it. For the first time since leaving the outskirts of Karlovac she sat up, wincing in pain, and leaned over the seat to tap the horn.

They drove on to the wilderness of Plitvice, the rugged high coun-try before the land descended to the coast. Bogdanov seemed to have a particular destination in mind, rejecting the escorts' desire to stop at an abandoned cottage and, farther on, a bivouac of local partisans. At the driver's insistence, they spent the night in the open, camped a short distance off the road in the hilly forests near a waterfall rumbling over the brim of a turquoise lake, arriving an hour before sundown, the sky overcast and threatening. While her son and the young soldiers collected firewood and Bogdanov wandered away into the forest with a tin pail to gather mushrooms, Marija walked along the lake until she was out of sight and removed her dress and waded into the frigid water to wash herself with a brown bar of soap, her teeth chattering and the sting in her breast and shoulder easing with the cold. When she looked back at the darken-ing shoreline she noticed smoke curling out of the trees not only from the direction of their own camp but throughout the wooded headlands and thought, of course, the forest is filled with runaways like us.

Back in the clearing, the soldiers had slit the throat of the little goat and were yanking back its hide and Stjepan heaped branches on the fire as if it were All Hallow's Eve. She sat on the running board of the car and called him over to dry her hair, telling him, Careful, not so hard, pain streaking through her right shoulder, and then Bogdanov emerged from the shad-ows between the trees with a companion. I found this Jew hiding in the forest, Bogdanov announced. He says he's trying to get to the boat to go to Palestine and he says he's hungry. Is it a problem? he asked the two soldiers, intent on butchering the goat, who looked up at the haggard man with more indifference than suspicion and said they didn't mind. The man nodded his appreciation and dropped his duffel bag at the rear of the car and sat down on a log, head bent, staring at his cracked shoes. Where's Palestine? Stjepan asked his mother. Is that where we're going too? Look, said Bogdanov proudly, dumping chanterelles and wild onions on the hood of the car. That's the stuff, eh? and he sent the boy down to the lake with the emptied pail. Marija, he said, stepping over to her, are you feeling better? With paternal tenderness, his large hand alighted on her right cheek, below the swelling where the captain had struck her.

What happened? The bastard hit you.

Yes, she said, pressing into the warmth of his palm, this small reprieve from the poverty of touch.

What can I do for you? Perhaps brandy?

Yes, she said. Thank you, Bogdanov. Brandy.

Grandpa, don't forget us, said the soldiers.

He went around to the trunk and came back with two bottles and a metal cup, which he filled and gave to her and gave the partisans the unopened bottle for themselves and a pack of cigarettes and took the first bottle to the man on the log. Rabbi, a taste? he said with strange joviality, and the fellow took a long swallow and then Bogdanov took a long swallow and the bottle was soon finished. Stjepan returned with the pail of water and Bogdanov helped the soldiers wash the carcass of the goat and took a jackknife from his pocket and trimmed what little fat he could find and put it in the cook pot the soldiers carried in their kit, along with the mushrooms and onions. Son, he said to Stjepan, stop putting wood on the fire, let it burn down, and the partisans cut forked branches for the frame of a spit and Bogdanov skewered the goat through the gullet and anus and Marija drank the cup dry and asked if there was more and out came another bottle. The last of it, said the driver. The last of everything, she whispered bleakly.

Nightfall was upon them and blackness hugged the campfire where the men prepared their rustic dinner. From her perch on the running board she watched her son enjoying this adventure, poking at the coals with a stick, seemingly oblivious. She sipped her brandy, welcoming its burn, the relaxation of the hard knots that held her perseverance together, which could be loosened but never untied, and thought about her husband Andre and about Davor and Andre, what firebrands they had been, what spirited boys, ardent and enlivening, unlikely but devoted brothers, living poems of courage and passion.

She and Andre were university students and Davor a street-corner recruiter for the Organization, the cafés of Zagreb the mixing bowl between the intellectual activists and the uneducated paramilitaries. They were young together in a world they agreed was no good and could not be allowed to persist. Was that it? she wondered, to which all the energy and glorious intensity of their youth had been dedicated, was their common cause that banal?—and not their idolization of the hard-line nationalists who, within a few short years, would become the government of Croatia. Why had they become such good friends when so little in their backgrounds recommended it?

So Davor, she concluded, I see. Your joke was not a joke, when you hectored us for being bourgeoisie. How do you spell that word? she had once teased back, everyone laughing at the hick's expense, but she had wounded him and never teased again.

Davor, she said into her cup of brandy, saving my life won't prevent me from hating you. I don't have the luxury of choosing my protectors.

It was Davor who inspired Andre to cross the ideological threshold from talk to action, to put aside his books and join the uprising, and then they were running from the police and when Mussolini allowed the Ustashe to set up training camps they fled to Italy, an effortless transition for the two of them, newly married, both Dalmatian-born and schooled in Italian, foreigners yet not absolute outsiders. Davor, however, felt shunned as a philistine and mistrusted the Italians, a mistrust that would spare the three of them twenty months of internment on the island of

Lipari with the hundreds of Ustashe exiles imprisoned by Mussolini after the assassination of Aleksandar, the king of Yugoslavia, during a state visit to France. As the training camps closed and the roundups began, the three of them had already embarked on a ship bound for Buenos Aires, Davor having persuaded Andre to answer the Organization's call for volunteers to establish Ustashe cells abroad. Embraced by the Peronistas, Andre lectured and administrated while Davor drilled recruits; the children of German businessmen and the Argentinian military became her students at the piano. Before the year was out the leadership issued a decision that Andre's talents could be applied to greater benefit in the United States, and so she began English lessons and two months later there they sat, the three of them, for the last time together, in a steak house behind the wharves in Buenos Aires, their farewell dinner, making plans to reunite in Zagreb but they never did, never the three of them together again, although the two men saw each other frequently that year, back home before the war. She never understood Davor's aloofness, never fathomed why he would not make an effort to see her and the baby, his godson, or participate in a second christening in the national cathedral, but now, sickened by her first smell of roasting meat since that day her husband's head was booted into the fire, she understood.

Twice the traitor, she told the brandy before taking a gulp. Even in friendship and love, a turncoat and double agent. She should have known then, in Buenos Aires, when he kissed her good-bye—the way he kissed her good-bye—and she let him, turning, gasping and confused, from the flare of the embrace toward her smirking husband, the only man who had ever measured her passion.

She shifted her gaze toward Stjepan and the boyish partisans, the three of them squatting like Indians around the red coals, the glint of a knife passing from hand to hand, taking turns carving fistfuls of meat from the goat and stuffing their mouths. The Jew sat hunched on the log, slowly chewing, the fire's glow sliding along the muscles of his jaw, and she watched him for a moment and then looked away, not wanting to think about Jews or imagine their troubles or anticipate tomorrow, when her fate would pass into their hands. Then the archbishop's driver came toward her with a full plate of meat and steaming mushrooms but she shook her head no, groaning from the noxious fumes, and he opened the driver's door and sat sideways, his feet on the running board next to her, and began eating the meal himself.

Bogdanov, she said after a while, did you know Davor Starcevica? The colonel. I mean, before today.

Not well. I saw him around with the others. The Home Guard. The police.

He called you bagman, she said. I don't know this word. This is a gangster word. What does it mean? She waited for him to reply but he didn't and she continued. What did he want from you? Money? Information? What did you give him?

Marija, said Bogdanov, life is complicated now. What he gave us is what's important.

She felt the urge to reprimand him but could not make sense of her feelings—he had risked his life to undo his mistake, taking her to the captain—and she had no desire to examine her continued value in the bartering that took place among enemies, which, she was learning, was how the temperature of war cooled down to a state of tepidness.

Bogdanov, she said, tell me about killing people. You know about this, yes? Are we all going to hell?

The sin, he told her, was to not protect those you love.

War is a sin, and I chose it, she replied. Who did I protect by killing that man?

I would have killed him myself, and been happy for it, said Bogdanov. He was a Turk, an animal.

Happy, she said. Yes, I understand now. That's the sin. I won't lie, Bogdanov. That's what I felt. A war has come and gone and today was the first I felt it.

Happy, or sinful?

I'm talking about the blood on my hands, she said, the brandy gone, her voice beginning to slur. I'm talking about the satisfaction.

In God's eyes, you are without sin, he said. How is it possible to sin by resisting the devil?

You know what we need, Bogdanov, she said, suddenly drunk. The campfire was blazing again and there was her boy, illuminated by the towering flames, a cigarette in his mouth, brandishing one of the partisans' rifles and the older boys showing him how to hold it but Davor had made sure their two escorts were Croats and so she was not alarmed and did not disapprove when they let Stjepan have some fun and fire into the trees, the blasts swallowed by the forest as it began to rain.

What we need, Bogdanov, she said, is another war.

CHAPTER EIGHTEEN

The roar of the rain woke her at dawn and she opened her eyes to fibrous woolen light inside the car, afraid to move, anticipating the swell of pain throughout her body. Bogdanov and his foundling Jew were crumpled in the front seat, snoring, and the boy was huddled back against her womb, encircled by her arms, her left arm underneath him and tingling and she slowly realized her hand was tucked under the waistband of her son's pants, cupping his scrotum like a warm toad. She concentrated on moving her fingers until the sensation of feeling returned and she withdrew her hand and the child moaned and shifted and the rain came in angry spasms that made her feel trapped and hopeless and finally stunned by the desolation she felt within her. God give me strength for one more day, she prayed, as she prayed every morning since they had fled Dubrovnik. Then the pain awakened from its bed of brandy and she could think of nothing else until the engine started and she heard the *ticktock* of the wipers across the windscreen and Bogdanov, hacking as he lit a cigarette, was driving them out of the deluge.

Down through the mountains the rain slowed and changed to rolling mists and Bogdanov stopped on the side of the road to allow everyone to empty their bladders. She sucked in her breath and sat up with tears in her eyes and took the boy behind a chestnut tree and made him squat with her, despite his resistance to this embarrassing intimacy, and insisted he move his bowels but for the third day in a row he couldn't. Back at the car the Jew

was in the front seat, waiting, frozen with gloomy patience, and Bogdanov
had opened the trunk, where he had stored her luggage sometime during
the night to keep it dry.

Bogdanov, she said, looking up and down the road, the mists above
and below. Where are the soldiers?

I don't know, said Bogdanov, shrugging. They left in the night.

We heard music, said Stjepan. In the forest.

I told them not to go, said Bogdanov, offering around a cone of olives.

She prepared toothbrushes for herself and Stjepan and afterward wet
a washcloth and wiped his face and rubbed salve into the cut on the top of
his head, which had become infected, then took her hairbrush and lipstick
with her to the front seat to use the mirror, saying as she sat down, Good
morning, to their passenger, getting a good look at him for the first time,
his haughty topaz eyes, the narcissism of his bloodless lips, and thought,
since when do Jews have eyes like this? He snickered with cold amusement
and she said, Tell me, what's so funny.

It's possible they will accept you as one of their own.

Who?

The Jews on the boat. You and the boy, eh, you look like you've come
crawling out from the camps.

What camps are those? she said, not trying to be disingenuous, knowing instinctively without knowing literally. You could listen to British pro-
paganda forever on the BBC and still not know the truth or harvest its
attendant verities. The first time she ever heard the word at her dinner
table she had naively accepted the image it conjured, rustic holidays, family outings in the mountains, happy children, uncomfortable bedding. She
turned the mirror and saw herself, her skin sallowed by malnourishment,
her face waxen and hollow-cheeked, the ghastly bruising, her limp hair and
the ringed flatness of her eyes and, resigned to the irony of her position,
looked back at the man. And what about you? she asked.

Me? he laughed darkly. Oh, yes, the Jews will welcome me with open
arms. We will share fond memories, the Jews and I.

However they receive me, I don't care, she said. If they let us on the
boat, God bless the Jews.

244

Your husband was a Jew lover as well.

You don't know what you're saying. Who are you?

Oh, yes, said the man. You didn't know? So I will tell you. Many times the SS complained to the Ustashe leadership about your husband's lack of appetite for exterminating Jews.

Where might you have heard such things?

The Germans claimed he was insincere.

Insincere?

Racially and spiritually.

Who are the Germans to lecture Croatians on race or spirit?

Oh, yes, said the man, slapping both knees for emphasis. Here's how it was with your husband. If a Jew joined the Communists or the Chetniks and fought against us, then your husband obeyed his orders. Otherwise, he allowed the kikes to escape to the Italian zone, where he looked the other way.

I see, she said. It's your opinion that my husband is to blame for losing the war.

Perhaps he was too busy converting Serbs.

Who are you? she asked again, warily, not knowing what to expect anymore from anyone, when all the loss her world had suffered merited not consolation but seething resentment and recriminations. Another priest with bloody hands?

She heard Bogdanov's footsteps approach and he held the door open and with his free hand he reached and lightly took her elbow and helped ease her out of the car. It is our duty, Bogdanov said, to survive, and the sad reprimand of his voice disheartened her. The rueful cast of his eyes moved beyond her, over her shoulder and back up the road they had followed out of the clouds. What is it? she said, alarmed by the sharpening concentration of his face, and, turning, she saw the black outline of the motorcycle and its sidecar emerging soundlessly from the fog. Oh, Davor's boys have come, she said uncertainly; whether their belated reappearance was good or bad she could not discern from Bogdanov's stony lack of reaction.

Like an apparition from a twilight world, the shape of the machine and its riders floated toward them, announced by a dull tapping that grew in

pitch and volume until it pulsed in concert with her body. A sudden brightness of color, a vermilion flag, began to snap in her vision and then came the
freezing dread of impotence, a new danger hurtling their way and nothing
to prevent it. The boy in the sidecar slumped awkwardly, head lolling at an
angle like a village idiot. Then she could see he was near death, his throat
slashed, the front of his blouse glazed with blood, and the other boy, the
handsome moon-faced driver, wept red tears, blood striping his tortured
countenance from a wound plowed across his forehead.

Where are they? the young partisan demanded wildly, steering the
motorcycle to a stop behind the car. Have you seen them?

Seen who? said Bogdanov.

Goddamn you, he sobbed breathlessly.

We've seen no one, she said. My God, what happened?

Roma, the teenager panted, swiping the blood from his eyes with the
back of his sleeve. Roma! Let's go. Get in the car. Let's go.

The motorcycle leaped ahead, absorbed into the oblivion of mist, and
Bogdanov followed but without urgency, as though nothing unusual had
happened or might happen. Only Stjepan talked, no one taking the trouble
to imagine answers for his questions, the road descending through swirling obscurity until the mists cracked open like an egg and there was the
blinding barbaric sun and there too was the motorcycle, abandoned by its
driver who stood in the center of the road firing his rifle into a plodding
oxcart filled with Gypsies, several of the men among them with rifles of
their own, shooting back.

There was a bang inside the car and a glittering hole flowered in the
windscreen. Bogdanov reversed violently, skidding out of the line of fire,
and they watched as the young partisan advanced, aiming well, and methodically dropped his foes, the men with guns first and even the heedless ox,
then the women as they shielded children, and then the children too until
a single survivor remained, a screaming teenage girl with parted waves
of black hair that fell almost to her waist, perhaps a few years younger
than the partisan himself, whom he dragged out from the cart and lost no
time tearing off her embroidered peasant's dress until she stood in tattered

underclothes in the road, trembling, and he tore these last rags of modesty from her as well.

That's how it's done, said the Jew who was not a Jew, nodding with appreciation.

Bogdanov, she said, as they all saw the young partisan lay down his rifle to unbuckle his belt and his pants sink to his boots. Make him stop, dear God. But she felt nothing, her shame hidden, her compassion voiceless. Why bother to believe in her own goodness or anyone else's when the very idea of goodness had come to seem nothing so much as a useless thought? Bogdanov quietly slipped the car into gear and drove forward, neither the soldier nor the Gypsy, on hands and knees like two dogs in the road, aware of their passing, the girl's hair like an executioner's hood hiding her face, the men in the car—yes, her son too; even the boy's dead comrade in the sidecar—craning for a look, and Marija examined the moral curiosity of the nothingness she had come to contain. My God, look, they cut that boy's throat and almost killed us, she reasoned, fixated on the bullet hole in the windscreen, and what did we do to them, and what finally was left to believe in except the horror of existence?

Stjepan, she commanded. He knelt on the seat cushion, facing backward to look out the rear window, the canine image of the teenagers receding but never the mystery of what he had witnessed, nor the mystery's implicit temptations, which he had no language to describe yet somehow understood must be guarded from adults and preserved, unspoken, feelings you gazed at wordlessly like strange animals in the zoo.

Stjepan, she repeated in a voice he could not ignore. Turn around, sit right. Take out your rosary. Say it with me.

Nearing the coast their progress slowed, the sedan required to halt at partisan checkpoints in each maimed and ravaged village, the route clogged by a grim exodus of refugees fleeing the boundless treachery of the *kamenjar,* the stone fields of Dalmatia's interior, its ethnic Italians to be slaughtered by the thousands in the coming year and thrown into *foibe*—sinkholes—until Tito secured the zone for Yugoslavia.

At a crossroads above the entrance to Zadar, in a landscape of olive groves and vineyards and a rosemary-scented sea that for much of her life had been home, Bogdanov swerved around a horse-drawn wagon piled high with household furniture and parked, blocking its path. Please, one moment, he announced and walked back to speak with the drover, a conversation she could not hear. Nor could she discern the consequence of its outcome when Bogdanov opened the trunk to pay the drover with a hundred dollar bill and transfered her luggage to the bed of the wagon. Behind her the trunk clicked shut and still she had no sense of what was happening.

Marija, please, he said, may I speak with you a moment.

She began to lower the glass of her window but Bogdanov went to stand in front of the car and when she approached him she could not catch his eye and followed his distracted gaze down the limestone slopes to Zadar, which appeared half-eaten by some leviathan, the red-tiled roofs and Venetian bell towers, the ancient stone facades and whitewashed walls bombed seventy-two times by the Allies. He told her the next checkpoint at the city's gates was operated by the British and he dare not risk it but she and the boy would pass through safely with the drover, who would carry them the remaining distance to the wharves. She was too dumbstruck by the abrupt finality of their parting to do what she wanted, which was to embrace the fearless old man to whom she owed what could not be repaid, to grasp and kiss his hand like a daughter, to press for a few seconds against the warmth and shelter of the flesh of the last person on earth except her child who knew her name and might say it with the smallest light of affection. Instead she bowed her head and whispered a promise to keep him in her prayers.

Take this, he said, making her conceal the five hundred-dollar notes in her shoe.

Bogdanov, she asked, what will happen to you now? Where will you go? And he told her it was better not to know.

She retrieved her handbag from the seat and Stjepan became obstinate when she called him out of the car to say his good-byes, demanding to know why, burning an accusatory look into the archbishop's driver, seeing what she herself refused to see. Son, take care of your mother, said Bogdanov, but the boy, showing only rancor, told him go to hell and stomped away, clambering up the footholds to sit on the wooden bench next to the drover, who chastised the child in Italian to climb in back and give the seat to his mother.

Bogdanov, she began, but the old man interrupted her to ask her forgiveness. But Bogdanov, she protested, and he interrupted her again to ask that she open her handbag and give him the envelope.

Envelope? she said, although she knew perfectly well what he wanted. Her eyes begged him for a different end to their story but he had become distant and aloof.

Please, he insisted, taking it from her.

What are you up to, Bogdanov, you and this man in the car? Was I ever the archbishop's envoy?

Yes, Marija. God and the saints watch over you, he said, and with that he was on his way.

The drover, not a farmer but a scavenger picking clean the ruins, was good to his word and brought them down the last few miles to the medieval walls of Zadar, rolling to a stop behind the crowds assembled at the Land Gate thronged with British soldiers, whom she despised but feared less than the partisans, who were there too among the hapless Italian police. Behind her she heard Stjepan say in awe, Look, Momma, and she thought Dear Christ, how could the planes have missed this mockery of Croatia's soul, the triumphal arch crowned by death to ward off death, a harrowing row of broken-beaked skulls meant to be cattle but more recognizable as satanic predators in perverse collusion with the monumental winged lion of Saint Mark reigning above them.

As they took their place in the queue to enter the city her heart raced remembering the laissez-passer Davor had written, still in the pocket of Bogdanov's coat. She had forgotten to ask for it and likely he would not have given it up anyway. But look at all these wretched people, she told herself, and why should anyone care about two more castaways, a harmless boy and his battered mother. It was the boat she could not stop worrying about, the Zionists would surely care about who they were, ready with the questions for which there would never be an adequate and acceptable response.

249

The morning had turned muggy, windless. Exposed to the Adriatic sun she lapsed into a trance of anxiety, startled to feel her knee poked and hear the word *Madame* wrapped in an alien accent and her first thought, looking down at the British soldier inviting her attention, was, *How ridiculous, how absurd, this pink-faced man wearing shorts like a schoolboy,* her contempt for the great liberator immediate and unconcealed. In stilted Italian, he requested her documents and, with regal exasperation, she rummaged through her handbag as if searching for a coin to dismiss a beggar and handed him an expired passport, issued by a government that had ceased to exist even before the war. He stepped away to consult with a partisan officer who became animated with nervous excitement and she understood what would happen next and then it happened. She and the boy were ordered off the wagon, their luggage tossed into the street by Carabinieri, the drover told to go on, an escort assigned to take them a block into the city to a small cobblestoned square where she found herself penned with veritable scarecrows, scores of sagging button-eyed dispossessed made to stand in the sun's wilting rays throughout the paralyzing hours of the morning, Marija holding her son's hand in hers knowing only the archipelago of pain rising from her flesh multiplied by unbearable thirst and thinking one thought, ceaselessly, that we are all bobbing on an ocean of death, clutching and unclutching our fears, and who might save us, and why, and then what, and where was the haven that would allow her mortal self to rest. Gradually they mobbed the bar of shade cast by a roofless building and then, sometime after that, a partisan appeared behind the cordon, calling her name, and she staggered forward, squeezing the boy's hand to reassure him of her pride in his forbearance.

They were taken a short way down a narrow alley through a portal leading to a rubbish-strewn interior courtyard and through an iron-strapped wooden door that opened into a vaulted chamber, a dank cave illuminated by an electric bulb dangling from the ceiling. She saw a chamber pot and smelled moldy excrement and stale beer and saw a bare tick mattress that seemed to be a repository for every possible human leakage. At the back of the room were four mismatched chairs, an empty desk, a mound of ashes from a fire that had scorched the blue plaster above it, and graffiti gouged into the walls. Italian, Serbo-Croatian, German, English. Names, dates, obscenities. *I fucked your little sister,* and she stopped reading.

What now? she turned to ask the soldier.

Sit, if you like, he said, scratching his unshaven cheek. Stjepan asked to pee and the soldier said he would take him but she refused to let the child out of her sight—Use the pot, she said—and when she asked for water the partisan said I'll see and left and never came back.

Then they sat, rosaries in hand, counting Hail Marys like divine seeds to temper her misgivings until the boy dozed off, and she could smell how death surrounded them and imagined she smelled much the same. Minutes or hours later, she heard the yawning cry of the door and hammering boot steps and asked God for a miracle. Two men entered the chamber, one of the partisans deposited their ransacked luggage next to the desk and went away and the other, an officer with a pitted face and freshly ironed uniform and a ridiculous visored cap that dwarfed his head walked behind the desk and stood looking at her with a perplexed but not unfriendly expression and did not speak for a very long time.

She saw the red star on his cap, a revolutionary ornament that would soon infuriate Stalin as a needless provocation of the Western Allies, and she supposed he was OZNa, one of Davor's OZNa agents—the Department for the Protection of the People. OZNa's growing efficiency had given birth to the rhyme she had heard on the streets of Zagreb, *Ozna sve dozna,* Ozna finds out everything. OZNa itself was to be transformed by Colonel Starcevica into Tito's UDBa, the Office of State Security, with its own spine-chilling motto: UDBa, *your fate.* Prepared for his questions, she looked with challenging directness into the officer's close-set, intelligent eyes, and he exchanged his querulous expression for a courteous smile as he came around the desk to pull up one of the empty chairs and, facing her, knee to knee, took a seat.

Are you well, Madam Kovacevic?

Yes, thank you, she said, relieved to hear his accent—not Bosnian, not Serbian. He's a Croat, she thought, he understands that one day we must all stand together again.

And the boy? he asked, with an avuncular wink at Stjepan.

251

Yes.

And your journey?

Has not ended.

Of course, he agreed, and continued amiably. Colonel Starsevica had written her a pass and entrusted to her a correspondence, and he had attached an escort for her safe deliverance. Strangely, she and her son had arrived alone in a peddler's wagon. I find this very troubling, he said. May I see the pass?

Without hesitation she told him she didn't have it, not the pass, not the correspondence, none of it.

I see, said the officer, his mouth pursed with commiseration. And where is Zarko Bogdanov?

I don't know, she answered. He abandoned us.

And the escort? he wondered aloud, folding his arms across his chest. The soldiers? Where might they be? She told him they had fought with Gypsies, one was dead, one was . . . she didn't know.

And Bogdanov, said the officer, his eyes contemplating her, focused intently. When he put you out. He took the road north or south?

She felt an irrational craving here to speak and be spoken to truly, to have honesty restored to her affairs with her countrymen, imagining in her interlocutor a similar hunger for a world stripped clean of its compulsory lies. *If only we are honest with one another, all will end well*, she thought, but could not convince herself that such a thought amounted to anything but self-delusion.

South, she said.

No sooner had the lie left her mouth than the officer, having earlier interrogated the drover, catapulted to his feet, his fist landing square under her chin, the very tip of her tongue bitten off and several teeth chipped from the blow. She fell backward in her chair to the concrete floor, unconscious, unable to prevent or even know or ever know what happened as she lay thrown into the blackest depths of darkness. She awakened dazed to the nightmare of herself and the boy alone within the vile skirt of piss-colored light, swallowing her own blood, the boy next to the desk shuddering and speechless and once again lost in place, his face pummeled, nose broken, one eye puffed into a slit and the other open but lifeless, pants dropped to his ankles, shit on the floor, shit caking down the spindlebacks of his legs. Ears ringing, she crawled to her suitcase, spitting blood, and began as best she could the desperate act of cleaning him without water, wiping him with the last of their clothes, trying to speak clearly through the pain, to offer the lisping comfort of her blood-thick words, begging the mother of God to repair this irreparable damage to her only child, terrified to look upon her son's profound absence, terrified to ask, to know.

When Stjepan finally spoke again that night as she cradled him in her arms and rocked him on the mattress he confessed he didn't remember what happened, there was nothing he could tell her to ease her conscience or cool the fever of her hatred, and for the rest of his life the only memory he carried with him of his ordeal in Zadar, on the eve of his leavetaking from wartime and Yugoslavia, was of being strangled by a soldier, the clarity and consequence of the overpowering grip of death on his throat, his boyhood emptied of life and destroyed and then, because he would not surrender, refilled and resurrected.

All she asked from Davor was water when he came the following day, the last word he would hear from her coveted lips for many years, Marija determined to teach him a lesson about the intractable lack of submission, the unforgiving obstinacy of Croatian women, to deny him the guilty sympathy of her mangled speech, consonants skating over the jagged precipice of her tongue. At first he tried to flash a smile but she would have none of it. He selected his words to placate and soothe her, to draw her away from her resistance to his solicitude, but gave up soon enough, his only accomplishment the reinvigoration of her God-invested hatred. She refused to listen to the glib evasion of his apology—*Marija, please understand, this is how peace begins*—to justify the psychopathic behavior of his minion, a blind extension of Davor's own homespun cruelty, as unprincipled as it was useful, here at the end of her war but not his. Finally, without further sentiment or insipid nostalgia, the colonel transferred them personally to a room in a hotel by the port with shattered windows and a staff of cheerless old women in smocks, sent for a medic to tend their injuries, and instructed his aide de camp to find clean clothes for the boy and his mother.

At the end of the hall was a bathing room with a rust-stained claw-foot tub where she washed her son with feeble strokes of tenderness and let him remain posted like a sentry, his remote eyes floating the length of her body, lingering only briefly with equal fascination on both her wine- and mustard-colored bruises and soapy breasts as she soaked in tepid water and thought of Davor's duplicitous attempt at kindness—even the memory of kindness a boneyard where she felt tempted to lie down and rot—and she could not remember if she had once loved him because she could not remember love and saw how she was bereft of earthly prospects, destined for a loveless life in which she would love God and only God and, of course, her son, the last remnant of an answer to the question, Where is my joy?

She dressed in the black dress of crones and widows that had been brought to her room and fixed her hair in a severe bun that bared the lividity of her abuse for all to see. Davor returned in the evening to take them to a café for dinner, an offer it was not within her heart to decline, knowing the boy must get some food in his stomach if he was to stay strong. On the street-side patio she sat at their table and sipped cold tea absentmindedly and said nothing and could barely look at him because there was nothing he could make right and she would not give him the chance. Men's brains grow big with war and their hearts small, he told her, a needless prelude to his resolution of mysteries for which she summoned not the slightest curiosity.

The price of Bogdanov's freedom had been the betrayal of the passenger he had collected in the forest of Plitvice for Starcevica, executed on the road to Senj by the colonel himself. The man's name surfaced like a crocodile with a corpse in its mouth—a murderous criminal, the Ustashe police commander in Slavonska Pozega. The recovery of the church's stolen wealth, intended to fund an insurgency against the state, now the property of the patriots devoted to protecting the people. She sat facing east, not quite listening to him, lost inside the waning light, watching the night bury itself in the death throes of her nation's independence, the slaughterhouse that would always be Croatia, its endless bloody-minded pageantry of violence, thinking, the devil can be found anywhere, in anybody. She thought, *I am sitting with a repugnant man who represents a curse upon the world.* She thought, achingly, *I will never have sex with my husband again, or any man who imagines I might love him.* She thought, *our hatreds are not invented,* and she thought Davor, once a simple truant, had finally succumbed to the unenlightened worship of power.

She clicked her fingers and gestured toward the fountain pen clipped inside Davor's shirt pocket and he gave it to her with a glance of trepidation. When she snapped her fingers again he tore a blank page from the small diary he carried inside his jacket for note-taking and passed it to her and she stabbed out her words and pushed the page back across the table and he read its message, *In this world you dreamed of, only weeds shall grow,* and she snatched the page away from him and flipped it, scribbled furiously on its blank side, and pushed it back again across the table, and he nodded dispirited acceptance, reading the annotation, *My happiness awaits your destruction.*

Night fell and he took them to the quay and reached for her hand to say don't give up on us but she turned her back to him. Here she was, finally, a Ustashe widow engulfed by Jews and the mortifying expanse of their silence. But the Jews were like herself, haunted emaciated women, physically ruined, with exhausted rag-doll children who owned nothing but the unspeakable pain of living. She had never lost all sense of who she was and neither had these Jews, she realized looking at them, custodians of epic shattered histories like herself. And yet not like herself because they were victims and she was not—to lose and survive is not to be a victim, just a loser with a God-given right to try again, and potentially more dangerous than ever before. Not like herself—her leaving was not surrender. Their kind weren't coming back, her kind—God help us—were. Who knew they would remake the world—or make the ancient world new again? They were going to Palestine. In the cowed silence of their own survival the haggard women hooked their arms with hers and together with each heavy plodding step unbinding them from the barbarity of Europe they went aboard.

In the morning the ship docked at Ancona to refuel for its voyage to the Holy Land. British soldiers checked the manifest and afterward took her and Stjepan ashore, the only passengers required to disembark, where the Vatican's ravens, a pair of laconic priests in black cassocks, thankless in manner and spirit, relieved her of the diplomatic pouches returned to her safekeeping the night before, thus ending her brief, corpse-strewn career in the service of the archbishop of Zagreb and the postwar intrigues of the Holy See.

Then, dizzying confusion. Ships arrived throughout the morning, off-loading beleaguered refugees like chattel, and they found themselves queued together with the swarm and at the end of the day trucked to a displaced persons camp on the outskirts of the city, where they remained in narcotic-like monotony throughout the autumn and winter until the advent of spring, 1946, when their own exodus began the day two jeeps carrying American soldiers drove through the gates of the camp. His mother ran to them, gobbling words he could not yet understand, waving a document he could not yet read, Marija struggling to pronounce the language that was his birthright. The jeeps stopped and one of the soldiers took the folded paper from his mother and looked at her and looked at Stjepan running to her side and looked to his buddies.

Hey, get a load of this. The kid's an American.

G'wan, said one of the GIs, she's pulling your leg.

Nope, said the soldier holding Stjepan's birth certificate. Says right here, kid was born in Pittsburgh.

Pittsburgh, said a GI in the second jeep, who would become Stjepan's stepfather. Whaddya know, I'm from Pittsburgh.

That night she took the boy to the tent of the Roman Catholic priest who heard their unremarkable confessions, a brief litany of sins that in no way resonated with the evil world from which they had been expelled, and, after the recitation of their modest penance, she smothered her son with kisses and told him she had not forgotten her promises nor her duty nor forgotten his promises nor his duty and in the flurry of his mother's blessings the boy bowed his head to accept his heritage, and she draped his father's gold chain and crucifix around his neck.

We are leaving soon, she said, and into eternity she whispered in her husband's ear, *It's done, my love, good-bye, what more can I do or say?* The boy wondered, Will we go to Palestine as well, with the Jews, and she said no, we are going to the only place strong enough to defeat the enemies of

Christ our savior and he told her, Yes, I think God wants that and he told her, as she had taught him in English and encouraged him to say again and again, *I love you*, and he told her he was ready.

In Zagreb she had promised, You and I will talk about this, and so they did, for many years, submerged together into a vision that was timeless, where history reigned and was immovable, one monolithic and unchanging thing with its roots sunk into the fault lines of the earth and summit far above the clouds. The mountain was never not the mountain, beckoning them forward. Memory alone, with its random chords and puny awards, could never be as alive or as full as this dream. They embraced the union of their pain; their defeat would have anniversaries to be revered. Planning the supreme duty of vengeance, calculating its inevitable unfolding, imagining its satiating honor would become her way of focusing him, creating his center of gravity. The umbilical cord of vengeance pulsed with the fidelity they would share completely, mother and child, until the end of her life, until the child himself would go forth on his quest to breed the living mountain's legacy of grievance into another generation.

This is how peace would begin, Colonel Davor Starcevica had told her. One beating at a time.

Book Three
Tradecraft
Istanbul, 1986

If any question why we died, tell them, because our fathers lied.
—*Rudyard Kipling*

CHAPTER NINETEEN

Dorothy Chambers's father flew in from Ankara to spend another weekend with her but this trip, his second visit in April, was special and tonight she would be having dinner with him but *where* was the question, always the question, his habit of mystery, his idea of fun, turning simple things into a challenge and a challenge into something simple. She knew only that their rendezvous involved, as always, a game, well-known and practiced between them since she was a child in Kenya, yet this late afternoon as she left her school in Uskudar and took the ferry across the choppy, breeze-swept Bosphorus, the game had become for her a source of increasing ambivalence, here on the occasion of her seventeenth birthday. She was in a hurry, or rather a state of hurriedness, her body tense with teenage urgency, already anxious to turn around and ride the ferry back to Asia, where her friends would be waiting for her in a coffeehouse on Baghdad Street. But, as always, there was no denying her father.

And now here was Europe and the busy mouth of the Golden Horn— *Hello, Europe!* she sang to herself, reciting the mantra she had composed to express her utter joyous wonder with the magnitude of this city and the delicious fumes of its landings, brine and diesel and grilled meat and jasmine— *Asia begins, Europe ends, Asia ends, Europe begins*—the ship rumbling as the captain reversed engines and the ferry nudged against the quay of Eminonu and the crew threw out the heavy ropes to men with outstretched arms, seagulls shrieking and the gangplank rattling into place. She pressed into the crowd of dour Istanbullus streaming ashore with the by now familiar exhilaration of having so easily crossed continents, ignoring the hateful stares she had grown accustomed to from some of the men, although sometimes she would stare back brazenly at the boys her age, defying their clucking tongues and vulgar gestures, and wondered what, on this most important occasion, her father's present might be, thinking she should have come right out and told him her world would be perfectly complete if she ever were so lucky to own a Vespa. But the bus system is excellent, he'd say. Or: Take a dolmus. Her mother would just say scooters are suicidal, why not jump off a bridge, but that wasn't what her father would ever say.

She was to approach the donar kebab vendor on the east side of the terminal but, preoccupied with her post-dinner, après-daddy plans, she forgot what she was to ask him and had to dig her father's note from her shoulder bag and read the instruction again: *His name is Mehmet. He can see the future. Give him fifty lira and ask him for your fortune.* This jug-eared Mehmet, like most Mehmets, was very happy to make her acquaintance. With the same hand that he used to slip her money into his windbreaker he withdrew a deck of cards, fanned them in his two hands, said pick three, and laid them out on the cutting block of his kebab wagon, pointing at one card and then the next. They were not the tarot cards she had expected, their faces printed instead with calligraphy, which she could not yet read although she was becoming sophomorically fluent with Arabic in its Latinate form.

Ah, he said, squeezing her right hand in both of his and raising it in the air. Happy birthday. Happy happy. Allah sends you as his bright angel to this earth.

Far out, she said in English, as if she were one of the old hippies passing through the Pudding Shop on their way to Kathmandu with the Rock and Roll Raj; as if she were her own mother at seventeen, her clueless, ex-flower-child peacenik-turned-astronomically uptight mother, a xenophobe who would insist on seeing an ID before letting her own shadow through the door.

This card, number two, said Mehmet. This card says you will leave here and go to Kumkapi, to the place called Karaca, and speak with a man who plays the violin.

Yes, okay, she said hopefully, finding her pen and scribbling in the margins of her father's note—*Kumkapi, violin,* and the familiar name of the restaurant. Maybe tonight there would be no more to the game than this, dinner at the Sand Gate near the seawalls along the Sea of Marmara and then back on the ferry, but it never paid to underestimate her father's addiction to trickery and practical jokes and object lessons meant to be eye-opening. Mehmet lifted his chin toward something behind her and she looked over her shoulder to see a silver-haired man with black horn-rimmed eyeglasses, professorial in his tweed coat and baggy trousers, yellow V-neck sweater and shiny black necktie, standing next to his shiny black Mercedes-Benz, waving a brisk hello.

And number three? she asked.

Number three, he said, studying the remaining card and turning it facedown with a frown. Number three says you will have a prosperous life.

No it doesn't, she said. What does it really say?

You are clever, little sister. *Yok.* It says nothing.

Mehmet, are you really a fortune-teller? she said, cocking her hip, resting her hand there, posing, not thinking she was flirting with him but she was. I'm sure my father told you what to say for two cards but maybe not for three. He's not *that* controlling. What does the third one say?

It lies, miss, Mehmet said. It says what is untrue. It says you are my enemy.

That's crazy, she said with shocked laughter, lifting up on her toes. Why would we be enemies? I love everybody in the world. Love, love, love.

It is a mistake, miss, said Mehmet. I am very sorry.

Sometimes these people enlisted by her father into the game worked for him in a capacity she no longer bothered to imagine, and he seemed to have access to an endless supply of conscripts from all walks of life, businessmen, scholars, tradesmen, tough guys, police, bureaucrats, vagabonds. Sometimes they were simply people he had met on the street, at a newsstand or tobacco kiosk, in the library or at a barbershop or café, and charmed or perhaps bribed into service. And who could resist a man so genteel and sunnily handsome and affable, a textbook case of the charismatic diplomat circa Camelot and American goodwill, well-groomed and dressed in an Italian suit and always smiling, always a spark of sincere curiosity in his gray-blue eyes, or the twinkle of mischief that made people relax and laugh with him and agree to do him a favor. She did not look like her mother, thank God, she looked exactly like him, but as she slid into the backseat of the sedan that had been waiting for her, she thought that maybe the game was something she was now too young for or too old. The game had a life of its own, of course, full of odd surprises, but by her father's design it evolved in unpredictable and obtuse ways and throughout the past year she had noticed the game change in a pattern that made her think he meant it to be more to his purpose than to hers or theirs, less entertaining, less of a lark, more fashioned toward a different kind of education now. It was hard to say, but then she had sensed a similar shift away from clarity with all the boys she was coming to meet and find interesting in the bistros and lycées and colleges.

The game had started in Nairobi, her favorite place on earth before Istanbul, when she was ten years old. *I'm going to turn you into a flaneur,* he said, making her look up the word in the dictionary. Why he chose her for this project and not her brother Christopher was obvious to anyone. The first time they played, what she privately liked most about it—that it was their game, no one else's—never seemed diluted but instead only enhanced by the many strange and prodigious characters to whom her father led her. When she finally tracked him down they would sit at a table in a sidewalk café and she would sip her soda and eat her french fries or plantain chips or noodles and he would drink his glass of beer and they would talk with loud disbelief or hushed admiration about this one or that one, the man who, the woman who. Was he actually a chief back in his village? Did you see her scars! Do you think that old man really was a sorcerer! That guy said he killed a lion with just a spear! How do you know them, she asked, and he said, Oh, you know, friends of mine, and she said, Dad, you're friends with *everybody!* As they took a taxi back to the new American compound in one of the residential areas of the changing, modernizing city about to be transformed by Big Man politics, he leaned over to whisper in her ear, *This is our secret, let's keep it to ourselves, we'll say we went to the zoo.*

Quickly, the stage expanded from its original four blocks downtown to eight blocks and then doubled again, her knowledge of the once-intimidating city and her comfort with its people growing accordingly, but then one day—by now she had turned eleven—he sent her off on the hunt into the squatter settlement known as Mathare Valley, where people were too friendly and clinging or not friendly at all, and she was intelligent enough to be amazed and angry that her father would let her wander unaccompanied through such dangerous quarters. But when she finally found him drinking beer with a throng of laborers in a bar with thrown-together walls and roofing tin, the place erupted with a cheer. The men patted her on the head to run their rough hands across the golden silk of her hair, praising her bravery, giving her small presents of beads and marbles and all the roasted groundnuts she could eat, the troubadour among them making up a song in her honor. Remember, don't tell your mother, he said, hugging her onto his lap, letting her take a sip from his cold bottle of Tusker. She wouldn't understand our game.

She'd disapprove, said the eleven-year-old, sounding sophisticated and wise with insight.

She'd disapprove, agreed her father with mock severity. You've certainly got that right.

But a little blonde-haired American girl walking by herself through those poverty-stricken neighborhoods, talking to vendors, stepping into shops to receive the next installment of her father's instructions—*Go to the open-air market three alleys south and one street west* (he had given her a compass on her ninth birthday) *and speak to the man who sells monkey meat* (*Oh, gross!* she had thought, reading the note), stopping to ask directions in Swahili (which she called dog language because the dogs would obey her in Swahili but not English)—of course her mother found out in no time at all. One of the *askaris*—watchmen—on the way home to the room where he slept during the day with the other *askaris* who had immigrated to the city from the countryside had seen her. The next day when her mother heard the reports she went ballistic and Dottie escaped to her brother's room.

Are you out of your mind, letting a child walk alone through those filthy slums! What the hell were you thinking?

She's an American, and I want her to know that she can go anywhere and do what she wants, within reason. I don't want her growing up to be afraid of anything.

She sat on the edge of her brother Christopher's bed and entertained him with her tales of the city, which he seemed to appreciate and always kept her confidence. But she could not stop herself from pitying him his fate, not because he had been ill for two months with malaria, not because walking home from school one day he had been attacked by a pack of wild dogs that came charging over a hillside, not because he'd rather go to the movies than go on safari and take pictures of the animals or better still, learn to shoot the rifles, not because she had to personally save him from drowning in the waves the year before when their entire school went on a field trip to the embassy beach house in Mombasa, not because he absolutely hated the martial arts class they were made to attend together, and not because he was his mother's son just as she was her father's daughter but because she knew that her brother, two years older, had indeed grown up afraid of everything and was becoming the unmentioned disappointment to her father that she could never allow herself to be.

And this was one of the huge and irreversible reasons why she loved her father, loved him beyond tears though not beyond torment, because she had never heard him once express regret over having spawned a wimpish son, never heard a word of criticism directed at her brother's caution or shy reluctance than what was sent her way—*clean up your room, finish your dinner, homework, homework*—had never seen him humiliate her brother, had only witnessed her father's unqualified encouragement that her brother find his own path, however timidly, through the hazards of the world, her father standing guard over them all.

She's eleven years old, for God's sake! There are people and things she needs to be afraid of. And if she gets any more independent, why not plant a flag on the kid and declare her a sovereign nation.

Later that evening when he was in his study she had asked her father about a sensation she had felt at times during the game, when she had stopped at a crossroads and looked around, trying to get her bearings—was someone following her?—and he said, yes, now next time I want you to see if you can lose him, and he bet her a dollar that she couldn't. She lost four before winning four, and then that part of the game seemed finished.

In Africa her father encouraged her in the rich extravagance of her freedoms. At that age she experienced the vague feeling that it must be difficult for a person like her mother to have a child as willful and unaccepting of boundaries as her daughter had proved to be, but for as long as she could remember, she had neither her mother's attention nor yielding affection. She was, of course, daddy's girl, but then so was her mother.

In the Mercedes with the chauffeur she remembered that when she was younger she'd loved hearing the story about how her father, the young consulate in Morocco on his first foreign service assignment, had rescued her mother, a twenty-two-year-old Peace Corps volunteer raised in Fulton, Missouri, from imminent injury and perhaps a thousand deaths at the hands of tribal heathens massing outside the mud-walled house where she lived. She was staying with a family of eight in a backroom without windows and ventilation and just a squat hole in the yard for a toilet and was served her breakfast of bread and cheese and yogurt and her dinner of couscous and cauliflower by a silent wife watched over by an ever-changing number of teenage boys who, when the mother wasn't looking, rubbed their groins when she made eye contact with them. This disgusting tableau was garnished with a soundtrack of cackles emitted from an ancient grandmother covered head to toe in blue robes, planted on her cushions in the corner of the kerosene-smelly kitchen. In truth, these heathens were no more of a threat than can be posed by a well-behaved room of doe-eyed Berber schoolchildren who mechanically repeated every syllable of English that left her mouth six days a week, including, after just two months in the country, the declaration, *I think I'm losing it.*

It was well-known throughout the expatriate community in Morocco that her father exercised an open-door, open-phone policy at his villa for any volunteer in from the countryside for R & R or medical treatment, plus use of his chlorine-saturated swimming pool and the twenty-four-hour attention of his three domestics who came with the lease (there was no getting rid of them). On the day he returned home from the consulate to the panting sobs of an attractive young midwestern girl in the throes of a nervous breakdown, he ordered his housemaid to soothe her with an almond oil massage and his houseboy to supply food, drink, and, should she want it, a pipe of hashish (she wanted it, but being stoned only magnified her distress), then walked down to the city center and had his supper irrigated with several rounds of gin and tonics. He walked back up the cobbled streets to the villa to find the volunteer on the phone in his study, hyperventilating transatlantically to her parents in Missouri, and he took the phone from her grip and spoke calming, reassuring words to her family and replaced the receiver in its cradle and asked, *What can we do to make you feel better?* She said she wanted to go to church, and he said do you want to wash up first and she nodded tearfully and it took the rest of the night for her to scrub herself free of the germs of hysteria and disorientation. By Sunday dawn they were side by side in a pew at St. Eusti's, celebrating first mass, the immediate bond of their devout Roman Catholicism overshadowing the differences that would make them an unlikely couple. By noon they had changed into bathing suits to retire poolside for a service of tea and fruit. By twilight her father-to-be had discovered what her mother-to-be most needed, which was to be held in the tender unquestioning arms of the familiar.

That was how the story of her mother began, she thought, noticing that the driver had begun to circle past Hagia Sophia a second time, and only God could say how the story would end, though the ending already seemed to have taken place some time ago. You could not conceivably pack more irony into a life than had been stuffed into her mother's, a woman who desperately wanted to escape the exoticism of faraway worlds, yet she had guaranteed her exile from her own by falling in love with the one person who would keep her from returning home. And how could her mother ever live in the States again, her daughter thought unkindly, without her legion of servants, without the accumulated privileges that only came from living overseas, the viceroy's wife.

They had married, one had to think too hastily, in Casablanca, her father undoubtedly expecting her to be the virgin that she was, her mother having never given procreation a thought. Then he surprised her on their honeymoon in Paris by leaving her there in a walk-up apartment on the Left Bank, a war bride and freshly pregnant, and flying away to his new assignment in Saigon. She liked Paris but despaired of being alone, found the student riots thrilling but almost everyone she tried to talk to was an insufferable snob (she had only to mention she had a husband in Vietnam to be held personally responsible for the war), and often she forgot that she was pregnant and imagined instead that she had contracted some awful African disease. After her son was born, her husband visited his new family like clockwork for ten days every other month, for a year, then three months in, one month out, and then she reclaimed him full-time, starting with his recovery from a bullet he had taken to his left shoulder during the Tet offensive. Then eleven months back in the States in the suburbs of Washington, DC (where her father purchased one of the new town houses mushrooming through the cow pastures of Vienna, Virginia), followed by two years in New Delhi, where their daughter was born and her mother stuck her with the name she would come to abhor, Dorothy—Tell Daddy there's no place like home, baby—as if to punish them both for not being somewhere else where they belonged. Soon afterward she sunk into a postpartum depression, withdrawing to a room she took as her own at one end of the sprawling humid house where she lived in bed all day, listening to American folk music and smoking vast quantities of pot out of a chillum. When she finally emerged she had, in her husband's words, *gone hindu*, wearing saris, visiting gurus, making a pilgrimage to the Ganges and returning to an infant and a small boy who seemed, perplexingly, as much a part of the house as the servants and rented furniture and peacocks in the yard and just as removed from her sense of responsibility. Her brother remembered the *ammas* and nannies—even the ambassador's teenage daughter, Maura—and sometimes their father changing diapers and dressing them but never their mother.

Cairo, her mother was fond of saying vindictively in the years ahead, made her come to her senses—she might pretend to *go hindu* but she'd never *go muslim*—and for the first and only time she fled all the way back to her parents' cozy redbrick bungalow on a quiet maple-lined street in

Fulton, arriving thoroughly exhausted, international travel with two small children clearly a message from God that God hates you. Her alcoholic but good-natured father an agricultural extension officer for the university in Columbia and her book-loving but narrow-minded mother tenured in the poli-sci department at Westminster College offered their *tsking* admonitions and unplacating concerns—*But honey, this is the life you've made; I would think an annulment is not something the Vatican makes easy. What is it you want? First it's save the world, now it's ruin yourself.* She answered always with two minds, self-doubt the only common trait between the pair—*But you don't know the things he does,* she'd say direly, unable or unwilling to explain, and then in the next breath, *He's the most altruistic, dedicated man I've ever known,* and then she'd wedge in a half-formed unconvincing diatribe on American imperialism that would cause her parents to shake their heads at the naïvéte that had driven her overseas in the first place.

Think of the children, her mother would tell her quietly as they stood at the kitchen sink, washing up after meals. *But that's what I've been trying to tell you,* she'd say back in a rebuke to her own mother. *These places we have to live, they're no place to raise children. It's their attitude about things. Poverty doesn't have to be so dirty, does it? And the way the men treat women—don't get me started.*

Well fine, said her mother. There was no lack of decent folks here in Calloway County who would appreciate a helping hand. But she had felt called as a freshman at Washington University, watching television when JFK, campaigning in Michigan, had said if he were president he would create an agency for young people just like her, bursting with unshaped idealism but ready to help, bit by bit, to make the world better, and now here she was, knowing the call had been a mistake, crossed wires, and she felt her life had been misassigned and she was doomed to be forever remorseful that she had not succeeded in her callow passion to make a better world, or make even one life easier. Instead, she had made her own worse.

Dottie knew what she was meant to know about the story, knew her mother's point of view, her father's, her grandparents'. Her brother's, who could only remember that mom cried often and that their grandfather had taken them fishing in the Ozarks and that their grandmother had pulled from the oven tray upon tray of oatmeal raisin cookies, which she distributed parsimoniously. She herself only recalled the golden image of their father showing up at the door, come to retrieve them from what came to be known in the family as the Vacation. Although he had phoned his wife frequently during their separation, he assiduously avoided probing her thoughts and did not ask the questions she was not ready to answer, and so had left her alone for three months, three months being the limit, he liked to say, on losing touch with your old life and creating something new. Three months was long enough to have thought about everything and discuss it with her parents and decide what she wanted. Now that he was here she saw her error, not in leaving him but coming to Fulton, realizing her parents were going to see him as God's gift to mankind, not solely because of his princely good looks or unstoppable charm or provenance in the world but because walking into church together to attend mass as a family they were, in everybody's eyes but especially her parents', the ideal family, a blessed family, and any failure to appreciate this condition surely meant that you were yourself a dismal failure, without virtue or hope. They had raised her to be grateful for her blessings, and honey, what in the world did you think a blessing was, if not this husband, these children?

But he had come with a secret, a real secret, one that it was against the law to share, he explained, as he initiated them into the government's intrigue. The president was going to China. Part two, you can tell anybody, he said: So are we. Not the mainland, naturally. Hong Kong. Her mother, this once but never again, enjoyed the posting—the overlay of British culture, urban amenities, rational people, Filipino domestics, clean beaches, the flocks of snow-white cockatiels in the air, excellent shopping.

And the rest, as her family liked to say with the tacit understanding that they had been swept away into its current, is history.

She loved her mother but her mother was not lovable; if that paradox didn't exactly make sense, she did not want to think about it anymore tonight, definitely not tonight. The driver was trying to edge around a stalled dolmuş and force back into traffic past the Topkapi Gate, apparently to skirt Hagia Sophia for a third time. Dorothy knew to be patient and trust the game and not second-guess her father even if his behavior sometimes puzzled her girlfriends Elena, Yesho, and Jacqueline (whose name she envied), who understood most everything about her. Finally, she couldn't keep herself from saying, with a slight tone of annoyance, Excuse me, and the driver's glass-covered eyes jumped to meet hers in the rearview mirror.

How many times are we going to go around the *cami*?

Not *jammy*, he said, correcting her pronunciation of the Turkish word for mosque. *Jahmy*. And it hasn't been a mosque for fifty years. Please, you can speak English, he said to her, and already she was interested in his schooled British accent.

But Muslims go there to pray.

And Christians go there to pray, but it is a museum.

Shouldn't we just go to the Kumkapi? she asked.

He took his right hand off the wheel to pull back the cuff of his woolen jacket and tap his ostentatious wristwatch. Faulex, she thought immediately. It's fake.

There's a problem, he said. No, not a problem, sorry. There is a delay.

We have to kill time.

Is that how you say it?

It's a funny expression, isn't it?

It makes good sense, he said. Killing is wasting. He twisted around to look at her and offered a cryptic modification of his axiom—but when it is necessary to remove waste, this is different—and then asked if she wanted to park and go inside and she said no thank you and he nodded and turned back to his driving.

Have you ever been inside? he asked.

Yes, she said. Several times.

He was silent for a while, maneuvering through the swarm of cars and pedestrians and pushcart vendors, and her mind drifted inside the elephantine dome, through the ancient majestic spaces of the cathedral that soared above Istanbul like a stony rose-colored knob of mountaintop, goose bumps rising on her arms as they did when she first saw the Pantheon in Rome, the other place where she truly began to comprehend the words *sublime* and *mystical*, the basilica a mysterious world of its own floating between earth and heaven. Standing within the Hagia's echoing mysteries, she had to admit, made her want to pray, but it also spooked her, its magical sweating column and holy hole and, worst of all, the column with the power to reveal whether or not you were a virgin—she wouldn't go anywhere near it.

Your father will not pass through the gates of Hagia Sophia, the driver said, interrupting her thoughts.

Really? she said. You've come here with him then?

Yes.

And he won't go in?

No, he won't go.

Do you know why?

I don't blame him.

She said light-heartedly, Sir, you're being very mysterious, her thoughts drifting toward some of her friends, Turkish and foreigners, fun, hip, brilliant but smirking pseudointellectuals when the mood suited them, who wouldn't bother to visit Hagia Sophia or the Blue Mosque or Topkapi Palace or any of the other fabulous sights of the city, all clichés, they said, manifestations of Scheherazade fantasies for Western tourists although, of course, they loved the Grand Bazaar, the biggest freaking shopping mall in the universe, refusing to see these grand edifices as she saw them. When a particular boy that she liked despite his arrogance had condescended to join her on a visit to the Blue Mosque, she had huffed and said in amazement, *Cliché? How stupid! You might as well call the breasts on a woman clichés. And why not the moon as well?* And the boy, mocking her, said he wanted to sell her a rug.

My name is Maranian, said the driver. The intimacy of revealing his name seemed to open a door between them and now he wouldn't stop talking. In Greek, he said, Sophia means divine wisdom, and the church, the centerpiece of the first Christian capital in the world, sat at the epicenter of three great empires, enduring the rise and fall of these empires, the obliteration of their wealth, the decline of their power, the sufferings of their peoples.

But tell me, Mr. Maranian, why my father won't go inside.

Because he is a very religious man, he said.

He is, she said. But Hagia Sophia is a holy place, isn't it?

Your father will not pray inside a church that has been defiled by the Turks.

Oh, she said, but you're a Turk, aren't you?

I am an Armenian, he said.

I thought you were all dead, she said thoughtlessly.

And so we are, he said with a sigh. And so we are.

Oh, God, I'm sorry, she said, mortified by her insensitivity.

Your father says he will return to the Sophia to pray after the next Crusade.

I think he should just go inside and say a Hail Mary, she said, and not worry about it.

I want to show you something, said Maranian, and sped off in the opposite direction from Kumkapi, across the Ataturk Bridge and up along the Bosphorus toward Beşiktaş, slowing when they came to a tree-lined avenue passing through a neighborhood that did not hold much interest for her. It was one of the first to modernize—which meant scramble to westernize—when the city began to reawaken from the stupor that had overwhelmed its citizens as the century turned and the Istanbullus realized that, once again, they had been crushed by history, shame and its lethargy imbuing in the population a trait known as *huzun*, a collective sadness and painful sense of loss, which she had heard her father liken to the *saudade* of the Portuguese. He even accused the city of stealing its angst from Europe: *the black passions of the French,* she had heard him say, then sharing the phrase with her girlfriends, who adopted it as one of their favorite jokes, laughing hysterically whenever they found cause to use it. She herself had felt the city's melancholy but resisted it, except sometimes on a ferry or walking the cobblestoned alleys when she would be overtaken by a piercing sense of déjà vu, the feeling that she had already lived her life a thousand years ago and that she was now a phantom spirit—an angel, perhaps, or a reincarnate—who existed for the sole reason of bestowing eternal compassion upon her past selves.

But this neighborhood Maranian had brought her to with its depressive hues did not lend itself to romanticizing the past. Winter would sit with a terrible gloom on these streets, yet this time of year the light flowed up from the Bosphorus in the late afternoon like warm syrup through the channels of the tidy street-level shops tucked into the uniformly high six-story buildings, row upon row, each one as anonymous as its companion to the left and its neighbor to the right, with the same glass entrances and minimalist facades plated with glass or polished granite and the same late-twentieth-century bourgeois respectability that—she clearly saw the cause and effect—suffocated personality and devalued culture. These buildings told her with a dry murmur that she was being invited to be an ordinary person in somnambulant possession of an ordinary life, a nowhereness of cloned identity that you could insert here or anywhere, what's the differ-ence, Paris or Berlin or London or the District of Columbia or Rome or a modestly affluent district in Istanbul. *Inauthentic,* she thought, which for her was a synonym for not worth preserving, not worth the trouble one might take to care. Not for her, at any rate.

That building, there, said Maranian, slowing to point out a particularly unremarkable piece of white-collar architecture, its ground floor housing a bank. I am the man who made that building.

It's very nice, she felt obliged to say. You're a builder?

I was an architect. 1962. My first and last.

Oh, like Sinan, she said. Why did you stop?

Here's something you do not know, he said. The famous Sinan was a Christian. Did you know that? An apostate.

No, I didn't, she said. What's an apostate?

Listening to Maranian, she understood that he had brought her across the Golden Horn not to see the building but to hear his story about the bright young student on scholarship at Istanbul Technical University who, upon graduation, discovers that his design and engineering skills mean less and less in a city yearning for amnesia, its reinvention inspired, like a school-girl's, from pictures and ideas borrowed from foreign magazines, learning to despise its former diversity and embrace its rising nationalism, hail the Turks and to hell with the Greeks and the Jews and the Gypsies and anyone else who imagined here was where they belonged. The westernized rich were not comfortable with an Armenian and his smoldering grievances in their employ, and the soon-to-be-rich Turks from the Anatolian provinces coming to rebuild the city practiced a robust mix of incompetence and corruption that pushed decent men into bankruptcy. These commissions were like eating dung, said Maranian. So the star-student-turned-young-professional returned to the Technical University to join the faculty as a junior member, yet by the 1970s the Armenians who remained in Turkey after the century's wars were being made to disappear again through a different type of cleansing. But an Armenian always knows who he is, said Maranian, and without regret he left the university to teach at a private boys' school for fifteen years and then, because of his passion for the city, retired to enjoy himself as one of the city's many freelance guides, a guild famous for its arcane obsessions.

And now you work for my father? she asked.

Now I work for the future, said Mr. Maranian, turning the car around in the direction of the Flower Passage, and she said to herself, Well, if working for the future means driving me in circles on my seventeenth birthday, then tally ho. She sat back against the seat, liking the grandfatherly Mr. Maranian, who did not treat her like a helpless child, and liked his answer. The future was every person's business, everybody's occupation. Well, it should be, certainly, she amended herself.

So how's the future looking these days, she said cheerily.

Much like the past, he said. New forms for old misery.

Tinker, Tailor, Soldier, Spy, she said in a rush, recognizing the quote from her father's repertoire of le Carréisms, and maybe that's where Maranian had picked it up as well—*Cultural attaché—Balls!* another of her father's favorites—*he has military written all over him.* Her memory for languages and names and whatever she read or heard was the thing that made people think she was smart, not realizing her skill (and her brother's) for recall was something their father had drilled into them with games at the dinner table, car games, campfire games, waiting-in-line games—Name That Song, Weird Discoveries, So and So is the Author of What, Who Said Blah Blah, or the game they played at embassy receptions, Who's the Spy.

That's John le Carré, isn't it, she said. Daddy had him over for dinner. When we lived in Rome.

Maranian took his eyes off the road to give her an appraising look. Have you read *Stamboul Train?* he asked.

No! she said with a purity of élan for which she was often adored by adults. Tell me.

He double-parked at the intersection at the top of Kumkapi, saying he would wait for her, and as she walked down the lively street webbed with festive lights and lined with crowded bistros, smiling at the touts in front of each establishment trying to coax her in, the sea air made even more delicious by the aroma of garlic cooked in olive oil, she realized she had not asked Maranian if he meant he'd wait for a few minutes while she collected her next clue, or wait until she had finished dinner with her father, whom she eagerly imagined just up ahead, sitting at a linen-covered table in front of their favorite seafood restaurant, sipping a glass of red wine and savoring a bowl of fried mussels. He better be, she began to whine to herself, because he must know that by now she would be ravenous, anxious for the conclusion of the game, today's version uncustomarily anemic, almost haphazard, last-minute, and she was mildly disappointed, yet no sooner had her mood darkened than it brightened again—here was the restaurant with its big red umbrellas and here was the violinist, a large mustachioed man wearing a tuxedo, his instrument like a toy in his hand.

Good evening, she said respectfully. Can you help me? I am looking for my father.

Barbie speaks Turkish, he said beaming, exaggerating his delight, and she sighed, having heard this everywhere she went in the world from men this man's age, fathers coerced by their daughters into buying blonde-haired American dolls. The violinist snapped his fingers and a trio of aproned waiters escorted her to a seat at a candlelit table, brought her a flute of French champagne and a single white rose, then warm bread, a bowl of the famous fried mussels, a smaller bowl of bright green olives. As the waiters stepped back the musician stepped forward, tucking his violin beneath his chin, his head tilted and his eyes pinched shut, the violin now his heavenly pillow, the bow angled atop the D string without a squeak, the violinist inhaling loudly through his nose, all very dramatic but not without grace, she thought, and then his eyes opened wide and he dipped his broad shoulders and played for her.

Oh, she gasped, having recognized the piece after the first four exquisitely sad notes he pulled from the violin. Her father's eyes often brimmed with tears when he heard it, because it was his most beloved piece of classical music, how could it not be hers as well, Pachelbel's Canon in D Minor, and her heart swelled, how achingly beautiful sorrow sounded, and she relished this, being drawn to the very limit of her capacity for sentimentality, her feelings so overpowering at times, this place inside you that would allow life everything, and thus risk everything.

She gulped her champagne to keep from crying and picked up the long-stemmed rose to smell the memory of those other landmark days in her life, Confirmation and First Communion, when her father had also given her one white rose, and then she looked at the violinist and laughed as he held and then contorted the last note of the Canon and made it squeak like a mouse while he grimaced and his eyes became clownishly wild and she wanted to jump up and dance as he segued to a mazurka, an insanely exuberant, reeling version of Happy Birthday, all the waiters, the diners, people passing by, clapping their hands to the fiery rhythm. Then the song finished, the violinist bowed, and she did jump up, unable to contain her pleasure.

That was awesome! she said in English.

Awzume, he echoed in his gravelly voice, and then reverted to Turkish to tell her she must go now to the fish market on the Bosphorus and perhaps there she would find her father.

Oh, man, she said, reverting to girlish frustration. When was this going to end?

Maranian shrugged when she told him to take her to the fish market and with darkness falling and the muezzins calling the faithful to evening prayers they drove a short distance to the shore and she got out and marveled at the scene, the smell pungent but not unpleasant, the fishmongers lighting scores of candles and small clay oil lamps to illuminate their stalls, mackerel and bluefish piled high like loaves of bread in enormous baskets, the light a shimmering flow like water across the fish, and behind the market out into the strait the ships passing like broken-off pieces of the city sliding away toward open water, unperturbed. Her light-headedness felt like the warmth of spring and how true love might feel but also slightly champagne loopy, the waiter refilling her flute once or maybe twice, and she walked with a bounce from stall to stall, the men calling to her as they would any customer or any pretty girl, until midway through the market she heard someone address her in Arabic and stopped.

Inti bint meen, welaadee?

She peered into the shadows behind the baskets and could detect a face but not its features, seeing only the oracular shape of the smoker, who sat cross-legged atop a crude wooden table, presiding over the flaring red eye of a water pipe. Then a ball of fragrant smoke, smelling of hot apples, and the voice asked again, *Inti bint meen, welaadee?* Whose daughter are you, my child?

She almost snapped, Excuse me, I am not a child, but collected herself and composed the sentence in her head and answered properly. *Ana bint Abu Theeb.* I am the daughter of Abu Theeb.

Abu Theeb, eh? the voice said, sarcastic, switching to English but carrying the same tone. Daughter of the son of the wolf. Who knew that Americans could have such names?

His face loomed forward into the egg of candlelight, his mouth stretched expansively into a grin that revealed the gleam of his teeth, and she saw that he was only a few years older than she and, she thought giddily, gorgeous in the way Arab boys could be—smooth-faced with a full-lipped sensuality and eyelashes like a woman—when they weren't shouting their idiot heads off and complaining about the most piddling thing and trying to be despicable little thieves.

I am Mohammed, he said.

Of course you are, she said, tossing her hair. Who isn't?

Don't be blasphemous, *welaadee.*

Stop calling me your child.

You must choose a fish, he said, getting down to business, and she pointed to one in the basket and he said no, choose another, and she pointed to a second one and he said no and she stamped her foot and demanded he choose a fish himself.

This one, he said, lifting a mackerel that seemed to her the same as all the others. This is a number one fish.

I can't tell the difference, she said.

Ah, he said, you will never know the difference until you look in its mouth.

Her reluctance came not from squeamishness but from the thought of having her fingers stink of mackerel. You do it, she said. You open it and I'll look.

Oh *welaadee,* he said, prying the jaws. If we could only see what this fish has seen. This fish has swum through the sunken ruins of a lost city, fabled Tanpinar. This fish swam through the portal of the emperor's palace, past the great hall containing the mosaics of paradise, swim swim, and into the queen's chamber, where it swallowed a treasure.

Yeah, sure, she said, looking into the mackerel's mouth. There's nothing in there.

Really? said Mohammed, aghast, raising the fish to examine its mouth himself, becoming more alarmed, shaking the fish, tail up, as if it were a Christmas stocking with one last chocolate inside the toe, saying one moment, please, one moment, while her face began to hurt as she tried to keep from laughing and then couldn't stop herself.

Maranian was out of the Mercedes, pacing, and when he saw her returning from the fishmonger he glanced at his wristwatch and opened the rear door for her and even though he did not smile when she declared they were friends now which meant she should ride up front, his face turned kind and he allowed her what she wished. Look, she said, excited, fluttering her right hand in front of his nose, and he switched on the overhead light to admire the gold-banded ring, mounted with an unusual pink pearl like a lozenge set in a cage of braided gold wire. Isn't it fabulous!

They call this pearl baroque, he said. Very rare. He turned off the light and said now they must go, her father was waiting. Super, she said, not having eaten the mussels or olives to avoid being disrespectful to the violinist. I'm starving. She chattered as they sped back toward Sultanahmet, saying that boy was so funny, he had stuck the ring inside a fish but couldn't remember which fish until he grabbed the right one and out came this lovely ring but dripping slime, ugh, and he popped it into his mouth to wash it and she thought she would gag. Then he put it on her finger and said now we are married, *welaadee,* and she said in chiming tones, *Don't think so,* and he told her she must always buy her fish from him and she told the boy but didn't tell Mr. Maranian that perhaps one day she would buy his fish and cook it for him *à la français.* Agreed, he said. From this minute on, I wait for you, *welaadee.*

Never marry a Saracen, said Maranian. The Muslim man will make you his slave.

That's harsh, she said, but there was no time to discuss Mr. Maranian's backward point of view because the ride, and today's game, had come to an end. What's going on here? she asked, frowning at the flashing lights of police vans, the line of Turkish soldiers, a row of limousines. What happened? What is this place?

Your father is inside, said Maranian.

Is he all right? she asked, her heartbeat rising in her chest.

He is very well, I think, said Maranian.

Are you coming? she asked, hoping he was, because what was happening outside on the street seemed terribly ominous, so many awful things kicking you in the gut these days: Libyans arrested in Ankara last weekend outside the American Officers Club before they could blow it up with their bombs, the embassy urging Americans in Turkey not to leave their homes except for necessary business, the bombing three weeks ago of the discotheque in West Berlin, the assassination at the embassy in Khartoum, the bombings and kidnappings in Beirut, the hijacked TWA flight in Greece, which ended with the execution of an American sailor, the massacre last year at the airport in Rome two days after her father had been reassigned to Turkey, and, just a few days ago, the bomb outside the bank here in Istanbul, enough to give anyone what her mother called a major case of the nerves, not to mention the government's nasty attitude toward students, planting MIT agents and undercover finks throughout the universities and cafés. She certainly didn't like the looks of the men in black leather jackets milling around, smoking their cigarettes with unsavory expressions, plainclothes whoever, secret whatever, nothing more obvious than their brutish instincts.

No, said Maranian. I am not coming. I am invisible again.

But what's the military doing here? That's not good, is it?

He is waiting for you, said Maranian. Go. You will be happy, I promise you.

The army was the source and protector of secularism in Turkey, but to go among these uniformed men it helped, she knew, that she had dressed conservatively, changing after her afternoon swim team practice into an ankle-length skirt and bulky sweater that concealed her breasts. The Turkish girls at school, obsessed with Western fashion, lived for the weekend hours when they could shuck their gray skirts and white blouses and squeeze themselves into jeans and short skirts and busty tank tops, but the Muslims in the neighborhoods of Uskadar were old-fashioned and disapproving, the women in their head scarves hissing at any girl they thought immodest, and the men were worse, unable to decide what they wanted from females—celestial virgin or gutter whore—and the infuriating impossible answer seemed to be *both*.

She walked as her father had taught her, as a free person fully in her rights to do what she was doing. Behind the cordon on the sidewalk were two policemen and one asked her name and then relayed it to the other one who held a clipboard and crossed out her name on a list and she thought, *How stupid.* The first policeman said please wait and descended a set of stone steps to a large wooden door and went in and she asked the policeman with the clipboard what was happening, why such heavy security, and he said he did not know, and she said respectfully, why won't you tell me? I think you should. The first policeman returned and said please follow me and they went down the stone steps and through the old wooden door and down another set of shadowy steps to another old door within a stone wall, the policeman's voice echoing slightly in the musty, cavelike air. Please go ahead, he told her and she put her hand on the door pull but turned around uncertainly and said please tell me where we are.

A Byzantine cistern, he said. Rented for occasions. You will see, and he nodded for her to open the door and she did, stepping out onto a landing that resembled an interior balcony suspended beneath the vaulted brick ceilings of a magnificent cavern, torches in sconces making an undersea light that danced over the long communal dinner tables attended by tuxedoed waiters balancing trays of drinks and across the cheering, whistling faces of the crowd below, these wonderful people, dear God, applauding, her father and a large group of men in dark suits on one side of the room underneath a blue cloud of cigar smoke, her best friends from school and it looked like her entire class on the other, her favorite teachers, even some of the entel boys (the self-styled *entellectuals*) from the lycée and cafés, surprise, surprise. Oh, my God! she said under her breath, a rosy heat spreading on her cheeks. Her eyes, now misty, returned to the commanding presence of her father, his hands stuffed into his trouser pockets, and met his sparkling eyes and she knew that look better than she knew herself, the boyish radiant smile under lifted eyebrows that said, *Look where we've found ourselves this time, Kitten!* and he winked at her and she flew skipping down the last set of stone steps and into his arms.

CHAPTER TWENTY

It took some minutes to understand that her birthday party had been attached to a second event, not a celebration but an unfolding crisis, something disastrous that the men were reluctant to discuss in her presence. Her father took her elbow and introduced her to his circle of special guests, the type of distinguished, soft-spoken, and elegant men who were always appearing on the periphery of her life, clean-shaven faces (except for the mustachioed Turks, this general, that general, so many generals) dilated with an attention that was soon withdrawn, the wineglasses and champagne flutes in their manicured hands tipped her way ever so briefly in royal salute, their smiled murmurings fading behind the gravity of their eminence. One was her father's colleague from Ankara, a gangly dweebish man she knew to be the embassy's station chief, the resident spy-guy actually, as unlikely as that seemed to her. Two were the fathers of her schoolmates, one a businessman but the other, like every one else, a member of the diplomatic corps of their respective countries. Only fat Mr. Kirlovsky, the émigré businessman who was also the father of her best friend, wrapped her up for a much-appreciated hug, providing her the opportunity to ask under her breath, It's not another bomb, is it? To which he replied while kissing her moistly on each cheek, Worse, but not to worry.

I'm sorry you had to drive around, her father whispered in her ear, his warm breath making her shiver. There was some difficulty rounding up all these gentlemen, he said, and he didn't want her surprise interrupted by the Swedish ambassador's grand entrance, you know how these fellows can be. Join your friends, have a good time, we'll talk later, he said, letting go of her arm and turning back to his mysterious conclave of statesmen. Bathroom, she said to herself, and asked a waiter for directions to the toilet as she slipped a flute of champagne off his tray.

The door to her stall banged open and there she was, squatting, one hand holding her skirt bunched at her waist, sipping champagne with the other, looking up into mock-scolding eyes, her best friend Elena dressed as usual in a style Dottie called Soviet Goth, military boots and black Levis from the Kapalıçarşi and a lilac angora sweater, ghoulish makeup emphasizing her cadaver's paleness, black nail polish and chintzy red plastic barettes from Eastern Europe pinning her wavy hair at her temples. *There* you are, said Elena, speaking English in her thick accent, her voice hoarse and deep, almost mannish, like a man trying to sound like a girl. You *never* lock the door. Because you have *no* shame, eh? I am thinking those men with our fathers *never* let you go. You should see the look on your *face* when you come in the door, oh, my *God*. All week, it was *so* hard not to tell you, and make the other girls not to tell you. Your father is so *fucking* handsome and nice, you know. My father is like a slobby bear. Now tell me, how did you get this champagne? The waiters only bring children's drinks to our side of the room. Okay, stop pissing already. How do you carry so much piss, like a cow. Where is the old woman with her scrap of tissue to scream at you for ten lira? Okay, stand up and kiss me now.

Laughing, she rearranged herself and they embraced, her blonde head and Elena's glossy black curls bobbing sideways as they kissed each other's happy faces.

Dottie pushed them out of the stall. I can't believe I keep the secret, said Elena. I never keep the secret.

Dottie paused to check herself in the mirror that hung above the sink, a wistful searching gaze, balling her golden shoulder-length hair behind her head, the experiment ending in frustration. I've looked this way since I was thirteen years old, she despaired. She twisted to inspect herself from a different angle and dropped her hands. I want to cut my hair, she said, but my father won't let me.

Tell me about, said Elena, misstating one of the American expressions she had learned from her friend. My father, he would be furious.

Daddy wouldn't be angry, she said. I think it would just make him sad. She whirled around, her unsatisfactory moment of reflection dissipated. Wow, speaking of secrets, she said, what's going on out there?

Some bad thing has happened in the Soviet Union, said Elena. Too bad, yes? she added facetiously.

What kind of bad thing?

An explosion, something, I don't know.

Where? In a city? In Moscow? Are you worried about your relatives and friends?

It is the Soviet Union, they are Jews, said Elena. I am always worried about my relatives and friends. Now listen, she said as they walked arm in arm back to the party. You are the queen. You must get me a glass of champagne.

Hidden below the world, the ancient cistern seemed to her a glowing chamber of lovely secrets and concealed passions, its warm wavering luminosity—the image struck her as curiously religious—like the light encircled within a communion chalice. With Dottie's arrival, its sonorous buzz had increased in volume, a festive trio of musicians playing traditional music, the bell-like ringing of tableware, the high-pitched melodies of raucous schoolgirls, like entering a shop that sold songbirds. There was caviar and kebab and every kind of meze imaginable, her piggy school chums cramming it in, and she floated merrily down the length of the tables, accepting a lifetime's worth of double-cheek kisses, thanking everybody, accepting salutations and little gifts, a cassette of seventies rock and roll, a pack of highlighters for studying, a bottle of bubble bath, makeup she wouldn't use, a beaded change purse, and sat for an awkward moment with jolly Mrs. Naslun, her history teacher, and the *très bohemian* French instructor who was the object of her infatuation, unable to be anything but shy and formal in their presence, exceedingly Turkish of her she knew.

Then, with Elena and Jacqueline and Yesho in tow, she broke the vestigial stricture of purdah etiquette—ladies sit with ladies, et cetera—and moved on to the corner of the room where the lycée boys had a table to themselves, some in coats and ties and others in jeans and leather jackets, most too young to be served beer but all of them drinking anyway, blowing smoke rings from their Marlboros, arguing soccer. The American boys struggled to be cool and the Muslim boys struggled to imitate them and the European boys were too cool to even bother, all of them sweet puppies but her interest inclined more toward two of the older boys from the university: Osman, who had somehow gotten an invitation, and Karim, who had somehow not. Osman, the classic *entel*—long hair, the Ortakoy leather bag on his shoulder with at least one book inside—who shared her love for photography, and the always sulky, sleepy-eyed Karim, the son of a Moroccan father and Turkish mother, who dreamed actual dreams of going to Afghanistan and joining the mujahideen to chop off the heads of Russians. Just by looking at her Karim made her muscles bunch with tension and sent fantasies through her mind she couldn't begin to explain.

Another barrage of kisses, less polite, more grabby. Osman, the least polite, who quickly wiped her cheeks with a serviette—*What are you doing?* she laughed nervously—before kissing each one, and then stood back apologizing, *I'm sorry, the general.*

What are you talking about? she said, and he stammered, *He kissed you, the pasha, the chairman of the Turkish army. Excuse me, you understand, he is a criminal, and how could I, I cannot—*

She rolled her eyes at Osman's weirdness, which she forgot about the moment he handed her a present, a stranded bracelet of Turkey's ubiquitous dark blue beads centered with white circles to ward off the *nazar,* the evil eye. Oh, how sweet! she said, slipping it onto her left wrist, pecking him on the cheek as she swirled away.

She tapped a waiter as he walked by and asked for a round of champagne and returned his stern look with a bright boldness and said, This is my party, please just bring a bottle and glasses and when he still seemed to hesitate she said, my father's over there if you need to speak with him, and that took care of it.

The four girls toasted one another again and again, and the lycée boys talked rock bands and boasted about colleges they would be attending next year in the States and France and Germany or England or here in Istanbul

287

and lamented with borrowed nostalgia that the revolution in Iran and the war in Afghanistan prevented them from the summertime adventures they had dreamed of having on the Silk Road. They compared notes on connections for hash and opium until Elena and Jacqueline stopped ignoring them and began to flirt. Osman pulled a chair up next to Dottie's and asked if she wanted to go with him to the secondhand book market in Sahaflar next weekend (yes) and the music bent itself into contortions, a slithery Middle Eastern cadence punctuated by the bash and rattle of a tambourine and *darbuka* drum.

Oh, my God! the three foreign girls said at once, their hands flying to their mouths and then grabbing at Yesho—Sit down! My God!—who had jumped to her feet and exposed her abdomen—She is auditioning for school slut, said Jacqueline—its muscles performing an undulating rise and fall beneath her taut skin, the smooth tawnyness of her flesh defiled by a hedgerow of coarse black hair that began at her navel and disappeared beneath the belt of her jeans. Their Turkish schoolmates squealed on cue, the boys hooted and jeered.

That is called *gobek atmasi,* Yesho said proudly, sitting back down. Throwing the stomach. Men become sex maniacs when they see *gobek atmasi.*

I want to learn this dance, Elena said, looking at the boys for their approval. Yes? It's good?

All belly dance is not *rakkass,* with the sparkle bikini and shaky ass, said Yesho. Every Turkish person dance with the wrists like this—she demonstrated, twirling her hands—and the arms like this and the ass like, I don't know, happy. But if I teach you, she said, you will require bodyguard.

Okay, guys, said Elena wickedly, slapping the table to get their attention as she rose to her feet with an erotic tilt and glide of her pelvis. So who is getting erection? Dottie blushed, Yesho smirked knowingly, Jacqueline spit her mouthful of champagne back into her glass, shrieking, and the lycée boys laughed nervously and Osman put his lips to her ear and whispered I am, but it is because I am sitting with you. Under the table he placed his hand on her knee but when she didn't respond he returned to her ear and said have I offended you and she seemed to reenter reality and smiled at him and said no, taking his hand off her knee but holding it loosely in hers and she sighed, thinking, these girls, every time someone touched them between the legs they couldn't stop themselves from proclaiming *I love you*, but not her.

At the other end of the room, she watched a courier deliver a message to her father. Then the waiters appeared with an immense cake and she heard her father's clear tenor begin to sing and the room joined in but when she tried to focus on the candles they swam like fireflies in her vision and she almost set her hair ablaze when she leaned forward to blow out the flames. By the time the word passed around that a fleet of taxis had arrived to take everyone to the ferry station or back to Uskudar she had forgotten what she had wished for, peace on earth or going steady with Osman or getting accepted to Yale—her father's alma mater—or still the Vespa. Her father came to stand behind her where she sat with her uneaten slice of cake and massaged her shoulders, telling her we can't go yet, honey. Our most important guests have informed us they'll be a few minutes late.

How's mom?

Didn't she call you?

Daddy, she said circumspectly, I want you to meet Osman, and Osman stood up with congenial good manners and shook her father's hand. The two other fathers came over to the table to tell Elena and Jacqueline to take taxis if they didn't want to wait, but the girls—except for Yesho, who was headed off to a club with one of the European boys she fancied— announced they would keep Dottie company. She insisted on walking Osman out to the street, for some reason thinking she needed to protect him from the authorities, and on the sidewalk saying good-bye he tried to kiss her but she turned her face so that he kissed her cheek, knowing that to do otherwise was not smart in public, and really dumb with all the cops standing around, any one of them ready to go fundamental on you. Then she went back inside, her concentration set on not falling down the steps, reminding herself she had forgotten to thank her father for the pearl ring—well, he hadn't asked about it anyway.

He was still at their table, talking to Elena while he stood behind Jacqueline, rubbing her shoulders as, minutes before, he had his daughter's and she could see that Jacqueline—what a clotheshorse she was, with her Benetton scarves and water-colored dresses and enviable short hair and self-absorption—was enjoying his touch and the sight upset her. Are you okay? her father asked as she sat back down and because he seemed to expect that she was she simply nodded and manufactured a pleasing smile and he said our guests should be here any second now and there will be a short meeting and then off they'd go. As soon as he returned to the men she waved to a waiter for another bottle of champagne but there was no more champagne and he came back with three glasses of sugary white wine.

Osman, said Jacqueline slyly. *Très* hot, yes? You think so?

Yes, but, said Elena, her accent making the words sound like *yizboot*, an automatic way to make her friends giggle. Turkish boys have repression.

What?

The sex repression.

It's true, said Jacqueline, lowering her voice. They won't eat the woman, yes?

Stop, said Dottie. How would you know?

Yesho! Elena and Jacqueline said together.

And which one of you was in charge of inviting the guys? What happened to Karim? Why wasn't he here?

I don't like this Karim, Elena said. This Karim has murder in his eyes.

Yizboot, Dottie said mockingly, you say that about—

Yes, but it's true, protested Elena. I am a Jew. What do you expect me to say? Have you noticed? Muslims are very happy to kill the Jew.

That's just not true, Dottie said. You spend every minute of every day surrounded by Muslims.

And what about the bombs? Elena said. Who is killing people with bombs? Oh, yes, I forgot. It is the Eskimo.

And what the Jews are doing in Lebanon? countered Jacqueline, her English beginning to fail with the wine.

I think you must be anti-Semite, said Elena. You are French and the French are this way.

The Jews have all the money, pouted Jacqueline. Everyone know.

Jews know how to make money. They work, said Elena. Arabs know how to get money. They steal.

You are a paranoid, Jacqueline said.

I am not speaking now, you bitch, said Elena, and turned in her chair away from their familiar quarrel in time to see the long-awaited guests arrive, a hush spreading through the haze of the room as they stood gruffly on the landing sending a grave regard down toward the group assembled below, a civilian and a soldier, or rather a high-ranking officer judging from his uniform, the red epaulettes and peaked cap and tunic adorned with service ribbons and medals. Oh, shit, said Elena, Soviets. And of course she would know, thought Dottie, since Elena's family had emigrated from Leningrad four years earlier, yet it seemed improbable that the bow-tie-wearing civilian of the pair, who more resembled a florid-faced British schoolmaster than an iron-hearted Stalinist apparatchik, could bear any responsibility for the crimes of the president's evil empire. As if to prove her point, Comrade Bow Tie's somber expression dissolved into warm collegiality as the two men descended the steps side by side, Bow Tie's flat-footed shambling bonhomie almost a parody of the military officer's rigid movement, his arms clenched out from his body as though there were tennis balls clasped in his armpits while Bow Tie extended his hand to greet old friends and calm a fresh crop of adversaries. Elena decided they had come to arrest her father.

Chairs were offered but declined. Bow Tie explained they were needed elsewhere in their duties and regrettably could stay at most a few minutes, and the diplomats and Turkish generals formed a half-circle in front of the Soviets and questions were asked in English and French. Her father, unusually subdued, apologized for the American ambassador's absence and then deferred to the interlocutors. The military officer remained silent as well, confrontation etched into the lines of his face, while his civilian counterpart offered breezy answers basted in optimism that only increased the chorus of questions from the diplomats.

The three girls sat quietly nearby, titillated, keen to hear every word of the dispute. Chernobyl, Dottie finally whispered, where is that? The

Ukraine, Elena whispered back, you have been given nuclear meltdown for your birthday.

Someone said his country's monitors were reporting radiation levels that were alarmingly high. Each repetition of the accusation found itself paired with the same cavalier denial. Offers of assistance—technical, humanitarian—were brushed away with an effusion of insincere gratitude. The questions turned into admonishments. Catastrophic, said a deputy from the German embassy, his voice disturbingly loud. Winds. Fallout. You understand? Europe, humanity.

Mais oui, said Jacqueline, *exactement,* nodding sagely when she heard her father's emphatic interjection to own up to it.

Our business, said Bow Tie. No problem. Small problem. Routine. Under-control problem. How is your wife? Under control. How are the children? Under control. Comrade Kill-You-In-Your-Sleep sends his best. Comrade Slit-Your-Throat remembers you fondly.

Good, let's go, she thought, watching the grim-faced statesmen reaching for their coats and hats—who gave these pinko a-holes license to interfere with her seventeenth birthday?—but the other man, the military officer, suddenly came to life, barking in a language so aggressive she felt it in her stomach and thought, *so that's Russian,* an eruption that froze everyone in place, heads rotating slowly to search out the one among them who seemed to be the object of the officer's outrage.

Elena said as if to herself, Oh, my God, Dottie, this bastard is yelling to your father!

Bizarro! she managed to say, the room trying to float into separate planes and beginning to pinwheel in front of her.

I don't believe, said Elena, leaning into her friend conspiratorially. This lying Communist says your father kill his son in the mountains of . . . some place. Ah, a place in Afghanistan. Sorry, I hope it's true.

Look at their eyes, she said, and in them Dottie saw the searing hostility, the sadistic refusal to allow forgiveness or entertain its possibility, the ferocious intolerance for mistakes, their deadly honor, unshakable allegiances and loyalties, the blend of mutual hatred liquefied in her whirling vision, sloshing back and forth.

Your father, Elena said haltingly, his Russian is not so good. There is a misunderstanding, maybe.

Daddy's never even been there, she said. Okay. He goes to Pakistan, she added, thinking, *that's a little white lie,* because her father had been spending much of his time in Pakistan, and last year, when she asked him why they didn't just move to Islamabad she had been embarrassed by the irascible outburst and unexpected bigotry of his answer. You and your mother don't deserve a place like Pakistan, he had told her. No woman does. These are disgusting countries, barbaric. The worst. The Africans are better than these *Mujos*—a Slavic word he often used, which she more or less understood as something like *Muslim niggers.* Jesus, she had said to herself, backing away from him, confused.

Your father is agreeing, I don't know what, Elena translated. Okay, I am not following. To think in this language gives me headache. My family wiped off this language, like snot from a pig. Ah, he is admitting that Americans give weapons to mujahideen, the Russians give, gave, weapons to Vietnam people, this is war, be a big boy and accept this, but the Soviet says I am speaking only of you—your father. Yes, but—your father and mujahideen. The Soviet says you, you, you. You hold a weapon . . . missile. He is saying this missile hit some helicopter and everyone is dead, maybe, and his son. And saying don't be stupid to think an American who shoot a missile can be secret. Your father is saying the Soviet come to make trouble and make lies and maybe everyone forget this Chernobyl and the Soviet must give apology.

She remembered thinking, *That's enough* and getting up from the table to defend her father, thinking, *Oh, they love this, don't they,* and she remembered Jacqueline insisting Dottie, stop, don't, and Elena's attempt to hold her back and she remembered chanting, *Bullshit,* but she didn't think anyone heard because she thought she was only saying it to herself. She could remember just those things, and then feeling sick and her father loading her into a taxi, saying it's very important you learn how to hold your liquor, Kitten, and the last thing she remembered, when she woke up naked in her father's suite on the top floor of the Hilton, was the absolute importance of making herself not remember.

Daddy, she made herself not remember asking, *did you really fire a missile? Bullshit, right?* she had slurred. *Crazy.*

Right, he said, undressing her, lying as he would always lie, as protocol, as policy, as a matter of prudence, because not to lie placed lives in jeopardy, and to tell the truth exposed a weakness in character. To not lie was an act of vanity.

Daddy, don't, okay? she would not remember saying, the sick confusion of her hands intercepting her father's hands at the waistband of her panties. With a spinning glance she saw his ring, Osman's bracelet—better not to know or even imagine what passed through her father's mind as he purchased a rare baroque pearl, pink as a girl's innocence, to celebrate her seventeenth birthday. What do daughters truly know of fathers? Their fingers paired, then interlocked.

Okay?

CHAPTER TWENTY-ONE

Always the opera buff, her father stood at the window humming *Carmen*, fresh from the shower, a white towel girdling his athletic hips, scanning the Hilton's famous view of the Bosphorus, a favorite pastime, monitoring the sea traffic, hoping to spy a Soviet warship or the menace of a submarine's conning tower, a black slice of shark fin branded with hammer and sickle in the private pool of his relentless obsession with Communists. Daddy's Red Menace . . . but the very idea . . . coming to get us. They're creeps, okay, but . . . really, *ugh*.

Rise and shine, kiddo, he said, his ability to sense her watching him a skill she had accustomed herself to early in life. His voice prodded her toward the shower with a reminder, Let's not be late for church.

Looking around the room strapped a headache across the general sense of anxiety she had awoken into and inside her queasy stomach she felt a balloon of nausea inflating and when she opened her mouth she couldn't keep her voice from sounding pitiful.

Daddy, where are my things?

What things?

My clothes.

Being cleaned, he said, looking over his scarred shoulder with a sunny, complicitous smile. You probably don't remember.

Did I get sick? she asked, closing her eyes on the vile pain, not wanting to know and he said, I'll say.

She whimpered, But I can't find my—

Your what? he said.

My underwear.

In the bathroom, he told her, with her overnight bag, and she pulled the sheet up to her neck and swung her feet out of bed to the carpet and pleaded halfheartedly, *Don't look,* the refrain of her pubescence. Silly kitten, he said, and she sprinted across the room to the shower without a second to lose, retching into the drain as the water belled over her pounding head. Toweling her hair she heard him announce the concierge had returned and the door opened and he held out into the steam her skirt and blouse and sweater, hangered and draped in crackling cellophane. Her elbows bracketed her head and the towel like a hijab, framing her flushed face and he looked up and down the length of her with an impossible love in a way she understood a father does not look upon his daughter and she said a bit provocatively, What? and he said, You are the most beautiful thing God ever put on earth and she exhaled chagrin and frowned in protest and said, Daddy, come on, go away.

Gule, gule, he said in Turkish—*smilingly, smilingly*—and she dropped the towel chastely across the top of her breasts. I need you so much, he said, stepping back through the door, and his humility when he told her this always weakened her and she softly admitted, I know.

Most often when he came to Istanbul it was all embassy business and they would meet for dinner somewhere excellent in the city and after dessert he would check his wristwatch and disappear—did he go to a mistress? she wondered possessively—but if he stayed the weekend she would rendezvous with him at the Hilton Saturday evenings or Sunday mornings and they would grab a taxi down through Taksim Square toward the Golden Horn. They often bypassed nearby St. Anthony of Padua and its straw-colored steeple, as they did this Sunday, Istanbul's largest Roman Catholic cathedral—too modern, her father complained, run by lefties—in favor of the smaller, more distant sanctuary, the imposing medieval hulk of the Church of St. Peter and Paul. Built in the fifteenth century by the Genoese, her father preferred its esteemed congregation, the local Maltese community, heroic people, fighting men, descendants of the Knights Hospitallers—Knights Templars, Knights of Rhodes, Knights of Malta, the last stand of the great crusaders.

The Angelus bells rang brightly. She bobby-pinned a white lace mantilla to her hair and stored her sunglasses in her purse. They slipped, latecomers, into the dimness of the vestibule, her father's hand removed from the small of her back as they paused to dip fingertips into the marble basin of holy water before slipping down the nave into a half-empty pew and kneeling side by side. Her father's daunting piety was a perpetual fascination to his daughter. It had an intensity that, as a child, she tried to emulate but now considered too eccentric and even backward, something of the Old World she imagined had flowed into him from his Yugoslavian mother, his clasped hands lashed together with the ivory-beaded strands of her grandmother's rosary and nailed onto the rail of the pew in front of them, his forehead dropped like a penitent's atop his hands, facedown and eyes closed with a degree of concentration that seemed to hint of agony, his lips in constant motion with a passionate burble of Latin, regardless of whatever language in which the mass was being celebrated. He would rise in a fervor to knock his breast during the Kyrie, the first and the loudest to sing the congregant's response in the liturgy, the first to line up in the chancel with his tongue stuck in the air to receive the consecrated host, the last to slide out from the pews in the aftermath of the benediction, still on his knees and head bowed, remembering the dead, the grandparents she had never known, relieving himself of his limitless surplus of prayers. He was meant to be a priest, she sometimes thought growing up, and so wasn't surprised the day her mother confided to her, as if here was a fairy tale about a prince mysteriously required to forfeit his kingdom for the call of duty elsewhere, that as a young man her father almost had been, dropping out of the seminary—Jesuits? Dominicans? she couldn't remember—six months before he was to be ordained, to pursue instead a secular career—grad school, a year of overseas work with the AFL-CIO, then the government. The revelation immediately explained at least one of his disquieting habits she recalled from childhood—her father's nightly appearance in the doorways to his children's bedrooms, his last act of vigilance before he retired for the evening, a faceless silhouette backlit by the hall light, wearing only jockey briefs glowing ghostly white, his right arm slowly quartering the darkness with the sign of the cross where his son and daughter lay with the covers pulled up to the slits of their eyes, feigning sleep, his deep-voiced patriarchal Latin not the comforting voice they knew—*In nomini Patri, et Filii, et Spiriti Sancti*—the blessing entering her drowsiness as a somewhat frightening and supernatural visitation. And how he sobbed at her Confirmation and First Communion and made her pose, immaculate, for a thousand pictures.

The mass ascended, unlocking its miracle of transubstantiation, *My Body My Blood*—my goddamn head, she moaned to herself, her body tightening into her misery. The thought that she had repressed throughout the ritual pushed through the loose weave of daydream and rote prayer and memory that had occupied her during the service and she told herself firmly, *I can't*, at the same moment her father stepped into the aisle and stood, waiting for her to join him in line to the altar—so handsome and debonair: who could not go to him?—the puzzled expression on his face recalibrated to the bland curiosity of questioning eyes when she failed to move and instead sat down, impassive, staring at her hands folded in her lap and her new ring and the ring's pearl in its gold-ribbed cage, suddenly forlorn and forsaken, unsure of God's judgment upon her, an insecurity that made her aware of the impossibility of receiving Communion in any state where she had not calmed her doubts with an appropriate penance. She couldn't do it, she realized for the first time in her life, just because she was supposed to do it, and this breach of loyalty, like a splitting away not from God but from her father, seemed extraordinary and paralyzing and she feared her father's reaction. Then he was back, announced by the rustle of his crisp suit, and she could smell him again, his aftershave and peppermint breath and shoe polish, even before she felt his nudge, the side of his body warm against hers. His hand crossed to her knee, which he patted reassuringly yet she knew once he swallowed the melted wafer he would say something but then he didn't and the hurtful thought of his disappointment became unbearable to her and she kept her head lowered.

I'm sorry, Daddy, she whispered, unable to raise her eyes to him, her fingers worrying the ring he had given her. He whispered back, asking what was wrong; she told him she hadn't been to confession. He pressed his left hand compassionately over hers and bent his head to whisper into her ear something she did not readily understand, that confession was contingent upon the commission of mortal sins, but otherwise an unnecessary emotional indulgence. Not a problem, he counseled her, for those who are blameless.

The priest at the altar issued a declaration of peace, the mass ended, and she considered what her father said and thought, *That couldn't be right, could it?*—wasn't she to blame, too?

Between you and me and the Man above, he assured her. Not a problem.

If he wasn't in a rush for the airport, after mass they would taxi back to the Pera Palace in Beyoğlu and drink chai in the patisserie or eat a hamburger in the American Bar, her father an encyclopedia of anecdotes about the Orient Express and the hotel's roster of celebrity guests, Agatha Christie and Mata Hari, Hemingway and Graham Greene, this king and that dictator. Or, depending on the weather, they'd stroll as they did today from Pera to Karakoy, down steep and narrow cobbled passageways flanked by cracked sidewalks and busted steps, laundry fluttering overhead, banners of commonplace drudgery connecting seedy apartment buildings filled by a rising tide of tenants swept in from the Anatolian countryside. Their enterprise turned the formerly prosperous neighborhood into a junk-shop sprawl of low-end vendors, spare parts, pirated tapes, and smutty lingerie everywhere and urchins twisting through the crowds with their circular trays of tulip-shaped tea glasses or a load of fresh-baked sesame *simits* balanced on their heads, a less grand bazaar than the one across the Golden Horn but no less invigorating. Her hangover was eased by the walk and her dour mood uplifted by the boisterous humanity massed in the Byzantine streets, a liberation she felt as she emerged from the claustrophobic lanes below the Galata Tower to encounter the glorious waterfront and its rioting seagulls, anglers with buckets and rods lining its stone promenade and its spellbinding view of Old Istanbul, minarets rising from its three central hills like rockets aimed at the sun.

Their destination, as always, was the iron footbridge spanning the banks of the Golden Horn to Eminonu. It seemed all of Istanbul tramped across the Galata Bridge on Saturdays and Sundays or gathered below its surface, and the dam of its unfortunate pontoons made a smelly lake of inland water slopping back into the metropolis. But the dark recesses beneath the bridge's roadway housed a fragrant honeycomb of ramshackle restaurants, smoky nargileh joints with bubbling water pipes, teahouses overrun by backgammon addicts, and hideaway dens packed with burly unshaved men devoted to political argument and the unIslamic pleasures of raki and Johnny Walker.

They wandered happily into the bustle and its singular exuberance, investigating the gastronomic possibilities, until her father poked his head into a cramped *lokanta* they had overlooked on previous visits, saying, Oh, man, that's the stuff! hooked by the bountiful selection of meze displayed like a doll's banquet on the wooden counter. Let's give it a try, he said, but five of its six tables were colonized by families and in the back the sixth had been commandeered by a single patron, a swarthy man whose coal-black hair had been pasted against his scalp with something oily. He wore a blue tracksuit and warm-up jacket, the uniform of the city's uneducated working class, and sat like a guard dog over a plate of chicken bones picked clean, drinking beer from a bottle with a look of loutish self-absorption and she thought, *Ugh, let's not,* but her father went ahead, shining with affability, exclaiming, *Yemek, yemek!*—Food, food!—and she followed with a tolerant sigh, the good daughter.

Her father asked, Do you mind? The man at the table nodded without apparent objection but remained indifferent to their presence and when they sat down her father winked at her and said he was so hungry he could eat a camel, and she stifled a laugh and the man took a final gulp from his beer, scraped his chair back from the table, and stood up fishing into his pocket for lira to pay his bill.

Allow me, said her father and she thought, *How bloody rude,* watching the man accept this generosity without a word or gesture of thanks, flicking his wrist to snap open a pair of wraparound sunglasses, slide them on his unpleasant face, and leave.

Dad! Why did you pay for him?

Random act of kindness.

Then she noticed he had forgotten something, a large brown envelope the size of an unfolded sheet of paper, on the floor next to his chair. Oh, hey, she began to say, but her father caught her eye and she felt an inward thrill and clammed up, pretending she had not witnessed what she understood amounted to a more sensitive level of her father's world of games, hidden in plain view.

He seemed kinda greasy, didn't he? she said, playing along, excited about the drop, an occurrence he rarely allowed her to observe, but more than anything relieved to have her father again all to herself.

Yes, he did, agreed her father. What would you like to drink? How are you feeling?

Better. Thanks, she said shyly, her act of contrition.

After the waiter had memorized their elaborate order, her father added water to his glass half-filled with raki and told her, Dot, I have some big news.

She marveled adolescently at the trick she had seen countless times, the liquor turned cloudy by the water, and he chided her for not listening. She twizzled a straw in her glass of Coke and to prove she had indeed been listening said, Well? Aren't you going to tell me?

Your mother's not coming back, he said.

This isn't another vacation, is it?

No, he said, it isn't.

So, is this like a divorce or an annulment or something?

No, he said. Not at all. She wants to be in Virginia, now that your brother's in college.

She can't handle it anymore.

She wants to be there for Christopher.

I'm not surprised.

I didn't think you would be.

What did you think?

I thought, Dottie is seventeen. She knows how to take care of herself.

That's so true, she said, pleased.

The invasion of the meze began, the surface of the table disappearing beneath an advancing army of small bowls and saucer-sized plates, three

301

varieties of *ezme*—carrot, smoked aubergine, and chilies with tomatoes—
fasulye, stuffed vine leaves, yogurt with grated cucumber and mint, cubes
of grilled white cheese rubbed in olive oil and oregano, paper-thin slices
of smoked tuna called *lekerda,* a salad of charcoal-grilled octopus, humus
topped with fat slabs of grilled red peppers and pine nuts, mussels in beer
batter—Dad! Enough! she said. No way you'll eat all that—spinach balls
with yogurt, fresh anchovies—Ho ho! he said, just watch—a disgusting
lump of fried brain salad, an obscene fig dribbled with gunk—and she said,
Stop already, you are definitely crazy—his enthusiasm for food verging on
the pathological and sometimes when she felt her father's appetite enclosing her she would remind herself of the pertinent family legend deployed
to justify his gluttony, that his parents were dirt poor and he had almost
starved to death as a kid in Pittsburgh during World War Two.

By the time the waiter brought her order—a cheese and tomato *pide*—
there wasn't space for it on the table. Oink, said her father, making room
by wolfing down two of the dishes, and she picked up her knife and fork
and cut a tiny bite of her pizza and stared at it hopelessly, not expecting
her empty stomach to appreciate the intrusion, and tried not to care about
her father's big news, telling herself, Okay, it doesn't matter, the season for
her relationship with her mother had come and gone and she could never
trust her mother to keep her safe anyway.

Try some of this, said her father and she shook her head no in slow
motion, remote, distracted by her awareness that she wasn't as sanguine
or cavalier about any of this as her tone suggested, in fact she was actually
pretty good at denying herself permission to think about these things at
all—the folly of her parents—and she lifted the bite of pizza to her closed
lips, lost in thought, exploring the renewal of an old feeling, that she had
been born motherless.

After all, she told herself, would somebody please tell her what she
was supposed to do?

After all, she never wanted to be inadequate like her mother and as
a teenager found it increasingly impossible to conceal her disdain for
her mother's deficiencies. PMS, migraines, panic attacks, paranoia, crying jags, selfishness so consuming it sometimes seemed like a form of

amnesia—*Whose children are these?* She had never stopped being afraid of the world, which made her anathema to her daughter, who did not like women who rejected, however sensibly, a dangerous expansion of their world. The way she hid herself behind walls she might as well have been a Muslim woman. She took too many pills. She was anorexic before it became fashionable among the girls of her daughter's generation. She was freaked out by the topic of sex, welcoming her daughter's first period with a box of Kotex and silence, and totally insane about cleanliness and hygiene, dirty countries, dirty food, dirty people . . . after all, her mother allowed her father to regularly administer purgatives to his children, and even, Dottie suspected, to her mother herself, sudsy enemas that horrified her with shame until the onset of puberty, when she became headstrong and learned too late to refuse him.

Oh, man, this octopus! said her father, chewing rapturously. Try some? It was like . . .

. . . no secret to her that women were an open field, a free market for her glamo father. He could have had anybody, chosen anybody, but the woman he chose was her neurotic mother and as she grew older and kept asking herself why, even knowing her parents truly loved one another despite their obvious misalignment, the only good answer she could come up with was that it all came down to the fact that in a time of crisis he had rescued her, and the object lesson was self-evident: be careful who you rescue because you're likely to be stuck with them.

Oh, boy, said her father, holding out a nose-wrinkling anchovy like a flatworm speared on his fork. These are fantastic. Here. But she jerked her head back, miming revulsion, and quickly ate her forgotten bite of pizza to make him stop.

After all . . . she had watched it happen, her father attempting to be playful with her mother—a tickle, a kiss, an impromptu dance in the kitchen, a pat on the rear end—and had noted her resistance and later understood that her Catholic parents would not use birth control and her mother was adamant about no more kids but then her mother became jealous of her father's affection for her until his physical displays of affection became clandestine and she had to hide everything, which is what her father wanted.

303

Going, going, gone, said her father, popping the last of the meatballs into his mouth and she pushed away her plate and its uneaten pizza, her own appetite waning as her father's multiplied beyond comprehension.

Groaning for the waiter's benefit, he wiped his mouth with a paper napkin and looked at his watch and said, Great, we have a few more minutes. She ordered another Coke to settle her stomach, he a coffee and strawberries, and they chatted about her studies and life at school and he asked, What about boys? She avoided the question with her standard dismissal—Turkish guys are weird—knowing better than to open a window for him into the topic of dating, and she shuddered seeing how instantaneously the wrong topic could rip away his charm and make him scary. Hatred flashed through his eyes when she asked about Chernobyl and she saw the hatred enlarge pleasurably with satisfaction—They've done it this time, Dottie, it was the beginning of the end for those bastards—and just what was radiation? she wanted to know, because she wouldn't dare bring up the incident with the Russian general, and any mention of the envelope on the floor, which had come to rest against the legs of his own chair, would be a violation of the rules, but he wasn't paying attention.

Hey, he said, making an expression like a dumb cluck, How could I forget? and he reached across the table, his hand asking for hers, to examine the ring on her finger, Dottie sensing his desire before she recognized its proprietorial determination molding his face.

Do you love it? he asked, and she did not always like to hear such eagerness in his voice, the intense need to please her begging the question of her need to please him, sometimes trapping her in appeasement and lies. But she did love the ring and told him she loved it yet when he stretched forward, quickly and circumspectly, to brush his lips across the pearl's gold cage, she hissed, Daddy! and tried to pull her hand away but for one long second he would not let go.

He sat back straight, smoothing his necktie, his guileless expression not to be trusted. I know you wanted a Vespa for your birthday, he said, grimacing at his failure to fulfill her wish. I'm sorry, he apologized, and as she rushed to assuage his guilt—Really, Daddy, I adore the ring—she hesitated, her impulse to forgive him interrupted by the leap of mischief into his eyes, the cunning sparkle that introduced the reentry of the game, and she said smartly, Okay, Daddy, what's going on?

Will this do instead? he said, disingenuous with uncertainty as he plucked the envelope off the floor and unfastened its clasp and withdrew a photograph from its sleeve, placed it upside down on the table between them, and, with a tentative, teasing index finger inched it toward her. It's not a Vespa, he cautioned, flipping the photograph triumphantly like the card that wins the game.

She's a beauty, don't you think?

Daddy! she squealed, not quite sure of the meaning of the photograph she was looking at—an unpainted wooden-hulled sailboat, varnished to a gleam, its upswept lines and wind-filled sail frisky to the eye, skipping across the turquoise-colored water of the Bosphorus.

She's all yours.

Oh, my God!

Don't I get a kiss, he said.

On the return trip to Uskudar, her imagination ran wild, susceptible to the enchantment of unleashed possibility. In the middle of the Bosphorus she edited her farewell to Europe to include a giddy good-bye to the ferry as well, her future already aboard the boat that he had given her, sailing across the strait for an evening in Sultanahmet or Karakoy, dropping anchor to picnic with friends on one of the islands or taking Osman for a romantic cruise to the Black Sea, utopian expeditions that would make each of their lives perfect and lovely and there she would be at the helm, in command of all happiness. But as the ship approached the shores of Asia her mood lost its elevation, her inspiration graying, her thoughts becoming clouded by reflection, and she wondered what she had to complain about—that her father loved her? That his sin was loving her? That he loved her too much? I have big plans for us, he told her, and she thought, you always do.

And what do daughters truly know of fathers? Too little perhaps, perhaps too much? What secrets do their mothers guard, what secrets have they simply missed, overlooked, refused to acknowledge? The answers—given and taken away and returned as mysteries or just as often as lies—were a perilous confusion: too much, too little, too late, too soon.

And what do daughters truly learn from fathers? To understand, or misunderstand, love?

Forgive me Father for I have sinned, she said to herself, without hearing an inner tone of the repentance she had thought would be there, when she searched her soul.

I confess, she said without remorse. I want his love too.

CHAPTER TWENTY-TWO

In June, the *poyraz*, a gentle northeasterly wind, blew in from the Black Sea to cool the rising heat of Istanbul. One Friday afternoon she and Osman took advantage of cherry season to stage a photo shoot in an open-air *pazar* in Balat, the city's old Jewish Quarter on the southern shore of the Golden Horn, inspired by their common passion for the photography of Ara Güler. Osman, of course, like any Turkish guy she knew even remotely, wanted to learn everything about her, and the day was exalted with clear blue skies and marbled with heavenly light and she felt like telling the history of her happiness in bits and pieces, which is how happiness wandered in her memory, fractured and incomplete, uncertain of its destination.

In the perfect early days of family and childhood, she had loved throwing rice at embassy weddings, touching the noses of camels on a trip to Egypt, sleeping stretched out in a row of empty seats on airplanes hurtling through darkness to some unpronounceable place, going to kindergarten with doll-like Chinese children, picnics on the beach in a half-dozen countries and swimming in the waves, painting her toenails shocking colors like Black Ice and granny-apple green, safaris and camping trips, gin rummy with her brother on rainy holidays, baking sugar cookies with her mother at Christmas, exploring strange cities, saying her prayers in each new language she acquired, doing the polka with her father, and, rarely but euphorically, the jitterbug with her mother, and dancing spasmodically with native kids on the ceremonial fringe, and disco alone in her room. She wrote poetry about the animal kingdom, which her father Scotch-Taped to the refrigerator, next to her brother's drawings of robot men and gremlins from outer space—*Crocodiles are mysterious/Because their tears aren't very serious; The animals are wild/They even ate a child*—and sent countless postcards to the playmates she was always leaving behind, outlandish declarations of fidelity . . . *love you forever, best friends until the end of time.*

Oyle mi? Osman kept saying, *Really?* his eye squinched against the viewfinder of his Nikon and his left hand adjusting her pose, Dottie in a tangerine-colored starburst-patterned sundress and black high-topped sneakers standing in the *pazar* surrounded by dried slabs of rolled apricot stacked like amber tiles. When she frowned about the artificiality of modeling Osman explained he was trying to create *the goddess effect. Whatever,* she smirked, knitting her hands in the air like a belly dancer, and he said, *That's it!* making her suddenly self-conscious. He wanted to know everything, though she demurred to his appetite for more intimate details about family and boyfriends and emotions and then it was her turn and she led him down the path past the hefty, rosy-cheeked women with their snow-white cotton head scarves and long-sleeved sweaters and baggy *salwar* pants to the *kiraz* stalls and stared at his lovely lips through the viewfinder of her own camera, the dangle of Hellenistic curls at his jawline, zooming in as his teeth nipped at the purple Napoleon cherries and the sweet juice stained the mesmerizing tip of his tongue.

Me? he scoffed, self-effacing, sampling the fruit at another stall. No, I can't remember. My childhood was boring.

No it wasn't, she said, which made his lips tighten into a pained smile as he spit out the seed of another cherry and she pressed the shutter and he began an intense discourse to explain to her how it was for him, growing up in Istanbul.

The most important thing to know about his childhood, he told her in facile but heavily accented English, was the jarring symmetry between noise and silence, the tyranny of public space in a perpetual state of tension with the dubious concept of privacy. Your family did not like it when you closed the door to your room, but neither did the government; secrecy was a privilege reserved exclusively for authority. What he remembered most about his childhood, he said, was his stubborn solipsism, the incuriosity and righteous disregard he had for others, paired against its likely source, the claustrophobia of overpopulation, his parents and grandparents and two older brothers and two younger sisters sharing the upper floors of a four-story apartment building on the hill near Istanbul University. His strict Kemalist father was a professor of economics and his status-conscious mother an administrative assistant for the school of law. The residence turned into a hostel for extended family flocking in from all over the map like homing pigeons—Frankfurt, New York, Paris, Geneva; lemon farmers from the Aegean coast, head-scarved aunties from Trabzon—the omnipresent huddle of relatives multiplied by his sibling's unruly friends, his father's didactic colleagues and obsequious students, his socialite mother's stream of lacquered guests and distinguished visitors, the cook and her ignorant children, the *kapici* and his family, and the neighbors stopping by for tea, the pandemonium within the building a full dress rehearsal for the greater pandemonium erupting throughout the ever-spreading metropolis, his fate inside and outside to be unnoticed, voiceless, and overwhelmed.

You were just shy, I bet, she said, snapping frames that married Istanbul's human wealth of opposites, the eastern Mediterranean profile of his gorgeous face, nose to nose with the merry-eyed Asian profile of the scarved, porcine vendor, a cigarette jutting from the corner of her wrinkled mouth, as he paid for a kilo of cherries and she lowered the camera, moved by the beautiful contrasts of the image—*classic,* she told herself—and they continued walking.

I think I was probably a snob, he laughed. My brothers enjoyed toy trucks and glue-together airplanes and sports where you kneed each other in the balls, my sisters loved American pop music and soap operas and I loved books, you see, and I was pretentious about them. I would not tolerate being disturbed, and my brothers would not tolerate my preference for solitude. And so, he said, with a tarp and old cushions he created a refuge for himself on the roof, below the grove of Süleymaniye's minarets, or in bad weather or winter escaped to the library, feeling himself on more of an equal footing with the chaos of life when he encountered it sealed in the no less lively silence of books, a delicious potent silence that would occasionally seize the entire city for days and weeks when the military felt compelled to remind everyone who's boss, curfews emptying the streets, martial law like a headmaster's command to Istanbul to pipe down, get back in your seats, put your nose in the book of secularism and modern thinking.

Leaving the *pazar,* they returned to the leafy streets of Balat, photographing its collapsing wooden houses, the visual romance of aging geometry—tilting roofs, cracked bow windows, swaybacked balconies— pausing frequently to pop cherries into the other's mouth, a slow amble in the general direction of the water, where the new mayor, a post-imperial sultan of urban renewal, was in hot pursuit of the city's future, tearing down everything in sight, stripping the landscape, razing thousands of buildings, peeling back the grimy industrial crust of the old tin and concrete factories from the littoral, leveling slums, obsessed with transforming the shorelines of the cesspool that was the Golden Horn into a network of public gardens, parks, and playgrounds—camps, Osman foretold derisively, for Gypsies and migrants.

Yes, Osman continued after she assumed he had finished describing his boyhood estrangement, a tale with a resonance she found instantly familiar, reminding her of her own brother's self-involved state of withdrawal.

Oh, good, she said, leaning into him, looking up into his brown eyes with encouragement. You're going to tell me more.

Yes. When I was ten, one Saturday I packed my school bag with bread and cheese and boiled eggs and, of course, a book—*The Ring Trilogy.*

You read that when you were ten!

Of course. It's a children's book. I don't know why because I didn't think about what I was doing but for some reason I became restless and walked down the hill to Eminonu and I purchased a token for the next ferry, which was going to Uskudar. I had never ridden the ferry by myself and I wasn't sure where Uskudar was but these facts did not concern me. I sat alone on a bench near the front of the boat and began to read and when the ferry docked I got off and purchased a token for the next ferry. This one was going to Beşiktaş. I read my book and was very happy with the hobbits and such. The next ferry took me to Ortakoy, the next to Arnavutkoy. What were these places? I didn't even look at them. I didn't notice the oil tankers and freighters, I wasn't interested in the dolphins jumping in front of the boat. I didn't look at the magnificent palaces along the shore or the *yalis* of the rich people or the passengers getting on or off at each stop. Finally, I was almost to the Black Sea and had to turn around. By the time I arrived home it was very late and I expected to be punished. My hands trembled as I removed my shoes at the door and walked into our flat, dreading the scene to come. My mother was entertaining a houseful of frightening ladies hidden beneath layers of jewelry and cosmetics and silk and she made me introduce myself and said, Darling, where have you been so late? I said the library and she beamed and announced to everyone I was going to be a doctor, although I had never indicated any such desire, but one of the guests said skeptically, *How does the boy get such a sunburn in the library?* And then the truth came out. My mother became very dramatic, beside herself with anxiety because I had journeyed all day long without an amulet to protect myself from the evil eye.

Dottie didn't interrupt but raised her left hand to display the bracelet he had given her for her birthday. Yes, he nodded. Exactly.

The point of my story is this, Osman said. I became infatuated with Istanbul's ferries, not for any practical or aesthetic reason. Every Saturday I would ride them back and forth, back and forth, from somewhere to somewhere to somewhere else, restored by the constant stream of air and water, suspended in a sublime state, moving across the water with everyone else but unlike everyone else, going nowhere, because I was already where I wanted to be, which was turned inward and facing outward at the same time. I was happiest in this place called Between. Between was not the space of separation everyone imagined it to be. On the contrary, actually. Perhaps this perspective is the difference between you and me. So, yes, I was talking about books. I read dozens of books on the ferries. Hundreds. No, I'm not exaggerating.

So, he said, and her stomach fluttered as she let him take her hand. You might think that my love of books transformed me into an excellent student, but that was not the case.

Oh, crapola, she said, and he gave her a sad glance, his customary response when she contradicted him. You passed the entrance exam to Robert College.

Okay, did I say I wasn't intelligent? The problem was, the books had made me a dreamer, an inhabitant of every world but my own, and because of this it is very clear to me the day my childhood ended, six years ago, when I was fourteen, and I began to see how I would have to adapt or perish.

But childhood should end at fourteen, don't you think? she said.

Yes, he agreed. Perhaps even sooner. I was immature at fourteen. But at whatever age childhood ends, it does not end naturally, it ends with a blow.

She thought about Osman's theory as they crossed the boulevard toward the bulldozed shoreline and agreed—childhood's demise was truly painful—but did not say so. They walked through an unsod plot of newly planted saplings, mangy stray dogs sniffing the scraped soil.

Why do people call the dogs Arabs? she asked.

Ask your Mister Lawrence.

Sorry?

Mister T. E. Lawrence. And when she didn't understand he laconically explained, We don't like the Arabs.

A horde of boys played soccer on the bare ground where not long ago had stood a dilapidated row of warehouses. She felt Osman's mood shift and asked, What's wrong? and here was that strange blend of his, passion and gloom, fueling a smoldering rant about the popular mayor—the ringmaster for the ruling elite, he lamented, granter of wishes for invisible people while the working people and artisans, who had lived along the waterways for generations, were thrown out of their homes and displaced to the goat pastures beyond the farthest suburbs, and she did not intend to argue when she said, But, Osman, the pollution here was so gross.

Listen, Dottie, he lectured her, the real pollution is the way the government runs this country, and she sighed, not wanting to ruin everything with politics.

Do you think the radiation from Chernobyl has come here?

Yes, he said ruefully. It's obvious. We're all fucked.

Far up the quay, a small white-hulled ferry had docked at the terminal below the iron church and she said, Come on, let's run for it! and took off trotting before he could object. Osman caught up to her and then their brisk steps became a foot race, the two of them leaping from the dock to the boat as it pulled away into trash-swirled water, crumpling together onto a wide bench near the bow, breathless and laughing and Dottie tortured by the looming possibility of love.

Fourteen, she said. You promised.

I never promised.

Beginning a story is like a promise that you'll finish it. Otherwise, it's not fair.

Okay, he said. Trust me. I promise you when I finish, you will wish I never began.

How old do you have to be to be a terrorist? Someone whose very existence makes the *devlet*—the state—fear for its own survival. Is fourteen old enough? Twelve? Six? What about six months? The answer is yes, even babies are terrorists if the *devlet*, in its obligation to preserve the nation, determines the existence of a baby is a threat to security and stability, if not today then certainly tomorrow. How does the *devlet* make this determination? Is it a reasoned process, or a caprice of the moment, a paranoid and arbitrary whim? How many mistakes are made? How many mistakes can the *devlet* afford? I don't know the answer, he said. Perhaps we should ask the Kurds or the Armenians.

Do you know what *tevkifhane* means? A house of detention, a prison. In the heart of Sultanahmet, there you will find Tevkifhane Sokak. Tourists pass by this place every day on the way to the Blue Mosque and Hagia Sophia but don't see it. It's nothing, an old Ottoman building, big, impressive, but not special for foreigners. The way I found out about Tevkifhane Sokak was by a simple mistake, and you can ask, Whose mistake? but since the *devlet* is beyond reproach and does not make mistakes, and therefore cannot place itself in the absurd position where it must acknowledge mistakes it has not made, I find myself in the equally absurd position of acknowledging the mistake as my own.

My parents were delighted when I was accepted to Robert College— my brothers both failed the entrance exam—and naturally were disappointed I did not share their enthusiasm for the best secondary school in Istanbul. They didn't understand my reluctance, but I hate getting out of bed in the morning—not much of a problem when your school is only a short walk up the street, as mine had been. But you know Robert College, yes? Way the hell up in Arnavutkoy. If I overslept I missed the ferry. If you miss the ferry, there's nothing you can do but take a bus or dolmus. Don't say taxi—who has money for that every day? Rush hour on a bus—have you tried it? Maybe it takes fifteen minutes, maybe an hour, who knows? I suffocated. The clouds of perfume would make me want to vomit. My days often began and ended this way, a horrible slow-motion rush, your insides crying because it's early in the morning or late in the day and you need a toilet—which, it embarrasses me to confess, was my first step on the road to becoming a terrorist. Apparently, my body understood my true nature before my mind had any idea.

Oh, it's funny, is it? Yes, you're probably right, but trust me, now you must stop laughing.

Do you know what happened in this country in 1980? Yes, of course you do because you see it everywhere still—the soldiers, the police, the fear. Military coup. One day in the autumn of 1980 I left school late and missed the ferry to the Golden Horn and took the bus instead but traffic was very bad and I had to piss so when we reached Taksim I jumped off and ran to a *meyhane* to use the toilet. When I came back outside the square was overflowing with students, mostly older kids, university students. Where had so many come from all of a sudden? I couldn't believe the noise, the uproar they made, shouting, chanting, drumming, whistling—the sensation was very much like a thunderstorm, the demonstration seemed able to create its own gusts of wind—and I had never seen anything like it. You could feel the city shake with the power of the mob. Instead of catching the tram to Galata, as I had intended, I began to walk toward the mass of students. Let me see what's going on, I said to myself. Just for a minute, yes? Suddenly, I heard glass breaking and the sound of sirens and people were telling me to run and then the police were everywhere, beating the students with batons and I began running, too, it was like a stampede, but in a box—what's the word in English . . . corral? No matter which way you ran there were the police. Somehow my shoes were no longer on my feet and I fell down and before I could get up they were

314

beating me and there was nothing I could do. Then I was lifted into the air and tossed into a van atop many bloody, moaning students and then more students were tossed in atop me, the door was shut, and in the blackness it felt like we had all been buried alive. Someone beneath me began convulsing and everyone was crying and groaning and I passed out until I woke up freezing on the wet concrete of Tevkifhane Sokak, in the company of hundreds of students who were as bad off as me or worse. I sat up with my back against a stone wall and didn't talk to anybody and closed my eyes and kept them closed, waiting to be rescued from my inexplicable persecution. My father will come, I kept telling myself. My father will come soon and I will go home. You see, at that moment I was still a child.

Dottie, many people in Turkey can tell you this same story. It is part of our culture, our history, our system—the cliché of injustice—and I think sometimes we are almost bored by it. What did you expect? we say. From all directions, Turkey is besieged by enemies committed to ripping apart the nation. The *devlet* must respond to all threats with an iron fist and unforgiving heart. Too bad for you, we say, if you step in the way. Being in the way means you are either stupid, a criminal, an anarchist, or a fanatic. If you are any of these things, you cannot also be a victim. You cannot be innocent, even if you are fourteen, even if you are a baby stupid enough to be born to the wrong parents.

So, all night long and throughout the following morning, while I waited for my father to come to take me home, the guards marched back and forth and took the students one by one—the older ones first, especially those advertising their guilt with beards or long hair. Our police are very proud of their ability to produce confessions. They believe in the utility of torture, they guarantee its benefits to the state. The screams echoing from the depths of the building hour after hour seemed unreal to me and I could not quite imagine I would end up in one of those rooms, howling like an animal. My reaction was strange. Or normal, I don't know. I felt dizzy, light-headed, the soreness of my body vanished along with hunger and thirst and I became simply hollow and numb, waiting.

Finally, a guard walked past me and stopped and turned on his heels, noticing me for the first time. He grabbed my hair, which was not as long then as it is now, and yanked me to my feet and pushed me ahead of him, up a flight of bloodstained stairs to the second floor. I can still remember the feeling, stepping in a patch of fresh blood in my socks. I looked down and there were my own footprints in blood.

Eventually the guard deposited me in the passageway at the end of a line of other wretched detainees waiting to go into a room to be interrogated. No one spoke or met each other's eyes but a group of guards stood nearby joking and talking about football and at intervals the door would open and out would come a cringing student, one of the guards would slowly pull himself from the group to escort him away, and in would go another student, shitting his pants. No, not really, but you understand.

Now, after an eternity, my turn. The room was gray or green, I don't remember, and nothing on the walls except, of course, Atatürk. I sat in a chair facing the investigator behind a metal desk, a bald-headed man who had loosened his necktie and opened his collar and for a moment I had the surreal impression that a tarantula was crawling out of his shirt onto his throat, but it was just tufts of hair, his chest must have been matted with hair. Perhaps he wasn't bald at all but had shaved his head to appear more menacing. He sat at the desk, writing, as if I wasn't there. After a while he sighed and put his pen down and closed the folder he had written in and opened a new one and at last he looked at me with weary exasperation, such tired, bloodshot eyes, and picked up his pen and looked back down at the new folder and then came the questions. Name, father's name, age, residence, occupation. Student, I said. School? Robert College. He tapped with his pen on the desk before raising his head to truly look at me and I could see from his expression that I had become a waste of his time. Why were you in Taksim with the extremist troublemakers? he asked. As I told him, he rubbed his eyes and yawned. Are you a Marxist? he asked. Sir, I said, what is a Marxist exactly? Is your father a leftist? Sir, I said, what are leftists? Are you trying to be impudent? he said. The questions were ridiculous, but he asked them anyway, as if reciting from a note card. Are you a trade union member? Do you believe in theocracy? Are you an activist? A radical? An agitator? Are you a Kurdish sympathizer? Are you hostile to the general interests of the country? Why do you hate the army? Are you

316

this, are you that, are you determined to overthrow the state? Would you like to confess or should I send you back downstairs with your comrades? Okay, I said, I confess that I'm a worthless flea—fourteen, ignorant, unable to hold my piss.

No, I didn't say that.

A guard entered the room with a glass of tea for the investigator. He stood up to stretch his legs while he sipped his tea and smoked a cigarette, paying me no attention. My mouth was parched and I cleared my throat and he stopped pacing and looked at me, surprised, as if he had forgotten I was there, and he smiled and said, Ready to confess? and I was bewildered by the playfulness in his voice. Sir, may I go home now, I asked, but before he could answer there was a knock on the door and another guard poked his head in and gestured to the investigator. They whispered, the door closed, the investigator came back and leaned against the front of his desk, looking at me with . . . how should I describe it? As if I had managed to trick him, and he admired my cleverness.

That guard was searching for somebody, he explained. He had a name on a piece of paper. Want to guess whose name?

I don't know.

Your name, of course. Why are the guards looking for you, do you think?

Sir, I don't know.

Your father is here, he said to me, cocking an eyebrow. Your father seems to be friends with every fucker in my chain of command.

You can imagine my relief—life came surging back into me, my thirst and hunger returned in an instant, and I began to obsess about what the cook was preparing for dinner. The investigator came over and clapped me on the back and said, Kid, why didn't you tell me that your father was such a big shot in the party, eh?

But now, Dottie, nothing I have told you so far amounts to much and now you shall hear the worst of it.

The door opened. There stood my father, a big man in shoes shined every morning by the same old man on the same street corner by the university and a custom-tailored business suit and carefully trimmed hair and mustache. His face looked boiled, crimson, and his eyes were insane. He paused for a moment and glared at the inspector and then looked at me and charged as if he were entering a boxing ring. With both hands flying he began slapping me on the face and head and shoulders. A cut on my ear from the day before reopened and blood sprayed onto his suit and the inspector's white shirt. I was so stunned I made no attempt to protect myself. The inspector, thank God, jumped between us or I think my father might not have been able to stop—he had lost his mind. The inspector dragged him back and my father was breathing so violently it took him a minute to catch his breath. He pointed at me, shaking his finger in my face, his breathing slowed, and I knew he was going to start shouting but when he finally spoke his voice was quiet and restrained.

He said to me, I wish I was dead rather than to have spawned a son like you.

In Turkey, it's impossible to believe a father would say this to his own child. Family is everything. Even the investigator was shocked. Tears began to roll from my eyes. I tried very hard not to add to my humiliation by crying but I could not stop myself. It was several years before I was able to comprehend why my father had expressed himself in this manner. His impulse, I am convinced, was to brand and cripple my conscience with the crime of patricide. He wasn't going to kill me—I was going to kill him. *Baba, devlet baba*—the father, the state, they are the same organism, you see. They perceive threats through the same pair of eyes. The failing of one automatically means the failure of the other.

Come on now, Professor, said the inspector to my father, don't be so hard on the boy. He's not a bad kid. He's free to go—no charges. Take your son and go home.

But my father would have none of it. He stared at me as if I repulsed him and said, You have done me a great wrong, stay out of my sight, and then he left me there in Tevkifhane Sokak.

Dottie was about to speak and Osman said, Wait, gently barring her lips with his index finger. Don't say anything yet. I'm almost finished.

Incredibly, the inspector was deeply affected by my rejection and abandonment. He did his best to comfort me and, perhaps to ease his guilt for his complicity in my situation, he personally assumed responsibility for my welfare. By now it was late in the day and the city was about to be placed under curfew. He sent for a guard to take me to the police canteen where I was given tea and something to eat and after a while the inspector himself came and escorted me out of the building and drove me home through the deserted streets. I looked out the window at the police car's flash of blue light through the emptiness and felt nostalgia for the silence of my innocence. The inspector tried to talk to me in a sincere way. What are you studying at school? What they tell me to, I answered sullenly. What's your goal? he asked. What do you want to make of yourself? I had never really thought about it and I said I want to write books. Ah, he said, very good. What kind of books? When I said poetry he seemed disappointed, when I said science fictions he seemed to think this was an excellent idea. Don't worry, he said as he dropped me off in front of our building, your father will have calmed down by now and realized his mistake. You'll see. Everything will be fine.

I was very grateful for the inspector's sympathy but he was wrong. Despite my mother's pleading, my father refused to allow me to return to our flat. I was banished to my grandparent's apartment, one floor below, and permitted to finish the semester at Robert College but then sent away to school in London after Ramazan. London wasn't so bad but compared to life in Istanbul the city lacked energy and joy. I rode the ferry once to Calais and back but couldn't even read the *Guardian* I had bought at the terminal and the water was ugly. After I matriculated, I was allowed to return to Istanbul to enter university. Like every other student from the city, I live at home, but home still means my grandparents' flat. The difference is, now it's my choice to stay with my grandparents. I will never live with my father again. It's very strange, of course. I see my mother and brothers and sisters all the time and our relationship is normal. I see my father too, but only in passing. We do not speak. We have never reconciled. Does he forgive me? What am I to think? Do I forgive him? You understand—I cannot. But I can tell you, your world fills with pain when you find it impossible to forgive your father, your worst suspicions about life confirmed.

Despite his daring behavior the night of her birthday party, Osman's boldness had receded to something more gentle and patient. They dated in a mannerly, cerebral fashion, chaste and sweet, with guarded hearts and cautious optimism, for less than two months, tacitly avoiding their respective friends, not secretively but perhaps selfishly, and she had never done these things before—taken his hand into hers and held it, thrown her arm around his neck to kiss him fully, with a fevered eagerness that seemed to blot out her mind. With their lips pressed together, in the back of his throat he began to laugh, a tender chuckling that seemed to express to her another type of fondness, as if he were offering a caress not just to the fact of *her*, but to the reality of *them*.

What? she whispered, releasing just enough pressure to let him speak without separating her mouth from his. You should kiss me again, she said, encouraged by the approach of twilight, and they embraced until the ferry docked in Besiktas, the hillsides rising above the coast snowy with pink-flowering Judas trees.

CHAPTER TWENTY-THREE

She let him know that in the morning she had a swim meet with her school team and shouldn't stay out late and when he said he would come to cheer her on she told him, Sorry, no men allowed.

They walked along the shoreline of the silvery Bosphorus, its surface quilted with spangles, and she fancied each gleam off the water a knowing complicitous wink in her direction, an affirmation of the newfound full-ness in her heart. Following the promenade below the gardens of Yildiz Park, they turned eventually back into the city to Ortakoy, to the cafés where everyone they knew could be found on a Friday night, wedged like electrons around the sticky nuclei of little tables, playing chess or backgammon, strumming acoustic guitars, sipping tea, floating in the heat of laughter and conversation, arguments and prophecy delivered with outlandish gravity.

Sometimes she and Osman would meet up in Ortakoy on weekends but would never arrive together as they did tonight. They climbed the stairs above a gift shop to a café named Gizgi, a preferred hangout, a tiny place with only ten tables, all low to the ground. Two of the tables were pulled together nearby a third occupied by Yesho and Jacqueline, hosting an invasion of older boys whom the girls seemed to be snubbing—or vice versa. They were Osman's friends, she saw, Karim among them, and Osman greeted them warmly and wedged into their circle. Most were university students she didn't recognize, not the usual pack of lycée puppies taunted by her brazen girlfriends, who yanked her down between them with a theatrical sense of urgency.

Uh-oh, said Yesho, murmuring but sounding dire, waggling her head side to side with misgiving—perhaps teasing, perhaps not. The minute you walk in with this guy, I see it in your eyes.

Jacqueline leaned forward and tilted her head away from the boys, looking past Dottie to Yesho, nodding agreement if not approval. She is in love, yes? she said, speaking behind her cupped hand. Oh my God. Terrible.

Yes, Yesho concurred. Terrible.

Dottie laughed without admitting anything and tried to accustom herself to Yesho's new look, her haystack thatch of yam-colored hair dyed back to its original raven black and cut à la Cleopatra, her forehead a full chop of bangs, helmetlike swoops on each side of her chin, the effect pushed to its extreme with kohl-lined eyes, fake eyelashes, and butterfly blue shadow, glossed lips, a half-buttoned gauze blouse over a red sports bra, gold harem pants—a performance that had earned Yesho a new sobriquet from Elena—Queen of the Vile. (And where was Elena? Dottie wondered. Still with family at synagogue?) As for Jacqueline, she seemed to be firing back at Yesho with a Parisian dominatrix fantasy, mostly done in leather—miniskirt, thigh-high boots, elbow-length gloves, studded biker's jacket over a black camisole, black lipstick and nails, a beret atop her lengthening Goldilocks curls. To Dottie, tonight they both seemed trapped in the flamboyance of their provocations, since the boys weren't paying the slightest attention to either of them. Even Osman seemed to have defected to the island of male indifference, and she felt a twinge of peevishness at the sudden push of distance between them, realizing that in all likelihood he had arranged to meet his friends here tonight.

For a moment she looked around, until her eyes met Karim's, mercurial and sunken with permanent suspicion yet pooled deep with a desire she could not fail to notice, and she averted her gaze from his before he misunderstood her curiosity as encouragement—she had chosen Osman, hadn't she?—and lowered her head, intrigued but uneasy. Except for Karim, she knew not one of them by name, and none appeared to be card-carrying members of the *entel* crowd, the chums she would expect Osman to rendezvous with on a Friday night to discuss books and art and music. A few of them had grown the thin ear-to-ear beards of the imams—strange but okay, Turkish men had a fetish for facial hair—but the bumpkin clothes, chosen without any deference to style, and crude haircuts like you get when you're a child, and just the mood, there was something about the mood she found bothersome.

Where's Elena? she asked, and Yesho sat up straight and said loudly that Elena had left because Karim and his friends had insulted her.

Seriously? said Dottie, and Yesho told her, Don't play so innocent, exchanging smirks with a boy who looked over at her. Yes, seriously. Because she is a Jew.

Jacqueline, still whispering, interjected to declare it was Elena's own fault, unable to hold her tongue when the boys, immersed in politics, found themselves suddenly being made fun of. Hey, ayatollah, Elena had badgered them. Ayatollah, hey—when you are going to Afghanistan? So they say dirty kike, Zionist bitch, explained Jacqueline, and she leave.

You know very well why this is disaster, said Yesho, dropping her voice again so the boys would not overhear. Osman, he is a Muslim.

But this objection made no sense to Dottie; almost everyone in Turkey was a Muslim, devout or not, yet the only religion she had ever known Osman to practice was as an Atatürkçu, a follower of Kemalism, which made him a rather ordinary Istanbullus. He was committed to progress (or so she thought, until his rant about the mayor) and secularism and the enlightened modernizing ideals of Mustafa Kemal Atatürk, the man she had heard her father describe as the greatest revolutionary of the twentieth century. The Turks spoke of Atatürk as a god, though you could say whatever you wanted about God. Osman a Muslim? Hardly . . . at least not with any apparent level of allegiance. Osman liked his beer and raki and cognac, and she had never seen him enter a mosque, or prostrate himself toward Mecca when the muezzins called out *ezan* from their minarets five times each day, and his regard for females was nothing, she could report firsthand, if not healthy, liberated from the absurd sanctions of Islam.

What are you saying, said Dottie. You're a Muslim yourself!

323

Yes, of course, said Yesho, technically we are all Muslims, but not like these Anatolian shepherds, who want to dominate the woman and keep everybody ignorant and throw us backward. You have been in my country long enough to understand.

You can't possibly be talking about Osman, she said, but Yesho snorted and rolled her eyes and shrugged as if to say, Wait and see.

Coup, coup, coup, said Jacqueline like a shrieking bird. She was not born to suffer the disaffection of men. I am bored with this coup. Six years and they can't shut up about the coup, and she lit a cigarette and stood up, exhaling a beam of smoke at the university students, who leered back at her audacity, eyes violent with lust, and went to the other end of the room to flirt with a German hippie, one of the regulars at Gizgi, playing a guitar.

They are stupid, these boys, said Yesho, obviously too impassioned to care that Jacqueline was abandoning them. They don't want to be Turks. Turks like Israel. Why not? The Arabs are no good for either of us. These boys dream to be Saudi or Afghani or something uncivilized. They want to hate. And don't tell me nonsense about head scarves. This is a trick to make all the women live under a black sheet. I can't believe, you know, that Osman join this stupid group. *What group?* interrupted Dottie, but her friend was not listening. Temper rising, Yesho spoke directly to the student who kept staring at her with undisguised contempt. Hey, you stupid boy, she said, parroting the opinion of her father, a colonel in the army. Who are the humans whose rights we are abusing? We don't abuse true humans, only animals.

Yesho, my God! Dottie protested.

The discussion among the university students stopped and they glowered like stage villains at the girls' table until, a moment later, Karim smiled, his hollow-cheeked expression black with ridicule, looked back at his friends, and said in his high-pitched voice, Excuse me, did someone hear a whore speaking? and so the feud escalated, Yesho and Karim trading slander and imprecations in English and Turkish, several of the other boys enjoining the battle while Osman, who would not look over at Dottie, appeared moribund, seemingly dazed by the cannon bursts of hostility, lost between factions.

324

And then like falling dominoes the *chirr* of conversations throughout the café went silent with the spreading awareness of a pair of newcomers looming a step inside the doorway. Two brawny gendarmes exuding a cocky sense of authority began working their way down the line of tables to check IDs, their boots resounding on the wooden floor, their hands outstretched like mendicants demanding alms, a harassment of the city's youth that routinely meant you were sent home if you were unable to prove who you were.

Which everyone in the club was able to do except, for some inexplicable reason, Osman, who riffled through his shoulder bag and dug through his pockets but could not find his government registration card. Dottie, waving her American passport at the police, tried in vain to vouch for him, then insisted she would go along too when it became clear that the police, each with a hand clawed on Osman's shoulders, seemed intent on arresting him. He turned once to look at her, signaling with a jerk of his head no, his eyes warning her not to get involved, but she had not been raised to accede to a position of helplessness in the world.

This isn't right, she said to Yesho. Is this what you were defending?

Calm down, said Yesho, unchastened. It's normal. It's no problem. It's his own fault, yes?

What has he done? she demanded, bounding to her feet, her eyes briefly pleading with the two tables of hapless students until she understood how cowed and useless they were and she turned away with a grimace of disappointment, shadowing the police to the door, the agglutinated Turkish words tumbling awkwardly into her mouth from the top of her throat. Where are you taking him? He's my boyfriend. He did nothing wrong. He lives near Sultanahmet. I will take him home.

Osman stopped, his expression desolate with resignation, and looked slowly around, over her head, back into the café, to tell Karim to please accompany her back to Uskudar but by now her defiance was full-spirited and she could not hear this request as anything but an empty patriarchal mannerism—*I can take care of myself*, she seethed, spinning around to reject Karim's assistance—and followed the police as they nudged Osman ahead onto the stairs and down to the street. They marched to their patrol car and she skipped in front of them to ask their names and ranks, her hand

325

fishing in her camera bag for a pen and scrap of paper. Osman turned on his heels and rasped, *Dottie, go home, please, I will telephone you. Please,* and she said, *This is such bullshit.* He saw her begin to pull her camera out and commanded her to put it away. *I'm going to call my father,* she said. The police opened the rear door and Osman, as he ducked into the backseat, met her eyes fiercely and said, *Dottie, no. Dottie? Listen, promise me you will not do that,* and then the car was splitting the flow of pedestrians as she scribbled the number of the license plate on the inside of a matchbook and a hand was pulling her arm and she wheeled around infuriated to confront whoever it was and there was Karim.

Come, he said. I will take you back to Uskudar.

She ran into the street, flagging taxis until one stopped, and Karim, nonplussed, scurried in beside her. She told the driver to follow the police, but the patrol car had disappeared up the avenue, and she said she wanted to be taken to the nearest gendarmerie. Karim, finding his voice, asked her sardonically what she planned to do, and Dottie said, I'm going to get him back.

Please, said Karim, you cannot understand. These police, they are like criminals. The regime imprisons and tortures thousands of people. They do what they please.

No, she said, you don't understand.

The taxi dropped them at the Ortakoy police station, where Karim pulled her aside and tried to persuade her that her attitude was dangerous, asking to get them all in more trouble than she could guess, that the best thing to do until morning was what Osman had asked them to do, and she stared back at him wordlessly and then shook free from his grasp and went inside.

Behind the front desk the duty officer, an older, jowly man with benevolent eyes and a droopy salt-and-pepper mustache, greeted her as if her presence before him was an unthinkable pleasure, and she said, Please, can you help me, and explained her situation. My dear, he said graciously, I can tell you for certain, your friend is not here. She produced the matchbook on which she had written the number of the patrol car and he studied it for a moment and handed it back. Not our boys, he said. This must be a Besiktas registration.

She thanked him effusively for his kindness and left, whisking past Karim-No-Balls, Karim-the-Pigeon-Hearted, son of Abu Jellyfish, as she stepped, waving, back into the street, yet hesitating before she closed the taxi's door, her voice cold as she asked Karim if he was coming. He came but sat pressed against the door like a bony mannequin, more high-strung than virile, this guy, not venturing to speak, his eyes straight ahead and she offered him nothing. At the Besiktas station she paid the driver and dashed for the entrance but Karim outpaced her, blocking the way, and they looked into each other's angry eyes until she, haughtily, said, Well?

Do you know what you are doing?

Do you? she challenged.

Okay, so, he said, tentative, then summoning enough nerve or pride to open the glass door. *Allahu akbar.*

We'll see how great, she said, mostly to herself, and Karim, following behind, hissed at the back of her head, You will not be blasphemous. Please.

Inside the public area of the station, a blaring television with snowy reception was tuned to a soap opera. Ordinary people sat crowded together on a bench, watching along with the gendarmes. This time the officer on night duty performed predictably, his arrogance flaring, tersely explaining that the Ortakoy streets were beyond his station's jurisdiction and he could assure her that the license number she had copied down was registered to the Ortakoy station.

Excuse me, sir, she said with stiff politeness. Someone is lying.

The accusation had the effect of shifting the policeman's regard from Dottie to Karim, who appeared jolted into servility by the gendarme's scathing eyes. Who are you? he barked. Why are you here with this disrespectful child?

Thank you, sir, Karim said, tugging at Dottie as he retreated. We are leaving, sir. Thank you. May God protect you.

Go to bed, little girl, said the duty officer, satisfied.

They argued during the ride back to Ortakoy, Karim unable to convince her that her persistence would doom them both to a night in jail or worse, but she thought such an outcome ludicrous. She was a girl, had committed no crime, she was an American coming to the aid of an innocent friend.

He accused her of astonishing naïveté and she called him frightened, a challenge that seemed to spur him out of his humiliation directly into a show of crazed recklessness, as though he had willed his sanity into the background in order to prove himself to her.

With Dottie hurrying to keep up, this time Karim was first inside the Ortakoy station, shouting irrationally and demanding Osman's return, slapping the counter for emphasis, the police like twitching alley cats watching a wounded bird, their amazement progressively more lethal.

It's him, Dottie cried out. There behind the desk smoking a cigarette with the older duty officer was one of the gendarmes who had taken Osman into custody. *Why did you lie to me?* With an embarrassed smirk, the previously avuncular officer answered her question by offering her his upraised hands, as if to show there was no blood on them, but the younger gendarme smiled in disbelief at their impertinence. He ordered Karim to show identification. Karim remained insolent; casting an I-told-you-so look at Dottie, he plucked his ID from his wallet and tossed it on the counter at the gendarme, who snatched up the card, glanced at it homicidally before ripping it in half and throwing the pieces at Karim's inflamed, unflinching face. At the same moment, Dottie had placed her passport with its red diplomatic cover on the counter where it was shoved back to her, unopened.

Just tell us, okay, she said, undeterred. Where is he? and with no answer forthcoming, issued an illogical ultimatum. Okay, she said, fine. We're not leaving until we see him.

Suit yourself, said the duty officer, retiring into weary impassivity. Wait outside.

So he's here, isn't he? said Dottie, as though she had managed to hoodwink them into a confession, but the order was merely repeated—Wait outside. When she said she would not, the younger gendarme came around the counter forcefully, reaching for her, and she shouted in English, *Keep your hands off me, you asshole,* and when Karim, burning through a final spasm of wildness, lurched forward to intervene she realized her mistake and heard her voice go screechy, *Okay, stop, don't, we'll wait outside,* wrestling Karim with her toward the door before the gendarme could latch on to either of them.

My God, she said, the two of them back out on the street, Dottie in a state of nervous hilarity. Holy shit.

Air whistled harshly in and out of Karim's flared nose and he looked at her severely and said, I don't understand you. He flicked his hand with a dismissive gesture. There is a teahouse across the street, Karim said. We will wait there.

Oh, she said, regaining her composure with a quick look over at the shop, the bronzed aura of sanctuary captured behind the glowing squares of paned windows, candles on the tables, a scattering of friendly-looking adults. Subdued, she looked back at Karim sheepishly, her instinct like a clock's alarm, prodding her to reverse roles, but when she tried to transfer over the leadership she had assumed earlier, he would not have it.

How long should we wait? she asked, and when he answered, As long as you wish, she had to admit the possibility that she had no idea what to do.

They sat opposite each other at a table next to the windows with a clear view across the street to the gendarmerie, watching one another fidget, Karim's legs as restless as her fingers crab-walking from spoon to napkin, waiting for their tea, sipping the bulb-shaped glasses self-consciously when it came, their exchange no more than an awkward release of monosyllables until Karim, straightening his spine, cleared his throat, confessing he was ashamed to have forgotten that a woman could be as strong, or stronger, than a man. My own mother, he said, is like this, like you . . . but of course, I should say, nothing like you.

Really? said Dottie eagerly, wanting to relax into a bath of peaceful conversation, be a boy and girl together, just talking, as this night was meant to be. Tell me about her. Are you Moroccan? Someone told me that.

No, he said, his father was Moroccan, but Karim himself, by matrilineal tradition, was considered, at least by the government, a Turk, a citizen. Dottie asked why his father had come to Turkey and Karim, his closed body like a fist unclenching, now seemed to appreciate her interest and was not averse to sharing his family's story of broken traditions and unrealistic expectation and the loss that invariably accompanies change.

My father came from an old family, respected, but not very powerful, Karim began, but immediately she interrupted.

What did they do?

They were tradespeople.

Of what?

Okay, he said. Cooking oil, cooking fuel . . . for many years charcoal; afterward, gas. I mean to say, bottled gas.

Where?

Where?

Where did he live? Like, a village? A city?

A neighborhood in Casablanca.

Oh, she said, her left hand splayed below her throat, as if she had received bad news.

What is wrong?

No, nothing's wrong, she said quickly and her face expanded with a playful smile. Pearls of candlelight swam in her eyes. I'll tell you later. What year was this?

My father's family has always lived in this place, said Karim, puzzled by Dottie's conspicuous reaction to his father's birthplace. No one can remember when they did not live there.

Okay, I'll tell, she said. It's possible that our fathers have met.

The world is not this small, said Karim, acting as if he would be horrified if indeed it were, and when they compared dates, it seemed improbable that their fathers' paths had crossed.

It's not like it would mean anything anyway, she said. Go on. I want to know more.

Throughout the centuries, the family was the family, each generation the same to the one before and the one after, Karim continued in a didactic tone she associated with the self-importance of university students. But the war, the Second World War, he said, switching to Turkish when he was unsure how to express a word or idea in English, had for the first time in the family's memory made them prosperous, and so his father, firstborn of the postwar generation, was viewed as an opportunity, a chance to lift the family to a long-desired level of wealth and status. His life, in other words, was theirs; the decisions, theirs. And then, of course, he rebelled. Perhaps it would have been so anyway, said Karim, but the family saw his father only as a lottery ticket for influence and . . . and (he paused, searching for the word) esteem. No longer would they be simple merchants; they would slip through the back door of the elite class by sending their children to the best private schools, then overseas to Europe or America to be educated—they did not understand this, you see—in a manner that would cast their children out from the family, far beyond their ability to be a living part of the family organism, to be anything, I suppose you must say, than—she stopped him to look up the words in her Turkish/English pocket dictionary and offered, *cherished phantoms?* and he continued, nodding uncertainly.

Yes, they would remit money home. Yes, they would visit on holidays. Yes, the family could boast of their accomplishments, but the family would still be required to sell its cooking oil and know its place in society and not imagine that its place was any higher than where it was. So that is my father's story, Karim said, and Dottie said, Well, what happened?

What happened? said Karim. My father studied in America and made his PhD and became an engineer. He came to work in Turkey. He met my mother.

Where? How? asked Dottie, anticipating a much different narrative than this, Karim's underfed provincial look suggesting a story more familiar with poverty than middle-class affluence and professional careers.

I feel you are like the *devlet*—you want to know everything, Karim said. Why?

Why not? she chirped. Maybe I'm a spy. Or just nosy and superficial.

Maybe you are a superficial spy, he said, the first joke he had ever made in her presence. She marveled at his smile, how disturbingly beautiful it was, perhaps because of its rarity or its surge upward into his eyes, soaking through their hardness, and she said, Oh, that's so much better, you should smile more. But come on, she said, tell me the rest, and Karim told her his father, when he finished his doctoral studies in the United States, applied for jobs in many places in the world, none of them Morocco, and eventually accepted a position in Turkey, because it was an Eastern country that was modern and Islamic, but not too modern and not too Islamic for his taste, which had been corrupted—Karim used the word *sickened*—by the West.

This was many years ago, said Karim, that my father came to Erzurum, to build roads and bridges throughout the countryside, and it was there I was born. Do you know it? Erzurum?

No, she said, but she had a classmate from Erzurum, who told her that wolves came out of the surrounding forest and wandered through the campus of the university, and Karim confirmed that yes, this was true. Yes, many types of wolves, he added cryptically.

How long have we been here? she wondered out loud. Should we order more tea?

Summoning the waiter, Karim looked at his wristwatch and declared he had a plan. Let me ask you, please, he said to her. Do you have money? I mean, dollars, and she gave him the twenty she kept hidden in her wallet for emergencies, which he then gave to the waiter, with instructions to take a tray of tea and the "gift" across the street to the gendarmes. And tell them, he said, Osman's friends are waiting.

I should have thought of this before, Karim said after the waiter left to conscript one of the kitchen boys for the mission.

Yeah, of course, me too, said Dottie, impressed by Karim's belated maneuver, right out of her father's playbook. I wasn't thinking.

And you? he said, his eyes mirroring hers, lambent with flame, her uneasy attraction to him like a radio's poor reception, the signal wandering in and out through a soup of static created by Osman. I thought you were an American but your passport is red.

Red, she explained, was the color for diplomats and their families. Then she sat back as if to see him more completely, her head tilting with consternation when he asked who's daughter she was, the question spoken in English yet she had shuddered at his use of the Arabic phrasing, wondering if it were possible that Karim too had been enlisted somehow by her father.

Why are you asking me that? she said, attempting to sound nonchalant but frowning with suspicion.

Because you are asking the same of me, he said, perturbed. Is it not allowed?

Sorry, Dottie said automatically, telling him her father was posted at the embassy in Ankara. She was unable to rid herself of the nagging thought that some relationship existed between her father and Karim, given her dad's spidery habit of weaving webs. I know this might sound weird, she said. You don't work for my father, do you?

Is it possible to work for your father? said Karim, his interest sharpening. You mean, as a driver? Or . . . what?

I don't know, she said. Maybe.

With your permission. I wanted to ask about your father . . . I mean to say, before. At the café. What does your father do?

I don't know really, she said, reluctant to pursue this line of inquiry and uncomfortable with the intensity of Karim's eyes upon her, inquisitive and mesmerizing. He's a diplomat. He talks to people.

Tonight, he said, before you and Osman came to the café, the Jew—

Don't say the Jew, said Dottie, bristling. Her name's Elena.

Yes, okay. That one.

What's my name? she needled. I've never heard you say it.

Dodi.

Thank you, said Dottie.

That one was bragging about your father, to make us feel weak.

What did she say?

She said your father goes to Afghanistan to kill Communists. Could this be true?

Of course not, she said with a supercilious guffaw. That's so incredibly insane.

Yes, I myself said to the Jew she is lying, but this other girl, the French *yabanci,* confirms the Jew is speaking the truth.

Her name is Elena. Stop saying the Jew.

But your father. It is true about him, yes? The Americans are in Afghanistan against the Soviets. This is no secret.

How would Elena and Jacqueline know what's true or not true about my father? said Dottie, infuriated with Elena for spreading a specious rumor and with Karim for his unacceptable display of prejudice. Do diplomats in suits and ties go around shooting people?

There was a missile, yes?

No.

I am sorry to have bothered you with the Jew's lie.

She bucked in her chair and said, Stop saying that.

I was hoping this story was true. If such a story were true, I would take your father's hand to kiss and pray for God to protect him. Tell me, can your father help me to reach Afghanistan?

You don't listen. Say Jew one more time and I'm leaving.

Really? To go where? We are waiting for your boyfriend, yes?

Enraged by his smugness she said, Say it one more time and I swear—

Forgive me, he said, his smile this time patronizing and not beautiful. I did not know this girl's name. Elena.

Forget it, she said, but her mood had turned precarious. She forgave him and then changed her mind and then changed it again, her emotions seesawing with exhaustion and the telltale cramping low in her stomach. She wanted everything at once—to cry, fight, sleep, scream, telephone Daddy, smoke hashish with the lycée boys, see Osman, be held, be alone, be hateful and be in love and be mad at Karim or maybe make out with him down by the water. Karim's jealousy was shockingly transparent, the way his lips had curled around *boyfriend,* the word she had blurted out to the gendarmes to try to get them to listen to her, but perhaps Osman himself would no more accept or validate this word than the police. Or, Jesus H Christ, her father, whom she had once overheard telling a colleague he loved Turkey because it was impossible to kill one billion Muslims—whatever he meant by that, other than his completely irrational loathing of Islamic people, another reason she found it difficult to believe he had become a comrade-in-arms with Afghans, despite the incriminating fact that her father was committed heart and soul to the downfall of communism, that he carried the scars of that endless battle on his own flesh. She could not calculate the slippery algebra of enemies (if the enemy of my enemy is also my enemy, then *what?*) to predict her father's actions and responses in the world, except as they applied to her, and certainly, absolutely, to her use of *boyfriend,* that word she could not yet imagine a place for in the reality that was the two of them, father and daughter, where even the word *mother* had a radioactive existence. The movie, already in her head, was, *Um, Daddy, I have a present for you, for those hang-ups of yours. Muslim boy. We're going steady. Check out this cool abaya he gave me to wear. Peekaboo, Daddy-o.*

They both turned their attention to the aproned kitchen boy returning from across the street, coming to their table to deliver a note, which Karim unfolded and read. What's it say? she asked, and he showed it to her—*Go home*—and she said, What should we do? Perhaps we should go home, Karim said, but she wanted to stay and he said, then, for a while longer he would stay as well. But it is pointless, you should realize, he added.

She had a moment's lucidity, a revelation that she and Karim were incompatible, irreversibly and until the end of time incompatible, yet she did not like this feeling of permanent volatility and, grasping for common ground, tried to switch the conversation back around to his own family.

Your mother, she said, reaching across the table toward his hands, an unconscious but sisterly gesture, a spontaneous coaxing touch, which she saw too late was unwelcome. You haven't told me anything about your mother.

She is a very pious woman, said Karim, his face darkening as he withdrew his hands from the table to his lap. Not like my father, who salutes the *ezan* with a bottle of whiskey. And not like your friends. Why do you choose whores and Jews for friends?

Excuse me, said Dottie. That's so obnoxious.

Excuse me, please, he said. You are Christian, yes?

Catholic.

Ah, I mean to say, a Roman. And in the eyes of believers an infidel. He saw she dressed with modesty and did not behave in a manner he found impious. Please, I respect you, Karim said, although I do not live like you, nor do I want to live like you. But your friends, they bring disgrace to your reputation. You should understand they make you less than you are.

Why are you getting angry? she asked, angry herself, and she struggled to smother the incendiary heat of her own temper, one of the pieces of her personality she did not own, or refused to own, because these parts were not her, or not herself, or made her feel like she wasn't herself, and they did not exist until they did, rising to the surface as her true self sank below, and afterward they were just gone, like a dream, which is what she told herself they were. Selves that seemed real until you woke up, or until, like a saint's visitation, God began speaking.

Angry? No. I am giving advice. Because I respect you.

Okay, she said. Sometimes Yesho doesn't make it easy to be her friend. But it's really none of your business who my friends are.

The impure behavior of women, he told her, was the business of all men.

You need to get over yourself, she said. What's your problem? Are you some kind of religious freaks, you and your friends?

You do not know my country or my faith well enough to say these things, said Karim. The military and the elites are the ones in Turkey who are illiterate and backward, not the religious people. The parliament—filled with idiots. They believe people are not mature enough to make their own democracy. For the *devlet*, religious tolerance is a crime. Tolerance spreads the disease of democracy throughout society. The *devlet* says we want to destroy democracy by asking for too much of it. Tell me, how can you have too much democracy? The *devlet* insults my intelligence, and these girls you call your friends are the enemies of God. These girls could not walk the streets of Erzurum as they walk the streets of Ortakoy. The faithful would strike them with stones.

Tolerant! she said. Is that what you think you are?

God willing, I would throw the first stone.

I cannot figure out, she said, why you and Osman are friends. He's not like you.

How do you know what Osman is? said Karim. You are a *yabanci*. How do you know what any Turkish man is? You are Christian.

Nice guys are the same, she said. It doesn't matter what else they are. Remembering Yesho's inadvertent and unanswered disclosure, she asked Karim to tell her why Osman had joined his group.

What group are you speaking of?

Your religious club or whatever it is.

Religious groups are forbidden by the *devlet,* he said. Maybe you did not know. There is no group. We are Mehmets who served together, he said, but she did not understand what he meant.

Recruits. In Turkey we call them Mehmets. We are friends from the army.

What!

Could it be Turkish men do not find it necessary to tell the girlfriend everything?

I can't believe it, she said. Osman, a soldier?

Every Turkish boy must give one year to the military. Three years ago, he told her, they were conscripted and sent to Diyarbakir, to fight against Kurdish insurgents. We killed no one—Osman, me—but I will confess, he said, we were often cruel. What choice did we have? Osman, who had just returned from England, was unhappy in the army, said Karim, but he himself discovered something he had not anticipated, that he enjoyed a soldier's life very much.

But you left, she said.

Because the Turkish army is no good, he said bitterly, building steam for a tirade, stabbing his finger into the table. Because I cannot agree with their mission. Because I admire the PKK.

I don't know what that is, she said.

Of course not, he said, continuing. They are the Kemalist nightmare. Because the only mission I agree with is jihad.

Lost me again, she said.

Because it is the duty of the faithful to recapture Jerusalem. Because I admire the mujahideen. Because I admire Abdullah Öcalan. Hezbollah. The Algerians. George Washington and Mister Lincoln. Abu Nidal. I admire Malcolm X. The PLO. The Malaysians and the Vietnamese. I admire them all because they submit to no one.

I'm sorry, she said, finding his harangue tedious and fatiguing. Go to Afghanistan, whatever. What the fuck's stopping you?

Fuck! he sputtered, his eyes livid, bulging. You say this unclean word to me, *fuck*?

Yes, fuck, she mimicked him, wickedly. Fuck fuck fuck.

You wish to fuck? This is what you are saying?

He intercepted her wrist as she tried to slap him, tightening his grip, her hand frozen in the air in front of his face, and she did not know how long the two of them remained like this, frozen in an eruption of hatred, or how long Osman had stood outside on the street looking in,

337

his eyes frozen wide with alarm, watching their wretched little skit of ugliness unfold until she began kicking at Karim under the table and Osman rapped his knuckles on the glass and in unison they jerked their warring faces toward the noise and there was Osman's head framed in a windowpane, his lower lip split and swollen, his own face thunderstruck with incomprehension, and how terrible, in the first hours of her first love, to feel her heart so clouded.

CHAPTER TWENTY-FOUR

She had been expected to dominate the five-hundred-meter freestyle against a field of more inexperienced swimmers, including a Turkish girl who swam spastically with her head above water, but frazzled by the vicissitudes of the day before, feeling puffy and sluggish, she finished an unprecedented fourth in the race and first in humiliation, a poor loser who could not bear the stain of defeat, deaf to the consoling efforts of her teammates, abandoned at poolside as she stormed off to the locker room to shower alone and flee their pity. Then she returned to her room in the dormitory, forgoing lunch to flop on her bed, half asleep and half on edge, until the house mother knocked on her door to report that her father was trying to get in touch and her mother had called again from the United States and someone else was waiting to speak to her right now.

She went down the hall to the telephone cubicle to take Osman's call, which began with congratulations for a victory that had never happened, though she did not tell him that, her thoughts still fixated on the shame she felt for being such a child, running out of the teahouse blubbering past a bewildered Osman calling her name and diving into the nearest taxi before he could reach her for an explanation—an opportunity that must then have fallen to Karim, and God only knows what he had said.

About last night, she said, offering a meek apology, but when he took too long to respond she thought, *Oh, God,* and asked, How's your lip?

My lip? It's nothing, he said. It's not what you think.

339

They hit you.

Not at all.

We should file a complaint.

To complain about what? he asked, making light of his arrest. It was nothing serious. The police are like mountain dogs that guard the sheep against the wolves. But it's not bad, like before, when they would bite anyone. These days they lift their heads to growl and go back to sleep.

He had not yet thanked her for coming to his rescue and she held her breath waiting, wondering if he understood he could depend on her whatever the circumstance and, hungry for both his gratitude and forgiveness, she apologized again for her juvenile performance at the teahouse, for quarreling with his friend, for running away without a word, and she asked what Karim had to say and he laughed and told her Karim and the gendarmes had said the same thing, Your girlfriend is a pain in the ass.

Very funny, she sniffed. Is that what you think, too?

I think you are this girl in the American comic book. Wonder Woman.

Wonder Woman has black hair.

Of course. I am thinking of Supergirl.

I'm not the kind of person who can just stand there.

Of course.

Not like your so-called friends.

Of course. But Dottie, you must promise. If you see the gendarmes take me, don't interfere.

No, she said, hardheaded. Why?

Please. It's very complicated. Very sensitive.

To appease him, she agreed, and again waited for his gratitude, until finally she turned petulant and wanted to know why Osman had never told her he had served in the army. He said of course he didn't think it was important and she said, But that's why you and Karim are friends, right? and he was silent for a moment until he said, Yes, that's right, and she wanted him to tell her why he had joined the group.

Unlike Karim, he did not deny its existence but he paused before answering and his voice became guarded. How do you know about the group? he asked and she told him Yesho had mentioned it. Okay, he said, how does she know?

I have no idea, said Dottie. Is it supposed to be a secret?

Yes, he sighed, explaining a certain level of secrecy was necessary. He had accepted Karim's invitation to join because its members were his friends, bonded by the same hardships from their days together in the army, and he thought they had an interesting perspective on the nation, although he did not share many of their opinions.

Opinions on what? she asked, and he said, Life, but she had more questions. Religion? and he answered, Sometimes. Afghanistan? Sometimes. Worried, she asked him, You don't want to go to fight in Afghanistan, do you? and he laughed and told her, Definitely not. Never.

She could not understand why the government would outlaw guys with little else to do but sit around bullshitting about life and he revealed that the *devlet* had invented an official description—illegal Koran school—for a group like Karim's, a revelation that she grappled with, but he anticipated her question before she could form it and told her to stop fantasizing that he was an extremist or a militant or any brand of fanatic.

Can I trust you? he said.

Yes! she answered, as if it pained her to be asked such a question.

Then you must trust me as well, he said. Believe what I tell you, not what you see. Not what you think you see.

More than anything she wanted to say she had fallen in love with him but the sentence came out haltingly: *I think. I might.*

You think? he teased, feigning dismay. Dottie, he said. When I dream, I dream of you, I dream only of our happiness.

The relief descended through her muscles like a blissful sedative and she returned to her room to sleep soundly throughout the afternoon, waking slowly and lusciously until her mind whipped back to the other thing she had forgotten to do after speaking with Osman—*call Daddy.*

Which was never easy. First, there were the chauvinistic Turkish operators to overcome, their deliberate misunderstanding of her careful pronunciations. Secondly, now that her mother had jumped ship and returned to the States, if she couldn't get an answer at her father's villa in Ankara she had to call the embassy switchboard, which would connect her to her father's longtime secretary, Mary Beth, his selfless appendage. She was a camp follower dragged around the world by Dottie's father and who would never put her through to him but instead ask for a call-back number and Dottie would have to sit tight wherever she was waiting for the phone to ring, which meant don't call Daddy without a book to read. Dottie dressed in jeans and a T-shirt and walked barefoot down the hall to the telephone cubicle and dialed his villa—no answer—and then called the embassy switchboard and left a message and began to concentrate on a chapter in her geometry textbook. Fifteen minutes later the telephone rang—*Hello, Kitten!*—and she said, Where are you, you sound far away? and he told her Belgrade, and she said, That's Yugoslavia, right? Correct, he said, and she asked, Is it pretty? and he said, Not to my eyes.

When she asked what he was doing there, his answer was what she had come to expect from him: *Oh, you know. This and that. Prepare a few things. Make new friends, visit old friends.* Drumroll, please. *Piss on the graves of our enemies.* There you have it, Karim, she thought, the previous night's conversation still rattling around in her head. What Daddy does.

It's getting very interesting here, he said. There's a new sheriff in town. That suggests a certain rearrangement of the doable.

Daddy, she said in a tone she relied on to ignite his concern. Speaking of sheriffs.

What's wrong? he asked. What happened?

Do you know someone in the Turkish government I can make a report to about police brutality?

Whoa, back up. What's going on?

She possessed the teenage knack of extemporaneous editing, trimming or tweaking a story into a version more suitable for the ears of parents, omitting inconvenient details, understating relationships, transforming the primary colors of questionable behavior into blameless pastels. In this new and improved story, she arrived at the café with her girlfriends, Osman was demoted to this guy she knew, her attitude toward the police mellowed into ladylike behavior, Karim and his secret group banished from the cast of characters, and Osman's split lip just one consequence of a pummeling that might very well have sent a lesser man to the hospital.

Okay, he said, neither sharing her indignation nor dismissing it, a quality in her father she grudgingly respected, his habit of withholding comment or judgment until he was satisfied he had gathered up the available facts—an investigation that occasionally exposed a fault line in her own credibility—and he asked her to spell Osman's surname, promised her he would see what he could find out, and moved the conversation along to his original reason for calling.

He was catching a late flight back to Istanbul and would send a car in the morning to bring her to mass. After mass, whaddya say, he said, and his proposal had not lost a scintilla of its capacity to thrill her. Let's go sailing.

At the end of the month, school was out for the year and the dormitory echoed wistfully with the absence of her classmates, the Turkish girls scattered back to their families, leaving behind Dottie and a few remaining foreign students, excluding Jacqueline, who a week ago had returned to France with her mother for the summer. Dottie had weighed her father's invitation to move into his newly leased penthouse in Ankara (the villa had been shed when her mother left), but there were practical reasons (some actually discussable) not to, given his erratic travel schedule, her lack of friends in the capital (she'd be stuck with all the embassy snots glued to their parents, suffering their condescension toward all things Turkish), and most of all there was the tension she felt begin to ball in her stomach when she tried not to think about nights alone with him in the apartment, his trespass submerged in the invisible depths of her childhood underneath a sediment of her father's private confessions, more adamant than guilt-ridden, that *he loved her too much*. And yet he had his way still of easing into certain liberties she did not know how to prevent, or even how to measure as right or wrong or neither. Most of all, her unwillingness to be separated from Osman and the rapturous adventure of their secret (perhaps not so secret, she suspected) romance.

The problem was, one evening at the beginning of the summer after the surprise of her first solo sail, her father had minced his words, as though he had a plan, and the plan this time seemed designed to bait her into her own intimate world of subterfuge and deception—another one of his myriad games. He had distinctly not forbidden her from seeing Osman; instead, he had warned her away from getting too close. Too close? She would not ask whose privilege it was to define what might constitute the difference between close and too close. Where was the divide, Daddy, the threshold, the line not to be crossed?—somewhere he himself could not define. Too close to a boy meant what—the same as being too close to your father? If it was meant to mean the other thing, her emotions, the grafting of one heart to another, then her father's injunction against it had come too late.

After mass that Sunday morning, they had taxied north along the European coast, bypassing the more fashionable yachting centers to the south, to Altinkum, a sleepy fishing village with a public beach and a stupendously marvelous marina, now home port for her beloved twenty-six-foot *tirhandil* she had christened *Sea Nymph*, anchored in the pristine cove among a fleet of traditional *gulets* twice as large, which Dottie thought of as the *Sea Nymph's* harem of big sisters. They were identical to the *Nymph*, with the same smiling, sexy roundness of their classic lines and saucer-shaped hulls, feminine curves in every direction, large wooden rudders, the emphasis on style rather than cabin space, although her *tirhandil* was beak-nosed, double-ended, sloop-rigged, and sturdy as a dance floor, a luminous work of art and eminently seaworthy. Now, of course, they all had motors in them, the addiction of Turkish yachtsmen, who seemed to equate hoisting a sail with some type of punishment or masochism, but originally the *gulets* were sailing cargo boats transporting goods throughout the eastern Mediterranean since the Roman Empire, and the pedigree of the *tirhandils* was even more distinguished, descendants of the oldest style of vessel to ply the Aegean Sea, and she felt herself an heiress to this history, given license to indulge in endless role-playing fantasies—a female Argonaut pursued by Hercules, the Grand Vizier's most favored wife, handmaiden to a knight's lady. *Ladies and gentlemen, I give you* Dottie of Troy. Anybody but Io, poor girl, Zeus's bitch, turned into a fat cow to hide her from his wife Hera, more than a little vexed by Zeus's philandering. Hera sent a gadfly to torment the transformed Io, who plunged into the waterway that would be forever named for her inglorious swim—Bosphorus, the ancient Greek word for *cow's ford.*

But no one in these waters had ever seen a girl or woman mariner, and so her ownership and growing mastery of the *Sea Nymph* had made both Americans—the diplomat father and his captivating Turkish-speaking blonde-haired teenage daughter—instant celebrities in Altinkum. The Poseidon-like dockmaster himself insisted on rowing them out in his skiff to the *Sea Nymph*'s moorage, as he did that Sunday morning, and the moment she climbed aboard she felt what she would always feel on a sailboat, a sublime sense of newness, defying the physics of one's life on land. Always on the boat there was an inner breeze of excitement, a happy gratitude for the water and its strong promising scents, the *Nymph*'s proud sail set against the sliding panorama of facing continents and their ghostly empires, crusted one atop the other like gobs of paint on a giant canvas.

She was a quick study and impressed to learn how accomplished a sailor her father proved to be, his nautical skills acquired while growing up in Pennsylvania, a boy capsizing racing dinghies at a summer camp on Lake Erie, and later in college a member of the sailing club at Yale. Their initial weekend outings on the *Sea Nymph* were cautious, his lessons methodical. They quickly began to gain a feel for the boat, though, and increasingly comfortable with the clutter and pace of the sea traffic in the busy, busy Bosphorus, developing a sense for its shift of winds, teaching themselves how to read the riffles and eddies of the trickster currents. On their first sail together, they wobbled out of the harbor into the sweeping channel and then, with the wind on their stern, trimmed the sail—only the mainsheet, that first time—and galloped on the crystal blue racetrack south toward the surreal span of Bosphorus Bridge. Coming about in its cool shadow they threw themselves into the high-alert exercise of tacking back to Altinkum through an oncoming flotilla of tankers and cruise ships and warships, ferries and hovercraft, water taxis, fishing vessels, paddleboats, and the occasional psychotic windsurfer.

Each time he came to Istanbul to take her sailing they swooped a little farther south down the straits, below wooded hillsides violet with flowering jacarandas, past the yacht basin and the well-to-do crowds of Tarabya, perhaps docking in Kanlica on the Asian shore for a bowl of its famous yogurt, past the towered ruins and crenellated walls of the magical twin castles, Anadoluhisar and Rumelihisar—one each for Asia and Europe— the gates to the Black Sea, built by the conqueror Sultan Mehmet during his final siege of Constantinople in 1453. Then drifting past Arnavutkoy to admire its surviving wooden mansions, fire-spared relics of Ottoman aristocracy, perhaps stopping for a lunch of grilled *lufer,* back in season for the summer, at a waterfront *meyhane* in Bebek or Ortakoy, where on one sail they had arranged to pick up Elena, Jacqueline, and Yesho for the afternoon.

This turned out to be not the best idea: Elena, her colorless skin turning a greenish hue, was immediately seasick; Yesho, who had spent her lifetime plying the straits on the public ferries, was terrified by the petite *Sea Nymph,* afraid to move off her perch atop the cabin hatch; and Jacqueline pouted like a brat after Yesho, noticing Jacqueline pretzel her arms around behind her back to unclasp the top of her bikini, squawked that this wasn't St. Tropez, she'd start a riot, she'd get them all arrested, the police would rape them, what was she thinking? Jacqueline, her hands holding up the cups of her unfastened top, turned to play the wounded coquette with her father, batting her eyes for permission and Dottie could see, in his sunny expression of regret that poorly masked what he truly wanted, that he would die for a good long look at Jacqueline's pointy breasts, but thank God even Yesho, the Queen of the Vile, had enough sense to stop it.

That Sunday morning in June, the *poyraz,* like an old family servant, met them at the cove's entrance, its freshening kiss of wind a bolt of cool velvet drawn across her bare shoulders and the backs of her legs. She stood braced in the cockpit, commanding the wheel, while her father cut the motor—a tiny inboard diesel with a toyland *chug*—and raised the mainsail. The *Sea Nymph* took the wind abeam until they were midchannel, the Byzantine battlements of the castle Yoros straight off the bow. Her father told her to fall off and inched the boom out over the azure water and they went flying ahead in a sizzle of foam, south toward Istanbul, her father in the bow hoisting the jib, letting it billow out portside, wing and wing with the main, the *Nymph* in the prettiest of downwind canters.

She called forward in her happiest voice, *Where are we going?* And he answered, *To the sea, my captain. To the sea!* They plunged through the cresting wake of a naval cruiser like children on a rocking horse as the implacable elephantine mass of the other vessel flashed by, a Union Jack snapping in the wind off its stern. *Ah, our esteemed allies,* said her father. *Hail, Britannia.* Then he added what sounded like a curse in a language she had never heard and she asked what he was speaking. *Serbo-Croatian,* he told her and she said, *Oh, like Yugoslavian?* naturally assuming he had picked up a few phrases on his trip to Belgrade. *What did you say?*

I said, *Shit on your dog-faced queen,* and she feigned disapproval, saying, *Dad!* and into their banter he slipped a teaser—*This Balkans project. I may need you to give me a hand*—and how could she have known what he was suggesting.

They sailed past the ivory jewel box of the Ortakoy mosque and its twin minarets, the Bosphorus rolled out like a turquoise carpet between rival continents, bottomless only in its histories. Dottie could not conceive of a world more enchanted or generous in its offerings, and she never tired of being on the glorious water, in love with its ever-changing moods and peacock colors, and would not mind if she never touched ground again.

Soon the coastlines of Asia and Europe began to widen and swell outward, the minarets of Suleymaniye and the city's five hundred mosques shrinking into matchsticks off the *Sea Nymph*'s stern and here they were, finally, at the top of Marmara Denizi, the cerulean Sea of Marmara, and over the horizon at its other end the Dardanelles emptying into the womb of the timeless Aegean. She fell off the wind just enough to create a slight lull and flutter in the sails and said, *Daddy?* And he answered, up in the bow facing out toward the daunting openness and its haze of infinity, *What are you waiting for—Let's go!*

The waves were bigger, the winds cuffing, and it scared her at first to not be bottled up safely by the land, but the receding shores gave her an adult sense of daring she had never quite experienced, and with less traffic and a boundless stage her father hauled the jib to leeward to match the main and they practiced jibing, zigzagging like a water beetle, coming about into the wind and swinging off, accelerating into a beam reach, spray fountaining over the bowsprit, her acrobatic responses gaining more precision on each tack and her happiness ascending toward some sort of trigger point, an exhilaration that seemed to be the culmination of yearning, purely alive and complete and confident, as if that day she stopped becoming and started, for all her life ahead, the impetuous, immutable act of being.

Eventually, bearing down on the Princes' Islands, they turned upwind and stayed there, beating back against the current. Her father relieved her at the wheel while she went down below into the stuffy cabin to pee into a bucket, fetch drinks from the cooler, and grab her camera. When she climbed back on deck her father had stripped to his Speedo bathing suit, his boating shorts and Hawaiian shirt folded neatly on the chart shelf, and was singing snatches of opera at the top of his lungs, his gold—wristwatch, chain, and crucifix—bouncing glints of light back at the westward sun. He threw her a kiss and she snapped his picture.

Given a reprieve from duty, for the next hour she sat quietly in the bow, taking photographs, sipping from a container of cherry juice, and watching Istanbul rise again from the sea, her thoughts wandering to her studies— half-day sessions with tutors (Arabic and chemistry, the extra credits allowing her to advance to her senior year)—and then, with a throb of lust, achingly to Osman, who she would see the next day, and with another more maddening throb to Karim—she told herself she didn't care if she ever saw him again—and with melancholy toward the missing half of her family, her brother—but he would not love sailing, drenched with spray, at nature's mercy—and to her mother, who had unlearned how to appreciate the pleasures available out on the edge of convention, tossed against the unexpected and the unknown.

Her father was suddenly behind her, lowering the jib, which he left her to fold and stow as he scampered back to the wheel and they funneled into the strait and beat upwind in a northeasterly tack toward the tower of Kiz Kulesi. Up in the bow, she watched a sleek motor yacht swing out from behind the tower, headed south, and, a minute later, worried that the boat was on a collision course with the *Sea Nymph*, she called out her concern.

I see it, honey, said her father. Come back here and take the wheel.

Where should I steer? she asked sensibly. We have the right of way, don't we?

Glancing at his wristwatch, he told her to stay the present course and went below. In a minute, the diesel puttered to life, and she wondered what was going on. The motor yacht, as big as a city bus, was closing at a reckless speed and she could see, below the crescent and star emblazoned on its red flag, its captain on the flying bridge dressed in whites and the smoked-black windows of its salon. Then her father was back in the cockpit, his cigarettes in a plastic baggie, which he stowed in the compartment below the compass before leaning over to release the mainsheet, the boom swinging over their heads, the transmission in neutral, the *Sea Nymph* in a slow-motion glide toward the oncoming yacht as her father dropped the sail.

Daddy! They're going to hit us! she said, just as the yacht, sounding its horn, throttled back and cut its engines, its fearsome bow sitting down in the water. The yacht's captain hove to, swinging his vessel parallel to the *Nymph*, a hundred feet off their starboard side, and now she could see the soldiers on its stern, a pair of Turkish commandos, armed with compact submachine pistols, Israeli-made Uzis. She knew the name because her father had once taken her to a shooting range outside Ankara and she had fired one. Where did you get it? she had asked him, digging out her yellow earplugs, and he told her, Well, it's mine.

Okay, she said, turning to her father but not returning his impish smile. Will you tell me what the heck's going on?

I have a meeting to go to.

Now? On the yacht? Really?

You have three options, said her father. She could wait for him, drifting and circling alongside for the next hour or two while he attended to the business at hand; he could send over a crew member from the yacht to help her get the *Sea Nymph* back to Altinkum; or, if she felt up to the task—and he would not suggest such a thing, he emphasized, without his supreme faith in her ability to handle the boat—she could stay at the helm and motor up the Bosphorus by herself.

Are you serious? she said. Can I put the sail back up?

Better not. Think you can do it? and she told him, Sure I can do it. You afraid? he asked, and she said, Of what?

That's my girl.

He grabbed his baggie and stepped up on the starboard rail, pausing to bless himself with the sign of the cross. Bon voyage, he told her, I'll see you back at the marina for dinner, and then he swan-dived over the side, breast-stroking with the bag in his mouth toward the ladder attached to the motor yacht's transom. She waited until he was safe, clinging to the first rung, waving back at her with his free hand, to engage the transmission and tap the brass bar of the throttle forward, steering for midstream to claim a lane of her own, her legs trembling not from fear but from a staggering pleasure.

That's like so double-oh-seven! she shouted into the breeze, her voice ending in a squeak.

In the throes of independence, she became all-seeing, her senses tethered to the boat but her soul transcendent, soaring in light, and she prayed, not as supplicant but as seraph, ecstatically: *Dear Lord, the sea is so large and my boat so small, please protect me on my journey.* Her confidence unwavering, even as the sky blackened horribly, north of the bridge, and a tiny squall dropped like a bomb on top of her, a direct hit, shredding her visibility for a disorienting minute before it blew past, its stinging glitter of rain pellets leaving her chilled and shivering but also invigorated. The strait scoured by white caps, she motored ahead toward a sunbeam like a celestial column prying open gilded clouds.

She moved on through the coppery splatter of waning sunlight, threading the Bosphorus to the entrance of Altinkum's tiny harbor, where she throttled back the engine and scrutinized the crowded moorage and thought, *Shit.* Earlier in her education, she and her father had spent an entire morning in the confines of the cove, dropping anchor, raising anchor, docking and casting off, but what seemed a routine pas de deux impressed her now as a challenge easily failed by a single novice sailor.

But she had not been paying attention to where she was going and, in a mild panic, had to swing about before crashing the *Nymph* onto the wave-slapped mossy rocks of the harbor's northern headland. Drifting back for a more central approach, she had an eerie feeling that something was wrong, and however hard she squinted, trying to identify the source of her uneasiness, she could not see it until she grabbed the binoculars and scanned the shoreline. At first she thought the beach and marina had been abandoned, which made no sense on a Sunday evening when people usually crowded into its dockside restaurant, and then the soldiers came into focus, a loose ring of armed sentries forming a perimeter from the sand up to the highway, where she could now see in the distance the strobe of blue lights, and she knew immediately, being her father's daughter, the basic scenario and thought, *What's Daddy up to now?*

She lowered the binoculars back toward the water, the dockmaster popping in and out of the oval frame, and raised them back an inch to see him clearly, signaling her to come ahead, and she steeled her nerves, turned the bow landward, relocated the *Sea Nymph*'s moorage, and headed in, side-slipping with the current, dashing to the bow to gaff the float line but missing the first pass and reversing, missing the second pass as well, crying in frustration as the third pass, too, went awry, and on the fourth pass, with the engine in neutral, drifting in high toward the float, she jumped overboard with the bow line, which she clipped to the float and then swam frantically back to the *Nymph*, clambered aboard, teased the engine into reverse, and set an anchor off the stern to prevent the boat from swinging with the tide. She collapsed in the cockpit, gasping with relief, then went below to change into dry clothes—jeans and a T-shirt and sneakers—and the dockmaster rowed out to bring her ashore.

Well done, *kizim*, my daughter, he congratulated her in Turkish. I would have come sooner but I feared you would sink me.

An hour passed but she hardly noticed the time, pampered by a staff with little else to do, gathered at the small bar with the dockmaster, garçon, and bartender, who she had conned into mixing her rum and Cokes, the anxious cook coming out of the kitchen every few minutes with plates of meze, the military officer in charge of security stepping over to flirt and practice English after inspecting her bag for bombs or daggers or God knows what and trying to confiscate her camera.

Twilight deepened and the dockmaster switched on the fairy lights strung along the outline of the open-air restaurant and throughout its arbor of sycamore trees. The army officer's walkie-talkie crackled and he put it to his ear and then back on his belt and announced to the staff, *Ten minutes*. When she had asked the dockmaster earlier about the giant yacht he told her, exasperated by the disruption of business, that this yacht was the pasha's. She asked which pasha, as if she knew them all, and he said, the Big One, and she said airily, Oh, that one. He was at my birthday party. But now she had a better idea of why her father had chosen such an out-of-the-way home for the *Sea Nymph*, the last ferry stop on the European coast, directly below an off-limits Turkish military base that stretched to the Black Sea.

She was chattering with the bartender about life in America, of which she knew very little, when someone tapped her shoulder and she turned— *Mr. Kirlovsky!*—and threw herself impulsively into the plump and sweaty embrace of Elena's father's arms. Then, as if by command, everyone at the marina stopped what they were doing to observe the yacht's arrival, its carving-knife silhouette sliding into view out beyond the harbor, a police launch bringing its passengers to shore.

CHAPTER TWENTY-FIVE

She had been there on the landing to greet him, ignoring the soldiers' half-hearted order to stand back, but as soon as her father had come ashore that night, dressed now in chinos and a blue oxford shirt (planning, *planning*—how many extra sets of clothes had he stored around the city?), she knew, despite his ostensible bonhomie, that he was in an impervious mood she would not be able to enter. Bravo, Admiral! he saluted her. How'd it go? but he had no time for her answer, stepping aside for the thickset pasha, in baggy swim trunks and a khaki pullover, to double-kiss her cheeks and anoint her with quick flattery. The other passengers—an aloof pair of men in Bermuda shorts and golf shirts she took, given their blue-eyed hauteur, to be Americans; a second pair, Middle-Easterners, one virtually a caricature of an ostentatious high roller, his swarthiness adorned in thick strands of gold jewelry and the other his opposite in every way, lean and severe with a malevolent smile slashed through the circle of his closely trimmed beard and mustache, outfitted in black combat boots and army greens with no insignia—expended nothing in their acknowledgment of her existence. Their eyes simply registering with indifference her virginal fuckability as her father tugged her away, whispering in her ear, *These other shitheads aren't worth knowing,* and walked her back to the bar, distracted, apologizing mechanically for asking her to stay put.

Triple-top-secret horseshit on a boomerang, her father said later in the car, riding with her back across the bridge to Asia. *Sorry, Kitten. Better if you don't know. Dirty business. I wouldn't mind seeing those bastards go to jail for it.*

Jail? she said. *Really? The pasha? Mr. Kirlovsky?*

No no no. The pasha was a man of immeasurable qualities—a necessary and discreet host, a great ally, trusted friend, fundamentally honest, commander of an army larger than any in Europe, a militant anti-Communist and fellow admirer (with the White House) of Saddam Hussein's strongarm secularism, a universalist and mullah-basher though, sorry to say, unbaptized (but we're not here saving souls). Exceeding folly to imagine he could be left out of the loop. Our pal Kirlovsky was a businessman—*I don't hold it against him,* said her father. *The man's been helpful on some projects we have going out in the east.* Her father, it seemed, was the reluctant matchmaker valued for imperturbability, and the Iranians—*Did I just say that? I didn't say that. Never tell anybody I said that*—were customers, extortionists might be a more apt choice of words, and it was clear her father would as soon stick a knife in their backs as sell them a shoelace. *No,* he said, *I'm talking about those fools from Washington, those fucking idiots and their neat idea.* He had become pensive then, staring out the window, the lights of Uskudar down below pressed against the Bosphorus, gleaming like an obsidian snake—or staring at the specter of his own reflection in the glass. *Just because they're our guys,* he added a moment later as they were descending into Asia, *just because they're on our side, doesn't mean they have brains. Never forget that.*

She had risen at dawn to prepare for church and now the day's splendid accumulation—the fresh wind on her face, the joyous showering of the water, the unanticipated gift of liberation, the illicit rum—seemed to suggest a nest, immediately available if she slunk down into the leather seat and leaned against her father, who smelled tranquilizingly like sunshine, and she closed her eyes, just beginning to doze off, when she heard him refer to calls he had made, something about your friend Osman, and Osman's name pinched her erect, wide-eyed and fully conscious.

This boy, her father continued, still gazing out the window into the sparkling night of the city, *is a very interesting fellow. He associates with some very interesting people.*

Uh-oh, she thought.

Bad children, the government calls them. The newspapers call them the lost generation—the kids who came of age under the military's control. This bunch calls itself the Committee of Democracy and Brotherhood.

But that's beautiful, she said, confused, expecting something apocalyptic. *It's like . . . inspirational.*

Yes, he said wryly. *Inspiring.* He turned away from the window to meet her eyes but in the flickering darkness of the car she could see only his cool detachment. *There's a code at play here, Dottie. Democracy translates into Islam. Brotherhood can be interpreted as a cadre of frat boys willing to go beyond the limit.*

Daddy, he's not a terrorist.

How unbelievably dumb—that's what she had said, guilt by association, just blurting it out like a simpleton, but her father, agreeing, had mystified her by being amused and omniscient. *I know, Dottie,* he had told her. *As a matter of fact, I've been led to believe he has redeeming virtues.*

What's that supposed to mean?

It means he has redeeming virtues, he said, and closed the gate with his riddle about closeness, *Just promise me you won't get too close to him. That could turn out badly, I'm afraid.*

She had not wanted a confrontation but was quick to take offense. *It's because he's Muslim, isn't it?*

That might be something to consider, her father said. *Do you think his family wants him marrying a Catholic girl?*

Maybe they don't care. What's the big deal?

His answer, she felt, had been beside the point and although she heard his coldhearted and uncharitable words their effect was deafening, only reminding her of Karim, and she had not listened. *You know why I like Turkey?* he said. *Because it has a divided soul. These are the front lines out here, Dottie. You might want to keep that in mind.*

God, Daddy, she whined, *I don't get your problem. I really don't,* and then the driver had pulled over in front of the academy's gates and she said, *What about Osman? The police beat him up,* and her father said, *You should know by now, that's what the police do.*

Piqued by how the day was ending, her triumphant sail forgotten behind the screen of her father's preoccupations, she delivered a hasty kiss to his cheek, grabbed her day bag, and opened the car door. He told her he was flying back to Ankara in the morning and would call in a day or two and she asserted her claim on the *Sea Nymph,* pressing him for permission to take the boat out by herself, and he said, *Let me think about that,* and she had slammed the door much harder than she intended and stomped back to her room.

Later in the week, he had telephoned with rules. I've already called the dockmaster to fill him in on the program, he said. Stay between Altinkum and the bridge. Motor only—no sails unless the engine breaks down. Watch the weather—winds over ten knots: remain in port. Daylight hours only. No overnights. Can I take friends? she asked and he told her not until she had more experience. How much more? she had wondered but did not ask, smelling a loophole in this particular prohibition, which she soon exploited, taking the *Nymph* out twice by herself before sneaking Osman aboard, picking him up at the dock in Ortakoy, a pattern of subterfuge established not that day but the day her father had returned to Ankara in late June and continued throughout the summer, the best of summers the summer when she was seventeen, she and her boyfriend finessing a citywide game of hide-and-seek with the men she imagined her father had assigned to keep watch on her, accidental meetings (*hah!*) at museums and cinemas, clandestine rendezvous at the clubs and bars where she and Osman danced throughout the night, anchoring the *Sea Nymph* in secluded coves to smoke hash and make out and begin to learn what her body had never truly known beyond her father's indecent tutorials in sensation—the anxious passion, the slow, tense curriculum of love.

There were picnics at Yildiz with Yesho and her noisy magpie family or just the girls themselves hanging out by the Blue Mosque or Taksim Square to absorb the kinetics of the surging crowds or ridicule tourists or bargain with the hucksters or just sit with Elena gossiping, consumed by laughter, fending off a queue of smitten boys and creepy, badly dressed hairy men. Also the mind-clearing hours of swim practice in the academy's pool, the quiet mornings with her patient teachers, walking home through the cobbled alleys of her neighborhood saluted by the smiles and nods of the old women hijabis, the vendors on the streets selling spears of salt-sprinkled cucumbers, going to sleep sticky-lipped or sore-lipped from her twin indulgences—wedges of watermelon, the juice dribbling down her chin; the rash of wild kissing—the rapturous consumption of meze and music and the ingrained fatalism and lusty overblown passions of the Istanbullus, interrupted only by her father's infrequent visits to Istanbul and their addition of an old familiar rhythm to the shining new forms of her happiness.

One day in August when she went early in the morning to Altinkum for a day of sailing the *tirhandil* was not there in the cove, a heart-stopping discovery until she found the dockmaster and heard the explanation. At her father's request he had sent the *Sea Nymph* down to the boatyard at Tarabya to have a cooking stove and toilet stall added to its cabin.

When she telephoned him that night, her father announced his intention to take a much-deserved vacation at the end of summer, just the two of them aboard the *Sea Nymph*—more than a vacation, something he had dwelled upon in prayers and dreams throughout much of his life: a pilgrimage. He had traveled to Israel frequently, could wander the streets of Jerusalem and Jericho, Nazareth and Bethlehem or the shore of Galilee in his sleep, yet it was his conviction that the true birthplace of Christianity was not its cradle but its nursery. That sacred honor fell not to Rome but to Turkey, Asia Minor, and its first-century provinces, the ancient Anatolian coastline a trove of New Testament sites, and, in the peripatetic footsteps of his favorite apostle, Paul, the Jewish tent maker from Tarsus turned evangelical Christian, he planned to visit as many of them as proved possible before her school returned to session the third week in September. Such a trip, he promised, no matter what else happened in the years ahead, would be a highlight of her life, and in the years ahead she would think about this often, meditating on transfiguration, Christ risen from the dead, though Dottie was not able to convince herself that resurrection could in any way be described as one of life's salient moments of ecstatic affirmation. What was the point exactly, once you had come to the end of what is necessary? A second chance to die again? How long could the resurrected Christ endure it? Not very.

Her reluctance to spend so much time apart from Osman was mitigated by her reluctance to maintain the pace at which they seemed to be hurtling toward the moment that she had so far resisted, irrationally but morally, pragmatically but neurotically, her contradictory impulses a source of panting confusion for both of them, but she needed more time to think about this—sleeping with Osman, giving (abandoning? submitting?) herself to him, shedding (or magnifying) her impurity, restarting her sexuality in a postpubescent body, inventing the permanence of her sexuality, splitting the difference on domination, overcoming the danger of asserting herself physically, overcoming the numbing terror of being *not there,* reduced to a one-dimensional flatness attached to a three-dimensional hole—although what more time offered to someone poised on a cliff other than heaps of anxiety she had no idea. It was all too much to actually think about in any deliberate and logical way and her father's plan to sail away presented Dottie with a respite from her ambivalence and hormonal dementia and her lingering fears of the darkness in men. Some of them, most of them?—she didn't know.

Early in September it was her old friend Maranian who appeared at the academy gates in Uskudar to chauffeur her to the boatyard in Tarabya, where she met her father overseeing the *Sea Nymph*'s short journey from dry dock back to the water. He looked worn down, his face drawn, his tan turned sallow, ungroomed and wrinkled and underweight, half-circle scoops under his eyes, and he said, of course, that it was nothing, a bug he had picked up on a trip out east. On top of it, he assured her. Got it beat.

Her first assignment was to go with the uncustomarily cheerless Maranian back to the hotel room in the village where her father had spent the night and collect his gear and the boxes of supplies he had purchased the day before, along with a plastic tub of books that snagged her curiosity: several travel guides, a pocketbook Bible, three volumes of poetry—Eliot, Brodsky, Rumi—and a small library of Christian theological writing— separate editions of the four Gospels, the Acts of the Apostles, and the

Pauline Epistles, the Gnostic Gospels, and a thin leather-bound, heavily annotated text entitled *St. John's Book of Revelation* (or, alternately, as the cover suggested, the *Book of Apocalypse*), St Augustine's *Confessions*, and a text she could not categorize at a glance, the *Meditations* of Marcus Aurelius that had a quote handwritten neatly on its title page: I do my duty. Other things do not trouble me.

Penny for your thoughts, she prompted Mr. Maranian as they loaded the Mercedes, yet he was no more receptive than he had been on the drive over from Uskudar, his responses clipped and his mood unsocial. Dottie persisted, asking about his family, only to be chastened to learn that he was alone, his parents dead, his two siblings dead, his wife likewise dead, his only son a teacher halfway around the world in California. That's so sad, she said, but he grunted in an ironic manner that seemed to pander to her sentiment. They finished packing the car and he stood by the driver's door, hands jiggling coins in the pockets of his summer trousers, looking at her with a lugubrious expression of farewell, as if he might not ever see her again. She met his eyes with an inquisitive look and said, What? and he seemed to bring himself back with a weak smile and said, I have something to give you.

He removed his left hand from his pocket and extended his arm toward her. It's so beautiful, she exclaimed, taking the tiny gold coptic crucifix and its chain from his palm to examine its Byzantine workmanship. Very old, he said. Antique. Armenian. Wear it, please—taking it back from her to noose the chain over her head, kissing the cross before he dropped it through the neck of her T-shirt. For protection, he said, tapping the blue beads of Osman's evil eye bracelet on her wrist. Better than a superstition. I love it, she said, and he responded brusquely, Please, get in the car.

The boat was in the harbor, tied off to the wharf, by the time they returned, its tanks being serviced with diesel fuel and fresh water and the coolers with blocks of ice. Her father sent her with cash to the marina's store to purchase foul-weather gear and candy bars and anything else she might have forgotten to pack. Before she finished shopping, however, the car was out front honking and she quickly paid and found herself driving with the men to a stone chapel in the village, where they went inside and lit votive candles below icons of Our Lady of the Sea and Nicholas, the patron saint of sailors and she knelt between Maranian and her father in front of the altar to pray for a safe voyage. Then her father offered to take everybody to lunch but Maranian said moody good-byes and drove away. Dottie said, Is Mr. Maranian all right? and her father told her that Maranian had a lot on his mind.

He's sweet, she said, pulling the gold cross out from her T-shirt. Look what he gave me.

Take good care of this, her father said, fingering the pendant. It was his *babaanne*'s, his paternal grandmother's.

Oh, my gosh, he didn't tell me that!

He's like an old mother hen, said her father. He worries about our trip. But he's not a sailor, is he?

When they sat down in a café for lunch her concern for his health returned. While she ate a Niçoise salad he drank two beers, claiming he had no appetite, and waved off her suggestion that they postpone the trip for a day or two. I'm fine, he insisted, as trickles of perspiration began to pour off his forehead in the steamy heat of the season. He took a pen from the pocket of his shirt and said, Here's the plan and began to sketch it out on a paper napkin, a route that would take them through the Dardanelles— he preferred Hellespont—and into the Aegean to Smyrna, Ephesus, and, ultimately, the island of Patmos, where the Lord unveiled the end of the world to the apostle John. They walked back to the quay and went aboard the *Sea Nymph* and minutes later were out in the shipping lanes, Dottie at the helm, wearing a violet-colored billcap and her black one-piece, the engine cut and the silence a seductive whisper. Her father raised the mainsail into moderate winds, heading south on their grand adventure, but as they slipped beneath the span of the Bosphorus Bridge he said, I'm going below for a little nap. That was the last she saw of him until late in the afternoon, when he appeared bleary-eyed in the hatch opening, bare-chested and glistening with sweat, his scarred shoulder a garish pink crab of molten tissue, a cigarette dangling from his lips.

We there yet? he said, grinning sleepily.

Almost.

The wind had fallen off and they were a mile or more from Kinaliada, the first of the Princes' Islands, and he told her to steer farther west toward the green hills of Buyukada, the largest island in the group, where they would anchor for the night and be ready for the morning's fresh start for their longest sail of the expedition, westward across the Sea of Marmara.

Let me know when we're ten minutes out, he said, flicking the stub of his cigarette overboard and withdrawing to his bunk.

It was a lazy sail through heat-drenched haze, the sky above an orange-tinted screen, that last hour until she was close enough to Buyukada's northern headlands to see the gingerbread villas climbing its slopes. When she called her father to come on deck he popped up transformed, face washed, hair combed, eyes lucid and teasing, all jolly, one hand rattling an ice-filled silver canister and the other holding two tea glasses, each containing an olive, surveying their position for a moment, saying to himself, *Well done*, until he turned to admire her at the wheel and announced cocktail hour. I think it's time you learned to drink martinis, Kitten, he said, prying the lid off of the shaker and pouring and then relieving her at the wheel.

But by her second awful sip—*Yech! This is straight vodka!*—she could feel her senses swirl and she rescued and ate the olive and offered the rest of the martini to her father. I think I'll start with cherry juice, she said, and went below to change out of her bathing suit into cotton shorts and a tank top, used the toilet and figured out its saltwater flushing system, rubbed lotion on her sun-tendered skin, and tied back her hair in a ponytail, noticing her father had fallen asleep with St. Augustine. She returned topside in time to help drop the sail and fire up the engine as they approached the channel toward the harbor and ferry terminal, lining up with the island's unmistakable landmark, the bulbous cupolas of the Splendid Otel.

Let's reconsider, her father said, back at the helm, frowning at the boat-jammed harbor. He tapped the throttle into neutral and they bounced in the wake of a passing ferry. It looks like a frigging regatta in there.

Whatever is fine, she said, though he must have sensed her disappointment, assuring her there would be an abundance of places to explore in the days ahead, but tonight he hoped for solitude and quiet in preparation for their dawn-to-dusk sail across open water, the two of them together beneath the stars, undistracted. *Getting*—he said with emotion—*to know each other better.*

Like, how much better, Daddy? she wanted to say.

He pointed the *Sea Nymph* south and they motored down along the hilly coast over mottled shallows, teal and greenish brown, Dottie a statuesque Aphrodite in the bow keeping a lookout for shoals, a blushing sun lowering toward the European mainland. *That looks fabulous!* he sang out as the headland they rounded fell away to reveal a perfect cove, its privacy walled by cliffs dropping to a pebble beach. She shouted out the depth and they anchored fifty yards from shore. Then a splash startled her until she realized her father had jumped overboard, the bobbing humps of his naked ass and shoulders visible as he butterflied toward the island, pausing once to somersault around, dog paddling while he called back to her—What are you waiting for? Jellyfish report: zero—and she said she had just changed out of her swimsuit and he said, You don't need a bathing suit in paradise, baby, and she told him maybe later, itchy with the embarrassment of her newly shaved crotch, her pubic hair dispatched by a disposable razor with the guidance of Yesho, who had finally coaxed her into a hammam, where such a thing was de rigueur. *Fistik gibi*—like a nut, said Yesho; the other Turkish women in the bath nodded approval. In wide-eyed disbelief she watched several of them—thick-waisted, saggy breasts, shockingly bare pussies—scoop up the floss of her curls and pass them, marveling at their fineness, from hand to hand. *Like a little girl,* she thought uncomfortably, now imagining beneath every conservative Muslim female's head-to-toe *carsaf* loomed the private contradiction of exposed genitalia. *Not for Daddy's eyes!* Afterward, she and Yesho leaning into each other, bent with uncontrollable laughter, waiting outside the hammam for a dolmuş, joking in English—*The clam has lost its beard. Poor clam! Cold clam! Scratchy clam!*—the queue glaring as if they were retarded, these girls.

But as she watched him swim to the beach and strut around like Adam, the audacious freedom of the sight spurred her envy and she changed her mind, stripped, and dove in, knifing through the underworld, relishing the taut glide of her flesh, seeing how long she could hold her breath, going farther than she thought she might, eyes wide open in wonderment, a deb mermaid, boundless.

Well what do you know, said her father as they climbed back aboard the sailboat and she quickly wrapped herself in a towel. By the looks of it I'd say you've been to a hammam. His droll tone caused her to stiffen and snap—*Don't say anything else. Just don't*—a rare rebuke of her irrepressible father for a minor offense that, minutes later, she had not so much forgiven but pushed away and forgotten before she admitted what she sometimes felt, the obvious answer to the question, *Who's to blame?*

Twilight arrived with the land-scent of rosemary seeping onto the water and an exquisite coolness exhaled from the sea and encouraged her to join her father in the cockpit, on his second round of martinis, with a rum and Coke in her hand, dressed to feel not quite dressed, braless under a scoop-necked sleeveless aqua-colored shift. Here's to us, he said, saluting her with his glass, a toast she echoed back to him. Dear God, we are blessed, he said, this is certainly the life, isn't it, and she stood up in the well and bent over to hug him, her nose pressed against his neck, breathing deeply the smell of him, which she knew so well but could never describe, saying how much she loved him as his hand rose and fell soothingly along her spine.

There's a baguette, he said. Olives, cheese, tomato, some prosciutto. Marinated eggplant. How's that sound?

While he went below to throw together dinner, she watched a raucous flock of seagulls pinwheel through the glassed surface for fish, a luminescent halo crowning Europe, the sea traffic light up on the Sea of Marmara, like flickering clumps of drifting villages, her consciousness soaked in a divine silence the absence of which she now realized had been a mistake in her life, one of the last missing pieces of the puzzle of complete existence. She reflected upon love, how she was in love with love, its presence crazy and sweet, the center of all yearning. Wasn't it true that when you fell in love you had done the one thing that no one could explain to any satisfaction? If she were to have Osman here right this second by her side, they would swim ashore like electric eels in the inky phosphorescent water and without a doubt and absolutely she would give herself to him body and soul, her

363

readiness for love, all of love, never more apparent in her life than at this moment, and yet the back of her mind muttered Yesho's folkloric admonitions, *Loving too much invites envy, bad luck, nazar*—the evil eye. *When things go well in your life, remember danger walks behind you. Protect yourself. Eat onions. Wear the bracelet.*

Up through the galley hatch he handed her another drink, a battery-powered lantern, a red-and-white enameled tin platter piled with food, shallow ceramic bowls, the silver cocktail shaker, and, finally, his own glass—*How about some Verdi while we eat?*—and she heard him slip a tape into his portable cassette player, the volume low, the opera like an imperceptible murmur blended into the lap of the sea against the hull. He climbed the steps into the tent of buttery light where she sat on the side of the cockpit and poured himself another martini, sipping thoughtfully, eating little while she gorged herself. She nagged him to eat more and he told her his stomach was not inclined at this time to accept her superb advice.

You know, he said in a hushed voice, back there at the harbor, when I saw that old hotel, it made me think of Pittsburgh.

Really? she said with a full mouth, voracious, a little animal with a huge appetite. Why?

There were smokestacks, as you might imagine, he said. But just as much, in my memory of Pittsburgh, there were the onion-shaped steeples of the Orthodox churches. You couldn't get away from the Eastern Europeans—Ukrainians, Slovaks, Serbs, Polacks, Czechs, boatloads of them come over to work in the coal mines and coke furnaces or the steel mills, but there was a bigger reason. They were running from the Russians, they hated the goddamn Communists. I used to resent them as a kid—a hick is a hick, no matter the country of origin—but you can't hate them and love the American dream at the same time.

My grandmother was Eastern European, right?

Not at all, he said. She was a Croatian from Dubrovnik, which is nearly the same as being an Italian. Better, I would say—less emotional. Roman Catholic, well educated, and worldly. She was no peasant, I can tell you that. When I look at you . . . well.

I'm like her, aren't I?

Yes.

And your father? All-American war hero, right?

Anglo-Irish-Welsh-Franco-Germanic stock, a full house, as they say, fourth generation. A hardworking man with a ferocious sense of right and wrong. Unfortunately, he was an Episcopalian. Your grandmother fell in love with him anyway, proving once again that love, as they say, is subversive and one might even say willfully blind.

So how did they meet? Dottie asked.

Well, he said, pausing to sip his martini, did I ever tell you your grandmother was the organist for St. Paul's, the big cathedral in the center of Pittsburgh? Hired by the bishop, who adored her, as did everybody who ever met her. Every other morning but Sunday you'd find her over on the east side at St. Nicholas's, the Croatian church. All the Roman Catholic Croats from the old country understood each other in a way other people would never understand. After what they'd been through, they understood the Communists and the *mujos* better than anybody. And after the war Pop worked in the mines as a union organizer. You'd never know it from looking at him—he was one tough bastard. If he smelled Red on you, run for the hills. He'd crack your head in a minute. He took the Cold War very personally. As did your grandmother. As do we all. Beware the Bear, or it will eat you.

His elbows on his knees, her father drifted into silence, staring down at the glass in his hands, until finally, well supplied throughout her childhood with her father's ideology but underfed on ancestors, she said *And?*

Pittsburgh, he said, as though he had forgotten the story he had begun. Great place to grow up. Muscular, self-confident, visionary. I had what would have to go down in the books as a wonderful childhood. The classic edition—delivered newspapers on my bike, had a home away from home at the movie theater. The three Ps—picnics, polka, pinochle—at the Knights of Columbus hall. The wedding parties at the Croatian Club—man, you would have loved those! Me and my pals went to the CYO dances. I was an altar boy and proud of it. Call me a mackerel eater and I would sock you right in the nose. I sang in the boy's choir—and not just because my mother was the director. Fished and camped and hunted with Pop up in the mountains, joined the Cub Scouts and the NRA and then the Boy Scouts. After the war, Korea, McCarthy, when it became apparent yet again that the union and the mine owners were of the same mind about the resurgent Communist threat, they thought, correctly, it would be in their best interest to cozy up to Pop and the other district leaders, and so they began to invite him out to Mellon's Rolling Rock Club in Ligonier—the Mellon brothers were famous bankers, you know—to play golf and talk business and share the common ground of their patriotism. Pop would take me to caddy, and by the time I was in high school at St. George's I was one of the top caddies at the club, the boy all the Ivy-League educated executives, all the presidents and operators of the companies, wanted carrying their bags on weekends. If Pop wasn't playing, I'd hitchhike out to Ligonier myself. I knew the links. They loved me, and when I learned the game and started kicking their ass, taking their money and dating their daughters, they loved me even more. There's a lesson there, Dot, if you can see it. Generation to generation. By their example, those men showed me what it meant to be a true American. Not just on the Fourth of July. Every fucking day of your God-given life.

She could hear this all night, sponging up the spill of details from his hidden past, which, by extension, was her hidden past, its dormancy throughout her life a vague frustration, but the cadence of his voice had begun to swing and pull and slide and she watched him empty the shaker's contents into his glass, waiting with undue patience for the last drops to emerge, and worried out loud if it might be bad for him. *Dad, martinis with antibiotics . . . is that a good idea?*

Rule number one, honey, he said. Never admonish a man on vacation that he is drinking too much.

She listened carefully for what was not there, the slightest hint of anger or irritation in his tone, and said, Fine with me, and, already tipsy, went below to mix her third rum and Coke.

Rule number two, her father said as she climbed back into the cockpit. Sacrosanct. Thou shalt not vomit belowdecks.

I know that, she said. Is there a rule number three?

Ah, he said, feigning deep consideration. Rule number three takes us to a much different place. Rule number three: Dedicate your life to something larger than yourself or you will never be fulfilled and you will never be happy and you will never be worth a damn to anybody.

Do you think that was Mom's problem? she said innocently.

Your mother, he said. She certainly didn't like the rules. I have to say, for almost twenty years, ever since you kids were born, your mother never gave me a day of happiness.

Wow, she whispered.

You are my brilliant, beautiful daughter, he said, gesturing toward her with his drink, sloshing vodka on her bare feet. I want to ask your permission to ask you something very, very serious.

Okay, she said, watching his head begin to droop in increments. Permission granted.

Rule number three, he said.

Have a cause to live for.

Live *and* die, he said, revived with a sloppy gush of exuberance, and his head snapped upright. Correct, beautiful. Live *and* die. Rule number three.

We've done rule number three.

Correct. Rule number four. The oath of secrecy. Thou shalt not tell. Ever.

Tell what?

Tell anybody.

Tell them what?

Vows are sacred. And, in my case, legally binding. Between us, okay, but that's as far as it can ever go. Classified.

Okay.

Promise.

I promise.

Very well. Excellent. Otherwise, you know . . .

I promise. Stop worrying. I know how to keep my mouth shut.

You are my beautiful, courageous daughter, he said, the words tiptoeing from his mouth. You are of an age. You have reached the age.

For what? she asked warily.

You have a grave responsibility, an imperative . . . praying for peace is not enough. You have to take risks. Act.

I know that, Daddy.

Okay . . . right. How do you know that?

Because I'm your daughter. Because of the way we live. Because, I guess, of what you do.

Ah, he said. Exactly. That's what I mean. You're old enough now to know what it is I do.

I know what you do, she said with a confidence that was not unwarranted. Like so many others in the diaspora of Golden Ghettos spread across the globe, she was a member of a family that existed in proximity to the headlines, tonight's dinner table conversations more often than not the morning's breaking news. In her father's office, prominently displayed, was a photograph of him shaking hands with the president (not Carter—anybody but Carter, who once described Cold War warriors like her father as *paranoid*) and another of her young father laughing with a team of Green Berets at their outpost in the Vietnamese highlands. The list of family encounters with VIPs was impressively and tiresomely endless, especially considering that, after pleasantries or cocktails or dinner, she and her mother and brother were frequently asked to leave the room. Counterterrorism—she was aware, vaguely, that the official focus resided there, floating atop an unabashed hatred for the Soviet Union and its proxies. Her dad had a boss, a guy named Dick, who answered to someone who answered to a presidential envoy named Bremer, whose boss was the president himself. Somewhere embedded in the program were the ambassadors and the secretaries of state . . . mostly, she got the sense, on the sidelines, official parents you maneuvered around, hid things from, interacted with only on a need-to-know basis, which meant almost never.

You work for the government, she said. Special assistant to the ambassador (which was how she had been instructed to answer the question, *What does your father do?*).

Correct. Yes and no. And what is it I do?

Stop the Communists, I guess, from taking over the world.

Grind them to dust.

And you're winning. We are.

I think you should understand something about the world we find ourselves in, he said. Until Armageddon. One war moves aside only to make room for another. Until the Day of Judgment, I should say. Peel back Communism and the *mujos* await. Okay, okay, he said, waving off an imaginary rebuttal. That point is contested, but hey, if you liked the Stalinists, you are going to love the Salafis. *Badda bing.* Hey, how 'bout that Islamic bomb! *Badda bang.*

Dad, she said, you're lighting the wrong end of your cigarette.

The fuck, baby.

Here. Let me light it for you.

I would hope to find you receptive. Simple matter. Good and evil.

I'm not sure I'm getting this.

Let me ask you a hypothetical. Can I ask you a hypothetical? If you had the opportunity, you'd help me out, right?

If I had the opportunity? Sure.

So you'd help.

Just say the word, she said, humoring him. This was the second time her father had seemed to solicit her participation in something shadowy and she still had no premonitory sense of what he wanted from her.

You are at the age, he said, struggling to his feet, and she held her breath, waiting for her father to fall, while he managed the steps down to the cabin to sprawl unconscious on his bunk.

She awoke in the middle of the night to a stream of terrible gibberish coming from him in a language she did not understand and tried without success to rouse him from his nightmare and comfort the trembles of his fever. She awoke again sometime later to an overpowering gagging stink infusing the cabin and wrapped her pillow over her face and tried not to breathe through her nose. In the morning she found herself alone and went on deck to discover her father hunched in the water off the stern, his body orbited by minnow clouds of tarry shit.

Good morning, sunshine! he called out in a wretched attempt at cheer. Having a little episode here.

369

CHAPTER TWENTY-SIX

The morning seemed to contain an implicit lassitude, without energy or desire, but even the fuse of her enthusiasm failed to ignite her father's spirit. *Come on!* Dottie encouraged him, singing Madonna lyrics into an invisible microphone, dancing on the bow with campy provocation to no avail, her vitality diffused into an inert atmosphere. The seabirds themselves refused to fly.

Listless, her father cleaned himself and his soiled bunk, had a spartan breakfast of coffee and bread, then held hands with Dottie as they prayed silently together to God, Saint Christopher, and Saint Nicholas for safe passage and with particular attention to Stella Maris, the Star of the Sea, and he recited out loud the *Sub Tuum Praesidium—We flee to your protection, O Holy Mother of God.*

The spread of the sky was yellowed and creased like old parchment, the sun blotted into an edgeless ochre smear. She had never before heard about the *lodos,* a southwest wind fabled for its virulence, born out of the Sea of Marmara in the last months of summer and known to gather in its gust-blown skirts plum-colored clusters of malignant squalls. Her father knew of the *lodos* and its fearsome reputation among sailors, yet motored south out of the cove anyway, the mainsail hauled optimistically into an eerie humid calm. Once past the island he had given her a compass heading and retired, spending the morning belowdecks, inhaling *naswar,* opiated

Afghani snuff, to ease the assault of his double-barreled malady, an uncharacteristic bout of depression added to the dysenteric churn in his gut. Later in the morning the wind strengthened and shifted head-on and when she sensed the change in weather she called for him, then shouted out for help, but he did not come.

The seas began to stand up higher than she would have thought possible, and then out of the swells a thick dark monster with a sudsy crest butted against the bow, washing the deck with warm blue water, and she could feel the boat buck and shudder and pause beneath her feet, a slow second's sensation of backwardness before gravity returned and the vessel dived into the trough, a motion that seemed to catapult her father into the cockpit, grabbing her shoulders to steady himself.

All right, he said, ordering his daughter to keep the boat pointed straight into the wind. Then she watched his off-balance performance as he slackened the mainsheet from its cleat to reef the sail, scrambling ape-like on all fours beneath the furious dragon wing of slapping fabric, tying square knots down the length of the boom, and then told her, as if he were suggesting something mildly interesting, to try falling off twenty degrees to port and he let the boom scythe out and, once secured, the *Sea Nymph* heeled over confidently into angry water, rocketing at a diagonal through the bludgeoning waves.

The breeze has picked up, hasn't it, he said, the assertion, like his expression, a bit daft and lordly, standing with her, shin-deep in the cockpit, water boiling through the scuppers. She stood in combat with the wheel as her strength and confidence returned, the boat a great-hearted warhorse splitting the advancing ranks.

Sorry I screamed, she said.

Listen, he said, sitting down on the deck with his legs in the cockpit's well, and then he quizzed her—What if he wasn't here? What would she have done?—and nodded with lethargic agreement at her answers, embellishing them with advice. As he spoke, she stared in dismay at twin lines of brown slime draining from his nostrils, imagining for a second the harrowing possibility that her father was discharging shit from every orifice, and

371

she said with great concern, *Dad? There's this stuff coming out of your nose,* and he told her about the *naswar* and its medicinal benefit but did not try to reassure her that all was well.

Last night, he attempted to explain, his head swaying morosely with the pitch of the boat. *Talking about Pittsburgh . . . honest to God, it made me miss my mother terribly.*

He told her he didn't mean to put her in a bad position and she said, Stop thinking that, okay? I love this. But her arms had grown tired, her bladder ached, she was thirsty, and he told her to hold on a few minutes longer and he would take over for the afternoon watch.

He disappeared below and cut the engine and returned with her grandmother's ivory rosary draped around his neck, a notebook and pen and a handheld device he identified as a GPS, something new from the military, a hookup to outer space, and with blank, hunched indifference to the moment, keyed sequences and copied down coordinates like a deskbound bookkeeper and staggered back below to consult the navigational chart. The promised minutes grew to twenty and then he finally came back on deck and relieved her at the wheel, adding an afterthought as she clambered below, the disheartening news that the head was out of order, use a bucket.

Once inside the cabin, however, a claustrophobic stench of confinement immediately magnified the faint sensation of queasiness she had been feeling for the past hour and she buckled over with nausea, instinctively lurched for the head, and vomited bananas and cereal into the vile soupy clog of her father's excrement. When she tried to pump the bowl clean, the toilet flushed upward with a surge of seawater, spewing out its abomination onto her ankles and feet, a horror to which she contributed a fresh pint of vomit, her convulsion so violent that she pissed her swimsuit. She made a mindless dash to her bunk only to discover that lying down made everything worse and she puked a spoonful of yellow bile onto her pillow and curled into the slope of the hull, her cheek pressed against the thunder of the wood, the misery she felt organic and elemental and enslaving, the boat's heaving stitch her body's own, her cowlike moaning syncopated with the cymbal crash of cooking pots in their cabinets. Immobilized, she closed her eyes, suspended in vertigo, and thought the only thought possible under the circumstance, that dying would be better than this.

She lay folded in, hugging herself like a mummy buried in a jar, her sentience wrecked, unaware of the passing hours and her father's headlong race for the distant shore. Then she felt her consciousness summoned, water splashing in her face, sputtering in agony for her father to stop, yet when she opened her eyes her father was not there. When she made herself sit up her feet dropped into a slosh of floorboards and books, their wet pages waving underwater like anemones. Her confusion evolved to fear but nothing like the petrifying fear she experienced after wading aft on rubbery legs to the cabin steps and hauling herself out of the flood halfway into the roar above, deafening and all-engulfing, her father struggling at the helm with blazing eyes and the euphoric look of a deranged prophet. The *Sea Nymph* exploded through mountainous seas as the heart of the storm, still a mile away, bore down on them off the starboard bow, a bloated twisting octopus that consumed the sky, evil purpled tentacles whipping forward, dragging behind a curtain of white rain seamed with incandescent bolts of lightning.

She clung to the handrails of the open hatch and hollered until she broke the suicidal focus of her father's charge into battle. Daddy, there's water down here, she yelled and he shouted out instructions, his attention swinging between her and the onslaught of the storm, telling her to go back down, start the engine, turn on the bilge pump, put on a life jacket, strap into a safety harness, tie herself to a secure line, get back pronto, and help him drop the sail. She did these things in a seasick frenzy and as she began to climb out of the hold she felt the concussion of an ear-splitting crack of light, the hair on her skin standing, and received a vision—an incandescent matrix, at its intersection her crucified father surrounded by a pale nimbus—that burned on and then off in an instant.

Then the *Sea Nymph* was absorbed into a whipping malevolence, her deck listing steeply to port, its gunnel submerged, the boom like a crusader's broadsword hacking the waves, and she screamed into the din, believing the boat was about to roll over. The blinding rain came then like a firehose in her face and she heard her father's unearthly grunting and his command,

Hold on, Goddamn it, Dottie, hold on, and she felt herself in a void being spun and torn, her father bellowing inside a noise as loud as jet engines, and she shrank into herself and breathed a stinging spray into her lungs and after an eternity felt the boat right itself in obdurate, infinitesimal increments and there was the solace of her father's voice again, reciting *Hail Mary, full of grace* with lunatic serenity. She opened her eyes and raised her head to a universe of wonders in their wake, the octopus transformed to a dark green toad, urinating a waterspout as it sat tucked beneath an archway of rainbows, the rain turned to transparent wet moths, soft lustrous kisses, and the sun dialing up and down like stage lights. She dared to step higher on the hatch ladder and looked forward across a deck littered with sparrows, dead or weather-beaten, and a shoreline to the west, jagged with majestic summits toward which the *Sea Nymph* rocked bravely ahead, sinking.

Daddy, she said to her father, who was sagged into the wheel, clasping his rosary. Her voice was tremulous and rainwater ran down her cheeks with her tears. *I saw you glowing blue.*

The *Sea Nymph* slogged toward the darkening coast, the land's center receding as its sides tightened to expose the expansive horseshoe of a bay, a montage of shadows and sunlight. For too long now her father thrashed about belowdecks waist-deep in the rising water, failing repeatedly to plug the breach where the toilet's outlet had been installed, the bilge pump malfunctioning as the batteries submerged although the engine puttered on, Dottie on deck trying her best to keep the boat steady, the *Nymph* wanting to wallow every time she nudged the wheel in the direction of the headlands. Deeper into the emptiness of the huge bay, she heard the engine gag and die and the dense, awful hush that replaced its reassurance.

Her father pushed a red dry bag out through the hatch stuffed with what he could recover of their personal belongings and she heard him on the radio, calmly pronouncing Mayday, switching channels—*no one's there,* she thought, *or it's broken,* listening to her father's steadfast repetitions of longitude and latitude. Afterward she heard him slip Dvorak's Slavonic Dances into the cassette player and he came on deck, grease-streaked and smiling weakly, and said, It seems we're missing cocktail hour.

At least put on a life jacket, she said, and felt her faith refreshed when he muttered another joke—What, and stand accused of pessimism?—but made an effort to find a vest and strap into it.

He scanned the water and studied the ring of coastline, nearby but still miles off, encouraged by their shoreward drift and the twinkling of lights to the southwest, which he guessed to be the town of Bandirma, near the base of the isthmus linking the ancient island of Arctoneus with the mainland. He thought they might just be lucky enough to bob along into an anchorage, and he sat on the edge of the cockpit's well, then lay back, staring at the sky. What about firing a flare? she asked and he said impassively, almost in a whisper, *Patience.*

By twilight, though, the waves lapped over the stern, bathing the underside of her father still sprawled on his back, his unnatural complacency almost like an abandonment to Dottie. The gunnels now sat perilously low in the water, and she strained her eyes searching the littoral where she predicted they would wash up, able to distinguish nothing useful in her survey, and when she asked for the binoculars he did not respond. In the dusk she observed something new, a bulbous fist of blackness, like a bull's head rearing above the ridge of the peninsula off the starboard bow, thunderbolts spiked from its nostrils, and a moment later a lazy fat wave of colorless water swelled across the deck, pouring down through the hatchway and lifting her father awake from his open-eyed dream to prop on his elbows and declare resolutely, *I'm sorry, Kitten, time to go.*

She watched, momentarily stupefied as he sat upright to fasten the dry bag to his ankle. The thought of crying seemed welcome and true and necessary, but it was only an idea, not a feeling. Trust was what she most felt, linking hands with her father as they stepped without fanfare into the sea, nothing dramatic about it, like exiting a bus when it had pulled up at your stop, and then, ascending back to the surface in a ticklish flue of bubbles, what she most felt, and felt deliriously, was an imperishable sense of the life within her. The game, their game, had been reissued, her father no longer its author, she imagined, but another player on the board.

CHAPTER TWENTY-SEVEN

Take your time, he told her. Pace yourself. This could take a while.

She flipped on her back to gaze at the sad receding outline of the *Sea Nymph* still afloat, wanting to witness the exact moment she went down. Backstroking, she checked on her father breaststroking, his head up like a golden retriever, then rotated her own head to get a better sense of her bearings out in the bay, the current already tugging them past the solitary clump of lights on the southern shore, the storm paused atop the northern peninsula, its interior roiling with belches of sheet lightning. My God, she thought with callow reverence, swimming idly, *We're so alone.* She rolled on her stomach and with a sudden burst of energy raced ahead for the pleasure of it, just to the addictive point where her body exerted predominance over her mind and then she stopped and treaded water, waiting for her father to catch up but he was not there. She called out to him in the darkness and swam back toward the beacon of his muffled voice.

The length of his image was wrapped in a snowy shroud of phosphorescence, greenish flakes of swirling light, and she heard him speak—*Let's stay together*—before she could read the strain of his face. Her father's condition, as it had throughout the day, distressed her, and when he groaned she made him confess to leg cramps and relieved him of the duty of the dry bag and tied its cord around her own ankle. She tried to grab the collar of his life vest to tow him to shore, but he brushed her aside with the cavalier insistence that he had so far found their evening dunk in the sea to be rousing and rather enjoyable. After a few minutes swimming side by side she noticed the night growing more impenetrable, the seas higher, the bounce and slap of sounds more threatening. Surf, her father barked, and moments later her ears were assaulted by a booming cannonade as the storm advanced from its redoubt atop the peninsula. The first flash of lightning brought with it a scary glimpse of her father's face painted in wide-eyed cold insanity, his jawline hidden underwater below an expression of homicidal determination.

The second blaze of lightning revealed an image more viscerally horrifying: directly in her path spread a garden of small ghostly craniums planted in the water like translucent floating skulls of infants, and she gasped, reeling backward, feeling a slithery graze across her left forearm, suddenly afire with stinging, as the current swept them into the school of jellyfish. She swam frantically and then stopped abruptly, pulling in her legs and paddling back with her hands, realizing she was being sucked forward by the crest of a breaking wave. She pivoted to swim back toward her father, splashing and cursing somewhere in the darkness, and found him faltering.

My lips tingle, he murmured as she grabbed his collar, dragging him southward parallel to the shoreline, determined to escape what would surely result in slamming mutilation among the rocks on shore and the next thing she knew they were being flushed out into deeper water by the riptide.

The current seemed to bulge inward around a promontory she could sense but not see. Then they were captured back into the coast-bound swell and there was nothing she could do about it. Lifted and catapulted precipitously forward, she tumbled down the curling face of a wave, her hand torn from her father's vest and her body yanked backward through the wave's base by a deadweight suddenly attached to the dry bag, the following wave breaking on top of her before she could catch her breath, gyrating in a chaotic sliding vortex until she felt the toes of her free leg scrape the bottom—first crusty stone and then sand—and she popped back into the air, her father floating facedown behind her on a mattress of ebbing white water, his right hand snared in the dry-bag line. Trying to stand up she was knocked down by still another foamy surge, which she bellied into and rode to the beach, her father rolling behind her.

In the next flash of lightning she saw her father expired, done in, immobile, his face nuzzled in sand, his limp and swollen hand leashed to her ankle, and in a final bolt before the downpour began she saw him return to life, his shoulder blades laboring to lift him.

Her heart thumped wildly when she turned him over and heard his urgent but incomplete command—*Pill*—rattle behind his clenched teeth and the choking gurgle of what she feared might be his last breath. For a moment she was paralyzed by the riddle of what was required of her and then she pounced on the dry bag, freeing her father's tangled hand, and began clawing furiously through its contents. Her blind fingers groped among a mash of clothes and toiletries for a flashlight or the first-aid kit, whichever came first, and then she had them both and stuck her head in the bag, snapping open the plastic kit to find her choices blessedly limited— aspirin, Benadryl, an empty vial of penicillin—and ripped an antihistamine out of its foil sheet. Lashed by wind-driven rain, she pried down her father's clasped jaw and slipped the tablet onto his tongue but instantly determined he could not swallow and rammed the pill into the warm cavern of his throat with trembling fingers. In the rain-shredded cone of light framing his streaming face he looked at her with fluttering eyes and rasped, *More*, and she stopped when he shook his head after five doses, squatting over him, panic-stricken and helpless, observing his struggle to breathe, until finally he began to smack his sandy lips and snort water from his nose and she watched the slow and then greedy rise and fall of his lungs, only now aware that she herself had been hyperventilating.

On his feet again in the pelting rain her father was unsteady and she insisted he lay an arm across her shoulders for support. Like a pair of drunks they careened ahead, the yellow beam of the flashlight hopping erratically through the liquid darkness. At the top of the beach they discovered a path leading into the rocks and scrub and followed it to a grove of gnarled and ancient olive trees where, unable to discern an exit, they found instead a low wall of quarried biscuit-colored blocks that disappeared ahead into the brambled undergrowth.

Her father said, *Up,* and they picked their way over the uneven spine of stones, Dottie behind him, aiming the flashlight into the rain, the wall like the path leading them to a confusing end—not olive trees this time but rubble, which they descended haltingly back to the ground. He took the flashlight from her hand, swinging it in a half circle across a field of ruins, and seemed to give in to their predicament, his body stiff and surrendering, and he lowered onto the fluted marble drum of a collapsed column. Not good, she thought, get up. In desperation she took the light from him and left the bag at his feet, begging him not to stray, and began to probe deeper into the site, searching for anything that would serve as shelter. What she found instead, between a channel of half-fallen walls, was a narrow alley of overgrown flagstone and she retraced her steps back through the mounds to collect her ravaged father.

He walked with a sightless man's grip on her shoulder as she trudged a serpentine route back through the heaps sprouted with wind-whipped thistles and tufts of wiry grass, rediscovering the crumbled outer walls of what tomorrow he would tell her was Cyzicus, a city once heralded as a wonder of the ancient world, and followed the paving stones into its labyrinth of destruction, a phantom architecture of indiscernible fragments and toppled hulks, until their dogged meander brought them to a clearing and the raised platform of a former temple landscaped with scattered remnants, like abstract pieces on a gigantic chessboard. They arrived at the base of the temple, Dottie's light sliding over the terraced layering of its enormous foundation, up to the shorn mesa of what had once held the grandness of its roofed structure, and down again along its length to a series of marble steps like subway entrances descending into black mouths, the closest of which she edged them toward with increasing caution. The beam of light from her hand crept toward the opening, her adrenaline stirred as she realized the steps went steeply down to vaults embedded beneath the temple's floor, a honeycomb of underground space that beckoned and repelled.

Inexplicably, her father dropped his hand from her shoulder and resisted this, their first and only chance to get out of the weather, until she

379

said, Dad, I'm freezing, and he let himself be guided down the cracked steps until she stopped abruptly and pressed back against him, aiming the light beyond the vault's threshold, the beam jittering across a lumpy array of shit, broken glass, ouzo bottles, animal bones, cigarette butts, a spew of bricks beneath a gouge in the back wall, and a dead cat decomposing in a puddle. She hurried him back up the steps in disgust and took his hand to lead him down to the adjacent vault, scouring its spooky interior with the flashlight but spying nothing more offensive than spilled scoops of round goat turds and the rubbish from a shepherd's meal. When he balked again she said, *Come on!* forced to yank her father's arm to make him budge and they stepped through a fluid curtain of crystal beads out of the rain, properly shipwrecked and stranded, their ordeal perhaps in recess for the remainder of the night.

I remember this, said her father dully. By now she was shivering uncontrollably and had no idea what he was talking about and did not care.

They had stripped out of their wet suits and dressed in the clothes her father had jammed into the bag and got down and tried to sleep. Sometime during the night the rain stopped and she awoke scrunched against the back wall, in the same position in which she had nodded off, knees drawn into her chest and arms clasped around her folded legs and head wilted forward. The pain was back where she had left it before accepting a calming double-pinch of *naswar* from her father—a cut on the bottom of her left foot, the bracelet of raw tissue from the burn of the dry-bag cord on her right ankle, the scoring of welts across her flesh, identical to but less numerous and inflamed than her father's—and she did not open her eyes, letting her ears take responsibility for the state of her consciousness. The rain's harsh monotone had splintered into a much less intense dripping, plinking, splatting, pattering like tiny feet. She strained to hear what should also be there—her father's breathing, which she seemed to have misplaced. Wasn't he next to her, within touching distance? When the batteries failed, she had leaned her head against his shoulder for warmth and comfort but found neither, his body prone to excruciating adjustments—reflexive kicks and twitches and endless unsatisfying shifts, as though insects had gotten trapped under his shorts and T-shirt—and she had little choice but to scoot away from him, just far enough to separate herself from his intolerable torment.

Sometime later she felt a spreading caress soft as flannel along her skin as an exhalation of warm moist air pushed into the vault, its soothing breath laden with a potent myrrh-like fragrance that assaulted her nose with the strangeness of its arrival, and then her head snapped up alert, her eyes open but unseeing, and she heard her father's throaty croaks across the vault, a mad oracle mumbling nonsense, though his lilting inflections and pauses seemed credulously engaged and conversational, a man on the telephone.

Daddy, she hissed, her hand instinctively searching for the flashlight. Who are you talking to?

Can you see it? he said, the surprise of his lucidity making the hair stand up on the back of her neck.

What? she said. I smell something.

Yes, yes.

Where are you?

You can see him, then? her father said, the words stretched and clutched with emotion.

Him what? she implored. You're scaring me.

The frantic sweep of her hand located the flashlight and she switched it on, casting a receding glow of pink light across the vault before returning them to darkness, but not before her eyes had composed an image of her father on his knees, his arms flung out to embrace or receive the emptiness at his fingertips, silver rivulets of tears etched down his cheeks and his face expressing a contorted pleasure so beyond happiness she shuddered.

Dad, she said. I'm totally freaked. Was somebody here?

He chuckled knowingly and said, If I said an angel, you'd be worried about me, wouldn't you? and she heard herself asking more with reluctance than disbelief, What did the angel say?

Nothing I don't already know, he said.

It was weird and exhausting talking this way, like two glaze-eyed converts exchanging heavenly revelations in a Roman catacomb, yet she forgave him with a gush of sympathy when without a sound he transported himself across the room with dreamlike ease and she felt the tentative touch of his hand exploring her arm, her heart absorbing his great weary sigh as he sat down next to her and bent her head to his chest, whispering with the pure sweetness of paternal love into her damp hair, *Go back to sleep now, baby*.

Okay, she mumbled, half-asleep and falling away, wondering was she entering a dream herself or leaving it when she heard him say, thought he said, imagined him saying, they had been summoned by God to Ephesus.

You were dreaming, right? she mumbled again, drifting down into his warmth.

Get some rest now, her father said. We've been called.

What awaited her in the morning was not what she anticipated—his supernatural recovery, her father restored to an even more vibrant and contagious version of his former self, outside in the ruins singing like Caruso, his gusto a questionable tonic for her own low mood, its thirst and famished appetite, its itch and ache. Grotty hair and exasperation. She complained to herself, wanting her hairbrush, carelessly emptying the dry bag onto the floor and repacking everything in a fit of sullenness. He had at least bothered to rescue her drawstring pouch of jewelry, from which she removed Osman's evil-eye bracelet to slip over her wrist, feeling no better for its belated protection.

She watched him with waning impudence from the top of the vault's steps, analyzing the transformation that had occurred, his nose in the ruins like an archaeologist at his first dig. When he turned and saw her, she was hailed with a barrage of manic exclamations. *Fantastic! Tremendous! Look at this place!* He laid his hands reverently on an intact slab of cornice to examine its pattern of ovoid carvings. *What about that fucking storm! Never seen anything like it!* He stooped to pick up a pottery shard, rubbing off the grime with his thumb. *Hercules! Hadrian! Marcus Aurelius! They were here!* He spun around, marveling at the surpassing novelty of their good fortune. *How's this for an adventure!*

Daddy, she said. What about my poor *Sea Nymph*?

The boat was fun, wasn't it? he said. Done, finished—every epitaph a non sequitur.

But I'll miss her, Dottie whimpered, a mawkish invitation to be consoled, an abject useless desire immediately discarded when he began to clap his hands provocatively, like her swim coach, challenging her to fly into high gear.

All right! Big day! Let's go!

Without any affectation of modesty, she unbuttoned and dropped her blue jeans to her ankles and peed. As she pulled up her pants she chided him for forgetting to pack toilet tissue and then voiced her most serious grievance—her purse and camera were missing. He lavished her not with apology but offhanded rationale; he had grabbed whatever he could find to stuff into the bag and here they were, two very lucky castaways, alive and well and in God's care. Nothing had been lost, Kitten, that could not be easily replaced. My address book, she whined, my passport. We'll replace them, he repeated cheerfully. Don't worry.

She was, after all, a teenager and willing, when properly seduced or inspired, to exchange one attitude for another, without a mature dislike of contradiction or the need for introspection. *What a perfect little bitch*, she reproached herself, shamefully aware that she had awakened prepared to hold her father accountable for all things beyond his control—the squall, the badly installed toilet and its catastrophic leak, his diseased intestines, his untimely slump into grief, the poisonous jellies, his almost dying, and the unsettling hallucinatory cameo of his resurrection. On the verge of genuine tears, she ran to hug him, clinging to his waist with gratitude, and when they separated she asked what was the plan and he looked at her with tender-eyed derangement, his neck a rashy swelter of stings, and answered, *Ephesus.*

Oh, she said uncertainly, I thought that was something I dreamed, and his right eye twitched—or was that a wink?—adding ambiguity to his constricted smile.

A muddy goat trail flanked by nodding sunflowers led them away from the ruins into a ravine where they wandered into the ancient city's amphitheater, scaling its broken rows of seats to the top of a windswept hill from which they could see the arched remnants of an aqueduct leading past a nearby village ringed with poplars, its dirt track connecting to a narrow road winding back toward the mainland. The lonely, primitive cluster of whitewashed cottages seemed abandoned until a large mastiff sent out an alarm of rabid barking at their approach and a gaunt churlish man with pants held up by suspenders opened his door to stare at them. She asked if they could stop for water but her father said I don't like the looks of that dog and they went on. Following the path to the track, and the track to the scabrous paved road, they found an elderly peasant woman sitting with her linen-covered market baskets on a simple wooden bench, who pointed to where the next bus to Edincik would arrive. She wore a faded blue dress cut like a grocer's smock, her white hair frizzing out from beneath a yellowed head scarf, and seemed to accept their company as an unremarkable event.

The bus was unexpectedly sleek and modern, an air-conditioned first-class coach with high windows and tall reclining seats that allowed for privacy among its unlikely manifest of shabby peasants. She and her father passed down the aisle to the empty seats at the back of the bus and slid into a row, Dottie taking the window.

Tourists? someone asked, but when she started to answer her father jumped in, telling unctuous little lies, alternate but plausible identities and circumstance fabricated out of habit, she supposed, and she began to feel cheated, realizing his intent to leave their incredible adventure a private affair, a decision she did not understand even as she remembered her father saying more than once that fame was a curse he could ill afford. That's you, she argued silently.

She was relieved to be off her injured foot but immediately vulnerable to more mundane discomforts—she craved water, her toothbrush, a shower; she wanted a tomato and onion omelet and a telephone, aching to spellbind Osman and her girlfriends with tales of personal disaster and, increasingly, with each passing minute stuck next to him in their upholstered booth, she wanted to retch from the suffocating vileness of her father's breath. The next thing she knew he was shaking her bad foot and she woke up ugly and snarling, saying, You're hurting me.

They had backtracked to Bandirma, Dottie asleep during the brief stop at the Edincik market. Their bus had been chartered by a travel agency for an excursion to a nearby national park, her father said, they had to get off with everybody else and find another bus going south. He paid the driver with lira from the dry bag and they stood in the sunlight of the insipid provincial depot, looking for a kiosk or vendor, anyone selling anything she could drink or eat, even a pack of mints would be heavenly, until she spotted a police station across the car park and said, pointing, Shouldn't we go there and report? and her father gave her a look that made her feel dense. Report what? he said. I think by now you would have learned your lesson about Turkish gendarmes. He was right, of course, but she felt disappointed again, her role in their survival negated, the act of telling someone, anyone, essential to her need to be rewarded somehow for her mettle, for not being a helpless baby, a reward not forthcoming from her father, who ambled off to make inquiries about schedules and destinations.

She sighed heavily and wandered around dragging the dry bag until she saw a kid lugging a jerrican sloshing water from its uncapped spout and he directed her to a public standpipe. Grateful at least for this, she removed her sunglasses, washed her hands clean and tossed water in her face, ignoring the vulgar catcalls of several pimply adolescent boys lounging against a nearby wall. Bent over the spigot to rinse her mouth, she listened to the taunts rise in volume and specificity—*Stick it in! She's waiting, she wants it!*—and sensing someone behind her she wheeled around to confront a handsome boy holding at his groin a priapic loaf of bread, previously aimed at her ass. They seemed for a moment disarmed by one another, her contemptuous smirk softening with sly and interrogating curiosity, sweet chagrin replacing the loutish arrogance in his sea-green eyes, before her gaze shifted over his shoulder and her expression became deadly serious and she said with fair warning, *Get out of here, my father is coming.*

Throughout her life, her father's outbursts had been rare but devastating, meant to destroy, his victims never his own family, thank God, but house servants who had stolen, cabdrivers who had cheated, rude strangers who pushed things too far. Never pardon or forget an insult, he once told her on a street corner in Rome, standing over a man he had just knocked down for groping her mother's breast on the crowded sidewalk. The boy turned, the self-deprecating grin that a moment before she had thought cute erased by her father's right hand with the speed of a guillotine, his fingers clawed into the throat of the boy, the boy gurgling for air. She stepped back, petrified, then lunged after them, her father strong-arming the boy across the oil-stained macadam to slam him against the side of a bus, Dottie crying for him to stop, inhaling her father's shit-breath seeping from the ice-cold hiss of his English: *I saw you, mujo. I saw you.*

But it went no further than that. He raised and cocked his left hand as if he meant to strike the boy yet his murderous focus turned sensible, businesslike, he was only checking the time on his wristwatch and the almost comic reversal of his personality left her giddy and dumbfounded, the boy released and forgotten, her father grabbing her hand, her other hand snatching the bag. *Wait! The bread!* she blurted, her emotions thrown aside by her unfailing instinct for self-preservation. Her father snatched up the baguette from where the boy had dropped it and the two of them were off and running like muggers to a bus beginning to roll, its doors closing behind them as they clambered aboard, breathless and, in Dottie's case, silly with laughter.

They sat near the back, her father at the window because she didn't want to be barricaded in by him again. She knew it was out of the question to object to his behavior. The boys in Istanbul are a lot worse, she could tell him, but he would find the comparison meaningless.

Where are we going? she asked and he told her Izmir and she said she wanted the bread, which she ate, relaxing into a lazy acquiescence, well-suited for daylong bus rides, toward everything strange and extraordinary that had happened, or might yet happen, on their journey. Her father, for the most part, occupied himself with his mother's ivory rosary, interrupting his prayers frequently to scratch, abstracted, at his welts.

CHAPTER TWENTY-EIGHT

They arrived in Izmir at dusk and she was thrilled to smell the sea again after a day spent motoring through the interior, fertile countryside rising steadily into a range of savage mountains that formed the backdrop to the city and its steep hills and the terminus of the Aegean waterfront where they now walked along the Kordon among a stream of pedestrians and cyclists, the cafés alive with noise and gaiety. The first two pensions they scouted were grungy and inhospitable, but the third, above a fish restaurant, seemed good enough, its rooms plain but comfortable. She went directly to the shower while her father registered and paid, leaving it to him to bullshit the proprietor, if the man cared at all, about her lack of identification.

Because she had not heard him return to the room, she shrieked when the bathroom door swung open, his intrusion a predictable surprise, saying, Don't use up all the hot water, kiddo, but he withdrew before she had to tell him to get out. She wrapped herself in scratchy towels and attached her narcissistic scrutiny to the mirror above the sink, admiring the sun-cooked tone of her complexion until he glided behind her into the stall, and she slipped away to the temporary privacy of the room.

Bracketed to the wall was an old television and she turned it on while she dried her hair, plopping down on the edge of the twin bed she had claimed as hers, her attention divided between the toweling and inspecting the wounds of her journey, hoping for at least one scar to brandish as a badge of honor, half-listening to both her father's bubbly croon of

387

pleasure and the transmission from an Istanbul station, a snowy static-smeared installment of a game show.

When she heard the shower stop, she jumped away from her towels and dressed hurriedly in her only clothes, worn throughout the night and now all day and sat back down, her fingers combing out her tangles, waiting for her father, wishing he would hurry. The show ended and the evening news began in garbled, urgent Turkish and the bathroom door slammed open and there was her father, nude and frowning and riveted on the broadcast.

Fuck, he said, who gave them that picture?

She turned in time to see a cutaway from her father's face to a Turkish coast guard helicopter lifting off from its base and then a map of the Dardanelles, an X north of the entrance to the straits, the commentator describing the unsuccessful search for the American diplomat and his daughter, lost at sea.

Oh, my God, that's us!

Son of a bitch, said her father.

They think we drowned. But they're looking in the wrong place, aren't they? said Dottie, bewildered but no less fascinated to be the subject of the news. She looked at her father for confirmation, startled with pity to see his flagellated body up close and in its entirety, the scarlet crisscross of whiplike markings on his shoulders, stomach, and thighs, but all she got from him was a guileless smile.

Let's get something to eat, he said, blithely lighting a cigarette before tugging his pants on over wet legs. It looks like we have a lot to talk about.

She wanted to sit outside at a sidewalk table but he chose a less crowded area in the rear of the restaurant. He sat not opposite but next to her and they ordered a bottle of red wine, her father leaning on his forearms, speaking in an earnest but confidential voice, falling silent each time the waiter arrived with a new round of meze.

It seemed reasonable and likely, he speculated, taking occasional small bites while she ripped through everything on the table, that whoever had answered their Mayday call had copied down the wrong coordinates. She swallowed what was in her mouth to say, But now they think we're dead.

Ah, he said, exactly, and there's the opportunity.

She did not understand his thinking and it seemed wrong and hurtful to everyone who cared about them, to pretend they had drowned when they had not. Not clever and romantic—irresponsible. It was, she realized, taking the game too far, and he said, First thing, you have to imagine that everyone's pretending everything except us. We're the ones only pretending to pretend.

Why would we pretend we're dead?

To be just you and me, he said, completely and absolutely free, the last two unencumbered people on earth. You see what I'm saying, don't you? No obligations, no responsibilities, no concerns. To be anybody you like, to be anybody you desire. It's a wonderful opportunity, don't you think? We answer to nobody and nothing except ourselves, like it was on the boat. Just until we return to Istanbul in ten days, where everything will be the same, except we'll be resurrected, won't we, returned from the sea. It's an experiment I've always wanted to try, and now, as I said, here's the opportunity, heaven-sent.

She remained unconvinced, unable to perceive how their freedom was enhanced or their liberties multiplied by playing dead. Tell you what, he said with the aplomb that always tempted her with provisional assurance. He raised his wine to toast, pausing until she did the same, and clinked her glass as if she had already consented to his plan. We'll try it for a day or two and if you feel it's not working out I'll call the authorities and say, Hey, you dopes, here we are, quite thoroughly alive. What do you say, Kitten? The possibilities are damn intriguing.

She felt the impulse to maneuver around her allegiance to their solidarity, careful not to fracture it with an excess of doubt or haggling but trading what she could afford to lose. Okay, she said, but on one condition, she wanted to make a phone call first. He wanted to know to whom, she told him Osman and Elena, it was only fair to let them know, she could make them swear to keep their mouths shut, and he said, Let's compromise. I'll call Mary Beth to let her in on the scheme and I'll have her call your mother and Christopher and your two friends and let them know what we're up to and that, I think, he said, standing up with his palms flat on the table to whisper in her ear, solves our problem, sweetheart. And then he was off to requisition a telephone.

She poured herself another glass of wine, emptying the bottle, and drank half before stopping to consider what her father was proposing and why, another game but this one improvised toward a purpose that seemed superfluous and a bit zany. Together they had never been anything but free—perhaps too free, she thought, trying not to dwell on what she meant, the implication of her submissiveness. And yet the thing about playing with Daddy was she always felt more herself, unshackled and granted immunity from the deepest part of her interior. All the blind alleys of self-discovery were, or had been so far, most securely investigated in the company of her father. Was that normal? she wondered, knowing she did not care to answer her own question, and then he was back at the table, making no effort to mask his consternation, and she said, What's wrong? Something's wrong, right?

He said, Should we order another bottle of wine? and when she said if you want he summoned the waiter and they chose identical entrées— grilled sea bass—for their dinner, Dottie abandoning her craving for a hamburger. When he lit a cigarette she asked for one too, waiting impatiently for the wine to be opened and poured, glancing at his new and unshaped beard, which had begun to look wolfish, she thought, a definite change from his physical trademark, the well-groomed presentation of reliability, and then free of the waiter she said, Okay, I know that look— are you going to tell me?

Perhaps our plan is being outpaced by events, he said cryptically, stabbing out his cigarette and lighting another. Or, he said brightening, one can finally see God's hand in the plot.

Earth to Dad, she said.

Right, he said, smiling apologetically. Mary Beth was distressed, as you might imagine, to be falsely informed of our fate by the Turks, and damn happy to hear otherwise. Then she was right back to business, something in the works for months, and now, apparently, we are looking at a green light, all systems go as they say in Houston, except for the lack of one, most crucial player.

So, can you tell me, asked Dottie, or is this one of those hush-hush things?

I think we can say this is very much one of those hush-hush things, he said, pausing for the waiter to deliver their plates of grilled fish before adding, Can I tell you? Actually, I've already told you.

Oh, you mean—

Believe me, I've thought long and hard about this, the risk involved, et cetera—I'll ask once more and I promise never again: Would you consider helping us out?

You mean the Pope thing . . . somebody trying to hurt the Pope. That thing?

He picked up his tableware, methodically deboning his fish and then switching plates to debone hers, and thus began his rant, sotto voce, deliberate, unbreachable except by a forkful of sea bass, the obsessive unscrolling of his universe, the politics and theology of its underpinning, which she barely listened to as she ate, not bored but restless, her attention not quite synchronized with what he was telling her. She had been overly inducted into his sophistry, its sideline audience for so many years, his beliefs invading and occupying her metabolism until they had become, without the virulence, her own.

With that with which you cannot compromise, she heard him say, it is impossible to be too aggressive, and her attention sprang back at the shift in his tone, the serene marshaling of details, as he finally resolved to lead her through the gates of his conspiracy. Of course she did not need to be reminded of the man who shot Pope John Paul II—Mehmet Ali Ağca; a Turk. Her Turkish friends, when they learned she was Roman Catholic, were embarrassed to say his name. Did she know why this man attempted to assassinate the Holy Father? I guess so, she told her father, whose heavy-lidded eyes seemed to smolder with impersonal anger as he corrected her: No, the crime was not religious except ostensibly; here was a case of a contract gunman recruited by government security agents. My God, said Dottie, what government would want to kill the Pope?

And he told her: the Soviets, the Soviets, the Soviets. The Soviets, who will stop at nothing to eliminate the Almighty's presence on this earth;

the Soviets, who instructed their surrogates in Bulgaria to orchestrate this diabolical crime; the Soviets, who, having failed, are prepared to try again, this time with a more effective cast of puppets, the blood-sucking Yugoslavs, some of whom I know very well, he said, and you must never breathe a word of this, what I'm telling you . . . and the fish would be better with raki, I think. Would you like something else? he asked and she said, Just water.

Her mind was empty as blue sky. She picked absently at the last spice-laden morsels of crispy skin on her plate while they waited for the waiter to leave. You have questions, her father declared, but she did not, not yet. The magnitude of what he had asked her seemed beyond the scope of her direct involvement, although it amazed her to think of her father as the one person in the world employed to stop this terrible thing from happening.

What am I asking you to do? her father rushed ahead. The man the Yugoslavs are sending to Istanbul to organize this atrocity has a well-observed weakness, and I need the assistance of someone like you, I need *your* assistance, to exploit that weakness. Why you, you ask, rather than someone like you? Here is the answer: to keep it in the family, so to speak, makes everything easier to contain.

Someone like me?

I will say it straight out, keeping nothing from you, said her father. The weakness they would exploit—he started to explain but succumbed to a quote. *He liked green fruit, imported from the west.* Who wrote that?

I have no idea.

That's our man Conrad, one of the Asian novels. It means this Serbian bastard I'm referring to has a taste for young women, young Western women, most notably blondes. I hope to God I'm not offending you, he said.

She scoffed at his presumption. At times her father was shock incarnate.

Now is the time to say you'd rather not get involved. There are alternatives.

But you have to tell me, she said, what the operation is, and when he finished describing the plan she said, Oh, you want me to pretend to be a prostitute.

Pretend, he assured her, was the operative word. Honey to trap the bear. The man only has to believe he can have his way. I would kill him before I would ever let him lay a hand on you.

No kidding, she said facetiously.

I've never been more serious, Kitten.

God, she said, I know.

He took the napkin from his lap to wipe his lips. I'm having a coffee and cognac, he said. Would you like some dessert? Without any hesitation she said yes, a chocolate fudge sundae, and when it was put before her she held her spoon in the air, turning her wrist with alluring dips and batting her eyelashes in a parody of a coquette.

So Daddy, she said, feigning radiant breathlessness, how would a prostitute eat her ice cream? and her father smiled enigmatically and said, Good question, assessing her with incipient prurience before he seemed to remember himself. You're a natural, kiddo, he told her, but I think you might be overplaying it.

In her bed an hour later she lay on her back with her eyes closed, wondering who the woman was, the winner of his nocturnal competition, as she listened to the sounds of her father's surreptitious jerking off, the barely audible piston-like rhythm, the familiar soft methodical pump of friction climaxing in a sharp suck of air as if he had inhaled a hot ember and she thought, sarcastically, *Glad that's over with,* and turned on her side away from him, tense and agitated, her left hand sandwiched idly between her thighs, a finger rolling the tiny hard pearl, thinking, Who's behind the door—prostitute or daughter? *Well, not Mom, that's for sure.*

CHAPTER TWENTY-NINE

His quick sidelong glance her way warned of discretion and she watched him sign the hotel receipt, *Lawrence Budd,* his copperplate penmanship a beautiful thing, an airy old-fashioned cursive—*Lawrence Budd?*—understanding the mission had been initiated prior to her own induction, a revelation that made her feel and act capricious throughout their breakfast on the promenade. Sitting at one of the café tables under a blue-and-white-striped umbrella, she was jealous of the sea and its sailboats, her sunglasses obscuring only half of her morose expression, grumpy monosyllables all she offered her father who, trying again for an insight into her mood, solicited a lie. I'm getting my period, okay? she said, unwilling to declare he should not always count on her to say yes to everything, and after that he had the sense to ignore her as she crumbled a pastry into her untouched tea. Then a white Mercedes-Benz sedan, a much older model than Mr. Maranian's and not well-kept, edged slowly up to the curb, and the driver lowered his window and stuck his head out—*Excuse please . . . Mister Budd?*—and her father said, Time to go. *And like who the fuck am I?* she thought. *Rose Budd? Very funny.*

She had lost track of the days and did not realize it was Sunday morning until her father told the driver to take them to a Catholic church—*No, no, this one's Orthodox,* he said, and they eventually arrived at the cathedral of St. John the Evangelist at the top of the city, the two of them dashing inside to the ringing of bells, joining the shuffle of an oddly mixed congregation, elderly women, European bureaucrats, and military personnel, toward the richly decorated altar. NATO, her father whispered. I believe they have a headquarters here. With love flowing in his eyes, her father pulled her to her feet as the mass ended and they walked arm in arm outside into the Aegean sun and back to the car, his voice cracking with emotion, recalling that here in this city, Homer's birthplace and apostolic sanctuary, once stood the first of the seven churches of Revelation. Without Turkey, her father reminded her, there would be no Christianity. Not without Rome, not even without Jerusalem, but *without Turkey*. And then they were on the road south to Ephesus, the once-great city of Asia Minor, where her father seemed to have a nervous breakdown.

Except for her father's sole instruction to the driver—*Meryemana, House of Mary, my friend*—no one said anything for three hours, her father content again to fumble with his mother's rosary, his lips sipping the air with nine repetitions of the *Memorare*. Dottie stared out the window at the elysian countryside, her thoughts flitting around, unable to settle into even a rudimentary coherence, feelings attached to a parsimonious minimum of words—Osman, the *Sea Nymph*, prostitution, angels, shopping, evil, the storm, her lost Nikon, Jacqueline in France, Karim's malicious sensuality— the elliptical survey of her reverie interrupted by the blink in her vision of a signpost announcing the archaeological preserve of Ephesus and the sudden wrenching heaviness of her father's breathing. When she looked at him, his eyes and mouth were closed tight and twisted in a grimace and he had broken into a crosshatching of sweat. Daddy? she asked, brushing his knee with no response. The driver turned off the main road onto a narrow serpentine route looping up a pine-forested mountain and she tilted her head toward her father's quivering lips to determine that he was asking her to tell the driver to stop.

In our hearts are the words, he said, scrambling out of the car, and she thought he was going to be sick but something else was happening. He told her with a deeply pained look that he would walk the rest of the way, to arrive at the house of the Mother of God as a penitent on his knees. Join me, he said, and she asked the driver how far it was and told her father her foot hurt too much to walk six kilometers up a mountain and he simply knelt down on the side of the road to pray, a mortification that made her stretch across the seat to shut his door. See you up there, she said, the heat of the afternoon and her father's overheated faith and the length of these final miles intensifying her disapprobation. The chauffeur turned into the car park at the summit and kept the engine running as he got out to open her door, then unlocked the trunk to remove the dry bag and, without a word, got back in and left. She looked around, figuring it would take her weird-ass father—*Saint Dementia,* she had dubbed this stranger—the remainder of the day to crawl the distance, and what was she supposed to do in the meantime?

A busload of Muslim tourists disembarked, a preponderance of women in head scarves and black raincoat dresses, whom she trailed down a walkway into the pines, the air laden with golden motes. Her body began to respond, feathery shivers of electricity absorbed in her chest, some ancient lingering energy flowing up and through the limbs of her spirit, tendrils of holiness like climbing vines. Her heart felt gripped by this modest stone cottage ahead in the trees, a hut really, a woodcutter's shelter, a place to hide from the world, where St. John had brought the Virgin away from the unforgiving barbarity of Jerusalem. These mortared walls in this lovely forest where Mary ate her bread and studied the dome of stars, wrestling with the miracle of her child, and, finally, died from so much yearning. In everything she looked at she perceived a mystical shimmer that could only be the mingling of auras, hers and Mary's. Their feet on the same ground, the baked fragrance of pine needles the same, century after century; their ears buzzing with the same isolation, the Virgin's parched throat cooled from this sacred spring whose water Dottie now drank from the cup of her hands. How could she have possibly foreseen what was being asked of her, what she had gotten herself into? Had she been carefully chosen or had it been more like, *Okay, you,* one womb as good as the next to carry light into the world? And whatever miracle could make that happen, Dottie thought, if a virgin has a baby, he better be the Son of God.

Her father had told her this: God sent his Son to experience time, the Achilles heel of creation, known only through the tribulations of mankind. The Virgin birth was meant to establish the bridge back across the cosmic

396

chasm—time's correction. Understand? The universe was not whole until Mary, the mother of our completion. Dottie was still a child when her father told her this and she had failed to comprehend why God didn't just have the baby himself—why trouble poor Mary? And when she was older, and more understanding, Dottie wondered skeptically, *Wait, did God rape Mary?* which is when she stopped going to confession, afraid to confess the mortal sinfulness of such a thought.

But how crowded it was, she felt, entering the queue into the T-shaped building, peeking around the horde of bodies into its austere vaulted bedroom and dank kitchen and kneeling with so many others on the cobbley roughness of the floor, candles guttering in the dim light, at the shrine dedicated by the Polish Pope himself, *her* Pope. She stood up in a daze of profundity and walked back out into the dappled shade of the trees to find a place to sit down—a low stone wall to the side of Mary's house, the mountainside plunging behind her—and sat there without being aware of anything much, her eyes blurred, staring at panels of an abstract fresco made from chicken wire fencing, its mesh crammed with the petitions of the devout—colorful bits of rag, scrawled notes, flower puffs, inscrutable totems: anything to make a wish—until the tranquillity she had discovered was blown apart by her father's arrival.

Wary-eyed pilgrims began to crane their attention toward a disturbance and when she stood to see what caused them to nod and point there was the spectacle of her father on the terrace, on his knees, shirtless, his torso slashed with angry stigmata, fists clenched over his weeping eyes, his chin wobbly with lamentation. My God, she thought, how did he become such a mess? She knew she should run to him but could not. And when he rose to his feet she gasped—can someone so dignified and handsome possibly look this wicked and unhinged?—tourists giving him a wide berth as he began to shout in English at the blameless Mary-worshipping Muslims—*You fucking motherfucking* mujos, *you filthy wild beasts, you cockroaches*—until a nun came flying like a raven out of the shrine and seemed to swoop him up in saintly wings and somehow pacify him.

Dottie held her breath, dreading the return of this crazy person to her side yet when she saw him straggle out the low doorway at the rear of Mary's house at least his shirt was on and he no longer required a chaperone. His puffy eyes searched the terrace, spotting her on the wall. He tried to smile but failed, his face disfigured by renewed bawling, coming toward her with outstretched arms, streaming tears.

Daddy, just sit down, she said coldly, estranged by his psycho display of weakness, and he did as he was told. Stuttering in a strangulated voice, he said that today was his mother's birthday, and Dottie pinned herself onto his tormented chest to console him and he clung to her until he regained his composure, the tremble of his hands receding, his jaw firm, eyes increasingly alert to here and now, the pathos draining out of him. I thank God for the joy of this day, he announced, a king's proclamation, sealing his emotions back into the deep reaches of his darkness. I've waited all my life for this, he said. *This what?* she wanted to ask but instead said nothing and watched him stand resolutely and walk to the chicken wire panels and pluck out from its collage a black scroll of paper, its tube containing keys and directions to a house in nearby Selcuk, and she followed after him to search the car park for a green Toyota sedan and then they got in and left.

Disorder was still an illusion—there was and always would be a plan. Sometimes she forgot, but she had learned long ago to count on it. *Never underrate Daddy.*

In the days ahead she would sometimes complain about being stashed away, sequestered in the dreary bungalow—bare stuccoed walls, sagging beds, spattered taupe curtains suggesting a house with a history she would rather not know, cracked linoleum floors, smelly kerosene stove, cobwebs and spiders, mouse shit and the stink of rotting onions everywhere. They could have easily rented something fabulous—a hip villa with a swimming pool—in the bustling seaside town of Kusadasi, some twenty kilometers southwest, where she was finally allowed her shopping spree and a trip to a bookstore (she picked out a used copy of *Fear of Flying* based on a startling chapter title—"Arabs and Other Animals"). But her objections were tempered by the return of her father's happiness, his unflagging upbeat mood and his love affair with the village, Ephesus a thirty-minute walk through the dust and heat and fumes, their quiet neighborhood only a few blocks east of a hill crowned by a Byzantine citadel, which she could see from her streaky bedroom window, and the shorn ruins of the Basilica of St. John, containing the disciple's grave—ground zero, the Ur-church, her father never tired of saying, John wrote his gospel up there. Her father's newly acquired habit to awake and shower before dawn for a circuit of reverent wandering around Ayasuluk Hill before breakfast, returning in time for coffee and scrambled eggs with the man he called his uncle, her trainer or helper or whatever, the person readying her for what she prosaically called the Pope Thing.

Her indoctrination began the evening they drove down the mountain from Meryemana into Selcuk and found the house at the back of the village. The minute she walked through the front door there was Mr. Maranian, her eyes gladdened by the sight of him, his herringbone jacket and sweater vest (doesn't he know it's ninety degrees out), yellow tie, rumpled trousers, steel-framed glasses, dignified posture—Maranian, her mirthless surrogate grandfather. The dry bag fell from her hand and she skipped to kiss his cheeks but he accepted her affection rigidly, eyes slitted and his palms out flat at his waist to keep a tense distance between them.

This is a dirty business, he said by way of greeting, scowling over her head at her father, a disaffected salute, but she refused to be chastened. *My boat sank!* she was finally able to blab but he already seemed to know, dismissing her excitement with a grimness she would not heed. He stepped out of the way of an elderly man coming from the kitchen, his beige linen suit protected by a flowery bib apron, the collar of his black shirt open beneath the stringy wattles of his throat, a shoulder oddly slanted, his face like chiseled stone with robin's-egg-blue eyes sunk below a skull squared by the brush-cut wheat stubble of his hair. He was good-looking, even at his age, a raw handsomeness more virile than alluring. He frightened her a little even as he met her with the warmest of disconcerting smiles, his lips parted across gold-capped teeth, looking at her as if she were a beloved ghost he had spent a lifetime chasing. Then he bowed at the waist like a clownish gallant and she gawked at the old man's mangled ear and he moved forward to embrace her father with one good arm. The two exchanged a hug more brotherly than formal, conversing in a language she had learned to recognize since her father's trips to Belgrade, but his apparent fluency in Serbo-Croatian surprised her.

Come, meet my daughter, her father said in English, taking the old man's hand. Dottie, he said, this is Davor, a friend of our family for many years.

The old man spoke to her and she looked from Davor to her father, who told him to speak Italian, and then, her brain flipping switches and rewiring to Rome, she understood: she was the . . . something—reincarnation? . . . of her grandmother.

You knew my grandmother? she asked, and then in English—Is that right?

He knew her very well, said her father, and she watched this man Davor wag his head yes, yes, yes, with rueful sweetness.

Maranian, forgotten and abject, cleared his throat to excuse himself, saying, Steven, documents I leave in the kitchen, good night.

Hey, no, her father protested. Stay for dinner, but Maranian withdrew with a morose glance in Dottie's direction, saying he would return in the morning with the lady.

Come, eh? said Davor to father and daughter, oblivious to the Armenian. Eat. A good time.

His English is baby talk, said her father. Italian would be their lingua franca, and in Italian she asked—a first sentence learned in any language—*Where is the toilet, please?*

He had cooked a wonderful supper—veal parmigiana and fried artichokes and a tossed vinaigrette salad of pine nuts, *finnochio,* endive, and mesclun greens and as they ate the old man could not take his eyes off Dottie, his fixation quickly unnerving, drawing a shade over her curiosity and its myriad questions. *Why don't you just take a picture,* she thought, not knowing that was the plan for tomorrow. The meal was *so good,* a culinary echo of living in Trastevere, and she concentrated on that memory, walking up the hill, ponytailed, with her uniformed schoolmates to the Janiculum, leaving the two men to talk sparingly between mouthfuls in their private language, until the old man winked at her father and reached across the Formica table to cuddle her hand, a papery touch of paternal kindness, and declare in Italian his wish to rub honey on her _____ and lick it off.

Honey on my what? she asked in English, looking to her father, puzzled. I don't know that word.

Your nipples.

Oh. She frowned but did not take her hand away from the old man as she processed the intent of this outlandish vulgarity. He's joking, right?

He's helping you, said her father. We've boarded the train. This is what we're doing now. Tell him anything you want. Tell him, Maybe later. Tell him to go fuck himself.

She locked her eyes on Davor's but they had changed, darkened with sexual aggression and she bunched her lips, staring back bravely at him as she lifted his speckled bony fingers from her hand and said with a shallow tone of promise, *Maybe later, okay?* and the old man snatched her hand back, squeezing her fingers with increasing pressure, saying, *Show me strength, girl,* and he was hurting her but she squeezed back stubbornly, between them now her resistance and his sphinxlike silence, assaying her value, until his eyes relaxed and he jerked his hand from hers to slap the table with a volley of applause.

In English, he told her he loved her very much. Not joking, he said, and she thought, *Fuck you.*

He told her she was beautiful and added in Italian: Beautiful women get away with murder.

Why is that? she said innocently.

The old man smiled, feigning his own innocence, and scraped his chair away from the table, grabbing a bottle of Slivovitz off the counter. From Croatia, he said, the best, but she did not want to stay up all night to drink with them and playact or fatten her Italian vocabulary with anatomical parts and she kissed her father's forehead and went to bed.

In the morning after breakfast she was given a large brown envelope fastened with a metal clasp, which contained her new identity—an Italian passport with the same photograph used for her American one lost at sea, issued in the name of Carla Costa, stamped with a student visa.

Is it legal? she asked and her father said, You bet. *Now put Dottie out of your mind,* her father insisted, *Do not answer to Dottie.* You are Roman-born, the child of an expatriate American mother and Italian father. Her make-believe mother: an art historian; her father a statistician for the Food and Agricultural Organization near the Forum—it was all there in the documents in the envelope, imperative that she memorize every last word, to live, breathe, dream *Carla.*

At first being someone else did not seem like much of a problem. Her assimilation of Carla, her Carla feelings, felt real enough yet then what initially felt genuine would end up feeling pretentious and fake—but her father, when he caught a whiff of her misgivings, would tell her, Let Carla *be* you, you don't have to be Carla, see the difference?

Not really, she said.

Try this, he said. Think self-replicating, self-affirming.

Okay, she said, dubious, but gradually she began to submit to the deeper temptation, an acolyte in her father's black zone of secrets. She would *be* the secret, penetrating the less overt layers of stealth only to find at the very bottom of the game, through the game's last unopened door, herself, the starlet of enigma, the mystery made flesh.

Changing oneself, however, was a facile trick, a practice not unfamiliar to ordinary teenage girls and their looking-glass wars. But Dottie glimpsed the real challenge at the end of the masquerade—changing back was not so easy if your former self no longer interlocked cleanly and separated effortlessly with the shape you had assumed, and when you retraced your steps searching for your original self, maybe that wasn't enough, because self-possession would now mean *what?*—a sharing—or a refusal to share—between two selves. It was giving her a headache to think this way.

Inside the packet as well were a from-the-shoulders-up photograph and a sketchy profile of the target, her nemesis, the villain she would lure into the trap where, it was carefully explained, he would be taken into custody, interrogated, and, after confessing the names of fellow conspirators he had traveled to Turkey to recruit, deported. Why not just grab him off the street? she asked and her father said, We've considered that—too many things could go wrong. But the option remained on the table if she got cold feet.

Despite his beribboned military uniform with its epaulette boards and oversized peaked hat, the donnish appearance—an oval face, the wisdom creased at the corners of his hooded eyes, the prominence of his Semitic nose and full, sensuous lips—of the target did not resemble any image she had of bad guys, she thought, scrutinizing the photo of a man somewhere between the age of her father and Davor. What's his name? she asked and her father said *Signori . . . for you he has no other name. Languages spoken,* she read: *Serbo-Croatian, Russian.* Do you know him? she asked. Davor said yes. Her father claimed a passing acquaintance. *Other languages: English, Italian, Turkish. Fluency level: Poor.* She looked again at the photograph, the solemn undercurrent in his features that for some reason she associated with a European academic, a teacher of philosophy, perhaps. Yet of course he was despicable, a rabid Stalinist and puny anti-Christ, a colonel in State Security, a thug plotting to murder the pontiff, a pedophile (if high school girls counted . . . she wasn't sure about that) and God knows what else. Certified by the devil. He would want to fuck her—it would be so arranged—and she would encourage him to believe in this absurd sicko fantasy and accompany him to a secret location and *then what?*

Not to worry, Carla, said her father. We're going to rehearse the *then* and the *then what,* and once we're finished, we'll rehearse it all again. Step by step. Minute by minute. You'll have all the help you need.

She kept telling herself. I'm Carla. Carla, the schoolgirl who knows how to make ends meet.

Maranian returned midmorning with the lady in tow, an officious middle-aged Armenian woman with the short, burly body of a laundress-wrestler, her muscular legs protruding from the black sheath of her skirt, plump feet wedged into leopard-spotted high heels and tits like footballs jutting beneath her pink rayon blouse—an artless arrangement of chic and frump. She carried a small vanity suitcase packed with lingerie and enough gunk to paint the face of every whore in Istanbul. There is no good light in this house, she declared, taking Dottie by the hand out the back door, ordering Maranian to bring two kitchen chairs to the patio. Set them there, she instructed, gesturing to an enclosed area shielded by a tall hedge of oleander. Now go away. You, she commanded Dottie, sit down, please, and sat down herself, hitching her skirt up her thick pasty thighs, her knees straddled around Dottie's, who sat like a coiled spring while the woman evaluated the structure and coloring of her face, opened the vanity case, and went to work, chewing cloves to sweeten her breath. What's this for? Dottie finally bothered to ask. The woman took a small sponge and smeared her cheeks with foundation and said irately, Please, no talking, and Dottie closed her eyes, not knowing where to look, saving herself from having to look at the ludicrous grill work of wirelike bangs on the woman's low forehead. Her father came out once to check on their progress, saying We're just going to take a few pictures, honey, while the woman waved him away like an interloper.

The application of cosmetics seemed both endless and invasive and Dottie whipped her head violently out of reach when the woman made an attempt to pluck her eyebrows. She was given a manicure, her broken nail repaired, talons glued onto each finger and lacquered the color of geraniums, and then the woman began to fuss with Dottie's hair, teasing and spraying, Dottie visualizing the trampy style, hating it without needing to see. When she had finished the woman said, Okay, inside, please, following the girl back into the house, the emotionless expressions of the three men in the kitchen—even Maranian—mesmerized by her sleazy transformation. Your bedroom, please, said the woman, closing the door behind them, and then, Please, your clothes, remove them. She stripped to her bra and panties only to be told, Sorry, everything, the woman's raised eyebrows clearly a reaction to Dottie's shaved mons, turning her head away with meaningless courtesy to hand Dottie a matching set of fire-engine red underthings, lacy silk panties, and a sheer teddy. Put on, please . . . Okay, sit please, and Dottie plopped down on the edge of the bed blinking, suppressing her humiliation, the funny weight of mascara on her eyelashes driving her nuts but determined to maintain her equanimity. The makeup artist appraised her handiwork, smoothing a few blonde strands of stray hair, snapped closed the vanity case, and called out in her husky voice to the men that the job was done.

She was replaced by Maranian, carrying a camera fastened to a tripod and a spotlight pole with extendable feet, her father and the old man close behind. When Maranian rebuffed her with a censorious look, she could only think, *Why are you the one looking so put upon?*, watching him set up the camera, exclaiming out loud, Oh, my God, is that a Minox? trying to be a good sport, a reliable member of the team with a positive attitude and yet understanding Maranian's impulse to protect her—but from what? She wished he would just come out and say. From danger? But danger was *what*—your boat sinking? Men with vile intentions hitting on you? Having a run-in with the police? Terrorist bombs going off in banks and restaurants? If he meant to exclude her from danger, if he found her lacking because of her age or gender or inexperience or some other unspoken belittlement, then who, she wanted to ask him, was misjudging whom?

Maranian left the room to gather up the lady and leave the house, not to reappear in her life, the two of them, until four nights later in Istanbul. She had no choice then but to accommodate her father and Davor, her non-chalance withering when she stole a glance at her father, slightly bug-eyed and lips clamped as if a bumblebee had flown into his mouth. Her nerves tightened and she registered the charged air, prickly aware of the impression she made, the crude taunt to any male in hot possession of a libido. *He wants to finish the job,* she thought, chasing the idea away as soon as it came to her, abiding by its ambiguity so she did not have to acknowledge what she meant. She began to shrink from the motionless assault of her father's desire, crossing her legs in a vise, shielding her veiled breasts with her arms, eyes downcast, and huddling, on the edge of being overwhelmed by the moment's unexpected hazard, the animal force uncontained even by fatherhood. Then she heard the old man tell him to leave the room— *Naturally, you make her nervous*—and her chin was gently raised by Davor's steady hand and he said, My dear child, relax.

I will take a picture—two, three, nothing bad—to stimulate the *signori*, he told her, and then she could wash this nonsense off her face.

She was fixed in his crinkled gaze and its uncritical priestly solace, finding nothing there to shame her and, in fact, she felt the truth of what he had told her the night before, that he loved her without a price for his love. For some reason she was cherished by this strange man, broken and old but also unbreakable and spirited in a way that made any man seem young. When he seemed satisfied that she trusted him he moved back from the bed, not to the camera but to the plain wooden chair where she had thrown her clothes, folding them with care, placing them atop the cheap dresser with its curling veneer, returning to the chair to sit, smiling at her with benign expectation.

What now? she said.

Tell me something, he said impishly, nothing bending his voice or manner except a carbonated eagerness.

You mean, something dirty?

No, no, he protested, looking sadly offended by this misunderstanding. Tell me about yourself. Whatever you like.

Can I ask questions?

Ah, of course, he said, his face lighting up. Curiosity is the difference between the dead and the living. I have been waiting for your questions.

What was your relationship with my grandmother?

Relationship? he repeated, reacting with shrewd amusement, as if this word's very existence harbored a ploy, an ill-disguised snare one must learn to spot and step around. I believe you ask if we were lovers, Marija and I.

I only meant, how did you know her?

We were not, he said, and we were. I had the joy of one kiss in the city of Buenos Aires—one kiss to make last a lifetime. Is it enough? It must be. If not for that thing that separates two people who are destined to be together but are not—I mean duty, I mean love of homeland, for which no sacrifice is too great—in my heart I know—*I am sure*—we would have married. You, precious girl, you would have been my granddaughter. Your father—yes, my son. Instead, he is my godson.

Why do I not know this? she said and he told her that because it was impossible to know everything, the definition of grace was to be at peace with what you did not know because you could not. This is a family secret, agreed? he said. Between us. It would cause trouble for your father, for me, with the people we serve. She nodded yes and asked, So who do you serve? and he paused, ironically reflective, before answering, For now, the wrong people. She wanted to know when he had last seen her grandmother and he told her not long before she died, in the city in America where her father was born, Pittsburgh, a very nice place. Now I know what this term means, and in English he said melting pot. But your grandmother, he said, she was not happy in this nice place. She did not wish to melt.

What did she want?

What did she want? A free Croatia, an independent Croatia. To come home to such a place. She never lost her devotion to this beautiful dream. Nor has your father. We share this dream.

So you came to Pittsburgh to visit them?

I came to eliminate a traitor.

Davor. Why did you tell me that?

But my darling, why do you think?

I don't know.

But perhaps you do.

Because my grandmother helped you, I think.

Yes, precisely. In her way. Up to a point.

And my father too? Do I come from a family of murderers?

A family of patriots. Your father was very young then, not much older than you. Perhaps he would have joined us, but he was indisposed.

What does that mean?

In custody.

In jail?

Yes. Correct. Jail.

What did he do? Will you tell me?

Nothing so bad. As a boy your father was very angry. When young men have this anger, they walk the streets always looking for a fight. In Pittsburgh, your father did not have to look hard to find an old enemy. Serbs, Russians, Albanians, Czechs, Bosnians. Not melting pot. Garbage bin. The trash Europe swept out after the war. Anybody who did not respect him, he would fight. Look at him the wrong way, watch out. His mother approved of this belligerence. She was proud of her son.

And what about my grandfather?

He was a weak man, a drunkard. He never understood your grandmother, he was not kind to your father.

This is not the story I heard.

407

Very well.

These things . . . I had a different—I thought—and in English she said, You're blowing my mind.

Enough for now, said Davor, his good hand patting a knee for emphasis before he stood up. We have business, he said, turning on the spotlight. Are you ready? He stepped behind the camera and then stepped out. You are thinking too much, he said. Stop thinking.

I'm trying.

Forget this trying. What is necessary is Carla. Bring Carla, please.

She angled herself into a sluttish pose but it felt too severe and her flesh seemed to turn insensate and she let her body droop back into its neutral form, shaking her head at the clumsy phoniness. The obstacle in her mind was all too apparent: she was not voluptuous, she would never be voluptuous, she was something else, lithe and spontaneous, something that did not present well when amplified, overstated, underlined, an organic wholesomeness that could not be shopped out or made over or repackaged.

We are not thinking Dorothy, said Davor, gently. We are thinking Carla. It is very simple for Carla to do this.

Honest, she said. I'm trying.

Do you have a boyfriend?

Yes.

Think of this boy. Look to the camera and think of this boy.

She could not say how it happened—Davor's advice was irrelevant because Osman would fall apart crying or maybe laughing if he saw her this way—but she felt the paradoxical facade of Dottie dissolving, an out-of-body release, and there was Carla, no longer an erotic parody, posing for her soft-core shoot, a breezy pinup girl who adorned the walls of sexed-up boys. She propped a leg, canted her shoulders at a diagonal and glanced back at the camera, sleepy-eyed, a modest girlish invitation, not too coy, for the cocks to come out. She had only to smile and not look bored or cynical or dissimulated—Carla's smile on Dottie's face.

Excellent, said Davor. One more. Finished.

You know what I want most? she said. Tenderness without bullshit. Is that possible in the world? Can I have that? She amazed herself—who was this talking, Dottie or the other girl?

In the bathroom she stood bent at the sink with the taps gushing and summoned the courage to confront herself in the mirror, appalled by the lurid puppet who stared back at her with garish eyes, how little girls make themselves vampy on Halloween. What her father said—You don't have to be Carla, Carla has to be you—she finally understood. *Buon giorno, Carla. Arrivederci, Dottie.* In Istanbul she would do a touch of lipstick, she would agree to kohl. Beyond that, Carla and Dottie were of one mind.

CHAPTER THIRTY

Regarding carnal relations, said her father, agitating his daughter with the pretense that they shared between them a proper ignorance on the subject. It was the only time he ever spoke to her directly about sex— usually something just happened in a tense space of pooling silence.

Once you had his undivided attention, there were many responses you could, as a woman, anticipate from a man, her father told her, but only two that you could reliably expect—lust and rage. These were subsets of the greater order of behavior, the biological imperative, the battle for control. As for desire, her father said, there are no traps except the ones we build for ourselves. I mean to say, you do not want to anger the *signori*, understand?

Wait, she said. I'm not having sex with this guy.

We've been clear on that from the beginning. But you have to make him believe, of course. That shouldn't be difficult.

He made her supremely uncomfortable talking this way, agitated with suppressed revulsion, his sweaty little lectures on the science of seduction, clinically sterile chessboard insights into a skill a young girl first practiced and honed in a years-long pantomime with her father, the come-hither teasing, the nascent eroticism like a seedling sprouting tendrils beneath the translucent surface of innocence, the drift of hugs and kisses toward the edge of some mind-stopping power to be tested or rejected, the child herself seduced by seduction, *What an exciting game!*

410

Then one day Davor drove himself to the airport and the next day after lunch she and her father left for Istanbul. The thrill of the escapade started with a seaplane, which picked them up alongside the quay in Kusadasi and flew them north back across the Sea of Marmara, Dottie glad to be returning home but frustrated about remaining barred from her real life, forbidden to contact Osman or any of her friends or return to school for a few more days. They landed at a private dock on the southern outskirts of Istanbul, where Maranian waited for them with his spotless car, his manner once again ironed by the formality of loyal service, masking the tension that remained between them with solicitude. *Look,* she said to make her peace with Maranian, pulling his grandmother's gold cross through the neck of her T-shirt, *We saved it when the boat sank.* He bowed and called her Carla and took the dry bag from her to stow in the trunk of the Mercedes.

Alone in the backseat riding into the city, she listened to the men up front and felt excluded, the weeklong center of attention shifting away from her to other business she was not privy to, something that had happened or would happen in Germany, imagining they were talking in code until her father asked Maranian about Davor and Maranian said, Yes, your man arrived this morning from Belgrade and Davor is with him now. Then her father shifted around in his seat to examine her.

Tell me how you're doing.

Fine.

Let me say it one more time. Walk away and that's understandable. We'll come at this from another angle.

I'm fine.

You see, he assured Maranian. She's fine.

Let me remind you, her father said, craning around again, his hands gripping the back of the headrest as though he might climb over the seat on top of her. When you see Davor again later tonight—

I know, she said with a trickle of annoyance. Who's Davor?

Right. And remember, there'll be another man with him.

Marko. Not our friend. Age, thirty-one. I know. If there's something I don't know it's because you didn't tell me but you've told me everything fifty times.

That's right. But now I'm thinking a couple of things. When we enter the apartment, you must leave immediately. I mean in a flash. Get out of there and get back to the hotel room and wait for Maranian.

You told me, she said.

It's very important. Also, the *signori* sometimes likes to smoke opium during his liaisons. Let's hope he does tonight, but do not do this with him. Fix him a drink, fix yourself a weak one to play along, get him relaxed, get him to take off his jacket, and that's it.

I know.

You won't see us but we'll be right there.

I know.

If he tries anything funny, I want you to run like hell out of the room. Okay. What kind of funny?

Anything at all. It won't be a problem, he said. We'll be right there.

Maranian pulled over to the curb in front of a drab pensione on a side street a dozen blocks north and west of Taksim in a neighborhood she did not know. The Hilton, she learned, was temporarily off-limits—*We drowned, remember,* her father said, promising her again he'd straighten that out in the next day or two. She, Carla, had already been checked into a room. Maranian gave her the key and told her she would find the lady waiting for her there and said in an oddly demanding tone, *Good luck,* raising his hand to his forehead in a military salute. She said it's not like I'm a soldier or anything and he looked at her and replied, *You are.* Her father scrutinized her with an intensity so harsh she knew he was trying to frighten her but her steel nerves were his own creation and she would not be frightened. *Okay,* he said finally, his face satisfied. *This is the right call. You're ready. This will happen like clockwork and, swear to God, the world will be better for it*—and he got out of the car with her, scooping her into his arms, his eyes uncustomarily misty, and repeated his father mantra, that she could never imagine how much he loved her, and she said, *I know,* not the same rueful, soul-weary acceptance of his unfathomable love in her voice but instead a frosty acknowledgment, her face unaffirming, and she felt her body not pliant as she meant it to be but stiffening against his.

And then she stepped away with a lewd wink and taunting smirk. *This is pretty weird*, she heard Dottie thinking from far away, *Carla finds Daddy's love intolerable.*

Carla in ascendance, mocking the game, disappearing through the glass door.

There was something darkly enchanted about coming into the cheap pensione and its blunt custodial emptiness, inhaling its stale air, the dimly lit corridors and creaking stairway a type of passage through a netherworld into another reality, like arriving backstage and being tucked away in a dressing room to prepare for a performance, detaching incrementally toward the ultimate absorption of character. Cherries, she thought, that's what I want. A white bowl of cherries. Champagne.

She keyed open the door to an interior darkness flickering with the grainy light of a television set, the pumpkinlike silhouette of the Armenian lady planted on the foot of a single bed, the lady unresponsive even as Dottie switched on the overhead bulb and said hello and realized the lady's shoulders convulsed with noiseless sobbing and she said in a resentful tone, *What's wrong?* and the lack of any answer at all summoned forth Carla once and for all. She crossed the room and turned off the set, hearing enough of the broadcast to learn its significance, the death of some great man, one of the Young Turks who had outlasted everybody, Ataturk's comrade, a former president of the Republic. Sorry, she reproached the woman on the bed, do you mind? Let's get this over with.

I hated him, the woman said, squashing away tears with the back of her plump hand. I am crying with joy because this bastard is dead.

Oh, said Carla. Good riddance then.

Rising to her feet, the woman pushed past the surly girl into the bathroom where she blew her nose with a snot-rattling honk and fixed the runny makeup around her frog eyes, readying herself for a battle of wills with the teenager, Carla wrongly assumed, but the recomposed Armenian instead acquiesced to Carla simply putting on lip gloss and kohl and a careful spritz of hairspray. She poked at the *nazar* bracelet above the girl's wrist—*I'm not taking it off*—but again, intent on her own defiance, she had misinterpreted the woman, who approved of the bracelet and wanted to compliment it with a gift—evil-eye earrings, which Carla accepted with a chagrined nod.

She obeyed a clipped mutter of instructions, stripped out of her T-shirt, jeans, and underwear and put on what was handed to her, a new set of bra and panties, green silk, a white blouse with a Peter Pan collar, a schoolgirl's camel-brown skirt, shiny black patent leather pumps, the studious illusion of fake eyeglasses. The taxi comes now, the woman said, checking her wristwatch, and they went downstairs to the street, the woman carrying a plastic tote bag containing the things Carla would need later in the evening.

Passing through Taksim Square she stared out the window at the mass of humanity on the move at day's end, this victorious march of ordinary freedoms, her vision glazing over, registering cameos of people going about their business—a man selling lottery tickets, a boy setting down bathroom scales for a customer, a melon vendor—and felt herself overcome by a feeling of calm, the streets a soothing blur of life as it should be, the promise of twilight drawing her forward into the night that lay ahead, a night inviting her induction into its greatest of secrets, understanding as never before what her father had always understood—when the time is upon you, you are never too young, or too insignificant, to choose sides, we are all born to choose sides, and therein lay the true power of adulthood, the self shorn of frivolous alliance, immune to decadence.

In a burst of pure clarity, she also understood her entire life—its plurality, the challenge of its basic improvisations, the assortment of homes and places and friends, the languages she readily acquired to mute her foreignness—had been designed to shape her into a professional changeling, and she resolved that this was the way she was destined to live, a type of actress in a theater without walls or boundaries or audience. Like other precocious adolescents who became pop stars or sailed across oceans solo or went off to college years ahead of everybody else, she was seventeen and self-possessed and old enough now to know something so fundamental about herself.

She realized the Armenian lady was jabbing her knee and repeating her name like a curse, *Carla! Carla!* and the taxi had stopped in front of the gates of the Italian consulate. Take this, said the woman, giving her a small embroidered clutch containing her counterfeit passport. I am waiting down there, she told Carla, pointing ahead to the corner of the block.

She presented her passport to a gendarme, who handed it back through the window of the gatehouse to an Italian security agent who checked her name on the guest list and she was allowed to enter the vibrant interior of the consulate, the staff directing her down a high-ceilinged hall toward a gilded ballroom churning with muffled conversation, the noise louder and flared with laughter but no less intelligible as she entered the room and its hive of glamorous people—*the shining class,* she called them—honey-skinned divas and military attachés and captains of industry, a clattering spangle of bracelets, gold jewelry and pearls, starbursts of diamonds.

She, Carla, glided toward a waiter carrying a tray of prosecco, stepping back against a wall to sip from the flute and savor a pulsing lucidness like a drug making her stoned with focus, something that made alertness and pleasure the same internal process, aware that she had announced herself to the room by her light-footed youth and proud erect body, a random pattern of heads swiveling to mark her arrival, which was exactly why her father and Davor had argued about this moment, the risk of her exposure to an assembly of people likely to contain at least several from the city's resident diplomatic corps who might recognize their American colleague's daughter. But this entrance was what the *signori*'s ego required, her public appearance allowing him the private knowledge that of all the men in the room who would want her, he alone would have her.

(Stage direction: Reception at Italian consulate. Speak to no one. Establish contact with Marko. Exit in two minutes.)

But her connection with her new identity seemed unassailable—anyone approaching her as Dottie Chambers would turn away, she was sure, flummoxed and apologizing for his mistake. She stared into and through the crowd, not seeing particular faces, always looking beyond, watchful but abstracted and static, until she saw Davor and their eyes met and she could feel the plaster of her expressionlessness, the satisfying lack of receptivity in her face. She lowered her gaze as she drank her sweet bubbles and when she lifted her head again she looked straight at the man

Davor was speaking with, the surprisingly diminutive *signori*, a frail gimlet-eyed gnome whose face sagged across the collapsed contours of his former vitality. He cocked an eyebrow imperiously but Carla revealed nothing before she swept her attention elsewhere and then to the man approaching her. The bodyguard, Marko. Not weaselish as she had imagined from his photograph but sharklike and gladiatorial. He was dressed like the *signori* in an expensive but more elegant business suit, his shaved head vaguely malevolent above his dark eyes and long, triangular nose and weight-lifter's body, the pursed asshole of his mouth and weak chin strengthened by a condescending regard, which made her feel bold and righteous, and she defeated his self-importance by handing him her glass and turned to leave.

Hello, he said in grating English, you are Carla. She replied in a hush of Italian, sticking to the script: Thirty minutes. Behind this building. The service entrance.

Then she was walking away and he said, Wait, one moment, but it was easy to guess from his tone that he had nothing he needed to say, he was grasping for a thread of intimacy to have as his own, perhaps a type of investment to cash out in whatever ridiculous future he imagined for the two of them, Carla on call for men like him and their aging masters, bureaucrats of primitive treacheries, and in English she answered, I don't think so, still walking away, and he made no effort to stop her.

Back on the street, night had freshened the late summer air and she walked to the end of the block and turned the corner and got back into the taxi with the driver and the Armenian lady, both of them staring raptly at the dashboard radio, listening to its gobble of seditious demands. Here, said the lady, thrusting the tote bag onto Carla's lap. Here? said Carla indignantly, thrusting it back. No, not here, and she asked the driver to pull farther up the alley out of the crude amber light of the streetlamp.

This was what the *signori*, a Bosnian Muslim, was willing to spend lavishly for and risk entrapment, costuming nearly-naked fair-haired Christian girls in Islamic dress, draping them in a shroud of piety to both emphasize and mock their forbiddenness, then peeling off the fraud of their modesty and chasteness to expose them for what they were, corrupted vessels of wanton infidelity, leaving him no choice but to further defile their pollution, their heretical debasement of the feminine. Then redressing them in Western haute couture and escorting them to the nearest three-star restaurant for a late-night dinner and the finest bottle of wine on the menu while the sticky coolness of his semen dried between their legs.

She removed the eyeglasses and toed off her pumps and tugged her skirt over her hip bones, kicking it away toward the lady's side of the car, then stopped, distracted by her own mood of insouciance, and asked the driver for a cigarette but he had none and she told him go to the kiosk back on the corner and buy her a pack. The woman hissed that there was no time to waste on unnecessary errands and Carla, bristling, snapped that the *signori* would certainly wait. The driver left to do her bidding and she unbuttoned her blouse and slipped it off her arms and said to the woman, Okay, give it to me, and the rustling black fabric rose from the tote bag like the skin of a phantom widow. She opened the door and the woman squealed in alarm trying to prevent her from disgracing herself in the street, Carla leaping agilely out into the dark in bra and panties to cloak herself head to ankle in the *kara carsaf*, fastening its endless row of buttons, which began at her throat, her fingers made clumsy by her luridly exaggerated nails. Come back inside, ordered the woman, and Dottie covered her head and ducked back onto her seat.

My shoes, she told the woman. Give them to me.

When the driver returned she puffed halfway through a cigarette, flicking the ashes on the floor near the woman's feet until the smoke made her high and she tossed the remainder out her window and turned toward the lady with a smug smile and said, Well? Don't you think we should go? The dress made her feel charmless and witchy and chafed against her bare skin, her irritation countering the flutter of anxiety that began in her stomach, muscles clenching as the taxi turned the corner. Midway down the block the men, all three of them standing off the curb, their expressions equally hollow and punitive, glared back into the headlights. The taxi stopped and the men peered inside like carnivores hoping for a meal and Carla exhaled.

Then, according to plan, the Armenian lady was out on the street, huddled with Marko, taking care of business, the exchange inexplicably interrupted by Carla, impulsive and unscripted and adamant—*she was*

Carla and Carla didn't like this—demanding her share of the fee now, or she wasn't going anywhere except home. The woman gaped at her impertinence and Davor furrowed his brow slightly but then smiled at Carla's brazenness.

This is interesting, said the *signori,* his unctuous inflections of Italian almost like a parody of the language's emotive power, and she realized he was being facetious. His air of refinement seemed like an ill-fitting mask worn over lowbrow oafishness. He cocked his oblong head, looking at Carla with mild curiosity, then spoke in Serbo-Croatian, questioning Marko, who questioned the Armenian woman in Italian, Carla breaking into the conversation to disagree over the amount, pressing her luck until the *signori* finally grasped the nature of the problem. Give to me, he said, this time in English, snapping his fingers for the woman to hand over the envelope she had received from Marko.

No one had bothered to openly suggest Carla's actual value, which now impressed her as astronomical. She watched him remove eight American one-hundred-dollar bills from the envelope's pocket, counting off four for her and four for the madam, but she stacked her hands on her hips and shook her head, crazily insisting that the agreement was sixty/forty in her favor. The *signori's* mouth began to flatten with impatience, he was finding her feistiness irksome, Davor was sending her cautionary signals to back off, and she faltered, not able to purely connect with Carla's next move, which proved to be the faltering itself.

Like Solomon, eh? the *signori* said, a shrewd gleam enlivening his eyes, expressing his sympathy for Carla's position with an act of inspired meanness. He plucked a hundred-dollar bill back from the Armenian woman's fist, tearing it down the middle, the halves split between the two females. On cue, Marko laughed at the *signori's* cleverness. Davor struck the pose of a man bored by the contretemps of whores. Carla stuffed the money next to the passport in her clutch, elated with the success of her outrageous performance.

Now, please, he said, his hand extended, summoning her, clasping his hand atop hers to lead her to the car, his touch gummy and repellent but not in the least forceful and Carla smiled with compliance, the *kara carsaf* wafting medievally around her legs and arms, her high heels clicking on the pavement like a time bomb hidden beneath its tentlike folds. She said to herself, jeering with contempt, *God hates your fucking guts, old man,* the first time ever she had a hard look at the someone in her, of her, always there with her, who was heartless and sordid and probably wicked, an inscrutable self inhabiting a void.

(Stage Direction: Stay in control. Let him believe.)

CHAPTER THIRTY-ONE

The long black automobile seemed gangsterish and she thought it must be American-made although she knew little about different models. To her relief, the *signori* maintained a discreet distance between them in the backseat, his hands atop his knees, reminding her of a boy told to stay put, waiting for his name to be called. Along the boulevard north the streetlights popped and dissolved like heat lightning throughout the car's interior and for the first few minutes no one spoke except Davor, who rasped directions in Serbo-Croatian to Marko, his muscled body grown testy and disgruntled behind the wheel, yanking the car from lane to lane in traffic that flashed everywhere like a school of mackerel in the nearby straits.

She stared directly in front of her at Davor's crooked shoulders and the feathery back of his head, mesmerized by the broken elegance of his injuries, the morbid appeal of the mauled ear, the dangling arm, evidence of a spirit able to endure the most excruciating pain. Even so damaged, there was nothing weak or soft about him—in Ephesus he had exercised daily, sit-ups, knee bends, tremulous one-armed push-ups—and despite his easygoing nature, a cunning tension seeped out of his most casual gestures.

Some fantasies seemed accidental, unbidden—she certainly never asked for them—like imagining the *signori* dead, torn apart by lions, but she fantasized now about Davor as her grandfather and herself a child surrounded by the gentleness and humor with which he regarded every-thing, even things that were not gentle or humorous. He seemed the most romantic and honor-bound of men, sustaining a love beyond the grave through the implicit lifelong union of one exquisite kiss, strong love the provenance of strong people.

The *signori* struck a match and her mind came reeling back to the car, the drive, the men, the game, and what the game had become, a fiction turned inside out, like watching a movie starring you that wasn't about you but there you were anyway. She glanced sideways to observe the *signori* in profile, a satanic flame flaring at the center of his face, the gnome transformed to gargoyle. The hand-rolled cigarette crackled and spit and seduced her nose with the aroma of burning rose oil. I like very much this, he said, exhaling in pidgin English, inhaling in baby-talk Italian, alternating bursts of rudimentary communication, *Me, Tarzan. You, Jane*, a stumbling fugue of language that might as well be played with drums and whistles.

You smoke, yes? he asked, extending a soft pawlike hand, the red eye of the ember jumping toward her face.

She was curious and held the drag in her lungs for several heartbeats, a warmth rippling through her body like the faint, out of reach beginnings of an orgasm that might never arrive without gigantic concentration, more potent than her father's Afghani snuff or the lycée boys' blend of cheap tobacco sprinkled with crumbs of hash.

I like mine better, she said, coughing out a tiny ghost of smoke, handing it back to him and tapping out one of her own from the pack in her clutch, tilting across the seat for a light, looking not at the cigarette and the match in his hand but at his face, filmy-eyed now and his full lips almost blubbery, his bemused countenance swollen by his own pleasure; his words, like his attempt at rakishness, muddled. Name is, of course, you are, Carla, yes? Young, beautiful. He landed a hand on her knee and she took it off and said, Wait.

Do I frighten you?

Of course not.

Say to me, he said dreamily. Tell me.

What?

You. You.

She heard herself talking, the neurotic pace of her sentences, reciting the things she had rehearsed and memorized and said without thinking,

So now tell me about yourself, *signori*. Are you an important man? I think you are.

You think? he asked tonelessly. Why?

I don't know, she said, and abruptly his hand was on her again, in her lap, a badger's snout pressing between the clamped roots of her legs. The contact was not caressing but matter-of-fact and fairly pointless, target practice. She felt a zippery jolt from her loins to her breasts, an unwelcome sensation and not the least pleasurable. She slapped at his wrist, scolding him with the exaggerated indignation of a tease, until he withdrew.

That's bad, she said, lowering her voice. Wait.

Yes, come on, he said, the mischievous twist of a smile rupturing his offended air. What for, wait? Give me your hand.

Wait, she shushed.

The hand, okay?

She didn't know how to respond effectively to his persistence but said, Say please, which made him snicker yet he said it and she let her right hand spider-crawl to the middle of the seat to be captured and drawn to his groin and for the first time then she felt disoriented and confused. His hand mashed down atop hers, scrubbing her palm against the detestable contrivance of his penis. Her impulse was to recoil but she kept on, held on, her puzzled fingers half-curled along the trousered shaft, beginning to recognize her body's transformation, the cold sensation of submissiveness that led to numb endurance, imagining she actually knew something that she was sure she did not know, what it was to be inside the head of a prostitute. Like swimming in a race where your body became a machine, feeling both liberation and imprisonment at the same time.

This is so sick, she thought, trying to tug her hand away, the *signori*'s veneer of civility flaking off into aggression. Wait, be nice, she said sharply, loud enough to alert Davor, who rotated around and barked a rebuke at the *signori,* allowing her to retreat back across the seat into the gleaming nimbus of her dress, reprimanding herself for the failure of Carla's attention, then satisfied by the contempt and disgust of Carla's defense—*This awful thing in his pants!*

Yes, yes, okay, the *signori* told Davor, slumping just a little. No problem.

Wait, *signori,* Carla said, cooing in appeasement.

She looked out the window at the buildings, blocked and functional, clean-faced like barristers, and knew they were only minutes away from Maranian's safehouse. Soon, she promised, her voice smooth and viscous and enticing—Carla's voice, perfectly attuned to duplicity and deceit—and reached across to pat the hand of the *signori,* the light blanching his face to curry-colored wax molded into terrible straining immobility, the cunt-thirsty look that preceded devouring, the mind-lost expression of an imminence she had been able to defer or escape or negotiate in the past, a cock hovering, nuzzling, probing. For the remainder of the ride she stared ahead, all but her nose hidden in the recess of the *kara carsaf,* feeling the dark bloated pressure of his lust. She had only known nervous self-conscious boys, not men like this, nothing at all like her father, filthy bestial creatures preying on girls.

All right, she grudgingly corrected herself, girls for hire, twats like Carla.

(Stage Direction: Marko enters building to examine location for security risks. Marko returns. Davor and bodyguard remain with car. Carla accompanies *signori* to elevator and sixth-floor apartment above bank.)

In the final seconds before he disappeared from her life, Davor was a courtier, opening her door, gracious and noble in his bearing. He bowed his head in tacit allegiance, saying under his breath as she arose from the car that her grandmother would be very proud, fortifying gestures she absorbed in her blood with the deepest gratitude. By the assurance of his manner he had dignified her performance.

On the other side of the car, Marko held open the door for the *signori,* whose sulky mood changed as they crossed the street together, his hand fastened to her elbow, steadying his doped legs with a ruse of gallantry to compliment her ruse of subservience, somehow managing to radiate spry anticipation, a delightful secret about to be shared with his darling whorelet, as though he were taking her upstairs to show her a puppy. His face creased with merriment and carved the flaccid skin around his mouth and eyes into an impression of libertine benevolence. Inside the foyer, as they waited for the elevator, he offered her a cautious half-formed leer that was almost vulnerable and almost bashful, yet when the door opened she felt panic swoop and dive at her like a demented bird, the elevator no bigger than a shower stall. He stepped ahead into it and turned around, facing out, his back against the wall, and beckoned playfully for her to come along and she hesitated before jamming into the narrow space, coffinlike and claustrophobic, turning face out herself, her back spooned against his front as she inserted the access key for the top floor and the door rattled closed, the nasty thing in his pants poking her ass.

His breath batted at her covered ear like a moth and she smelled cumin threaded with disgusting wisps of something old-mannish and rotten. His hands snaked over opposite sides of her rib cage to seize her breasts and she closed her eyes and fought against her body's skittishness, telling herself this was not a big deal, she was not an imbecile who could not foresee the scenes implied in her character's role, she was not unwilling to go this far, an eight-hundred-dollar consolation—let him believe what he wanted because it would never matter.

Wait, okay? she said. One more minute. Let's have a drink first. I'm thirsty.

You fuck how many?

Only you, *signori,* she said, uncoached, unscripted.

His damp liver-spotted hands went to her throat to pry at buttons at the same moment the elevator door opened onto the vestibule of the apartment and she twisted forward, buttons popping along her chest before his greedy fingers released the fabric. Ah, he said, triumphant, mocking her, gloating. *Wait, eh?* Scurrying into the soft lamplight of the front room, she sensed the clock of her masquerade ticking down, inwardly frantic to get her bearings in a space she had only experienced as a diagram—an antique Victorian sofa and two overstuffed wingback chairs, coffee table and breakfast table, an open door leading to a bedroom (stay out) and bathroom. A closet door. Another door, the important one, its bolt controlled by an electronic release with a remote trigger operated by her father. Behind this door at the rear of the building a short interior hall (Maranian's position, her vigilant sentinel) leading to an exterior fire escape (her exit route). To her right, against the northside common wall shared by the neighboring building, was a wide, waist-high sideboard replete with liquor and highball tumblers, a silver ice bucket and pitcher of water, centered beneath a large mirror with an ornate gilded frame, a trick mirror, she had been told, the kind you could see through from behind. Her father was positioned on the other side in an abutting apartment—this, too, Maranian's property—monitoring the entrapment, reinforced by the necessary authorities, her father had told her, never anticipating she would enter that room.

She heard the clop of the *signori's* footsteps behind her and whirled around with a beguiling smile, flipping back the hood of her dress to shake out the incitement of her golden hair. She planted her hands on his shoulders to interrupt the momentum of his accelerating desire, then dropped them to play for time with an inspired faux-striptease meant not to provoke but stall, slowly unfastening the buttons remaining above her breasts, confident that only the *signori* could see what she was doing. It was exciting, a bit thrilling, really, persuading herself her decision meant her control, a conditional power to be carefully tested and exploited until the calvary arrived. She unhooked the butterfly clasp at the front of her bra, bending forward just enough, the *signori* hypnotized by her presentation. He allowed himself to be guided backward toward the sofa, starving vacant eyes drilled onto her breasts. She let her pull off his suit jacket (no concealed weapon, thank God) and loosen his drab necktie as she said, breathlessly, *Signori*, relax, we are here, sit down, let me get you something to drink, I want a drink. At the sofa she urged him down, shuddering when his lips brushed a jutting nipple as he sank onto the velvet cushion and she told herself it's time, get out now, it's time, time's up, what the fuck are you doing? but he said Okay, very good, a vodka, and it seemed like the smart move, cross the room to fix him a drink to create a lulling distance between them, a safe unobstructed zone for her father and Maranian to bring down the curtain on this insane audition for a role exceedingly more radical than the one she had played to this point.

With resurgent modesty she clutched the top of her dress, closing the seam over her bare skin, and approached the side bar, her four-inch heels cracking echoes on the wood floor. She stole a glance at the door to her left, her body tensed in preparation for it to fly open any second now but it did not fly open and she stood at the side bar, peering at her supplicant reflection in the mirror, telepathically summoning her father, his face on the other side of the glass, those ungodly inches of separation, *Daddy! Get in here!* and in frustration she let go of her dress and her breasts floated into view while she unscrewed the cap from the vodka.

Carla, said the wheezing *signori,* to fuck, which way you like? From behind, yes?

She shifted her eyes to his image in the mirror, a colorless salamander contemplating her body, his white dress shirt rolled out over the swell of his paunch and his hands fumbling beneath the tails. She shifted her eyes back to her own image so she would not have to look at him directly and then looked down to pour his drink. I like to be on top of the man, she said foolishly, knowing immediately that something in her voice had invited this, the scene she had been persuaded would never have a chance—stage direction deleted: an implausibly athletic explosive charge, the *signori* attacking like an enraged animal. She saw her face caught in the mirror, flat with disbelief, as she received a disabling two-fisted blow between her shoulder blades and collapsed across the surface of the side bar, glass shattering on the floor. In an instant the dress's skirt was bunched above her hips, her panties a taut green span between her kicked-out ankles. He mounted her back with demonic strength, his body draped atop her torso like an old leopard, cords and tendons and sinew like animated iron cables beneath his age-loosened skin, her heartbeat lunging upward underneath him.

In a daze she registered a stabbing at her anus, then a searing nova of incandescent pain as the broomstick of his Soviet-made prosthesis ripped through the clenched ring of muscle into her rectum, sawing back and forth, lubricated now by her blood. She had stopped breathing and then when she started again her lungs expanded and emptied like bellows and each time she tried to press up and away he sank deeper into her and she felt a live coal stoked forward into her bowels.

She screamed once, suspended in agony, but did not call out for help, help itself arriving anyway but not before she had regained some of the control she had forfeited, as she had been duly warned. Her neck strained to lift her head to see better. Bending her arms above her to claw at the *signori*'s hovering face, she raked bloody cat-whiskers across his cheeks, several of the glued-on fingernails broken off and implanted in the furrows. For a moment he seemed uninterested in protecting himself but then he snatched one of her hands as her other found the full bottle of whiskey, her frenzied backhand, swatting hard at the dome of his skull until the bottle connected with his forehead, the force not enough to bust the glass but strong enough to stagger him back a few steps, off her and out of her and against the looming tower of her father as she wrenched herself upright, yanking her panties back in place before she turned into a pillar of stone. Someone took her arm and began to pull her toward the door but she fended Maranian off without truly seeing him or realizing what she was doing, her befuddled eyes fixed only on her father and his prisoner.

The *signori*'s blood-smeared phallus bobbed in the air, a hellish divining wand, ghastly in its prominence. Her father was certifiable, his madness a shimmering aura. His forearm collared the little man's throat and dragged him backward and his free arm swung in a half-circle to bring the silenced barrel of the gun he held to balance at the base of the *signori*'s everlasting erection. For a split second the eyes of both men focused on her as if she might pronounce judgment but her thoughts were muddied and she had nothing to say, the tremors in her thighs made it a struggle to just stay on her feet, and then *phfft*, her father pulled the trigger. Except for the quick sharp spit like a cobra strike the pistol was noiseless and the spray from the shot flecked her chest and face and the ceiling and walls with crimson. Her eyes were wide and open and her remarkable calmness lay blanketed over the hopeless truth that she felt nothing at all. She stared with empty astonishment at the *signori* and the gory stub in the fly of his trousers and the lump of the blown-off part like a garden slug in front of his bloody shoes. He did not appear to be in great pain, maybe the nerves there dead long ago, maybe the opium, but she felt at sea with the lack of stage directions. What to do next? What to say next? Stand where?

Her father gestured angrily with his head for Maranian to get her out and this time his touch felt clarifying and she looked at Maranian and then at her father with fierce complaint. But her father was too far fallen, unavailable, into some other universe of reasoning to absorb her grievance or even

427

its existence. She watched as he released the *signori,* who crumpled down into one of the wingbacked chairs cupping his blasted groin and tossed his head back to squint with pained wonder at her father and asked in chopped English, Who are you?

Maranian pulled her to the door and she turned on him with blistering scorn and became senselessly combative, pushing him away and slapping wildly, his failure as her guardian as incomprehensible as her father howling a name she had never before heard as she fled into the hallway.

I am Stjepan Kovacevic. That's who I am, *mujo*. Kovacevic. What do you think of that?

On the opposite side of the hallway was a door identical to the one that closed behind her and behind this door her father's stakeout. She knocked twice tentatively with quivering hands and listened for a moment, despairing because she had not known and could never have guessed but she knew now, no one was there to call to except the ghosts of her father's past and he had been alone in the room. Daddy was the only one there, a man with a camera, watching, eye to eye, filming his daughter's violation, her face separated from his by a looking glass, his heart on a five-second pause.

The heels were impossible on the steel mesh of the fire escape and she flung them off down into the darkness of the back alley below where they thudded on the roof of the waiting taxi. By the time she had descended to the street her entire body had begun to tremble and her teeth were clicking and she ignored the taxi, whisking past it and then stopping to pull out her earrings, thinking she had to give them back and then she would be done with all this, but her fingers did not seem to want to do this simple thing and the taxi started and eased up next to her. When the Armenian lady saw her condition she hauled Dottie into the backseat and held her throughout the delirium of sobs and convulsions, the lady petting the girl's hair as the tears stained her blouse and the girl's racing breath moderated and she whimpered for a while longer and then stopped.

Sit up now, she heard the Armenian woman tell her. Let me look at you.

I'm bleeding, Dottie said, staring blankly at the red blots she left behind on the woman's blouse.

Please, let me see, said the woman, taking Dottie's chin and turning the girl's head out of the shadows to examine her face and neck. Here, you are cut here, she declared, pointing to a small purple gash on the girl's breast-bone. It's not so bad, I think, and she took a handkerchief from her purse to dab at the wound. Here, she said. Without asking she rehooked Dottie's bra and then began to extract her arms from the sleeves of the *carsaf* and when the girl began to resist this she said, What's wrong?

I don't want—I want the dress. Leave it on, please.

Yes, okay, said the woman, but let me see, and she continued carefully to pull her arms free until the top half of the dress was down at her waist and the woman gave her a once over until she was satisfied the girl had no other visible injuries.

Your legs?

My legs are okay.

She convinced Dottie to put on the blouse she had worn earlier in the evening at the consulate and then the girl hunched her arms back into the sleeves of the *kara carsaf* and pulled its hood over the top of her head and the woman reached again into her purse and dug around and removed a hair barrette and nail file and made a hole in the buttonless seam of the bodice, inserting the clasp of the barrette through that hole and a buttonhole in the opposite seam and fastened the two sides together and said kindly, Okay? I think this is better.

I want to see Davor, said the girl.

The woman sighed heavily and spoke in Armenian to the supernaturally aloof driver and they drove out of the alley and back to the front of the block and cruised the street and Dottie asked, Where did they go?

I don't know.

That man wasn't going to hurt the Holy Father, was he?

Maybe. I don't know.

They know each other, don't they?

Who?

My father. The *signori*.

I cannot answer these questions. I don't know.

He's going to kill him, said the girl. I don't care.

Here, put on your shoes.

Don't you want to know what happened?

Do you want to tell me? said the woman but Dottie did not respond and the woman said, No, what happened is not my business.

The woman quietly explained that it was her job to return Dottie to the pensione where she could change back into her own clothes and be herself again and safe and when her father came to get her maybe he would have the answers to her questions or maybe not, maybe it was best to forget these questions and so the girl remained silent throughout the ride, neither Carla nor Dottie but some other unknown and forsaken self. How easy it now seemed to perceive the essence of men, their irreversible consummating need not for sex but for the cruelty sex invited, vigorous but impersonal, the domesticated savage rediscovering primal rapture reminding you, the female, of his fundamental wildness and the impossibility of that wildness lying dormant forever. This lunacy males contained—she was sure she was right about this, the absolute prevailing truth of men, every one of them complicit in the infinite perversions of desire, a brute or a secret brute.

No, she contradicted herself. That's so wrong, and she repeated his name to herself, the sound of it like an unwanted invitation for her heart to awaken: Osman, Osman.

The sting in her bottom would not abate and still it bothered her less to have been sodomized by a depraved Yugoslavian freak than to have her thoughts skitter around the inconceivable notion that her father was, in some way she could not yet put her finger on, liable for her rape. Of course there was the inexpiable delay in sending Maranian into the room and it was connected to that blunder but it was something more than that, arguing to herself against what would be evident to any human being, even the worst people on earth, Okay, he's gone too far, this is too much. He fucking watched. He sat there with his face inches from hers and would not stop. Could not. Five seconds of unthinkable depravity before he pressed the button that unlocked the door for Maranian to enter the room. Five seconds, five strokes. Did he sink the *Sea Nymph* too? Was that his doing? Why didn't he just turn her into a cow to swim the Bosphorus?

When they dropped her back at the pensione she tried to return the *nazar* earrings but the Armenian lady stopped her hand and said with sad eyes I want to give them to you, please. And wait, this too, she said as the girl opened the taxi door and she gave her the other half of the torn one-hundred-dollar bill.

Whatever inside the pensione had seemed intriguing to her hours before now seemed desolate and eerie and as she ran up the stairs to the room she became aware of a rivulet of blood sliding down her thigh and in the bathroom she left the light off and showered in darkness and dried herself and lay naked on the bed sucking her middle fingers, her body curled and catatonically tucked into fetal limbo, waiting to be born or born again, craving Dottie yet willing her to go away.

Every so often her muscles tightened and she felt a low moan vibrating in her throat, an intermittent release of an injury greater than her body reckoned with. No one came but it was hours before she understood that she did not want them to come. In the predawn light graying the room's window she jumped up suddenly and dressed in her jeans and running shoes and T-shirt and replaced Maranian's grandmother's gold cross around her neck, the tiny weight of the crucifix pecking at the cut in the center of her sternum. Then she covered her clothes with the black shroud of the *kara carsaf* and wrapped the hood over her hair and grabbed the clutch with Carla's passport and crazy money and flapped out into the city like a damaged bird. Only her green silk underwear with its shameful bloodstains remained on the bed, something for her father to find.

CHAPTER THIRTY-TWO

The muezzin sang from a nearby mosque—*Turkish roosters,* one of her father's less noxious insults—and for a moment she yearned to slip off her shoes and go inside and pray and find solace among the women, covered and segregated in their balcony and shielded from the maniacs below, but the impulse, she realized, recoiling from the entrance, was sinful and as a sinner she had outspent herself. Aimless only briefly, separated from everything and existentially out of reach, she advanced like a small pillar of black smoke through the brightening streets slowly filled with Istanbullus at the start of their day, a specter in a billowing dress descending through Taksim Square and Pera and down the hill to Karakoy and the Golden Horn and the people clustering at the ferry docks, crowds of businessmen drinking tea in the sharpening light of the new day, the night's violation like a switch thrown off in her soul. Of these things, the events, her history, the pain, the secrets of her life, no one, she felt, would ever or could possibly know.

Then staring into glittering haze, watching seagulls dive into the water and understanding her father's mendacity, to which she was no stranger and often an accomplice but had never once believed could be so perfidiously turned against her and her life held hostage still, as some lives everlastingly are, by relentless love. Battered by a love contaminated with all manner of immortal feuds. Her father's claim—*I am Stjepan Kovacevic.* What did this mean? Another nom de guerre, like Carla Costa? Knowing this: shackled to his obsessions, her father could not stop no matter what, always betting on the consequences breaking his way—short term, certainly; long term, if God so deemed. Repercussions? Not to worry, Kitten. He could separate people and events and missions and affairs and yet, she would eventually understand, he could not separate the bigger things in his life that sorely needed separation: patriotism and hatred, love and violence, ideology and facts, judgment and passion, intellect and emotion, duty and zealotry, hope and certainty, confidence and hubris, power and fury, God and retribution, dreams of peace and fantasies of war, one's devils and one's angels. The past and the future, upon which he asserted ownership. Righteousness and a moral compass that had never been galvanized to true north.

But of course it wasn't his fault, what had happened—How could it be? she argued to herself. Surely there was an explanation for his inexplicable failure. And wasn't it true that Carla was asking for it, Carla had it coming? No matter what else was true, wasn't that true too? Imagining herself sealed inside a bubble of unswerving guardianship, she had goaded the *signori*, whoever he was, the embodiment of some wickedness out of her father's past. And what would it take to unlearn Carla, relearn Dottie? Here she was in Dottie's real life again but not really because that Dottie did not exist anymore and the Dottie reemerging could only be a pathetic fake and how was it any longer reasonable to be either of them?

Crossing the bridge on foot because her lira and whatever else remained from the boat were in the dry bag in the trunk of Maranian's car and it was impossible to buy a ferry ticket with a hundred-dollar bill and then hiking up the hill behind Eminonu weaving through the busy streets, nothing in her mind but the cough of indecipherable voices and the beep of horns and the clank and jangle of shops unshuttered. Not aware of time or place or direction or anything at all until she found herself at the crest of the hill across from the university, standing at the corner of the block she believed was Osman's, the block where he always asked to be dropped if they were sharing a taxi, standing to wave as she was driven away. Strange for a Turkish boy to never invite his girlfriend to meet his family, but not so strange perhaps if the girl was a *yabanci* and the son and father would not reconcile with one another. She stood for some time gazing trancelike at the row of squat turn-of-the-century apartment buildings and then went up the block, door to door, asking the *kapicis*, the doormen,which one belonged to Osman.

Ah, yes, my daughter, said the third *kapici,* two doors farther on they live. At the fifth building on the block, she hesitated, staring at the glass door until the *kapici* noticed her and came out.

Buyurun? May I help you?

Evet. Yes.

Then, before she could explain herself, Osman's spindly little sister Saniye appeared over the doorman's shoulder, stepping onto the midway landing of the cement stairs leading to the ground floor. A few times during the summer she and Osman had let Saniye tag along with them to the cinema, the fourteen-year-old more interested in spying on the lovers than watching the action on the screen. Now she wore her school uniform, a backpack over her shoulders, a fat textbook cradled in one arm while her free hand stifled a sleepy yawn. Then the book dropped and her mouth stayed open and her hands pressed the sides of her face as she stared at the girl entering the foyer and exclaimed her disbelief, *How could it be? How could it be?*

In her excitement, Saniye ran down the steps to kiss the cheeks of the wet-eyed ghost and pull her by the hand up the stairway in a cloud of Sweet Pea perfume, her breathless squeaky babble rising with them all the way to the top floor and an open door flanked with shoes and plastic slippers, *We saw you on television, my brother has been inconsolable, where have you been, you look like a ninja, why didn't you phone us, why are you in this ugly dress, what happened on the sea, Osman now will die of happiness, come in, come in, shhh, say nothing, he is in the kitchen, shhh, oh, my God, shh.*

Hand in hand they went at Saniye's insistence stealthily to the threshold of an expansive kitchen at the back of the apartment and peeked in upon Osman and an older man in a business suit across the room preoccupied with their breakfast, sitting at a small table in front of a bank of windows looking out over the city. Osman, she saw, was growing a beard, or else, too distraught, hadn't bothered shaving, and had hacked off most of his beautiful curls. But the thrill was too much for Saniye, who began to hop

434

up and down, shrieking the news to her brother and—a shock in turn for Dottie—her father.

Osman! Baba! She is alive! Look!

Jumping out of their chairs, the men turned toward the girls in the doorway, the father wiping his mouth and mustache with a cloth napkin, his eyebrows in a quizzical arch, and Osman's grimace struggled through a series of contortions, arriving at befuddled astonishment. The silence between them filled with paralyzing wonder and she saw his ashen-faced countenance darkened by the bluish circles under his eyes as a measure of grief and her eyes welled up and still no one moved or spoke until his father said, *Salaam alaikum. Otur*, sit, and held out a chair for her and she went to the table and sat down and Saniye said, *Tell us what happened!* and her father clapped his hands affably and ordered her off to school.

Tea?

She nodded with a shiver of gratitude at the father, who stepped toward the stove, and Osman found his voice. My God, he gasped, sitting down across from her with a look of terrified confusion. I don't understand this.

I know, she said meekly. I'm sorry.

What happened?

She told him about the boat and the storm, about how they had nearly drowned but didn't and then had just continued on in innocence with no idea they had been reported lost at sea and only last night when they returned to the city did she find out everyone thought they were dead and she couldn't sleep waiting for the morning so she could come here and tell him it wasn't true, she wasn't dead, and she was sorry sorry sorry.

Sorry? No! he said almost angrily. You have given back everything to me. I was dead too, you see. You cannot be sorry that we are alive again.

In her heart she felt the reassurance of these words and yet something was wrong. There was an awkwardness between them, and no lack of reasons for it, but the immediate source, she guessed, was Baba, Osman's supposedly estranged father who seemed unable to glance at his son without revealing an unwavering paternal investment in pride. He regarded Osman with masculine affection, gruff yet slightly worshipful, and he was kind and

435

courteous to his son's oddly dressed, newly resurrected girlfriend, behaving with the utmost circumspection, bringing her a glass of tea and then, to her relief, bowing his apologies for running away to teach a morning class at the university.

But left to themselves, the awkwardness in the kitchen only intensified. She stared at a hard-boiled egg abandoned on the father's plate and couldn't remember when she had last eaten. Can I? she said, reaching for it, and Osman said, Please, take it, and they both fell silent again while she peeled the shell, thinking she had made a mistake maybe, coming here, her faith in Osman perhaps misplaced. She had been certain he would know exactly how to respond to her with the sweetness of comfort, what she most needed, but now she saw he did not know how to respond but instead was causing her to feel primed for heartbreak. Somewhere deep in the apartment she could hear his father preparing to leave and then a telephone was ringing and then Baba had stepped halfway back into the kitchen to say the call was for her.

Are you sure? she asked with streaking panic, already sensing it was true.

Two doors down to the right, said Osman with a complicated, leery expression.

Shaking, she went down the hall to a small sitting room and sat in a brocaded armchair next to the phone and stared blankly at the framed photographs of Osman's family and fez-wearing ancestors arranged on a credenza and then picked up the receiver and said hello, her father's voice swinging into her stomach like a fist of humiliation. He said he wanted her out of there now.

Where are you? How did you get this number?

I want you to go down to the street and wait for Maranian to come get you if he's not there already. Do you understand?

No. Why did you lie to me?

About what?

About everything.

Let me speak to this kid Osman.

No. Why? Where are you?

Listen—

But before he could begin the sentence she hung up on him. When she stepped back into the kitchen, Osman didn't wait to get the issue of the *kara carsaf* off his chest, but she buried his question under another mystery. She had to leave right now, she told him. Would he come with her?

Where? What's wrong? Yes, of course. One minute, okay? I have to use the phone.

Too many questions that she promised to answer later. She walked him down the hall to the sitting room and then she left him there and kept going to the front of the apartment into a living room decorated with gilt-trimmed satiny white furniture that overlooked the street and parted the lace curtains in time to observe a black Mercedes coming up the block in a crawl of traffic. Leave me alone, she whispered to the window, turning with an indescribable pang of loss back through the immaculate room. Down the hall Osman spoke in a furtive voice that grew lower as her footsteps approached and the receiver clacked into its cradle just as she reached the door. He spun around with guilty eyes, withdrawing his attempt at a smile when he saw the prosecutorial look on her face.

I need to know, she said. Do you have another girlfriend?

How could you think this of me?

You thought I was dead, she said.

No, no, he protested. Well, yes, but still I had hope. There was reason to hope, he said and finally held out his arms to her and she pounced into them and fought back an incipient rack of sobs threatening to undo her, resting her face on his shoulder, her nose burrowing into the earthy affirmation of his smell, ploughing her fingers through the curls remaining at the back of his head, saying I love you so much, saying it over and over again until he repeated the words to her, which made her brave enough to ask about the phone. It was just Karim, he told her, they had planned to meet later in the day. She was placated though not pleased by this answer and reluctantly ended their embrace.

We can't go out the front, she said. My father sent someone to get me.

Tell me—

I've told you before, she said. He hates Muslims. He doesn't want me seeing you.

437

But—
Please, please. Let's just go.
Tabi, tabi. Of course.

They tried to do what could not be done, to resume their familiar summer game, giving the slip to Daddy's spies, only this time there was no light-heartedness between them and no honesty and nothing to laugh about, this time was not an adolescent lark, and Osman, enigmatic and clearly paranoid, seemed to her somehow preconnected to this overtly dire shift in circumstances.

She shadowed him up a narrow staircase at the back of the kitchen to a hatch that creaked open onto the storied roof of his boyhood, no evidence in sight of its former role as sanctuary, and she allowed herself the luxury of turning in a circle, imagining him there as a child, huddled with his books, and she thought she glimpsed the shine of melancholy ebbing into Osman's eyes and the truth she had long dismissed became visceral—she would leave Istanbul because she never stayed anywhere and he would stay because that was what he was meant to do.

Now what? she asked anxiously and he explained they needed to cross the rows of low walls dividing each apartment's property from the next to reach the end of the block, where the afterthought of a single fire escape had been added onto the building after the Second World War. The stucco walls were belly-high and easily climbed and when they had come to the end of the complex she peered over the edge at the metal ladder, reminiscent of a swimming pool's, bolted to the exterior of the last apartment, straight down to the alley four stories below.

You must take off this dress, I think, said Osman with a nervous step backward. But why are you wearing religious clothes? It shocks me, this dress.

It's a disguise, she said, hoping such an obvious answer would mol-lify him, and she removed the *kara carsaf* and pitched it over the side and tucked her clutch into the waistband of her jeans and then, grabbing the curved handholds at the top of the ladder, maneuvered her body to face the building and stepped one foot at a time onto the rungs. This is a little hairy, she said. Shit. The blood drained from Osman's face and he admitted he had never dared to use the ladder, although when they were kids his brothers monkeyed up and down it all the time. It's not really so bad, she said, her encouragement halfhearted. Come on, she said, and continued down, focused and methodical, feeling her way with her feet, not looking up to check his progress until she found herself on the street, in a small group of spectators who had stopped to watch such a curious show.

Osman was on the ladder but near the top, petrified. She called and waited but when he didn't move she climbed up again and grabbed a quaking ankle to calm him down, feeling the fear in him like a reverberation of thunder through his flesh. Come on, she wanted to say, you can do this, but thought of her brother, how wise her father was to push his competitive daughter and lay off his son, and she remembered what she already knew about Osman, that he was not physically bold, how she would tease him when they would anchor the *Sea Nymph* to swim on a hot day, Osman a good enough swimmer but in dread of venturing into water over his head. She said now what she said then—It's okay, you're doing great—and when that didn't work she understood he had completely lost his nerve and told him to climb back up to the roof and go to his apartment and put on a hat or something to conceal himself and she would meet him at the Spice Bazaar as soon as he could get there undetected.

It's okay, she said, go back. There's a guy in a black Mercedes. Don't let him follow you.

If you fall, she said to herself, we fall together, a romantically morbid thought, the residue of girlhood that appealed to her expiring belief in perfect endings.

She waited until he was on the roof before she descended again to the street, retrieved the black dress off the pavement, and began her march through the labyrinth of hillside alleys that twisted and turned back down toward the Golden Horn, looking over her shoulder at each intersection before deciding left or right or straight, her choices deliberately random, her pace brisk but not brisk enough to stand out in the flow of pedestrians.

At the entrance to the Spice Bazaar she ducked into a public toilet and covered her blatant westernness again in the *kara carsaf* and then

439

blended into the ever-present sea of jostling humanity that occupied the dim interior of the market. She wandered in a state of jittery exhaustion, her head down and heedless, bumped and bumping back in the stream of people until somehow she found herself circulating in an eddy of modest tea stalls, single-vendor enterprises recessed into a wall of stony earth, like dens in a catacomb, each occupied by a kettle steaming atop a brazier and two or three rustic footstools and every kettle attended by an almost identical old crone with a head scarf knotted under her doughy chin, stoic and shabby, roosting on one of her stools. She heard a croak of Turkish directed, she slowly realized, at her, a sympathetic beckoning—*Come, come, daughter. Come, sit. You are lost. I can see. Come drink my tea and rest*—and fell gratefully under the crone's spell, folding herself onto the low stool in the gouged-out hole that contained the austere world of this white-haired woman.

Yet when the old woman handed her a glass of apple tea, her clouded eyes stared inhospitably at Dottie's face.

Yabanci?

Evet.

Are you a believer, my child?

Yes, she answered without hesitation, recalling Peter in the courtyard of Jerusalem's High Priest; Peter, the apostle who proved you could lie your head off about Jesus and get away with it. But he was a coward, she told herself, and I'm not. This was different. The crone spoke to her in Arabic and she answered appropriately.

There is no God but God.

Her brief sanctuary among the believers ended roughly, though, someone's fingers sinking into the flesh of her upper arm and hauling her to her feet and there was Osman, just as she had last seen him, nothing incognito about him, his face burning with disapproval. Quick! he snapped and tugged her, stumbling, back into the crowds, and refused to say a word or release his angry grip until they were back on the street, squinting at each other in the sunlight. She asked if they were being followed and he said he could not be sure and he demanded to know everything. Why was she behaving this way? Why was she pretending to be a Muslim? Why was she being strange? and she asked him Please don't be mad at me.

440

Her lower lip jutted out and she studied his gaunt unhappy face and helpless eyes, wary of offering even the smallest detail of her tribulations to pacify him, the train of deceptions she shared with her father, hers coerced or impulsive, his either compulsive or calculated in cold blood. Could Osman ever understand Carla? But then, yes, why not, what was so difficult to understand about a whore? Islamic men took it for granted this was a woman's indelible nature. His intractable rejection of her would be the inevitable result of the truth, added to the compounding of her own self-hatred, which she had no appetite to indulge, nor time. It too would have to wait. Still, she began to whimper, and when she saw his own eyes reflect her pain she blurted out a perilous confession, telling him she had been attacked by a man.

He was struck dumb, his body tightening with outrage. Say something, she pleaded and began to hiccup and Osman sputtered more questions. Attacked? Who did this? Was it him? The man in the car?

Yes, she hiccupped.

We will go to the police.

No!

Yes, they are my friends.

What does that mean? What are you saying?

What did he do to you? I myself, then, will kill this man.

We have to go, she said. You have to protect me.

He brought her into his arms then and kissed her face and wiped away her tears with his thumb and promised. She wasn't asking much, she told him. Take me back to the academy in Uskudar, where she could feel safe again in her own room. They would talk and she would answer his questions and then they would make a plan. A plan for what? he asked and she told him, A plan for being together.

Tabi, tabi, he assured her, yet the set of his lips seemed indecisive, and he said he'd need to place another call to Karim.

She was cheered to see the ferry station at Eminonu still jammed at this late hour of the morning and they lurked inside one of the souvenir shops on the perimeter of the square, keeping an eye out for Maranian's black

Mercedes, and then made a dash for the Uskudar ferry, sliding into the push of last-minute passengers. The Eminonu-Uskudar route was Istanbul's most traveled, requiring the fleet's largest ship to carry thousands of commuters daily between Europe and Asia, and it took them several minutes to press through the passageway to the bow and squeeze in alongside other passengers on one of the open-air benches on the forward deck. They cuddled together, Osman's arm around her shoulder, pulling her into him with tender mercy, as the ferry churned away from the Golden Horn into the once-magical waters of the Bosphorus.

I'm really, really sad, said Dottie.

Then I am sad as well.

I miss my sailboat, she said.

Yes, Osman echoed her. I miss it as well.

There was this thing troubling him and she thought she knew what it was and she thought if she mentioned it it would go away. Your father seemed nice, she said, feeling Osman's body tense as he automatically agreed with her, like a recorded message on a machine. She held still and waited for him to explain but as the silence became uncomfortable she allowed herself to wonder if the estrangement between Osman and his father had been a lie, a dramatic fabrication, a better story than the real story. He had been reading her thoughts, it seemed, because he turned from watching the approaching shoreline of Asia and met her eyes with a look of surrender and said what he had told her about the situation with his father was true until about six months ago.

You mean, before you met me?

Yes, he nodded.

What happened six months ago?

I took a position with the state, said Osman. This pleased my father, and he welcomed me back into his home. My home.

What does that mean—a position with the state? Have you dropped out of school?

No, no. It's nothing. But it made my father happy.

But why did you not tell me? she said and, plaintively sincere, he told her that the story of his estrangement with his father had never felt like a lie but felt more true than the reality that had replaced it, the years of bitter rejection and self-recrimination more vivid and alive than the past few months of eating breakfast each morning with his father, the two of them acting like those years were in the past, or had never happened. He asked her to understand and she said she did and she loved him and then the ferry was tying up to the dock and Osman went inside the terminal to telephone Karim.

Is everything all right? she asked when he came outside again and they began to walk up the slope to the academy.

Yes, fine, he said. It's nothing. He and Karim had arranged to meet today. Perhaps later, I told him, and he said okay.

Classes were still in recess for summer break, the new semester a week away, and the campus seemed unnaturally abandoned. Her keys lay in the mud somewhere on the bottom of the Sea of Marmara and she had to buzz the resident attendant to come unlock the door of her dormitory. The RA came down, not the one Dottie expected or liked, a gormless dull-faced stork too lazy to change out of her pajamas. Through the half-opened door she gawked stupidly at Dottie and told her it had been kind of weird having to think of her as drowned and then, like, not-drowned, and if Dottie needed something she should go to administration, the RA said, because she wasn't authorized to let her into the building.

Osman's face reflected her own dismay. She knew you were alive, he marveled as he trotted after her toward the academy's main building. How was that possible?

I don't fucking know, Dottie snarled and then stopped in her tracks, turning with a cringe of apology for her tone but then she was screeching that her father was sick, not sick like ill, sick like insane, and Osman finally managed to settle her down sufficiently to enter the central suite of offices for a visit, unannounced but apparently anticipated, with the headmistress, a Canadian educator with a gray bob and pale, worried eyes who decades ago had fallen in love with a Turkish man and decided to make her home in Istanbul despite getting what the students called The Big Heave-ho. She came out from behind her desk and swept Dottie into a consoling matronly embrace and piped, What an adventure you've had, eh? adding with dry amusement, You haven't converted, have you, my dear? her eyelids fluttering at Dottie's torn outer-dress. They sat in adjoining upholstered chairs opposite one another and the headmistress rested her chin in her hand pensively and examined the confusion in Dottie's inchoate eyes and said, I'm positively delighted you found the time to come say good-bye but I'm beginning to suspect that wasn't your intention.

Dottie forced her voice to be steady and asked, Have you spoken to my father?

Indeed, I have. He didn't say, but he seemed to be calling from the airport. What he did say was that he thought you might be stopping in this morning for one last look around and if I saw you to tell you to call your mother in the United States. Would you care to use the phone?

What she wanted, and wanted desperately, was to go to her old room and lie down and yank the bedcovers over her head but the headmistress received this request with a wide-eyed expression of pity. You poor thing, she said. That bastard. He didn't have the balls to tell you, did he?

The headmistress said she had been terribly relieved to get a call from Dottie's father the day after the newspapers had reported the two of them lost at sea, and then quickly disappointed to hear him say that his daughter would be attending her final year of secondary school back in America, a consequence of Dottie's decision to live with her mother.

No, said Dottie, stunned. That's not true. It's not right, it's not true.

True or not, said the headmistress, at your father's instruction, your room has been emptied and your things shipped to your mother's address in the States. I'm sorry, Dorothy. Would you like to make that phone call now?

She nodded through tears and without being asked, the headmistress stepped discreetly out of the office for a few minutes while Dottie placed her call, not to her mother in Virginia but to her father's secretary, Mary Beth, in Ankara, who responded to Dottie's histrionic demands with mechanical calm, explaining that her father was traveling and could not be reached and that she had a reservation at the Hilton under the name of Carla Costa and in the morning she should wait in the lobby for Mr. Maranian, who would drive her to the airport to catch a midday flight to Dulles. That's all

I know, honey, said Mary Beth, and Dottie lost control, shouting through her tears, You're not telling me! Where's my father? What about that man, the *signori*? The one who was supposed to kill the Pope! Tell me about him!

Mary Beth said her father had never mentioned such a man and she was sorry to hear Dottie so distressed and Dottie told Mary Beth to tell her father that she would never forgive him. You tell him, Dottie sobbed and stammered. Tell him *never*. Be sure to tell him that. You fucking tell him.

All right, said Mary Beth, her voice infuriatingly neutral. There's one more thing you need to do. Call your mother, please.

You call her, said Dottie. Tell her I'm staying here. Tell my parents to go to hell.

Okay, said Mary Beth. Will do.

CHAPTER THIRTY-THREE

She had slammed down the phone and stamped out of the building and found Osman waiting for her on the marble steps, forlorn and smoking a cigarette with manic puffs, his face as bloodless as it had been throughout the morning and he would not say what was troubling him. Perhaps it was only a particularly bad case of *huzun* yet by now she knew she had arrived back into his life as a complication. She took a ragged deep breath to calm herself before she explained the calamity of her situation and told him what she wanted to do, although it wasn't much of a plan, as plans go, and waited for his reply. Yet her fate was not what she had in mind at the moment—she only wanted an answer. Osman, seeming to understand the power she had assigned to him, looked stricken.

I don't understand what is happening, he said. It's simple, she told him. I'm choosing you and I'm choosing Istanbul.

It will be very difficult to do this, he said but his eyes gradually warmed and he took each of her hands in his and gripped them and that was it—that was their pact. They would be together, coauthors of a fairy tale about a boy and a girl and a brilliant place called Istanbul and happiness and love and defiance.

They walked across the campus of the academy and through its gate back into the city, farther inland up its slopes and into Asia until she began to feel light-headed with hunger and they bought fish kebobs and bread rings and cherry juice from a kiosk on the edge of a children's park and sat on a bench in a grove of pines and ate in silence while they watched the mothers scamper after their laughing toddlers through the sunny playground. It would never have been the same anyway, she said as they stood up to leave and he said, What wouldn't be the same? I just mean school, she said carefully, mentioning that the headmistress told her Jacqueline would not be returning from Paris for her final year, either. But if you don't go to school, what will you do? Osman asked and she shrugged and heard herself laugh in a way that was too giddy and unbalanced and told him she didn't want to think about that today.

They turned back down toward the center of the old city and its scribble of alleys, looking for a small hotel or pensione where she could rent a room for a few days but there were immediate obstacles she had not considered: the nature of her relationship with this young man by her side, the suspicious absence of luggage, her sudden absolute fear of exposing the counterfeit passport to Osman. She began to make Osman wait outside while she inquired at the desk, but her inability to pay in lira or with a card and the very fact that she was a teenage *yabanci* dressed in a strange manner made even the most open-minded proprietor leery of taking her in. The streets were filled with women shrouded in black, though, and wearing the *kara carsaf* seemed like the right tactic in this ongoing game, staying as low as possible under her father's radar, and she refused to take it off no matter how much Osman despised the garment and what it symbolized.

I need to change some money, she told him, and the search for a bank or black-market hustler took them closer to the train station and its squalid neighborhoods. Osman objected when she slowed in front of a decrepit hulk of weather-beaten clapboard taking up most of a block, a shabby Edwardian mansion grafted onto a structure resembling a warehouse that had been converted, according to a sign above a ridiculously pretentious entrance with curving balustrades and a grandiose portico, into a nightclub. F. Nightengale's, surely a joke on the nurse who became famous in an Uskudar hospital during the Crimean War. Another, less ostentatious, sign advertised rooms for rent.

Osman said no, this was not a place for reputable women.

447

She could not tell if he was being prudish or merely condescending.
I have to sleep somewhere, she said, her voice stripping away the frustration she felt because he had not offered her a room or a couch or anything
in his family's building and, too proud or just too unwilling to trap him
into excuses, she would not stoop to ask to be taken in, she did not want
to become anybody's responsibility. Here, she said preemptively, removing a hundred-dollar bill from her purse. Lira, okay? Before he could say
anything else, she moved up the warped steps and disappeared through
the establishment's massive oak door, its panels graying and blistered with
old varnish, her mood lightened by the stuffy, cigar-smelling, old-fashioned
atmospheric campiness of the salon in which she found herself.

A beautiful Ottoman-era rug covered most of the floor, muffling the
tread of her steps. Period furniture: leather armchairs and divans upholstered in melon-green velvet, tea tables and ashtray stands, water pipes on
brass trays, everything arranged in cozy groups along walls that had been
papered a deeper green with flocked patterning. An impressive cut-glass
chandelier hung from the high tin ceiling, a banistered, foot-worn stairway
ascended to a second story. The mahogany reception desk, a grand survivor
of more opulent times, was unattended, the convenience of a small brass
temple bell left on its countertop. She picked it up and rang for help and
waited, admiring the freakish voluptuousness of a row of framed divas, their
photographs hung on the wall in front of her, a gallery of belly dancers,
sinewy feline flesh and man-smothering tassled tits and prized sequined
buttocks and grotesque gobs of circus makeup and swooping Roman coif-
fures circa the 1960s.

A woman's unfriendly voice asked what she wanted and when she
turned to answer she found herself confronted by a big-boned giantess
nearly twice her size, thanks in part to the woman's outlandish hair, corn-
colored with platinum highlights, stacked and lacquered into a Babylonian
ziggurat of seashell whorls towering straight up off the top of her skull. She
wore an equally outlandish caftan, broad-striped purple and orange, pink
ballet slippers on her large feet, her very long fingers ringed with clusters of
jewels, a hardware store of bangles above each knobby wrist, her pouched
dark eyes outlined with flaring tails of kohl and her face, glistening and

heart-shaped, had been denied its natural beauty by an outsized Levantine nose hooked over the hypersensual protrusion of her lips, camel-like and scowling. She barked at Dottie as if she were an intruder, her presence an affront to a virtuous person's sensibilities.

You. What is your business here?

Unlike her mother, Dottie was capable of planting herself, undaunted, in the face of unexpected hostility. And indeed the woman's rudeness seemed arrested by what she saw as she peered more closely at the girl, the severity of her countenance cracking open with wonder and then tightening with acquisitive interest. I am Zubedye, she declared without further prejudice, and then the questions flowed in a more amiable tone.

Are you a religious person? No. Are you lost? No. Dancer? No. My dear, don't take offense—are you a prostitute? No, said Dottie, but I need a room where my boyfriend can visit me.

Ah, I see, said the giantess Zubedye, her rubbery lips stretching into a prurient smile. And for how long would you like this room?

Dottie took a hundred-dollar bill from her clutch and asked how many days it would buy and the woman, used to the cowering pliable obsequiousness of girls who came to her from the poverty of the countryside, eyed her shrewdly and snatched the bill from her fingers and said five. It was also necessary to show proof of identity to register lawfully but as Dottie began to hand over her passport she hesitated and sighed. There's a small problem, she said. It's a long story, but my boyfriend doesn't know my real name.

The woman reached out and took the passport and opened it. Italian? Yes.

Carla Costa?

It's better for me if you call me Dottie.

I will call you Dottie, the woman agreed and then frowned and corrected her. Not a small problem, she said. You are only sixteen.

Seventeen.

Where are your parents?

Rome. They come here all the time. To work.

And what am I to think about this? You have run away from home?

449

She almost said if anyone had run away it was her parents but the story she told was close enough to the truth—she was a student, enrolled in the girl's academy on the other side of town, determined to enjoy a week's liberty with her boyfriend until the new term began and she was locked up like a nun in the dormitory. Mmmm, purred Zubedye indulgently. Okay, I understand. You are a very clever girl.

But still there was a problem. The proprietress of F. Nightengale's enjoyed a good relationship with the police, a relationship, for obvious reasons, essential to preserve. Dottie was not of legal age, too young, in fact, to sit in the nightclub and drink alcohol. My business has many hidden costs, said Zubedye, rubbing the tips of her fingers together.

Osman inconveniently reappeared, casting a look of extreme disapproval in Dottie's direction as he shouldered open the heavy oak door and stopped, gaping at the spectacle of the flamboyant Zubedye and then moped, a hangdog droop to his face, his authority somehow unmanned, when both women glanced his way and then quickly ignored him. Without protesting Zubedye's extortion, Dottie slipped her passport back inside the clutch next to all that now remained of the perverted *signori's* money. There was yet one last problem, the giantess told her. You must remove this garbage you are wearing. People who come here to my club don't like to see this on women. Osman returned to life, agreeing vigorously and self-importantly, his judgment finally honored. Dottie tried to explain— it wouldn't do to have a schoolmate or teacher or a friend of her parents recognize her on the streets—but Zubedye remained adamant. Okay, I have a solution, she said, now we go upstairs and I will show you your room and I will introduce you to Dena and Dena will help you. You come, too, she commanded Osman, who plodded upstairs after the females with glowering reluctance.

Then they were in a nondescript book-lined room with a wardrobe and dressing table, not much different than her drab dormitory room except for the double bed and the darkly attractive, wispy-voiced Dena sitting on its edge in jeans and a football jersey, painting her toenails, her coal-black hair tied back with a white ribbon, sloe-eyed and sleek and unremittingly cheerful. If she had a tail, Dottie thought, she'd never stop wagging.

Osman, though, was not the least receptive to Dena's effusive friend-
liness. Smirking, he scanned the titles nearest him and said, Excuse me,
picking up a copy of a textbook on Marxism from a stack on the floor. I
am confused—*You* are a prostitute?

Dottie whipped her head around and seethed in English, Why are you
being so uptight?

Dena gave him an inquisitive look, not unlike an adoring pet ready
to please its master if it only understood what its master wanted. I am a
university student, Dena said with a flicker of self-consciousness. Second
year, okay?

Also a hair cutter, said Zubedye. To pay her education, she added with
her jaw thrust accusingly at Osman, pronouncing each word with an inflection reserved for someone unusually dense. She snapped her fingers to
order Dottie out of her torn black dress and gathered it into a ball as though
it were the hide of some repugnant animal and stepped back through the
door to leave the three of them alone. Dena began spreading newspaper on
the floor and centered her desk chair on the paper and arranged the tools of
her trade on the cosmetic-laden dressing table, talking all the while, playing an adolescent version of a game called Dreams Come True, a fantasy-
scape of accumulation—cars, villas, travel, clothes, shoes, jewelry—Dottie
politely approving all the elusive luxuries that inspired a girl from the slums
of Bursa to flee to the metropolis. I like this very much, chirped Dena,
tracing her index finger along the cheap *nazar* bracelet on Dottie's wrist.
Osman gave it to me, said Dottie, and Dena beamed at Osman, hapless and
brooding on the edge of the bed, as though he were the most exemplary
of providers. Dottie dumped herself into the chair on the paper and the
banter continued and finally Osman had had enough of it.

Be serious, he said. What university do you attend? What are you studying? and Dena responded to his skepticism with answers that required
Osman himself to abandon his ridiculous sense of superiority. The scissors snicked away while Dottie half-listened to the two of them engage
in a spirited discussion about the transformative miracles of secularism
and modernism, not exactly what she was accustomed to hearing from
Osman. On they chattered like flag-waving cousins elected to parliament,

Dena deftly lifting Dottie's chin as her head nodded forward, woozy with a fatigue that crept up on her from every direction in her life.

After a while she felt the wetness of the henna dribble down the back of her bared neck and the exquisite toweling and brushing and then the nuisance of blow-drying and from far off she heard Dena say, Finished! What do you think? and Osman's answer, amazed, It's like another person—do I know this gorgeous girl? Dena shook her shoulder gently and she opened her eyes to a hand mirror held in front of her face and saw Carla incarnate and Dena was asking in an opportunistically timid voice if it was okay if she kept the hair on the paper. You know, said Dena, to sell. For my education.

Yes, take it, sell it, said Dottie, blocking a sarcastic impulse to say, *for your education.*

She stared into the mirror and thought, I am the invention of other people.

They went across the hall to her own room and flopped on the bed and Osman was suddenly afire with erotic zeal, flinging his hips against hers, madly kissing her face and kneading her breasts and she wanted to lie in bed with him but not for sex, she did not want to have to think about sex for a while or feel sexual or let her body be itself. When he slipped his fingers halfway under the waistband of her jeans she stiffened and gripped his wrist instinctively and was stunned to feel the insistence of his hand, pushing down beneath her panties.

I want you so much, he said with such heart-tugging sincerity that to be fair, a translation from Turkish to English would have to flip a coin between *want* and *love.*

She did not doubt the nature of his desire or his determination to have what he had truly earned or arguably deserved, but she was appalled to find his touch unbearable. Now she was turning the person she cared most about in the world into a beggar as his fingers advanced without any consideration toward the stumpy forest of new growth atop her pubis.

Stop, she said. Osman, please stop. Tomorrow or the day after, she promised, he could spend the night and do what he wanted, have all of her, claim her, take her virginity. Or what was left of it, if anything, she said to herself.

She awoke in the late afternoon to an empty room and a full bladder and dashed down the hall to use the toilet and when she returned Osman was back, his smile open and sweet with gratitude but his eyes betrayed a twinge of guilt and she noticed her embroidered clutch on the dressing table had grown plump in her absence. The lira, he said, gesturing. I put them in your purse, and she searched his face for any indication that he had unearthed her alter ego, disconcerted by the sheepishness that crept into his self-involved expression, not the reaction she might expect if he had spied at her phony passport.

I have to go, he said, taking her in his arms. I'll come back later tonight.

But where are you going? she cried. I'll go too.

It frightened her that he did not immediately consent to her company, weighing her potential for being in the way. She understood better after his explanation—he was taking the ferry to Karakoy to see Karim for a meeting he could no longer delay. He'd be back in two hours, he said, and they would have dinner and would come back to this room and he would spend the night—*Like brother and sister, I swear*—and at that moment she wanted to confess everything to him and start again from there but instead she found herself clinging, pleading to come along, she absolutely had to see Yesho and Elena, she'd call them from the ferry terminal and they could get together and grab something to eat in Ortakoy. The boys were up to something, that much was clear, but so what? and she promised she wouldn't start anything with Karim.

Osman looked into her eyes, making a decision, she could tell, against his better judgment, and kissed her and said, It's crazy, okay? Something is definitely wrong with me. You should wait here, but always with you, why is it I forget this very good word? This very good word, *no*.

CHAPTER THIRTY-FOUR

They got to the terminal early and she had time to find a telephone to call Yesho, holding her breath while she listened to the rings, rehearsing the miraculous story of Dottie risen from the dead. Instead, Yesho's mother answered, and Dottie's nerves failed and without identifying herself she left a message for Yesho to join her friends later in the evening. She fed more coins into the slot and dialed Elena, who picked up and, immediately recognizing Dottie's voice, began shrieking, *Yes, but, you fucking bitch, why you didn't call sooner, I love you, you make me so sick, how is America?* Another consequence of her father's tomfoolery came to light—the day after the news reports that her best friend had been lost at sea, a sobbing Elena had gone to the academy to speak with the headmistress about organizing a memorial service for her classmate. *Guess how pissed I become,* Elena bellowed into the phone. *Gone to America! But it's the same thing as dead! I'm crying to her. What is the fucking shit I am hearing? Our Dottie is gone!*

She had to interrupt Elena's cascade of lamentation and reproach, saying, You're never going to believe it, this is just insane, I'm calling you from Uskudar, and the squeal coming through the line so high-pitched she held the phone away from her ear. Outside the windows of the terminal she could see the ferry about to dock and they made a joyous plan to meet at Gizgi in a couple of hours and Dottie said, *I have to go now.*

She went out on the quay and slipped to the front of the queue next to Osman and they boarded with ample time to have their choice of seats in the bow and she picked the bench all the way in the front to be able to watch the sun go down with an unobstructed view. While the ferry loaded up, Osman flirted, pretending she was a stranger, *Excuse me, have we met? What is your name? You are the most beautiful girl I have ever seen. What country are you from? May I please kiss you?* and she teased him back about the tenacity of horny Turkish boys and their annoying belief in love at first sight. Then the boat was filled with people and the engines throttled forward out into the rejuvenating Bosphorus and they leaned into one another and committed the small scandal of making out in public. They spent the crossing being what they were—young lovers, indefatigable and silent in each other's arms beneath the sunset, in motion and one and the same in their gratitude. She couldn't remember what else they might have said to one another until they were near the entrance to the Golden Horn and Osman told her he'd be right back, he was going aft to use the bathroom and grab a cup of tea at the snack bar. Did she want anything to drink? Sure, she said. Cherry juice.

Did she see Maranian then, when she turned to watch Osman go? Which silver-haired man was he in the crowd packed into the glass-enclosed sitting area behind the benches? Did she even see a silver-haired man? Did she see a dozen of them? If she saw him she could not possibly have really looked at him without panicking, so it never made sense that she saw him, even if maybe she did. But of course he was there, somewhere, tracking them, unable to save them or anybody.

The ferry cut ahead into the Golden Horn toward Karakoy and she waited for Osman to return and then the ferry was docking and he had not come back and a patrol launch with its siren howling sent a wonderful rooster-tail of water into the gloaming air as it sped away from shore.

She did not ask herself where Osman was because the lines at the snack bar and toilets were often notoriously long and nothing was unusual about finding yourself separated from someone on the jam-packed ferries, especially at this time of the day. The ropes were tied to their stanchions and the gangplanks attached and she became part of the disembarking herd shuffling toward the exits, not bothering to look for Osman because if they didn't bump into each other haphazardly getting off the boat she knew he would be there waiting for her, or she for him, on the quay.

Watching both gangplanks, her heart sank when she spotted Maranian in the crowd on the second one, near the stern, frantic now to find Osman and get out of there and disappear, and then in a panic, silently pleading for Osman to come and the last passengers left the boat and where was Osman? She whirled away, spinning in circles, looking for him in the throng of humanity on the landing, not seeing him but the sweep of her eyes catching a man with a camera—she specifically remembered the camera and its telephoto lens—talking to several police.

Maranian was calling her name—*Dorothy! Dorothy!* he must have known she had gone to Uskudar—and she saw him shoving through the crowd, red-faced and apoplectic, shoving and pushing and coming to get her and she pinballed around person after person across the square, still desperate to find Osman before she herself vanished into the refuge of the city. Then, near the car park someone else was calling her and it was, *thank God,* Karim. She ran toward him hollering Osman's name.

We are waiting for him, Karim said. I thought he was with you. What happened to him? asked Karim in a voice both defensive and accusatory and she said, Please help me, there's a man, please. I think he did something to Osman. What man? asked Karim, his mouth seized with a crooked smile and his eyes shifty and craven. She saw another man standing there but did not realize he and Karim were together until the two of them began to speak too rapidly in Arabic for her to understand what they were saying. Then Karim looked at her queerly to ask why she thought this man had done something to Osman and she cried, her voice ranging toward hysteria, I don't know, where's Osman? *Where is he?*

Karim's eyes went suddenly cold and shifted over her shoulder and she knew someone was behind her and she knew when someone grabbed her arm to drag her away that it was Maranian. He was winded and trying to catch his breath, never saying anything but looking crestfallen as she gyrated and fought and kicked at his legs, shouting for him to let go and then the person with Karim, whom she had never seen before, forced himself between her and Maranian and then Maranian had toppled to the ground and she was in the backseat of a car staring out the window at Maranian as if he had plummeted from the sky wearing a rosebud of blood on his shirt and she said, dumbstruck, *What did you do?* as Karim started the engine and they drove away, tires squealing like bank robbers.

The two men talked nonstop, she remembered, but again she could not fathom what they were saying in Arabic, the words had a pressurized velocity like spray from a fire hose, arguing—*she, she, she*—until it finally dawned on her that *she* was her. Please, she interrupted them, Karim, take me with you! but neither of them responded and she rode along limp and mute with shock, deep into the treeless hills of the western slums where she had never been before and Karim, yelling at her, slammed on the brakes and stopped with the engine running. Get out, he said, but she didn't move. Benumbed, she was hardly cognizant of being spoken to, and he repeated his command, this time furiously, Dottie, get out of the car! *But why?* she whimpered and then the other man had turned in his seat and leaned back to land a punch on her jaw and kept slapping her face until she had sense enough to find the door handle and she tumbled out into the street wailing and the car sped away.

The first night on the streets she had walked past a police station and a minute later wheeled around and went back and went in and the duty officer asked what she wanted and she trembled trying to find the words and the words themselves quivered when she finally said a friend of hers had told her about a friend of theirs who had had an accident on the Uskudar ferry, did the officer know anything about that. No, not personally, the officer said and pointed behind him to the ubiquitous television broadcasting soap operas. There had been a news bulletin, he said, earlier in the evening. A student had fallen overboard off the Uskudar ferry. They found him, didn't they, she said. He's all right, isn't he? and the gendarme gave his head a sympathetic tilt and said, Sorry, I must tell you, this person drowned.

Because of her own experience on the Sea of Marmara at first she refused to believe that Osman had actually drowned, assuming, instead, that he had managed to swim ashore or had been rescued and they were hiding him for some reason but as the night went on she began to believe it was true. Osman could not swim well enough to survive plunging off the ferry and who pushed him and why was certainly no mystery to her. The farther she walked the more she began to feel herself enclosed in a fog that threatened to suffocate her if she stopped moving and she began to obsess on the thought that she was having a strange mystical experience, like she was tripping or in some drug-induced trance and floating, an ashy, scorched rag of a spirit, and for the next day or two or three she was unable to extricate herself from the incapacitating stupor that accompanied her weightlessness, a pervasive numbness that left her ambulant but without a sense of free will, and when she tried to make her mind operate lucidly it would function in no other way except through the simple logic of hatred, a searing, linear, easy-to-connect design that created an isosceles triangle from which her father reigned at the flaming apex, and she and Osman thrashed underfoot, and off to the side of this pyramid lay the stick-figure body of Maranian, a cast-off extension of her father's power, and the antidote to this power and its unspeakable effect was a secret beyond her knowledge but what she instinctively knew was a daughter's formula to mete out punishment for his control over her, her mind and body welded into a perfect communion and her unholy peregrinations through the city guided by her quest for revenge. A perfect communion, until her lust for vengeance expired, defiling what should, by right and by love, have been Osman's, and would have been, but became instead, by default, the property of hatred.

What happened next? the man across the table asked. He was dressed in an army officer's uniform but had removed his hat and jacket and rolled up his sleeves as if he were trying his best to suppress a natural inclination to intimidate the people brought to him. She looked down again at the black-and-white photographs he had spread in front of her an hour ago and then up again into the artificial kindness of his eyes, the perfunctory gestures of compassion, *Would you like a tissue? Tea?* Not what she expected from a colonel in the Turkish military and in stark contrast to the ugly treatment she had received from the gendarmes when they had taken her into custody the night before in her room at F. Nightengale's. They had delivered her here from Uskudar in the morning in a windowless van but she had soon guessed where they were, across the Bosphorus on the army base north of the marina where her cherished *Sea Nymph* had once been moored.

What happened next?

She remembered most vividly the apricot spears of light breaking through the clouds, lanced into the Bosphorus off the bow of the ferry, but what happened next she was unclear about and lay crisscrossed and tangled in her memory, or, astonishingly, nowhere to be found. It sickened her, this inability to remember clearly, the fear that she had blotted out crucial moments, because what happened next, after she had been told and shown days later what happened next, had been seared precisely into another part of her brain separate from her memory, her version. The problem being, as she saw it, that the two versions combined should make an inevitable whole yet they did not, each instead conspiring to sow doubt into the other.

Their version: Maranian was on the ferry that day from Uskudar to Karakoy. Karim and the Palestinian were also on the ferry.

Her version: Maybe she saw Maranian on the ferry. She was 99 percent certain she saw him getting off in Karakoy. She never saw Karim on the ferry, or the man they said was with him. She saw them, though, when the ferry docked in Karakoy.

Their version: The Palestinian shoved Osman overboard.

Her version: Daddy. How could it not be? Who else was so medieval that he would remedy his daughter's refusal to cease dating a Muslim by drowning the boy? Her father had become a sword attached to the hand of an avenging God, striking down the guilty and the innocent alike. But this version had caused her to do foolhardy, degrading things to herself that she never wanted to remember as long as she lived.

Who was right and who was wrong and did it matter? After much deliberation she arrived at an answer that provided the self under construction with its most vital component. If it was true that the dead lived on, or carried on, in the living, then another more consequential truth had to be accepted. The dead mattered, the dead cared, as long as

459

life mattered, and the living cared. The heart, one learns, whenever one learns it, early or late, is a depository for the dead, a private necropolis. There is no other, really. Where are they? Here, or nowhere. That was what the heart shared with history. The holding, the preservation, the remembering—an eternal present.

What happened next?

August twenty-fourth was . . . ? Or was the twenty-fourth actually the twenty-fifth?

She would stare at September first and see absolutely nothing there. The day before and the day after were interchangeable in their fickle, wretched vacancy. September fourth was the police station and questions questions questions and the morning of September fifth still more questions after they had transferred her to this place and then the terrible humiliating shock of learning how wrong she had been. Stupid, stupid girl.

Try to remember, said the colonel. Take your time.

I don't know, she said. I mean, nothing happened. I was lost. I didn't know where I was.

Who did you contact?

What do you mean?

Someone to help you, perhaps?

No, no one. I wandered around. Walking felt like something I needed to do.

And all those days, where did you go?

Nowhere, really. I would just keep walking until I got tired. Then I would sleep wherever I ended up, in a church or a doorway or the backseat of a car or somewhere.

I find this puzzling, the colonel sighed. You asked no one for help. Why not? You have friends in Istanbul, I think.

I don't know, she said. I didn't know what was happening. I was afraid, she said, nodding dull-eyed at the photograph the colonel had placed in front of her of Osman and Karim having a furtive discussion at the railing near the ferry's stern, the Palestinian lurking nearby.

What were you afraid of? The terrorists?

Yes. I don't know. I was confused. Which terrorist?

And why was this man we know to be an Armenian terrorist chasing you? asked the colonel, tapping the photograph she could not bear to look at, Maranian lying spread-eagled on the tarmac of the car park.

I wish I could tell you, she said anxiously, her voice weak and despairing. Honest. I have no idea.

And you called no one? Is this correct?

I phoned Osman's apartment. I told you that already, didn't I?

No.

His mother answered the phone and said there had been an accident with Osman on the ferry and she said I had to hang up because she was waiting for the police to call. But how did the authorities know, it seemed instantaneously, that it was Osman, fallen off the ferry?

Dorothy, why did you cut your hair that day and change its color?

Really, I don't know. It's just a coincidence. I thought it would be fun.

Dorothy, I want you to tell me the truth, okay? I want you to believe me—the situation we have been discussing is very serious. Why did you disobey your father?

Because I loved him, she said.

You loved?

Osman. *Osman.*

Before they could be stained by her onrush of tears, the colonel reached across the table to gather up the photographs for safekeeping, evidence of crimes committed and yet to be committed. He replaced the first set of photographs in his briefcase and brought out a second set, which he arranged before her like a fortune-teller's cards.

You were watching me, she said, unnerved by the proof of her flagrancy and carelessness.

Yes.

How long?

Not long, said the colonel, pointing to a photograph. Can you tell me, who is this man you are speaking to?

I don't know, she said, embarrassed. Maybe I was asking him directions.

And the man in this photograph?

I don't know his name. Someone I met in a café, I think.

And this man?

That man. He sells fish. I forget his name.

His name is Mohammed, said the colonel wearily. I believe you spent a night on his boat.

Yes. He's not in trouble because of me, is he?

Only with God.

But what was I supposed to do? she said. She had succumbed to a juvenile whim, returning to the fish market to tell Mohammed that the queen at the bottom of the sea had, in her inconsolable jealousy, demanded she give back the treasure of her pink pearl. Whoever stole my passport, she told the colonel, stole all my money too. I had to sleep somewhere.

If you were my daughter, said the colonel, pausing while he retrieved the photographs and stood up with his briefcase and tunic in hand. If you were mine, he continued, I would lock you in a room.

There was much she had not told the colonel, much she could not tell him, but nothing she might have told him that would have made any difference. The chance to save everybody, she was about to find out, had been lost with Osman.

Can I get you anything? the colonel asked as he prepared to leave.

Pistachio sorbet? she said, the request of an unreasonable child and slightly naughty, her coyness like an encoded beacon signaling from inside the shell of her wreckage.

The colonel smiled, momentarily beguiled, and she observed him closely, registering the change in his eyes as he measured her as a potential object of desire, the gleaming surge, the ebb and flow of heat that temptation caused in a man. This man too, she understood, would fuck her if he could, and probably every man in the building, the trade for sorbet.

We don't have that here, he said, his voice a gentle reprimand punctuated by the closing door. A few minutes later the door opened again and there was Mary Beth, the can-do saint of her father's underworld, her decency exceeded only by her discretion and competence, holding Dottie's new American passport and a ticket to an alien place called home. Dottie dashed from the table into Mary Beth's arms, a spontaneous act of

462

surrender and an end to fear, the way tormented children run helpless to their mothers.

Grudgingly, during the course of his interrogation the colonel had remarked that she was an exceptionally lucky girl, and grudgingly in return she had replied that she supposed she was, congratulating herself on the single piece of good fortune that she could accurately gauge, packaged in the irony of misfortune—the theft of her clutch, resulting in the depressing loss of her money but the altogether propitious separation of herself from the passport of Carla Costa, a document that would have proven instantly self-indicting, catastrophic evidence of her participation in unknown conspiracies, an advertisement for her manifold guilt, when she was picked up after she eventually circled back to her rented room at F. Nightengale's. It was there, thanks to the perfidious disloyalty of Zubedye and Dena, that the police were patiently waiting for their suspect to finish her rounds with the males of Istanbul, her lascivious manhunt a parallel universe to the one being conducted by the authorities for Karim and his homicidal cohorts. *She's a fucking liar,* she screamed and screamed at the police, disavowing the giantess's insistence that the girl carried a fake passport. *I made up a name and she took all my money and wrote it down.*

But naturally the colonel could not have been thinking of the fortunate disappearance of Carla's passport when he judged her luck. Nor, from what she could discern from his manner, was the colonel overly impressed by her vulnerability as a teenage *yabanci* tramp prowling the streets of his city, a danger she herself did not acknowledge, operating in a zone of magical thinking, the disheveled and unwashed reflection she glimpsed in shop windows of no more concern or connection to her than the scuzzy hippies who liked to hang out at the Pudding Shop en route to nowhere and its banal enlightenments.

The colonel's true assessment of her luck was made apparent through a pair of revelations that rendered her air-brained and queasy and, for a short time, bawling, her tears interrupted by awful intervals of psychotic chortling that circulated through the austere room like the sound of a demented bird and elicited a period of dismayed but tender solicitude from the colonel, who displayed great sensitivity to the portion of her emotional pyrotechnics that was the outcome of her introduction to a second Osman, a shadow Osman stepping forward into an all too familiar cone of light already shining on her father. How strange to see him there in the sizzle, an Osman to be both adored and detested. How weird, how crazy, how clichéd and scary that on her first foray into the realm of love outside the palace gates of her father's kingdom she had in oblique but indisputable ways fallen in love once again with her father, Daddy's unlikely double, the rookie Turkish version, and of her own generation, a patriotic college boy working undercover to save the world or at least his own piece of it, one of many patriotic students selected by the state as members of a secret unit, infiltrating the clandestine Muslim brotherhoods germinating in the universities, stepping right into shit.

I believe you know this group of radicals your boyfriend was investigating, yes?

I don't, she said. I saw them once in a café. Osman was there. Karim was there. Can I ask you something? Osman was arrested that night.

Correct, said the colonel, anticipating her question. The arrest was a ruse.

I just had that feeling, she said.

The colonel had showed her the pictures taken by another undercover agent assigned that day to tail and photograph Osman as he met with Karim and a foreigner subsequently identified as a Palestinian terrorist, the suspected mastermind of a forthcoming but unspecified atrocity. The Palestinian had flown from Syria to Turkey to locate and collaborate with a group of like-minded fundamentalists, Jew haters who would provide logistical support—reconnaissance, safe houses, transportation, weapons, explosives—for his bloody mission. Whatever that mission was, Osman, as an agent of the state, was attempting to determine but had failed. She looked at the photos, weeping.

Dorothy, you can help us, yes? asked the colonel.

She shook her head wildly, voiceless, unable to speak in any language to describe what she saw or felt, devastated by the ghastly expression on Osman's face in the photo, a blur of horror, of total betrayal and total surprise, a mouth gulping with the instinct for self-preservation, his eyes enlarged not with fear but the promise of a repudiating, obliterating violence as he tottered backward into the sea. What she read in Osman's eyes convinced her that the colonel was telling the truth, and she began to perceive the hidden message contained by the truth, that no matter what seemed to an ordinary person to be the odds against such mythical human symmetry, people who are meant to be together find each other, enemies no less than lovers, throughout space and time and the sea of eternity.

Help me understand, said the colonel. Why did these terrorists let you out of the car? I think you are very, very lucky.

I don't know, she said, but she knew that the answer was Karim.

In their room in the Hilton that night Mary Beth gave her a note from her father that she unsealed from its envelope and read, a single handwritten page in her father's immaculate script, and then refolded and returned to its envelope and gave back to Mary Beth to be disposed of properly—following the instruction in the note's postscript. *I believe there is an Argentinian saying,* the note began, *that the past is a predator.* Without apology, he asked for forgiveness. For what, he did not bother to say, only adding this cryptic explanation—*There was a malfunction. I was the malfunction,* a non sequitur followed by a brief lesson in family history that left her mystified: Her grandparents and her father, she read with astonishment, had lived in Croatia during World War Two. Near the end of the war, Communist soldiers had killed her father's father and raped her father's mother. Three of these partisan soldiers did not survive the war and the carnage of its aftermath. One of the remaining three had been executed during a purge by the Tito government. Of the surviving two, one was lured to Pittsburgh where he met his just fate at the hands of Davor and your grandmother. The last living member of the six criminals responsible for these sins against our family was the *signori.* The note concluded with her father's profuse expression of gratitude to his daughter for fulfilling *her sacred duty.*

What duty? she asked herself.

One day I believe you will agree that the obligation and the grace to serve are in your blood, he wrote. There was no mention of Osman or

Maranian or the lethal consequence of their own commitment to this all-consuming, ever-hungry monster named *duty*.

See you in Virginia at Christmas, Kitten, her father ended. *God bless you.*

The hotel room was crammed with Mary Beth's luggage and Dottie sat humped over on the bed, watching her father's assistant open a suitcase and explore its neatly folded contents and slowly abandon the armor of her taciturnity. What size are you? said Mary Beth. We need to find you something to wear. Why don't you hop in the shower while I pull out some things.

Why did you bring all this stuff? Dottie asked. Are you going somewhere?

On her knees bent over a pile of skirts and rayon blouses, Mary Beth straightened up and sat back in a thoughtful pose, ass atop heels, and tucked her light brown hair behind her ears and cocked her head at Dottie with a vaudevillian shrug. Would you believe it? she said, her voice mocking a perky version of herself. I actually *am* going somewhere.

Where? Like a vacation?

Well, yes, I guess you could say that. I'll visit my family in Ohio for a while and then, who knows?

What's wrong?

She made a stern face, peering at Dottie judgmentally, but again she appeared to be mocking herself. Off the record, okay, she said.

I can do that.

I'll bet you can, honey, said Mary Beth, not unkindly. You are Steven's daughter one million percent. Here's what I know. I believe your father is out of the office indefinitely. He has, apparently, gone off the reservation—I suspect you know more about that than I do, and I don't want to know anything more than I know. So, okay, bad boy, naughty naughty, but it seems his friends in high places are both understanding and forgiving. That said, I seem to be the one left out in the cold. At least for the moment.

Where is he?

Stirring it up in Belgrade, with occasional excursions to pursue his hobby in Peshawar. Now, you understand what I just said, don't you, because I'm not going to say a word more.

Yeah.

How about this? chirped Mary Beth, holding up a very unlike–Mary Beth paisley minidress. It never fit me anyway, she said. I'm afraid the hemline will cover your knees. It'll probably hang on you like a bag but we can belt the waist. Whaddya think, honey? Your mother will kill me if I put you on a plane in those filthy clothes. And by the way, I shouldn't say anything, but whoever did your hair—

I know, said Dottie, it's gross.

She wanted more than anything to apologize to Mary Beth for being such a brat on the telephone, all those many days ago when her life with Osman was the only thing she had imagined she could believe in. After, *I'm sorry,* her voice cracked and Mary Beth held out her arms and said, *Baby, come here,* and she got off the bed onto her knees and crawled to this woman who knew her and held her and told her that her own heart was bleeding with the knowledge of a young girl's juggernaut of loss. Mary Beth let her cry for a while and then eased Dottie's head from her shoulder, telling her to go jump into the shower and she would order from room service and they would eat and then lights out for the big day tomorrow.

Outside came a boom, far away but strong enough to rattle the windows. What the hell was that? asked Mary Beth.

That's just the cannon in Taksim Square, said Dottie, drying her eyes. You know, they shoot it off every day at sundown.

Of course, said Mary Beth. The cannon. It must be time to pray.

Her dreams that last night in Istanbul were waking dreams where she watched herself watching a conveyor belt of images—Maranian with a hand line fishing along the quay, her father genuflecting before the Pope, Karim riding a miniature donkey, Osman eating the pages of a book (the Koran?), Elena giving a blowjob to an Arabic man wearing a suicide bomber's belt—crazy things, and everything unreachable except through unwavering sorrow.

What happened? Even stuck in the middle of things, you don't always know.

Sometime during the night there was a phone call that awakened her. Is that my father? she had mumbled into the darkness. Mary Beth said yes, go back to sleep, which must have happened because she had no memory of any conversation after that. Then, in the taxi on the way to the airport, she suddenly remembered. Did my father call last night? Mary Beth said yes, he had phoned to warn them to be careful. Why? she asked and Mary Beth said because yesterday a Pan Am flight in Karachi had been hijacked. Sixteen passengers were dead.

For days she would keep trying to refasten herself to the old calendar and its shattered trajectories. August twenty-fourth? August twenty-fifth? The calendar was not telling her what she needed to know. Sixth, seventh, eighth? September sixth!

September sixth was the Istanbul airport, soldiers with machine guns posted everywhere as she queued up to enter the international terminal.

September sixth she didn't know about until Mary Beth escorted her to the airport for their midmorning flight. September seventh was early morning in the airport in Frankfurt, saying good-bye to Mary Beth and waiting alone for her connection to Dulles and a headline in the *Herald Tribune* about the assassination of a Turkish diplomat in Bonn, an alleged retaliation for the assassination by police in Istanbul of one Raffi Maranian, identified as a leader of an underground organization of terrorists, the Commandos of the Armenian Genocide. Without buying the paper, she scanned the lead paragraphs of the story at a kiosk and then stopped reading because what it said happened in Istanbul was not what had happened and apparently journalists too were licensed to lie like anybody else.

Oh, God. Saturday September sixth was the Istanbul airport swarming with soldiers brandishing automatic weapons because the morning of September sixth was a pair of Palestinian terrorists who locked themselves inside the synagogue in Karakoy during Sabbath services and slaughtered everybody and blew them up with hand grenades and burned them with gasoline and in the terminal she began shrieking, *The Kirlovskys! My God!* because the Neve Shalom synagogue near the Galata Tower was their synagogue and she ran to a telephone cubicle and called Elena and kept calling until her flight was announced and then she called again from Frankfurt and whoever answered said Mr. Kirlovsky was dead and after the funeral and shiva the family would be emigrating to Israel.

September seventh was late afternoon in humid Virginia and the ugly satisfaction of the look of repressed revulsion on her mother's face when her emaciated listless daughter emerged from Customs wearing an ill-fitting paisley smock, Dottie's cheeks and forehead an angry hatch of acne and old bruises, and her golden hair chopped short and badly hennaed. Her mother's bright blundering, neurotically insistent—*I know you'll just love your senior year at Madeira, you'll just love your new room. Gosh, wouldn't you love to stop for a good old American cheeseburger*—on the drive down the access road back to Vienna and the ivy-skirted white-brick faux-colonial town house that served as the command post of her mother's dubious liberation. She was a disaffected ex-liberal who, like her newly adopted guru, a neocon pundit acquired at a Georgetown dinner party, had been mugged by reality. And Dottie was unyielding in her hostility, refusing to acknowledge the irony or shorten the distance. What she wanted didn't even make sense—to go home, but where was that? To be healed by her mother—but who was that? She had learned at an early age that she could get along very well without a mother.

August twenty-fourth.

August twenty-fourth was the cruelest joke anyone might ever imagine and in her memory she would sidestep away from its indistinct serpent-like manifestation with a startled jerk, stumbling in horror, her torment expanding until she was crying so hard she would wake up hours later, her face buried in a pillow still wet and cold with slobber.

The girl who drowned really didn't but the boy who drowned really did—this was the joke of August twenty-fourth and it kept returning her to Istanbul and exiling her to America and pitching her right back again into the lovesick clutch of Osman. And then she would find herself curled into an icy glob of space where she accepted she would remain forever, rocking in his lifeless arms and then not rocking at all but frozen by the immensity of loss and the immensity of the world's malevolence and its dim reverberation in her blood.

Day after day after day, a refugee in Virginia and ostensibly an invalid and certainly disabled by the savage loop of time playing in her head, as the season shrank toward winter, she did little else but stay in bed and count the calendar, those days from the end of August to the day in September when she was delivered back to the West, trying to unscramble the blood-curdled lump of time that seemed like a perpetual infernal day in hell and a single permanent night at the frozen edge of the universe, the sun rising and setting simultaneously out of Asia and into Europe or maybe she had that backward like everything else and all that was the world as she knew it had vanished and was condemned and ripped away, her mind blank from rage and incomprehension and the abysmal indigo depths of shredding grief. It was as if somebody had smashed her head with a crowbar.

In mid-September, looking around her room in her mother's town house, she slowly realized why her father had shipped her off to Virginia. Dottie was being offered back to her, like a coat she had left at a party the year before and wasn't sure she wanted to wear anymore, even if it still fit, which it did not. But losing Dottie was his mistake, not hers.

Whoever she was now about to become, that self would be a solitary creation, patented and inviolable, cobbled together and pounded into shape from its kaleidoscopic shamble of bits and pieces. Henceforth as her mother's ward she would practice the art of hibernation, subservient to her studies, passive in a social life that amounted to singing in the choir at St. Luke's, waiting for the light and growth of a new season and her happiness in finding herself alive again. She had wandered in the wilderness and mingled with its natives but she would come back, she kept telling herself. I will come back.

September seventh was that first terrible night in her mother's town house which stank of chemicals, geriatric potpourri and pukey air freshener and toilet bowl cleaner, her mother standing in the kitchen in a coral-colored linen suit and stockings and heels and her brunette hair permed into motionless waves, opening a bottle of white wine for herself and offering Dottie a ginger ale. Let's go sit in the living room, her mother said, grabbing the bottle and a wineglass and Dottie drifted behind her like a wraith into a purgatory of inanities. The living room seemed to be a midwestern celebration of chintz and the walls were churchy with evenly spaced icons and crucifixes with strands of dried palm leaf tucked behind Christ's sagging head and her mother plunked down on the sofa and kicked off her shoes and straightened her skirt over her shiny knees and slurped her wine and wouldn't shut up, reborn with the freedom to express herself uncontested, striving again for her emotions to embody substance, to suddenly contain genuine political meaning or stir involvement, trying to attach this resurgence of powerful feelings to an intellect she did not possess.

All great love affairs are tragic, her mother told her, trying to justify the less than dramatic fraud of her own marriage. I'm sorry about your friend, that boy who got himself mixed up with the wrong crowd, her mother had said the night of their unhappy reunion. But you know, your father tried to warn you, didn't he, and you wouldn't listen.

But Dottie found her mother's voluble insights unworthy of love and despicable and whining. I'll never understand, said her mother, why some people just can't let other people go. People shouldn't always have to live with their mistakes. And she breezily explained her child-rearing philosophy—I didn't pamper you for a reason, and it took everything I had to keep your father from spoiling you. Unlike your brother, you were quite a headstrong child. Disobedient, self-centered—beyond my comprehension, honestly. Show weakness? Not a chance. Ask for help? No, ma'am. And later, slurring and loose-lipped, the bottle empty, the cadence deliberate: As a woman, well, let's just say I allowed myself to be made a mother.

And then as she guided her daughter to her room: When are you going to stop being mad at me? Goddamn it, Dorothy, what is the point of this shunning? Dottie paused, hollow-eyed as a prisoner being led to her cell, absorbing the soulless chill of her new bedroom, peaches and cream, ivory-colored trimmings and good-girl tidiness, before she turned around to look at her mother without any discernible emotion and said, I think I have syphilis or the clap or something, I don't really know.

Hate me if you want, said her mother. You're still my daughter, no matter what.

In late September she was admitted to Fairfax Hospital for observation, nourished through a tube, and the nurse who came to monitor her IV drip talked about how it looked as though Virginia's Indian summer was a goner and then went away. In the opinion of the so-called experts she was anorexic but she wasn't. Eating seemed irrelevant at the moment and could not hold her interest beyond a bite of this and a sip of that. She was definitely not trying to kill herself—quite the opposite; she was determined to get on with her life, if she could only resolve the question of which self would end up being the lucky person who walked out of there. The competition was not fixed, the winner not a given. On her only weekend there her brother Christopher came and brought her flowers and they played a game of backgammon and she apologized for being so weird and when he began to talk about their life in Africa she foolishly dared to confide her biggest secret, how everything had started back then in Kenya. You know, touching and stuff, she tried to explain but Christopher cut her off. Dad? he said, owl-eyed, stunned, offended.

I don't believe you.

She contemplated the riddle of love, creating a dissonance in her thoughts that she found ferociously appealing, a mental form of self-scarring that seemed to validate the high cost of her experience and the exhausting struggle to understand. However you go about explaining it, she thought, love was what diminished you when it was not there.

In October she watched the maple tree outside her window in Vienna release its leaves with each fresh gust of winter-laden wind, like flocks of red birds scattering away to the gray horizon to become gray themselves and then nothing.

In mid-December she rode with her mother and Christopher to Dulles to meet her father's flight from Europe. The shuttle brought him from the plane to the terminal and there he was and she was staring at him, abject, lovelorn, and he waited, with hopeful eyes, for his daughter to take the first step forward, back into his arms.

Book Four
The Friends of Golf

I'm pleading with you, with tears in my eyes: If you fuck with me, I'll kill you all.

—*General James Mattis, US Marine Corps*

CHAPTER THIRTY-FIVE

They slipped Eville away from his unit in Haiti and brought him up to Miami for a few hours to caddy for Steven Chambers, the first of numerous occasions in the following years. Something Chambers said to him that first time put everything in perspective afterward. *We don't fly under the radar, son,* he said. *We* are *the radar. We're not operating with situational values here.*

True leaders did not look at a fire and ask, *What should I do?* True leaders were those men who know what to do and how to do it and, with or without policy, do it, and so it gets done, and it was to them that Master Sergeant Burnette had always owed his allegiance.

You could find them some days between temperate equinoxes on the links outside the District, convened on the first tee in these final years of the millennium, chins tucked and heads bowed and testicles snug, smacking their drives two hundred and fifty yards and beyond toward the middle of the fairway. They made the game look easy and natural and powered by grace, dialed in to the sweet and the straight, their balls nested in a little egglike cluster out at the edge of your vision. It was the kind of perfect placement you get from guidance systems orbiting the planet and that tempted you to think they had the course wired up, had punched the coordinates.

What they called themselves with wry half-smiles was the Friends of Golf, FOG, perhaps an advertent self-parody—a permanent threesome with a rotating fourth, selected guests invited on some other basis than handicaps or dead-eye putting, although they would not abide hackers given the tightness of their game. Hackers would be told to pick up their ball at some point along the front nine, or they would pick it up themselves when the scorn became too much to bear, and heaven help you if they caught you cheating, an inevitable reminder of the commander in chief's sleazy penchant for mulligans. They could not forgive the ineptitude of arrogance, the cavalier stupidity of players who voluntarily exposed their weaknesses and their commensurate need for forgiveness and let themselves be caught.

Eville Burnette saw the humor in that, a round-robin contest of the unscrupulous, the sly and the underhanded, the touts and the rogues, fox versus fox. Whatever anybody thought he was, Burnette was not a dumbass, although it took him an extra beat to sniff out what the chefs from FOG had cooking on their collective burners.

The course they preferred was west out on Highway 50 toward Front Royal and the Blue Ridge Mountains, a club called International Town and Country on a post-revolutionary estate known as Chantilly, far enough beyond the beltway to allow for the secure privacy they would never find at the metropolitan courses like Burning Tree or Congressional, where every golfer had ears. With the earth tilting against them around Halloween and the harvest moon, they would migrate south with the snowbirds to their fair-weather favorites—Pinehurst and then Augusta and then the Doral, their midwinter haunt in Miami. When the Friends of Golf dreamed of the game they dreamed of the balmy January morning they would dance on Castro's grave and tee up on the course Rockefeller had built in the glory days along Varadero Beach. You're in fine company, Chambers liked to joke with Eville Burnette. Che Guevara was a caddy down in Argentina, before he bought a motorcycle.

The three regulars had nicknamed themselves after some of the legends of the sport—Undersecretary Chambers was Arnie, Undersecretary Milliken from DOD was Ben (Hogan, of course) and Sammy, after Sam Snead, was the alter ego for the player formally attached to the Agency, whose real name and title Master Sergeant Burnette was never told and never troubled himself to know, but titles were often misleading in the league where these men played. Their fourth might be anybody with a useful skill set—lawyers, bankers, congressmen, arms dealers, patriotic celebrities, psychics, moguls from the media or defense industries, lobbyists, syndicate capos, cyber-engineers, oil men, narcotraffickers, professors, contractors or their subs, collectors, retainers, cowboys, or call girls—whoever you were, if they needed you they found a way to work you into the picture, foregrounds and backgrounds cropped and bleached and classified far beyond mortality, the image simple proof of their existence and nothing more. Anybody who came to them bearing a simplistic back-channel mentality only earned FOG's derision, since they operated quite a few levels beyond or below or behind that, in an endless hallway of locked and unidentified doors that opened into nothing until one door in fact opened into everything, but you were never going to have access to that door.

Burnette would learn a few things, though—Arnie was Roman Catholic, Ben a Southern Baptist, Sammy a Jew for Jesus who had accepted Christ as the Messiah and been saved. Eventually Burnette would come to understand the importance of their faith. They were graduates of Yale. He could see how that was important too, their vanities starched and pressed just so. They were not grizzled, not brawny or physically intimidating—Chambers was like a silvery elm and the other two short and sinuous with cabled sheaths of muscle like rock climbers, spider monkeys, trapeze artists—little guys immune to both weight gain and criticism. Little guys with big dicks, or at least big-dick syndrome. Phallocrats. The three of them together cast a glinting aura of sunny optimism, come to conquer, the self-confidence of men accustomed to the winner's circle.

The world, the Friends of Golf were fond of saying, is not run from a house on Pennsylvania Avenue. They were the architects of the unseen, the fabrication of interlocking subterranean networks and processes that formed the human infrastructure of what are known as deep events—multigenerational efforts routed together into a fusion that seemed to hold together everything in the cosmos of power, the continuum of power, the throb of ancient algorithms, an almost mystic coming together of forces converging across a grid of specialties. Deep events evolved in deep time and produced tectonic shifts in human affairs. Something happens, something obviously cataclysmic, where even the unexpected was not to be mistaken for a coincidence. There are no coincidences, and everything counts.

It all depended on the science of applied pressure and counterpressure, making sure that when things break—nations, ideologies, economies, atoms—they break to your advantage. And break they will.

In the final years of the twentieth century, the Friends of Golf were the Shakespeares of two events, the first in 1989—to which they had devoted every ounce of their energy and intellect and merciless ingenuity throughout their careers—and it turned out pretty well, in Kabul, and then, before the year was out, Berlin. The end of the wall begat what some happy fools had called the end of history and served as a vindication of more than just their methodology—it was a validation of their most sacred beliefs, a validation of their souls, yet an incomplete redemption for Steven Chambers until Croatia declared its independence in 1991, fulfilling the lifelong dream of Stjepan Kovacevic. There were anxious thinkers in the family who fretted that the end of communism left a void in the West, which would require the development of a new enemy—UFOs and aliens were being tossed around as candidates—but the Friends of Golf knew otherwise, and they were obsessed now with the second event, the eternal one ascending out of the twilight of the centuries—what the Muslims would come to call the Narrative, the hatred awakening into the bigger abomination under the eyes of God, not the end of ideology but the reanimation of the conflict between ultimate good and ultimate evil. The Friends of Golf believed themselves to be the true playwrights and producers of the Narrative, adapted for a new generation of bloody thespians. The old firestorm the same as the new firestorm, the sky opening to disgorge flumes of liquid death down upon God's enemies. Funding it, steering it, smashing it headlong through the bureaucratic clog into the wall of illusions and cowardice otherwise known to them as diplomacy, a waste product of gutless politicians, the short-term thinking of moral invertebrates.

What Eville Burnette did not know—but what he would come to know—was that they were all hands of the Company, the commissars and satraps and water carriers of the Deep State, a familial nexus of assets and adjuncts, overt and covert and beyond into a netherworld of unidentifiable phantoms, daylighters and midnighters and cave dwellers. In any combination spread they constituted the dark matter of the world of intelligence. They lived in two realms at once, like a certain kind of particle in quantum physics, simultaneously occupying the moral antipodes of a universe looking back at itself in a mirror, the entire world a shell company for another world, one reality a parallel for still another reality.

They had been poised for war since they were kids shagging balls at the practice range for a nickel a bucket, listening to the veterans back from Europe or the Pacific or North Africa, who'd warn the boys of the unfinished nature of the job of freedom. The poison was out there still, shape-shifting, flowing through the cracks in civilization. *It's in your hands now, boys,* which is not unwanted news to a gung-ho kid, an inspiration to grow up fast and be the future. That, in any case, was how it was for Eville Burnette, when his father returned from Southeast Asia.

Not many people ever knew that a generation of Montana smoke jumpers had been snatched up by CIA recruiters like Paperlegs Peterson and Big Andy Anderson in the sixties and sent to Indochina. The rationale was obvious enough—young men this far out on the edge of sane behavior, willing to dive out of the sky into a flaming forest, were an ideal resource for the clandestine death-match rodeo the Agency was running in the jungles of Laos. Crazy winged wranglers with nothing exciting to do in the off-season but keep the cattle fed or go to college. You could not train people to be fearless nuts like the Missoula smoke jumpers were—by Western birth and inclination. Not to mention the money—the Agency stuffed their saddlebags with tax-free cash. And they made the best *kickers* in the world, pushing cargo out of C-130s and C-46s and C-47s for Air America, payloads of weapons and food meticulously weighed and rigged to chutes and rolled out the doors over a drop zone in a matter of arduous seconds, hosed with adrenaline. A bad drop was worse than no drop at all, a gift to the enemy, and they didn't make mistakes.

Dawson Burnette had been hired as a C-130 kicker in 1960 with ten other smoke jumpers from the Missoula and McCall base camps for a mission called Operation Barnum. Barnum was about a place Eville Burnette's father had never heard or dreamed of—a Himalayan kingdom called Tibet, invaded by the Red Chinese, where the Agency was running an insurgency with Tibetan fighters known as Khampas. Dawson flew the Himalayas that winter in an unbroken fever of joyous wonder, kicking men and supplies out onto the ice-walled plateaus north of Annapurna, and then he returned to Missoula for the fire season. By the time the snows were blanketing the Bitterroots in the fall, the Agency asked him to report to Guatemala, where he joined a pair of other jumpers training parachutists and riggers for what they were told would be an invasion of Cuba. That was 1961, the year the US Army created the Golden Knights, an elite team of showcase jumpers designed to battle the Soviet pioneers in the clouds, the Reds a step ahead in world domination thanks to parachuting genius.

By 1962, Dawson Burnette was in Thailand, resupplying General Vang Pao's guerilla army across the border in Laos, but he made it home in time for that summer's wildfires and stayed put for the next two years to finish his university degree in forestry and start a family, marrying the sister of a smoke jumper from over near Bozeman, a ranch-raised girl named Paige who loved books and fly-casting and training Appaloosa barrel racers to turn on a dime.

Eville, the first of three sons, was born in 1965, the same month his father landed in Thailand, back in the Agency's fold, a branded maverick, part of a crew of smoke jumpers sent there to train PARUs, Parachute Aerial Reinforcement Units, and build helo landing pads and STOL airstrips on the ridgelines overlooking the Plain of Jars. For the next three years he'd pogo back and forth between his off-season secret war in Laos and the mountains of the Northwest, making babies and fighting blowups in Montana and Idaho, disappearing to Fort Carson in Colorado or Marana Airpark outside of Tucson for days and sometimes weeks to test R and D projects for special operations—a remote-control para-wing, a chute with a guidance system hooked to a frequency from a ground-to-air beacon, a Parachute Impact System that allowed pilots to stay out of the range of small-arms fire—then back on the weekends for barbecues on the ancestral ranch, home now to his own wife and his own children and most everybody else in Montana who proudly shared the worthy name Burnette.

Then for two years the family held its breath, waiting for Dawson to return. He claimed it was all about jumping, and probably it was, when he decided to join the Fifth Group Special Forces in 1968, a unit that had taken so many casualties that the qualification protocol to wear a Green Beret had been sidelined in favor of the expediency of warm bodies, jailbirds welcome, we'll redefine crazy ass for you, and the missions were the same ones he had been doing all along, the faces were the same, civilian and military, except now instead of training commandos to jump he was one of the warriors stepping out into the air fifteen hundred feet above the drop zone, nursing a desire to kill somebody to even the score for the friends he had been unable to haul back up into the air alive or unmaimed.

Eville knew the story of how they met, his father and Steve Chambers—both of them aboard a C-130 headed for the Laotian city of Long Tieng, one of the busiest airports on the planet at the time, operating the largest CIA field headquarters in the world, when the plane was shot down. For some negligent reason the new guy going up-country from the embassy in Saigon was wearing a rucksack instead of a chute, too green for words, and in the chaos of the moment Dawson cross-clipped the ruck's front straps onto his own harness and they rolled nose-to-nose out the door and away through the flak-peppered blue. *How is it, buddy? Where abouts you from?* They each sprained an ankle in the spastic dance of their hard landing. A Huey picked them up, along with the others who made it out of the 130 before the Pathet Lao could get there, and that night at the base in Long Tieng, drowning themselves from an ice-filled tub of canned stateside beer, they agreed that Steve Chambers's first jump had gone smoothly, all things considered. Guys would come up to Dawson saying, You did *what*?!

Year after year, the story was always the same—a nation of families, dying for one another, one way or another, bleeding into every benighted landscape across the planet. Not the arbiters of destiny, but its servants, entitled to the cemetery's solemn honors, the stars on the wall, the flags on the graves, wreaths redolent with sacrifice.

That was Burnette's America. Free the oppressed, oppress the barbarians. He turned in circles and looked around for some other way but was never able to see it any differently, and he submitted himself to FOG's game and the vast scale of its culpability and thought sooner or later it would be the death of him. Another Burnette hurling himself into the action, doing Lord knows what for his country.

> *On and on it goes.*
> *On and on it goes.*
> *Blood, dirt, death, horror.*

On a tape recovered during a raid on a Salafist safe house in Sarajevo, Eville would hear the jihadis singing this song, and agree that he, too, saw the world in the same way.

CHAPTER THIRTY-SIX

The Doral, February 1996

They stood there like arresting marshals on the first tee of the Blue Monster, eighteen beautiful holes of ankle-sucking bunkers and watery death, watching the colonel grind his cleats into the manicured pad of turf. His white leather shoes ripped into the greenness, some paw technique he seemed to have studied from Rottweilers and yet there was the effeminate counterpoint of his plaid buttocks, the incongruent wiggle, a little hula dance as he dug himself into place over the ball and addressed it like an ax murderer in a grass skirt. Swing, swoop, and a whistling slice into the oleander. The Friends of Golf stood in judgment, a tribunal of raptor-eyed old berserkers observing a terrible sin in progress, some kind of appalling character flaw in one of their minions, an overconfident sap with a bad knee and a miraculous God-mended arm once cracked in two by a .50-caliber round in Panama. They could attest to a little-known fact about military service—it wasted whatever style might have been there in your game before you buttoned on a uniform. The army, for instance, played like tank commanders. The navy, in the habit of letting fly, whacking balls off aircraft carriers into the waves, had developed a chronic shank.

Master Sergeant Eville Burnette fired off a perfunctory burst of praise, *Nice shot, sir!* because what was he supposed to say? Colonel Hicks, niched somewhere in Burnette's chain of command, was the notorious lunatic

Christian running the Combat Applications Group back at Fort Bragg, the unit that didn't exist, a ghost troop afloat in the martial ether with a name that wasn't meant to be a name, SOD-D, D as in Delta and Divine Intervention, and no one had yet bothered to explain to Eville why he had been teleported out of Port-au-Prince that morning to a freaking golf course in Miami. He figured the colonel had something to do with it, although that alone could not account for the surprise of Steven Chambers. The sadist echelon in the military went to a lot of trouble and expense to make an example of scapegoats, and Eville supposed he was about to be publicly chastised and stripped of rank as a proxy for all the hapless renegades who had screwed up the Haiti mission in a dozen goat-fucking ways.

The colonel bent over with a grimace of disgust and plucked his tee out of the grass. The überspook who called himself Sammy took his place, loosening up with slowed practice swings that were as butter-smooth as a tai chi routine and Undersecretary Chambers turned to the master sergeant with the diamond-blue-eyed smile Burnette had known most of his life and asked after his mother. She was fine, sir, off the ranch for a couple of months wintering in Santa Fe with her widow friends and the undersecretary said, Ev, when was the last time you called me uncle, and Burnette told him not since he was a boy. Sir. Right, said the undersecretary, and when was the last time you called me Steve?

Not since I joined up, sir.

How do you like the name Arnie? Let's go with that. Cocksucker.

Sir?

Wow, said Undersecretary Chambers, following the parabolic rise and fall of Sammy's drive with grudging admiration. That cocksucking son of a bitch Sam.

He's out there, sir.

Arnie, Ev. Tell you what. How about you caddy for me today?

Yes, sir.

And the next time you're up north let's drop over to Arlington Cemetery and pay our respects to your old man. Maybe I can get you out to Vienna so Joyce can treat you to one of her lousy home-cooked meals. Sound okay?

Thank you, sir. I'd like that.

Arnie. Try it out in this sentence: *Arnie, what in fuck's sake am I doing here at the Doral?*

Ben and Sammy plopped themselves onto the vinyl cushions of an electric cart and purred off toward the center of the fairway, the colonel headed off in a cold-blooded hobble toward the oleander hinterlands, and Eville shouldered the undersecretary's heavy red leather bag and followed a step behind his erstwhile Uncle Steve, listening to him tell war stories about the master sergeant's father. *Your dad, your dad,* this and that. Laos. The Secret War. Once virtuous youth wolfing down a lifetime of bloody unspeakable adventures.

About two hundred yards from the pin, Ben and Sam calculated wind direction and speed, sprinkling blades of grass into the breeze rattling inland off the ocean through the fronded palms. Chambers was to the side, about thirty feet behind them, his jaw grinding a pellet of nicotine gum. He turned to look at Eville standing back a respectful distance, a comic figure among the sherbet pastels of the gentry, his dusty black boots and blue jeans and T-shirt not quite the sartorial standard for the pretensions of the Doral, the golf bag slung like a big TOW rocket launcher over his collarbone. Chambers smiled warmly and asked for his advice—a lazy wood or an easy two iron or a full three?—and Burnette confessed he didn't know a damn thing about the game and Chambers said he had eighteen holes to learn, unless he was in a hurry.

You in a hurry, Ev? *No, sir.* You sure? *No, sir, I don't know what I am.*

The four of them waited for the colonel to profane his way out through the rough, chopping a shot that dribbled fifty feet beyond the pod, and then one after another the three Friends slapped their second shots onto the skirt of the kidney-shaped green. Burnette stoically readjusted the bag across his spine and they walked ahead and the undersecretary continued his tale of two young Americans ensnared in the dirty work of survival against an unlikely but all too familiar and persistent enemy—their own guys.

Your dad came out of the bush one day and showed up in my office in Saigon, said Chambers, and man was he pissed off. Ev, you've been around enough black ops by now to know a few things, am I right? Just because Dawson joined Fifth Group and put on a uniform doesn't necessarily mean he ever really left the Agency. That's easy to understand, you have to utilize talent, especially when you have covert business like MACV-SOG going on and you're drawing personnel from all over the place to put together missions and no one's ever going to get their hands on a paper trail or follow the money and you're running projects with a mix of soldiers and agents and paramilitaries that are so black and deep you think you're living in the Mariana Trench and you forget that there's something called sunshine back in the world.

So your father comes in and starts shouting at me, *You've got to fix this thing, Steve, pronto, goddamn it,* and I said, Absolutely, I said, Of course. I said, You can always count on me—but look, what the hell are you talking about? What happened? Well, what happened was just one of those things, right, but boy did it cause a stink among the ladies. Fifth Group, with the help of its best friends, was training and infiltrating South Vietnamese agents into the north and they sniffed out a double who was passing intel to the NVA. Time to take the guy aside for a heart-to-heart, but the conversation does not go well, and the agent expires.

Maybe the gook had a medical condition, I say to your dad. So what's the problem?

Well, some toff lawyer in the JAG's office started an internal investigation and was preparing to arrest Fifth Group's command staff, top to bottom plus two NCO bystanders, and charge them with murder. You father was one of those noncoms, and he believed his command was scrambling together a cover-up that would have made the two noncommissioned officers the fall guys. Essentially I'm describing a situation where the conventionals in the Big Army wanted to administer a spanking to the Special Forces, whom they loathed for all the reasons you're familiar with, I suspect. And maybe they would have gotten away with it if Fifth Group alone owned the project, but they didn't, which is why Dawson came to me. I'll get on it, I assured him, and I did, but I was under wraps myself, you understand. I had to be careful, and couldn't work it fast enough to keep all these guys from being arrested. Two months later we have the happy ending. All charges dropped by the secretary of the army. Lo and behold, the Agency told the JAG, in the interests of national security, go fuck yourself sideways on a barbwire fence. We refused to make our guys available as witnesses, and that was that. The war never blinked but kept flaming on, whether we were right or wrong or dead or alive.

Now, Ev, you're an intelligent man, just like your father. Why did I tell you this story?

I'm not sure, sir. Am I in trouble?

Why are you asking?

I kinda feel like I'm in trouble.

Not at all. Not in the least. You're the prize stud at an auction. Sound good to you?

Honestly, I don't know, sir.

But if you were, in fact, in trouble, I'm there. I can do that. Ben and Sam can do that. The colonel imagines he can but beyond a certain point he can't. That's why I told you the story.

Yes, sir.

Never a question. And I mean always, and I mean forever. I will stick you on the moon in an Airstream trailer to keep you away from the bastards.

Thank you, sir.

Ev, said the undersecretary, you remember my daughter, don't you? She must have been what, thirteen? The last time you saw her.

I think it was after that. She might have been fifteen.

I want you to do me a favor. The favor means I claim half of you, and the colonel owns half of you. Agreed?

All right, sir.

I want you to keep an eye on Dottie for a while. She's down there on that island waiting for you to get back.

You're shitting me.

I shit you not, son.

They reached the green and Chambers slid his putter from the bag and gave Burnette instructions on how to properly attend to the pin. Ev, said the undersecretary, squatting to eyeball the track of his shot. After we putt out, walk with the colonel to the next tee.

Can I request a heads-up, sir?

I believe he means to take you away from the easy life you're living.

Burnette groaned and said he guessed he was still living on the getting-fucked side of the tracks and the undersecretary said it's not what you think, Ev, remember what I told you. Now go stand by the pin.

Ben birdied the hole and Sammy and Arnie two-putted into pars. The colonel two-putted for a triple bogey and promptly claimed victory for his creed, spreading his arms toward the throne of heaven to declare, Look at me, Jesus. I've been in the battle. I've been fighting for you. Amen to that, Colonel, said the Friends of Golf, and Burnette couldn't fail to notice they were like some Latin ballplayers, their religion worn on their sleeves, blessing themselves before strokes, eyes upraised, pointing at God with a tip of their sun visors, *Thanks, God.*

Coming off the first green, Colonel Hicks marched prune-mouthed and unseeing right past the approaching master sergeant and Burnette thought, *Yeah, what's new,* a typical case of brass myopia, nothing personal, never a reason for an officer to pay attention to an enlisted joe unless he wants his ass licked or is experiencing some Zulu impulse to ram a spear through your chest. Yet after several more steps the colonel paused and waited for the caddy and then unnerved Burnette by pretending to be human, always a shocking transformation in a tyrant, his Tidewater features—preacher's face, southern lawman—moonbeaming brotherly love to the newest member of the flock. He spoke to the noncom like a confidant while Burnette suffered the earnest lock of gunpowder gray eyes, thinking the cleft in the colonel's chin sank deep enough to hold a candle.

He wanted to know if the master sergeant had read Auden, the twentieth century's most influential Christian poet, *English majors in the army, not many of them, not many of us, am I right, Top.* Burnette, nonplussed, wondered if he should mention Eliot or the eccentric religious impulses of J. D. Salinger, but instead mumbled the only line he could recall from Auden's work, *We must love one another or die.*

Bingo, said the colonel. Son of a bitch had the wrong conjunction.

They sauntered side by side toward the second tee, behind the Friends of Golf, the master sergeant wary of the colonel's outpouring of fellowship, the lion and lamb camaraderie, wishing the man would stop blowing sweet-heart bubbles up his backside and just make his point, which Burnette had to assume was considerable, given the trappings of its preamble. And here it was, but he couldn't decipher the colonel's tone, reason nuanced with prickish humor.

Now, Top, said the colonel, I want to know how you would assess our mission in Haiti.

Burnette said, We did our best, sir, and the colonel's mouth hung open, mildly stupefied, while he reflected upon this and then his lips clamshelled back together into a don't-bullshit-me smile. Our best, he chortled. Now, Top Sergeant, what the fuck does that mean? You did your best? I suppose I should give you a medal then.

No, sir.

Yeah, come over here, he said, stepping ahead, mounting the platform of the tee to join the other players with a wink. Come up here, soldier, and stand at attention. We're going to have us a little ceremony.

Burnette resigned himself to the order, placed his heels together, and straightened his spine perpendicular to the sod, eyes straight ahead, posted like a dry turd held upright on a skewer. His vision focused on the oily sheen of the colonel's cap of aluminum-colored hair and beyond that an honor guard of royal palms casting down a ribbed overlay of sunbeam and shade upon the deadpan expressions of the Friends. The colonel's hand noodled in a trouser pocket and reemerged with some sort of unidentifiable medal hanging off a wad of blue ribbon. He pinned the mystery award on Eville's T-shirt and back-stepped to cock an exaggerated salute, which the master sergeant returned, halfhearted and chagrined.

Thank you, sir. Permission to speak. What's this medal for?

Damn, you're an impertinent shit, the colonel snarled, feigning offense. I don't fucking know, Top Sergeant Burnette. Distinguished Zoo Keeper. The Kabuki Cross. What would you like it to be? A Purple Heart?

No, sir.

No, sir?

I haven't earned a Purple Heart, sir.

You are correct, Top Sergeant. But you will, isn't that right?

I have mixed feelings about being shot, sir.

You want this medal or not?

No, sir.

Correct answer. Top, let me tell you why you don't want this medal.

The colonel's rawboned fingers unpinned the clasp and removed the medal from the soldier's breast and sailed it out toward a duck pond behind the tee and explained that unless a man wore the uniform of his country, medals were a useless foppery.

How do you feel about that, Top? Being a man without a uniform?

Bewildered and uncomprehending, sir.

That it? That's your state of mind?

Aggravated, said Burnette, unclenching his teeth just enough to eject the single word from the herd of expletives stampeding his tongue, but apparently it was the funniest word he ever uttered, triggering a wheezing explosion of laughter from the Friends of Golf, the colonel himself rubescent with mirth, *hee-hee*ing the bray of a fat lady. A reliably enjoyable moment, good fun, fucking with a subordinate's mind. Okay, I get it, said Burnette, restraining a smile. This had been a jest, a type of court amusement, and he cheered up, allowing himself to imagine being tasked to babysit Steven Chambers's daughter would prove to be still another one of their pranks.

Okay, at ease, said the colonel, extending his hand for a congratulatory shake. Burnette, welcome to Delta.

Sir? Is that possible?

Anything's possible, Top. You want in, you're in.

The colonel never bothered to tee off on the second hole but walked with Undersecretary Chambers and Burnette down the fairway, briefing the soldier on the blackened peculiarities of his new mission, which would not switch on without sweeping up one more day's manure from the old mission, some mysterious crisis with a freighter and its crew held hostage in Gonaïves. The State Department and the DEA were interested in getting this thing resolved, said the colonel. Fucking nonsense but take care of it tomorrow and then I want you on this other thing, this Jacques Lecoeur thing, and keep in mind you work for us, just the undersecretary and me and not that goddamn godless Pakistani colonel down there, one more blue-cap pissant crawled out from the sewer of his own country, looking to put some notches in his belt. Another thing, the colonel said, start growing your hair out now. How about a mustache? Beards I can live without. And stop at Walmart or one of those places on your way back to Homestead and buy yourself some civvies.

Ev, the undersecretary told him as they all gathered again at the second green for a farewell, you can give me my bag back now.

The colonel requisitioned the electric cart from Ben and Sammy and chauffeured his newest recruit back to the clubhouse, explaining the protocol Burnette needed to follow subsequent to his special assignment in Haiti. I want to see you at Bragg, he said, parking the cart in the driveway near the main entrance next to a town car with government plates, where an army major sat waiting for him with the engine running. We bring you inside the fence, said the colonel, do an official selection, run you through some indoctrination courses, cut you with knives, upgrade your killer's license.

You ever killed anybody, Top?

No, sir. Well, maybe. It was the Gulf War. The gooks were too far away to confirm kills.

What are your languages?

Spanish. Creole . . . well, some.

Worthless shit, said the colonel. We'll get you speaking some sand nigger —Dari, Arabic, Pashto. You're going to need those before this is all over.

I look forward to it, sir, said Burnette, wondering what the man was talking about.

They have a spa in there, the colonel said, pointing at the clubhouse as he got out of the cart. You ever been to a spa, Top? You ought to try it sometime—get yourself a facial, pedicure, hot stones on your spine, get one of those herbal rubdowns. And listen, between you and me, the colonel said, keep a tight leash on the undersecretary's daughter. She was a rookie just off the Farm at Fort Lee, he confided, where she had managed to gain a reputation as a bit of a wildcat.

Yes, sir, Burnette said, watching the colonel disappear into the Doral. He tried not to think about how this day had become a watermark for strange in his life, the elevation to Delta Force delivered to him in the guise of a practical joke. He opened the passenger door to a blast of air-conditioned relief and sat down sighing, addled with elation. The major behind the wheel tossed a clipboard of paperwork onto his lap, reached over to give him a ballpoint pen, and said, *Sign.* Burnette scanned the first document and sucked in oxygen and looked at the major.

Hold the phone, I'm a captain now?

Looks like it, said the major, retrieving the signed paperwork and issuing Burnette a federal concealed-weapons permit, a corporate credit card—Omega Systems—from a bank in the Cayman Islands, and an envelope nine-months pregnant with twenty-dollar bills.

The next thing Master Sergeant Eville Burnette knows he's back in Haiti getting his forehead split by some coked-up banshee in Gonaïves and then he's Mister Burnette with UN press credentials hanging off his sweaty neck, up in the mountains with the girl and Tom Harrington, who was not so bad for a do-gooder, one of the few so-called humanitarians he befriended in Haiti who reserved a dram of their flooding compassion for the boots on the ground. How much the lawyer understood he had been cultivated as a pawn in other people's schemes, Burnette did not know, but it made him ache to see Harrington at this moment of dark enlightenment, crushed by his own naïveté, realizing his role in the northern mountains was to sow betrayal and be himself betrayed, and then the girl is a whirling tigress with eyes sealed shut in pain and he hits her and she crumples to the ground. It's Harrington who kneels over her while she gags and chokes and Eville Burnette punctures the trachea of the strangling Haitian and he's swearing to himself, *It should never go beyond this,* meaning his deal with the undersecretary and his daughter, and yet it does.

CHAPTER THIRTY-SEVEN

In the twilight, the Blackhawk became consumed by a cloud of rancid dust as the pilot put the helicopter down as close as he could to the medical tent inside the UN base in Cap-Haïtien. Jackie was first out the door and Burnette would not see her again until the following morning. Then the operation's tardy air support, a Chinook and a second Blackhawk, returned after their sweep through the mountains with their ignominious haul—the dead (three, including Jacques Lecoeur), the wounded (four, one of them an eight-year-old girl), the detainees, twenty-three in all, men, women, and children. Not a single blue cap with so much as a scratch. Lucky man, the twenty-fourth detainee was Lecoeur's second-in-command, Ti Phillipe, in surgery at that very moment to repair and close Burnette's hasty field tracheotomy. Seeing the dead rolled out in zippered body bags, it occurred to Eville that the undersecretary's daughter had, in all likelihood, saved Phillipe's life when she almost killed him with a gullet full of pepper spray.

Burnette had then made the mistake of trotting after the Pakistani colonel and grabbing his upper arm as he exited the chopper and swaggered toward a Humvee waiting to return him across the strip to quarters. What happened up there, colonel? he demanded, trying to control his breathing, which was how he controlled his anger, which was why he wasn't behind bars somewhere. What the hell did you do?

Digging out his yellow earplugs, Khan spun around into his face, enraged. To whom am I speaking, sir? he demanded, bellowing at first before dropping his voice into a lower but more sinister range of sarcasm. A journalist? A soldier? To the first I answer, the United Nations Pakistani attachment has successfully engaged and quelled the activities of a murderous band of reactionaries threatening the stability of the host nation. To the second I answer, you are insubordinate, my friend. You are impudent. And, should I say, a hypocrite? If you have an objection to my command, the colonel jeered, I want it written and submitted, and I trust it will include an explanation of your own role—and allow me to express my gratitude here and now—in our mission.

Look, sir, I'd just like to know. These people? They stayed in the forest, hiding. They were rabbits. Sir.

Excuse me, it was my understanding you were provided to us by your army as a field advisor. For reasons you perhaps know better than I. The operation was a success, Captain. Wouldn't you agree?

No, he would not, but he backed off the open confrontation, the impossibility of anything being resolved beyond his duty to obey. Colonel Rashid Khan, his ego inflated with carnage, killing, and murder, the mastermind and hero of the bushwhack in the mountains, saluted and Eville returned the salute and the colonel took his seat in the Humvee, leaning out to call Eville back over to issue further orders. After the International Police Monitors from Caricom had sorted out the detainees, the colonel told him, he expected the captain to monitor their interrogations.

Out on the helipad the next morning, Burnette noticed a taxi stopped at the chain-link gates to the restricted area and groaned and cursed to himself as he watched Jackie Scott flash her identification and be allowed through on foot and come toward the choppers, fiddling with her badass camera before she fixed it to her right eye and started shooting. He started to walk away, back to base headquarters to update the situational report he had cyber-filed last night with his chain of command at Bragg, still not understanding that there was very little chain left in the matter of whom he was obliged to answer to these days, when she dropped the camera and called to him.

Eville, wait, she said in a neutral voice, neither demanding nor upset by the obvious bloody consequence of their deceit. What happened?

He kept pounding on for several more steps but found he couldn't ignore her and stopped and stomped back until he was in her face. Why don't you tell me? he said.

I left the mountains when you did, she said. You forced me onto the helicopter, remember? Otherwise, I'd know, wouldn't I?

You know what, he said. Right about now I'm doing the best I can not to smack you again.

Hey, I knew what you knew, okay, she said, self-contained and formidable, stepping brazenly forward into his threat. So, go fuck yourself, man.

Their hostility enclosed them in a sickening bubble of mutual contempt that prevented either of them from being aware of the SUV speeding their way until it had slammed its brakes, honking superfluously for their attention, and Tom Harrington, almost in tears, was flying out the door on the driver's side, taking in the scene, the dead, the wounded, the flex-cuffed huddle of ragged prisoners left to sit in the dirt throughout the night. Then Harrington, wheeling on the two of them with a fire hose of accusations, was eviscerated by Jackie's calm autopsy of Tom's innocence. She pointed at his vehicle, the smashed windows, the bent front bumper and dented fender, and asked him where the huge splatter of blood had gone that she had seen in the parking lot as she left the hotel that morning. *I hit a dog, okay,* Harrington yelled back, flustered and unconvincing. *Yeah, you hit something,* Jackie agreed. Eville stole a sidelong glance at the vehicle and had to admit it was pretty messed up. In a faintly heckling manner, she reminded Tom that his own freely confided purpose in interviewing Jacques Lecoeur had been to determine, at the behest of unknown benefactors, if Lecoeur and his men were still operating on yesterday's agenda, the good guys versus bad guys program that was counterproductive to a liberated Haiti, or, just as bad, were freedom fighters who had dissembled into a gang of bandits. *Am I right?* she taunted. *Did I get it wrong?* Watching her performance, Eville found her undue confidence breathtaking, her implied assertion that she was disconnected from events and blameless. She wanted to make it clear to Harrington that she didn't really give much of a shit about any of these issues as long as she could continue to do her job, which meant take her

495

pictures without the interference of self-appointed censors. When she paused for a breath, perhaps for Round Two, Harrington exploded.

Master Sergeant Burnette, Tom Harrington's rant spewed on, I don't know what the fuck you're doing up here out of uniform with this psycho cunt—and everything the guy said Eville felt he had coming and it pained and discouraged him, having someone he honestly liked and respected, a civilian no less, vilify him and question his honor, but Harrington's tirade began to spiral and break apart in midair when he returned his outrage to the girl, readjusting his aim to her career, her sorry-ass future as a member of the press, making threats that he had no possible idea were ineffectual and quickly tiresome. In Eville's recollection of the scene, she had looked right at him with a dispassionate self-knowledge that was heartless and without mercy and asked, with what he could only describe as supernatural blitheness, *Where do you go around here to report a rape?*

Harrington lunged at her and Eville was compelled to intercept him, although he would have taken an immoderate pleasure in stepping aside and letting the two of them have at it, the primal male thing sunk in his brain stem curious to see how far Harrington would go. But he grabbed Tom, not roughly but with enough force to edge him back from the disaster of assaulting Jackie, who stood there with her hips cocked and arms folded, mocking both of them, *All the big bad men who get off hitting women,* and he jockeyed Tom back to his battered SUV while Tom pleaded with him, *Who is she, man? Who the fuck is she? I thought you were one of the guys in the white hats, Eville,* and what other option did he have but to lie to Harrington and swear he didn't know her. Eville nudged and persuaded him back into the SUV, where Tom's hands trembled on the steering wheel and he dropped his head as tears skipped down his face and he confessed he thought he had hit someone on the road that night at a barricade, coming out of the mountains. *I couldn't stop, man. It would have been suicide.* He drove off, wiping his eyes with the back of his hand. Eville heard he had gone over to headquarters to have it out with Colonel Khan, who refused to see him, and had left the north soon afterward, and soon after that had withdrawn altogether from the never-ending travails and tribulations of Haiti.

Burnette went back to speak with Jackie before heading to his assigned cubicle on the base where he could hook up his encrypted laptop and try to make sense of things to anybody in the States who might be listening. She had volleyed the first words, dismissing the drama in its entirety by defining Tom Harrington. *He thinks he's so much better than us,* she said. *He thinks he's Mister Clean. The go-to guy for moral intervention. The halo's a bit much, don't you think?*

But it had been easy to read her face when she garroted the lawyer's conscience—she was bluffing—and it had not been difficult either to read the wretched expression of Harrington's reaction—something had happened between her and Tom, and she had emerged from the encounter with aces to play for leverage.

So, he said, you're saying he raped you?

Did I say that? she said, unaffected by his curtness. For the first time that morning looking at her face he registered the fact that she had attempted to apply makeup to camouflage the bruise he had telegrammed her the day before. Did you hear me say that? She smiled with a sparking trace of wickedness in her captivating blue eyes, a bratty chime to her words, and Eville imagined that as for the fate of the undersecretary's daughter, he was beyond caring. There was nothing he found fundamentally right with her, nothing trustworthy or exculpatory—she was, instead, a human isotope. Every reproach earned the lash of her ridicule, every attempt to advise or help was rejected with juvenile recalcitrance, if not fury. At the same time, there was something too methodic about her intensity, a practiced sense of routine, as if she had been taught, or self-taught, to escalate the psychodrama, which of course was nonsense, because any training in black tradecraft taught you to cool down, not heat up. There seemed to be a fault line at her core, two different plates of the self, slammed together in perpetual grating that he could fairly guess would one day crack and heave and devastate.

And yet. That morning when her attitude morphed and reassembled in a transparent zone of seduction, his mind was disgusted while his body seemed to muster the minimal amount of forgiveness necessary to agree, tentatively, if he could make it—*yeah, right*—to meet her for dinner that night. Maybe, she said, they could get back into their own groove, like the other night on the veranda at the Oloffson. What he found so hard to parse though was that nobody, as far as Eville could determine, was exploiting Jackie; her behavior was unilateral—there was no one she had to defend herself against. On the contrary, he would continue to see, she was snatching up anybody who wandered into her orbit, which was A-plus behavior for the sneaky-Pete lot, but he generally had trouble thinking of her as an agency spook, and second generation, for Chrissakes, carrying forth some scary family tradition into the Darwinian future. True, there was nothing fragile about her, certainly an eye-catching trait for recruiters and trainers; undoubtedly she could and would launch herself like a wolverine into the fray, but then, he was learning too slowly, count on Jackie to throw an inner switch and reverse direction, her caprice jerking you around in your seat with a sort of highly engineered, clutch-burning torque of bipolar whiplash. She did not court his allegiance, not at all, although she summoned it cat-and-mouse-style, only to bat it away. There was nothing she seemed to desperately need except to screw with everybody, her game always the superior game.

It was an awakening of sorts for Captain Burnette, an acidic epiphany that seemed long overdue and willfully delayed—his complicity in the deaths and injury of innocent people, the casualties by no means collateral damage in what was by no stretch of the imagination a war or its attendant fog. And nobody cared. Poor and starving and nobody cared made more sense than gunned down and nobody cared, not counting Tom Harrington, for the little that was worth. The detainees themselves beseeching in their misery toward the shabby men, their captors, who considered themselves no more exalted than herders and therefore, logically, considered these pathetic specimens of humanity no more human than goats. He thought at first it was Haiti but he would come to know otherwise—the planet was chock full of expendable people, overflowing with targets, and genocide an organic event, as common as a wheat harvest. That day on the base his afternoon had not improved, helping a contingent of Jamaican police sort out the prisoners and stumble through a series of basic interrogations before they

498

were locked up for the night, simply trying to identify who these people were, the base translator's English not up to the job, Eville himself not up to the chaos and caterwauling, and he had arrived for dinner deeply distracted and brooding, in a dark state of mind that she put up with mostly not at all.

What is with this resentment? Jackie said within seconds of his ordering a bottle of beer. What did I do to you exactly? He could have said but didn't, Hey, get over it, not everything's about you, because in a way so far everything had been about her, not directly, of course, yet her involvement seemed difficult to separate from every jump in a situation from standard to calamitous. But after a couple beers, he leveled out and could see how his shitty mood was exaggerating her influence, her negative force field.

How did you get so tough?

She reached across the table without asking and her bitten fingers crabbed away his pack of cigarettes and box of matches and she lit up and said if she were a man, he wouldn't be wasting his time with such a fatuous question, would he?

Look, he said, my mother's tough. She had to be, the way she grew up, all right? But you grew up considerably more sheltered—

It might have looked that way to you, she said.

—more innocent maybe, and I know you've seen a lot of the world but the world you've seen and lived in has been basically good. If you were a guy, the question I'd ask you is how you got such a king-sized chip on your shoulder. If you're trying to prove you're as badass as a guy, you proved it, okay, so, like, stand down already.

By the time they ordered, the only dish still available on the menu was fried chicken legs with a side of black beans and rice, and when the waiter left their table Eville made the mistake of commenting on her seemingly overnight fluency in restaurant Creole.

Americans have a problem with this, don't they, she said, but it wasn't clear to Eville if she meant specifically a woman's intelligence or multilingualism in general. Cleopatra spoke nine languages, Jackie informed him with a distinctly peevish rise to her voice for what she obviously considered a set series of infinitely tiresome challenges to the perception of her specialness, the unfair excesses of her drop-dead good looks or intellect or courage or God knows, her very birth, as if she had somehow stolen these laudable parts of herself from someone else, an imaginary deprived person. My father the polyglot speaks seven or eight. So? Anybody who wants makes an effort and does it.

Don't be so sure, he said. I was trying to compliment you. Voice my admiration.

It was the first time either of them had mentioned her father since the evening on the veranda at the Oloffson when Harrington had stepped away. So anyway, he said, just as their food came to the table. How'd your day go? What did you do?

Walked around, she said, picking up her chicken leg and nibbling at it, halting her reply to chew and swallow a tiny bite of flesh. Checked out the port. Humint. You know.

Right, he said. He asked her if she was headed back to the States now that the Lecoeur operation was a wrap and she sent a surge of rotten electricity through his neck and shoulders by revealing that the Lecoeur thing was nothing more than a last-minute add-on to her primary mission, which would likely keep her on the island for several months.

Why are you looking at me like that? she asked.

Tell me right now that you're bullshitting me, please.

Nobody was sure that your buddy Harrington would let you tag along on his vision quest. You know what they say, right?

I haven't the slightest idea what *they* say. Who's they?

They is *you*, singular, plural. They say, *What money won't buy, pussy will.*

Eville, recoiling, asked her why she had to talk like that. Like what? she said and he told her like a hooker, an insult that made her eyes roll, clearly about as cutting as a butter knife.

I'm having another beer. Do you want one?

Last one, he said, dropping his voice to not be overheard by diners at the nearby tables. Look, it would help me to know some things about you. I'm pretty much in the dark here. Does Colonel Khan know who you are?

She shook her head no and reverted to being flip. Why would he? *You* don't even know who I am.

Man, he said. Man.

She reconsidered her attitude. All right, she said more evenly. We're on a separate track, behind separate fire walls. Ask anybody—I'm nobody. I can't speak for you.

Khan knew Burnette was army assigned to him as an advisor. Why the ruse, I can't figure, said Eville, but at this point it's plain ridiculous, right, he said. He flicked the laminated UN-issued press pass that hung from a lanyard around his neck, identifying him as a correspondent for some outfit called American Media Initiatives. Who else is in the loop, nobody bothered to tell me.

I don't think there's any loop, she said. There's a Gordian knot.

Eville gave a squinch-faced nod, not wanting to let her further into his ignorance. He'd get a green light and a wave-through whenever somebody needed to check a list, which meant he was not as abandoned as he felt. But you, he said, wagging his stripped chicken bone at Jackie, you're NOC—nonofficial cover.

Her eyes narrowed in contradiction. Bad form, she said. Don't say that.

Even in the spook playbook, that's extreme. No one there to catch you if you fall.

I guess someone had the bright idea that you should audition for that job.

Someone who happened to be your father, he thought, satisfied that their encoded conversation, in most ways resembling a random stroll through a minefield, had now arrived at a destination worth exploring, if only for a business-minded view of its practicalities.

What exactly are you doing in Haiti?

Surveillance and research.

Okay, he said reluctantly. Thanks.

She picked up her fork and stabbed at her rice and beans, toying with him yet again. What are these called? she asked and, acknowledging his quizzical frown, added, *in Spanish.* What are they called in Spanish? The dish originated in Spain, I think. Or maybe Cuba.

I have no idea what you're talking about, he said, completely and understandably missing her gist, which, in retrospect, would bang like a temple gong in his memory. There would be, in the years ahead, countless opportunities, more than a sane man would ever wish for, to revisit in grief this puzzling moment, Jackie pointing to her plate with a self-satisfied grin, Eville not comprehending her implication, that a world of hate, a world fully awakened by hate, was a lot further along in becoming what it would become than he could possibly have imagined.

Moros y Cristianos, she said. Isn't that a riot. That's what's on our plate.

You've lost me here, he said.

Best not to know. It's all you need right now. That could change.

Okay, he sighed, wearied by the riddle and all its sealed-lip smug cousins. What I think I'm hearing loud and clear, and what I know I'm seeing, is you don't need me, right? Your father was only being—what, a father—when he asked me to keep an eye on you.

Yes. Don't need you. Probably not. But that could change too.

He glanced down at his own empty plate and fixated on her partially-gnawed chicken leg and untouched mound of beans and rice and felt his appetite redoubled. Are you going to eat that? he asked, and she shoved the remains of her dinner across the table.

By the way, she said.

By the way? He could hear the exhaustion press down on his voice and he needed to take a breather from the high-velocity roller-coaster ride of Jackie's apparently sociopathic personality and retreat to his room, still booked for another couple of nights, where he could feel like shit in peace.

Have you been down to the harbor?

Which harbor? I'm not following what you're saying.

The harbor here in Cap. That ship from Gonaïves. It's anchored out there, she said, pointing beyond the secure glow of the Christophe's self-generated light into the darkness of the streets. After you liberated the ship from the bad guys, or the good guys, or the in-the-middle guys or whoever, they sailed up here.

Okay, he said tentatively. And that means what? I'm still not following you.

Friendlier waters, she said with an odd burst of gaiety, as if she had just revealed the emotional resolution to an excellent story, as if this resolution also described the universal condition of where they together now found

THE WOMAN WHO LOST HER SOUL

themselves. She asked him if he was ready to retire to the hotel's bar for a nightcap and instead of wishing him good night when he told her he really had to lie down she flashed a downturned expression of childlike disappointment and sniffed, *Suit yourself,* and walked away alone into the bar, the swing of her hips just another piquant ingredient in the way she mixed her message. Lust rose up through his weariness like a hiccup, up and out and gone and done, and he scaled the stairway to the second floor and keyed himself into his room, tossing his rucksack onto the tiled floor and emptying his bladder of beer before he toppled facedown in an inhuman sweat atop the yellowed sheets of the mattress on his bed to sleep unmolested until dawn. And as he slept in such sound oblivion, a demon-free celibacy much unlike his normal routine of dream-harried tossing, the ship from Gonaïves was being off-loaded, a fact that would elude him during his next two months in Haiti, its discovery delayed until he was back in the States, on a golf course in North Carolina.

CHAPTER THIRTY-EIGHT

In early April, after almost two months in the north of Haiti, where he had been braided into an operation he quickly realized was seriously fucked, someone at the bar at the Christophe bought him a drink, identified himself as State, counterterrorism, et cetera, and said all the right things to relieve him of his misery. The next morning he boarded a Blackhawk on the airfield for Port-au-Prince, where he was to reacquaint himself with the men he had once trained on the presidential guard, assess their competency and loyalty, make nice with the natives, and await further instructions. He hooked up with a pair of Delta boys already assigned to the palace and a sense of honor began to trickle back into Eville Burnette's blood, and what he had most woefully missed in Le Cap, camaraderie. Even with a stack of books at hand in his hotel room in Cap, being a lone wolf and set apart had bugged him more than he expected, and the solitude came with an insight that should have been obvious before now, that he naturally gravitated toward a world of buddies—once upon a time his own brothers, his teammates on the gridiron in high school and college, his fellow grunts in basic training, his platoon in Iraq, his A-team in Haiti. Going solo had put a crack in his alignment that the undersecretary's daughter only seemed there to intensify. They were not buddies, that's for sure.

Back in the capital, he had checked in to the Oloffson despite its liability—Jackie was living there—because it was downtown and close to the palace and the proper venue for a phony correspondent with murky credentials. Four days later at breakfast on the veranda the waiter passed him a note from the girl at reception, which summoned him to the military attaché's office in the embassy, where he was handed a voucher containing a plane ticket. *Don't know who you are, don't know what you're doing, but it's time to go,* he was told. Burnette flipped through the voucher, learning that he was on the afternoon flight to Miami with a connection to Raleigh-Durham. *Wait a minute,* he said. *I should be booked to Fayetteville. The connection's the connection,* said the attaché. *On whose orders?* Eville asked. *Not ours,* said the attaché. *We're not in the business of ordering journalists to do anything but fuck off,* and Burnette gripped the man's hand and couldn't stop saying, *Thank you,* like some imbecile. He took a cab back to the Oloffson to collect his gear and was standing at the front desk, signing his bill, when Jackie Scott—Dottie—came in off the street, drooping and empty-eyed and skanky beneath her cameras, looking like she had plowed through an all-nighter, which in Haiti could mean all manner of reckless or suicidal pursuits.

You're avoiding me, she said. Why?

He asked her if she still had a rental and she said yes and he asked her if she was still using Gerard and she said he was out on the veranda ordering lunch. Lend him to me, he said.

Where are you going?

Stateside.

Reporting to Daddy.

What's to report?

Whatever, she said, I need a shower, walking away toward the stairs and the second floor and her room.

He had waited for Gerard to finish his ham sandwich and lemonade and on the crawl through traffic to the airport he couldn't get the driver to talk much at all, Gerard's hard feelings burning bright from the day the two of them had met back in February, the guy still carrying Tom Harrington's torch, and fair enough, he thought, but by now the Haitian knew more about the screwball doings of the undersecretary's slattern daughter than Eville himself, and he had to ask.

She still wigging out with the voodoo priests?

Oui.

Taking pictures and stuff?

Yes.

Foo foo shit, my friend.

I don't like it. It's not good. Bad people. Why is she doing this?

Have you seen Tom?

No. Tom is gone.

If you see him—

He's gone.

At the terminal, Eville's guilt slipped five of his remaining twenties into Gerard's shirt pocket and they turned away from one another without anything more to say. In the Miami airport he rode an elevator to the rooftop bar above the hotel to smoke and have a beer and slam down a cheeseburger while he watched a trio of pubescent girls splashing in the swimming pool, faux tarty, showing off for the boys in their dreams, more serious about vamping than about their game of Marco Polo, and his mind drifted back to Dottie-Jackie-Dottie, in a temporarily flirtatious mood during their last dinner together in Le Cap, telling him, *You know, I used to have a crush on you,* and just as he scoffed and said, *When was that?* an image of her with her pants down, her fuzzy peach pudenda presented for display, flicked on in his memory. What was she back then, twelve or thirteen? Which meant he was probably eighteen, that summer in Rome before he started college, on the way to visit his father in Ramstein, Dawson on a three-month assignment teaching an advanced jump-masters class to NATO troops.

After tapping on the closed door and getting no response, he had walked into the bathroom in the Chambers's flat in Trastevere and she was standing there, posing, not getting up off the john or stepping out of the shower but just there with her shorts and panties around her ankles, the puff of her mons proudly thrust forward, glowing eagerly like a junior hostess at a birthday party—*Here's the cake!*—or some other happy occasion for exhibitionists entering puberty. He had a four-count of enthrallment, gaping, unable to tear his eyes away from what he had never actually seen, not live anyway, a female's mysterious real estate, though he could boast of no longer being a virgin, as of the last semester of his senior year. But the deed, twice done, had both times unfolded under musty quilts in the pitch black interior of a friend's family cabin on the Kootenai River, and he had only the vaguest visual sense of his penis's destination. He hadn't grown up with sisters, and even the times he saw his mother buck naked—not that rare, actually, when the family was on a river camping—all he could really absorb was the dark thatched triangle of her crotch, which impressed him as resembling nothing so much as a slice of blackberry pie. Her breasts, more exposed, more all there, were more interesting, in a science fiction sort of way.

In the bathroom in Rome with Dottie, the four seconds of bewitchment imploded into an awful, self-righteous, stupid disgust, as if somehow he were suddenly channeling Nathaniel Hawthorne, a sanctimonious schoolboy self with all the traits of a puritanical little prig. *Pull up your pants,* he said, *What's wrong with you?* and the expression on her face jumped from bright nymphet invitation to confusion to bitter compliance, as she bent over to do what he told her but kept her head raised in a bold challenge, hissing back at him a fierce accusation, *What's wrong with you?* He didn't regret his reaction then, but he regretted it soon enough, sitting down the next morning for breakfast with Dottie and her parents (her brother remained in his room, a hostage of Nintendo), his embarrassment no match for her unshamed buoyancy as she sang the praises of a girl's exciting life in the Eternal City, her self-confidence clearly not jarred by his scorning rejection of her precocious sexuality, even flaunting a mean smile when her parents got up from the table, to call him, in a voice that only he could hear, *Faggot.* Off he fled to the airport and by the time he landed in Germany, the image of her precocious middle-school crotch, untouchable and unthinkable, had buried itself so deep in the sedimentary muck of his own psyche that he could never, not once, in the years ahead summon it forth into his libido as an erotic picture-memory to fuel a jack-off fantasy. It was simply unavailable, not lost but repressed for a reason hard to fathom, and when he saw her again when she was fifteen her personality had surprised him with its chaste self-consciousness and sensitivities.

And then, to his dismay, another memory of Dottie, his earliest, oozed out of the confounding carnal world of his own childhood, not erotic but certainly sexual and not even partially understood at the time, yet perhaps exaggerated now in its lewd implication. The memory had popped up disguised in an innocence he had thought was genuine until it segued unexpectedly into another dimension.

I think the first time I ever saw you, he told her at the candlelit dinner on the terrace of the Christophe, *you were still a baby.*

That must have been when we lived in India, she said. *Why were you there? You must have been like what, five or six?*

Six, I think, he said, *my dad was on R and R and my mom decided to meet him in New Delhi, your parents must have invited them,* and then the tableau appeared out of the blue in his memory—walking with his father and little brother through a house fragrant with cardamom, following a man's voice somewhere ahead in the maze of hallways—*Back here, Dawson. Come on back*—and entering a bedroom where Mr. Chambers was bent over a baby laid out on the wide interior sill of a window, changing her diapers, tiny pink legs capped in lace-cuffed anklet socks, the feet pedaling the air above her father's head.

What? said Jackie, studying him, the inward veer in his mood.

Nothing. Just remembering.

There's not much I remember from back then.

Our moms were out shopping I think and our dads were sitting around drinking whiskey and telling war stories. That's all I remember, except for elephants in the streets, but in his mind now was a scene he was certain his six-year-old self had witnessed, ignorant of the code of its sordid meaning, Dottie's father slowly lifting his nose away from the infant and grinning at his own father and winking, *What do you know, Dawson, pussy smells the same on a baby.* The picture stopped right there and the words became odd clenched feelings and all that remained was a residual but still withering sense of his father's unexpressed disapproval. As a child, the moment had flapped away on wings of insensibility, meaningless until this new moment twenty-five years along into the future, when he tried to steer the subject into the relative safety of a parallel groove.

I guess you're pretty close to your father, he said, but his angling made her dour. What was he hinting at anyway? Now everything shifted and it became the sort of dinner endured by people who once knew each other intermittently as kids but were now required to have a professional relationship as grown-ups. She wasn't going to talk anymore about her father, maybe the taboo was nepotism or maybe something else, although the topic prompted her to mention his own. *Do you miss him?* she asked, and he nodded a long time before answering, *Every single day,* and then listened numbly as she revealed the strangest bond between them, the death of her own grandfather during World War Two, as grisly yet more comprehensible than Dawson's own demise, a one in a billion accident, his father's head clipped off on an everyday jump in Georgia when he exited a DC-3 not falling down but flying back, face-first into the plane's horizontal stabilizer. Of the rare and arcane things their families had in common, the most surreal was decapitation.

A mother rose up from her poolside chaise longue, extending the offering of towels, calling her nubile ducklings from the water. An arid sorrow washed over Burnette. He was back in America, always a nip of culture shock after a deployment. He never entertained the thought that his life could be different—the structure of it, the fundamentals, not the interchangeable parts like a woman or a place, or the harness of a narrow ideology or a religion—because he never once wished it to be different, swapped out for some ersatz lifestyle. If not today then soon he was going home to Fayetteville, back to an empty—and emptied—off-base townhouse, his domestic life once again a casualty of his service. He already saw himself ordering a pizza to be delivered, sitting on whatever piece of furniture his now ex-wife had left him, watching TV until he dozed off. I want my own kids, he thought, but their presence in his life was something he had only imagined. Their mother remained unattainable, a stranger somewhere off in the world carrying his heart around like an overripe and soon to be rotting apple.

A matched ebony and ivory set of gym gladiators came off the elevator wearing Oakley sunglasses and bone-white safari vests and pressed jeans and Eville recognized the type before he realized he knew them, flat-headed creatures who flourished on a diet of steroids and pain, in this instance special ops studs who hopped the fence to harvest the new money suddenly available everywhere for trained killers, working now for an outfit called Dyncorps, which hired them out to the Haitian president on two-month rotations as personal bodyguards. They sat down at a café table nearby and nodded with a studied sadistic coolness and Eville nodded back.

Burnette, said the black guy, that you underneath that 'stache?

They wanted to know if he was coming or going and they wanted to know, given his new low-key style of civilian, if he was in or out, and he said, *In,* and the white guy of the mercenary pair said, *It's raining cash out here, bro, everything's coming up green,* and Eville told them he would always be in.

Born that way, am I right?

Yeah, said Eville. *Born lucky.* He stood up, finishing his beer, and knew he should keep his mouth shut but didn't. *It's like this,* he said. *I fight for my country, not a corporation.*

Dude, said the white guy, *this ain't 1776. It's all the same.*

CHAPTER THIRTY-NINE

Pinehurst, April 1996

It was dusk when he landed in Raleigh-Durham and at baggage claim there was a curly-gray-haired fellow in a Blue Devils jacket holding a sign with Burnette's name on it who seemed to be exactly who he claimed to be, a man driving a cab for a living, and Eville just another customer, his fare prepaid. They drove south down Route 1 and after about ten miles, deep enough in the wooded countryside for Eville to wonder where they were going, the cabbie said, *Hell's bells, son, I thought you knew*—Pinehurst, America's first and oldest golf resort, down in the Sandhills.

You a golfer? asked the driver and Eville said he was a caddy and the old man said, *For some big shot, wouldn't it be?* and Eville said yeah but he couldn't talk about it, celebrity sensitivities and contractual privacy clause and crap like that. *Okay, none of my business,* said the kindly old fellow and Eville told himself sardonically, *Not if you're a taxpayer, bro.*

An hour and a half later the cab dropped him at the colonnaded entrance to the Carolina Hotel and he was checked in to a suite of rooms far beyond his pay grade. Rather aristocratic for his tastes and habits but why not, he thought, dropping his gear and picking up an envelope deposited on a marble-topped side table in the foyer, reading the message— *Relax and enjoy, have a drink, order room service, sleep in, we'll see you at the pro shop at 1000 . . . Arnie.* Also on the table was a bottle of Glenlivet scotch, but he had never developed a taste for his father's refreshment of choice.

Unaccustomed to the cold, he turned up the thermostat for a wave of semitropical heat, dialed room service to request a couple of beers and added a prime rib steak medium-well and fries without bothering to look at the menu. Then he stripped and showered away Haiti, a gritty pungent coating, a concentrate of body-organ sweat and woodsmoke and fatalism, shaving the stubble along his jaw but leaving his now bushy mustache untrimmed, put on the white terrycloth robe he discovered in the closet, and flopped on the king-size bed to phone his mother back in Montana.

My sweet boy, she said in the flat steady tones of the western mountains, *are you back in the land of the free?*

Not that far back, he said, wishing he were home on the ranch, helping her bring the livestock out of their winter range, calf-counting and vaccinations, saddle sore, wind-burned and all that, an honest hand. She talked about the haywire spring weather and her February escape to the tangerine desert light of Santa Fe. She talked about her most beautiful friends, her beloved horses, and about who died and who didn't or wouldn't and before she was done she gave in to a brief lament about his brothers, the youngest a meth freak who survived by poaching up in the Yaak Valley, the middle brother a go-get-'em real estate agent in Bozeman, a prodigal son of the Highline in thousand-dollar boots, busting up the old spreads into twenty-five-acre ranchettes, which he sold to the only enemy his mother had ever confronted eye to eye, the people she called lard-tailed shitbirds from California, advancing upon her homeland with an arsenal of lawyers smart-bombing the state with zoning and environmental litigation. But she was a military wife, military widow, and military mother, self-trained to believe it was not safe to feel a free range of sentiment, and she did not linger on her heartaches but stored them away in the root cellar of her solitude, there for when she felt deprived and needed the remedy of their cruel nourishment.

When you coming back? she asked when they were about to hang up and he said, *Don't know, Mom. Soon. I love you, too.*

Dad and I are proud of you, Scout, which is what she always said, the pet name, her sign-off, arm in arm with her husband, one voice forever, even after Dawson was terribly dead and terribly gone.

The food came and he turned on the television and watched a college basketball game, a rerun of Duke slaying some weakling Cinderella team during March Madness, and the steak was the best thing he had eaten in months and he ate every last fry on the plate, slathered in ketchup, and drank the two beers and felt well-treated by life and at ease with the sublime boredom of the cottony textures of peace. He woke up once in the middle of the night, listening for the drums, before he remembered where he was.

At the far end of a screened porch attached to the pro shop, affording separation if not privacy from the cleated traffic, a waiter had rolled in a linen-draped service cart bearing a flowered china pot and a six-cup setting for tea. Eville walked up on the mark at ten, wearing baggy cargo pants and an olive army T-shirt under a hooded pullover sweatshirt, his metabolism still adjusting to the underlying chill of a Carolina April morning. The welcome he received from Ben and Sammy and the undersecretary seemed authentically hale, the pleasure of his modest company clearly anticipated, although the fourth tea drinker, a black man with sulphurous eyes, whom Eville mistook as the day's invited player, did not step forward to shake his hand. Chambers introduced him to Sanders Coleman.

Call him Sandy. He'll be caddying with you today on the first nine.

How's it going? said Ev, withdrawing his hand as he met Coleman's gaze, hardened beyond an appropriate greeting. He stared back and understood, vaguely, that there was some history here. Do we know each other? he asked, and Coleman replied, Maybe you saw me around.

Where would that have been? asked Burnette.

Le Cap.

Oh, said Burnette, which black guy were you?

Coleman smiled and clapped Ev on the shoulder and that seemed to be enough to eclipse the strange tension between them. Chambers interrupted, intending to make a few points understood, he explained, before their guest appeared. First thing, he'll be arriving any minute now from Fayetteville, said the undersecretary, which, in case you were wondering, Ev, is why you're not coming from Fayetteville. The Friends of Golf wanted to see for themselves how things were between Burnette and their guest, lay fresh eyes on what they had reason to suspect was an unworkable relationship. You'll understand why as the day goes on, Chambers advised Burnette.

Who are we talking about here? Ev asked.

Second, said Chambers. We have a cat in the bag—he nodded affably toward Coleman—and he needs to stay there. Sandy is our eyes and ears in the DEA on this project. He never set foot in Haiti, all right, Ev? Wouldn't know it from his grandmother's douche bag.

Yes, sir, he said, and he noticed Coleman's eyes go slapstick wide as the agent looked past Eville toward the central screen door, its bell jingling as it swung open.

Check out Omar Sharif, Coleman said under his breath.

Burnette stepped aside, disheartened and incredulous, as the Pakistani colonel from Cap-Haïtien swept onto the porch and made a beeline for Undersecretary Chambers, chirruping, *My most honorable friend Steven, salaam alaikum, what a pleasure!* and Eville, floating away from the hallucination of their royal embrace, replete with an exchange of air kissing, wanted to puke his breakfast. Colonel Rashid Khan was dressed all in white, costumed like a paunchy cricketeer, a Raj version of the dashing sportsman, his coal-black hair shellacked with brilliantine and his mustache waxed to a plastic finish, his corporeal presence reeking of astringent cologne and his spiritual presence as foul as a sack of putrefied offal. Whoa, Burnette said to himself, what the fuck, ambushed and beginning to feel paranoid watching this east-meets-west pantomime of a love fest, Chambers leading the colonel by the hand to introduce him to Ben and Sammy, tasteless in their fawning manners and saccharine diplomacy, then the undersecretary directing the Pakistani's attention to Eville, who saluted as Khan stepped over to acknowledge the American soldier, his expression warm with condescension.

Ev, said the undersecretary, I believe you already know my old friend Colonel Khan, the lion of Peshawar, one of America's great allies.

514

Ah, yes, Captain Burnette, said Khan, the supercilious flash of his dark eyes accentuating the pretension of his empire lilt. He twisted his upper body to accept a cup of tea from Ben and turned back with a dry undercurrent of dismissiveness. We have adventures to share as well, wouldn't you say?

One thing I never understood, Colonel, said Chambers. What possessed you to put on a blue cap and drag yourself halfway around the world to handhold a bunch of spearchuckers? Things get too quiet at home, did they?

Burnette winced at the slur and Chambers turned the colonel away from Eville to introduce him to his African American caddy, Coleman, whose crisp, *Good morning, sir,* merited only a disinterested nod from the colonel, both viceroys ignoring Coleman to saunter back spikes a-clicking toward the tea service for refills, the Friends of Golf gathered around to be entertained by the explanation of the colonel's illogical assignment to Haiti. Burnette backed away a humble distance to stand with his fellow coolie, Coleman's eyes igniting like blowtorches aimed at Khan, muttering out the side of his mouth, *You're the nigger in the picture, asshole. Not me.*

Me?! Eville whispered back, stunned.

You? Not you, man. That Paki motherfucker. Agent Coleman paused with a crafty insider's glance at Burnette and snickered. *Well, maybe you too, the way he played you for the fool in Cap-Haïtien.*

What would you know about it?

I'd guess you're about to find out, Captain.

The colonel began his oration, identifying Somalia as the place where the story is born, this new story a wake-up call for modernity itself, the insufferable humiliation that struck his nation like the fangs of an asp, scores of Pakistani blue caps slaughtered by the renegade warlords before the first American Blackhawk ever went down smoking into inglorious history. With Pakistan's international reputation and honor and the blood of its sons flushed down the toilet of Africa, the colonel had said to himself that not just his country but he, Khan, had rested for far too long on yesterday's laurels, the blessed triumph over the Soviets in Afghanistan, and, with the time now upon them to be serious men again, he had petitioned his superiors for a transfer, temporary of course, out of Inter-Services Intelligence back into the regular army, with a specific request to command an overseas deployment to give proof to the world, or at least India, that the Pakistani military was a professional institution that could indeed be counted on and must in fact be reckoned with by all. Let Nepal be the joke, the cannon fodder. Let the Bangladeshis, the Salvadorans, the blasted Dutch. But Pakistan, said the colonel. Never again. You must have had a similar response, I imagine. To Mogadishu.

Rashid, my friend, said the undersecretary. That's a rusty bucket of crap. The way I heard it, you stepped on some toes.

Hah, yes, said the colonel, charming in the immediacy of his surrender to the truth. Only half bullshit. Always the disease of politics, isn't it? I took the cure.

Chambers looked at his wristwatch and announced, Start time, gentlemen. Eville couldn't read the undersecretary's voice one way or the other when Chambers told Colonel Khan that the undisclosed reason they had invited him to Pinehurst was to administer a caning to his Muslim rear end.

In that case, said the colonel with bobble-headed arrogance, accepting the challenge with a glittering look of malice, I propose we play for real stakes. One thousand dollars a hole. He looked to Ben and Sammy for indulgence, mocking his own apostasy. Steven knows, he told them, I am a bad Muslim, willing to gamble with Allah's blessings.

Too rich for Sammy and Chambers, who declined. Ben thought about it and said, *You're on.*

So tell me, Steven, said the colonel, how is our hero Charlie Wilson these days? Do you know, gentlemen, that there is a nifty little course in Peshawar, built by the British in an old lake bed? Tell them, Steven. You've played it. What a brilliant foursome, wasn't it? Zia and Wilson and Steven and myself? And what about you, now that you have conquered all your enemies? Are you awfully bored?

Not so much, said Chambers. Actually, I was thinking you and I might find a way to work together again. Develop projects of mutual interest. Something fun, like interior decorating. Rearrange some furniture. Open up the tight spaces, let in light, that sort of thing.

Oh? the colonel said, and away went his jesting smile, replaced by the guarded expression of a man snared once too often by the too-clever traps of his allies.

Some of your old friends back home have recently decided it's in their interest to start blowing up American property and personnel. Again. Issuing proclamations. *Jihad. Death to infidels, Allahu yoo hoo, the caliphate restored.* What have I left out, gentlemen? he asked.

My friends? said the colonel warily, his hubris drained to paler tones. You are mistaken, Steven. I am remembering correctly, yes? that the directorate made you a gift only last year of this airplane chap. That boy.

Yousef. The New York bomber.

Ah, yes, the airplane plotter. Yousef. Operation Bojinka, wasn't it? This word *bojinka*—curious, to choose a word from the Balkans. Why do you suppose?

The word is Croatian, said Chambers. A nation overrun with *mujos*. I was referring to your old friends, across the frontier.

Some of these hooligans were in Mogadishu, you see. They step on Pakistan whenever it suits them. My friends are not outlaw Arabs.

Well, let's talk about that. I think they mean to improve their game.

Yes, you're right. We should.

They were slow to get out of the pro shop, the colonel rejecting his first bag of rental clubs, filling a second bag with individually selected woods and irons, inspecting an array of putters as though they were hunting rifles, sighting down the shafts, before choosing one to his satisfaction. Okay, quipped Ben, good-natured in his mild but growing concern for what he had gotten himself into, I can see I have not been sufficiently briefed on the good colonel's talents.

Rumor has it you were swinging a club down in Haiti, said the undersecretary, and the colonel smiled and confessed to chip shots only onto an improvised practice green, unless of course someone was so insufferably stupid as to stand in his way. Then, chuckled the colonel, *I took out the wood.*

Eville tried to reconstruct the insights of the morning into a coherent picture of what had happened on the island, glue a frame around what he had long suspected was his unwitting role in events otherwise contrived for a purpose he could not perceive, into which he had been inserted not essentially as a Delta operative—he could see this more clearly now, but as a player working deeper, blacker, so deep and so black he himself wasn't quite sure what he was doing or why or for whom. The United States Army wasn't much invested in what went down or festered up in Cap-Haïtien. He was Chambers's boy after all, sent there for a still opaque reason, a reason ostensibly covered by his big-brother assignment with the undersecretary's gonzo daughter, whom he now had to assume was privy to more than one layer of the deception.

Wake Up and Smell the Latrine Fact Number One, he said to himself—the Pakistani colonel and Steven Chambers were old comrades-in-arms, orchestrating the cash flow and weapons shipments for the mujahideen's white-hot war out in Central Asia. Fact Number Two—the undersecretary had suggested to the colonel that the time had come to partner up again on the tilting, rubble-strewn dance floor of Fuckistan. *Fuckistan!* the colonel had guffawed, snorting a laugh through his fat Pashtun nose. *Hah, very good, Steven.* Okay, Eville said to himself as they moved out to the first tee, what does that mean?

We Pakistanis are a very competitive race, the colonel proclaimed, as though a mountain of data existed to back him up on the goofy chauvinism of this assertion. He chose a driver from the bag held upright by the sullen Coleman, and so began the nine holes of warfare, as practiced hand to hand among the ruling classes, between Kahn and Ben across the piney hillocks of Pinehurst #2, one of the world's most superior courses, Sammy bragged, and, circa 1898, America's first golf resort.

1898, was it? Colonel Kahn said to the ground in front of him as he leaned over between the blue markers to puncture the Bermuda grass with his tee and ball and strolled back to address the Friends of Golf. Latecomers, eh? he jabbed smugly. The Rawalpindi Golf Club, my home course, established 1885. Steven has been there and can tell you. In paradise, isn't it, Steven. The foothills of the Himalaya.

The colonel returned to his ball and set his stance only to relax it again for the sake of further illuminating the Americans about the benefits of a

Pakistani golfer's congenital volume of good fortune, athletes naturally gifted with excellent motor control but the secret to their success, said Khan, was an Asian mind-set that married competitiveness with a balanced inner calm. Then the colonel resumed his stance, threatening the ball with a flurry of quarter-swings before he cocked his arms fully into position and fired the white orb a mile down the skinny fairway, the ball sailing and rising and sailing and dropping centered on the lane between shoals of beachy sand that counted as rough below the channel of pine thickets shaping the hole. Sammy whistled and Ben snarled.

You bastards could have warned me.

The colonel's father, an Air Force officer assigned as an attaché to the foreign ministry, had taken his family from Islamabad to London when the colonel was a boy. Excelling through the forms at the elite private schools, not merely in the classroom but on the golf and tennis squads, the colonel had then entered Cambridge, matriculating out of the university straight into the Royal Military Academy at Sandhurst, the initial training center for cadets destined to become British Army officers, or, for cadets imported from the boondocks of commonwealth states, the promising youth meant to be fast-tracked into the higher ranks of their nation's armed forces. At Sandhurst as at Cambridge, Kahn was again courted as a scratch golfer, a token dusky-skinned champion out on the Hampshire courses surrounding the academy. After two years as a cadet, which culminated in Kahn being awarded the Overseas Cross for the all-around best wog in his class, he received his commission as second lieutenant and, in short order, Rawalpindi summoned him home, eastward into the service of his country and an entry-level position at the ISI directorate, where his rank rose steadily through the intelligence service according to his reliable performance out on the links with a heady eclectic assortment of the world's spymasters, arms dealers, and bagman princes. Most of them, sniffed Kahn, faders, choppers, and chokers, the kind of blokes knocking worm-burners off the tee.

Gee, that's quite a story, said Sammy. Goes to show you what you don't know. I had always thought golf was a Christian sport. I never imagined Muslims would take to it.

The colonel stopped and looked at Sammy with a nervous smirk. Let me ask you, said Sammy, not very convincing as an open-faced yokel, awed by the little mysteries of the big world. You ever played golf with the Talib gang? The Reverend Omar? Gulbuddin Hekmatyar? Or what's his name? Sammy snapped his fingers. Mr. Hakkadin? You know who I mean, Steven.

Jalaluddin Haqqani, Chambers said helpfully. Charlie Wilson called him goodness personified.

You ever played a round of golf with Goodness Personified, Colonel? Sammy asked.

He is not Taliban, said the colonel. He is Punjabi and will not accept Arabs telling him how to pray or fight.

All I'm asking, Colonel, is what does Sharia law have to say about golf? I'm quite certain, absolutely nothing.

Well, there you go, said Sammy. I think I can speak for all of us when I say our hopes and prayers are with you, Colonel, as the man we trust to bring the great game of golf to Afghanistan.

Ha-ha-ha. Kahn hammered his laughter as flat as the fairway. *Ha-ha.* That's very good. Let's hope the Afghanis appreciate our great game, isn't it?

Eville watched the curtain close on their thinning amiability, the duplicity of tight smiles and the wink of implied threats, not an exercise in affable one-upsmanship but a charade with insane implications, lives saved or lost depending on this sentence or that pun.

Here they were on seven and the Paki had just slapped a drive worthy of Nicklaus straight into the gut of Ben's sanguine and normally indomitable self-assurance. Goddamn it to hell, Ben howled on the seventh tee. Where does a Stone Age Muslim get off hitting a ball like that, son of a bitch, and Khan grinned viciously, handing his club back to Coleman, needling Ben, *That is your mistake right there, isn't it? In the nutshell, I believe you say. You think I give a shit about Islam.*

I want you to know, Colonel, said Ben, nothing on this earth would make me happier than to program a six-pack of Tomahawks to pay a visit to some of your madrassas.

Steven, the colonel protested. You promised me we were playing today with friends.

The undersecretary, penciling in his scorecard, glanced over at Khan with well-practiced sympathy. I apologize for Ben's rudeness, he said. I think Ben expected he was going to roll you over.

Apology accepted, of course, said Khan.

On the other hand, continued Chambers agreeably, look what happens when you put a white man's back against the wall. They don't take it very well, do they?

You right about that, said Coleman, paving the way for everybody to laugh again, and they went on to finish the round, Kahn and Ben trading holes seven and eight only to be rejoined in the self-canceling impotence of their identical talents on the ninth.

After Colonel Rashid Khan had pocketed a three-thousand-dollar check from Ben, he of the freshly striped Christian buttocks, the Friends of Golf sent him on his way back to Islamabad and his treacherous directorate, recommitted, he swore with his gloved right hand over his heart, to working in a mutually advantageous relationship with the Americans. Partnership, fellowship, you cannot disagree, Steven, this is our destiny.

Saying his farewells, Khan rubbed it in one last time, the win over Ben having affected him with a giddy infusion of bad sportsmanship, waving Ben's check above his head like a flag taken in battle.

American money is always put to good use in Pakistan, eh, Steven?

The gift bag is officially empty, Ben said. No concessions, no mulligans, no nothing.

And may I ask, Ben, how is your bum? said Khan. Perhaps my excellent caddy will be so kind as to apply some ointment to the lacerations.

Rashid, the undersecretary cautioned. Keep in mind we're not guys inclined to find the time to issue démarches. That's the message here. Deliver it to Islamabad.

Agreed, said Khan, shaking the undersecretary's hand as an electric cart arrived to whisk him back to the pro shop and the car waiting to return him to Pope Air Force Base. Lovely to play again, Steven. We should do it more often.

One more thing, said Chambers. This kid Yousef is very fond of his uncle.

Very good, said Colonel Khan. Done. We will keep an eye on him.

You know what I'm saying, said Chambers. I'm saying, share.

Yes, yes, said Khan. But I am dancing on snakes.

Understood, said Sammy. We're going to put their heads on pikes and we want flies crawling across their dead eyes.

Don't look so mystified, Ev, Chambers said. Friends kept close and enemies kept closer was the law of the shadowlands. He told Burnette the plan, although it was not a plan anybody was particularly wedded to, to send him out to Pakistan, a liaison for special operations that were about to enter an actionable phase in Central Asia. That had been their intent, the Friends of Golf and Delta's Colonel Hicks, and they had been willing to let the chemistry develop of its own accord in the laboratory of Haiti. There had to be some chemistry in these relationships or they quickly became untenable—well, it was a preference, not a law, and they'd find another mission to occupy Captain Burnette.

I can't hide it, sir, said Burnette, his relief at Khan's exit turned to gratitude. We weren't Simon and Garfunkel.

They had veered off from the tenth tee to walk in loose formation toward an isolated gazebo overtaken by blooming wisteria vines, its cedar-shake roof sheltering a picnic table where the resort's staff was finishing its prep for what would be their lunch—pitchers of iced tea, two silver chafing dishes containing warm Kaiser rolls and Carolina pit barbecue, a serving bowl with cole slaw, a bottle of Trappey's hot sauce. Chambers told Eville to drop the bag and come sit down before Sandy Coleman, his mouth already sharked around a dripping sandwich, ate up everything in sight.

Unlike the slow peeling back of the underlying mysteries of the morning, the ensuing revelations sprang forth like Russian nesting dolls in reverse—big, bigger, biggest—jolting Eville toward ever-higher states of both alertness and dread, beginning with the surprise of how nonblack—not white but processed, pasteurized mainstream, a federally owned civil servant—Sandy Coleman turned out to be as he got down to business, rushing with his food to clear his ravenous hunger from the agenda. Be right back, he said, as everyone else was getting started with the fixings, and he wiped red sauce from his hands with a napkin and gulped from his glass of iced tea and stood up to trot over to Ben and Sam's electric cart and returned carrying a large brown envelope and sat back down, shorn of any vestiges of jive, to deliver his briefing to the Friends of Golf.

What have you got for us, Sandy? said Sam.

Coleman opened with a date of prime importance to the culture of his profession, December 2, 1993, the last day in the life of Pablo Escobar and the Medellin cartel. Into the vacuum left by Escobar's death in Colombia's narcotrafficking power struggle had stepped the Cali cartel, the dominant organization for the past few years but under increasing pressure from attrition and rivals and armies and prosecutors and governments and in danger of losing its monopoly of the market. That freighter you boarded in Gonaïves, Captain? said Coleman. She was carrying what might turn out to be the last large shipment of cocaine the Cali people ever manage to pull together. Time will tell, but the trending suggests that these people won't be in business by next year.

Aw, cripes, said Eville, that ship showed up in Cap-Haïtien.

That is correct, said Coleman, explaining that, anchored in the harbor in Le Cap, the freighter had off-loaded seven tons of product, give or take a ton, which were, over the course of a week, broken down into smaller units to be loaded onto smaller vessels to make high-speed or low-profile runs into the coastal waters of Florida, Texas, and Louisiana.

How did I miss that? Burnette lamented, his forehead propped with the palm of his right hand.

Eville could read Coleman's unspoken recrimination in the man's eyes before the agent attempted to console the captain with bureaucratic push-offs. Cancel that thought, he told Burnette. Our interagency priorities are best addressed when we allow the product to flow through a completed network. Anything you might have done to intervene would have been counterproductive and we would have waved you back. We depend on the transshipment of those loads. We need to be able to track the supply and distribution chain and identify affiliates, okay? So let's get back on point. Why Cap-Haïtien? The answer is twofold, part one obvious and not so interesting, part two very interesting. The first reason is the endemic corruption of the Cap-Haïtien police department. The HNP command changed hands during this period—I know Captain Burnette, if he likes, could speak to that. Anyone falling out of his chair yet? The second reason is why you gentlemen asked me here today, aside from your fraternal impulse for playing practical jokes—not to say that I take no pleasure in my role in your little skits.

Nobody handed you a script, said Ben. You have a weakness for improvisation.

A dark genius for impersonating your inner Sandy, Sammy agreed.

Anyway, said Coleman, unruffled. First, some backstory. With the demise of the Medellin cartel, and the apparent weakening of the Cali syndicate, what we've been seeing is a shift of organizational and operational capabilities to the north, by which I mean Central America and, more pertinently, Mexico. We are at this time observing what still must be categorized as a transitional period, which, in the provenance of drug lords means a period of flux and anarchy. There's a cumulative effect we're observing, as the small-time operators step in and eventually are assimilated and consolidated—or annihilated—by more ambitious but still nascent organizations, primarily in Mexico, primarily on the Gulf Coast, with more manpower and more rapacity and more political clout, who have seen the future and staked a claim. Okay? Back to Haiti.

First, why Haiti? Answer: a lawless state with imminently corruptible functionaries and an unguarded coastline within striking distance of the United States. A slam dunk, as they say. Why specifically Le Cap? For all those same reasons but with a bonus ingredient—one of the world's foremost traffickers in the opium trade and heroin just so happened to be in Cap-Haïtien, exercising nominal jurisdiction of the northern districts under the auspices of a United Nations mandate, and in accordance with the nature of his entrepreneurial personality, exploring the business environment, researching the players, and essentially testing the waters for expanding his own geographically specific activity into an enterprise with significant outreach, an entity that would function more like a global conglomerate.

Agent Coleman, said the undersecretary with a low whistle of appreciation. Is that what a country boy sounds like after he comes home from a Rhodes Scholarship?

I'm from Oklahoma, Coleman explained for the captain's benefit.

You're talking about Khan! said Eville, aghast, kicking himself for his deficiency, his lack of situational awareness.

Yes, of course, said Coleman. Who else but Colonel Rashid Khan? What we all want to determine is why? Personal wealth? Khan is a rich man, yet we all know rich men never know when to stop making themselves richer men. And, since his illicit activity has back-channel approval by his C & C structures in Islamabad, we should ask ourselves, is there another motive that is not so obvious as greed and regional power? At the moment I would argue that the answer is not available. How might it make itself available? I would also argue that we have made a good start on narrowing and, with the evidence at hand, eliminating some of the variables.

One thing we know, said the undersecretary. The colonel is one of the best liars on this earth.

Eville found himself half-listening, mesmerized by the choreography of Coleman's fingers bouncing over the large brown envelope that had replaced the plate in front of him. The limber, flexing troupe arrived at a suspense-filled pause, the fingers poised to lunge upon the envelope's metal clasp. So, said Coleman, an unexpected character appears on the stage of the production in Cap-Haïtien. Who is he, why has he come? At first, no one seems to know. The fingers shucked back toward the clasp and unbent its flanges, removing the envelope's contents, a thin sheaf of eight-by-ten black-and-white photographs, the top image a portrait of a darkly handsome white man, his features faintly swarthy and cunning and his expression animated by a roguish charm. The man's name, Coleman told them, was Parmentier.

He looks Jewish, said Ben. Is he a Jew? What are we dealing with here? Mossad?

Coleman needed only a minute to exhaust his knowledge of Parmentier —a Cajun from Louisiana, a petty thief and addict who was lucid enough and smart enough to earn underworld credibility as a dealer in New

Orleans, gaining the trust of the city's crime bosses and flirting with the local mafia, which helped him relocate to Boston after some unpleasant business involving narcotics took him off the streets, the leniency of the sentence a result of outrageously expensive lawyers and a sealed plea bargain that seemed to infer he would be offering his services to the Federal Bureau of Investigation. Next stop Tampa, where Parmentier seems to have rendered the promised service to the Bureau in a rather reckless manner. His movements after the Tampa sting are not entirely clear, said Coleman. What is clear, though, he said, flipping over the top photograph to reveal the one underneath, a waist-up image of Parmentier and Colonel Khan, standing in front of the colonel's white UN-provided SUV, engaged in conversation, is that he came to Haiti, to Cap-Haïtien, where it appears he made a new friend and perhaps a new associate.

Time frame? asked Ben. Before the ship?

After, said Coleman. The product had already left the country. Perhaps its arrival in the States reminded Parmentier's people of Haiti's potential. That's a guess but a good one. Parmentier is likely representing Mexican interests who are capitalized to some extent by interests in New Orleans, though I can't document that. But let's assume it's true. We still have to ask ourselves, what's in it for our Colonel Khan? Short-term skimming? He's in town, he's the sheriff, he takes his ten percent, he rides on, end of story. So okay, said Coleman, flipping to the next photograph. This was taken a few days ago. Anyone want to speculate?

Who took these pictures? asked Burnette, already figuring it out, glancing not at Coleman but at Chambers who said, You didn't underestimate her, did you, Ev?

No, sir, said Burnette, and there was no more mention of the undersecretary's daughter.

The third photograph suggested the possibility of another ripening mystery, Parmentier and Colonel Khan together at the shabby porticoed entrance to an art gallery in downtown Port-au-Prince. Let's assume they're not collectors, said Coleman, flipping to the fourth and final photograph in the sheaf. This guy, he said, the pink moon of his fingernail tapping the platinum Levantine head of the man in the portrait, is the gallery's owner.

Always a pleasure working with you, Sandy, said Undersecretary Chambers, standing up from the table. Sandy said he forgot to mention the creation of a Haiti task force at the Treasury Department, a most undesired development—competition, interference, cross-purposes, hoarding, premature ejaculation, bureaucratic infighting and all the liabilities of a turf war—and Chambers told him not to worry about it, *We'll pump in smoke.* Then he instructed Captain Burnette to take the clubs out of the cart and ferry Agent Coleman back to the clubhouse, which Burnette did, and the Friends of Golf sauntered over to the tenth and teed up and played on.

CHAPTER FORTY

An unsettling shapelessness seemed to wash in on Burnette, a sluggish but relentless tide of gloom. His sense of direction and larger purpose blurred; the bona fides that formed a protective casing around his identity felt pocked and friable and he had begun to think it was possible he had lost his bearings, that he had been dropped into some barren worthless place he had never been before, without any recognizable landmarks, without so much as a north star to lead him out again and home. Whatever he had to report to the Friends of Golf about Haiti or the knavery and dereliction of the Pakistani colonel or his assessment of the field performance of the undersecretary's daughter had remained unsolicited and unsaid, a debriefing in search of an audience, and he had to guess his value to these men was either negligible or, improbably, overlooked.

And yet at the same time he felt strangely upheld by a countervailing force, the sharp attention paid to the details of his movement and support, an unfamiliar luxury of methodical thinking applied to his individual but lesser needs, a diametrically opposite pattern for how any military looked at and accommodated a single human being, as though he had undergone a metamorphosis into a more elite but insubstantial caste, less collective but also less productive, a more symbolic level of existence, an aristocrat without a grand calling, separate and privileged but essentially useless, attended to by an invisible network that anticipated the meaningless requirements of his day with astounding clairvoyance.

That afternoon in April, after he and Sanders Coleman had returned the golf cart to a Pinehurst staffer, an ordinary man stepped out of his ordinary car in the drive, hailed Burnette, and waited for him to check out of his room and then took him to the Moore County Airport in the nearby Sandhills. He drove Burnette onto the tarmac and parked next to a little bird—a red-and-white Bell 44—and, like the chauffeur in Miami, handed Eville a clipboard with papers prepared for his signature. Burnette asked what they were and the guy said finance docs and a speak-no-evil form and gave the captain a new credit card and a second card printed with a cryptonym (for Agency use only), access code, and password for another account opened in his name at a bank in the Bahamas. What's this for? asked Burnette and the man said, You're asking *me*? Whatever you do, don't file on it. All right, said Burnette, scanning the secrecy oath, which identified his updated TS security clearance, then scrawled his name at the bottom of the page.

What's level five? he asked and the guy said there was no level six. Burnette said, What's yours? and the guy told him three, see-no-evil, and he got out and strapped himself into the cockpit of the helo and before Eville knew it he was back at the Green Ramp at Pope, hitching a ride to Fort Bragg and his off-post town house, where his footsteps reverberated in the late-afternoon glare of uncurtained nothingness. He took an aggravated inventory of the shabby crap his wife had left behind—a veneer-nicked dresser, a yard-sale recliner, a folding chair, an old TV with rabbit-ears antennae, dust-covered stacks of several dozen books on the living room floor, a table setting for one but no table, a coffee mug with a Special Forces decal, a pot for boiling and a pan for frying, sugar packets from McDonalds, surplus moving cartons. Nothing in the bedroom but his weight-lifting bench and barbell and iron discs and, in the bedroom closet, his rack of uniforms and meager supply of civvies and, pushed to the corners, his personal cache of weapons and fly rods, boots and running shoes, and two wooden apple crates holding framed desktop pictures and photo albums of his beloved and the accumulated miscellany of a soldier's life. It almost felt like too much, just by the sad weight of its being so little.

On the kitchen counter next to the cliché of unopened bills he found the note she had penned in February—*Ev, I'm sorry, I just hated watching everything get smaller. Take care, xo Cheryl*—and he picked up the wall phone to call the firm where she had planted her tiny flag in the world as a paralegal and stood listening to the deadness in the line until he understood it as a mercy. He knew the immediate choice was to stay there and wallow in the misery hole of his lonesome domain or get out and so he located the keys to his truck and got out, driving over to the base, parking in the lot at Third Group and sitting there for a moment, disoriented, watching the snake-eaters come and go in their BDUs and Girl Scout caps, unsure of the many things that now confronted him as they had not before—Should he report to his old company or continue on to the compound where the D-boys assembled? Should he be in uniform or street clothes? Did he know enough now to know if he pussied out of Delta he would nevertheless live happily ever after among the brethren of an A-team, or would he kick himself down the road of his life for being a back-away slink, a quitter, not up to handling the full experience? At this point was it even possible to hit the reverse button, cancel the offshore accounts, sever his ties with Chambers and his cohort of overlords, and rewind the tape to where his ambitions were sweet fine dreams of higher callings but still only dreams, idle and weightless and not much more, prodding the drudge of a day's work, where *someday* was a story you made end however you pleased and not a confusing, potentially self-defeating reality in which you always played the weakhearted moron who blew it, a defeat made manifest by the poverty of your own character.

But he scolded himself then because he was a soldier who had never thought to ask himself how far is far enough. *Forward* wasn't a compass point as much as a vow. Therein lay his father's lesson—the intrepid never yearn, they fly right past on their way to the getting done. He scolded himself for trying to make sense of the layered shit of Haiti, one cover atop another stacked atop another, its pointlessness and contradictions, the totally fucked-up cast of characters, the setups he should have seen coming from a mile away, the intrigues right in front of his eyes that he never noticed come together into the switch-out. The amorphous mission—blob, not creep—had warped his mind and misaligned his thoughts and left him groaning inwardly with some genuine existential soulburn.

He let it all churn a few minutes longer until he had reduced the problem to a single lazy cause, blaming the girl for everything but for no better
reason than the fact that she rattled him to his core. There wasn't enough
training in the world to teach him how to get it right with Jackie—she
made him feel bad about himself, dulled and inferior in a way he never
imagined. That alone was what was so hard to let go and everything he
disliked and mistrusted about her had vectored into play the last time they
were together in the north, before she removed herself to the capital near
the end of March.

She hadn't connected with him for a few weeks and he let himself
believe he had seen the last of her. Then she was there one evening at dinnertime, sitting down at his table at the Christophe, wearing a robe-like
white cotton dress identical to the ones he had seen on a choir of Haitian
Pentecostals, hymn singers gathered like egrets by the water on Sunday
nights. Jackie said she needed him and he said what's up and she told him
she had been invited to a ceremony out in the countryside and she could
go alone but having an escort would be the wiser course. I want to know
more, he said warily, trying to read behind the appeal of her good-natured
smiling, the untrustworthy display of innocence, and she told him there
was a religious service near Grande-Rivière-du-Nord worth checking out
and he assumed she meant evangelicals and church and agreed to take
her in his banged-up CUCV, a handed-down Chevy Blazer from the US
military to the blue caps.

It was a fragrant, beautiful sundown drive past cane fields and sweet
potato plots and peasants moving steadfast toward a peaceful end to their
day. They traveled down a paved road lined by cacao groves and breadfruit
trees and the feathery plumage of coco palms, the air warmed and dreamy
with the aroma of woodsmoke and burnt sugar and orange blossoms, the
unhurried long procession of humanity along the shoulders like a stroll of
neighborly souls as the CUCV motored past respectfully in low gear, the
only vehicle on the darkening lane.

On the ride in, Jackie seemed a wiser, chastened version of herself,
shorn of the aggressive snip of sarcasm, even her camera put aside for the
night, surprising Eville with her straightforward and sometimes unguarded

reply to his cautious efforts to chat her up. She had stood down, he thought, retired her out-there hard-boiled Agency persona for a few hours and allowed him short glimpses of her bedrock sane self, a rational being named Dottie. Oh, she said with a soft thoughtfulness, when he asked, not expecting any honesty, why she had chosen to make herself such an active participant in her father's black universe and everything that path implied. Well, she said quietly, explaining her sedition against her parents had run its course.

I had my little rebellion against it, believe me, she said. You can ask, but trust me, it was all a prodigious bore. I was meant to do this, I was schooled in the trade. It could have been my brother, but he was timid, so it was me. Her father thought the males of her generation were more willing to let things go, to just forget about it, but females were less forgiving of that that was unforgivable. My dad says females are elephants, she said. He believes people who don't crave justice and vengeance are empty, that there's something vital missing from their spirit. I have my father's commitments, she said. Things are not unclear. He asked her then about schooling but she only told him her degrees—her undergraduate work at Yale in Islamic studies—*living in Turkey, you know, piqued my interest*—and a masters in ethnobotany at Harvard and he didn't have a clue what ethnobotany was. A lot of stuff, traditional medicine and altered consciousness and those areas, she told him, but ultimately, for me, she said, it was about primitive forms of biological warfare. You're messing with me again, he said, and she laughed merrily and said, Oh, come on now, Captain, have I ever? and when he thought about it, he flashed on Iraq and Desert Storm, enclosing his existence into a hazmat moon suit, and saw the logic, if not the motivation, behind how she had paired her studies.

I suppose that makes sense, he said, except when I try to plug it in to what you're doing here in Haiti.

I'm doing research, she said. I'm learning. Let's talk about something else.

They continued on for a while without words and he impulsively asked if he could ask her something personal and went ahead and asked without consent.

Do you trust your father?

I trust my father's cruelty, she said.

What's that mean?

I don't know, she said. It seemed the truest thing to say.

Then she said when they crossed the bridge ahead to slow down and go left and he turned off the paved surface onto a dirt track that followed a river he could hear but not see. They drove until darkness closed in, deeper into the bush, where the air began to pulse and he bent his head toward his open window, listening to the faint beat. Drums? he said, and the volume of the drumming swelled and then, farther on, pressed like thunder into his skull as they arrived at a clearing teeming with peasants. He killed the blinding offense of the CUCV's headlights but not before the drums fell silent and the beams froze a tableau of heaving dancers in the yard of a mud-walled farmhouse. Then all was blackness with stabs of flame from rag-wick torches and above the thatched roof a rosy slosh of sparking light from an unseen bonfire blazing behind the house. And centered in that arc of radiance, on rough-hewn flagpoles flew the rippled standards of a *houn-gan*, a sight Burnette knew fairly well. When she had told him *ceremony*, he should have known right off what she had meant. White-eyed silhouettes surged forward to engulf the vehicle. Say again, you're invited, right? he said, groping the cuff of his pants for his ankle holster and sidearm. Jackie said, Yeah, trying to push her door open against the gaggle of bodies swarmed against it. I think we're like the guests of honor.

After all the time he had logged with his A-team in the time-lost hinterlands of Haiti, he was inured to this, the sweaty glistening clamor of faceless humanity in the middle of the night, the raised chorus of anonymous voices and the ambiguity of their passions, never sorted out until you finally identified a ringleader or appointed a spokesman. The Americans were there to breach the villagers' barrier of fear, behind which they cowered and behind which they suffered. Yet *vodou* was no Halloween trick in Haiti, although it made some of the team members piss their pants to contain their laughter, just as it gave others the creeps. *What's the problem here? Werewolves,* would come the answer. *What's the problem here? A witch placed a curse on my sister. What's the problem here? A devil has taken possession of the dog.* Burnette and the team would nod grimly, stifling their amusement or disgust, at each fantastic fairy-tale account of supernatural mischief. They snapped off the tips of their chem-lites and swabbed phosphorescent crucifixes over the thresholds of families with infants, to ward off werewolves who would come at night to steal the children's souls. They'd track down the witch and put the fear of the Lord into her until the jealous scheming hag lifted the curse. They'd put a bullet into the heads of the devil-dogs, foaming with rabies. Sometimes it felt as though they had stepped back into a shroud-misted ancestral past to the birthplace of psy ops. As far as Burnette was concerned the *vodou* dramas were fascinations and part fun and gave him the blood-thrill of a medieval rush, summoning visions of Beowulf and Grendel, men who were giants and women who were swans and the venerable age-old tactic of magic on the battlefield.

Nothing truly bad had ever happened when he found himself among the *vodouiste*s and he didn't expect it now, lowering his pants leg back over his pistol and following Jackie out of the car. This was, in its style, an imperial conclave among an exiled tribe, a secret society's coronation of its new *empereur,* the final night of a two-day fete and a jubilant display of *vodou*'s three Ds—drunks, drums and jungle dancing. Burnette was not immune to the internal stir, the itch of the rhythms, the loosening of hips and heels. An elderly man with white sideburns, narrow-shouldered above his royal girth, his dignity uncompromised by bare feet and his wide-brimmed crown of woven fronds, stepped through the crowd and—*Ah, mon cher, ma belle mademoiselle*—clasped Jackie's hand in both of his.

He was the *gros neg* himself, the new *empereur* assuming the throne of the one recently expired, cloudy-eyed but vigorous, and as he conversed with Jackie in Kreyol Burnette again had reason to marvel at her quick fluency, two weeks further along and years beyond his own baby talk. The drums had resumed their artillery roar and from behind the farmhouse a chant floated out in clipped exhalations like a pounded song. Come, come, said the *empereur,* and they were led by the old man through the revelers past embered cookfires and children spooning callaloo from their gourd bowls and into the candlelit house itself, people resting on wooden benches against its shadow-played walls, no other furniture in sight, and they followed him to a windowless side room, where the *empereur* kept his household altar for his patron saint, the tempestuous succubus Erzulie Mary. In some other place, at some other time, the *lwa*, it seemed, had confessed her attraction for Jackie into the *empereur's* ear, and this was how Burnette learned that the undersecretary's daughter was running some kind of stealthy ops with the witch-doctor crowd.

From the altar's motley stack of bottles the *empereur* selected and uncorked one filled with clear liquid and dribbled a serving of its contents on the ground, quenching the great thirst of the *lwas*, then drank himself and passed the bottle to Jackie, who repeated the ritual offering and passed the bottle to Burnette, who did the same without hesitation, gasping as the tongue-cauterizing moonshine raked his throat, the *clairin* like an emulsion of fire ants. Another simple rural man appeared clutching a live chicken to his chest and the *empereur* received it into the bony gnarl of his own fingers and with a sudden surprising force twisted off the bird's head and sprinkled the altar with its blood and then bloodied the feet of his guests and handed the carcass back to the farmer. *Bon*, rasped the panther-faced *empereur*, kissing Jackie's cheeks and shaking Burnette's hand. *Bon*, he said, the *lwas* are happy, I am happy, and Burnette asked what had just happened and Jackie told him they had been presented to the spirits and, without objection, inducted into the *empereur's* cult. You don't have a problem with that, do you? she said. It's honorary. She took the bottle and another swallow of *clairin* and handed it back and he dared another gulp as well.

Far fuckin' out, he said. Do I get a tab to sew on my uniform?

The *empereur* left them there and disappeared, perhaps to attend to occult duties, and Burnette and Jackie wandered back outside with the incendiary gift of the bottle, behind the house to where the real jamboree unfolded on the foot-packed red earth beneath the thatch of a *hounfour's* peristyle—a rapturous danse macabre performed by a cluster of houris and a trio of bare-chested men with red kerchiefs knotted at their necks, a line of drummers enslaved to goatskin drumheads, whipped on in their mania by spectral masters and the dancers themselves ebony dervishes, slickened with spirit-energy. Jackie tipped the bottle skyward and lipped the neck like a glass trumpet and chugged and slanted her body against him, the side of her hip tapping his own with the salacious beat, a provocation not so terribly hard to reconcile with the moment. He could have moved away but didn't.

All was as it should be until a pair of spinning houris were seized by the gods, their eyes rolled back into their sockets as the bolt of possession passed into them like electrocution and the women fell, convulsing, to the ground, and flailed until each was claimed and taken—ridden—by a separate *lwa*, each a mortal horse with a divine rider, jabbering prophecy and esoteric instruction. Moved by the equally powerful spirit of overproof alcohol, Jackie surrendered herself to the show. Burnette tried to grab her back but she flung herself out to the peristyle, her gyrations an awkward white-girl version of letting go and Burnette stood appalled for the next few minutes watching her thrash around, Jackie oblivious as the object of far too much male attention, until she suddenly slumped to the dirt and Eville prayed, My God, stop her right now, do not let her rise up a mad-woman speaking in tongues.

But hello, Jackie was only stone-cold drunk, and when she didn't get up he rushed toward the heap of her, face-first in the dirt, to carry her out of the *hounfour* back into the darkness in the not-so-heroic cradle of his arms. He recoiled when he put her down to open the door to the CUCV and she wobbled and swiveled to her knees and vomited what smelled like rancid kerosene on his boots. Nice, he said derisively, shaking his unsympathetic head, and when he finally scooped her into the passenger seat she toppled across onto the driver's side as well and he couldn't make her sit back up. Which meant, for fuck's sake, that he drove the entire way back to Cap-Haïtien with Jackie's head jostled about in his lap and her mouth half-open.

The dashboard instruments cast a greenish velvet illumination and he looked down between his legs at the tarnished flax of her hair and felt her face pressed dead against his enlivened cock, a bad affair that he only made cravenly worse as he drove along and thought delicious, lust-tormented things. He watched the road and didn't watch the road, trying not to swipe any pedestrian looming out of the dark at the same time his eyes insisted on tracking the sublime curve of her torso to her legs, bare to midthigh where her dress had bunched. He stretched his right hand over onto her rounded hip, patting then stroking as if to comfort her. She didn't respond and he wasn't trying to comfort her and he reached farther and edged up her skirt until it was at the waistband of her panties and his hand was locked into a sequence of trespass, palming her butt, and she didn't wake up. By now he was trembling and he let his fingers glide along the veiled crack of her ass down into the crevice below and its patch of heat, where his fingertips rested on the sealed lips of her sex and when she still didn't move his index finger tested the tension of the elastic of the silky fabric and its rim of escaped hair and he realized with a shock what he was doing, about to stick his finger in the cunt of an unconscious woman, and withdrew his hand carefully from its scavenging path of violation and carefully rearranged her dress over her legs and drove on with her mouth lolling atop his hard-on, telling himself he was the lowest of indecent men.

In the Christophe's car park he dragged her inconvenient rag-doll carcass out of the CUCV and humped the load up past the disapproving night watchman and through the lobby and up the staircase to his room, muscling her over his shoulder like a sack of rice and cussing to himself all the way, into his ascetic's matchbox cell, taking her straight to the bathroom and slinging her down propped into the corner of the shower stall. He struck a match and touched the flame to a candle in its holder on the back ledge of the sink's basin and a small sphere of light jiggled into the room.

The water system was, as always, turned off at this time of night although as always the maid had filled a five-gallon bucket set next to the toilet for flushing. He was too exasperated not to pour it on her, for her own good, of course, but he picked up the bucket and put it back down trying to decide whether he should undress her first, the pros and cons of disrobing a knocked-out hellion who just might regain consciousness in midstripping, and concluded, *To hell with it, man,* and dumped the water over her head, jumping back as she woke up with a sputtering howl, lashing out with a flurry of blind swats and kicks overtaken by a bout of dry heaves that calmed soon enough to profanity-laced moanings as she collapsed herself into a soggy fetal position and fell back asleep. He retreated through the shadows to his narrow bed, satisfied that she would live to continue tormenting him another day.

But he should have known that wasn't going to be the end of it, that Jackie had a trick of resurfacing. Sometime before dawn her clammy naked body tried to wedge itself onto the single mattress next to his sweltering naked self and he played dead—there was no room for her in the bed regardless—and the next thing he knew she was kneeling over him, straddling his hips, tugging his penis into the automatic compliance of an erection, and he growled at her, the spontaneity of his rejection puzzling even to him. *What do you think you're doing. Get off,* and she said, *Oh, come on, Burnette, fuck me, let's just get beyond the sex, okay. Do it.* His cock was a flagpole, straight up in her grasp and she began to lower herself onto him when he pushed her sideways against the wall and rolled himself off the mattress, crawling on his hands and knees to find his sleeping bag and foam pad, his stomach knotted into a queasy spasm of wrongness. He spent the remainder of the night there on the floor feeling like a steamed dumpling, the heat too heavy and the air too close, the bag pulled over his face, listening to the swishing pant and muted snores of her breathing as she lay above him in bed, asleep again within minutes of their uncoupling, which he would never be able to explain to himself, lacking any real principle to account for his sudden unmanly priggishness.

In the morning as he dressed she remained asleep, her body contorted like a drowning victim, legs and arms broken wings jutting awkwardly, her brow knitted and face strained with frowning concentration, her lovely breasts exposed, the sheet wrapped at her waist like a toga in disarray. He tiptoed into the bathroom but when he came out she was sitting up, hugging her elbows, her head inclined toward him with an impersonal smile, her eyes hostile, waiting to hear what he might say.

See you around, he said, grabbing his kit and getting the hell out of there before she could open her mouth, say something to enrage him— conceivably even a *good morning* would do the trick. The beast of the field, the somehow guilty one, gnawed by his own conscience, the molester, the could-have-been rapist, the unsated victim, running away.

Was this how all men act and think? It would not console him if they did.

He shut off the truck's engine and followed the sidewalk across Third Group's campus to Bravo Company's headquarters and the hayseed non-com stuck on the desk greeted him with a knowing smirk and another collection of paperwork. Early on in the invasion, he had seen this kid sauntering around one of the FOBs in Haiti with a big-ass Bowie knife strapped to his leg and had asked him, Who are you supposed to be, Davy Crockett? Yuck, yuck, said the kid, my dad carried this evil blade in 'Nam.

Top, I'm not letting you go until you fill out every one of these suckers. You heard then?

I heard a rumor, sir. I heard you no longer exist, *heh heh*. Also I'm supposed to tell you to report inside the fence at the Wall tomorrow at 0700. Ask for Lieutenant Colonel McCall.

He told the staff sergeant he was looking forward to it and suddenly he was, anything to reestablish a zone of routine and daily regimen in his life where he did not have to think quite so hard about the rightness or wrongness of his actions, where his decisions were given the reliable bene-fit of a context, straightforward and practical, ABC, one-two-three, God and country, faithful obedience to the higher cause, and when he finished with the paperwork he walked down the hallway to the team rooms to visit with his former detachment, to say hello and say good-bye, but the only men he found there were the team's jug-eared choggies, Wascom and Boles, transferring gear and weapons from the permanent main locker into two footlockers and Burnette asked, You guys going somewhere? and they looked up, preoccupied but grinning, and Boles said, Hey, Top, back in time for the farewell party! and Wascom said, Yes, sir, Bosnia.

He walked out of there trying to remember who said it, an aphorism he would never forget, first because he had always thought it was nonsense and then because he came to know it was wise. *War is but a spectacular expression of our everyday life.*

539

CHAPTER FORTY-ONE

As the sun went down he went to Kmart to do a simple thing that would make him feel better, normal, human, real: shopping for his spartan comforts, a pillow and a two-pack of pillowcases, a plush bath towel, shampoo and soap, a coffeemaker and floor lamp, then to the supermarket where he bought a bachelor's ration of coffee and eggs and bacon and beer and a hand of greenish bananas and cigarettes and a copy of the *Fayetteville Observer*. On the way home he stopped at his favorite sandwich shop and took away a foot-long Italian sub and back at the apartment unloaded everything and stood up the lamp next to the recliner and sat down to eat the sub and read the newspaper, glancing at the headlines and then the sports section—and thumbed through the classifieds, used trucks first then real estate, acquiring a ballpark sense of the value of what was left in his name, mulling upgrades or downsizings or flat-out liquidation. Generals were materialists, not foot soldiers, who only wanted their due, hard enough to get as it was. He owned the town house but wondered if he should own a bed? At this point, probably not. *My bed* was subtext in the sentence—*This home*—and his life was trudging off in some other direction.

He read on, fantasizing about buying a motorcycle or a boat, scanning the job market with a sense of relief that he had not been put on this earth to be frog-marched through the adventureless monotony of a civilian's life, the unnatural atrophying blood-thickening safety of it all. Because it nuzzled keenly against one of his fondest dreams, he saved for last the listing for pets, the critter sales and giveaways, humane or something less, sniggering at the lady-favorite rodent breeds, Pomeranians and Yorkies and quivering Chihuahuas, vermin-sized lumps of uselessness, scowling at the much-maligned gangsta dogs, pit bulls and Rotties and Dobes, his blessing and empathy offered to the legion of mutts in need of anything resembling a home, missing the bold and stalwart heelers that you would find in any Montana paper, the habit of his search designed to mire his heart in nostalgia, hoping for (and dreading) a listing for a setter or a Lab, anticipating the pain and the memories, the dogs of his boyhood the most cherished of lost friends—the hunts with his dad and the dogs for grouse and duck, the true love of endless happy canine kisses, the furry spring of joy in every waking morning whatever the season. The perfection of his imagined life culminated with a dog, yet under the circumstances he could not have the dog unless he had a woman who loved dogs, or just a woman who loved him, a yearning as distant from his reality as the moon.

The beer and the sandwich and the sedative of the newspaper and the darkness falling beyond the lamplight had left him sleepy, and he pushed back the reclining mechanism of the chair to stretch out and close his eyes for a nap before going out to join the gang at Rick's bar and lay there thinking about the one good thing that had happened in Haiti in the past two months, or at least the only bad thing that had ended up all right.

The morning after the Pakis brought in the bodies and the wounded and the detainees, he was with the Caricom troglodytes when they unlocked the cargo containers where Lecoeur's people had spent the suffocating night. The Jamaican police herded the prisoners out into the glaring sunlight, the wailing and crying began anew, and the clamor excited the surly Jamaicans, who began a type of indiscriminate batting practice with their batons on the shoulders and buttocks of anyone not nimble enough to skip out of the way. He had stepped in and put a stop to it and made them separate the women and children from the men and then he ordered them to release the women and children. Go, he told them in Kreyol, you're free. Go where? a woman asked. Get out of here now, he said, pointing across the airstrip to the front gate, wanting them gone before the Jamaicans questioned his dubious authority to bark out commands. He exchanged hopeless looks with a young woman clasping the head of a little boy to her skirt, his limbs as insubstantial as twigs, and he understood she didn't want to move. He had to shout, to step toward them menacingly, *Allez, allez!* and they scuttered away like a flock of black geese, casting panicked glances over their shoulders at the fox on their heels.

The beefy captain of the monitors squared off in front of him, nostrils flared and glowering, his rotund face a graven image, a countenance like a vicious walrus—*Tell me who you are again, mahn*—and Eville realized at least here in the compound this undercover journo bullshit was out the window and he would need to present himself dressed in cammies, holster his 92FS on his belt, offer and receive salutes.

That day, though, and the days to come, left him with a lasting foul taste of complicity, as if he had been required to attend a workshop in the effective application of human rights abuses, and his opinion of Third World law-and-order professionals jumped to a more elite bracket of disgust and incredulity. Lecoeur's downtrodden men were marched to a small concrete-blockhouse isolated at the back of the compound, where they were told to sit in the dirt and be quiet. Within minutes the heat and the excruciating blaze of sunlight had become unbearable. He asked the Jamaican captain to explain the protocol and the captain said they were waiting for the interpreter to arrive so the interrogations could begin. One of the prisoners pleaded to use the toilet, several others began to beg for water. What are they crying about? said the captain. Eville translated their distress and the captain said, Tell them to shut up, tell them to shit in their pants. This is what we're going to do, okay? said Burnette, and he put three prisoners, sworn to take a hasty dump, in the back of the CUCV and picked one of the policemen to ride up front with him and ferried the Haitians to a line of port-a-johns across the base and cut off their flex cuffs and let them shit on the promise they would not seize the opportunity to overthrow the government. Water, water, the others begged, the lot of them unfed and dehydrated since being hauled out of the mountains. He got back into the CUCV and drove over to the UN mess hall and grabbed a couple cases of MREs and bottled water and by the time he returned to the blockhouse the interpreter was inside with half the cops who, from the sound of it, were beating the daylights out of one of the detainees.

All right, listen, he said to the captain with as much cool equanimity as he could muster. Stop this right now or I am personally placing you under arrest.

The captain laughed in his face and got on his radio instead and Ev himself stormed into the blockhouse to try to reason the Jamaicans away from their sport of official cruelty. Next thing that happens, a Pakistani aide de camp drives up respectfully requesting to escort Eville back to headquarters for chitty-chat with Colonel Kahn, who berates him for illegally assuming command of a UN-Caricom-controlled joint operation and sends him back to the interrogation follies under strict orders to observe and assist or run away home to the land of namby-pamby. The day proceeds and ends with eight more pointless innings of sadistic self-fulfillment for the thugs in uniform, pounding a gram's worth of intel out of a ton of cowering screaming flesh. He had never seen anything like it, a day of useless petty brutalities administered by such a surplus of defective people, and it crossed his mind that they continued on for the double pleasure of defying the precious oversensitivities of a white American arsehole. Now what? he says as the ignominious afternoon clots to an end. Back to the lockup for the wretches, and since no one else will do it, he drives back to the mess hall and returns to the cargo container with food and water before the detainees are chained in for the night. He doesn't feel like the good guy. He feels like the good guy who failed.

If he wanted, he could have bunked on the compound overnight in an air-conditioned officer's billet but he thought why punish himself and he drove out the front gate nodding at the mud-headed Paki guards, hankering for a nightlong lineup of cold beers back at the Christophe.

He doesn't recognize the girl—she was sitting cross-legged and humped over on the side of the road fifty yards outside the gate, her face concealed behind the shield of her hands as though she might be weeping—but he recognized the boy standing next to her—mother? sister?—rigid with unearthly patience, his clothes in shreds, his belly puffed with malnourishment, a small ebony statue meant to convey the fierce stoicism of survival branded into all the children in the world to whom the world has shown only horror, supernaturally resilient children who refused to perish, like burned roots that keep sprouting into an otherwise charred and lifeless wasteland. Children who would grow into adulthood singing songs of war.

He pulled over a few yards past them and put the CUCV in park and walked back and stood in front of the pair until she looked up, not crying after all but desolate and dazed with fatigue, her sad wondering eyes searching his for evidence of his intentions. He said, Madame, you were with the people taken from the mountains, yes? and she said, a birdlike peep, *Oui.*

Where did they go?

Back to the mountains.

Why didn't you go with them?

God has abandoned me, *monsieur.*

Naturally she was frightened by him, her shyness and her fear wholly appropriate to the mystery of his presence, yet he gently coaxed out the shards of her life—here's a piece, here's another piece. The boy was her son, his father had been a teacher murdered by the tyrant's army three years ago when the soldiers came rampaging up the valley into the mountains after Jacques Lecoeur, burning schools and houses and crops, hacking to death villagers too slow to escape into the sanctuary and subsequent hardships of the jungle. She had plucked the boy up from the flames and fled with the other refugees, joined by her older brother Reginald, her only living relative, a coffee planter who became one of Lecoeur's men, a brother who protected her and her son, and fed them, when they would not have been able to endure, as others had not endured, without protection and food. Now he was one of the prisoners rounded up by these foreigners who had come to Haiti—not the Americans but these other men, neither black nor white nor Christian—and it made no sense to her to return to the mountains without her brother and his guardianship. Why should I make such a difficult journey to starve there, *monsieur,* when I can starve here without the trouble?

I want to help you, he said. Will you let me help you?

She lowered her head without answering and so he sat down next to her in the dirt, watching the traffic pass on the road, and waited for her decision.

Finally she whispered to her knees, Why would you help me, *monsieur?* and it pained him mightily to realize why she would ask this question, that nothing might strike her as more poisonous than his star-spangled good intentions. And what could he tell her, how should he answer? Because I need to help *somebody?* Because I am an American and I can? Because God and my own mother would scorn me if I didn't? He wanted to sigh, Give me credit for being decent. Or trying. It was the thing he could do for himself. The purifying act.

She is not grateful for his attention; she is a woman, and hesitant with suspicion. He looked to the boy for an ally. Are you hungry? he asked, and the boy bobbed his head meekly once, *Oui,* his eyes flicking toward his mother, unwilling to assume that the acknowledgment of his hunger might actually contribute to its relief, and Burnette said to the woman, *Come,* his tone light and invitational, *Get into the car,* careful to not make it sound like a command, and she rose from the ground resolved to her fate, now deposited in this *blan's* hands, attempting to smile, the sinewy strength and childlike youthfulness of her body resurgent, taking her son's hand, and they came.

In the roadless mountains the rivers flowed undefeated, the color of lapis, as they had since time immemorial, but the tidal river below this bridge on the road from the airport to the center of the city looked and smelled like a channel of diarrheal sludge, its filth oozing toward the nearby sea through the middle of a dung-colored slum, a warren of repulsive miseries, constructed entirely of wreckage and garbage and degradation. Even the charity of a penny would not fall their way. He saw her gazing out the window into the twilight at its hovels and cook fires and children romping in its pestilence of mud and knew this was their squalid fate, the hell where she and the boy would be absorbed and vanish were they left on their own.

Across the bridge he turned toward the harbor and drove through the broken streets to the quay, where he knew vendors had claimed a sidewalk outside the gates of the port and its massive warehouses, hunched over their iron cauldrons stoking nests of fragrant coals, cooking the fare they would sell to the sailors and stevedores for their dinners. There were no stalls, no chairs or tables, just the market women and their steamy pots, and he stopped in front of one of the cooks because her plump face was creased with laughter for no apparent reason and he bought each of his foundlings a scoop of rice and beans ladled with conch stew and grated cabbage, the meals served on paper plates and eaten with a communal tin spoon. The kid and his mom sat together eating in the backseat of the CUCV, chewing rapidly, with the watchful vigilance of alley cats. The boy cleaned his plate first and his mother shared what remained on hers. He went to another vendor and bought them bottles of lurid-colored soda and leaned against the hood while they washed their meal down, trying to devise a plan, until she came out of the vehicle to return the bottles and the spoon and approached him demurely to say thanks and then raised the dark lambency of her eyes to his with a quizzical expression.

Awkwardly, because it was an afterthought, he asked their names. Margarete, she said, and Henri. And yours, *monsieur*? Burnette.

We have to find you someplace to stay, he said.

He didn't bother with the Christophe, which had for many months now been rewarded by the international crisis with a hotelier's windfall of no vacancies. Behind the Christophe, up the slope of a wooded hill, was the only other respectable hotel in Cap-Haïtien, the Mont Joli, but when he rolled into the Joli's car park Margarete seemed to shrink into her seat and her eyes darted across the scene—the hotel's tropo-modern multistoried facade of affluence, the swaggering flow of NGOs with their briefcases and walkie-talkies, the landscaping of an off-limits world where the young woman and the boy themselves would be considered trash—and she turned to him with a look of frantic appeal that required no exchange of words and he said, Okay, I think I remember seeing some places back on Route Nationale, and he whipped the CUCV around and drove out toward the southern gate to the city where they found a depressingly seedy roadside pensione, its run-down rooms exclusively for Haitians. *Bon*, she said apathetically, *no pwobwem*, but he couldn't bring himself to leave her there with the child.

He drove back into the city, aimlessly cruising its stricken neighborhoods, until ahead he saw the spire of a cathedral and eventually found its rectory attached to the backside of its hulk, the stern glow of light in its windows like a warning against intruding sinners. Let me ask here, he told the impassive Margarete. He went and rapped on the wooden door and heard from within a faint but shrill command to advance and so he advanced, stepping into the stark administrative space of Christ's earthly accountants, forced to smile because the brusque elderly woman behind the metal desk at the rear of the rectory, the bishop's secretary, reminded him of his own grandmother, a black-skinned bewigged version of her stout, no-nonsense self, reading glasses tilted on her nose, an earpiece mended with hospital tape. What is it, *monsieur?* asked the woman, scalding him from head to toe with her gaze, and he made a bumbling attempt to explain himself before his French, and the explanation's own logic, faltered.

Where are they? said the bishop's secretary. I want to see them.

He brought them in and tried to listen to the conversation, but the streaming speed of their language outran his comprehension. Okay, said the old bitch, switching to English, letting her eyeglasses fall and hang, fixed to a cord around her neck. Her face registered extreme doubt. You are keeping this woman, *monsieur?* she demanded.

Keeping?

I will not help you keep a woman for your own purpose.

It became clear to Burnette that the bishop's secretary—dangling the prospect of a solution before him, a recently vacated gardener's bungalow on church property, three month's rent in advance and in dollars, daylight visitors only—was going to take Margarete and her son and not give them back, for the sole purpose, not of altruism, but of defeating the imperial white, the Pope himself meriting the same hostility from the Haitian clergy and its die-hard Duvalieristes.

Dako, madam, show us the house, please, he said, desperate to escape back to the Christophe, and the old woman took a set of keys from her desk and a plastic flashlight and walked them down past the cathedral to the next block to a two-room clapboard bungalow and Burnette said to Margarete, Okay? and Margarete shrugged in agreement, Yes, why not. He promised he would come back tomorrow with supplies and he turned to leave, rubbing the head of the boy affectionately, when Margarete reached out to touch his arm and said *Monsieur,* please, my brother, but he would not raise her hopes on that account.

As things went for the next two months, he would never have known his ass from a breakfast biscuit if it hadn't been for this unlikely relationship, the serendipitous triangle between himself and Margarete and her sibling, their gratitude—fair enough—never forthcoming, the emotion instead replaced by their discreet unsolicited loyalty.

One day she would tell him, Mr. Burnette, do you know who Jacques Lecoeur was? He was what we call a *bayakou.*

I don't know that word, he said.

Bayakou. In Haiti, *bayakou* is the laborer who comes at night to clean out the latrine.

When he returned to the UN compound in the morning he dropped by the medical tent to check on the condition of the wounded. Two, including the gunshot girl, had been medevaced to Port-au-Prince, sharing the helicopter with the body bags of Lecoeur and his dead compatriots; the other two lay on gurneys, befuddled by painkillers and the vagaries of misfortune. Ti Phillipe, he was astounded to discover, had been released an hour earlier. Released? he asked the staff, no one saying much until he took aside one of the Haitian orderlies. Why? To whom? The answers he received were confusing. The police had taken Ti Phillipe with them. Which police? The national police. The HNP? Yes. Did they arrest Phillipe? No, the commander took him away in his Toyota HiLux. Which commander? The commander for Cap-Haïtien. Where were they going, do you know? I don't know, *monsieur,* but the commander was angry.

There was a standoff in progress when he arrived at the shipping containers, the UN's ad hoc penal colony, a half-dozen Haitian national police faced down by four Jamaican International Police Monitors, everyone armed but not quite dangerous, the detainees still locked in the oven, bellowing from inside and pounding on the metal walls. Both sides took it for granted the white guy had come to settle the conflict in their favor. The entire lot of them groused when he declared, I don't know what the fuck is going on here, but at least let those people out of there to get some fresh air until we get Colonel Khan or someone over here to figure this thing out, his neutrality only managing to combine each side's contempt for the other into a shared contempt for the interloper in the middle. Where's your commander? he asked one of the Haitian cops.

He is speaking with Khan.

What's his name?

Major Depuys.

Speaking was not the word he would have used to describe the interaction between the two commanders, the Haitian and the Pakistani, when he heard them inside Khan's office, Depuys shouting in high-pitched French, Khan responding in French himself but only to an interpreter in the room who parroted the colonel's supercilious tone. His entry into the fray had been denied by Khan's deputy, who asked him to please take a seat and wait. What's happening? he asked, and the deputy told him a newly commissioned police chief for Cap-Haïtien had arrived from Port-au-Prince bearing a militant jurisdictional grudge. Minutes later the door banged open and there was Khan, ushering out an enraged Major Dupuys, a tall lean man in an all-black uniform and a black baseball cap embroidered with gold letters, HNP.

Ah, Captain Burnette, said the colonel in English. Just the man I need. I want you to supervise the transfer of the detainees to Major Dupuys's prison, where they are to remain incarcerated—and Captain, I hold you, not the major, accountable for this—until I receive further instruction from Port-au-Prince. Understood?

Yes, sir.

Very well. Get this foolish man out of my sight. He is giving me a headache.

The issue, the contentious heart of Major Dupuys's grievance, was neither small nor inconsequential and it stripped away the illusion of his nation's fragile sovereignty and the restoration of that sovereignty by the powers invested in the mission. It took Burnette all day to begin to grasp the situation, and another week to pry out the nefarious details. Essentially, the government of Haiti had never authorized Khan's excursion into the mountains to take down Lecoeur and his men, although the palace seemed to have consented to a vaguely outlined operation to contact and assess the current status and activity of the evasive band of guerillas. When

549

word of Khan's bloody raid on Lecoeur reached the national palace, the government's reaction was as you might expect—outraged impotence, hollow threats, a formal protest to the United Nations Peacekeeping directorate, a clamor for the dismissal and deportation of the Pakistani colonel, a demand that the bodies of the slain be delivered to Port-au-Prince and the immediate and unconditional release of the incarcerated, a demand that the colonel finessed by remanding the detainees into the custody of his American advisor until further notice. Maybe somebody at UN HQ in Port-au-Prince wanted the prisoners sent down to the capital for further questioning. Maybe not. The conflict took days to resolve. Meanwhile, Lecoeur was given a state funeral at the National Cathedral, eulogized by the president as a freedom fighter and a martyr and interred in an already crammed mausoleum, the country's pantheon for assassinated and butchered heroes.

Seize the narrative. Cue the riots. He could feel the ground rumble under his feet and knew nothing here was bound to improve.

For Burnette, the story never really got any better. Work with me on this, he told Major Depuys that morning as they walked to their vehicles. I don't like it any more than you do. But he would learn this lesson again and again—mistrust was organic; trust itself Sisyphean. Waiting in the cab of the major's white pickup truck was Ti Phillipe, an immaculate bandage circling his neck like a priest's collar. *Como ye?* he asked Lecoeur's lieutenant. *Feck you,* Ti Phillipe said in garbled English, the clenched face, the black gleam of hatred in his eyes, making the curse superfluous. Burnette pulled the major aside. Okay, we need to talk. Phillipe was what?—a free man or the same as the other detainees? Major Dupuys had his own question.

You were there in the mountains. Why did the soldiers massacre these people?

No, that's not correct. I wasn't there.

You were there. You attacked this man.

No, I saved his life. We left before the soldiers came.

Why did they attack Jacques Lecoeur?

Honestly, major, I don't know. I just know that it was the wrong thing to do.

This colonel was doing the dirty work for the big *macoute* families. Maybe that's the reason. I don't know.

It would be some days later when he sat down in the UN canteen across from one of the Canadian pilots who had flown in the operation and heard a far simpler explanation that chilled him with its credibility. Anyone with a headset on, and that of course meant Khan as well as the flight crews, had listened in as Burnette radioed from the ground for a medical evacuation. The quality of the transmission, as was frequently the case, was poor, interrupted by static, open to interpretation. Khan's voice entered the commo, asking the American for clarification—Have shots been fired? How many wounded? You never responded, the pilot reminded Burnette. Were you receiving? No, said Burnette, trying to remember if he had that right. Well, you can guess what happened next, said the pilot. Khan got on the intercom and told his troops to lock and load. He told them the LZ was hostile, they were coming in hot. We were still out a ways, but when we put down a half hour later, the fucking Pakis were squirting rounds as they came off the ramp. One of those things, right, said the pilot, reacting to the crestfallen look on Burnette's face. Look on the bright side, Captain.

The bright side, Burnette said. That would be?

We're in Haiti. The Big Stinky, eh? Cheer up. It doesn't count.

To ease the tension, he let Major Dupuys dissuade him from going back into Khan's office to get it straight about what to do with Ti Phillipe. They requisitioned a pair of Humvees from the motor pool and enlisted Paki drivers and returned to the cargo containers and Burnette explained the transfer to the Jamaicans, who took the occasion to recompose themselves into bureaucrats. Let's see de paper, mahn. The prisoners broiled for another hour while Burnette returned to Kahn's office for a written order and Dupuys tracked down the IPM captain to obtain a copy of the roster of the detainees. Finally the door was opened, men stumbled into the sunlight, Burnette intervening when the Jamaicans lurched forward. Put the cuffs away, he said. Step aside, goddamn it. Call the roll. When Margarete's brother answered to his name, Burnette removed him from the group. Major Dupuys, he said, this man will ride with me. You guys are dismissed, he said to the Jamaicans. The detainees were packed into the open beds of the Humvees, the HNP climbed into the back of Dupuys's pickup, Burnette coaxed the reluctant brother, wary of being singled out, into the CUCV and they convoyed out of the UN compound, halting for fifteen minutes at the line of port-a-johns.

You are Reginald, *oui?* I'm Captain Burnette.

I remember you. From the mountains.

He wanted to explain himself, to apologize, but it was too soon—it felt that way at least, too soon to warrant the brother's trust, too soon to know what further trouble might insert itself between them in the coming days, and so he contained himself, offering nothing more than the one piece of information that could matter, that he was helping Reginald's sister and nephew and would try to arrange a visit. He glanced over to see the man's rearrangement of fear and suspicion into baleful mystification, Reginald finally lifting and tilting his head to look at him, study him, calculating an array of possible motives or possible deceits, trying to understand the white man's own face and expression but understanding nothing and asking, as his sister had asked, the question for which Burnette had no answer and many answers, *Why?* But the question was starting to bug him and his brain, held captive by the warden of a foreign language, had begun to fry.

Just accept it, man, he snapped in English. *Comprenez?*

Oui, noncomittal.

Comprenez Anglais?

No.

Okay then, pal. Let's just keep it to ourselves.

They arrived at the central police station downtown with its bullet-riddled exterior, shot up by the marines in the first week of the invasion. This was not the deliverance the detainees had imagined and they became unruly with resentment and everybody, even the police and Dupuys, looked at Burnette as if he were to blame. Eventually the men were processed and registered and taken upstairs and divided between two large cells. He told them it was his understanding they'd be out of there in a few days and asked them to be patient and said give me your word you won't try to escape and they narrowed their eyes and stared at him as if he were Mephistopheles reincarnate. I know you're innocent, he said, although the truth was that he really didn't know squat about any of them. He went back downstairs to the front desk and saw Ti Phillipe in an animated and unnervingly jocular conversation with some of the cops and he waited for Major Dupuys to get off the phone and said, What about Phillipe? and the major smiled and told him that Ti Phillipe had agreed to be his deputy. Burnette rocked back on his heels and said, Whoa, that's what I call a reversal of fortune. He borrowed one of Dupuys's men and returned to base and filled up the back of the CUCV with cartons of MREs and bottled water and drove back to the station and kept a carton of each for Margarete and unloaded the rest for the prisoners. The rules of the game, he told Major Dupuys. Unless you want me breathing down your neck night and day, I have to be able to trust you. You can trust me for three days, said Dupuys. Then I am letting them go.

He drove over to the cathedral and found Margarete sitting listlessly on the front step of the bungalow, watching her son playing in the yard with a stick and an empty plastic water bottle. She shyly redirected her attention to Burnette's approach, her face warming, the apathy erased, when he told her he had spoken to her brother Reginald and explained the transfer and the prospect for his imminent release. Here's food and water, he said, bringing in the cartons and placing them in the kitchen area that adjoined the second room, the bedroom, a curtain hung across its doorway. Let's go shopping, he said. He asked her what she wanted to buy first and she answered shame-faced, her eyes downcast, pulling at the hem of her soiled T-shirt. *Si vous pait, monsieur.*

Burnette, he insisted.

Monsieur Burnette. A bucket, please. Soap.

We'll start there.

Excuse me, we need to bathe.

They drove to an intersection where the money changers lurked and he unsnapped the Glock 19 in his ankle holster as a precaution and whistled over one of the boys, who passed him a grimy clump of black-market *gourdes* in exchange for his crisp twenty-dollar bills. Along a street of crumbling warehouses built by the French planters out of coral and limestone blocks, they found a neglected arcade with a dry-goods store and bought those few things she desired and more, a washcloth and a towel and a comb, toilet paper and a box of Kotex and toothbrushes; he bought her a cheap wallet and a purse to hold the cash he planned to give her. The boy stood mesmerized but selfless, not really like a boy at all, until Burnette asked if he would like something and his mother said, He would like books, please. To write in or to read? said Burnette. Can he read? Both, Margarete said. And a pencil. What about a box of those marbles over there? he asked the kid, and for the first time was rewarded with the daybreak flash of a smile. Then he said, You need clothes, yes?

In the *marché*, as they wandered from stall to stall, she picked through the bins of secondhand giveaways—the charity of humanitarian collection from faraway worlds, purchased by the ton by a network of middlemen and shipped to merchants in places like this—she held a dress or a skirt or a blouse to her body, this sensual tableau of public intimacy like a gentle step toward partnership, pausing, lifting, spreading the fabric over her breasts or hips, tentatively soliciting his approval, her chestnut eyes sparkling when he gave it. They filled a handled plastic bag for her, and another for the boy, and then found stiff pairs of Taiwanese running shoes for both of them. At the farmer's market Burnette had to leave when it became obvious that his presence inflated the price of everything and he sat outside at a two-stool kiosk, drinking a beer, until she and the boy appeared with their sacks of provisions, rice and flour and cornmeal and oil and spices and cassava and mangoes and, because there was no refrigeration at the bungalow, no other fresh meat than a plucked chicken, tonight's dinner and tomorrow's lunch and tomorrow's dinner.

Day by day he watched their purloined spirits revive, the shine of livable life return to their faces, their hearts less silent, opening to this new beginning. If he had wanted anything from her maybe he would have acted differently, maybe he would have felt some discomfort behind his actions, or the opposite, a sense of ownership; it could have gone either way, it could have become emotionally confusing, something less than straightforward, especially after her brother moved in with them in the bungalow, but it hadn't, because he wanted nothing from Margarete except her permission to let him help. She had to submit to him, the patron, the benefactor, in that way only, to collude in the availability of his goodness without reflecting back indebtedness or judgment, because it wouldn't have worked any other way than that way, their tacit agreement to just let it be.

He went to say good-bye the morning he was recalled to Port-au-Prince but couldn't find them in the time he had—the boy was in school, the brother somewhere on patrol in the city with the HNP, Margarete was wherever she was. At the rectory, the bishop himself poked his august head out from behind his office door, curious to have a visitor, sending a look toward the old woman at her desk, a more beatific version of a facial message Burnette knew all to well, *Glory be, a white man. Get his money.* Precisely why he had come, still toting around a fistful of cash, and he paid the rent for the bungalow for the next nine months—it wasn't much by home-front standards—and he made the self-important crone promise to tell Margarete he would stay in touch, however unlikely that seemed at the time. Very well, *monsieur,* said the bishop's secretary, her eyes round with skepticism, as she counted the bills a second time. *Bon,* she said tartly, looking up from her desk to mock him. *Au revoir.*

He was dreaming and he was waking and he kept his eyes closed until the final image of the dream slipped away and with it its illusion of healing, the bungalow shimmering in a dazzled aqueous light floated inland from the harbor, Margarete on her stoop happy, her ordeal in the mountains no longer the single hellish force shaping her present circumstance or her son's future, dressed in a sleeveless shift, canary yellow with a print of sunflowers, the color striking against the mahogany sheen of her bare arms, her nails a sexy red, her hair fastidiously cornrowed, her white teeth perfect between the swell of her lips; the boy on his bike out front in the street, pedaling hard with a look of orgasmic determination, other boys on foot chasing him with the same look of determination but less sublime, shouting, *My turn! My turn!* Between him and the woman, there is a fluency they never could manage, but now they have a conversation that is more than a conversation and Margarete's side of it seems to go like this:

When you were always a loser there was never any side to pick because the allegiance of a loser is worthless, and whatever seemed to hold forth the slightest possibility for survival, you attached yourself to it without questions and clung to it until, like everything else, it passed you by. She herself would never assign the indomitability of the human spirit to her actions, no more than she would ascribe a similar canine version of motives to a dog. What benefit might come from her own examination of her circumstances? She was alive, and for the living being alive and staying alive was a reflexive force that only death denied. And why would anyone choose that option when death, a tireless chooser, would work its way around to you soon enough. In the meantime, given life, there were always moments to live for.

Look, the boy is laughing, Margarete said. Come inside and I will fix you lunch.

The memories he carried of Margarete and her son were like a missal, a little black prayer book always there in his back pocket. Shit, Burnette said to himself, opening his eyes to the empty apartment in Fayetteville, I've been dreaming in Kreyol.

CHAPTER FORTY-TWO

Fort Bragg, North Carolina
0700.

Burnette stood outside the Wall, this nonplace among the pines, confronted by a singular, mind-bending catch-22, this one served forth as the army's special ops version of an unvoiced ontological riddle. He showed his ID to the sentry at the gate who shook his head nope and handed it back. St. Peter's challenge at the gates of heaven: *No authorization onto the compound without verifiable nonexistence—Kill yourself and come back.* Burnette insisted. The guard double-checked his visitors list. Sorry, go away. Burnette kept insisting until the guard phoned inside to the security desk and ten minutes later someone of unidentifiable rank strolled up and signed for him and escorted him inside and signed again and escorted him back out after his sit-down with the deputy commander and his briefest of meetings with the boorish evangelical superman, Colonel Hicks.

The second time Lieutenant Colonel McCall addressed him by his former rank, Eville had the sensation of sitting in an ejection seat, preparing for the explosive thrust that would catapult him out of this mystery tour. Are you familiar with the term deus ex machina, soldier? Har-har.

Welcome back, Master Sergeant Burnette, said Lieutenant Colonel McCall. The modest office like a guidance counselor's, and McCall himself requiring no more description than the stereotype he embodied to action-figure glam perfection, a magazine-cover SF operative, a brutally handsome

557

graying-at-the-temples brush-cut Caucasian male specimen containing a mountain of clear-eyed self-esteem, triple-X buff, squared-away in body, tightly wrapped in soul, a standard-bearer at the center of a superpower's cosmos. You could never be this man if you weren't born this man, and being born this man took centuries. He leaned over his government-issue desk and swung out his arm, gripping Eville's hand in a handshake, the squeeze a fleeting pressure, just right and nothing more, no unnecessary redundant muscle-message about his prowess, then motioned Eville toward the facing chair.

How was your Haitian vacation?

Weird, sir. Not fun in the sun.

How's that?

I guess I never felt so dispensable.

I'm thinking something like a kestrel. Alone, small, powerful. Built to strike but there's a problem. I don't know—fog, no visibility, hot winds blowing cold shit. Something like that?

Sir?

We're not sparrows or jays, right? We're hawks, falcons. I've seen eagles. I've seen pterodactyls.

Yes, sir.

Colonel Hicks encourages his men to use metaphors, said McCall, flex and stretch the gray matter, maintain cerebral agility. Think two ways at once, concrete and abstract. Embrace the binary but engage the spectrum. Yes, no. Life and death, creativity and killing. Think about it—it makes sense. Employ both sides of your brain, see the complete picture, see beyond the picture, use the Zen advantage. Have you heard of another outfit in the military that values a fucking metaphor?

No, sir.

Fucking right, Top. Show me them gobblers.

There it was, Eville told himself, the second time, *Top,* and no way on earth the LTC was making a mistake.

Yeah, so, I like what I've heard about you, Burnette, but here's the deal, said McCall, arching back in his seat and clasping his hands behind his head. Don't get me wrong. The colonel wasn't pulling the wool over your eyes or something like that. Okay? You weren't sent back to Haiti as a Title

10 operation, under the purview of DOD. You were assigned to a Title 50 operation, which meant for two months you were no longer officially DOD, and commo stays superencrypted within Agency channels, although it seems no one was explicit about that detail when they brought you in. When we lend you out to the Agency, we don't want to hear a word about what you're up to, but you probably figured that out. Am I right? Whatever you do for them is their business, not ours, unless it's ours too, if the ops are joint. Otherwise, it's their mandate, their budget, their lawyers, their scalps. Whatever blowback's coming, they own it. Anyway, the deal is, you were a captain when the powers that be needed you to be a captain, when the circumstance required an officer of rank. Anything less than a captain would have been taken as an insult by our exalted frenemies, okay. But okay, you're not a captain, Burnette, though we'll set you up on a fast track as a mustang, if that's agreeable to you. Okay? Okay. So listen.

Sir, I'm a little confused. Am I still in Delta?

Where you are is standing on a bridge. You want to go back to where you came from, get your life back as it was, okay. I can refer you over to JSOC and they'll do the deed. Or you could cross the bridge. Have you already crossed the bridge? Yes and no. You're in the middle of that bridge. The army's still the army, right? We can't just wave a wand.

Here for you, sir, said Burnette.

Fucking-A. All things are possible, said McCall. The bureaucracy can literally evaporate and we all stand around and say, *Gaw!* People tell me you're good. People tell me you belong inside the fence. That said, let me say there are no guarantees. You're going to have to go through the assessment and selection process like any other deadly dreamer. Your job is to qualify. If that happens, my job is to make all your best bad dreams come true.

Yes, sir.

Okay, Top. First things first. I have to demote you. It's a technicality. Don't think twice about it. My advice—laugh it off. When we bring you in, there's a big fade on rules and rank. But as a noncom you can't volunteer for Delta if your rank is higher than E-6. I have to bust you back a grade. It's temporary.

Yes, sir.

Good. Great. So, Sergeant Burnette. How's forty-eight hours sound? Get your affairs in order.

That won't be necessary, sir.

Wife? Kids? Gerbils?

No, sir.

You poor son of a bitch. That's what I like to hear. You're a phantom already, an outrider. All right then, the commander wants a word with you.

He was escorted down the hall to the office of Colonel Hicks, where he stood at attention waiting for the colonel to get off the phone. Then he was off the phone, scribbling intently on paperwork, speaking to the paperwork.

Burnette, you spoke with McCall?

Yes, sir.

Everything good to go?

Yes, sir. Thank you, sir.

I take it your golf buddies aren't shipping you east with that insidious heathen scumroach.

No, sir.

I don't know what the fuck is on their minds sometimes. The golf boys. You know what I should have done? I should have had you put a round in Khan's eardrum while you were down there on Devil's Island. That would have saved us a load of trouble down the road.

Yes, sir.

All right, Burnette, said Colonel Hicks. The colonel finally looked at him dead-on and his eyes turned hard and Eville knew he was being judged plainly and unapologetically as a killer, Hicks trying to gauge what Burnette figured was either there or not, and nothing he might say would ever change Hicks's opinion of what he saw in the depths of any man. The colonel picked up the phone again. God bless you, he said, stabbing a button for an outside line. This shit is like God and satan. It's place is eternity. We're going in and hell's coming with us. Go get yourself trained, son. Then get your ass back here and help me fight my holy war. We are a warrior nation.

For the next seven months he was an anomaly out on the bridge, half in and half out among a rich harvest of valedictorian ultrajocks and brainiac gunslingers. The only control he could exert over his identity came to the forefront when the instructors tried to paint him with a call sign he had resisted ever since grade school, teachers and teasing classmates alike mispronouncing his given name, his mother picking him up at school when he was sent home for fighting. It's all right, Ev, she would console him. No damn vowel will ever make you Evil, so don't be silly. You're Eville, short *e*, like Mount Everest, that's what you tell people, and it's a proud American name, your great-grandfather's name, and you have my permission to sock anyone in the nose who thinks it's okay to insult our family. Roger that, said the instructors, acknowledging the can of worms. Harassment and bullying were anathema inside the fence, no buffoons in animal skins, no flat-headed drill instructor sadists; even the twenty-something junior recruits displayed a level of maturity that came across as some strange generational defect of perfection, the selection process designed to create a force about as diverse as an Amish picnic.

How's Burn One? That work for you? Everyone had to have a nickname, too, but after his classmates saw how the call sign incident had ruffled his feathers, they took the easy way around this one sensitivity and let him be what he was thankful to be, *Montana,* and later, when his buds had a closer look into his life, *Scout.*

For a D-boy, free thinking and creativity abounded within the confines of how to find someone and kill him. That's what Delta did. That was all that Delta did. Back inside the Wall at 0700 that first morning he was grateful, too, to be a busy man again, quickly immersed into an all-consuming training curriculum. Through May, June, and July the program was keen on honing marksmanship skills, that talent brought with him from his boyhood that had allowed him to evolve into an ace weapons specialist in the Green Berets. One day in June, right after the Khobar Towers bombing in Saudi Arabia, the top instructor approached him and said, Montana, I'm making you my pet sniper trainee. You will leave here with a PhD in ticket-punching. You good with that? and he was, his nascent but still amorphous identity as a government-certified assassin snapping into focus by several more degrees, as did the larger panoramic focus of eventual targets, an expanded view provided by the smithereened deaths of nineteen of his fellow servicemen, out in the godforsaken alcohol-free, woman-bashing Arabian desert.

They taught him the hoodlum trades, how to crack safes and steal cars and break into just about anything locked down or up. They taught him the pyro-art of demolition, how to build an esoteric variety of bombs and how to blow them up in a variety of enjoyable ways, some spectacular and ear-splitting and others percussively hushed and eerily musical. They taught him the spook skill sets, the range of tradecraft essential to the universal rhythms and textures of espionage, the second oldest profession. An instructor from the Secret Service dropped in one week to impart his knowledge of executive protection, the bodyguard business and its counterintuitive appeal, the Lord calling you to take a bullet for a pinstriper who would never take a bullet for you. When he wasn't majoring in counterterrorism, Delta's raison d'être, he was cross-training as a medic, cross-training in cutting-edge communications, taking language classes over at the Schoolhouse, going back to the apartment most nights with a briefcase full of manuals, falling asleep in the recliner with homework in his lap, his wristwatch waking him at 0500 for a six-mile run. He had quit his pack-a-day only to replace cigarettes with an hourly dip of Copenhagen, one of the three ingredients behind the blend of smell inside the Wall: minty spit, whiskey sweat, and cordite.

Then, deep in the regimen's warrior-zone and not welcoming the inter-lude, in August he was summoned once again by the Friends of Golf for another walk-and-talk, this time to Virginia.

International Town and Country Club, August, 1996

They were on the back nine, Eville Burnette patrolling the sloped shore of a small green lake pressed down glassy smooth against the contours of the rising Piedmont, the fairway behind him flanked by magnificent groves of old-growth hardwoods, oaks and ashes and maples, hickory and walnut, the greenery wilted by the heat and muggy air that carried the moulder-ing cut-grass smell of deep summer sweetened by honeysuckle. With lazy futility he waved at the cloud of gnats in front of his face and scanned the shallows of the jade-colored water, wishing for his fly rod. The lake looked clean and came fresh and slightly cool into his nostrils and, suspended out over the drop-off, Eville could discern the long tapered shadows of a pair of dinner-sized fish.

He had lived in Carolina long enough to foster an appreciation for the pleasure of a large-mouth bass rising to the fight, a true satisfaction but nothing like the thrashing good fight of the native cutthroats or ten-pound rainbows that launched up out of the depths of his parents' lost world, his mother and father out on the crystal flow of those Montana rivers in his father's homemade wooden dory, the three bare-chested little kids, the brothers, high-siding in the bow. A wild brand of happiness only available in the West, uncensored and unregulated. His mother had taught her boys how to fly-cast but Dawson himself had been a meat fisherman, a man who preferred a baited hook held fast to the pebbled bottom by a wad of lead, and as an angler and as a soldier, he scorned the modern and so-called enlightened practice of catch and release. Whatever you beat needs to stay beaten, he liked to tell his sons.

He was developing some kind of dreamy feeling for this course, its swaths of antebellum forests, rolling vistas of the confederacy, Manassas just up the road, Winchester not far to the west, the old battlefields echoing in his imagination with the thunder of cannonades and the fearless charge of cavalry, sabers clanging like blacksmith hammers. Everything absorbed by his senses, here under the hazy white sun of Fairfax County, every mote of scent, every pitch of sound, reminded him of a beautiful pain within his rib cage, the tender hurt that was always there inside, mostly quiet, when you loved your country as much as Eville Burnette loved America. It wasn't a matter of being raised a certain way, although he was. It was a matter of gratitude, the thing that you were called upon to feel if you ever hoped to be a decent man, or a soldier.

Off at the end of the lake he watched Ben set his stance for his second shot and swing and he had to admit he was growing to love this moment as well, watching the liftoff of the balls soaring to their apogee, something in his spirit flying up with them. Then, coming toward him down the bank, he heard the crunching approach of footsteps on the patchy red clay and an exasperated release of breath. The undersecretary seemed unusually agitated today, excited but prickly.

What's the verdict, Ev? Did it roll in?

No, sir, said Burnette, unshouldering the bag of clubs. Calling his daughter Jackie was one thing but he could not bring himself around to the winking assininity of addressing Steven Chambers as Arnie. It just felt awkward, and the operational logic wasn't justified, at least when Burnette had been on the scene.

I mean, yes, sir, he corrected himself. It's in the water, but I don't think it rolled. See, he pointed as Chambers stopped next to him. It's there about four feet out.

Okay. Fuck.

What would you like me to do?

Ev, I want you to be open to your own potential.

You're talking Haiti, sir?

I'm talking your potential. Forget about Haiti. Haiti made you unhappy.

Yes, sir. I don't much like being on the wrong side of things.

Don't overthink it, Ev. Sometimes the right side of things doesn't feel much better. Let that second-guessing go. I'm going to put you in a stronger position for fixing what ails you. Something hands-on and out front. You ready for that?

Yes, sir. Thank you.

Now, would you mind terribly? Can I ask you to wade out there and get my ball?

Burnette bent over to untie his running shoes. Above them on the knoll of the fairway, the thwack and the shout—not *Fore!* but some foreign word clearly meant as a warning—arrived a second before the ball cleared Eville's head by inches, whistling past to splash twenty yards out into the lake. The golfer, today's exotic rotating fourth, flapped his arms in a dismissive manner that seemed to say, *Calm down, children,* and barked out an apology in broken English. His name was Drako or Draco something and he had been there waiting for them after the first nine holes, sitting in a black SUV with USG tags parked in front of the pro shop. All Burnette knew about the guy after a couple holes was that he was an officer in the Croatian army, some updated version of hypermuscled Ostrogoth from the Balkans, dressed in black paratrooper pants and jump boots and a taut black T-shirt that made his chest look like a gorilla's. Beetle-browed, shaven-skulled, small ears, blunt nose, frosty blue eyes, he could have been a prototype for the chain mail and broadsword crusader, not the prince but one of the lesser-born knights, in a video game popular with the troops down at Bragg, and, despite his intimidating brawn, or perhaps precisely because of his ridiculous strength, the worst duffer imaginable. Burnette had him sighted as a special forces nut job from a part of the planet that excelled in nut jobs, and it was anybody's guess, exempting the three gentlemen out here who knew everything there was to know, what he was doing in Virginia.

Now there's a fucking maniac, said the undersecretary, gazing up the hill at this fellow. Ev, I think you're going to find working with this guy interesting.

Draco Vasich was a colonel in the intelligence division of the Croatian military and apparently an associate or asset or perhaps just a friend of Steven Chambers. Their familiarity, their chummy interaction, had made Burnette begin to ponder the undersecretary's thought process and decision making, his impulse toward matchups. Maybe he was only imagining it, but he thought he could discern an emergent pattern—Dawson's son Eville, Chambers's own daughter, this guy Vasich—in the way the undersecretary chose his minions, built his secret family, his inner circle of Knights Templar, as if he nursed an intention to influence events by personalizing them, a determination to shorten the distance, the degrees of separation, between the action and his control of the action, the better to move the world in a direction he believed to be preordained. There was something cultish about it, something in the air that smacked of the royal point of view or, conversely, the mob boss, something that both engendered genuine loyalty and corrupted it with an inflexible form of obligation. But Burnette didn't know enough yet to be able to visualize FOG's extended family portrait, whether only a chosen few fit in the frame or the edges of its ranks blurred into infinity.

Everyone waited for Colonel Vasich to reach the green. Ev, tending the pin, heard Ben asking the colonel as he walked up if he had seen the latest fatwa from the sheik.

Hey, it was pretty good, I thought, quipped Sammy. Did our people consult on the language?

War declared. All over the front page.

Chambers smiled. I missed it. Remember that peacenik slogan back in the sixties? What if they gave a war and nobody came? Was that a poster or a song?

What's it going to take? First Iranians, now ragheads.

Bah, said Draco Vasich. Dogs barking. One by one, we shoot.

Life can be funny, can't it, said Chambers. You know, in 1984 I met this trust fund *mujo* at one of the guest houses he was running in Peshawar. He came from a family of contractors, builders. Khan introduced us—he wasn't a colonel in those days. The three of us had tea, the drink of *mujo* bullshit. This contractor sheik wasn't a warrior, he was never a warrior, his Afghan Arabs were clowns, the real mujahideen laughed at them. He was nothing more than a tour operator, this sheik, for all the punks across the Muslim world whose own countries couldn't get rid of them fast enough. But what I want to say is this, the pretender and I shared a vision, we were brothers in this respect. We converged, biblically speaking. We could see the future, and we did not see it differently. How many years ago was that? It's taken more time than I expected, but in the interim they have not been idle, have they? In the fatwa he said, *There is nothing between us that needs to be explained.* He's right about that, isn't he?

Ben said, They're opening the door for Christ.

Look at Bosnia, said Sammy. Am I right, Colonel? You try to be generous, be reasonable, be humane, overlook the negatives, and what happens? In pour the caliphaters from every corner of the globe.

Burnette's epiphany that day seemed, in retrospect, to be as lackluster as any platitude, its truth bleached out by the overwashing of its own consistency, that sometimes the interconnected spin of humanity revealed the axis of its rotation in the most pedestrian scenes, the fate of societies left in the hands of a few men playing a round of golf, a few men drinking chai in caves, hatching both sides of the same eternal plot, reversible good versus reversible evil, and God's way both ways, which was why, he had to suppose, God was a fucking mystery floating out there far beyond the binary.

Cowboys and Muslims, gentlemen, said Ben, grinning at Burnette and Vasich. Mount up.

CHAPTER FORTY-THREE

Camp Dawson, West Virginia

One rainy morning at the beginning of September, as a tropical depression scoured the Outer Banks and pushed inland to wring itself out on the Piedmont, he packed his full combat kit and his rucksack and stuffed everything in the cab of the truck and was on the road north by early afternoon to Camp Dawson in the mountains of West Virginia. Now came his chance and probably the only one he would ever get to prove himself in the crucible of ultimate manhood, born into a new life where you would be forever known for being unknown, defined by silence and exalted for the mystical self-restraint that made killing an honorable, even noble, profession, an almost spiritual task never to be confused with the chaos and random slaughter of a battlefield. A Jedi knight, tier-one warrior, like the hammerheads on Seal Team Six, Delta's waterborne counterparts, or Israel's Sayeret Matkal, France's GIGN, the British SAS, the neurosurgeons of state-sanctioned death.

Staring through the rain, though, Burnette began to brood, and as he drove he searched his heart for the answer he didn't have—How much do I want this?—and his heart kept referring him to his father and his grandfathers. As the miles accumulated in his rearview mirror and the sun broke through the overcast right on time for setting, he tried to command his brain into the zone but the effort only increased his anxiety.

The scuttlebutt had been anything but reassuring. Two guys he knew from Seventh Group, both triathletes and Iron Man contenders, had crashed

567

and burned somewhere near the end of last season's selection during their loaded-up forty-mile march through hellish terrain. Equally unsettling were the rumors Burnette had heard about the psych evaluations and follow-up interviews. Although you didn't have to submit yourself, as did Agency recruits, to a lifestyles polygraph, also known as the when-was-last-the-time-you-sucked-dick detector test, you were made to endure the excavation of all the emotional crap inside that you never wanted to mess with, as you underwent the Wonderlic Personnel (how close to knuckle-dragging is your IQ), the Jackson Personality Test, and the Minnesota Multifacet Personality Inventory (an in-depth personality battery, every question a variation on the theme of bed-wetting), the soft-science dicing of your id and ego then handed over to a series of personal interviews where bad things regularly happened to pretty good people if you somehow managed to piss off a member of the interviewing board. On the menu of self-inflicted wounds, the number one culprit was often described to Burnette as arrogance, one of those things visible to everyone but the arrogant themselves. Burnette had heard an anecdote from a captain friend of his, who had inadvertently expressed his hubris and a sergeant major from the unit showed him the door, just like that. I don't like his attitude, the sergeant major explained to the other taut-faced members of the board. He's finished, and he was, because if you're that fucking outstanding, keep it to yourself.

For Eville, that finished feeling, absolute and undeniable, came a few hours before his completion of the physical assessment's final exam when, in the starless deep-woods void before dawn he tripped over some root or vine at the top of a ravine and tumbled thirty feet down ass-backward until his rucksack snagged in an outcropping, his sudden arrest remarked upon by a vertebrae's dull pop in his lower back. And still, even though he knew he was out, crossing the finish line a half-dead and defeated man and immediately sent to the clinic for an IV and a gulping handful of ibuprofen tablets, none of the instructors seemed in a terrible hurry to cut him loose. Instead, they sent him trotting to another building to be tortured for a week straight by a humorless tribe of shrinkoids. *What's your favorite flavor of ice cream? How does it make you feel? Rate your anger on a scale of one to five, five being a raging white-hot desire to kill a homo.*

The first 3 a.m. session started off on sound footing, despite his groggi-ness and fatigue and a spasm like a wooden stake pounded into the base of his spine, the three-man board lobbing softball questions about operating procedures and techniques, quizzing him on the culture of operational security and his temperament for anonymity—*Consider yourself exhumed from the tomb of nameless souls at Arlington, and nameless you shall remain.* And then one of the D-boy evaluators said, Tell us about Haiti, and Burnette hesitated perhaps a second too long, tangled up by his two very disparate deployments, until his interrogator straightened his back and his face grew pinched and inquisitorial—You have nothing to say?—and Burnette began talking about the mission with as much tonal upbeat as he could fake, until another guy on the panel interrupted.

We're not interested in winning hearts and minds, said the panelist. For our guys, hearts and minds are targets. We shoot hearts and minds. Without notification. Any reason you can think of why we shouldn't do that, or why you couldn't do that? A religious reason? Are you squeamish? Are you walking around with a guilty conscience for blowing away your first squirrel? Do you think it's evil to assassinate someone who wants to destroy America, slay our children? You have two brothers, correct? Sup-pose one of them hijacks a jetliner full of passengers and threatens to blow it up? Could you take your brother down?

Five *nos* and one, *I don't know.*

For the record, nobody's going to ask you to shoot your brother. I'd shoot your brother. But suppose you were the only one there standing between the death of every innocent person on that plane and whacking your brother?

Okay, I'd whack my brother.

But you'd feel bad about it, right?

Yes.

All right, psycho-killer. Your brother's dead, you took him out. Then what?

Honestly, at that point I think I would say I had done enough and it was time to go fishing.

More than most people would get off their ass to do for their country, right?

I can't speak for most people, sir.

But you'd hold it against them, right? That's natural. They might just hold it against you too. Fratricide. Summary execution.

Yes. Maybe. Not the passengers and not the crew. Not their families. No, sir.

The evaluator who had yet to speak now chose to speak. Why are you here, Sergeant Burnette? he asked, his voice artificially genial, nonthreatening, obviously meant to conceal the bait, the trap, the coup de grâce.

Sir?

Your presence here puzzles me. There's the cart-before-the-horse factor—for the last three months, you're down there inside the Wall. Are you the prom queen or something, training behind the fence before selection? Some new brand of hot shit? You seem to have friends in high places.

Honestly, my friends mostly stick to the low places, sir.

I hear your father served in Vietnam, is that correct?

Yes, sir.

Was your father one of these crybaby 'Nam vets? Nobody appreciates us, nobody understands us?

The interview was meant to push him over the edge, he was aware of that, on guard for that, but the master sergeant had, with malice, fully awakened the one sure emotion in Burnette with the power to render him a murderous animal. He struggled for self-control, the muscles in his jaw flexing and his metabolism, strangely, appropriately, absorbing the sniper training leaked into his circulatory system. His heart rate and breathing slowed to a rhythm that became a coiling focus. The countenance of the other panelists made clear that they knew exactly what they were seeing, had seen this throughout their lives in uniform, this facedown between two modern-day triceratops at the prehistoric watering hole. The tension seemed to flashburn the oxygen out of the windowless room and the silence began to build until it roared like a tornado.

Stay cool, warned one of the board members but two words alone, regardless of their worthiness, were not enough to break the spell. The panelist tried again. Burnette, he said levelly, I want to hear you.

Yes, sir, said Burnette. His voice was barely audible and he was finished, he knew it. Speaking, interviewing—finished, done, toast.

Burnette, talk to me.

Sir. What would you like me to say? There's nothing to say.

That might be true. Let's work this out, the interviewer said, yet nobody volunteered another word and he began gathering up the documents he had removed from Burnette's dossier. Overcome by the futility, Eville found himself willing to forfeit everything he had not already lost for the sake of his father's honor.

I only want to say, Burnette said. You need to tie me into this chair.

The master sergeant's voice bristled. Excuse me?

You know what I'm saying.

Yeah, I know what you're saying, said the board member who had been trying to settle him down. I'd just like to know when you walk out of here, will you regret what you're saying.

No regrets, said Burnette, and that was that. The board members exited the room and left him there to contemplate his fate, a castoff sitting alone on shore as his ship sails away, struggling to remain upright under the awful downhearted weight of his tremendous weariness, his eyelids one blinking iteration away from being out of commission, and then the door swung open and Colonel Hicks was in the room, his evangelical joviality as offensive as the master sergeant's insinuations.

God led me into Delta Force, and He said to me, This is where you ought to be.

CHAPTER FORTY-FOUR

Fort Bragg, North Carolina; Missoula, Montana

October was more of the same back inside the exclusive domain of the Wall, Burnette training intensively, ingesting forty-unit bottles of Motrin by the week, rehearsing with a four-man assault team, fast-roping out of choppers or kicking in doors. There were multiple Lone Ranger and Tonto sessions with his long rifle and spotter, the arduous calculations of wind and elevation, dialing the scope and acquiring aim, yogic breathing and visualization, squeezing off hundreds of rounds. There was the daily language instruction, a class in fear management that made him feel bored, a continuing class in biometric data collection and, almost like recess, a Schoolhouse course in the history of Islamic fundamentalism, Burnette avidly consuming the assigned texts with a microwaved dinner back in his apartment at night. The notion of any ingrained, innate conflict between civilizations, between the Orient and the West, one of the authors argued, was a specious myth. What should we call it then, Burnette asked himself, when we turn on the TV and see Muslim wankers chanting, *Death to America,* and, *We hate your guts?* What was the proper response, the inborn response. *We love you?*

Reading accounts of the Gulf War brought to mind a diatribe of Steven Chambers, one of the more adamant voices from State who had lobbied against regime change in Baghdad. *What in God's name were we doing in Iraq? Saddam killed a million Iranians for us. He should have kept going, right through Kuwait to the peninsula. Muslims killing Muslims, my God, that was the beauty of Afghanistan after the Soviets left. All those weapons we gave the* mujos, *they turned on themselves. Abdul Hatfield and Abdul McCoy.* The last items on his reading list were a pair of manuscripts commissioned by the US Marine Corps, the first a collection of interviews with the Russian generals who had been humiliated in Afghanistan, the second a similar collection of parallel interviews with the victorious holy warriors who had handed the Soviets their ass.

Then in November he disappeared for three days, partnered with a lanky thatch-haired D-boy from Kansas everyone called Scarecrow, the two of them flying to Dulles and driving over to an office building in Tysons Corner where the Agency had established a working group on the fifth floor called Alec Station, a subsection of the counterterrorist center down the road at Langley. Alec Station's specialty was unearthing financial links between guys with banks and charities and guys with guns and bombs but it seemed to be giving all its love to just one person, a messianic war-declaring sheik hunkered down in Afghanistan. There was an odd duck posted at the station, a lone Bureau agent from New York sent to Virginia to check out the intelligence the Agency had collected on this obscure network of Islamic radicals. The Bureau agent and two US attorneys had just returned from Germany, where for two weeks they had interrogated an Islamic turncoat, an informer from Sudan with close ties to the Saudi financier and mastermind.

Division heads and subs were more inclined to pass around their wives than share their databases, but the command at Delta wasn't going to stand out in the cold while other people masticated the information that might one day get a D-boy his horse-drawn caisson and cortege at Arlington. And so Burnette and Scarecrow were directed to pay Alec Station a quiet visit and find out what they could to keep trigger pullers in the loop. Burnette had not been quite clear on the nature of the mission, but when he finally put it all together, he told himself, Okay, the colonel and FOG, the Cassandras of Western civilization, were way out in front on this.

In Germany, photographs had been presented, identities confirmed, organizational charts sketched. A few days into the benign interrogation, the Sudanese informer mentioned the name of a network none of the Americans had ever heard of—an Arab-centric group of extremists called the Base, with training camps, lines of finance, recruiting protocols, annual budgets, sleeper cells, and even a health care plan. On their quick mission to Tysons Corner, Burnette and Scarecrow became the first American servicemen to ever speak its Arabic name, eight years after the Base's formation. They listened and took notes and returned to Bragg having glimpsed the real enemy at Alec Station, the most powerful opponent of all and the ally of all others: the status quo. The looming war that Burnette and Scarecrow saw coming down the pike was what insurance companies called a preexisting condition and nobody wanted to underwrite it in any way that might hold them to account.

Ding-a-derry, said Scarecrow, his trademark critique of screwups. Life would be so merry, if I only had a brain.

In December, without fanfare, Sergeant First Class Burnette was informed he had successfully completed his training and, as required, would now enter a six-month probation period as a D-boy. Colonel Hicks stopped by his deputy's office long enough to open the door and shout Eville's way, *Outstanding!* He was issued a pager, reminded of his twenty-four-hour on-call status and his mandate to carry a sidearm at all times, then furloughed home for Christmas, flying out of chilly Fayetteville on a sun-teased morning and landing in Missoula in a gap between late afternoon squalls, the granular snow pelting down like rice at a Viking's wedding by the time he had retrieved his gear from the baggage area and walked out into the polar bite of winter to Joaquin Zertuche's late-model Dodge Ram, the manager of his parents' ranch treating himself to a new truck every spring, the only self-indulgence Burnette knew him to have. The truck was a perquisite for running the outfit—six hundred acres, two hundred head of cattle, a cadre of seasonal employees. That, a rent-free cottage, and four weeks annual leave, two in September for his family's huge Basque jamboree in northern New Mexico, when the sheepherders would drive the flocks down out of the high country, and two midwinter weeks, when Joaquin would take his wife Deolinda to the Florida Keys.

His mother could survive without her husband and three sons, but she couldn't make it all these years of abandonment without the man she addressed as Mr. Joe.

The twenty-mile drive northeast to the Potomac Valley took forty minutes on slippery roads and then he was home again on Camas Creek, the timbered ridgelines above the hay ground and pastures scrimshaw outlines in the falling snow, the summits of the Garnet mountains whited-out by the storm. The arthritic Sweetpea, Dawson's last living English setter, greeted him at the door, burying her old snout into his crotch. His mother had a pot of hot brandied cider on the stove when they arrived, stamping the snow off their boots in the mudroom and sitting with her at the kitchen table with their hands wrapped around the steaming mugs, Bing Crosby crooning on the radio. She couldn't keep herself from sneaking sideways glances at him until he said, *Okay, what?* and she asked, Where's the spit and polish, Scout? He told her without telling her much that he'd been upgraded to a unit with relaxed grooming standards, but she knew the military too well to find this answer anything but disingenuous, and she picked at it until she got him to say more—*Mom, all I can tell you is counterterrorism.*

Omerta, she stage-whispered. Isn't that right, Mr. Joe?

Mom, come on.

You're right, she said. I'm better off not knowing, a chatterbox like me.

She stared at him with maternal regard, searching his face for deeper truths, her flat mouth offering the hint of a forlorn smile, before she said, My God, Ev, it takes my breath away sometimes, you look so much like your father. Then she seemed to buck up, swat the emotion back to its hole, coming at him again with her sly formidability. During Vietnam, you know, Dawson was in that Phoenix program, she said, a laconic reminder to her eldest son that she wasn't born yesterday, and he told her he hadn't thought about it but yeah, *something like that.* Who's the enemy this time? she asked, her voice crab-apple-tart and facetious. I swear, I didn't know we had any enemies left. That'll be the day, he told her and she sighed and said, Have I not been paying attention? He said he detected an undertone of pacifism in her voice and she said she had always been a pacifist.

You? The hell you say. Now that's a whopper.

Half a whopper, she said, pushing her chair back from the table to come stand behind him and wrap him in her slender arms. Put your coat back on, she said, her unpainted lips pecking the top of his head, shaggy by her exacting standards of masculinity. I want to show you my new mare before the sun goes down. She gave him her hand, ungloved, as they walked to the barn.

The holidays with his mother were a balm massaged into his soul, a rejuvenating quietude of snow-hushed walks up into the foothills, horse-love and dog-love, the holiday scents of fir wreathes on the stone mantel and blazing piñon (the New Mexico connection) in the fireplace, the four of them—Paige and Ev and Joaquin and Deolinda—playing canasta, then Ev reading himself to sleep each night in his boyhood feather bed, the range outside bluish with freeze and pierced by coyote lullabies, a banshee music he found more soothing than any other. For the first time since he had left to go thirty miles down the road for college, returning home was not a chore marred by restlessness or boredom or tragedy or guilt but a restoration of place and belonging, a prescription for a deeper sense of serenity than any he could remember since he had walked off into the world, exchanging one hard center of gravity for another, equally hard, but here was the pull again of the first, renewed and not unwanted, emerging from his memory. He loved Montana's mountains, as plentiful as prayers inside the mind of a preacher. But it was possible for a life to be bigger than the mountains, and for Eville the possibility channeled into the tighter outbound path walked by his father, who showed him that the things and places and people you never wanted to leave you left anyway. And then managed the regret, if you found yourself with any.

After a gluttonous ranch hand's breakfast on Christmas Eve, he followed the shadow of his longing for his father into the den, where he unlocked Dawson's antique cherrywood gun case and spent the day on the lumpy brown corduroy couch cleaning his father's collection of shotguns and hunting rifles, taking a sweet luxury of time to do it right, his mother coming to the door at lunchtime, bringing him a brisket sandwich and a bottle of beer but standing there for a moment watching him with a reluctance of sorrow, finally saying in a terse whisper, *I was wondering when you were going to do that,* then bucking up again to give him his lunch and leave him be. Telepathically, she probably experienced the same blow as Eville when she turned her back, her son suddenly bent in half, gut-shot with the pain of his God-stolen father, and she paused perhaps to steady herself to come back to him. With the sun going down he asked her about church and she said she loved the singing but it was an ordeal for her to stay up so late these days and so they remained behind while Joaquin and Deolinda risked the ice-slick roads to drive to St. Francis Xavier's for midnight mass, his mother standing a moment before the crèche on the mantel, blessing herself with the sign of the cross, saying a silent prayer before she slipped off to bed.

The idyll with his mother endured a predictable but only temporary disruption on Christmas Day when his brothers and their people turned up for dinner, his mother waking at dawn to begin slow-roasting two wild turkeys she had shot in the fall, Joaquin's wife joining her soon after the birds were stuffed and in the oven, the willowy pair of cowgirl housewives shoulder to shoulder at the chopping board and stove, like two laughing sisters encamped in the kitchen throughout the morning, their shoulder-length gray hair pinned back in wispy buns. His middle brother Wayne arrived at noon with wife and kids; Ross, Ev's youngest brother, made a chaotic entrance just as dinner was about to be served, blasted on schnapps and meth. Since Ev had last seen him he had adopted a skinhead look, wearing a hooded camouflage parka and black jeans and motorcycle boots, towing along his latest female acquisition, a wan stringy-haired retro-hippie in a calico granny's dress draped over red longjohns, sporting a nose ring. Eville, bloated with cheer, surrounded by family and friends, found it impossible to stop smiling, even as the day's tidings of comfort and joy began to dissemble with the unaccustomed challenge of being all together.

That night after his brothers had left, Wayne for his in-laws in Missoula and Ross for an all-night rocket flight back to his hidey-hole in the Yaak, his mother came to his room in her terrycloth nightgown with her hair let down to sit on the corner of his bed and talk, the starting point of the conversation a present she had not wanted him to open in front of his brothers.

It was my dad's pistol in World War Two, she said, opening an old wooden cigar box and he took the weapon, kept in an oiled rag, in his hand with reverence. I never knew you had this, he told her—spoils of war, a German Luger. They're antiques now. You sure you want to give it to me?

I do, she said, sighing with a tired wistfulness. All my life I've lived with men who thought too much about something that does not matter to me, Eville. Glory. I think it was an instinct in them. They were always humble men, and you're just like them. They found glory I guess, and maybe you will too, but I never knew them to find a use for it. But anyway, your granddad's sidearm—he carried it during the Battle of the Bulge—should go to you. I was thinking the other day, when you were a boy and I yelled at you, you listened, thought about it, sometimes you experimented with sassing back but mostly you just looked horrified and nodded like a half-pint stoic and went away and thought about what you had done wrong, or were accused of doing wrong, and then you'd come find me and apologize, even if you had decided I was wrong and you were right. Your brothers only seemed to know how to yell right back at me, and Dawson would chase them all over the ranch to catch and spank them. Remember?

Ev, I came in here tonight to say I love you and to give you my daddy's pistol but I wanted to talk about the future too, if you'll allow that, and I'll start by telling you my health is fine, so that's not the issue, understood? But I've been thinking a lot about the ranch, she continued. Maybe I should sell it, maybe to Mr. Joe and Deolinda or maybe to another true soul who'll work it but not to Wayne or his crowd, who'd break it up into ranchettes to make an easy fortune off the shitbirds. And you saw for yourself, Ross is out of the question. He'd trade the whole spread for a month's worth of getting high. What if one of my fool horses throws me someday and I break my damn fool neck? Then the three of you would have to work it out, and I don't like to picture that one bit. You want to say something?

No, Mom, he said, although he was thinking that it had never crossed his mind that he was the good son, and that his brothers were not, for whatever reason. He was the absent one, they were nearby, on call, should they be needed. No, he said, you just say what you want to say.

Well then, I'll ask you, she said. How much time do you have left? In the army?

I'm committed to three more years. After that, I can't say.

Do you imagine you'd ever want to return? Here, I mean. To the ranch.
Just like Dawson, he said. I would.
You don't want to ponder on it some more?
Nope.
Your brothers will get some money. One doesn't need it, the other
needs to burn through it.
Whatever you want. It's your place. It's your money.
We understand each other?
We always have.
Merry Christmas, Ev.

The week between Christmas and New Year's advanced at the same luxurious pace as his first week home, the bracing freedoms indulged in mod-
eration by the fine laziness of books, coffee talks at the breakfast table,
helping his mother tend her stable of Appaloosas or riding snowmobiles
with Joaquin to drop feed for the herd, solitary walks toward the Camas
or up into Ponderosas and Lodgepole pines along the ridges, Ev and his
mother on no particular schedule one afternoon when they joined in a
sentimental pawing through Dawson's desk, searching for the man in his
papers and scrapbooks, then candlelit dinners at the oak table, the warmth
and pine-glow of sheltering against the elements, sensible talk about their
country and about their world and outrageous gossip ripped with fits of
laughter, and they talked about the future too, both resigned and hopeful, on the cusp again of separation. On New Year's Eve the grand dames
spent the twilight hours holed up in their respective bathrooms—boudoirs,
said his mother—preparing themselves for the big night out, a shindig at
the American Legion hall, dinner and a dance and midnight champagne
and noisemakers in the company of Missoula's finest, lifelong friends and
lifelong adversaries, both factions the real people, in his mother's opinion,
the homegrown permanent insiders indispensable to a place's identity and
memory and sense of trueness.
    You couldn't find anyone inside the legion's steaming banquet hall who
wasn't wearing a cowboy hat and boots, Ev's a Christmas present, made
from the skin of a rattlesnake disposed of by Joaquin's shotgun. You couldn't

find a female in the herd who wasn't decked out like a Queen of the West. Every surviving member of Dawson's old posse of smoke jumpers and veterans made it his duty to stand Paige and Eville a drink, Joaquin and Deolinda feted nearby with the same wet enthusiasm by Joaquin's Korean war legionnaires, which meant they were all mutually tipsy by the time the waitresses brought the steaks and fixings to the tables. With everyone tucked into their meals, a country and western band set up on the small stage at the far end of the hall, the group fronted by a female vocalist who, by ten o'clock, began belting out her repertory of Patsy Cline. At some point his mother grabbed his hand and hauled him out of his seat.

Dance with me, Scout. I need to smell you before you go away.

Then the music stopped and the singer's voice boomed from the microphone, *Yippee yay, you all, it's 1997.* Paige kissed him and looked balefully into his eyes and whispered, *Back to soldiering, soldier boy,* and lowered her forehead against him, tapping his rib cage with the crown of her skull, almost like she was asking to be let in. The band played "Auld Lang Syne" and he was slow to recognize his mother's surreptitious jag of sobbing until he felt the wetness of her tears spotting his chest. I don't know what's wrong with me anymore, she squeaked, childlike, between muffled gasps. I can't seem to hold my liquor.

CHAPTER FORTY-FIVE

Tampa, Florida
Sarajevo, Bosnia
Cairo, Egypt
Fort Bragg, North Carolina
Nairobi, Kenya
Kirkuk, Iraq
Uzbekistan
Panjshir Valley, Afghanistan
Mojave Desert, California
Augusta, Georgia, April 1998

His orders, when he arrived back at Fort Bragg, were to pack his full
kit and proceed with due haste to Tampa and report to CENTCOM for
a weeklong series of briefings and further instructions before catching a
commercial flight to Bosnia. He would be traveling under his real name as a
civilian defense contractor employed by an Agency shell company known
as Omega Systems. He would also carry two passports, blue and brown, the
blue one ready to hand over in an emergency so he would not end up facedown on the tarmac with his head blown off by a hijacker. A level below the
cover was his official mission, documented and classified, to assist NATO
operations in the capture of war criminals. Ride the elevator down to the
deepest level of the operational shaft and the mission went entirely black.

BOB SHACOCHIS

At MacDill Air Force Base, inside the offices of SOCCENT, Burnette was introduced to a major and his working group tasked with compiling a jihadi database, an intelligence mother-net of personalities, finances, and logistics that could be cross-referenced and matrixed with other servers and inputs. Burnette was provided with a Sony still camera that could burst digital pictures into the system by satellite, then given a block of instruction on how to access the biometric database resident on servers in Tampa. They sat him down in front of a screen for a day to familiarize himself with the list of high-value targets that might be out there with their camels and scimitars wreaking havoc in the Balkans. He was made to memorize the top-five high-value capture/kill targets, names and faces, and download to his computer another longer catch-and-release list of suspects whose activities had yet to come into focus. He watched films captured from AQ operatives and Chechens, recording the torture and murder of prisoners of war in Bosnia and Chechnya, scenarios and images of unadulterated horror twisting in his intestines that prompted him to recall the SERE class back at Bragg, the Kennedy School instructors warming up the trainees to the possibility of being beheaded on international television.

During his last intensive morning with the task force, something happened that he knew to expect but it had never happened before—his twenty-four-hour pager went off, buzzing like a June bug on his belt. Hey, that's a first, he said sheepishly to the guys in the room, who seemed to be waiting for him to dash to the bathroom and reemerge as some comic book superhero. Burnette excused himself off to the side and stared at the pager, which flashed with the number of his own cell phone, which he retrieved from his briefcase and activated and up popped the novelty of a message in text. *Your attendance requested. Tonight, 1945 hrs,* and then a street address in Ybor City, and the sign off, *Arnie.*

Can Chambers hack my pager? Burnette asked himself, feeling naive.

The SOCCENT guys called in pizza for lunch and he worked straight through with the group until the end of the day, when the major shook his hand and said, That's it, Sergeant Burnette. You are now switched on, and gave him a mini-dictionary in Serbo-Croat as a going-away present. At 7:15 he took a cab up along Hillsborough Bay through downtown Tampa and

582

over to the historic, gentrified neighborhood of Ybor City, where the driver let him off at the bottom of Seventh Avenue, the nightclub and entertainment district closed to traffic. He joined the happy flow of Friday night, the prosperous mob heading to the bars and restaurants, tracking the numbers on the buildings until he found an old brick cigar factory, restored to house a cooperative of artist studios and galleries. Okay, Burnette said to himself, stepping through the main entrance, now what? The answer was announced by a placard displayed on an easel outside the plate glass front of a well-lit gallery.

Meet The Artist
Voodoo Spirits: The Houngan Priests of Haiti
Photographs by Renee Gardner
Exhibit Opening: Tonight, 8, wine and cheese

He peered through the window at the row of black-and-white photos mounted on the wall, waist-up and head shots boldly enlarged to life-sized scale, darkly luminous portraits of Haitians at some stage of ecstatic derangement, and he looked at the three people visible inside the gallery, two women and a man setting up a refreshment table, fussing over snack trays and uncorking bottles, and he looked at his wristwatch—1950, five minutes late or ten minutes early—and tried the door but it was locked. The people inside looked his way and one of the women smiled and came to let him in and he could hear the gunshots of her stiletto heels striking the polished wood flooring and he thought whoever she was—in that little black dress, its décolletage cut to showcase volcanic breasts, the dangle of diamond earrings matched by the toothy sparkle of her lipstick smile, the pixie-cut auburn hair à la Audrey Hepburn, her beauty earthbound but her glamour stratospheric—she could not possibly be the photographer, the so-called artist. Owner, patron, celebrity screw-on hood ornament—anybody but somebody who crawled in the dirt of the peristyle with the *lwas*.

As she approached the door she held out an arm, enticing him with a set of keys. He noticed her bracelet of eyes, the three rows of dark blue beads, but the glass cuff didn't register in a memory that rarely cataloged or valued jewelry. She inserted the key into the lock. The door opened inward and she held it, posing. He stared at her and he stared at her, straining to see what he wasn't seeing but sensed he should, and she returned his stare with an audacious lack of guile. Then she stepped forward in an envelope of knee-weakening fragrance and kissed him on the cheek.

Hello, Eville. Thanks for coming.

He sputtered something inarticulate, and she winked and said, Come on, come in.

He stared even harder.

She raised a plucked eyebrow and said, Maybe it's the boob job?

Dottie? Dottie Chambers?

Renee Gardner, she drawled, holding out her hand. A pleasure, she said, and offered to guide him through a quick private tour of her work before the public arrived.

On Saturday's transatlantic flight he tried to read one of the books his mother had given him for Christmas, a collection of Twain's writing from *Innocents Abroad,* and he put on his headset and tried to watch the movie being shown, and he tried memorizing some sentences in Serbo-Croatian, and he tried sleeping, but whatever he tried to do to pass the time in a peaceful and ordinary manner, there was Dottie galloping into his thoughts. He couldn't get far past the truth that this version of Dottie—her metamorphosis into Renee Gardner—had reeled him in. In less than fifteen minutes. By the time he left the gallery he was enchanted and, much, much worse, he was jealous, both fairly reliable signs that she had invented effective new ways to drive him crazy. He had stood in front of her photographs in awe.

Did you really take these pictures? he had to ask, and she spoke to him in a lowered voice from that moment on, establishing the confidentiality that made room for her to play her repertoire of personas simultaneously, until the gallery filled with people and she was Renee, completed, invincible, and perfect.

Tell me the truth, she said, and he noticed her eyes were a bit too incandescent and her voice became sweetly southern but manic the longer she talked. What was your opinion of me?

Unformed, he said, and she laughed at the lie.

You thought I was just fucking around. The camera was a prop, right. Like I was in my own little action movie or my own little spy novel, entertaining myself, pretending to be a photographer. There are one hundred photojournalists covering the story, the war, the invasion, whatever, and only one who's not real, and that was me—except I *was* real.

Hey, he said, leaning to speak in her ear, are you high?

Yes! she said with gleeful disregard. I'll tell you more about that in a minute.

They shifted their position to the next photograph and he asked her why he was here and her expression fielded the question like a small wound and she said because you're my partner. Then she told him her secret, parts of it, and he asked, Why are you telling me this?

Well, who else can I tell? she said. I knew you were in town and I know you're leaving tomorrow and I wanted you to come to my opening, I really did. But listen, Ev, I'm serious now. This isn't Daddy talking.

Who's talking? he asked tersely.

I know you hated Jackie Scott. And I hope you never get to know poor little cokehead scag Renee Gardner. This is Dottie talking. I need to know you'll come rescue me if something goes wrong.

When are you going back down? he asked.

I don't know. Soon, I hope. It depends if I'm lucky in love, she said, her eyes darting toward the door, unlocked and opened and the gallery owner greeting people. Renee took Ev's hand and it seemed she had no intention of ever releasing it as she drew him ahead into the space of the next portrait. Remember this lovely old man? she asked.

Eville studied the portrait, the background darkness of the world and the darkness of human flesh, both incipient and corpselike and natural and animated, interrupted by the diabolic and overpowering radiance of the subject's eyes.

The guy from Grande-Rivière-du-Nord, said Eville.

Right, she said. The *empereur*. Isn't he beautiful? He died four days after I took this photograph. Nothing nefarious, he was just old and sick. There's a new *empereur* now up there, Honore Vincent, and I'm afraid he doesn't think very well of me. And by the way, you've heard about the interim commander of the police, Major Dupuys? He was recalled to Port-au-Prince.

I didn't realize he was interim.

There's a new chief. You haven't heard? It's Ti Phillipe.

They moved to the next photograph and he made the observation that although she did not seem inclined to let go of his hand, he would not run away if she did, and she said, You're not surprised?

About Phillipe? he said. No, in a country where nothing makes sense, what makes the most sense is being an opportunist. When did you say you were going back?

Soon. Back and forth.

Do you think you'll be going up to Le Cap? he asked. I need you to check on somebody for me. Her name's Margarete. Margarete Estime.

Definitely, she said. Done.

There were perhaps two dozen people in the gallery now and even as they talked she could not keep herself from watching the door and then he saw by the way her eyes jumped back to hide with his, underscored by an excited if unconscious lock on his hand, that whoever she was expecting was there and she preempted his natural curiosity as he began to pivot.

Don't look, she said. Wait a minute.

Who is it?

There were two guys, she said, easy to spot, sunglasses and gold chains and Hawaiian shirts and linen pants, not the type of guys you'd think would come to gallery openings. One was a nickel-and-dime dealer to the college student/office worker crowd, who imagined himself as her boyfriend. Jackie Scott had seen the other man around in Haiti but never met him. He was a supplier, with influential friends, who was increasingly powerful himself. The dealer liked to talk to her about his friend who spent a lot of time in Haiti and she had gambled on the validity of the connection to send an innocent message. Bring him along, I'd like to meet him. Jesus, thought Eville, I should have known. Narco-traffickers, Haiti—wasn't this Sandy Coleman's case?

I explained this to you in Cap-Haïtien, she said. It's not about drugs. The drugs are something you keep staring at until you see what it's really about.

Where's this heading?

A honeymoon in Haiti would be nice.

She raised her left hand, her fingers fluttering an acknowledgment, and whispered, Here they come, and she threw her arms around him and kissed Ev hungrily and he closed his eyes and kissed her back. Then her lips were at his ear and she was saying thanks and she was saying, Go.

He opened his eyes and stepped away from her with his blood racing and said, I'm sold. How much is it again?

Which one? Renee said. She cocked her head coquettishly and looked at him with mild surprise.

The *empereur* priest.

Fifteen hundred, Renee answered with a level gaze.

What! Burnette said, genuinely taken aback.

You don't think I'm worth it?

Excuse me, one of the men behind Burnette interrupted, stepping forward to introduce himself. Honey, from the looks of it I'd say you're worth every penny.

Why, aren't you sweet, Renee cooed.

Jack Parmentier, he said. If every sale is sealed with a kiss, I'm buying them all.

Aren't you a riot, said Renee.

The sleepless gap between energies—slow and fast, passive and kinetic, Florida and the Balkans, the good son of his mother and the good son of his country—proved to be a fertile space for another invasive round of mind fornication by the daughter of Steven Chambers, his obsessive reverie of Renee Gardner, breeding in the darkness over the ocean and fading with the European dawn, the turmoil of his private thoughts as good as banished by the stricture of his mission as the plane descended through the fog into Sarajevo's airport. On the ground she was gone, out of his head, and she would stay gone throughout the following year, when he would neither see nor speak to Dottie Chambers, a year of leap-frogging around the planet for Burnette, constant travel marked by all-consuming but infrequent intervals of sudden violence, which would remain with him not as memories but as cinematic clips, shown daily against the screen of an untroubled, abstracted conscience. Even her photograph of the *empereur* would remain in the packing it was shipped in from Ybor City to Fayetteville, propped against an empty wall in his barren living room.

In Sarajevo, at a freezing safe house in the bombed-out city, an almost hallucinogenic revisitation of his grandfather's war, Eville sat at a wooden table with Colonel Vasich, who gave him a crumpled pocket notebook opened to a blank page and said, *Write for me the names*. Burnette wrote the targets and pushed the notebook back to Vasich, who scowled at the list and pronounced it junk. *The Egyptian doctor, two months, gone. The Yemeni, dead. Number three, not in Bosnia.* He proceeded to contemptuously edit the candidates. *Okay, this guy, the Iranian, he is here. The Libyan, no.* He ripped out the page and crossed the room to toss it into the smoky flames of the small fire in a large woodstove and then recaffeinate himself from the lukewarm pot, burnt-tasting although it had never boiled. *Good,* he said, *your intel is very bad. And where are the Saudis? America should eliminate Saudis. Saudis wish to kill your country. But, okay, what Kovacevic asks to do, I will do.*

Kovacevic? said Burnette, hearing the name for the first time, but Colonel Vasich only looked at him like he was a big joker and slapped him heartily on the back.

Burnette knew these things: America was at war behind the drapery of shadows and secrets, almost everybody in the government considered the very idea of the war one big fucking lunatic stunt, and he, Burnette, was himself at war but only halfway, given his countrymen's near total indifference to the conflict, which could reverse itself in a bloody second but not in his favor, should he be publicly exposed as an American who was actually fighting the war in a manner ladies and gentlemen might consider dirty and underhanded. The disconnect existed in his body like a low-grade influenza, an infection that wouldn't go away. So here he was in Bosnia, like Afghanistan a wartime proving ground for jihadis, a graduate school for slaying giants, and now a lawless haven, on a hunter-killer team with no license to kill, although Vasich operated under his own flag as an agent of vengeance, unfettered by legal niceties, free to fire away to his heart's content at his mortal enemies, the Mohammedans, the ancient Turks in all their modern incarnations.

Thirteen months later he was in the Mojave Desert, his training now specific to the harsh ecologies of Central Asia, when he was pulled off the team and put on a flight to Atlanta, connecting to Augusta, and delivered to the Friends of Golf for the second time that year. By now he found the ritual irksome, on the verge of disruptive, hauling the undersecretary's bag in a game he knew, despite the fresh air and exercise, he would never enjoy, but this time he arrived on the course in the late afternoon to find the Friends—minus one—off by themselves in hooded insulated jackets on a windblown patio, their eighteen holes long finished, drinking Irish coffees while they awaited his arrival from the other side of the nation.

Ah, Eville, said the undersecretary, standing to greet him with a slack handshake. He seemed off-kilter, mildly disoriented, and later in the conversation would mention the incident—a spell of vertigo—he had briefly experienced on the ninth hole. Sit down, will you, he said. Thanks for coming.

Where's Sammy? asked Burnette.

He's been scrubbed, said Ben.

Okay, said Burnette. How was the round?

Not the same, said Ben.

Sorry you missed it, said Chambers. I could have used you. For moral support, at least.

Ben reached into a gym bag at his feet and unzipped it and set one of the new, small, DOD-developed satellite phones on the table, which the three of them stared at for a moment until Ben explained, We're waiting for a call.

It's complicated, said Undersecretary Chambers.

Sir.

It's complicated, Chambers repeated. Trust me.

It's cockamamie, if you ask me, said Ben.

The phone began to ring and rang three times while they each looked at it and Chambers nodded for Ben to answer it and Ben said into the receiver, Hold on.

Ev, said the undersecretary, I need you to go back down to Haiti.

Okay, sir.

We have a situation. I need you to get rid of Renee Gardner.

Excuse me, we're talking about your daughter, sir?

Chambers sighed and planed the middle of his forehead, pinching and massaging a pressure point with two fingers. Yes, he said, my daughter, I need you to take care of my daughter.

Take care how?

You know what I'm saying.

Eville understood there was a game and, behind the game, very committed people practicing a level of seriousness and decision making in which nothing could be discounted. Burnette looked up at the sky and the clouds horsetailed in the sky and then back at Steven Chambers and at Ben with the phone to his ear and back at Chambers and said, Negative, sir. That's not going to happen.

Ben, said Chambers, give him the phone, and Burnette put the receiver to his ear and said, Burnette, and there was Dottie's voice saying, Eville, you promised. I need you down here.

He listened to what she had to say and hung up and looked at Chambers and Ben, their rictus smiles anchored beneath unsmiling eyes, and asked, What's Plan B? and Chambers said, We want to avoid Plan B.

CHAPTER FORTY-SIX

They streak down into Le Cap late and spooky and prepped for a firefight, no landing lights, no rum punch, and the welcoming committee is Dupuys. Eville is not even clear about his present rank so he calls him colonel and that seems to work, and there's a happy surprise, of the two men with Dupuys one is the portly Brazilian commander of the UN police training mission but the other is Margarete's brother, Reginald, who tugs at his sleeve, wants to speak in confidence, but Burnette says later, and they pile into the back of Dupuys's HiLux and drop the pilots at the darkened Christophe and drive to the safe house where Dupuys has a half-dozen guys from the palace guard dressed like ninjas, trying to pull together a hostage rescue mission, the hostages being three Brazilian police trainers and the newly appointed governor of the northern cantonment.

Burnette shakes hands and introduces the ninjas to his team. Hey, I know these men, they're squared away, my own ODA trained them after the invasion. Ti Phillipe and his force have gone rogue, grown treacherous, creating mayhem throughout the north, allying themselves with the narco-traffickers and criminal gangs like *Armée Rouge,* recruiting the old *macoutes* and accepting financing from several of the elite families to build a little rebel army of their own. The squad listens to the skinny and starts working options and Reginald's so agitated Burnette takes him outside and Reginald says, She is in danger. The woman your friend.

Renee? says Burnette.

Oui, Renee, they are going to kill her and her husband tomorrow.

Who's going to do this?

The drug people, says Reginald, foreign people, but Ti Phillipe organizes.

When? asks Burnette. Where?

Tomorrow evening, Reginald tells him, at a ceremony in Saint-Marc, and when Burnette hears that his alarm goes off, because the ceremony in Saint-Marc is where he and Renee have arranged to rendezvous and nobody knows that who isn't supposed to, and Burnette feels lashed with a sense of urgency as his Title 10 and his Title 50 begin to bust out of their little compartments and collide into one glommed-together mess of a single frenetic mission.

You know the guy, Phillipe's guy? he asks Reginald, and Reginald says there are two guys, a Mexican and a Haitian.

All right, says Burnette, we'll go to Saint-Marc tomorrow and stop them, okay? and back inside the house Burnette shakes up the planning. Listen up, he says, something has come up and I'm on a tight schedule here, so we're going over there now, to police headquarters, and bringing out those hostages. Colonel, he tells Dupuys, you got a phone here? Get on the phone and call Ti Phillipe and wake him up and tell him we're coming down there.

Who put the firebug up your ass? says Scarecrow. What happened to dawn?

You and I have somewhere else to be, Burnette tells him.

Scarecrow says, Okey-doke, but it's past midnight, you don't want to surprise these ass-clowns?

No, says Burnette. Colonel, get on the horn and tell them we're coming and we're not happy and if we see anybody point a gun at us we will drag out every last person in that station and hang them upside down in the street.

The squad kits up, strapping on body armor and headsets and night vision goggles and chambering 40mm grenades in the launchers on their MP5s and bandoliering themselves with ammo and tear gas and they cram themselves in two Toyota pickups and caravan downtown, the D-boys divided between both trucks, a most fearsome sight through the dark empty streets and they split when they're almost there so the pickups approach from opposite ends of the block, stopping near the corners and the men flowing silently into position, establishing a kill zone, Tilly and Spank setting up on a diagonal behind the Haitians so they won't be doused by the ninjas' Uzi spray, then Burnette backed by Scarecrow walks across the street toward the blacked-out headquarters and pounds on the big wooden door and steps to the side because it's hard to say what's coming.

You know what you're doing, right? Scarecrow's voice hisses in his earpiece, and Burnette says softly, Yeah, but I could be wrong, and then he shouts, Phillipe! We need to talk, and it seems he knows his man well enough, because Ti Phillipe cracks the door to peer out, armed and ready with his own machine gun pointed knee-high, and Phillipe looks at Burnette in bitter astonishment and says, You! and Burnette says, Yes, me. How's your—he says, tapping his throat because he can't remember the word in Kreyol.

Phillipe, with a murderous pop-eyed glare, says, Why are you here? To invade my country again? To make war with me?

I'm your guardian angel, Burnette says, and I've come to save your life a second time.

At each end of the street more pickup trucks careen to a stop, armed men flying out into a firing line, the D-boys including Scarecrow go flat on the ground and the ninjas press into the walls and doorways and Burnette says to Ti Phillipe, Tell them to lower their weapons and we'll work this out, and Burnette can see Phillipe calculating the odds and gives the command and Burnette says thank you. Here's the deal. You have four hostages inside. Just push them out the door.

Tell me why I would do this, says Phillipe. If I do this then you will kill us.

If you don't do it, we're killing everybody, the hostages will probably die too, and I don't care, they're not my people, says Burnette. If you do it, we'll just take the hostages and leave and everybody can go back to sleep and then tomorrow you and Dupuys will sit down with the Brazilian commander and work this out. I give you my word. For the next three days, no one will fuck with you, nothing, as long as you don't fuck with them. You have three minutes to give me the hostages, okay. Then we go away. This is a good deal. You and I made our peace long ago. I've got nothing against you and you know I didn't come all this way just to tell you lies or screw around. Let's not have a bad night.

Ti Phillipe says he's going back inside and Burnette says three minutes but Phillipe has them stumbling out the door in their underwear in less than that, clutching their clothes and shoes to their stomachs, and Burnette sends two one way and two the other, to the ninjas who get them down the street and into the trucks and Scarecrow back-steps to Tilly but Burnette stands a minute longer in the middle of the street and then turns his back on the station, if a bullet takes him now the cause of death would be listed as *disrespect,* and he walks to Spank's covering position and they get out of there, Burnette yelling at Phillipe's reinforcements to return to their trucks, and that's how it goes.

When they arrive back at the safe house Scarecrow jumps down from the bed of the Toyota wildly aggressive, and chest bumps Burnette harder than he should, bellowing, *Ding a goddamn derry! No cover, no advantage, no surprise! That was the stupidest, fuckiest action I have ever been dumb enough to enact!* and Burnette sticks his hands in his pockets so he won't punch him and sighs with contrition and concedes that indeed it was, a style of insanity that would have inspired his father to sign on the dotted line.

Burnette and Colonel Dupuys pull up chairs for a tête-à-tête, closing the door in the face of the cowardly Brazilian commander who had begged off the raid to stay behind and take a dump, and Burnette tells Dupuys that he and Scarecrow have some other business down south but half the squad will stay and he'll be back in three days, three days should be enough to negotiate some reasonable outcome with Ti Phillipe. And Dupuys says three days will be enough, yes, but he doesn't say enough for what, his eyes are shifty and his voice distant and his answer sounds unnecessarily cryptic. Burnette makes sure Tilly and Spank are set for the night and he finds the chickenshit Brazilian and says I need a vehicle.

There's only my own, says the commander, a brand-new UN-purchased SUV, and Burnette says I'll take it and the guy asks for how long and Burnette tells him he'll have it back right away and the Brazilian cop reluctantly gives him the keys.

It's 0400 and Burnette tells Scarecrow snag a nap and I'll be back at
sunrise and he leaves with Reginald and at the darkened bungalow near the
cathedral he sees the curtain move when the vehicle stops in front and it's a
good feeling poking through the venomous haze, knowing Margarete's there
waiting for them, and it's good to see Margarete, something he waited for
without knowing it. By the time they come inside there's a golden welcoming light from a lantern and Margarete has water heating on the stove and
her relief is a palpable mix of joy and lingering fear, embracing her brother,
kissing Burnette's hand before he can stop her. I listened for the shooting
but it never came, what happened? she says. *Monsieur* Burnette, thank God,
you have come again, things are very bad here. Ti Phillipe has grown wicked,
I don't understand him. He wants to fight the government. Thank you for
sending the money with the woman, she has been very kind to me, but my
brother told you, yes, these men are going to kill her husband and kill her.

The three of them sit at the rickety table drinking Margarete's thick
black coffee and Burnette asks about her son and asks about her and Reginald says, *Monsieur,* I must tell you, I fear for our lives. Burnette raps the
surface of the table with his knuckles, trying to think this through, and says,
Bon, let's make a plan, and they talk for another twenty minutes.

Outside the windows the night begins to lift, it's time to go, and Burnette leaves them there while he drives back across town to collect the
grouchy Scarecrow and then return to the bungalow for the family and their
sad suitcase and plastic bags, a blanket wrapped robe-like around Henri,
the sleepwalking boy. Reginald is out of his cop's uniform into the casual
prowl of D-boy fashion, just us guys, jeans and T-shirt and journo vest, all
those pockets hanging empty with the bare meaning of his life, carrying
his service revolver in a paper bag.

As she's getting into the backseat with Henri and her brother Burnette gives Margarete a clip of money, which she accepts without remark,
a manner he most appreciates, tucking the dollars into her bra. The kid
and Scarecrow drop back to sleep and by sunrise they are on the outskirts
of the city, dodging chickens and goats on Route Nationale One. Fifteen
minutes later Burnette pulls over at the turnoff to the unpaved road that
heads up into the northwest mountains, where Margarete and her son will

seek refuge for the time being until it's clear the danger to her and her brother has passed. They leave Henri and his mother and their meager heap of possessions there on the side of the road in the tap-tap queue and drive on, south through the central range of mountains, his passengers' heads lolling with fatigue, jarred by potholes, then straining erect on the hairpin turns. At Gonaïves they stop for gas and cold sodas and Burnette makes Scarecrow take the wheel across the mud flats and rice paddies of the Artibonite Valley, Ev zonked and snorting at the havoc of his dreams before they make it out of town but even in the depth of his unconsciousness he smells the coastline and the freshness of the sea as they approach Saint-Marc and he straightens awake clearheaded and anxious, striving to rehearse the op in his mind but he might as well be a blind man because he can't visualize any of it.

The next decision is coming fast upon him—sooner or later the police in Saint-Marc will have a role to play in the mission and although he knows the command pretty well, trustworthiness has never been their virtue. Should he bring them in now? Avoid them until they're unavoidable, then entertain them with song and dance? Fuck, fuck, Burnette says to himself, because he doesn't have the answer, and they've crested a hill and can see ahead a half-mile or so to the next bend, cars pulled over and parked on the shoulders, and atop the low mesa on the inland side of the road, the temple flags and Haiti's own red-and-black high in the windless air, hanging without glory, limp on their poles. This is the place and he knows he's driven past many times but can't remember ever paying a courtesy call when his A-team was bivouacked there all that time ago, two gritty sleepless months wasted in the center of Saint-Marc.

He tells Scarecrow to pull over and give the wheel to Reginald and they sit there for a minute double-checking the armory they have strapped onto their various parts and discussing what they came to do and how it might happen and Reginald has the jitters and Burnette tells him don't worry, we do grabs like this all the time, and Reginald confesses he's not worried about the bad guys, he's nervous because he has little experience driving a car but on he drives, a little goosey on the pedals, and Burnette tells him keep going around the bend until there are no more parked cars and let us know if you see the Mexican's wheels and they lurch down the line, Burnette offering Reginald driving lessons, but never seeing the Mexican's black SUV and they park in the thin shade of an acacia tree and Reginald says, Sundown will be their time, and Burnette says, Okay, Scarecrow, ever been to a voodoo ceremony? Scarecrow says, I don't care if they're fucking nuns up the ass as long as they sell cold beer.

They climb the bank to the top of the little mesa and there's a pathetic mud-walled *hounfour* with beautiful murals and dozens of people but the drums are farther on and real action is unfolding behind the temple in the dusty expanse of a barren field, hundreds of people, a thousand probably, buzzing around, and at the center of their orbit are two enormous bulls, wide-horned and black and frothing in the heat, tethered twenty feet apart to separate stakes, and behind the animals, peasants stacking branches for a bonfire. They split up, Scarecrow and Reginald looking for the bad guys, Burnette hunting for Renee but she finds him first, hurling herself into his arms, her legs off the ground and wrapped around his thighs, and he pries her off to explain.

Her reaction is airy and cavalier and she tells him she's there with Gerard and her husband Parmentier's up in New Orleans on business but will be flying back to Port-au-Prince in the morning (Eville knows every one of these details). Ti Phillipe talks big, she says to Burnette, and Honore Vincent detests me, he's jealous not to mention insane. She wanted to attend a sacrifice ceremony and had to pay a bundle for it, and I didn't choose him, she tells Burnette, I chose the priest here in Saint-Marc, his arch enemy, but hey, relax and enjoy the show, she says, Honore will not show his face here, this is not his turf, these are not his people, and he would never come this far south to fuck with somebody he could fuck with up north with a lot less effort, but by the end of her reasonings Burnette is only convinced that the hit is not a joke—which is truly messed up, Phillipe's hit on Renee competing with his own. Reginald and Scarecrow come back from their recon with nothing to report and Burnette sends them out front to watch the road. Then it's late in the afternoon, the crowd's drunk and raucous, the bulls have been beheaded with a great pulsing outpour of blood, skinned and disemboweled and quartered and hacked into purple chunks, people shoving and clamoring for a piece, the fire lit like a bomb, leaping up in a sheet of red flame and showering sparks, his teeth are rattling from the drums—and now cue the shit, cue the fan.

He might have expected a heads-up from his boys on the road, but suddenly the woman says to Burnette with cool amazement, Oh, my God, there's Honore Vincent, and Burnette looks and this jumbo-assed black guy is coming their way with wild-eyed ferocity, the crowd parting to let him pass, and Burnette wants confirmation from Renee, *You're absolutely sure?* and Renee seems puzzled, not by his identity but by his audacious presence, and Burnette yells out the monster's name as a question, *Honore Vincent?* but gets no reaction, just an unbroken deliberate stride of sheer menace, not a threat one needs to stand back and ascertain. Burnette can smell the alcohol, the guy's been bathing in *clairin,* he's like some android demon pro- grammed to reach through a brick wall for Renee's throat, the all-powerful *gros neg* come to teach a lesson to the world's white bitches. He steps in front of Renee to shield her from the assault but Renee instantly switches places, herself perhaps a *gros neg* stuck in a puny woman's body, and at the same moment she boots Honore Vincent's scrotum into his spleen and bends him over, Burnette hops aboard trying to wrench Vincent's arms behind his back and ends up riding him for a short distance until they topple to the ground, Burnette flipped underneath the monster and into a stranglehold until Renee seizes his flailing leg to release his sidearm from its ankle holster and cracks the brute into semiconsciousness with one flat-sided swing, at which point Burnette heaves and Vincent releases and Burnette rolls over and pins Vincent's wrists behind his back to get the cuffs on.

The thing could have gone better but okay, it's done, and now Burnette realizes he and Vincent are at the center of a surging uproar, surrounded by a shrieking mob and it's not clear what component of the spectacle has them so inflamed but the sight of a white man beating the tar out of a black man in Haiti has never qualified as a dependable crowd-pleaser. Renee's being jostled in the frenzy but she's still holding the gun and doesn't seem concerned and then a man, not old but resembling something smoked over a brazier, is standing next to her, a skinny little guy wearing white pajamas and a *houngan's* crimson sash—this is Bòkò St. Jean—and St. Jean says,

Shoot him, and Burnette, with dumb innocence, asks Why? and the old wizard says, *He serves the devil. He brings the devil here.*

The crowd cheers the verdict of their priest but Burnette retrieves the pistol from Renee and says, Maybe next time, and hauls the dazed Honore Vincent to his feet, keeping one hand in the waistband of the giant's pants as he wrestles him through the crowd and out to the road, wondering Where the fuck are my boys? prepared to fire upon anybody who approaches with a hint of Mexican in the family tree, and he's pushing Vincent down the middle of the road in the direction of Saint-Marc when he sees two vehicles: the Brazilian's SUV and the Mexican's black SUV, and there's Scarecrow and there's Reginald in the middle of a shouting match with four members of Saint-Marc's finest, on a patrol out of the city to check out the big party.

Reginald spots him coming down the road with Vincent and says something that Burnette can't hear, something like, *Look, here comes the boss,* because the police turn to look, saucer-eyed, and by the time he gets there, the cops are rambunctious, their guns drawn, intending to arrest the lot of them, and Burnette quickly realizes they're in trouble because he doesn't recognize a single one of these men. Recruits, newbies—therefore trigger-happy, terrified, and dangerous. He pinpoints their leader and takes the initiative, calling him out, *Corporal, attention, I need to speak with your commander, Captain Joncil, immediately.* The corporal recovers enough to say he wants to see IDs, he wants some explanation for this wild cowboy shit and Burnette tells him to send a man to find Captain Joncil and bring him here.

What's your name? he asks, and the kid, a brave and competent kid, says Corporal Antoine. Do we have an agreement, Corporal Antoine? and the kid mulls it over and they do. Burnette's awareness of the rest of the scene enlarges enough to hear a woman crying and he finally turns and peers over to the black SUV and sees the Mexican slumped in the driver's seat with his pants open and wanger exposed and a skeletal mulatto woman, much distressed, in the passenger seat. Burnette looks to Scarecrow, Did you whack this guy? and Scarecrow says, Nope, after your big man there walked away, I approached the vehicle and this dude here was getting a blowjob from the female and I knocked on the window and when it went down I darted the guy just as the cops pulled up. We have about five more minutes to get some cuffs on the dude before he wakes up.

They ignore the three policemen and order the woman out of the vehicle and go about their business of securing the Mexican and Honore Vincent and transferring them to the backseat of the UN SUV and then the truck returns from town with Captain Joncil and it's long-lost brothers when he sees his American army friend and Burnette walks him down the road away from everybody and tells him what he needs to know and slips him ten very beautiful one-hundred-dollar bills. One mind, one heart, one currency.

Back at the vehicle, Honore Vincent is kicking and thrashing in the backseat and the Mexican is coming around and Scarecrow and Burnette cuff their feet as well and tape their mouths and Burnette asks Scarecrow if he wants one of these uniformed Saint-Marc cops to ride with him and Reginald back up to Le Cap and Scarecrow says, Nope, I got it, bro, and he bangs both perps with morphine from Burnette's med kit and takes off before the police have second thoughts about further matters of legality and profit.

Everybody's on buddy terms now and the cops join Burnette back at the fete, their mouths watering from the pervasive aroma of grilled beef, and Burnette checks in with Renee, who is enjoying her elevated status as a kung-fu goddess. You're okay then? he asks her and she says, Sure. perfectly fine, although she thinks she might have given herself a mild sprain, kicking that ugly son of a bitch, and they stick around for another hour as the sun sets and the dancing begins and she says, Okay, I've had enough, and he gets a lift down to Port-au-Prince with Renee and Gerard, who drop him at the Hotel Montana, and she tells him, Sorry for the trouble. Thanks. See you later. And of course he does, the following night, on the road south of Moulin Sur Mer.

The second night, shortly before dawn, he's been in his room at the Montana for thirty minutes. He's washing up and the phone rings. It's the defense attaché from the embassy, he's down in the lobby and he wants Burnette to come down with his gear and the attaché is driving a van hauling the dead

600

girl and they head to the airport, the attaché tells Burnette the embassy wants him to accompany the body back to the States, and when they arrive at the airport the DCM is there with an honor guard and he pulls Burnette aside and tells him a C-130 has been diverted from its regular supply run to Gitmo to pick up the girl and he wants Burnette to get on that plane and not come back. Burnette says, Sir, I'm just following orders, and the DCM wants to know whose orders and Burnette says, Sir, I work for JSOC, and I've told you everything I can.

We'll see about that, Sergeant, fumes the DCM, and the bird comes in, they load up the casket and fly to MacDill and Burnette catches the first flight available down to Miami and back to Haiti into foreign policy hell, a madness co-produced by a squabbling, elbowing rowboat full of US government agencies, battling over a single oar. DOD seems to be playing it straight, happily mired in its doctrine, blithely committed to the ideal, standing up an indigenous quasimilitary police force to defend and protect (or one day overthrow) the freely elected government of Haiti. The DCM, suited up for the team at State, has a low opinion of the elected government, finds himself persuaded by the arguments, if not the morals, of the elite families, and is intrigued by this warlord up in Cap-Haïtien, a former comrade of the guerilla hero Jacques Lecoeur, a messianic braggart who claims he has been chosen to bring true democracy to his nation. The CIA has been funding this guy, Ti Phillipe, the commander of the Cap-Haïtien police force, but they've been funding him on the sole principle that the Agency funds everybody, and they know this guy has serious, perhaps insurmountable public relations problems, plus there's an issue with his mental health. The DEA is in play too, lobbying its interagency counterparts to preserve the status quo.

Whoopee, Burnette says to himself with the blackest cynicism when he's back that night on the island, driving north with Gerard toward a possible coup supported by half the embassy, with the other half supporting a countercoup, which Burnette himself and his D-boys have been sent in to assist. By the time they reach Plaisance, thirty miles south of Le Cap, Burnette observes solid evidence of how Colonel Dupuys has spent the past three days negotiating with Ti Phillipe, the talks no more than a stalling technique while Dupuys musters loyal forces from throughout the island, the roadside through Plaisance lined with cattle trucks and pickups and SUVs ferrying north a hundred members of the national police and palace guard. End of story, really. Burnette hooks back up with Tilly and Spank, who have almost succumbed to boredom, and the next day and the following day the D-boys are in discreet attendance of the rout, Dupuys and his men driving Phillipe and his men out of the city west to Fort-Liberté and then, after the gesture of a last stand, over the DR border into exile.

Dupuys reconstituted the Cap-Haïtien force, installing loyalists from the capital and the central plateau, outsiders destined to indulge in their own salad days of abuse and corruption. Burnette got on the satphone and called in a ride home for Tilly and Spank and then cajoled Gerard to take him up into the mountains to track down Margarete and her brother, found them well and safe and Reginald determined to rebuild their lives on their own land, in their own place, and Burnette vowed to help.

On his last day in Haiti, in Port-au-Prince, Burnette paid a visit to the American consulate, checking on a visa application for Gerard and then, his request spurned, paid a visit to the American embassy, where he was made to wait at the receptionist's desk until he found himself suddenly flanked by a pair of marines and a flak from State, his escort to the airport.

Au revoir, Haiti.

Book Five
Prelude: Enough Is How Much?

Oh, but the end of safety comes to us all. Right to where we live. My dear, someone once said, security is superstition. The fearful are caught as often as the bold. And only faith defends.
—*Jacki Lyden, Daughter of the Queen of Sheba*

This is how the dead come back to us, he thinks, rotting angels, bagged and tagged and shipped home to America in the deceptively clean and shiny crates of their uselessness. Dispensed, expired, return to sender. The sight, its mimicry, feels vaguely sacrilegious. He has never seen a flag-draped coffin loaded onto a C-130 before and the fact of it this time is wrong but how to say something about that to the marines from the embassy and now he's not sure what to do with the flag, the thick stiff starchy cloth like a pup tent or bistro awning folded sloppily in his hands and in his distraction he drops the flag to the floor of the aircraft, unaware of it underfoot.

They are in the dark deafening tunnel of the fuselage, securing the metal casket to the bolts sunk in the deck and Burnette wants this crazy thing, this demented harebrained scheme, over with right now, there's a Navy doctor in perturbed attendance who came in on the plane diverted from Gitmo, nervously agreeing, and as soon as the cargo officer gets off the intercom to the cockpit he raises the ramp on the C-130 and they're rolling thunder across the tarmac and Burnette and the doc open the casket.

Mother of God, says the medical officer. What the fuck is this?

For the past twelve hours she has not spent more than sixty minutes out of Burnette's sight but the blood still sickens him, dried in her hair and on her face and chest, necessary for the subterfuge on Route Nationale One and the Saint-Marc police station and at the Haitian coroner's, and she looks genuinely dead and miraculously beatific, an early Christian saint pierced

605

by pagan arrows or skewered by a legionnaire's lance, her hands folded above her womb and the rosary she asked for recovered from her purse in the car and interlaced between her fingers like a binding web of pearls. Start talking, Sergeant, says Doc, pulling a stethoscope out of his black bag. I get a call from my command in Gitmo at 0430 telling me to get my ass on this bird and go to Haiti to monitor and assist in a NASA field test.

NASA? Now it's Burnette's turn to be shocked. N-A-S-A?

Correct, says the doc, poking a digital thermometer into her ear canal. Now what in God's name is going on, man?

Look, sir, says Burnette. I need to know your security clearance.

I'm good on that, says Doc, trying to draw a blood sample from the crook of her arm. I was told I'd be monitoring a TS project in suspended animation. Give me a break, I told the guy. NASA's doing long-term space travel experiments in Haiti? I don't fucking believe it. Now I really don't believe it, unless the idea is to send dead people to Mars.

Is she dead?

Pretty close. Who shot her?

It was staged. That's all I can say.

Burnette tells Bòkò St. Jean to step up and revive her and Doc says, Wait, wait, wait, who's this guy? He a doctor?

Yeah, sort of, says Burnette. A bush doctor.

Mother of God.

Doc watches speechless, standing by with his stethoscope and a syringe full of atropine and another with epinephrine to plunge into her heart in the event of the *houngan*'s failure, but St. Jean prays and separates her blood-caked jaw and he takes a chicken feather and dips it into an old aspirin bottle and sprinkles the antidote into her mouth and steps back, praying still, a soundtrack of reverent mumbo jumbo to accompany the secular grand magic of chemistry. After a while her lips bunch sourly and her eyelids twitch though they remain closed and Burnette leans over her, waiting and holding his breath, terrified by her etiolated appearance, watching for her lungs to refill.

Hold me up, she says from inside the coffin, the weakness in her voice causing him a twinge of despair. Eville? And her eyes are still sealed but her forearms lift and she gropes to be taken up, she gropes like a sight-less infant for the support of his arms, fingers clenching and unclenching, the gold crucifix dangling between them in front of the faith of his own believing eyes. They are taxiing and turning into the wind and the engines scream and then they are in the rumbling air. He works his hands under her shoulder blades and his face is in the coffin his cheek to hers, his body radiating heat like a lamp, and he says, Ready, here we go, and lifts her to a sitting position and her chin cradles loosely on his collarbone. She feels like a corpse too, not rigid but inhumanly cold. Pulse is not great, says the leery Doc, who has seized one of her wrists.

Burnette?

I'm here.

I don't want to open my eyes, she says in a sick little girl's voice.

Why not?

I like where I am.

Where are you?

I don't know.

Let's get you out of this fucking box, he says. It's giving me the creeps.

He stands her upright, her arms still monkeyed around his neck and she says, I'm freezing, where are my shoes? and immediately her teeth chatter and her frame quakes and now he remembers the flag and knows what to do with it and she opens her eyes, which are vacant but then gradually her irises seem to collect the sun flaring through a port window, golden splinters of consciousness, an upwelling lambency of returning life, the opposite of what he had upon occasion observed in the eyes of the dying, dog or person or horse or elk all the same when the interior light flicked off in their eyes. Gone in an instant and you knew it.

Can you stand on your own? he asks.

Keep me warm, she stammers, and he makes her sit in one of the canvas seats along the fuselage and wraps her in the flag and she becomes giddy, makes a sound like an unhinged giggle that worries him, and he borrows a flight jacket from one of the crew and drapes it over her shoulders and sits down next to her and hugs her close and she says, That is so much better, Ev. The doc presses in with his stethoscope and examines her pupils with a penlight and says, If this wasn't classified, boy, this would be one for the books, and Bòkò St. Jean nods sagely from his seat farther down along the wall and says, *Pa pwobwem, pa pwobwem, Ayibobo, amen.*

I can't believe you wrapped me in the flag, Dottie tries to joke, the words chopped through her busy teeth. I'll never hear the end of it, she says, feigning some category of sartorial irritation, and Burnette is so relieved he momentarily chokes up before he pulls himself back together enough to croak, You look like hell.

Thirsty, she says, and the doc comes back with a bottle of water and Burnette asks him to find a rag or hand towel or something and what she doesn't drink he uses to begin a delicate cleansing of her face and throat, finally dabbing around the circumference of the real wound he fastidiously plugged into the side of her head with the empty sterilized brass casing of a .357 round, a tiny cookie cutter to stamp a precise hole, his frantic night-vision surgery the night before on the roadside near Tintayen, removing the perfectly round bullet-sized flap of skin with a scalpel from his medic's kit, trying for a credible volume of her own blood without nicking a vein, St. Jean splashing a bottle of pig's blood on her clothes and car seat to add to the illusion of gore, the police captain and the *bokor's* nephew keeping Parmentier at bay across the road in the quarry.

Ow, she says, jerking away from him. That fucking hurts.

Your feeling's coming back.

And you thought I had none. Fuck, Ev! I said that hurts.

As much as being dead?

Being dead, she says and her voice trails.

Every few seconds like a slowly blinking light she moans and he asks Doc to bring another bottle of water and his SF med kit which he opens and then twists the cap from a prescription and gives her a tablet and takes one for himself and she swallows it before asking what is it and he tells her oxycycontin, which is how he treats his back injury, and Doc, overhearing, says Go easy with that stuff and Burnette says, Roger that.

They doze off together in the opiated warmth of their awkward cuddle and wake up on the touch down at MacDill and she squeezes his hand with a force that tells him her strength has returned and she says softly, Thank you, and tells him, Your gift to me is my death, and he doesn't like the tenor of that and doesn't know what she means and maybe she senses his puzzlement and disapproval because her attitude springs headlong forward to the self he knows best.

I am your zombie bitch forever, she says, and he says that's the last zombie joke he ever wants to hear. She looks at the aluminum casket, shuddering, and says I have to climb back in there, don't I? and it's different now and she doesn't want to and asks for another one of his pills and then he lifts her back into the box and tucks the day pack with her personal effects next to her side. He's already feeling queasy himself when she says she might throw up and it's a grim moment when he lowers the lid, her eyes watching his as it brings its darkness over her, and then the ramp is down and he can see the hearse out there and the reception of another honor guard and they take her away as a Jane Doe to the morgue, the Navy doc riding with her, and they clear the area of all personnel and here she is again, popping out of the death cake and onto a gurney to be whisked to an isolation ward at the base hospital for two days of observation and interviews, access restricted to a small cadre of wide-eyed doctors, military neurologists and psychiatrists joined by her professor from Harvard and an agency scientist, a biochem specialist from a disbanded DOD team formerly tasked with conducting psychotropic experiments on enlisted men at Fort Dexter, Maryland, during the 1980s, and, yes, some space agency geek from Hunstville, the calculated decision to use the *houngan's* powders a natural outcome of a highly classified research mission that from the beginning carried a NASA imprimatur. Her final visitor, at dinnertime on her last night there before discharge, is her father.

Whatever she and Burnette were working out with each other in the past they worked out this time in Haiti and so in her day pack is an envelope with the address of his town house and a key because she can't be seen in Florida, especially Florida but anywhere, and she needs to stay dead until she can be reassembled and baptized anew into the midnight flock and he wonders if she'll turn up in Fayetteville or disappear from his life altogether back into the Agency's nethery vortex. He stands at the top of the ramp inside the bowel-like cavern of the fuselage as the soldiers slide her into

609

the idling hearse and Burnette turns and recedes into the dimness of the plane to get his gear, stopping to stare mindlessly into the empty place that had contained her coffin. After a moment Bòkò St. Jean is there next to him, looking, also, into the dreamless afterglow of it all, and Ev swings an appreciative arm over the fellow's shoulders and helps him down the ramp to deliver him to his escorts, his American rainmakers, some suit from State and someone, maybe INS or maybe US marshalls, and the master *houngan* is driven away in a town car, about to rise from the dead himself, a soul in search of asylum, reincarnated as a bureaucratic conundrum.

Then Burnette finds a ride over to the commercial airport to catch a plane to Miami, where he connects with the late afternoon flight to Port-au-Prince and tracks down the immensely distraught and grieving Gerard and tells him, It looks like a nice night for a ride up north, my friend.

The woman is dead, the woman is dead, Gerard laments, wagging his head in disbelief, and there's nothing Eville can tell the driver to assuage his sorrow.

I heard, man, says Burnette, switching from Kreyol to somber, almost angry English, feeling like a coldhearted prick but not ashamed about it either, not truly, because the truth could only console Gerard up to the point where his own life was cheapened by it, radically devalued; worth, in fact, nothing at all. I heard, he says again. Her husband whacked her.

But she is protected by you! How can this happen?

You know her better than me, Gerard. She told me to go away.

She sent me away as well.

Go figure, says Burnette.

I do not cry, Gerard insists, but then, astonished by himself, he does, a little.

CHAPTER FORTY-SEVEN

Beginning to end, with Renee Gardner sandwiched in between, his unfinished business with Ti Phillipe in Haiti had taken five days and on the sixth he returned to the States, arriving exhausted and stinking at the town house in Fayetteville well after dark, unlocking the door and hitting the light, instantly aware of a scent in the air that was not sweet but not his own. The flame-eyed *empereur* of Plain du Nord hung all by himself on the off-white expanse of a living room wall, staring back at him. Eville's eyes swept the space: a café table and two nice wrought-iron chairs in the breakfast nook, and on the table, yellow tulips in a blue-glass vase next to his truck keys and a Toughbook laptop computer and a clipping from the *St. Pete Times*, two paragraphs of Renee's obituary. In the big room an expensive black leather sofa—an upscale companion to his tattered recliner—and an oak bookcase for his books. No curtains on the windows but wood-slatted blinds, another high-end improvement in his monastic habitat. He dropped his duffel and his flight bag, taking in the domestic statement, wondering what exactly it was meant to mean. And then he heard her before he saw her, her voice playful with mock concern, saying, Burnette, how long have you lived here without a bed?

She was standing in the half-shadow of the hallway that led back to the bathroom and bedroom, a figure of rumpled sensuality, sleepy-eyed and vulnerable, dressed in an olive T-shirt that said Army and wearing a purloined pair of his flannel boxer shorts, large enough to fall off her hips like culottes. Even in the dimness where she stood there was ample light to see the blonde reclaiming the roots of her hair, the punkish fading cinnamon color of the rest of it, and her expression, something he had not yet learned to fully trust, advertising a smile for her new campaign, said she was pleased to see him, he was a good thing, coming home.

I'm not here that much, he said.

There's beer in the fridge, she said, padding barefoot into the light, her painted nails—toes and fingers—neon orange, a vividness matched only by the flowers. She removed the vase and computer to the kitchen counter and sat at the table one bare leg swung over the other and he opened two bottles and came around the divide to sit with her.

So, he said, raising his beer and they clicked a toast, you look, you know, okay, I mean you look good. How are you?

Good, she said. Nothing to it.

Her gaze seemed guileless and direct but he could only look straight at her for so long without becoming self-conscious and his own gaze drifted beyond her to float around the adjoining rooms.

You've been shopping.

You have to expect that. From a girl, she said.

Some of them. You?

It was fun. I bought you a bed. It's freaky not to own a bed.

So, he said again, too travel-weary to be shy about talking but ready to change the subject, holding the here and now reality of their arrangements in escrow for the time being. I heard the Feds have Parmentier locked up in Miami.

My poor little Jack, she said, the blade of her sarcasm slicing down. But her tone dropped, lower in the scale of her octave of mockery, when she said, I don't think my father's particularly happy about that.

Okay, said Burnette. Okay, this is where I get lost in this whole thing.

Well, she said. Yeah. I don't think he thought this thing through far enough. That's not like him.

I want to ask you something, said Eville. Tell the truth. Did this guy Parmentier ever play golf with your father?

Honestly? I don't know. Everything's possible.

Let me ask you this, he said. Was your father running Parmentier or this other guy, the Pakistani guy?

You mean from Germany, that guy? Maybe. I don't know for certain. If he was running either of them, they probably wouldn't have known. I know the DEA had Parm in the mix and a guy from the Bureau, Singer, was keeping an eye on him. Maybe they just co-opted him. Or Jack's working for everybody, right? Jack has an interesting history with the mob, he's from New Orleans and I know he answers to one of our own assets there, typical player conflict of interests but there you go. Colonel Khan's one shipment of heroin landed in New Orleans, and I'm guessing that was a trial run, you know, to check out transit routes and networks for moving people out of Asia. But I think my father overvalues Parmentier, which is why I had to go and Jack got to stay. Only he didn't, did he? Daddy's worried that now that the Feds have him he'll cut a deal and start talking and, at least for my father and the Agency, certain people in the Agency, that's a problem. So he's got someone, ex-Bureau, private investigator, who knows Jack, who was compromised by Jack when he was a special agent and Jack was his informant. My father has this guy pushing in the opposite direction. Not hard, but just enough for Parmentier to shut up and wait. It's still a murder case, I'm still a dead girl. The guy, his name is Dolan, doesn't know otherwise, and has no clue about my father's involvement, but I'm afraid he does know his wayward daughter, Renee. I wouldn't be surprised if he believes Jack shot me in the head.

Man, said Burnette, I'm still not seeing this.

Which part?

Most parts.

She asked him if he wanted to have another beer or if he needed to get some sleep and he said let's keep talking and when he went to the fridge she slipped back into the bedroom and came back with a soda straw scissored to three inches and a glassine packet of cocaine. Don't say anything, okay, Ev, she said, laying out a short line on the tabletop. I thought, you know, being in the hospital and being here alone would give me a chance to kick it over, but that isn't happening. Not yet, okay. It seems I'm still Jack

613

Parmentier's cokehead wife. But see, look, it's just a little taste, that's all, her cheery rationale, and he set her beer down next to her preoccupied hands, watching the powder go up her nose, her changing eyes.

I love that feeling. When your two front teeth go numb.

I love it when the snot runs out your nose. Very attractive.

Ha ha, she said, not laughing.

I thought I threw all that stuff out of your kit, he said. Where'd you get it?

I'm good at hiding things, she said. And anyway, it's not that hard to find. Just don't be mad.

I'm not, he said. I understand.

With a pained look of hope, she studied his face until he watched the pain shift, hope clarifying to belief, now a pain that came when you were unprepared for another's trueness and kindness, and she whispered, Thank you.

That day in Haiti in Saint-Marc, he said, I was convinced you were a mentally deranged person and you said, Trust me, Burnette, and I trusted you and it's worked out pretty well so far.

She brightened. Second wind? she asked, tapping the gram of coke with her index finger.

Not for me, he said. Help yourself, but she didn't, sipping from her beer instead, and he said, How come you're not wired?

It's strange, she said. It affects me in a different way, it calms me into alertness, wakefulness. Well, not always. Unless I overdo it.

Can I ask you something?

Have you heard me say no?

Damn right I have.

But not tonight.

Right. So, who are you now? Are you Dottie now?

Yes.

I can call you Dottie and you'll be Dottie?

I actually *am* Dottie, Ev. But Dottie can't always come to the door.

I should get this by now, he said.

He returned to the table with round number three and a can of roasted peanuts and Dottie finished off her second beer in one hurrying gulp and said with an energized air of resolution, All right, I should tell you some things I didn't tell you in Haiti. First, about two months ago, I ran my mouth off to this guy Dolan at a restaurant in Tampa. I told him—I implied—what Jack was doing, not the drugs and the counterfeiting but something new, basically running a ratline for people we don't want on this side of the Atlantic. At least a few of them were known terrorists and the others you could assume were on the same team, and Jack was supplying the paperwork and documents they needed to slip into the country, right, and I told Dolan if he had any influence over Jack to tell him to stop. After that, I don't know, everything got a little weird, and then this guy Karim shows up in Port-au-Prince, at least I think it was him, although he was traveling with a German passport issued under the name of Ahmed Sidiqi. And when I passed this information on to my father, his reaction was, *It's not Karim*, and, *Stay the fuck away from him.* And then he had his visa and was gone.

Uh-huh, said Eville. What's that about? Who's this Karim, exactly? He's not Paki?

When I lived in Turkey, Karim murdered a boy. She stopped for a moment in the telling, her face blank with memory.

A boy I knew, she continued. Karim and another man pushed him off a boat and he drowned. Then he went away to do jihad in Afghanistan during the time that my father was in and out of Peshawar, Operation Bags of Money or something, you know, that big game, and if you told me my father met him there I wouldn't be surprised. Daddy knew all the jihadists sooner or later. Actually, if you told me Karim worked for my father—in what way, at what point, I don't know—that wouldn't surprise me, either. Anyway, if this guy who showed up in Port-au-Prince was in fact Karim, my father was worried I might lose it and blow the op by going after him.

Like how? Going after him?

To avenge my boyfriend.

You would have done that?

I've considered it, she said, frowning, digging a peanut out of the can to throw at him. You still think I'm psycho, don't you. I'm Jezebel or somebody.

My opinion of you is—they both said *unformed* simultaneously and erupted with laughter.

He excused himself to use the bathroom and when he came back she said did you see the bed and he said it's big, is that a king? Queen, she said and told him she figured he might barf if she went for anything fancy.

I like it, he said. That style. A platform or whatever.

Oh good, she said, happy and high. Sit back down and I'll tell you my big confession.

Maybe you should wait until tomorrow, he said, sitting back down.

No no no. This is important. Jack Parmentier really was in love with me. Yeah?

Yes. And it was becoming clear to me that my father and I were working at cross-purposes and that was just not going to end well. The op had to shut down and Jack would never have let me walk away from him and I knew my father would never agree because he wanted these fuckers to come in so he could put them under surveillance and see what they're up to, they had cells in Florida and California and other places, and I want to keep them out, period. They are evil, period. Why let them in, period. It's as simple as that, really.

Wait, hold on, said Eville. Am I hearing this right? You did this thing to protect yourself from your father?

Protect is the wrong word, she said. I had to step out of his way.

Nope, not simple, said Burnette. Not making sense.

It's not like Americans are sneaking around in trench coats murdering each other. She tweaked herself again with the coke and raised her eyes to his face and said, Come on, don't look at me like that. I'm not lying.

You're hard to follow. How are you going to get any sleep, putting shit up your nose.

Don't worry about me, she said.

Let me get back to you on that. Your father might still have me on the worry-about-you clock.

Oh, fuck you. Let's try again. Did I tell you Jack was in love with me? Crazy in love?

You did.

So maybe love's the wrong word, too. He was obsessed with me, totally. The relevant point is this. I see what's going on down there and I don't agree. My father says ridiculous, forget it, I'm imagining things, just like I once imagined he was involved in my boyfriend's death in Istanbul. I tell him to pull me out and I'll just disappear, but my father says that won't really work because Jack knows too many people who know too many people who know the right people and he'll do what he never really bothered to do when he took up with me, which is look below the surface at who I am, and that makes sense to me because of Jack's obsession, you know, he wouldn't have let me vanish into thin air. So I let my father persuade me I have to go. I want to go. But be a clever girl, he says, and come up with a plan that leaves the ratline intact. So what happens next? I don't remember everything I told you in Haiti. Should we have another beer?

Last one, he said, getting up.

Where was I? she said. Oh. Ti Phillipe is plotting something dramatic.

Phillipe knew who you were?

No, he knew I was Renee, Jack's moll, uncontrollable bimbo addict—let's not forget, white—who knew too much about their trafficking and he had people try to check me out but didn't know who to believe. Even Jack began to suspect Phillipe's intentions. Now there's murder and mistrust in the air, and I need to devise a scenario for my exit. My father gets involved and he has this inspirational flash from Jackie's original mission, her scientific focus, her research into the potions and the powders, the ethnobotanical aspects of *vodou*, right, remember? Traditional medical applications but more specifically, the secrets of the *houngans*' apothecary, and Daddy said, What about that? Is that a possibility? What are the risks, et cetera, is it worth considering? And so I thought about it, you know—trusting Daddy doesn't always work out—but I talked to St. Jean. Not to say I wasn't personally fascinated.

What you're telling me, he said, shaking his head with disbelief. You always do what your father says? That's it, isn't it?

My father's a great man.

There's a big thick file of daddy issues.

You have no fucking idea. But come on, you have to admit, it was pretty cool.

My solutions come ready-made.

Oh, right. Look, a problem—*bang*. Look, another problem—*bang*. Oops, there's a bigger problem—*boom*. Not very creative. One size fits all.

He yawned and rubbed an eye with the ball of his fist and told her it was time to pack it up for the night and began untying his boots, Dottie looking on, something behind her facile curiosity that seemed imploring, though it wasn't in her voice, which held its edge.

Ev, can I ask? Are you glad I'm here?

Yeah, he said, glancing up from his shoelaces. I'm glad you're alive.

Take the bed, I'll take the couch, she said.

Negative, babe, and off went his socks and boots and his shirt and his trousers in an odorous pile on the floor—The pecs! she teased. The glutes!—and by the time he reached the leather sofa she was back from the hallway with a sheet and pillow.

Are you sure? she asked.

About what? he said, closing his eyes, and she kissed him chastely on the forehead and the lights went out and he began to doze off with the weight of grave disappointment in her self-absorption, that she hadn't asked how things had turned, better or worse, in Haiti and she hadn't wondered about the fate of Margarete and her brother, two people with some responsibility for saving her life from Ti Phillipe and his thugs, and she hadn't been fully forthcoming with the truth, or maybe she had told him everything she knew, which amounted in the end to partial truths and confused ripping crosscurrents of bad agendas and perfidious motivations. Then he heard her walk back into the room in the darkness and stand in the quiet looking at him.

I wanted to say, she said, and maybe it didn't matter to her if he was awake or asleep. I wanted you to understand. It's not just my father. It's him and his cohorts, his friends, his associates, his affiliates. His congregation. These powerful men, if you disagree with them, it's like you've made a heretical assertion. Challenged the will of God. Questioned the divine mission. Dissent in their eyes being the equivalent of disloyalty.

Without opening his eyes he told her he knew, and he told her good night, but she was not finished.

That's what worries me, she said. I know you know, so you know where this is going. He kept his eyes closed and his mouth shut because she wasn't making sense again, and let's get real, he said to himself, wasn't it a bit belated in her universe for second thoughts and soul-searching? He heard her there breathing for another minute, holding out for a better answer than his silence, and then she went away and then he heard her stop, more silence expanding, pressurizing the air, but the cocaine's there, the beers went down fast, and she's still not finished.

He wants the gloves off, he wants to hurry up, she says but she's muttering to herself. I'm saying, she said more lucidly, he's creating you. That's different than teaching. That's not the same.

Speak for yourself, he would have said, if he had anything more to say.

CHAPTER FORTY-EIGHT

At five he sat straight up and stared at his wristwatch, waiting for his brain to get the call, good message or bad, the pain is here? not here? which is how he awoke most mornings since his induction into Delta, getting his feet on the ground, and when he walked down the hallway to the bathroom he saw her light and kept walking into the bedroom to take the book from her chest and put it on the new nightstand and turn off the new lamp, these ambiguous investments, and withdraw without ever truly looking at her because looking at her now was something he desired.

Back in the bathroom he performed his ablutions and dressed in his running shorts and wife-beater top and then tiptoed back into the bedroom for clean clothes, which he folded into a daypack and strapped over his shoulders and wrote her a note saying he'd be back by dinnertime and then hit the road for the ten-mile jog to the Wall, where he showered in the gymnasium locker room and redressed himself and walked over to the clinic for HIV and drug tests, mandatory after every deployment, then gathered up Scarecrow and the other two members of their four-man squad and reported to command for an after-action debriefing.

They took their seats around a conference table, joking, getting settled, slurping mugs of coffee, spitting vile tobacco juice into paper cups, and Burnette asked Scarecrow how was Panama and Scarecrow made a face of exaggerated incredulity and said, Dude, don't tell me you've never been. How does one explain mango pussy to an Eskimo? The major jumped in, Any hitches down there, Scarecrow? And Scarecrow said, Same old, sir. Temper tantrums and snits. The agency contractors, the Bureau, the DEA, the DIA and the League of Women Voters squabbling over jurisdiction, butting heads over interrogation techniques, swiping fountain pens. But if you ask me, sir, said Scarecrow, this rendition doesn't pass the smell test. Who are these bozos—the Mexican and this Haitian? Why was this a Delta mission?

Sir, if I may, said Burnette. The capture and rendition of the two suspects was a last-minute OGA request to provide assistance during a developing emergency, a confirmed and immediate threat against an agency asset. At every level of our original mission they were in the way, magnets for blowback, and the plane was on station. Sorry, man, he said to Scarecrow, the tempo was fucked and I told you what I could.

Bad karma, Bernadette, said Scarecrow, smiling wickedly. Squad keeping secrets from one another. You could have whispered in my ear.

For the record, said the major. Burnette, because of a previous but tangential commitment under Title 50 authority, goes dark for two days, ends up in Tampa with a dead US citizen, female—

Off-limits, sir.

—turns around, heads back to the AO and completes the mission. What about you two guys? he asked the other squad members.

Tilly and I remained behind in Cap-Haïtien, said the broad-chested D-boy from Perth Amboy called Spank. We monitored the situation until Burn returned to theater, sir, and then it took us a few more days to successfully conclude, or fuck up, the mission—take your pick, sir.

Let's talk a little about that, said the major. JSOC got a call from some fuckwad at the PAP embassy complaining about American special forces in Cap-Haïtien operating in support of a coup d'état.

Horseshit, sir.

It would have to be, Burnette, said the major, since we sent your squad down there to stop one.

I think some people at the embassy might be confused, sir.

Wow, said Scarecrow. Zow.

What the fuck were you thinking, Burnette, said the major. Where'd you get the idea you can walk into an American embassy and start threatening people?

No threats, sir. Just miscommunication. I was trying to do the right thing.

There you go, bro, said Scarecrow. Sink your ass in boiling water.

That day at Augusta with FOG, no sooner had his call ended with Renee when his pager buzzed and he asked to borrow the satphone and Ben gave it back and he called Fayetteville and the major said where are you exactly and Burnette told him and the major said wait a minute and when he came on the line again he told Burnette he had until 1800 to get himself to Daniel Field, an airstrip operated by the city of Augusta, and when he got there the flight manager said, Get your gear, son. Your ride's on approach and they already cleared for a turnaround. In comes a Gulfstream with his squad aboard, Scarecrow pops his head into the hatchway and hollers, Party! Tilly's behind him waving a bottle of Courvoisier and Eville takes a minute to feel the love, let's all just go off together to Hell Central and die for each other and be one thousand percent forever beautiful.

The final score, ladies, said Tilly. Ass-clowns, one; Cacaville, nothing.

Permission to speak, sir, Spank said, grinning at the major. We need therapists.

I'm gonna say something, Ev, said Scarecrow.

Yeah?

There's only one little thing wrong with your story, said Scarecrow. The story about the chick.

Just say it.

How much time did I spend with these skunks, on the plane, listening to their blubbering in Panama. Right, but I don't speak Haitian-speak, so this witch-doctor boogeyman might as well be talking to the moon. *Mi español*, that's another story. I listen to this greaser on the flight and then I listen to his crap when they start hammering on his ass in Panama, and here's what you should know. The Mex worked for this guy Jack Parmentier, not that punk Ti Phillipe. The hit was not husband and wife—the hit was wife. Ever wonder why she was alone down there at the party? Your man Parmentier put the contract on her. We fucked up, Burn, said Scarecrow. The girl's dead, her husband punched her clock, and we could have stopped it.

That's not right, that's half right, he said, his despondence suddenly genuine.

What say to a seven-day furlough, gentlemen? said the major. I think you need to catch your breath.

She was at the little round table in the breakfast nook with her laptop and a cup of coffee, tapping out the final draft of a report that would join a cyber-queue or paper stack in someone's cubicle at Langley, perhaps to be perused and discussed for a few ephemeral minutes of geo-pol banter between a desk officer and a case officer or deconstructed by a lonely analyst and then locked away in the agency's vaults, joining the millions of field reports in a climate-controlled institutional subconsciousness, a shuttered discouraged id, its self-defined and unacknowledged secrets lapsing into a deep, fecund sediment of meaninglessness, the hubris of the past identical to the hubris of the present and as unremembered as its sacrifices. The shit comes in and never flows out, where it might contaminate. She found the process oddly reaffirming

When Eville sat down across from her she closed the file and key-stroked the computer down with a half-smile of apology and he asked about her plans—short term, long term: what was she thinking about? She was welcome here. He was curious, that's all, he said.

I want you to know everything, she said, her voice raspy and her mind still dense with introspection from writing, although of course she wasn't being as honest as she sounded. She didn't feel ready yet to reinstall herself in northern Virginia. Practically, physically, professionally, emotionally, she told him, she remained for the time being unprepared, not fragile but not sure-footed, either. The practical was obvious—stay on the rolls of the dead, at least for a few more months until the various investigations would inevitably become sclerotic. Her health and strength were normal, but she was not at the moment up to the challenge of what the Agency would demand for her if now, after two years as a rookie in the field, she accepted their offer to be part of a new wave of tactical application, a favorite fantasy project for the terminally frustrated belligerents, an Agency-owned and operated boutique of paramilitaries, the Agency's first generation of sanctioned gunslingers since the OSS and the early years of the Cold War, and she was still considering that option, still undecided.

Some guys—my father's one of them—want to see the Agency transform itself into a DOO, Department of Offense, no more hired guns, let's do it ourselves but, you know, I'm not sure I'm made for it, she said. I can't seem to control my anger. You know this better than me, Ev: If you're going to be a killer, character matters.

There was the real possibility she could switch directorates, work for Ben's counterpart at Langley, develop into one of the young superstar analysts on his team at Alec Station. Maybe instead she would go back to university—the Walsh School of Foreign Service at Georgetown had its allure; maybe she would follow her father's footsteps and slip out of the shadows into the diplomatic corps, dress nice, make nice, or maybe she would return to the Mideast and study classical Arabic to develop a deeper perspective on the cult of millennial revenge. These were the options that Renee's death had given her the time to consider, to reason through until she could tell herself with confidence, Okay, there it is, my life, the arc of it, the contribution one is called upon to make. She explained, tried to explain without getting into it, her mother's mother was dying, which meant her mother was in Missouri tending to her grandparents, which meant that if she, Dottie, went back to the DC area she'd be coerced into living with her father at the town house in Vienna until she accepted a new assignment, at the very least she'd have to fight with him about getting her own place, and she couldn't manage the complexities of that right now.

You know what I mean? she asked, and he nodded, she could tell, just to nod and agree and let it pass.

I have a proposition, he said, his tone and countenance rather too formal for her to look forward to what he might say. What do you think about getting away? Going somewhere?

You want me out of here, she said, frowning at the idea, how it felt, the sink of disappointment.

No, sorry, not what I meant, he said. I'm off the hook for seven days and I was thinking it's probably not good for us to hang around Fayetteville and be seen together. So what do you think? Want to go somewhere?

Together?

The word *together* had a heart to it, moved her own solitary heart with a faint sting of impossibility. He nodded cautiously and she said I like that plan and he asked her what appealed to her most, the mountains or the shore, isolation or something in between.

Going off someplace away from everything, she said. Can we do that? I want to be the only two people in the world. Can that be, just us—leaving unspoken her true concern, the relentlessness of their intimacy, that being alone together would eventually challenge his tolerance for her, summon his puritanical hostility and spoil this unexpected chance for something restorative and perhaps lovely.

The shore, she said. The ocean.

There was a place he had wanted to explore since coming to Fayetteville, an uninhabited island on the Outer Banks, but here's the deal, he said, it's primitive, no bathrooms, no showers, no stores, no phones, no nothing, just the sea and the burn of the sand and wind and at this time of year, thanks to the southward springtime migration of redfish—mammoth red drum—some of the most awesome surf fishing in the universe. How's that sound? he asked her pointedly. Sound boring? and she responded with girlish ebullience, telling him, *What are we waiting for?*

When he dumped out the contents of his duffel onto the bedroom floor and began to repack she asked him with some timidity if he minded and he said, Go ahead, and she threw her own clothes and stuff in with his, sequestering her toiletries and laptop and her agency satphone in her own day pack and he paused, down on his knees, looking thoughtfully at her things and his snuggled in the duffel and said, You've heard the phrase cognitive dissonance? I'm staring at panties in my kit. They seem to be getting along, she said. So far, he cracked, and thank God he smiled again and again crookedly, which made shyness gather on the left side of his mouth, settling up toward his eyes, something he would hate about himself if she ever told him she found it quite adorable.

The town house had a modest unfinished basement where he stored his voluminous camping and fishing gear and while he was down below puttering around she took the truck and followed his directions to the sandwich shop and came back with subs and chips for their dinner. Afterward they each showered and headed out together into the town to shop—a big-box store first, where she wandered off to buy a bikini and shorts and something loose to wear at night around the campfire. He stood in the sports department, examining the surf-casting tackle, not his style of fishing, before he decided to purchase a rod for Dottie. Crab net, clam rake, bait bucket. Frying pan, a large pot for steaming shellfish, a pair of blue-speckled enamel plates like shallow bowls. She was wearing Hello Kitty sunglasses and a flouncy pink sun hat and a truly ugly purple and green muumuu when they caught up with each other again with overloaded carts at the checkout. Since when did it become so easy to make you laugh, mister? she said, lowering her sunglasses to perform a peering scrutiny of his mirth.

Next stop groceries, then onward to ice and liquor, two cases of Rolling Rock, an irresistible bottle of Barbancourt and, her last minute impulse, a fifth of tequila. Back at the town house they opened beers and heaped all the gear in the living room and mulled it over and Ev said, impressed, that's a lot of stuff for seven days, and she said, seven days *with a girl*—and most of it's yours.

He turned on the television, hoping to catch the weather on the late local news, but the broadcast was wrapping up with sports and she said, Let's not worry about the weather, let's just go. Drive all night, be there in the morning—doesn't that sound great? she said, watching him consider it, watching him waver. Come on, she said, tell me one good reason why we should wait until tomorrow? Are you too tired to drive? I'll drive. Or, she said, we can pack the truck and do what's left of the coke and hit the road. He blinked at her, nodding uncertainly and then just nodding, giving in and not unhappy about his surrender, saying, As influences go, you are definitely not good for me.

They hauled the gear out and stowed it and stretched a tarp over the truck bed and tied it down and came back inside and split the last of her coke and she went to the fridge and opened beers for the road and he took his beer and said, I believe there goes my life, I'll be busted before we're a mile out of town and she said, thank God we're not risk takers, right, or who knows what the fuck we'd be doing.

As soon as he felt the coke sear the membrane in his nose for the first time in more than a year he craved a cigarette and when they stopped to gas up he went inside to buy a pack of Camels. I want one too, she said as they drove off. Let's be bad in all the normal wholesome ways. Reprobates, he said, is what we are. She turned on the radio and spun through the dial until he said, Stop, that's my parents' tunes, they loved that fifties stuff, and she slid across the seat next to him and he said, Yo, seatbelt, we're already asking for trouble and she quoted from *Romeo and Juliet,* all the world will be in love with night, and told him she wasn't driving to the beach at midnight with an attractive, kissable hunk of a soldier boy—Did we ever kiss? *No.* That's what I thought—listening to sock hop music and feeling so good only to strap herself in on the other side of the cab, a thousand miles away from her mood.

They headed away from the city lights, east on Route 24 toward the coast. When they weren't singing along with the Shirelles or Leslie Gore or the doo wop groups, Ev, amped up and unusually talkative, riffed about some new experimental type of D-boy training he had begun out west before he was yanked for Haiti—aikido, a martial arts regimen on the surface but something a bit New Age queer the more you sank into it, he said, developing your so-called inner technology. You heard anything about that? Biofeedback? Meditation?

Meditation? she snorted. Now there you have two things that don't go together—meditation and killing.

I don't know, he said. The longer I had to sit still, the more I wanted to shoot the instructor.

She could feel the bigness of his coyote grin before she turned to admire it and be uplifted, the harmony of the alcohol and the stimulant, the cigarettes and music, the flirty patter and the mellow springtime air and the lunar gleaming and the motion, all the fine small things in the world simulating a sense of romantic buoyancy that she hadn't experienced, or granted herself, in ages, without pretending.

It took an hour for the station to fade and by then they were deep into the Tidewater, past Roseboro and Clinton and out into the farmscape of old plantations where America first practiced being America, the moon-lit antebellum mansions now timeworn anomalies between the more regular intervals of less-old sharecroppers' shacks and lesser old trailer homes and featureless brick houses, the big estates parceled among the many, this field of new corn and this field of cotton and this field of tobacco and this pasture fallow, overgrown with abandonment or dispute, the land sandy and honeysuckled, wrapped in kudzu and flat as a lake encompassing a vast archipelago of pines, stray covens of fog along the bottoms where the sluggish rivers and creeks lay like serpents. Without asking, she turned off the radio and the middle of the night pressed into them and made them contemplative, smoking and nursing their beers, and after a long silence she said, Is it all right if I ask you about killing?

At first she thought the answer was no because he didn't answer her and the abrupt torque of his nerves was so tangible she felt it ratcheting into her own neck and shoulders. She said, Is that a weird question—knowing full well it was, even for people like them, the cause of chronic moral indigestion. I don't mean to sound depraved, she said. I just want to know what you know. Maybe you can't tell me. Maybe there's nothing to say, and she gasped as he swerved suddenly and pulled off the road, mad at her, she could only surmise, but he waited for the headlights far behind them to float past and got out to take a leak and climbed back into the driver's seat with another cold beer for each of them. I'm just trying to figure out how to begin, he said, and she nodded gratefully, her attention there for him as if it were something much more than just ears and listening. I guess the first thing I want to say, he said, hesitating, and they were on the road again, the truck accelerating through its gears through the countryside.

The first thing I want to say is SF black, if that's who you were, meant the stories were taken away from you, Eville said. Even without instructions and oaths he had little desire to talk about his missions anyway. Speaking would diminish them, shit begins to sound all B-movie, speaking would merely dilute the narratives into sensational tales that everybody loved and nobody understood.

Outside of the Wall, he told her, you're probably the one person on earth I can tell.

He had no desire to kill anybody, except sometimes he really did. In Haiti when they told him to get out there and train the detainees to be cops and the other cops to be better cops, some guys were ancien régime, some were guerillas, and they all hated each other and he tried not to hate them, but it wasn't difficult to come to terms with the feeling that the day might arrive when he would have to shoot one of them, somebody turning against him in an unacceptable and absolute way, the most likely candidate for a bullet being Ti Phillipe. The recruits seemed consumed by a shifting array of little moods, pinned to imagined slights, and it made him more combative, more volatile, more prone to petty aggression, until he began to see how it was he might become a person no one who thought they knew him well would ever recognize or accept.

When he was younger, before the military, he told her, my imagination, my tough-guy schemes, were about protecting every girl and woman from the man he himself might be without an imagination. That sense of vigilance, of being poised to step into the middle of something, never disappeared, it just expanded outward to the nation, but in Haiti I could see how easy it would be to shrink the whole trip down to an enraged redneck walking around purifying the earth of its infestations.

But here's what I want to tell you, he said. How many years have I been in uniform now? Since I was twenty-one. And I never killed anybody, at least as far as I know, until my command—your father was in on this—sent me to the Balkans last year to work on a hunter-killer team with a Croatian counterpart, a colonel named Vasich. I don't know why you asked about killing—okay, I suppose I do—but this is the only story I have. That's funny, right? Trained to kill for years and just one story. So we're in Sarajevo, okay. We have a list, some names, and we're tracking people. Terrorists.

Before they could get to the Palestinian with American blood on his hands, the Mossad got to him first. Then Vasich and Burnette sat shivering their asses off for two days in an urban hide, staring through their scopes at the windows of an eighth-floor apartment in a concrete building across and down a bullet-pocked block. Late on the second afternoon the Iranian appeared in the apartment and they watched him sit down on a couch in the small living room. Me the spotter (a legality issue), Vasich the shooter, and I'm the American talking through the steps with this guy—range confirmed, wind speed negligible, identity confirmed. Fire when ready—*Wait.* A woman dressed in cosmopolitan clothes entered the frame of Burnette's scope and sat down next to the target on the couch and then in the next instant her blouse and face darkened with a heavy splatter of her companion's brains and she appeared not screaming but stunned, her hands swiping at the pieces of flesh in her eyes while Vasich already had the rifle broken down and back in its case. You didn't wait, said Burnette as they walked to the stairwell at the rear of the hide. Wait for what, said Vasich. For them to make *mujo* babies?

The assassination of the Iranian exhausted the only target list Burnette was aware of but Colonel Vasich had no intention of ending their partnership, and Burnette soon understood why. In Bosnia, Vasich was a target himself, his presence as a foreign combatant unacceptable to the NATO command, which was still trying to separate the ethnic groups from one another and sort out the wholesalers, the bona fide war criminals, from the run-of-the-mill retail killers. I need your help, the colonel announced. It will be a good thing for your country, I promise. Burnette's encrypted e-mail bounced back an answer from Fort Bragg in less than an hour. *Stick with Vasich until told otherwise.* We need transport, said the colonel, and they took a taxi to the NATO motor pool at the airport and several hours later Burnette had persuaded the officer in charge to call a number at the allied headquarters in Brussels for clearance and they drove off in an armored SUV, back to the safe house to pick up their rucks and weapons and then up into the mountains and its still-smoldering patchwork of battlefields, staying that night with an American Special Forces A-team billeted in a ruined village, everything destroyed except the eternal hatreds.

In the morning, they headed higher and deeper into a zone of fluctuating hostility, a ravaged world haunted by its starving survivors, plunging along the slushy ruts. Do you have a wife? the colonel asked Burnette. Do you have a son? Vasich had traded with a Russian kill team—a clandestine cell of Chechens for the Bosnian Serb militia leader who had raped his wife and murdered his twelve-year-old boy. You fall on your knees thanking God, said Vasich, when God lets you bargain with the devil for revenge. For two hours they drove on back roads through the mountains, almost impassable tracks sometimes barricaded by snow drifts where they were forced to dig their way through, high into the subalpine wilderness, Burnette feeling strangely back home in the evergreens of Montana, until shortly before dawn the colonel said pull over by this stream and they stopped near a brook tumbling in white cascades down the mountainside and washed their faces with the freezing water. Vasich clawed through his ruck and emerged with bread and cheese and, already in his mouth, a bottle of slivovitz, which he passed to Burnette. Back and forth it went, the bottle emptied as the sun rose behind the eastern slope of the peaks and the colonel passed out in the backseat and Burnette was swirling in the front of the SUV, his eyes closed but his mind clamoring, much too jazzed to connect with sleep, thinking about something Scarecrow had told him, the Crow a Ranger during the Panama op and then deep behind the Iraqi lines with his A-team chasing scuds during Desert Storm. War, Scarecrow had said, it's just like pussy. You don't know why you want it but you gotta have it. And then afterward, you're looking at yourself asking yourself, Why the hell did I want that? And where can I get some more? and Burnette stared out the window at the serenity of spruce trees and their frosted needles and thought, *A little more would be all right.*

Vasich leapt awake looking ten years older saying, Let's go. They drove west, somewhere in the mountains three hours later crossing an unmarked border between Bosnia and Croatia, then driving south until they reached a Croatian town and Colonel Vasich announced, Now we are home. They drove to the scarred center, masonry spewed out into the streets as if the city's walls had vomited out their guts, and parked at a municipal building while Vasich went inside to find a working telephone. Good, he said returning a half hour later, we have now our appointment, and they drove on into a neighborhood of houses traumatized by shelling and close-quarter combat, chimneys vanished, facades herniated and bulging or slumped into rubble, stubborn flower gardens decorated with a glitter of glass shards, stucco cratered and blackened by scorch, families gathered under bright blue tarps, cooking their midday meals. Here, turn in here, gestured Vasich eagerly, and Burnette pulled into the yard of a cottage with half its roof of red tiles blown off and away.

His wife was named Dajana, a blonde-haired overweight woman with a pugilist's broken nose and dentures that caused her to lisp. She was wearing camouflage pants and a black flannel shirt and she sat on a decrepit water-stained couch, petting a sickly little white dog curled like a festering hairy fetus in her lap, cigarette butts crushed under her military boots on the concrete floor, her bowed head jerking up to register the presence of her husband and his companion. Vasich, physically effusive with his affection, sauntered forward to bend himself into an embrace and kiss her on the forehead, stroking her limp hair, and when he stepped back she remained as she was, vacant-eyed and unmoved, even as he introduced her to his friend the American. He spoke to her for a minute in their language and she pushed the dog away and raised herself with a wet sigh and went into the kitchen and Vasich went to the side table filled with family photographs in tin frames and picked one up to hand to Burnette—My son—first his son, a tow-headed, hawk-faced lanky kid in a soccer uniform, then his wedding portrait—Look how beautiful my Dajana was—although she clearly was never attractive, even as a bride, and then the third picture he wanted Burnette to see was Dajana in uniform, a guard at a detention camp operated by the Croatian army during the war, two knives strapped to her service belt and one protruding from her left boot. She did her duty, said the colonel, and now they want to charge her. Who? said Burnette. The Hague, those bastards, said her husband. She had been gang-raped by the Muslims, had lost a kidney to a bomb blast, and had shrapnel in her skull. Yes, of course, she killed the *mujos* in the war, he said. What do you expect? Sometimes hand to hand, and I am proud. Later, back in Sarajevo, Burnette would hear the stories of the colonel's wife in the detention camp, accused of multiple atrocities—carving crosses into prisoners' foreheads, slitting a man's throat and making his cellmates lap up his blood, forcing men to drink gasoline and then putting a match to their lips, cutting off the penis of a man she said she had witnessed rape and kill a teenage girl. She is a human being, said the colonel, she watched our son bleed to death before her eyes, she is guilty of being a mother and a woman, what do you expect?

On the kitchen table she had set out plates of cold sausage and hard-boiled eggs for the men and they ate while she stood at the stove, smoking an acrid-smelling cigarette while she waited for water to boil for coffee. Vasich spoke to Burnette in English with his mouth full. It was early in the war, the Yugoslavs were shelling Dubrovnik, and I was there with General Gotovina, organizing the resistance. During that time the Croatian Serbs attacked this town, do you understand, and I could not protect my family. His wife brought two demitasses of coffee to the table and the colonel talked to her and she left the kitchen and came back minutes later carrying the dog in one arm and a full gym bag in her free hand. Okay, said the colonel to Burnette. Finished? Let's go.

They drove south through the hills of Dalmatia for hours, crossing the border back into Bosnia near a place called Imotski, arriving at their destination, the Serb-controlled western half of Bihac, at twilight. Okay, my friend, beware, said the colonel, as they entered the town. Everyone here is the devil, and he advised Burnette to place his pistol at the ready in his lap. He followed Vasich's directions to a part of the old city until Vasich said, Okay, park here, please, engine running. Three doors down, you see there, we are going into that café. Count sixty, my friend, and then you must go. Go where? asked Burnette, and the colonel said, After sixty, leave. With us, please God, or without us, as God wishes, but you must go and find your way back to Sarajevo. As Vasich spoke Burnette's eyes were on the rearview mirror, watching the woman remove a handgun from her gym bag. You will be fine, my friend, said the colonel, reaching across the seat to squeeze his shoulder, a gesture Burnette would remember more than any other. Thank you, Vasich said. Sixty, and then you must go.

They each made the sign of the cross and got out of the SUV and his wife carried the dog hugged to her bosom, using its body to conceal her pistol, the colonel's own pistol—an HS2000, a Croatian-made polymer-framed semiautomatic—in the right pocket of his coat. Burnette began his count as they disappeared into the café, inching the vehicle forward, his left hand on the steering wheel and his right hand gripping his gun. By sixty, everything was as it had been at zero, and by ninety he was almost parallel to the entrance of the café when he heard the boom of a shot and then another and then the door flew open and a man with a pistol back-stepped out onto the sidewalk and began firing into the café and Burnette tapped the horn to draw his attention and when the man turned to face the street, Burnette waited a split second for the guy to aim at him and then lasered his breastbone and shot him. Even as he fell to the ground, it seemed, the colonel and his wife were leaping over his body and into the car. What is your count? said Vasich as they skidded away. Burnette said, One twenty, and Vasich said, My apologies, sorry to take so long.

Who did I just shoot? Burnette asked and the colonel told him, An asshole. Darkness cloaked the outskirts of town and they passed into the countryside without incident. The throttle of Burnette's heartbeat idled down, his brain stuck in an absurd loop, thinking about the dog. What happened to the dog, he finally asked and Vasich said, The dog was old. Right, said Burnette, somehow released and assured by this nonsensical answer. In the rearview mirror he scanned the gloom of the backseat, able to just make out the silhouette of the woman, wiping her eyes with the cuffs of her jacket.

Self-defense, said Dottie. Her spine was nailed against the passenger door, her legs stretched out across the seat and the soles of her bare feet warm against his thigh as she watched him talk, examining Eville's broad face, his gaze down the road, bluish in the moonlight.

You know, whatever, he said with a faint sneer in his voice, a hint of scorn. I've never worried about it.

Of course he spurned her facile offer of absolution. There would be no pardons or amnesty or exemption for someone like Eville. She had known this caste of man her entire life and they did not require expiation; perhaps they only needed this, the one thing different than a comrade or a priest—a woman to listen to them, at night on an untraveled road, with some truthful measure of sympathy, until the anger passed, and their doubts.

Right, she said.

Two men, both faced death. I lived, he didn't, and what more is there to say about it? You hear stories all the time, he said. Some you figure are sincere, there's dignity, self-respect, or they're rituals, you know, like penance; some sound plain phony, the hand wringing, the weepy confession, the self-justifying emotions. Guys whack somebody and afterward have a come-to-Jesus reckoning or something, they look at the dead guy and feel awful regret, they wake up in the middle of the night in a cold sweat, saying to themselves that miserable son of a bitch was my brother and I killed my brother. I never felt any of that. But what I told you really isn't the story I think I should tell, he said, turning toward her with a grim, furrowed look, making a specious impression, she thought, that he had challenged her moral universe, a place he should know by now was impenetrable. You want to hear the rest, or have you had enough for one night?

I want to hear it, she said.

I'll make this quick, Eville told Dottie, determined, it seemed to her, to unload and shut up and withdraw, his energy losing its boost in these early hours of their new day and its undefined togetherness, its potential for harmony not yet resolved and its pattern for volatility already established.

So, he continued. Got back to Sarajevo, checked in, and I find out my boys are there, my squad—Tilly, Spank, Scarecrow—tied in with some of your guys, SPECAT, Agency contractors, and a pair of investigators from the Bureau—man, that's oil and water—and they've set up surveillance on some jihadi safe house, they've reconned the target and are intercepting message traffic and developing a plan to go kinetic and so I hook up with the op and we take the place down, this apartment in some fleabag hotel on the edge of town. The entry goes fairly well, we have to tape a cutting charge on the door and blast it off, start clearing rooms, there's five gooks inside and one of them gets a round off at Tilly, who's right in front of me, and he's okay, it hits his body armor at an angle, cracks a lower rib and sends him sprawling but I don't know that he's okay and I'm a lightning strike on the shooter, I'm right there, I'm Cassius Clay in the jungle, man. Orders were we want them breathing or that guy was mailed to paradise. I swung the stock of my M4 into his face like a baseball bat and then kicked the shit out of him when he dropped to his knees. That should have been the end of it, right? I turned back to see about Tilly and he was huffing but struggling to his feet, and when I turned back to the shooter one of the SPECAT guys had already flex-cuffed him into a chair, he's spitting out teeth and he's bleeding from the nose and mouth, he's bleeding from a dent in his forehead, and I walked over there and walloped him so hard I broke his fucking jaw and somebody pulled me off saying, Hey, cowboy, save something for the Egyptians.

So I cooled down and we started going through the apartment, bagging up the haul. Computer files, fake US government ID badges, credit cards and European bank accounts, photos of landmarks in the States. Video tapes, man. Chem warfare on dogs, bomb making, kidnapping, not to say anything about the porno, and one video from a training camp in Afghanistan with these dirtbags in Sinbad pajamas rehearsing to kill world leaders at a friggin' golf tournament. Now listen to this. I'm checking out a pile of documents and crap and I find an envelope and inside are plane tickets, like five or six of them, most going to London or Germany but there's one that originates in Islamabad connecting in Madrid to Santo Domingo and the final destination—want to guess?—was Port-au-Prince. You heard about that, right?

No, she said. It never came through the pipes.

Yeah, well there it is, he said. Small world.

Daddy's world, she refrained from saying, talking to herself. Everyone against Dad.

The Bureau team is tussling with the SPECAT team over who has dibs on what. Meanwhile, we have five detainees and a zip-bag full of passports and my squad is trying to sort that out, snapping digital pics and uplinking them to our database, trying to determine the catch, who's who, you on our playlists or not, and we're working the stream, I'm fishing the passports, and suddenly the anti-cupid shoots me with a hate arrow, I'm looking at a match and it tells me the guy who winged Tilly is a Pakistani with connections and I just go off, for the third time I'm wailing on him, Spank has just put ten stitches in the guy's forehead and I yank them right out with my fingernails, I'm screaming in his bloody face, Tell me about Khan, tell me about this plane ticket, and I'm knocking his brains out and the Bureau guys are saying, Dude, he's defenseless, that ain't right, and the SPECAT guys are saying, Whoa, killer, save some of that for our friends, and finally Scarecrow gets me in a headlock and pulls me away, saying, Burn, come on, man, have you lost your mind? And all I've been thinking about ever since is something that aikido instructor told us out in California—the warrior must descend all the way into his body and soul and live in that gap where the world falls apart.

What I want to know is, what does that really mean, said Burnette, pounding the steering wheel with the side of his fist. I lost it in that room in Sarajevo. My mind—gone. No argument. What worries me is what I found, what remained after everything else. No more wondering who you are, because here you are, pal.

What was it? she asked.

My soul, man. That's what you find in the gap where things fall apart. You descend to your soul.

Tell me what you mean, she said. This interests me.

I don't know, he said, a rise of escaping anguish, squelched. I'm all over the place with it. What does it mean, *true to myself*? I feel righteous, the next minute I'm ashamed. Or just disgusted.

Ev, she said, you're a decent man, an appraisal that he, of course, promptly ignored. Can I say something, she asked with quiet adamance. So don't be a coward, don't be a hypocrite—choose your crime, she said. Isn't that right?

Right, said Eville. There's the rock, there's the hard place.

People who won't choose sides. They don't accept they're responsible for everything bad that happens.

Vasich's wife, he said. She shoved the dog in the guy's face. Kiss my boy's dog, you bastard. Pulled the trigger.

So what do we call that? said Dottie. Crime of war, crime of dereliction, abdication, passion? Crime of what?

I don't know, he said.

I think about this all the time, she said. I don't think everybody who hurts us should be forgiven.

Maybe that's right, he said, but it cuts both ways.

They approached a well-lit roundabout with an unmanned guard post at its center. Hey, said Eville, Camp Lejeune. He stuck his left arm out the window, pumped his fist in a salute, and hollered *Semper fi!* and seemed to feel better for it, the moment's interjection of esprit de corps, as they passed into the sonambulent confines of the marine base, sharing, it seemed to her, a tacit agreement to ride on in silence, meandering in the lowlands of their own thoughts, Dottie imagining tonight was her first encounter with an honest man. Everything's either cartoons or Tolstoy, she thought. Who's playing games? We die, they go to the movies. *No wonder the boys clam up,* she thought, stifling their doubts. *And who am I to blame them?* she reasoned with herself. In her own vocabulary of self and experience, exposure meant *to be extinguished,* and honesty meant a reliable hell-bent shortcut to extinction.

On the military base, the fields and their silvered crops vanished into the primordial forests and mossy blackwater swamps of the Croatan Indians and Walter Raleigh's Lost Colony, the road sandwiched by insect-pulsating walls of leafy darkness blinking with fireflies. They emerged from this wilderness into an all-night mile of off-base decadence, servicemen's bars and strip joints, tattoo parlors and bail bondsmen, patrol cars cruising past sidewalks clustered with Friday night brotherhoods of hooting, callow marines, invincible stumble-drunk boys with shaven heads and a deep yearning for faceless enemies. Then Highway 70 took them into Morehead City's deserted streets, then out onto the causeways over to Beaufort and north toward Cedar Island, one of the old fishing settlements they sped through named Smyrna, not that she was on the lookout for omens, Eville tight with fatigue as they turned off the main road into the watermen's hamlet of Atlantic and found the marina he had read about and turned down toward the harbor to park behind an industrial-sized pickup truck with balloon tires and a walk-in camper weighing down its bed.

I'll be damned, Eville said, his head craned out the window. There's already a line.

The moon had set into the westward spread of the continent and she could make out nothing beyond the vehicle in front, fishing rods rising straight up from its bumpers like a grove of radio antennae. A line for what? she said groggily, while still another truck took its place behind them.

She woke with the sound of the door closing and the engine starting again, half-conscious and feeling crappy, Eville, in a new kelly-green ball cap embroidered with a brassy fish, dog-faced tired but smiling as he handed her coffee and a sausage biscuit he had purchased in the marina store. She put the coffee in the cup holder and the sandwich in her lap and tried to focus, the truck in gear now and edging forward down a ramp. There were spartina marshes and the slate-colored expanse of Core Sound and out to the lavender mist of the horizon where they were going the low profile of the North Core Banks, and she thought somewhat obtusely, Water changes everything.

Then they were the last vehicle poised to be loaded onto the little four-car ferry, the *Green Grass.* Her heart was unprepared for this sight and, missing a breath, she said to herself in a breathless burst of despair, *Burnette, what have you done, where have you brought me?* because there was the water and the other side of the water and the ferry that would take them there, its sturdy classic lines identical to the upswept design of a Turkish *tirandhil.* Against her will, her memory had begun its bittersweet alterations, removed the ferry's cuddy cabin and replaced it with a mast, it had stripped the deck of the boat's white paint to reveal an expanse of varnished teak, and there lashed to the dock was her long lost *Sea Nymph,* the impossible cruelty of the happiness given and taken away, and here she was being a baby, a weakling, crying to herself, *Go away.*

Burnette, his smile collapsed, was looking over at her now, at the same time trying to obey the attendant's directions into the confines of the remaining space on board, asking her, *Shit, what's wrong?* And how could she ever open her mouth to tell him, in the guise of reminiscing, *I haven't been on a ferry in twelve years. Once upon a time I was a girl and my name was Dottie and I was seventeen and in love and I was real. I had a life that I loved and it was beautiful and the boy was beautiful and here I am again but once was enough, once is all you get to ask for, once is about all I can survive.*

They were securely on board and each sensation made her ache with sadness, the sense of imminent departure once so precious, the shimmy of the ferry's diesel engine, thrumming into her flesh. The attendant chocked their wheels to keep the truck from rolling and she said without looking at him or anywhere, Ev, do you mind? I need a few minutes. Alone, she said coldly, feeling hateful, and she waited for him to get out of the truck. It was a moment, a straw, that you would never get past unless you love someone.

CHAPTER FORTY-NINE

The sun rose red through a purpled cavalry of clouds marshaled along the horizon and after a while it spiked straight into her eyes and she could not look at it and looked away under the shield of her hand east along the ribbon of the island, thinking, It doesn't look like a safe place, which she understood for some would be the island's virtue. It could have been the Bosphorus, eons ago, before a cow jumped into the straits to break the diluvian spell separating east from west. The distance was approximate shore to shore, and the outer banks were in the purest sense borderlands, where you occupied the last footstep of a boundary and looked out beyond, facing the naked immensity of the unknown, impossible to see where it might end, plucking and shedding dreams until you arrive at the last dream and find that it is enough or it is not.

Dottie dropped her hand from her brow, looking out the windshield at Eville, his feet planted directly behind the low gunnel on the starboard side, no rail to prevent him from pitching overboard but the water was a slick calm and no traitors around to undercut him with a shove more consequential than the one he had just absorbed from her. Oh, Christ, she lamented, understanding the need to get out of the cab and speak to him.

This interests me, she had said to Eville during the night, her laconic catechist's response to the overwrought, slightly flaky topic of soulcraft, yet by her own accounting she had lost her soul and had given up the search as besides the point and probably chimeric, her soul elsewhere in

another unnameable realm, neither America nor heaven, not to be read-
mitted, believing that the loss was irretrievable but believing also that the
loss was not insurmountable but a circumstance to which life required
adaptation, a loss you ceased struggling with and learned—and it got easier,
didn't it—to live with as you learned to live without. Because in the end
you can't fight everything, she told herself. But how ironic, Eville finding
his soul in Sarajevo, as if that would ever do him any good, bring him any
peace of mind, secure his wholeness when he felt so condemned by the
blemish of an anomalous part. Because, because. Someone would have to
tell him—when you cannot be saved by love you must be saved by hate.
Drop the knife and turn the other bloody torn cheek? Follow Christ to the
cross? *Why?* Must we all be crucified? *Why?*

She opened the door and went to stand next to him, his face fallen with
a lack of sleep but also with misgiving, and stared down as he was doing at
the water, the reflections shifting over the shallows, the flicker of small fish
and scuttle of crabs, the swaying meadows of turtle grass and the solitary
whelks. After the silence became too much she said, It's not you, I'm having
these bad memories, I don't always know how to be myself, you can throw
me over if you want, a terrible joke she couldn't believe hearing from her
own mouth, unsparing, disloyal, but it seemed she had rendered him mute
and she had to apologize.

Her penance was to suffer his polite aloofness, cool and matter-of-fact,
his mouth opening and closing like a wind-up toy. He told her what he had
heard from the other fishermen and the people in the marina. The red drum
were running, the crowd would be down for the weekend and then the island
would clear out, there was a chance for bad weather Tuesday or Wednesday.
I got you five pounds of frozen mullet for bait, he told her, still reserved, his
eyes in the shade of his ball cap and his vision still fixed over the side.

I'm sorry, Burnette. I really am.

I don't get you.

How many times have you told me that? Why bother?

You gonna be okay?

I'll live, she said, relieved that he had met her eyes without rebuke or
animosity but open concern, trying to read her face and what it might tell

him about his fortune. I was having some weird past-life flashback, she told him, I was Julia or somebody, the daughter of the Emperor Augustus, being banished to an island. It doesn't make any sense, I know.

Eville said, Banished? Why?

I don't remember. Either for being a whore or for plotting against her father. Probably both.

She grabbed a beer from the cooler and sat back down in the cab, satisfied for the remainder of the voyage to watch Eville in his element, striking up conversations with the guys in the other trucks, grand sportsmen all, a native among his people, gathering intel for the vagaries of Operation Dottie. One of the older fellows strolled over to examine Eville's tires and she heard them talking, the man handing Ev an air gauge and advising him to deflate the pressure to fifteen pounds to avoid getting the truck bogged down wherever the sand was soft—the sort of practical butt-saving information Eville loved, and he spent the last five minutes of the trip in a squat, the tires hissing like reptiles. Then the *Green Grass* idled down into the channel of an austere cove staked with fish traps and they began to dock in what looked like the middle of nowhere, an osprey's insouciant nest of sticks right there atop one of the pilings, and Eville was back behind the wheel and despite her general feeling of shittyness, she gave him what she suspected was a daffy look, thanks to her breakfast beer and sleep deprivation, wanting to reignite his optimism and diminish his anxiety for the gamble he felt he was taking simply by being with her.

They followed the other trucks off the ferry and down a sand track through flats of yaupon and sea oats into a small hamlet of rental cabins on stilts, where the truck in front of them pulled off but the lead trucks kept on and so did Eville until he was called upon to downshift into first gear to navigate the looser sand on the rising barrier of dunes. The trucks ahead mounted the incline easily and disappeared down but Eville had to back up and gain more speed to power up to the top of the crossing, where he stopped to appreciate the sudden stark magnificence of the view, disciplined squadrons of brown pelicans on patrol, an offshore breeze throwing back the manes of frisky little pony waves trotting to the beach, the beach itself an unstained purity as far as the eye could see, out into the emptiness that was the fullness of the natural world.

Dottie looked at the ocean and exclaimed, It's blue! before she hung her head out the passenger window and quietly threw up.

The two other trucks on the ferry had turned south down the beach, heading, he supposed, to New Drum Inlet. Eville turned in the opposite direction and they motored along the tide line when they could, bouncing through the gullies higher up when they had no other choice. She began to feel like liquid, the sensation of her insides sluicing from head to gut with each gravitational dip and anti-dip. After several miles they had spotted only two other vehicles and their campsites and she asked where they were going and how much farther and Eville said he was just scouting around for a good place. It all looks the same, she said, her hands clamped to the dashboard, and he looked over at her, registering her distress and began angling up toward the dune line, slowing down at a hard-packed wash that formed a level cut between the hillocks back into the flats stretching beyond to the sound. He stopped and said, How's this look? but she was already out of the truck with the dry heaves, telling him between gasps, perfect, great, she loved it, and then she felt as if she were spiraling and falling, and she fell.

There was an unremitting harsh light suddenly obstructed by a low ceiling or shelf of darkness, a claustrophobic change until she realized this was Eville's doing, his work, taking care of her, blocking the sun. Later she felt her damp head lifted out of the sand and resettled on the comfort of a pillow and thought, self-satisfied, he was the one who didn't want to bring pillows to camp.

Somewhere further along in the jagged sequence of her awareness there was the unimaginable luxury of lotion-spreading hands gliding along the inflamed contours of her face, the hands moving on to her arms, then alighting erotically on her feet, the exposed skin of her shins and calves, stopping prematurely, stopping before she was ready for this useful pleasure to end, her flesh engulfed in wretched heat, everything burns, she said or thought she said, keep going, do everywhere, and she slipped away again toward some center of longing that seemed always to be receding from her thirsty approach. Then there were fingers at her swollen lips, trying to put something into her mouth and she heard Eville, exasperated, say, Goddamn it, stop fucking hitting me and swallow, and she heard herself making an awful noise and Eville saying, What! his voice latent with repugnance, and she passed out in the middle of her incoherent objection, asking herself, What did I say? Telling herself she had lost them all, her lovers, all being no greater than one.

Hours later Eville was able to sit her up and she opened her eyes to a plague of screeching seagulls diving at the camp, one side of her face coated with sticky granules of sand, her body in a cold sweat and trembling. Why are they doing that? she asked with a weepy voice, as if the riotous birds were a new brand of tragedy. He told her he had thrown out bread from his lunch and for some reason this struck her as a heinous act and she looked at him severely and said, Don't. You have a fever, said Eville. What do you think is going on? She told him everything aches, her teeth hurt, her hair even hurt, and she wanted to lie down again but he made her scooch onto the blanket he had spread under the shade of the tarp and drink a glass of water with two aspirin and told her to shout if she needed anything, he wouldn't be far. Aren't you glad, she said meekly but never finished what she meant to say and never said what she should have, revealing the very active remnants of her addiction, the cocaine, her pockets full of it in Tampa and Fayetteville, *I'm in withdrawal and I want want want,* tormented and ablaze with want, do anything, *anything,* just tell me what I can do, *fucking hell.*

Then holy suffering, the sensation in her mouth of a communion wafer welded to her tongue, which she could neither expel nor swallow, her delirium bombarded with irrational thoughts and lucid dialogue and hyperreal episodes that felt like dreams but were more truly hybrids, like satyrs, of the darkest memories she possessed patched together Frankenstein-like to bizarre tableaus, convinced at first that if only she said her rosary, it—the plunge of this sickness within; the hopeless moments, these helpless hours—would go away, but then she was reciting her rosary and her father was in some dirty dark place under Turkish ruins speaking with an angel who looked like a clear plastic bag filled with glowworms and Eville came dressed in a black cassock and white collar to sit on a cushioned bench behind an ornate metal screen and she was mumbling gibberish. You are not worthy of my confession—did she actually say that to him, to the Eville in his bathing suit and ball cap, cross-legged in the sand, watching over her? He wasn't the priest, but then someone else was, demanding to hear her confession, not a man after all but a woman and, of course, and fuck me, it was her mother. You don't know? she shrieked at her mother who seemed to be dressing for an evening out in DC, pulling on panty hose, shimmying into a floral-print satin gown with a hedge of ruffles sprouting from her bosom. I don't know what, sweetheart? she asked, apparently heartbroken by the look on her daughter's face. If something terrible happened, I swear I did not—*did not*—know. But let's face it, you were his girl, not me. From the day you were born. Do you want to hear about it? her mother said. He loved you more than anything, but Dottie knew that was as well not true. I put that man on a pedestal, said her mother. He could do no wrong.

Then her thoughts curled around her father who was sitting on the edge of her hospital bed in Tampa, just in from a round of golf with his uniformed chamberlains, his hand atop the sheet, stroking her leg. Let it go, he told her, but she couldn't possibly let it go. When she keyed Karim's name and pseudonyms into the TS datascape, she was rerouted to another base and denied access. Daddy would know about this, she had thought, but when she asked he told her Sidiqui's nom de guerre is Abu Masab. She persisted in believing that the man was Karim, she had spoken with him briefly in the Syrian's back room, he had Karim's malevolent dark green eucalyptus eyes. She had asked him disingenuously in Arabic, Is there a painting you would like to buy? and he had said to her, I knew a girl like you once, and she held her breath until he continued. Well, not like you, he explained. You are a woman. He questioned her about her fluency in Arabic, where had she learned to speak like this, and she repeated the cover story she almost believed herself, her father an oilman who had taken his family with him to Jedda when she was a girl in middle school. She had ended the conversation's roulette with a rude dismissal, shuffling the documents on her desk, blatantly ignoring his lascivious assessment, not bothering with a response when he asked if he could buy her a drink, thinking, If you want to be a martyr, asshole, say *Turkey,* secretly thrilled by the antimony, the hermaphroditic nature of espionage, two natures inhabiting the same body, the one space. Yet how odd it was to have the years go by to reveal her most enduring love from that time, her love for the fatherly Maranian, abiding and real, more faithful than her love for Osman, which now seemed to have been not much greater than a powerful teenage crush. But she always remembered what it felt like to believe she loved him, the exquisite forever-after unachievable purity of her heart, their youth inexhaustible and dead-ended.

Daddy, did you know what he would do to Osman? Why didn't you save Osman? We can't save everybody, her father said, but we can kill the Salafis. What's for dinner, Kitten? He asked her three times and each time his eyes grew duller and his look further away. Pharaoh's tribe, drowned in the tide, he said, sing-songy.

And wasn't it obvious to everybody in his alternate universe, not his desire for perpetual war but that a state of perpetual war was his congenital condition. His birthright, you could say. Don't be history's enemy, he would say. And if it came or not it would not matter, at least to him, because he had done everything possible, everything one man could possibly do, and *that,* finally, for him, was enough. And whatever happened, whatever might happen, did not require his presence, only the infusion of his spirit. You could step back, or be thrown back, and be gone, but what you had set in motion could not be rescinded.

Yet what mattered to the dead, *your dead,* what did they care most about? Could there be an answer other than justice, whatever its name, whatever the price? She had met a man in Haiti who professed to share this same conviction but in a manner weakened and diluted by his submission to procedure and evidence—transitional justice, he called it, his duty performed for the glory of abstractions and not for the necessity of blood—and after Haiti she finally understood that men like this left the door unlocked for defeat, on earth, in heaven, and, as death had taught her, the hell that contained the eternal present of everything in between.

Her dreaming self said, I want to see him dead, and she was startled awake by a real voice asking, *Who?* Something's wrong with my father, she muttered without opening her eyes to change the scene, her father saying, Do they deserve democracy? They deserve a cage, a whip, a flaying, he said and his hand stroked higher over the sheet to the top of her thigh, pretending to smooth the cotton wrinkles. What shall we have for dinner, Kitten? his eyes beseeching. But you've already eaten, she reminded him.

Did I? A blank stare before the inexhaustible charm of his smile resurfaced on his aging face and he clasped her hand and told her he wanted a kiss.

Enough. She had sensed he wasn't in his right mind but in many ways his right mind was not so radically different than the one he now inhabited. Enough, she said, unable to hold back her tears, but he wasn't going to listen. Enough, Daddy. You can't keep doing this forever.

Then it was as though she'd been parachuted into some lunatic scene out of Paul Bowles, one of her father's favorite writers, the blinding desert air resonating with a chant, *Keyfaya! Keyfaya!* A Muslim woman ululating. There, you see? said her father. You see how these sand apes treat their women.

September second was maybe September third and the middle of the night and she was naked and doglike on hands and knees in the grass somewhere in Pera Park and the Muslim boy—Muhammed? Mustafa? Murat?—was giving her a violent fucking from behind and she didn't care about that. The problem was Maranian's gold cross, batting against the festering stigmata on her chest and distracting her and finally she balanced on one hand and snatched the cross and put it in her mouth to prevent it from swinging against her wound like a pendulum of nipping shame. But the boy rammed into her with such force and unexpectedly deep against her cervix and the pain was dagger sharp and so excruciating that she bit through the links of the chain. The boy thrust again, harder and so hateful he knocked her flat, splayed on her belly, and the cross wasn't pooled on her tongue anymore because it had flown down her throat and she stuck her finger in her mouth and tried to retch it back out but it wouldn't come.

Then she was being shaken and she opened her eyes to Eville crouched over her, his hands relaxing their steel grip on her shoulders, his body outlined in the golden-furred penumbra of a modest campfire, shy flames caressing a bowl of embers. You were shouting, he said, you were having a bad dream, and it alarmed her that it was night and that her head was raving with Arabic.

He wanted her to sit up and drink something and she tried to clear her mind of its turmoil and confusion, telling herself what she told herself after Istanbul, and told herself again that night on the road in Haiti when she began to feel the turning-to-stone effect of St. Jean's powder coursing through her metabolism, I will come back, I will come back, I have not gone native in this world's darkness, and she did find the way back through the graveyard but along the journey something slowed and then impeded her progress, she found the gate of return and opened it but hesitated on its threshold, she came back halfway, where the shadows and light mingled in the beauty of impermanence, which seemed to be the right place, which proved to be far enough.

She must have said *sorry* out loud because Eville lifted her like a spineless creature, slumped over into a sitting position, whispering, it's okay, baby, everything's okay, nothing to be sorry about.

Sweetness, she mumbled. You're sweet, and she remembered something that wasn't in her memory, because she was outside the vision, located in a spaciousness not wholly contained by her body at the same time she was inside peering through a stationary lens at the starless firmament, her *ti anj* hovering above herself prostrate on the roadside in Haiti, her head seeping blood into the gravel, and she was cognizant of Eville kneeling over her, looking at her as if God were looking at her, she had never seen that look from a man but recognized it in an instant—the end of desire is named God—and behind him in the darkness was that dim-witted stealthy boy, did he even have a name, the *bokor*'s nephew, her erstwhile guinea pig, slipping Osman's bracelet from her wrist, stealing from the dead.

She had given the boy his own bull to be sacrificed, she had given him a red motorcycle, the only thing he ever dreamed about, to compensate and justify his own brief death the night of the ceremony, a rehearsal for the following night and her own submission to the sorcerer's chemistry. What she had given for a few hours of the idiot's life, it was enough, wasn't it, but he had taken more, he would always take more. Every counting comes up short. There was no *enough*, was there?

Eville tried to encourage her to eat, handing her a warm tin cup with broth and packaged noodles but the overriding strength of her craving allowed her no more of an appetite than a wish for cigarettes and beer and so, listless, she chain-smoked mechanically, lighting one butt off the other, and nursed a bottle of Rolling Rock, pressing the cold glass against her ruddy cheeks, slowly widening the circumference of her sensibility—the pitched tent, a cache of driftwood, the sand chairs set angled like a conversation in waiting, the tarp overhead, one end tied to the truck, extending out to two pieces of flotsam lumber erected in the sand.

You were busy, she remarked, apologizing for being no help, and he sipped on his own beer and said, True, if she meant short intervals of jogging, fishing, and beachcombing, constantly circling back to check on his patient. Did you catch anything? Wasn't trying, he said. He asked her if she was feeling any better and she said, This hole in my head is throbbing and maybe she had the flu. It's not the season, he told her, let me have a look, coming at her with a flashlight, brushing aside a flattened patch of sweaty hair to inspect the triplet stitches closing the wound. It seems to be healing fine, he pronounced, but rubbed on a dab of antibacterial ointment as a precaution.

The truck was parked parallel to the water and under the tarp they sat facing the dunes. She could hear now more clearly what had been there all along, the thumping crash and sizzle and shush of the waves, the ocean calling, and she began to crawl out from their tiny cave onto the open beach, her feet unsteady as she stood, her form instantly illuminated by the rising moon, erupting into the misty atmosphere like a single monstrous salmon's egg, the bright droplets of haze a steamy crystal dust magically wisping along the shore, not exactly the globs of cocaine her flesh thundered for, but for the moment an alternative, the best the world dare provide. It's full, she said, delighted, and Eville told her, Not yet but Monday night. Look, she said wryly, pointing at their elongated moon shadows in the pale blue nocturnal sand, there are our souls.

In the lunar light she saw him actually blush when he asked if she wanted to go for a dip. It's chilly, isn't it, she said, and he responded by placing his open hand on her glistening forehead, his palm overlapping her brow, a comfort closing her eyes, the elixir of his touch sending such a powerful current of solace and quickening deliverance through her body that she almost began to sob. He diagnosed the persistence of her fever and she told him despite her rally she continued to feel wretched and tomorrow would be better but she needed to lie back down, can we roll back the tarp and sleep outside, it's a beautiful night, and he brought out their sleeping bags and a quilt from the tent and arranged them on the blanket next to the dying campfire and in front of him she removed her garish muumuu, which was all there was to remove, and jammed herself into the bedding and fell asleep. Not very long afterward he woke her as he lay down himself and she said I'm cold, and he pulled her sleeping bag and their communal quilt higher up on her bare shoulders and she said to Eville, You can hold me, you know, and he said he knew but didn't move and she said, Hold me, and after a moment felt his iron body spoon against hers and smelled the rum on his breath. His arm came tentatively across her side to hug her breasts and she sighed so long and deeply and with such intense relief that when the sigh in fact ended she was still tucked under the lovely arching bridge of his arm and it was morning.

CHAPTER FIFTY

For a prep area he lowered the truck's tailgate and cooked breakfast on his fold-out propane stove and she took a bite of egg and a bite of bacon and puffed on a cigarette while she drank her orange juice before telling him she was still sick and lay back down on her sleeping bag, vaguely aware that he had leaped into action, refitting the tarp on its posts, protecting her, his new mission and his old mission, obeying orders, *tasked* with the viceroy's daughter, a mental case, the idea of his service affecting her like an unwanted infusion of melancholy. But she was eased away from her self-pity before the bitterness arrived, a tide of vertigo dragging her toward the mercy of unconsciousness.

When she cracked her eyes again it was not quite the end of the day, whatever day this was, the sun backing brightly over the sound, leaking elevation, the air hot and motionless but not so oppressive anymore and the silence hidden within the lulling rhythm of the sea. She called out for Eville but got no reply and she stood up and walked around to the front of the truck to look down the beach just in time to expose herself to a cadre of fishermen driving by. They honked, saluting her nudity with cans of beer; she waved, a small promiscuity that made her realize she must be feeling better.

She went behind the dunes, smiling in admiration at Eville's methodical private stakeout supplied with trenching shovel and bagged toilet paper and an unused cat latrine, one more reason to cheer the troops, and then she went to the tent, an oven at this time of day, and grabbed her new bikini out of the duffel—an off-the-rack purchase at Walmart, solid shouting electric orange—*my orange phase, okay?*—and the bottom fit just fine but the cups would not agree with her breasts. She stared down at her nipples erect in the loose fabric and no amount of tugging would alter the equation. She half-apologized to Eville and then she grimaced and sighed, acquiescing to her self-deprecation—Eville the Decent in association with a woman he already judged long past her apprenticeship as a whore. When that was a man's opinion of you, what chance did you have to be something more complex than slut?

She stepped over to the cab of the truck to rummage in her day pack for her toothbrush, thinking boy or girl, no one was walking away from their biology without considerable damage, but sometimes—many times—she found the best thing to do was to disappear during sex, some women do, perhaps every man does, to just let flesh fuck and forget you might be a person with any greater feelings than a baboon. Girl not there; girl too much there, possessed by an animal rage. A little humiliation, a bit of force—was that the answer to Freud's question? Eville'd been married what—once? More? Trust-building exercises, right? And how was he going to react to her if they ever actually slept together and he experienced the binary nature of her sexuality? Anyway, she thought, thinking about Eville was making her feel oddly lovelorn and romantically deprived and she set off on a stroll down the beach to find him, reminding herself of the obvious: for either one of them too attached meant just about any attachment at all.

She walked north along the tide line, her feet lapped by the last cool kiss of each wave, surprised by the temperature of the refrigerated water— swimming promised to be a bracing exercise—but the breakers looked ideal for body surfing and sooner or later, once she felt like herself again, rejuvenated, she knew she would have to do it, fling herself right in, to be reborn in the baptismal exuberance of the water. She walked at least a mile it seemed, passed by three trucks heading down to the ferry, the weekend over, honking, waving, hooting, the lustful faces of their occupants exaggerated in joy at the sight of her.

She walked on under the brilliant saline sky, cloudless and cobalt, forgetting about Eville in exchange for the bliss of the primal shore, the edge species whispering to her own identity. She stooped to pick up shells—a scotch bonnet, a cowrie, a fluted angel wing—marveling at the ugly buglike herds of sand fleas unearthed by the expiring waves, likewise the vivid shoals of tiny coquina clams like a child's glossy painted fingernails—yellow, pink, purple—each exposed community frantic to burrow back in before the shore birds snapped them up. Then just about the time she decided she had chosen the wrong direction, walking from him rather than toward, a man came into view headed her way and she knew it was him, Eville waddling through the sand in his heavy rubber waders, his fly rod in one hand, a string of fish in the other, a look on his face like he'd been blasted into the promised land.

The fish too were a conspiracy, more evocations of Istanbul—a pair of Taylor blues and a pair of mackerel but Spanish, a more flamboyant looking species than their Asian cousins, their sleek undersides lit up with a fluorescence of blue dappled with yellow spots. Oh my God, she blurted like her seventeen-year-old self as she and Eville came together. Your fish are beautiful.

They were running, he said, his eyes replaying the excitement.

You're happy, she said as they turned back toward the camp.

I'm topped out, he said. But hey, come on, how are you?

She said better but what she meant to say was, Yes, I'm happy too.

At sunset thunderheads gathered over the mainland, the gloaming exploded with columns of a whiteness more alive and grand than any primary color she had ever seen, and she crossed the beach from the water to camp carrying a filet knife and the scaled and gutted fish, Eville looking up appreciatively from his crouch, kindling his cook fire, saying, Where'd you learn to do that? and she arched her eyebrows and said, Seriously, Burnette? Clean a mackerel? She laid the fish out on a plank of scavenged driftwood and butterflied them along the spine and went to the dry box in the back of the truck for olive oil, garlic, salt and pepper, and a lemon. Cook two for dinner and save two for breakfast, Eville suggested, and when she glanced back across the fire at him, his eyes gleamed, his vision a hostage of her levitated breasts, escaped from their cups. She said she would put on a T-shirt. If you want, he told her, but he said he'd rather just enjoy the unobstructed view, and she reached behind her to unclasp the strap and said, *Well then, there,* letting him look as he wished, a symbiotic liberty, his look itself calmly arousing, until she slapped at a horsefly on her ankle and said the bugs were beginning to drive her crazy and she needed to put on that shirt.

Yep, he said, saying the wind had shifted, blowing in mosquitoes from the salt marshes.

I'm taking care of you tonight, she said, returning from the tent, her legs and arms shiny with repellent, and he helped her position the grilling rack over the coals where she set two unhusked ears of white corn to roast and then went to work at the lowered tailgate, slicing cucumbers, onions, and tomatoes for a simple vinaigrette salad. Want a beer? he asked, going to the cooler. She said, How about a rum and Coke, and he made them both Cuba Libres and they shared a cigarette while she finished with the prep. Burnette, she said, I should tell you why I've been sick, and he preempted her confession, he supposed it was the cocaine, hard to throw that monkey, and she told him it was nothing to be proud of, she had run through her stash, voraciously, deliberately, okay, but still, and if he set out a line right now—

Stop, he said. It's over.

But you should know.

You loved the dope.

Yeah, there's that. The Agency doesn't select homemakers to send out into Indian country.

Right. What were the other chicks like, in your training group?

Don't ask. You don't want to know. In a hand-to-hand exercise—actually, it was the final exam—one of them used her menstrual blood as a weapon. She wiped it on the instructor's face. Honest to God. We all stood there speechless. You have to admit, as a tactical countermove it was inspired. She was being dominated but she worked an arm free, stuck her hand down the front of her sweatpants, pulled out her tampon and swabbed the poor guy. He freaked out, like *gack!*, broke contact, and she beat the tar out of him.

Oh, man, said Eville, laughing uncomfortably. That's vile.

She didn't want to lose.

They sat side by side at the fire and she rolled the corn until the husks were uniformly blackened and then grilled the fish and fixed their plates, Ev given the Taylor blue, taking the mackerel for herself, each feeding bites to the other to savor the difference in taste. Burnette, finishing with a satiated groan, lay back in the sand to proclaim, *That fucking meal—now that's America,* as though this moment somehow represented everything he ever wanted in his life, and he propped himself on his elbows so that she could see the fullness of his face, the wordless addition to his thanks for the food, *To have a day and a meal like this,* to have these days with her, saying, trying to say, *this* is the land that I *love.* Were there ever better days?

Of course that's what he had meant, not quite what he had articulated, and she stared out at the darkness to the east as they waited for the moon to rise and said, I still don't feel at home here.

But it's your home, he said. It's who you are.

Is it? she said. I haven't lived in the States long enough to be sentimental about this. Out there—she gestured toward the ocean, across the ocean—it's like my drug of choice. It makes me high in a way that makes me real. You must have felt it, being deployed.

But you have to come back.

Why?

To take the cure. For being too real.

Yeah? Is that like a white people disease?

Montana's a good place for that. So's here. Let your life mean something else for a while.

Something less. Do you want to go for a swim?

He said excellent and when she returned from the tent with towels he was standing over the fire, his nakedness sculpted by the flickering light. She stripped too, quickly, with an unfamiliar self-consciousness for her body, shrunken and gaunt from abuse, not looking at him watching, her sense of humility appealing in a way she understood to be perverse. They pretended to race to the water and she dropped the towels above the tide line and grabbed his hand as they splashed into the shallows high-stepping toward the waves, unjoined by the first one that knocked them off their feet, the second one sending them under, but she knew how to resign herself to an undertow until just the right moment to scissor free. She swam ahead submerged in black and when she surfaced outside of the break she could hear Ev somewhere behind her in the fizzle of the last wave, calling her name.

I'm here, she said, treading in the frigid water, I'm here, she said, but not loud enough to be found.

In the morning she woke to the sound of a horn, a staccato double-bleat, and poked her bleary-eyed head through the door of the tent to observe Eville bent at the driver's window of an avocado-colored SUV, in conversation with a uniformed park ranger wearing sunglasses and a wide-brimmed hat, and she watched until the vehicle drove off and then scurried behind the dunes to relieve herself. When she came back Eville was pouring hot coffee into two mugs and she took hers with contrite gratitude and said, What was that about?

Guess there's a storm coming, he said, blowing steam off his cup, slurping, his eyes inquisitive as he tested her equilibrium with a smile. The ranger had advised him that the last ferry was leaving at four and then there wouldn't be another for a day or maybe two.

She asked if they had to evacuate and he told her it was up to them. There was no official order but they were going to get slapped by the tail end of a late-season northeaster, there would be wind and some overwash, they'd be wise to move their camp up a few feet to higher ground, but if they were prepared to be isolated without hitting the panic button, they shouldn't have a problem beyond a good soaking. It's your call, he said. You've had a rough couple of days. Maybe you want to get out of here. Maybe we should go, she said. You have to be pretty well fed up with me by now.

Nope.

I'm such a fucking wreck. I don't want you to hate me.

We checked off that option, he said. If you weren't here, doing what you're doing, what would you be doing?

Trying to score. Scoring.

What you're going through, he said. You need me.

No. Maybe. Is that okay?

Stranded with a needy woman? he grinned. Every guy's dream.

Yeah, yeah, yeah.

It was a gorgeous balmy morning, lethargic brush-stroked clouds above the ocean, and she looked around, sipping her coffee, refreshed, feeling at the end of something bad. Is this the calm before the storm? she asked.

Looks like it, he said, and she said then let's stay and he smiled and said, Yes, ma'am.

She withdrew to the privacy of the tent to attend to her neglected self, changing into her bathing suit and tugging a comb through her scary clown hair, opening her compact case to stare briefly into its mirror before she snapped it shut, a dismissal of Renee, who would have shrieked at her haggard unmade face and devoted the next inviolable thirty minutes to cosmetic repair. Renee, Renee and Jack—*God!* she said out loud, shuddering. Jack was sitting right this moment behind bars in the federal building in Miami and she thought, money laundering, drug running, extortion, world class venality, material assistance to the nation's enemies, murder, for Christ's sake, what more do you need? *Keep him there,* but she knew a half-dozen agencies in the government needed him out and gone before he opened his mouth. By the time she crawled back into the sunshine Eville had fixed a breakfast of delicious sandwiches, fried fish and egg and tomato, and they decided to spend the rest of the morning clamming in the sound, driving back down to the mouth of the cove behind the ferry landing, Burnette raking and Dottie meandering through the warm flats just using her toes, carrying her haul in the front of her bikini bottom until she had stuffed it so full of cherrystones her pants were falling down, Ev bent with laughter at the sight of her. When she hooked her thumbs into her waistband and lowered the front panel to let the clams plunk out into his bucket, he smiled, devilish, Cheshire rat, saying, Is there one more? and she looked at him sideways, sultry, and said, That one stays.

Afterward they explored southward until they arrived at the desolate inlet, empty of fishermen but its sand littered with the huge flyblown skeletons of redfish. Dottie was astounded by their size and

Eville, rhapsodizing, said before we leave the island, we're going to get you one.

They stowed their books and sand chairs and extra clothes in the back of the truck with the coolers and fishing gear and drove up the beach toward the unsettled horizon of the approaching weather, Portsmouth now their private sanctuary. They were alone, the first humans or the last, not lawless on the frontier, certainly, but readily succumbing to the temptations of the unwatched and unregulated, the happy delinquencies of life before the park service, passing the bottle of tequila back and forth between them on the joyride up the beach, their spirits synchronized and boisterous. At the end of the ride they had arrived at the limits of their world, the vast sand flats like a miniature Gobi Desert creating the northernmost tip of the island and beyond that the inlet beginning to churn with a rising tide and beyond that the smudge of land that was the pirate haven of Ocracoke.

They parked as far out onto the Atlantic side of the point as they could drive, where the treachery of shoals mounded and arced a mile out toward the entrance to the inlet's channel. Eville sat on the tailgate rigging Dottie's surf rod with a thick filament of forty-pound line, a wire leader and sliding nugget of lead weight, and a large barbed hook shiny with malice and baited with a hunk of thawed mullet. He asked if she wanted him to cast for her and she put her hands on her hips and said, Is this my rod? He said yep and she said, No, and took it from him, wading waist-deep into the shorebreak to heave the line out along the base of the nearest shoal and Ev said, What is it you don't know how to do? She walked the rod back up the slope of the beach, reeling in the slack and planting the butt in the holder he had staked into the sand, next to their chairs, and sat down with tequila and her book.

Nothing to it, he said, Dottie detecting a slight air of superiority in his voice. Eville hoisted the straps of his bib waders over his bare shoulders and spent the next several minutes fussing with his rod and tackle box. Then he was ready and clomped over to where she sat to take a gulp from the bottle, grinning down at her slyly, pleased with himself for having something clever to say. This is his and hers fishing, he said.

Yeah? She smiled crookedly. How?

658

You're on the bottom, I have the top.

She gaped at him, feigning astonishment, before she sniggered. God, Burnette. You just cracked another sex joke. I think I need to be on guard.

Something like that, he said, taking another slug before he strode down the bank into the inlet, stepping into a drop-off that threatened to fill his waders before he found his footing and lunged up onto a bar where the waves foamed around his knees.

She watched him for a while, mesmerized by his art, the backhand grace and looping precision that were the pride of every fly fisherman but when his luck hadn't turned she picked up *The Odyssey* from the sand to read and read until she began to doze as the clouds moved closer and the light changed. The next thing she knew she was wrenched alert by a incipient sense of emergency and she saw Eville, perhaps fifty yards from shore, waving his arms at her, his whoops barely audible, and then she heard the buzzy humming of her line, run out completely to its knot on the spool, before she noticed the rod itself, its stiff fiberglass bowed with the pressure of something strong and big. She sprang to her feet to grip the shaft with both hands as she released it from the holder but when she did the torque of the fish was overpowering, dragging her into the water, amazed that the line could withstand such tension without breaking.

She lowered the tip of the rod to gain slack but when she tried to crank the reel after two wraps she was locked again into a stalemate of resistance, the fish edging her farther into the water while Eville slogged furiously toward shore and then the bottom went out from under him and he disappeared, submerged by the deadly weight pouring into his waders, only the fly rod in his upraised hand visible, marking his position, and she had a moment to tell herself they were identical in their stubbornness, suicidal almost, neither of them willing to lose a rod or a fish or anything else. She lay on her belly and kicked, letting whatever was on the end of her own line help, sledding her deeper into the surf until she was close enough to angle her body sideways to Eville and snatch his wrist and in a few seconds their feet began to bump along the slope of a sand bar and Eville's head bobbed up like a hapless Poseidon, gagging water and half-drowned. She let go of him then and stood up and planted her heels, determined to carry on with her struggle against her leviathan, whatever monster this was on the end of her line. Eville tried to thrust himself higher onto the bar but the waders held him down. Drop your rod, she said. He sputtered back, Drop yours. Finally he managed to slip the straps from his shoulders and peel the top of the rubber overalls to his waist.

Let me have the rod.

Get away.

Take mine and give me yours.

No fucking way.

He was out of danger now, standing next to her, the draining waders down to his knees like a man interrupted taking a crap. Come on, he said, give it to me.

Hey, she snarled. Back off. No.

Just let me take it for a minute to get a feel for what's on.

The muscles in her forearm were corded from the strain, her biceps bulged, and no matter how much effort she threw into the fight she felt the fish would best her, the line snap, the hook shake free. Then they both saw the line slacken and Eville yelled, *Reel! Reel!* and she did, grunting through clenched teeth, saying, Excuse me, weren't you busy drowning?

But they were giddy now, sharing the exhilaration of the battle, and she reeled frantically for a moment before she began to think the fish was lost, Eville groaning with disappointment—Is he off? He's off—yet the line went taut again and flew out of the reel in a siren's pitch as the fish made its desperate run from the shoals toward open water. Eville almost tackled her from behind, laughing maniacally, wrapping his arms around her middle. He gripped his hands on the rod between her hands, saying, Come on now, share, and she thought, Oh, okay, I like the way this works, and together they broke the fish's run, Eville's stubbled jaw nuzzling her neck, Dottie feigning reproval, Stop it, the waves at the front of the bar slamming against her hips and the butt of the rod pressed at her crotch and Eville pasted against her backside.

Okay, okay, Eville cheered, we got the son of a bitch. She cranked forever, so it seemed, without seeing the catch until Eville said, Hold up, we

don't want him short-lined this far out, let's get back to the beach where he
can't escape, and so she opened the bail to ease out line and they dropped
into the cut and frog-kicked spastically back to shore and she resumed
reeling until the line angled down into the cut between bar and shore, the
fight gone from the beast, and she pulled and reeled until the widened jaws
slowly emerged like the prow of a submarine from the murky water and
Eville there at the water's edge, ready to pounce on the thing, made one of
those yodeling rebel yells.

The eyes emerged, big and dumb as a cow's, and then the enormous
bulk of the fish's head, an unearthly refulgence of the most dazzling orange,
a bejeweled horror although not so horrible as beautiful, and then, after
several more cranking revolutions, nothing—pale tatters of shredded flesh,
like a flag ripped apart in a high wind, streaming in the current.

Motherfucker, Eville howled. We've been robbed.

She walked the rod higher up the beach, dismayed and angry herself,
dragging the disembodied head out of the water. Eville dashed to the truck
for his handheld scale, speculating from the remaining twelve pounds that
the shark had taken forty. There's still good meat here, he said, carving out
the scallops of the drum's cheeks and the triangles at both sides of its throat.

I'll get it, she kept thinking about the shark. I'll kill it. Bait me up again,
she told Eville, but it was time to go.

Overhead, scudding clouds heralded the arrival of the front and the
afternoon, now late, cooled and darkened. The ride back to camp was filled
with the agonized jubilation of cheated fishermen, hooked into the dream
only to see it stolen. At the tent and without modesty they changed into
dry, warmer clothes, jeans and long-sleeved shirts, drawing their eyes along
the length of each other's bodies, her lust no more inhibited than his.

She started a fire with the last of the wood while Eville went behind the
dunes to scrounge more fuel, coming and going until he had a pile sufficient
for a bonfire. She melted butter with garlic and steamed the clams and they
popped them into their mouths and chewed, exchanging lame jokes about
the female attributes of bivalves, lewdly licking the labia, making pussy
puppets, chasing their merry vulgarity with the last of the tequila. She
was getting loaded, and so what? Why not? she told herself, her thoughts

boozy, zinging, swooping, mean little birds. This time he wanted her too, what could be more obvious, had in fact always wanted her as all the men seemed to want her, a man prize, alpha only need apply, their wanting no secret or mystery to a beautiful woman, beauty's curse until it wasn't, every guy on your leg like a glaze-eyed dog. A thousand, *Get offs!* for each *Climb on.* In Haiti in Cap-Haïtien Burnette had looked at her ruefully and asked, Are we friends? She was amused.

What's so funny? Eville said.

Nothing.

Why are you laughing?

I don't really know. Us?

Yeah, he said and chuckled along.

At sunset the wind began to rise and the ocean boom and she stood at the tailgate cutting yellow squash and onions into a foil packet with butter, which she threw on the coals to cook while Eville pan-fried the odd but substantial scraps of salvaged red drum. With the cooking done and the sand blowing, they were forced to retreat to the cab to eat their dinner, bringing along cans of Coke and the bottle of rum, Dottie's appetite returned with a vengeance that matched Eville's quotidian hunger. Jesus, *so* good. Damn right, they chorused, fuck the shark, slurping on their drinks between mouthfuls, watching sparks shower away like burning hornets from the fire into the gloom as night descended with the heart of the storm. By the time they put their empty plates out of the way on the floorboards and decided to retire to the tent they were, after hours of merry drinking, bad dancers interpreting the wrong disaster, more earthquake than gale, staggering out of the truck, Dottie falling over Eville falling down, the two of them hee-hawing, pretzeled together.

Rain spattered in intervals; the wet wind flapped and cracked like wool blankets shaken by giants. Lying down inside the tent they listened to the roar, staring like insensate beings at the dome above as it jerked and convulsed, as if someone stood outside beating it with a paddle. Dottie had just enough sense to ask if they should relocate their shelter higher up in the dunes but Ev, the boy from the mountains, thought they'd be fine where they were. Should I turn on the lantern? she slurred, but he rolled against her and her body seemed instantly a type of carnal sponge absorbing a superheated flow, the divine pressure of a man's length against her own, this heavenly thermal exchange of hidden energy, the body's best secret. My God, to be touched!

He began touching her, its specificity breathtaking, and she hastened to unbutton her shirt and his mouth followed his hand to a nipple and in the dark whether she closed her eyes or opened them made no difference. Light-headed and quivering, she pulled him hard against her. Kiss me, Burnette, she whispered, and he started to, his mouth smearing along her jaw until it discovered her lips, her tongue poised to go inside, one of his legs prying between hers. Then a downburst of wind seemed to detonate the tent, collapsing the dome, the rain raking the fabric like buckshot. A bolt of nearby lightning revealed a snapshot of Eville's face frozen above hers, cross-eyed with intoxication and exasperated with the interruption. Sober or not, he was a man who rallied to a crisis and he was up and outside in an instant, leaping instinctively around in the downpour, lashing the tent to the truck to keep it from blowing away while she lay on her sleeping bag, her hands folded atop the denim over her crotch, thinking, Hurry back, what better accompaniment than this, what better orchestra, the smashing urgency of it all. She undressed and waited and when he came back, thoroughly soaked and dripping, pelting her with shocking droplets, she helped him tear off his sodden clothes, saying, Here, pulling him back onto her, come here, let me get you, warm you, warm up, but as they kissed she wrenched her head away, alarmed and gasping, and pushed him aside because his weight had settled her down into the soaked bottom of the sleeping bag, the floor of the tent turned sloshy with the storm tide beginning its surge across the beach.

They threw everything but the ruined bedding into the duffel and sprinted through the flood to the truck, buffeted and rocking in the wind, flinging themselves into the cell of the cab, too stunned to say anything, naked and freezing and addled. She dug towels out of the bag and Eville started the truck to blow heat into the space and they wiped themselves off and struggled into dry clothes and sat back silenced in the din, exhaling their mutual impotence. Eville flicked on the headlights, the nearby tent barely visible in the downpour, soupy water streaming past its puny island. He put the truck in gear, forgetting the tent secured to its frame, and edged ahead through the maelstrom until he found a terrace higher up in the dunes and parked and cut the useless lights and pronounced them safe and secure. Crazy, huh? she said mirthlessly. The bad news was the beer was outside in the cooler and they were out of cigarettes. The good news was dry pillows and she gave Eville one as he reached behind the seat to extricate an old malodorous grease-stained blanket from a moldy heap of cleaning rags and tools, and there they huddled, the world outside seething with its violent harmonies, supreme and impersonal and mindless, the two of them, almost lovers, resigned to a squirming, fitful night—worse—of almost sleep, rousing themselves at dawn to behold a new world, an awesome world, midstream in the deluge, water triumphant everywhere below, the spine of dunes their Ararat.

What she saw, the entire beach, had the appearance of a washtub overflowing, snowy with suds, skittering balls of foam leaping into the air as far as the eye could see, the ocean a roiled slate-colored mountainscape of successive peaks, every summit hosting an avalanche, the atmosphere what she knew painters would call Payne's gray, the bluish dark gray color of a tempest gathering or expiring, the assault of the clouds slowed from invasion to occupation, the rain slackened to an apathetic drizzle. She gazed at the panorama in wonderment, feeling unexpectedly well, perhaps finally on the other side of the torment of her withdrawal, a little raunchy from the daylong indulgence of liquor and the night's accommodations but clear and unchecked in her overall sense of body and spirit. Eville, obviously, looking pale and hungover, was a different story in the aftermath of the night's excesses, shambling off behind the dunes.

Dottie exchanged her damp and rumpled clothes for the ill-fitting orange bikini, splashing across a slow river of ankle-deep surge to the ocean and its daunting upheaval, pausing respectfully at the edge of the spume, the furious shore break and its lethal riptide, before stepping in just far enough to yank down the bottom of her suit, relieving herself quickly, her pants still lowered when a wave she had not anticipated reared behind her, towering overhead at twice her height, sucking her up helpless into its bilous yellow-green curl. Then it broke and trampled her like an elephant, her body bounced and tumbling and pounded, the top of her head rammed against the bottom, seeing stars and tiny tendriled threads of lightning, having the strange panicky thought that she had lost her grip on her father, allowing him to be swept away, until the whitewater deposited her with a final flipping smack far up onto the beach, her fingers clawed into the sand to keep herself from being sucked back out. Her suit was somewhere else, ripped off, oh, well; where's my Botticelli? she thought, spacey and nonchalant, standing up with whimsical defiance, re-creating the Venus pose, shielding herself, an arm across breasts, the other dropped to cup her pubis, Oh, the shame! You little tramp! she teased herself, that thing that would have killed her long ago if she hadn't gotten rid of it, willing shame from her psyche, a smothering friend turned foe. She executed a girlish liberating half-pirouette, chortling, and began to shake the water out of her hair but stopped because the motion made her dizzy and her neck stiffened with pain.

She touched her forehead and there was blood, a small trickle from a small abrasion, not worth considering. Then, fully realizing the stark sublime beauty of her isolation, she began to walk up the flooded beach in a state of tranquil ecstasy, nearly out of sight of the truck when she began to sense something was very wrong, very confusing, existence itself disrobing, and she lay down in a few inches of water to quell her sensation of spinning but the spin remained and she closed her eyes but the spin accelerated. Maybe I have a concussion, she told herself. That would explain what's happening. When she opened her eyes again the clouds in the sky whirled into a vortex, melted and drained, leaving behind an express train of sunlight and shadows, strobing at a pace so rapid it seemed to hypnotize her and when she closed her eyes again it was a mistake, filling the vision behind her eyelids with uncountable flashes of simultaneous lightning, the balls of her eyes deflating. She felt sharp pellets of glass nick her teeth, like a rodent biting her mouth, she felt her lips stinging and a scream locked in her throat and time smashed into a million phosphorescent splinters of braiding memory. *Am I dying, did I die, am I dead?* she thought, reassuring herself, *No, that was a trick, dying was a trick, you're fine.*

Then, *what?*

She was being tumbled again, not by water but by time, which made no sense, to be time's prisoner and yet not, to be outside as well, beyond the burden of chronology, oblivious to the count of the days, where time was amorphous, porous, popping up here and there and everywhere, everything happening all at once. I'm naked and lying on the beach, she told herself, but she was aware of an impossible connection, there was one beach but not one *now,* the trick seemed to be time itself, you could *think* this way but it was not real to *be this way.* I'm lying on the beach, she insisted, but something's broken, something's wrong, how do I fix it, what do I do? Oh, she said with great relief, I get it, I'm dreaming this incredible dream and Eville was inside of her, they were nuzzling, smeary with sweat, the taste of him salty as she licked his chest, then she was poised to come and she was almost there and then she was there, her orgasm running like a shiver through the timbers of a ship. Wow, she thought, opening her eyes, if that wasn't real, then—but it was too real, the walls of her vagina swollen shut with pleasure.

She could see the sky again, the vestiges of the storm clearing off, and she had one of those rogue memories that didn't fit, which seemed to skip ahead, Eville telling her he didn't know how to love her and she asking why are you taking so long and Ev, laughing, saying sweetly, I guess I've run out of options.

I'm lying on the beach and I'm dreaming or I'm dead, she thought. Prescient, clairvoyant, hallucinating, delirious, insane. Then a compulsion to pray became irresistible, and she found herself in a familiar sanctuary, kneeling in St. Luke's out in Langley with her family, the church packed with a congregation of families much like hers, the ossified OSS crowd and the graying Cold War crowd and the new crowd and her crowd, the spiritually slothful and the divine firebrands, and she bowed her head and prayed, Dear God, I want them all dead, but a modern person could not pray for this. Pray for enlightenment and tolerance, pray for democracy and justice, pray for her father's salvation. Lord, forgive me, I am a deadly wayfarer, the means by which sin enters this world, the vessel willing to carry forth the corruption. Is it true, Lord, only angels can fight the devil? Has that worked well for you, Lord? I stand and face your enemy. What shall you have me regret? My father, Father? Where is the time for that? Would you replace my hate with nihilism, oh, Lord? What shall you have me sacrifice—but it was never a question of how far she'd go. Kill them all, she prayed, and paused, reconsidering a possible correction, a potentially definitive flaw in her understanding—perhaps a soul is what you have spent your life making, not a piece of metaphysical equipment shipped ready-made from the factory, another myth like original sin, which you were outfitted with at birth and could somehow lose, like men high and low somehow lost their humanity—and so she prayed that no god was listening, she prayed she hadn't been heard. At last she prayed, We must be patient until love turns. Amen.

The sun broke through the clouds to stay and warmed her body and the water began to retreat and she wanted to rise but for some reason could not until Burnette, dependable Burnette, the good soldier, came to her rescue.

I'm here, he said and stooped to take her hand.

I was waiting for you, she said. You found me.

Let's get you up, he said, and she never felt more grateful in her life, or properly loved, than when he pulled her up and they walked on, the headwinds fresh and ever lessening, the world receding in their wake, faded into haze.

CHAPTER FIFTY-ONE

Friday morning as he broke camp Dottie stood on top of the dunes, checking in on her satphone, and she skipped down after a few minutes saying, He wants to talk to you. Eville took the receiver and listened, confused, to hear her father rip him a new one for the vanishing act he had just pulled off with his daughter. Then abruptly Chambers changed his tone, assured him not to worry, *Remember I've given my word,* a gift like gold, incapable of devaluation. He had the situation in hand, he said, but for the moment they had to deal with a temporary glitch, an interagency overlap, Bureau agents down in Fayetteville knocking on Burnette's door with perfunctory questions about the death of Renee Gardner, nothing to be concerned about, trust me, said Chambers. An episode of miscommunication, not investigative zealotry. Inevitable that your name would come up but you're covered, said Chambers, your command is heads up on this. However, I think it wise you remain unavailable for several more days. Bring my daughter home and by the time you get here this inconvenience will have disappeared into its natural tangle of ego-webs and protocols.

Roger that, sir, said Ev, and the undersecretary said, Good, I'll see you tonight then.

He snapped the phone back into its cradle and disconnected the system, thinking, *Inevitable, right? Why didn't I see that coming?* and Dottie asked if something was wrong and Burnette said he wants me to give you a ride to Virginia.

Really? Why?

He didn't say. Maybe he wants us to have a chance to get to know each other.

That might take some time, she said, flashing a cagey smile and he told her it was beginning to look that way, wasn't it, and they finished packing and rode the *Green Grass* back to the mainland and caught the Cedar Island ferry to Ocracoke, where they drove out onto the beach again to fish and swim, an encore for their evolving dispositions, but the run had been pushed south by the storm, which had left behind magnificent rollers, the water transparent again and restored with an aquamarine tint. The day was hot and bright and the fish nowhere to be found and after several hours they decided to drive back down the beach a mile or so to a break they had noticed where the swells hit a sandbar about fifty yards offshore and popped straight up into a body surfer's version of paradise. She had been fishing in running shorts and a T-shirt but the weekend crowd had yet to arrive so they both stripped down and dove in and swam to the bar and walked out to where it dropped off again and lined themselves with the peaks and started riding them in, shooting out of the curls, human torpedoes propelled toward the beach in a joy-filled surrender to catastrophe, getting to their feet to hoot and cheer and going back out and doing it again and once more, once more. Then on his last wave he came smashing to shore, his back wrenched by the impact, and looked around for Dottie, who had pulled out of the same wave and held back. When he spotted her again he saw her mermaid's form suspended in the wall of a gigantic swell, her body vertical, hair like a crown of fire, her arms outstretched, not wings but the bones otherwise meant for wings and beautiful, she was so beautiful inside the wave, but then like a target flipped up at a carnival's shooting gallery, suddenly ascending to her right she had company, a mako shark, its split tail fin only a few feet away from her hip in the screen of the wall, its shape silhouetted in the refracted light, its length easily twice her length, and there they were, embedded inside the wave like objects in amber, beauty and the beast, the image frozen for a second before the wall spit its curl and collapsed and when her head finally bobbed up in the foam and he saw she was safe in the shallows, what he had seen remained like a panel in a painting, the otherworldly juxtaposition gesturing toward something mystical but profoundly unstable and hopeless—the girl, the shark, the rising curtain of underwater light, the moment of suspension, the cosmic wink, the clap of erasure.

When he told her about it she said, I'll bet that happens all the time. They're always out there. We just don't know it.

They head for the Hatteras Inlet ferry in the late afternoon, Dottie delighted this time by their day of ferrying from island to island, standing in the bow together here, now, leaning into him, Ev daring his heart to wait and see, looking at her and thinking with a vague uneasiness how normal she could be sometimes. She smiled and reminded him of what he had said back in Fayetteville about the cure.

A week ago I was a burnout.

Really? he teased. How did I miss that?

They stopped for dinner at a restaurant in Hatteras Village and arrived on the outskirts of Norfolk well after dark. When she said, We're not in a rush, are we? he readily let her convince him to exit off the bypass to spend the night in a roadside motel. They began in the bathroom, showering together, Dottie hooking a slippery leg behind his granite thighs, balancing on the ball of her left foot, *en pointe,* to let him enter her, the entering the strangest black magic of all, taking her away to an obliterating nowhere. She changed positions, facing away, her hands flattened against the tiles, arrested, her face upturned and contorted in the spray, the sound she made a wincing feral gurgle, like ecstatic persecution, as he slapped against her flesh, Dottie pushing back against the plunge with extraordinary force. Then on the other side of the blowout she sat like someone hypnotized on the edge of the tub to shave the week's growth of bristle between her legs and Eville, kneeling, asked if he could do it, his tongue replacing the razor after the final careful strokes along the puffed ridge of her vulva, then she was thrusting against him with a violence he would never have imagined from a woman, coming from there, the bone at the top of her pussy hitting his mouth like a mallet, his teeth cutting the inside of his upper lip, then they were flopped on the bed, Eville trying to hold on and keep his cock plugged in, her body in some type of convulsive escape trance thrashing from the foot of the mattress to the headboard, her hands blindly clawing the sheets until he had ridden her over the side and onto the floor and she shuddered and kept shuddering and thought she was done but the aftershocks would not stop coming. He shook himself out of his own daze and returned to the bathroom, wiping the steam from the mirror to trim his new beard to a more acceptable goatee, but his hands were unsteady and she came in and saw what he was doing and took the scissors and razor from him to repair his hack job. We're becoming a real ma-and-pa act, aren't we, he said and Dottie smiled, Yeah.

They went back to the bed for more and slower lovemaking, interrupted by intervals of reading and short immersions into the television, falling asleep snuggled back to back. In the morning they lazed around, stealing time, going to a nearby truck stop for a breakfast of biscuits and sausage gravy, returning to the room for another bout, checking out at noon and spending the rest of the day on the freeways, at the mercy of the weekend traffic, 64 to Williamsburg, then the stop-and-go torture of 95, the traffic bumper to bumper north of Fredericksburg, then the Beltway, she guiding him to the exit to Vienna on 123 until the two of them sat in the parking lot in front of a row of colonial-style town houses, hedgerows of unpruned azaleas in bloom, the brick walkways lined with tidy boxwoods, behind the building the tops of maple trees like green clouds poking above the roof, Dottie's mood swung low the moment he pulled into an empty space and turned off the engine. I don't want to stay here, she said. Okay, said Eville. Nobody says you have to, but tell me how this works. You're supposed to be dead.

I think it's a case of mistaken identity, she said, getting out. You must have mistaken me for somebody else, and when she says this senseless thing, for a moment he wants to throttle her.

She knocked and they waited, listening to the clicking release of multiple locks, Eville bewildered by her infuriating caprice, Dottie nervously fluffing her unruly hair, sun-bleached to a color resembling cantaloupe, mumbling that she hated this place and then the door swung open and there stood a reproachful, stern-faced Steven Chambers dressed in a navy polo shirt and crisp chinos and tasseled loafers with no socks. Eville observed her quicksilver change into loving daughter, greeting her father with a prolonged hug and a peckish bouquet of kisses, Steven Chambers looking gimlet-eyed over her shoulder at Burnette with a tight courtroom smile of parental displeasure.

I had expected you last night, said Chambers. Why on earth didn't you call?

Yes, sir, said Burnette.

You ignored your pager. We call that dereliction, don't we?

It's my fault, Daddy, she said, ending her embrace to come to Ev's rescue without bothering to explain the nature of her blame. Don't be cross.

Her father's mint-blue eyes rescinded their indictment as they fell back upon his daughter and he looked at her then directly, brightening with repossession, the graying bon vivant restored to his natural pose of conviviality and panache. You made it, thank God, he said. You almost missed your surprise.

The surprise made its happy entrance—her brother Christopher, a shorter, dark-haired, and less dominating version of his father, and a lovely woman with shoulder-length locks and a strawberries-and-cream complexion, dressed in a white knit top and printed cotton skirt and rubber flip-flops, stepping out from the living room into the foyer. Dottie, who hadn't seen Christopher in six years, walked into the invitation of his arms with an effusive spool of questions. Wasn't he supposed to be in Texas, working on his doctorate? Done, said Christopher, comps, dissertation, defense, the whole academic shitload, signed, sealed, delivered, done. Never again a schoolboy, his real life now beckoned, replete with an unexpected nostalgia for the wider world. Hey, this is Jocelyn, he said, and his sister seemed stunned when he made his announcement—they were getting married in August in Harare. Harare! It's where my parents live, explained Jocelyn in the sonorous lilt of an Anglo-African accent. It's where I'm from. Rhodesia. Zimbabwe. But we were neighbors, weren't we, in a manner of speaking. You once lived in Kenya yourself. Christopher has told me so many wonderful stories.

Forgotten, Burnette stood awkwardly on the front stoop, a teenager all over again, bringing home his date, waiting with no little ambivalence to be invited inside to the rituals and bigotries of another's family code; instead, the undersecretary joined him outside to speak confidentially. I have some good news, he said, lowering his voice. You're off the hook.

What hook is that, sir?

Chambers said Jack Parmentier seemed to have hired a private detective, who was down in Haiti snooping around. With someone I believe you know, a lawyer—Tom Harrington?

Yes, sir. We've met. Dottie knows him too.

Well, it seems they tracked down the actual gunman.

Sir? How can that be?

I've been told that the Feds in Miami plan to release Parmentier tomorrow.

Excuse me, sir. What the hell is going on?

Chambers looked Eville up and down, faintly patronizing, mildly dismissive and entertained, unruffled by Burnette's challenge to this ludicrous assertion that two plus two equals three. He shrugged and said, It all seems damn promiscuous, doesn't it, Ev? and then looked absentminded, glancing at his wristwatch, apparently lost in a swath of empty thought before he turned away and clapped his hands inside the doorway, collecting his children. Everyone, let's go, he announced. To Maria's first, a cramped little Mexican joint a short drive up 123, and then Christopher and Jocelyn had an international flight to catch out of Dulles.

The reunited family piled into Chambers's silver Mercedes and Eville followed unhappily in his truck, kicking himself for being a damned fool, screwing the boss's daughter perhaps the least of his transgressions in light of his apparent inclusion on the list of suspects in her murder, a decoy in their fucking games, the self-dramatizing schemes of overheated minds, unrestrained in power and influence and felonious inspiration. It all seemed a bit too diabolically fanciful and he felt once again shanghaied, made to join an absurdist theater troupe renowned for bloodshed, performing exclusively for kings and their unsuspecting subjects, the cast and audience equally at risk of cutthroating or mock executions or ironically, because it was less titillating, almost a disappointment in its imaginative deficit, wholesale slaughter.

Dinner passed without a hint of discord, save for the Chambers's collective inconsiderate bad manners, the group oblivious to their outsider and yet its mutual exchange of affections unexpected, given what Eville had been conditioned to assume about the family from Dottie's innuendos. The implicit unwholesomeness of her relationship with her father, aberrant by any rational standard, was a mystery Eville had no desire to solve. The tacit regret he had heard in her occasional remarks about her brother, who Eville had been led to believe was too weak to bear the harsher realities of life as an adult. But none of these assumptions seemed to hold up and he endured their ostentatious enthusiasm with a sinking of his own.

The meal's celebratory theme was water. Newly armed with postgraduate degrees in hydrology, the engaged lovebirds were off to southern Africa to launch an NGO, DrinkUp, the organization already hatched, chartered with the United Nations and the war-weary government of Mozambique, where DrinkUp had received its first grant for its inaugural project, drilling bore wells and designing irrigation systems in the arid countryside. (Chris is the engineer. I'm the queen of groundwater, quipped Jocelyn. My path is the one of least resistance.) This is so exciting, trilled Dottie, who vowed nothing would stop her from attending the wedding. Then without pause the siblings shifted the conversation to their mother, apparently reincarnated as a saint, whom Christopher and Jocelyn had just visited in Missouri on their journey east from Lubbock, where the mother had immersed herself in devoted care for her elderly parents. The topic of his wife the Samaritan seemed to produce a surge in their father's appetite, Chambers's fork set in a quickened rotation from plate to mouth, packing in the chicken enchiladas and carne asada quesadilla, his disinterested eyes watering from the heat of the chilis. Will she come to the wedding? Dottie asked her brother. It depends, he said. You know. If she can get away. You're coming, aren't you, Daddy, she asked, and he looked up distracted from his plate, chewing boorishly, a grain of rice stuck to his chin, and nodded, his affirmation unconvincing, but with his mouth again empty he declared with a receding smile, Wouldn't miss it for the world.

Is Mary Beth still in Nairobi?

Last I heard, said her father.

Mary Beth? said Christopher. God, how is she?

We should go see her, Daddy. On the way to the wedding.

There's a good idea.

Ev, said Dottie, shattering his invisibility, will you come?

Oh, grand, said Jocelyn, beaming belated curiosity toward Dottie's male companion, her inquiring eyes probing the unexplained nature of their relationship, preempted by the undersecretary's cursory introduction back at the town house; Ev, a friend of the family. Jocelyn reached across the table with a surplus of sincerity to lay her hand atop Eville's. Please come.

Let me check the dates, said Eville, more uncomfortable with the sudden attention than their preoccupation and indifference, the unconscious rudeness families seemed to generate when they gathered into their nucleus, orbited by outsiders.

Steven Chambers swiped his red-greased lips with a napkin and took out his wallet, setting money on the table, Dottie slipped away to the restroom, and Chambers stood up saying, Sit tight for a minute everyone, but motioning for Ev to join him. Let's get Dottie's things out of your truck.

Sir, may I speak? Eville said, once they were out in the parking lot, and Chambers said impatiently, For God's sake. About what? The transfer was messy, Burnette unzipping the duffel, yanking out Dottie's clothes, grabbing her day pack from the cab, Chambers flustered because he couldn't find his keys, left behind inside on the table. He came back out with the full crew, Dottie casting a chagrined doll's face at Eville, an offering for his plight or hers, hard to say which, helping him stuff everything into the available space in the Mercedes's trunk, already occupied by the couple's luggage. Numbed by the sudden opacity of Dottie's eyes and her father's irritable behavior, he reported wooden-voiced to Steven Chambers, I think that's it, sir. Chambers told him to head back down 123 toward Tysons Corner, take a right on Route 7, and go a mile to a Hilton, where a prepaid room awaited him. Burnette, flat-faced, nodded acknowledgment of these instructions and pivoted with the practiced precision of obedience, baffled and furious once his back was turned to the undersecretary, stomping to his truck and climbing in, shutting the door, Dottie running over to knock on the window. He took a breath, refusing to look at her, grimaced, and then sighed and rolled it down.

I have to go to the airport with them.

I know, said Eville.

I've been horrible, haven't I? she said, searching his face for consensus.

It's family, he said. It's important.

And then she was back-stepping away, her hand raised to the side of her head, fingers pantomiming a telephone, saying she would call him, and he started the engine and drove off, convinced he had just been inducted into the Suckers Hall of Fame, certain his episodic misadventures with the undersecretary's daughter had been permanently discontinued, his service ending in the customary manner, a sudden forfeiture of meaning and utility, the voiding return to irrelevance and banality, the personnel who previously found you necessary and vital staring at their feet at the mention of your name. He would never see her again, he told himself, hauling his cargo out of the bed of the truck to the elevator and up to his room, a severance that would have been almost all right with him were he able to forget or even dismiss their days out on the island, their night in the motel.

At midnight, though, she was knocking on his door at the Hilton, passionate with apology and outbursts of gratitude, rattling with fucked-up rationales and nevertheless a presence he welcomed as he never thought he might or could, his good sense unmoored by this alchemic mess of a woman and her countervailing force—you always know better until suddenly you don't seem to know anything at all.

Seeing my brother Christopher was odd, she said.

You seemed glad to see him.

We were really close as kids and then one day we just weren't.

What happened?

I don't know. Daddy. I guess that's what happened.

How's that? he asked, but she was thinking in another direction.

I always thought my brother was queer. Not that there's anything wrong with that. Do you have brothers and sisters?

Two brothers.

Are you close to them?

Like you, he said. I was and then I wasn't. I'm close to my mother.

So, can I stay? she asked, less manic, glancing around at the gear cluttered around the room. Is that a problem?

Am I aiding and abetting an act of home-front insubordination? he said, attempting lightness.

I told you, she said. I wasn't spending the night there.

Explain the rules. Dead? Not dead?

Explain an act of grace. I want my life returned to me. It's mine. I'm taking it back.

And Parmentier? What about him?

He's gone. We won't be hearing from Jack again.

You and your father—

We're not talking about it.

Minutes before she appeared he had taken an Oxycontin for the recurrent pain low in his back; now, after such a day of aggravation unscrolled from the ease of their splendid morning, he felt incongruently mellow, sloppy with tenderness, pleased that she came to him regardless of what she ran from. Hey. Honey, he said. Look. Shh. Sitting down on the edge of the bed. It's okay, I don't care, none of that matters, and, suddenly queasy but painless, he floated back flat and loose and she responded as he might have hoped but for the bad timing of the opiate's arrival in his bloodstream, leveling him out, deboned, Dottie occupying another spectrum of energy, recharged and moving forward, his jeans unbuckled and tugged from his legs. He fell asleep caressing her silky head, her mouth warm and wet around his grateful penis, startled upright in the morning by the room phone ringing, the operator announcing his wake-up call, Dottie undressed and clinging to his bare self from behind, mumbling, We have to get up, we have to get Daddy and take him to mass at St. Luke's, and all Burnette could think to say was, Fuck all that tradecraft stuff, huh.

Dottie keyed open the door to the town house to a sonic blastwave of *Rigoletto* playing top volume on the stereo from one of the upper floors, her father's unfaltering tenor joined in a duet with the soloist, Dottie ascending the stairs and descending ten minutes later on her father's arm, dressed for Sunday services but wearing a blonde shoulder-length wig and designer sunglasses, everyone behaving with the utmost circumspection, like coddled, overprotected amnesiacs, imminently vulnerable to the wrong word or careless action that might trigger the memory of old grievances, and so they drove to church like any other family carved away by time, incomplete in number and destined for further shrinkage, filing together reverently into their pew on Sunday morning.

Ev, Chambers stage-whispered, offhanded, wickedly, into Burnette's ear, stepping close with jaunty arrogance as they walked back out into the sunshine an hour later. You fucking my daughter? He chuckled, one cocksman to another, and clapped Eville on the back and said, You lucky dog, and Eville gritted his teeth and impulsively placed his open hand on Chambers's chest, over his gold necktie, his hand there and gone in an instant but the line irrevocably crossed, the slightest push of insolence, warning the undersecretary to never speak to him this way again.

Or you will strike me down, Ev? asked Chambers, his head tilted with a taunt of gleaming interest, and Burnette said, Yes, sir.

Dottie, ahead of them, turned around gaily and asked, What are you guys laughing about? and Eville, his face blanched and rigid, said, I'm not laughing, am I? But she laughed herself, scanning their confrontational expressions, ignoring them with a smirk, continuing to the car, not about to step between them.

They went to the Joshua Tree for brunch, an Agency hangout in McLean, where the undersecretary spent much of his time table-hopping among his fellow suits and their fleshy accessories, the painted wives sipping mimosas, big-haired ladies smelling of Paris, his clubhouse laugh of affability bubbling through the atmospheric clatter.

He's like the fucking mayor, isn't he, said Eville.

Yeah, Dottie said drily, of the underworld. So, she said, and changed the subject. What was going on with the two of you after mass?

Nothing, said Ev. He made an inappropriate remark.

You must have noticed, she said. His behavior, it's been strange. Lately. A bit mental.

Yeah, I don't know. I haven't seen him that much.

I can see it in his eyes sometimes, she said. Slippage. Something, anyway. Ev, give me some advice.

The wig is too much.

People up here know me as a blonde. That's not what I meant.

Okay. The eggs Benedict.

She swatted toward him with her menu.

Advice about what?

She explained to him that despite appearances to the contrary her professional relationship with her father was casual, advisory, and that her actual handlers, her case officer and the little group of people in the Ops Directorate who had been running her quite unnoticed from their closets had now flashed onto the radar of the potentates and suddenly people on the fifth floor were talking about, and I quote, she said, the death-wish flamboyance of what they call my stunt. They wanted her in from the field—not so cold anymore, is it?—secured behind a desk, exploiting her language skills, analyzing documents, fetching coffee.

Yeah? he said. And? What does your father say?

This is internecine. He's against it, but I don't think he has the clout. It's all too straightforward and petty. Inside the building, no one knows he's actually theirs, one of their own. More than one of their own, actually. Not just clan. More like a chieftan, you know, with his own faction. The guys on the summit with their oxygen bottles, two or three people—they know. Everybody else knows him as an ideological cheerleader from Foggy Bottom with impeccable connections.

Well, Burnette said with a tight grin. I'd advise you to go rogue.

They seem to think I already have.

Flow with the go.

I love that. Rock on. Everything is happening out there. I'm prepared to take the risks.

Copy that, he said, pausing for the waitress to set down their plates and leave. Didn't I hear you mention you wanted to go back east and study classical Arabic? He told her to request an assignment that fit the profile. Let them put you in an embassy somewhere in Indian country as an analyst and then enroll in a class in a local school or find a tutor or something along those lines. Have it both ways, you know. Let the bureaucracy reform you on your own terms.

Hey, she said, suddenly effervescent, will you go to Africa with me? For the wedding?

Go as what? he said. Your bodyguard?

Wouldn't that be great.

I was there. Last year. Short mission.

Where? You never told me.

Kenya, he said. Two or three days. Jihadi pest control.

Kenya? she said. I haven't been paying attention.

Chambers returned to the table and they ate their breakfasts garnished with Beltway small talk and the latest gossip about the president, specifically his famously careless propensity to knuckle-walk his way into scandals with women who proved to be stupendously insipid. With perverse optimism, Steven wagered that the commander in chief would one day soon discover a higher purpose for his testicles, their existence to date limited to slinging jism into the dentally challenged mouths of trollops.

God! Daddy! That's disgusting.

Eville's face reddened and he said, Sir, come on now, stopping himself from voicing any further admonishment. Chambers clipped him with an indulgent smile and continued on, mindless of his offense.

The undersecretary predicted the president would shoot his way out of this farce, his latest and most dire sexual folly. Watch, said Chambers. And that would be a blessing, don't you think, but God save us, consider the man's target list. Haitians? Timorese? Serbs? I'd suck him off myself in the Rose Garden if I thought it would wake him up. He's a weak sister, a little momma's boy from Arkansas.

That's really enough, said his daughter. Stop.

Rome's burning, Kitten. Christ almighty, what do we have to do?

Eville folded his napkin over his unfinished breakfast and said he intended to drive over to Arlington to visit his father's grave. Dottie said she wanted to go along, which she did, after her father declined the invitation and they dropped him back at the town house, exchanging the Mercedes for the pickup truck, and turned around, taking Dolly Madison Boulevard to the George Washington Parkway, exiting at Memorial Bridge and through the arch to sacred ground.

Like all family members of the interred, Eville had been issued a VIP pass to the national cemetery but it sat in his odds-and-ends box in Fayetteville and so they parked among the tourists for the long walk in. I've never been here before, she confessed, her voice wavering as they hiked from one acre of hallowed ground to the next, the nation's sorrow a city unto itself, its resources inexhaustible. It goes on forever, doesn't it, she said. Eville consulted the map he had grabbed at the entrance to the visitor's center and guided them forward. We go left here. Then, a few minutes later, Okay, right again and up a ways. Then he said with a catch in his voice, Two more blocks is Vietnam, and they counted the headstones down a middle row until they were standing above his father's grave, perfectly surrounded by the fallen, and Dottie took his left hand in hers, Eville kissing the fingertips of his right hand to touch the rounded white stone of the marble marker and pass the kiss to the dead—*Dad. Hey.*

They spent the night together again at the hotel, forgoing the talk they might have had about important things, what was around the corner, down the road, over the horizon—*fuck the horizon*—opting out for a last night of mutually assured dissipation, room service and pills and vodka, a long encore of slothful rutting, a surfeit of sloppy tenderness, these hours dumb and beautiful, themselves sustaining, falling asleep in a knot like tranquilized wrestlers, waking at sunrise to a *chirr,* slow to realize the source of the intrusion into their peace—Burnette's pager. Burnette was being buzzed, summoned to report for duty.

She phoned the receptionist, reserving the room for the next two weeks, and then drove with Eville to Andrews Air Force Base, Dottie clearly determined to have at least the front of the conversation they had sidelined the night before. What happened on that island, she confessed, admitted, declared, insisted.

Yeah?

It made me happy, she said. You've steadied me.

That's good, he said. I'm glad.

Then what do we need to say to each other, now? What's next, Burnette?

We should keep in touch, don't you think? he said, and she let the silence ferment and enlarge between them before she answered.

I've never been to Montana.

Let's do it then. Let's go.

He presented her with the keys to the truck before he walked out onto the tarmac for a flight to Kyrgyzstan, and they would keep in touch, more frequently than he could have reasonably hoped, exchanging encrypted updates of their whereabouts and doings and planning a rendezvous in Africa for the wedding. She would write to tell him that things continued to happen in the world that affected her deeply, personally, that she had enrolled in the Agency's clandestine service course but changed her mind about volunteering for a slot in the paramilitary special activities division. I'm putting on a dress and heels, she said, and heading for the desert, there's something in me that needs to go to the end of the world, and by midsummer she was in Yemen, working for the ambassador. A woman! she wrote. At first glance, she's not so much different than Daddy—*We're coming in and hell's coming with us*—you know the type, all faith, no fear, but I have a suspicion underneath the Amazonian veneer she is a Chamberlin. They don't bother with shitty little hatreds here, they want the West vaporized, every man, woman, and child. Sometimes I feel like I'm crawling on my knees, looking for a place where I once lived, trying to return to the place where I lost myself, or rather found myself, alone in the sea, so deep and so empty. She wrote that she was up to her neck in intrigue, donning a burqa to take a night class at the university in Sana'a, making enemies as fast as friends, both categories sharing an odd politeness. She wrote that a prince who owned Arabian horses was teaching her how to ride. At the end of July, she dropped him a postcard of a mud-walled fortress, saying, Love may be the only thing we are right about. They arranged to meet in Johannesburg in early August, rent a Land Rover, camp their way up through Kruger National Park and into Zimbabwe for the wedding. She never mentioned she would be flying into South Africa after a stopover in Nairobi. Burnette tried phoning her once from Fayetteville but couldn't get through.

CHAPTER FIFTY-TWO

He would not see Dottie again until August, not in Africa but in Germany, in the intensive care unit at Landstuhl Regional Medical Center, the largest American hospital outside the United States. This time with her surely the last time in his life, although he could not even say with absolute certainty that it was her and not somebody else swaddled mummylike in bandages from head to waist, her face hidden and misshapen, a breathing tube snaking into a mouth hole, but when he took her one unbandaged hand, its skin a raku of superficial lacerations rising up her forearm to a band of gauze and tape, he knew well enough, and when he squeezed her hand and said I'm here and felt a bird's wing beat of his own desperate affirming pressure reciprocated, he knew. I'm here, he told her and he held her hand then long after the machines sounded their alarms, an urgency that seemed to have no corresponding effect on the IC nurse in the room. A harried-looking doctor stuck his head in the door—Do we resuscitate?—and the nurse said, No, her father had signed the order this morning, and the doctor nodded grimly, no saving this one, and left to continue his rounds.

The nurse said, I see this happen all the time. People wait for their loved ones. She waited for you.

What's happening? he said. What happened?

It should have happened this morning, the nurse explained gently. It should have happened on the medevac. It should have happened in Nairobi at the embassy. She should have died in the bombing, like the woman she was with, the woman standing next to her. But she was waiting for you, wasn't she?

She squeezed my hand, said Eville. She squeezed my hand. I felt it.

The nurse was behind him, patting his back, and he could hear her whimper as she struggled to control her own emotions. Her brain was dead, said the nurse. She suffered massive trauma to her skull and upper body. She was in a coma. She wasn't going to pull through. Her father brought a priest this morning to administer last rites. It was only a matter of hours. But she waited for you, didn't she.

I felt her, said Ev.

Yes, said the nurse, her tenderness stabbing into Burnette's disorientation, her kindness destroying him. Okay.

All right, said Eville, still holding Dottie's hand, cold to begin with, cold now. His lips pursed torturously, jaw clenched, eyes beginning to glaze with devastation. All right, he said, aware just barely that he was repeating himself. All right, all right, all right. Nodding, just nodding like a reprimanded simpleton.

I'll leave you alone, the nurse said. Eville bent and kissed the palm of the woman whose name was printed at the top of the IC unit's chart, and on her baby-blue admissions wristband, Dorothy Kovacevic, and dropped her hand, beckoning in its curl of death, and said to the nurse, No, do what you have to do here, ma'am, thank you, I'm finished. Thank you, thanks. God. Shit. I'm sorry. Shit.

The sight of a chair in the hallway seemed to whisk away his physical composure and his knees twisted, sinking him onto the seat, and there he sat staring into space as two attendants entered the room and exited uncountable minutes later, wheeling out the gurney, the sheeted body sailing past him on its journey to the morgue. He was aware of the nurse, her angelic kindness enveloping her like an aura, and he had some sense that she had walked past him several times before she clicked into focus and he stopped her, wondering if she knew what had happened to Ms. Kovacevic's father, who had earlier escorted him to Dottie's bedside, wondering if he had been informed of his daughter's death, and the nurse told him, Yes, your father-in-law knows, he's down in the chapel. Take the elevator to the ground floor, said the nurse, and take a right and it's on the right.

Eville found his feet, confused, thinking, Father-in-law?

In the chapel there was Steven Chambers on a bench in front of an ecumenical altar, a man at peace with nothing and nobody, yelling into a mobile phone—*You hit first and let others complain!*—and Eville sat down nearby, paralyzed. Then the call was finished and minutes passed in silence, broken finally by the undersecretary.

Do you expect me to commiserate with you? he said, turning in cold appraisement of Eville's pain. Shall we commiserate with one another then?

Sir, said Eville.

Do you know what I want right now, Sergeant Burnette? said the undersecretary.

No, sir, whispered Eville.

I want you to remember who we are. I think it's worth a fucking try, don't you.

Okay.

Now it begins, said the undersecretary.

Yes.

This war will be a blessing.

Okay.

So keep your mind on that, said Chambers, his uncanny calm betrayed only by the tremble in his hands, the phone replaced by a rosary, and he asked the sergeant when was the last time he had checked his pager and Burnette said he didn't know. Turn it back on, man, said the undersecretary. I believe you have a plane to catch.

He missed her, but more truly he missed the person he was during those days with her, out there on the island in a life they could imagine as theirs alone, knowing that person might never appear again. Her absence became her daily presence, with a greater persistence than it ever might have been otherwise in his life, her most potent form of reality, and reality itself for Eville Burnette became more violent, the violence an altogether different order of magnitude, and thus more self-negating and life more tolerable, this hatred and this love dragging him deeper into the world and its madness, where he imposed his country's will but not its dream, for it had no dream to impose. He stood in the shadowed entrance of a mountainside cave in Afghanistan and watched cruise missiles rain into the valley below, the dust blooming like a garden of ochre chrysanthemums. He met up with his D-boy squad in southeastern Turkey and they crossed the border on a hunter-killer mission into northern Iraq to clean out a training camp of Arab extremists near a remote Kurdish village. Then he was in Tajikistan with Scarecrow and a pair of Agency outliers where they boarded a rattletrap MI-18 helicopter left behind by the Soviets and flew with an Afghan crew to the Panjshir Valley, looking out a cracked porthole at snowy summits that said, *Nothing here is worth dying for,* the spooks with a sack of cash to buy up Charlie Wilson's leftover Stingers while Burnette and Scarecrow acquainted themselves with the warlords of the Northern Alliance. Then Spain, where they pulled a trio of jihadi scorpions out of a hole in Madrid and delivered them to the secret police in Morocco. For the first three weeks of December, he trained at a clandestine site in the Negev desert with an international assortment of special forces operatives and Israeli commandos.

A week's leave during the holidays allowed him to slip away from the Delta cycle to the ranch in Montana, the family gathered again for dinner on Christmas Day, his mother a silvery rose, not yet acquiescent to her failing muscles, still breaking horses that might at any moment turn the tables and break her into irreparable old age, his younger brother much subdued after his autumn's residence in the Whitefish lockup on assault and battery charges, a barroom fight that accelerated into some stuporous zone of honor that brought out whatever lay murderous and ready in the kid's psyche. His mother came to him in the den on Christmas Eve where Eville sat on the crummy old threadbare couch, lost in the annual ritual of cleaning his father's guns, sitting next to him, close, legs touching, his arm bumping hers as he worked, quiet for a while before she asked, Why so sad, Ev? Aw, Mom, he said, quiet himself for a stretch before he could speak. A friend of mine was killed, in that bombing in Africa.

I heard about that, she said. She took his closest hand away from the rifle across his lap and held it in her own lap and he sat there with nothing more to say, wondering why he didn't tell her the friend was a woman. He could have said girlfriend, couldn't he? Maybe he could have said fiancée, as he had at the hospital in Germany, when they were reluctant to let him onto the floor at the IC unit, visitation rights restricted to family only. What if he said she was the daughter of Dawson's old Vietnam buddy, Steve Chambers? And what he really couldn't tell her was what he had been increasingly wondering about himself, like a miner toiling in an inhospitable desertscape, after years of coming up dry and empty, who had just discovered gold in the hills only to be ejected from the claim, forced by a grand robbery to flee for his life. He wondered about this sense inside him, not helplessness so much as resignation, that he might lose the world and it would not matter, a vision of perishability that seemed to inform him about a condition that was not war and life and death but just him, losing control of his feelings because his feelings—it was a slow, not sudden, process but each increment seemed irreversible—had been canceled, threatening him with a bankruptcy of spirit and conscience. He thought he could be better than that but now he wasn't so sure. Despite the loss he felt, which was intractable, he would not think about Dottie now, he wanted no memories, she was never his, and in all likelihood never could have been, their relationship fetal and miscarried, their weightless footprints vanishing as the world disintegrated. It was a mistake to believe otherwise. Did they ever exist? Was their time together worth anything? Prove it. Can you prove it?

Flicker, flare, gone.

Love, understanding, happiness.

He thinks, as he will always think, I can bring you close: an image, our time—but he will not and cannot do it, because it is too much to bear, her closeness, now that she is gone. I can remember, he tells himself, but he won't.

Why would he want to keep telling himself their story when it felt better, saner, to have no story at all?

Mom, it's late, he said that quiet unholy night, go to bed. And he kissed her cheek and she went to her room and he kissed her again on Christmas Day under the mistletoe and he kissed her after they finished dancing at the American Legion on New Year's Eve and then once more the following day when she dropped him at the airport in Missoula, a free and independent woman, his mother, her beloved eldest son like his own beloved father, off somewhere in the hinterlands of the world when in her loneliness she most desired their company and they most desired a higher cause, which she both acknowledged and despised with a buried impotent fury.

Back inside the Wall at Fayetteville he reported for duty and was told that the lieutenant colonel wanted a word with him and there in his office was McCall, half-hidden at his desk, the poor bastard barricaded behind dung heaps of paperwork. The lieutenant colonel scratched his brush cut and selected a folder from one of the mounds, using it to fan the air. Top, he said, a salutation Burnette hadn't heard in ages. With apologies for a nonsensical policy now defunct, the colonel informed him that his original pre-Delta selection rank had been restored. That ain't the end of it, said Lieutenant Colonel McCall. Burn, you still want to go mustang?

Yes, sir.

The major shuffled the dung heap and extracted another document that had him shaking his head. Man, Burnette, your file is one fucked-up bitch, I have to say. This piece of paper here tells me your direct commission as a captain has continued to mature. Your entire career path has been highly unorthodox, wouldn't you say?

I'd say so, sir.

Want to try to explain it?

I can't, sir.

I have the orders right here to put you in school—the Command and General Staff College out at Fort Leavenworth. Yes or no, partner. Choose your poison. You're eligible for a bump up the ranks.

School sounds pretty good, sir, said Burnette.

And so that winter of '99 he found himself in Kansas, sitting in Bell Hall, the schoolhouse at Leavenworth, scheduled for promotion to major off a special, never published list of candidates, a zebra dropped into the horse show, learning how to write operations orders to scale for a battalion or brigade, his classmates and especially his instructors mostly people who look down and see the top of their stomachs, guys with more degrees than a thermometer. For a while Leavenworth seemed like the right choice to Burnette, an idyllic respite from the regimens of killing (practice, practice, practice) and the adrenaline stream of the field, the blood drama, the screech of chaos and precision, the eerie calm, the hideous thrill. The classroom was a powerful antidote to his season on the warpath, a dismount into a restorative interlude, breaking the bad habit of not thinking beyond the absoluteness of the moment, not thinking deeper, deep enough to separate his life from its lethal existence before it became impossible to have a life beyond war that amounted to much. But after a few months, alone at night in his rented room, the episodes of doubt began—he was being shown an army he had never truly seen, the one worried about PowerPoint presentations, fonts on slides, men who can't climb the stairs without being out of breath. His workouts became fiendish as the classes struck him as increasingly worthless.

And it was there at the college that spring, after a heated morning's seminar in international humanitarian policy (topic: war as philanthropy), that he was pulled aside by an adjutant as he left the classroom and told that the head of the department wished to see him. In line with his scholastic immunity, he hadn't been paged or summoned to action in months, nor had he had any contact with Steven Chambers since the undersecretary's heartless dismissal in the Landstuhl chapel. When everything's that fucked up you don't ask questions, you walk away, you don't look back, you move on, you forget because forgetting is the only positive thing you can do. He took the stairs to the third floor, his footsteps echoing on the tiles past the long line of doors on both sides of the hallway, the length of a football field. He reported to the secretary in the front room of the administrative section, who gestured toward an inner door. He knocked and walked in; the colonel, bland as any civilian dean, stood away from his desk, forgoing a salute, waiting to greet him with a handshake. Burnette, he said, do you own a suit and tie? I mean a black suit, wool, formal? And a tie? Not any old hippie tie with flowers and polka dots.

No sir. Just a blazer.

All right then, said the colonel. When you leave here my adjutant will take you to the clothier in Kansas City.

Got it. What's up, sir?

You're on a Title 22 request for the next four days, he said, and Burnette, with a look of perplexity, admitted he couldn't recall ever hearing mention of Title 22.

It's State Department, said the colonel. They requested you, specifically. There's a funeral in Europe. They've asked that you head up the security detail for our people.

Why would they do that? State operates its own muscle-heads, sir.

What's the problem, Burnette?

Why me? Is there some reason?

I can tell you what I know, said the colonel. One, we're talking the Balkans. Two, State has received credible threats on the life of one of its dignitaries. Three, you seem to be acquainted with the chief of the host country's security service, some general named Vasich.

Vasich? A Croatian?

Yes, said the colonel. I think that's right.

With all respect, Colonel. Please advise State I'm unavailable for the assignment.

Not going to happen, Burnette. Given the possibility of your refusal, my orders are to ask you to pick up the phone on my desk and dial the number I read out to you.

Who am I calling, sir?

The Pentagon.

Who am I speaking to?

I can't tell you that, son, because I don't know. You getting the picture here?

He dialed the number, whoever picked up asked his name and rank and transferred the call to another person who asked again for Burnette to identify himself and he was transferred once more to a secure line and after a moment's clicking someone answered saying, Ev, how the hell are you? How's school? and he played along, answering politely, letting the guy talk, recognizing the voice but unable to place it until the voice said, We miss you out there on the links, buddy, and Eville said Ben? This is Ben, right? What's this all about?

You got a few minutes? asked Ben sardonically and Burnette said I don't know, sir, but Ben kept talking and Burnette tried to explain his reluctance to participate in the mission but didn't get very far. Ben euphemistically described the undersecretary's medical crisis, and then mentioned The Hague, ongoing investigations, potential legal complications. If Steve starts running his mouth, shoot him, said Ben, letting the silence on the line resonate before amending his directive. Hey, Ev, I'm joking, but you get the point. And one more thing. This guy from The Hague snooping around, an American lawyer. I think you might know him.

Everything settled? asked the colonel.

Oh, man, said Burnette. Fuck me, sir. Yes, sir.

Then the adjutant was there to take him downtown and then to his apartment and then to the airport for a flight to Andrews where he boarded a plane with Scarecrow and the team at sundown for a sunrise landing in Zagreb, Vasich a lone sentinel on the wet tarmac, dressed in winter-blue camo fatigues, a brass star pinned to each epaulette, bareheaded, his baldness aglow with pluvial mist, greeting Burnette with a bear hug and a happy growl, *My fucking brother,* ready to begin the advance work, two days hence, for the funeral of Davor Starevica, a man the general described to the Americans as the father of Croatian independence.

He was also very close to Kovacevic, your undersecretary. Chambers, I mean, said Vasich. Not the father but I think stepfather, godfather. It's not so clear. And how is he? I hear he is not so well.

Yeah, said Burnette, sleepwalking, helping the squad load their footlockers and garment bags into a panel truck. So I'm told.

The threats were manifold, generic, longstanding, and, to an undeterminable extent, an in-house ploy, the forthcoming state funeral and its high density of VIPs generating a widespread crackdown on dissidents and undesirables—Muslims and occasional Serbs—throughout the Croatian capital, roundups and detentions, interrogations and deportations and a small discreet selection of disappearances, a choreography of internal security that Burnette and his team mostly observed from the sidelines at the headquarters of the intelligence service. This was the Balkans, not

Scandinavia. No one forgets when you hurt their feelings, said Vasich, we are very sensitive, ha-ha. Here, the children are born already with enemies.

But we are accustomed to it, said Vasich, and with Chambers, who knows? He was very involved with things at the beginning of the war, he was very helpful with our leadership, he and Davor, you would always see them together, okay, so we Croatians love him, he is one of us, but the *mujos*, they dream to take his head off. But this is not a problem. The situation is normal, okay? and Burnette said, If that's the case, I don't understand why we're here, and Vasich threw his meaty arm across the American's shoulder and confided, I think maybe to babysit. I also think something serious. I think Kovacevic wants to send a message, to warn somebody not to fuck with him. Who? asked Burnette. The Hague? but Vasich shrugged and said, Perhaps. Or maybe someone in Washington, I don't know. Okay, said Burnette. Next question: Who gets through the door? Three hundred, said Vasich. By invitation. The public was free to gather outside the cathedral and along the route. Okay, said Burnette. Anybody credentialed from ICTY? No, said Vasich, The Hague is not so interested in us. They are not serious people. They take little fish and leave the whale. The lawyers, they like this game. They come like bugs to crawl on our suffering. You have someone in mind? Yeah, said Burnette, let's run his name, and they walked down the hall to another office to pull up the database for an aggregated master list. Type in Thomas Harrington, said Burnette to the technician, and they watched the screen switch to the roster for international media and then isolate ITN and there was Tom, with the film crew, identified as a consultant.

Hey, look, said Vasich. Your man. He is from the tribunal? Yeah, said Burnette, and Vasich said we can detain this guy or put him on a plane or pull down his pants, what would you like? and Burnette said, Nothing.

Exiting the building Scarecrow pulled Eville aside on the street and said, I smell it, bro. What's the deal? You pulling more of that voodoo wool over my eyes? And Burnette said, I smell it too, Crow, but it's not coming from me.

The Croats came for them at dawn the morning of the second day, grabbing the D-boys out of their safe house for a rehearsal, starting at the presidential palace, where Davor Starevica's body lay in state. Check it out, Burn, said Scarecrow as they ascended the spruce-lined drive to the modernist palace known upon its completion in 1964 as Tito's Villa, I was expecting a castle or something, some medieval vampire shit. Next, familiarizing themselves with the route the cortege would follow to the cathedral, the rooftop positions Spank and Tilly would share with Vasich's marskmen; last, a brief step out at the Mirogoj cemetery, a graveyard memorable for its sheer beauty, its ivied arcades and pruned shrubbery and domed chapels and tiled promenades and statuary more like a museum attached to a royal garden, a groundsman pointing down a pebbled path ahead to a black canopy erected among a grove of headstones. Do you want to see? asked one of the Croats. Nope, this is good, said Burnette.

At each venue Vasich's liaisons introduced them to an ever widening circle of counterparts composing the mechanism of the event, then they were back at the Ministry of the Interior, having their photographs taken for full-clearance IDs, linking them up with the ministry's commo network, trying to memorize faces of bad guys pulled up on the counterterrorism section's computer screens. After lunch, one of Vasich's drivers ran Burnette and Scarecrow back out to the airport to collect the advance man from the State Department's own protection detail, an aging former US marshal twenty years their senior, dressed like a Texan, unsubtle and agitated, miffed to be reporting to a pair of army hotshots who had usurped his authority. No offense meant, said the bland-faced gunslinger from State. What do you know that I don't? What the eff are you doing here? No offense taken, said Burnette, just give me the skinny, sir, and we'll bring you up to speed and show you around. First stop the US embassy, where tempers flared. I suppose you never heard of us, Scarecrow smart-assed the senior political officer, because we're like fairies. We only exist in a higher realm. The other possibility is we were never here. Deputies placed calls to the States, inquiries were made, egos chastened by denials of access. The ambassador dictated a memo to his staff—*Stay out of it.*

For Burnette, the read-in had yet to include the actual size or identities of the American delegation. Vasich supplied a preliminary list—the ambassador, the DCM, the station chief, the defense attaché, a Seventh Group colonel working with the UN peacekeepers, a visiting congressman—but no one could verify who the last-minute out-of-towners might be, if any, save for the undersecretary, whose inattendance, Burnette had learned from Vasich, would precipitate a scandal of mysterious proportions. Burnette's focus had been grapple-hooked to Chambers and he assumed that State's own security handmaidens had the broader responsibility. The issue was clarified immediately, however, as he and Tex sat down together to begin to orchestrate the next day's schedule and reality surfaced inside the scaffolding of logistics.

Transportation staging at embassy motor pool: 0600. Coordinate police escort: 0630. Airport arrival: 0725. Flight ETA (from Brussels): 0740. Roger that, said Burnette. Why two vehicles? How many people are in the box? Are we dividing VIPS and security? I'm not comfortable with that. Me plus one will be glued to the undersecretary. My other two guys are on the roof. Anything beyond that, it's your call. Tell me what you have, he said, and he was told. Got it, said Burnette, I'll take you over to meet Vasich and his people and then I'll see you here in the morning. They gathered up their notes to leave. Hey, Burnette, said the man from State, I appreciate that you're not trying to step on my toes. Come clean with me, partner. What are we walking into here? I figure you and your gladiators wouldn't be on deck without some kind of shit storm on somebody's radar.

You keep not believing me when I tell you I don't know, Burnette said equably. But I have an opinion—you want to hear it? Trust this general, Vasich. In this city tomorrow dogs don't bark without his permission. I think we're looking at clear skies.

0500. The liaison knocked on their door, dusted with snowflakes, bringing a thermos of hot sweet coffee and a towel-covered basket of cheese pierogies, still warm from his mother's oven. They rotated into the tiny bathroom, taking turns murdering its space with odious fumes after the previous night's strange grub and the hard-drinking excesses spurred by Vasich and his capos, slivovitz, a brutal Slavic protocol of toasting, fraternity and liberty, of course, then a litany of battles in towns and villages that might as well have been on the moon, then vengeance and retribution and its teary oaths. They took turns showering and meticulously trimmed their facial hair to revised standards, swiped deodorant under their arms, and began to suit up in layers of comfort and discomfort, lightweight thermal underwear first and then an array of strap-ons—weapons, commo units, body armor—laughing with locker room insults, Scarecrow and Burnette donning their formal wear, *Crow, you look like the undertaker himself; Hey, dudes, check out Burn, the dude can't tie a tie,* Tilly and Spank spared a similar ribbing, dressing in street clothes and parkas and watch caps, their rifles cased like electric guitars.

Then out into the metropolitan darkness to the waiting van, footlockers and all, the urban air windless with a furnace smell of sulfur and the winter mothball smell of crones and bitter diesel exhaust and the flurries falling straight to the pavement and melting. At the back gates of the embassy, the marine guards mirrored the underside of the van and checked passes and identification and cleared the vehicle through the maze of concrete blast barriers to deliver Burnette and Scarecrow and turn around and back out again, continuing on with Spank and Tilly. Tex awaited them with a nose drip and hacking cough and balled handkerchief, shivering in a trench coat, stoically miserable, unable to muster a collegial smile.

Which one you want? he asked, gesturing toward the two black armored 4x4 SUV limos parked on the apron, adorned with tiny American flags. Both the embassy and Vasich had offered to supply drivers but the head count wasn't going to work and Burnette was against the idea anyway, agreeing only to valets at the drop-off points. Let's fire 'em up and get those heaters going, said Scarecrow, I'm freezing my 'nads. I almost forgot, said State, reaching into his coat pocket for a folded note. The PAO asked me to give you this, and Burnette glanced at the message scribbled on the paper, crumpling the note in his hand. What's what? Scarecrow said and Burnette told him it was a request from ITN television to interview the undersecretary after the funeral. Ain't going to happen, said Ev. Out on the street, the police escort assembled without fanfare, two teeny cartoonish squad cars mounted with disco lights, four motorcycles ridden by faceless androids, and they were off to the airport across the gray city, the sunrise offering its inhabitants little more than spreading gloom.

695

They stamped their cold feet to take out the numbness, watching the Gulfstream land and taxi toward the general aviation terminal and stop in front of the idling motorcade. The D-boys's brains switched from hibernate to operational, a visceral zone of total concentration and reflex, the Oakley sunglasses coming out of their breast pockets, flicked open like switchblades and slipped over their eyes. The hatch opened, the stairway unfolded, and a black-suited fellow appeared and then a second, clean-cut civilian versions of Burnette and Scarecrow. Those are mine, said the Texan. Two of three. The undersecretary appeared next, beaming with affability, a hand raised in salutation, looking beyond his welcoming entourage into the middle distance to broadcast benevolence and affection to an imaginary crowd, the gesture merely premature, given the scarved and gloved throngs ahead and their reciprocal adoration. Behind him came a disheveled giant with a scornful grimace, his impatience nearly pushing Chambers down the steps. That's Holbrooke, said Tex. The famously abrasive special envoy, Holbrooke, the wizard of peace, grand ringmaster of the Balkans's fragile accords, clearly unwilling to put to rest a contretemps with his diplomatic colleague, interrupted but not ended by their arrival, something they got into in Brussels, at the NATO summit's deliberations on Kosovo.

At the bottom of the stairs Holbrooke stepped around and in front of Chambers, turning on him, jabbing a prosecutorial finger at the undersecretary's chest while Chambers stood there silently, taking it in stride, absorbing this browbeating with a respectful smile of promised compliance, nothing obviously defensive in his genteel veneer. In fact, Burnette thought, he looked the superior being in every respect, the model august statesman, the very embodiment of statesmanship in elegance and temperament, distinguished in his camel-hair topcoat and Savile Row suit, the knotted perfection of his silver necktie reflecting the sculpted crest of platinum hair. There he stood, dignified and composed, his demeanor vibrant with an easy understated presence of command, his visage bronzed with a year-round suntan, professionally handsome, a bit short on the gravitas associated with the word *noble* but not lacking in the impressions associated with the word *aristocrat*. And there he stood, in the grip of the choleric envoy, Holbrooke looking rumpled and slightly shabby, an unattended self, thickset and overheated, a boardroom pugilist with his tie loosened and the flaps of his black hair uncombed, displaying the mannerisms of a vulgarian and bully, snarling at Chambers, You're marching off a cliff with these motherfucking Serbs, when Burnette intervened.

Sir, he said, stepping forward. Time to go.

Not the slightest acknowledgment of his protégé, no indication whatsoever of registering Eville's presence. Chambers simply walked past Burnette with an expressionless gaze to where Scarecrow held open the rear door of the SUV and took his seat. Crow closed the door, obscuring the undersecretary behind the tinted glass. Who's Burnette? asked the special envoy, prompting Eville out of this stinging moment of invisibility, identifying himself and stepping away with Holbrooke toward the cockpit of the Gulfstream.

Listen, Burnette, said the envoy, dropping his voice. Major, right?

Not yet, sir.

This plane is yours. After the funeral, I want you to put Chambers on it and take him back to the States.

I don't expect he'll want to do that, sir. There's a luncheon—

He's not going. Under any circumstances. Chambers was being detrimental to peace, fighting the administration on Kosovo, bucking against the framework. This man is out of his goddamn mind, the envoy said. He needs medical attention.

Sir—Eville began to protest but Holbrooke interrupted, taking a cell phone out of his coat pocket, saying a name, a magic word.

Let's call Ben. You'll listen to Ben, right? You think this could happen without Ben's approval?

Sir, if the undersecretary resists. I mean—

Holbrooke seemed amused by the concern. Persuade him, Captain.

Braying sirens, whipping lights, radio squawk from walkie-talkies, Scarecrow behind the wheel, Tex's third man, Bill, joining him up front, Eville sliding anxiously into the back with the undersecretary, the special envoy hustled into the SUV behind them, and they were on the move. The motorcade made its way past the terminal and out to the highway and Eville thought for many reasons, *This is so fucked,* not the least of it the shunning, Chambers sitting erect with indifference, eyes closed, eyes open but blinking at the back of the driver's skull, *Who is it among us who exist for this man?* tormenting himself with that, the disavowal, this reinjury and its penance of emotional solitude that seemed to be the lasting consequence of Dottie's death, this totally in-the-way personal shit. Just trying to cope with the toxicity of it, until out of the corner of his eye he noticed Chambers staring at him, stalled in a genuine effort of memory, and when the undersecretary finally spoke it spooked Burnette. Dottie had voiced concerns and Ben had danced around it and now Holbrooke had been explicit and he had seen for himself peculiar vignettes of erratic behavior, the early warnings were out there but he did not entirely comprehend the undersecretary's condition, and now Chambers opened his mouth and words came out to carry on a conversation they weren't having.

These are days to look forward, Ev, said the undersecretary, an otherwise unctuous sentiment were it not so bizarre. Retain our optimism. I was hoping I'd see you here. Say, did you ever make it down for Christopher's wedding?

No, sir, he said, toneless.

What a shame. I thought you and Dorothy had it all planned out. Meet in Johannesburg, drive up to Harare, spend a few days exploring Kruger on the way. Fantastic.

Yes, sir, he said. That was our plan.

Fantastic, said Chambers, how was it?

How was what, sir?

I couldn't get there, you know. His mother went. Ah, that reminds me, Chambers continued but stopped, a fleeting panic in his eyes until the thought came skipping back and he reached across the seat, his fingers alighting on Burnette's knee and then springing away like startled birds, Burnette reeling at the sight of the unclipped index and middle fingernails on Chambers's right hand, their extraordinary womanish length, like a Chinese emperor's. There's something I must show you. Something of great importance. Don't let me forget, Ev.

Yes, sir.

698

Later, said Chambers, oddly relieved, it appeared, of an unspoken burden. Remind me.

His attention shifted, filling with delight, to the city and for ten minutes he talked nonstop, pointing out landmarks, sites that had been shelled in the latest conflict, attaching vivid anecdotes to buildings and neighborhoods and monuments, at one point leaning forward to tap Scarecrow on the shoulder, mistaking him for a national, addressing him in Croatian, Crow telling him, I don't speak that, sir, Burnette confronted with yet another riddle that slowly turned to revelation—apparently the undersecretary had spent some part of his childhood in Zagreb during World War Two.

Then Chambers's mood evanesced and he fell silent for a few moments and his gaze turned dreamy. You've been to Brussels, right? he said finally to no one in particular. Best *moules* on the planet.

Another extended pause and then a pronouncement, his voice enthusiastic, tallyho, as if the answer to a trivia question had popped into his head.

Maintain your convictions!

Yes, sir.

Ev, that man is an asshole.

Okay.

That's not the problem, you see. The problem is he's a *mujo*-lover. No good will come of it.

They were slowing down behind a processional line of vehicles as they approached the main entrance to the presidential palace. Burnette commo-checked his team's wiring, the cuff mics and earbuds, and began to rehearse the in-and-out details and timing, not solely for the undersecretary's benefit—Bill, the add-on to their detail from State, needed to hear it; straight routine for Scarecrow and Burn, this was SOP—but it brought a fiery irrational rebuke from Steven Chambers.

I know what to do, goddamn it, he said and Burnette stared at him in cold wonder. Goddamn it, Ev. After all these years.

His voice trailed, something new flooding into his blue eyes, unprecedented in the crossed connection of their relationship, at least to Burnette, Chambers showing what he made a point of never showing. Brokenness, pain.

You don't understand, said Chambers. I'm here again to bury my father.

The pager on Burnette's belt jiggled as they passed through the palatial gates, the undersecretary defying Eville, lowering his window to wave at a mournful crowd roped behind the cordon of police and soldiers, the people animated by their glimpse of Chambers, burbling with reverent noise—it would be wrong to call it cheering—for a native son's return. Up through the evergreened knolls to the esplanade of paving stones, its red carpet and ceremonial guard, at the front of the motorcade now, Scarecrow placing the transmission in park, Vasich's valet opening the undersecretary's door. Eville glanced at the screen of his upgraded model as he exited the vehicle to lope to the undersecretary's side, hitting the wrong keys until he hit the right one, reading the text message from Ben, *Green light. Bring Arnie home.*

He remembered—Yeah, Arnie, right. Call me Arnie.

What's he got? Scarecrow had asked the other day. That Alzheimers crud? The neurological term was multi-infarcted dementia, diminishing mental capacity signaled by intermittent cognitive blips and ruts due to a years-long series of tiny aneurysms, micro-explosions in the brain, too minuscule to be consciously experienced by the person being rerouted toward an impending abyss.

Arnie, strokes, *Christ.* It was too much. Christ's chosen one, handpicked by the Lord to serve as the supreme allied commander for Armageddon, going eighteen holes with the devil and a play-off round of sudden death. Says Lucifer, How many strokes you giving me, Arnie? *Zap, zap.* Keep 'em coming, my boy.

Inside the unheated glassed expanse of the palace, in a pale reception hall dim with dispirited light seeping through the plates of floor-to-ceiling windows, the air redolent with the viscid smell of Easter lilies, the receiving line looked to Burnette's uncongenial eye like a tenth reunion of the politburo. Severe jowly ministers in fedoras and felt overcoats that hung off their frames like Mongolian yurts; the high command of pigeon-breasted generals in uniforms of a cheap-looking green, plastered with medals and Croix de Guerre and campaign ribbons, their faces shadowed beneath large caps with peaked crowns; foreign dignitaries from across the Euro-zone and Eastern bloc who in their collective countenance openly displayed the belief that greatness could not accrue without a heavy investment in pomposity; the preening criminals subcontracted to nail a shell of drywall over the wreckage of Yugoslavia. Burnette walked a pace back, at the undersecretary's side along the long row of powerful men, acutely aware of his own unesteemed status. He had accepted his place in the order of the world long ago but something about today, in the presence of this critical mass of assembled pharaohs, rankled Burnette so that he had to remind himself that what he one day might give his life for was both more abstract yet more real than men such as these, men who killed and conquered but more pervasively corrupted, degrading the value of the blood they had spilled.

They had come to Vasich, the undersecretary and the general embracing, exchanging a double kiss, Vasich's shining eyes meeting Burnette's with a warning, his chin gesturing toward a high-ranking Canadian blue cap who a minute later asked to speak with Burnette and he looked to the end of the line and made a guess. I can give you thirty seconds, he said, motioning for Bill to assume his place, and stepped aside with the UN officer, affiliated he said with the peacekeeping mission's legal office, who confided, Heads up. There are some fellows from The Hague in town. I wouldn't like to see anything ugly happen. What is it exactly that can happen? asked Burnette. For instance, said the officer, there's some talk about the tribunal's subpoena power. Can't happen, said Burnette. No jurisdiction. Diplomatic immunity. American. Untouchable. Tell them not to waste their time.

There's a hitch, said the Canadian as Burnette began to slide away to rejoin his detail. It seems your undersecretary has dual citizenship. Honorary, of course, but I understand there's some legitimacy to it that could be tested.

Not on my watch, said Burnette.

He returned to position, Bill resumed his tail, the line ended and the moment arrived for the undersecretary to pay his last respects to the republic's hero, beloved architect of freedom and democracy, the former partisan Davor Starevica. Burnette and Crow remained where they were as the undersecretary took three steps forward to the raised open casket, flanked by the striped flags of sovereignty, red-white-blue, emblazoned with the republic's checkerboard coat of arms, a matched set of rock-faced soldiers as honor guard, Chambers peering inside the coffin with an incongruous pleasant smile, the dead man a disfigured gnomish fossil being buried in the bag of his uniform, four stars upon each shoulder board. Chambers bent in to press a kiss upon the corpse's opalescent forehead, reached into his own inner pocket, then wrapped an ivory-beaded rosary around the lifelong atheist's unpliable skeleton hands. The undersecretary looked daftly beatific, stepping back, straightening his spine, saluting and tottering away to become part of the line himself until the last dignitary had filed past and the casket was closed and flag-draped, lifted by the pallbearers and carried out to the hearse for its farewell journey through the drizzle of the city's sorrow.

The cortege was stop-and-go, the streets lined with solemn spectators. In the twenty minutes it took to arrive at the cathedral's gargantuan compound on the Kaptol hill—the southern Kremlin, some called the former archbishop's palace—Chambers, with eerie serenity, had occupied himself with a second rosary, fingers pinching along the beads, lips moving, an occasional phrase of Latin escaping into silence. Otherwise, he didn't say a word and his withdrawal began to bug Eville, the silence like a door left open for his thoughts to wander out where they didn't belong, nosing around in rubbish piles of melancholy and rage, here he was at a fucking funeral with the undersecretary and where the fuck was his daughter, his daughter's funeral? The son of a bitch never had the decency to let him know and he wanted to ask but wouldn't. Fuck him. Fucker.

Scarecrow nodded to a voice in his earbud and said into his collar mic, *Roger that,* and reported to his passengers, Three minutes out. Crowd estimate five-point-five-k. Then he glanced over his shoulder and said, Burn, you copied that, right? They have facial recognition on your guy, and Eville said, Yeah, I heard. Tan corduroy sports coat, black crewneck sweater, left side, press area. I'm going to step away and let Bill come forward with you. What do you think?

Don't get lost, dude.

Bill, you okay with that?

Sure, said Bill. What do I need to know?

Cockblock, said Scarecrov
We should be okay, sai
Then they were asc
rosary's crucifix an'
talgia of here and no
at the ancient crumblin
these walls were construc
invaded at the end of the fifte
many times with my mother.

At the top of the hill they inche
dropped off passengers at the plaza b
spires, the crowd split in the middle by a w
bike racks, lined with heavily armed police fa
rows of soldiers facing one other, standing at att
with shouldered rifles, and the towering cathedra
Alp at the far end of this temporary avenue, its entranc   ing
and ominous, an open black mouth. The undersecretary   out the
former archbishop buried now under the cathedral's flagst   tepinac, he
said, my father's cousin. Burnette half-listened, readying himself for their infil,
Tilly's voice in his ear saying, You're scoped, Burn. The story was something
about a tea biscuit, something about refugees.

Then the doors were open and they were out in the moist bone-aching
air and organized into the procession behind the president and his cabinet
and generals, the undersecretary flanked by Crow and Bill, Burnette a few
steps behind, his head on a swivel, scanning the ranks of Zagreb's citizenry,
Tex and Tex's detail and the special envoy behind him and behind them
the ambassador and the rest of the American delegation and behind them
a divided world.

From within the mass of bodies Burnette heard muted applause and
lamentation, an occasional outburst of bellicose emotion, patriotic slogans
or cursing—he couldn't tell. His vision swept past a grandmother weeping,
small rose-cheeked children riding their fathers' shoulders, grizzled old
veterans in partisan garb, young bucks in black leather jackets, decom-
missioned paramilitaries in camo, chic young women not inclined toward

despondence. About twenty meters from the entrance Tilly was in his ear again, saying your guy's on the left, five meters up, and Burnette spotted Tom Harrington and radioed back to say once he had the undersecretary inside he was turning around. Which is what he did, turning and just walking straight back to where the unsuspecting Harrington stood in the media pack behind the cordon next to a woman with a clipboard speaking to a cameraman and he walked past them a ways to a cop and flashed his ID and cracked open enough space between two sections of barricades to squeeze through and with as much politeness as he could manage muscled his way through and tapped him on the shoulder saying, Tom.

Tom, can I speak to you for a minute?

Yeah, what is it? said Harrington, his upper body twisting around until he could see who was talking and what he saw drained the color from his face although it was apparent to Burnette that Tom did not recognize him, a stranger behind the beard and sunglasses and dressed up like some bad-ass prince. What's this about? asked Harrington, his face wary, struggling for an answer that seemed just out of reach, behind a veil.

Funny thing. Going to a funeral carrying a briefcase.

What business is that of yours?

Will you come with me for a minute?

Why would I do that?

I don't know, said Burnette, pushing up the Oakleys to rest on his brow, squinting. For old time's sake, maybe.

Holy shit, said Tom.

Holy shit, Tom. Long time no see. I take it you're a friend of the deceased?

Did I see this right? Was that you bringing in Chambers? I mean, it's hard to distinguish one heavy from another. But what else would you be doing here?

Let's get out of this crowd for a minute.

Hell yes, Top. There's some questions I've wanted to ask you, man.

Me first, said Eville, but when they found themselves at the rear of the crowd and stopped in a newborn patch of sunlight, Harrington beat him to the draw.

All right, Ev, goddamn it, you tell me something.

Wait a minute.

I want to know who's buried out there in the Mirogoj cemetery.

What?

Right next to the grave for the bastard they're putting in the ground today.

I'm not following this, said Burnette.

The marker says Dorothy Kovacevic. It's right between this new hole for Starevica and a marker that reads Marija Kovacevic. That's Chambers's mother. He excavated her coffin from a churchyard in Pittsburgh and buried her here in 1995, after Operation Storm. Ever heard of that? The final assault? Ethnic cleansing? Have you talked about that with the undersecretary's buddies? The generals inside the cathedral.

Wait a minute, said Ev, flustered. Hold on.

One day these guys are going to end up at The Hague. You know that, don't you?

We'll discuss that in a second. What's this you're saying about Dorothy Kovacevic?

You tell me, Top. When I first came here last August—the fifteenth? sixteenth?—I was told by my minders, oh, too bad, you just missed Kovacevic, he came to bury his daughter in Mirogoj but now he's gone.

What? said Burnette. Wait a minute. Slow down.

So look, come clean with me. Who's in that grave? I'm thinking nobody. I'm thinking someone besides me was poking around and came too close and suddenly there was a necessity for a gravesite. Somebody like Jack Parmentier.

I don't know anything about this, said Burnette.

I hope whatever she was doing for the government was worth the cost of hooking up with a scumbag like Parmentier.

Tom. Look.

And who do you work for these days, man?

I can't talk about that.

Okay, said Tom. Let's talk about Jackie. Let's talk about Renee. Let's talk about Dottie, Dorothy. She's alive, right?

I can't confirm that.

Harrington mentioned discrepancies and Burnette mentioned due
diligence and they stared at one another until Tom shook his head, visibly
saddened.

You're in Croatia with her goddamn father. What do you think we're
talking about here? I'm talking about a human being, a woman, someone
I knew, okay. And I'm talking about Haiti, someone's life. I'm not asking
for the Agency's jewels. I really don't give a flying fuck what the game was.

All right, look, said Burnette. She's not.

Not what?

Alive.

I don't believe you, said Harrington.

Okay, all right. Have it your way.

Eville, we were friends. And Gerard was my friend. How did you get
Gerard to lie to me?

I didn't, Tom. Maybe she did.

You know what I do. You know I'm an investigator. You know I was
brought in on the case.

No, I didn't know that.

How about we dispense with bullshit, Top. Then one day I think I see
the priest, St. Jean, in Miami, Little Haiti, and I'm right, it's him, because it
takes me a while but I finally track him down, and guess what he tells me,
some wild fucking story about voodoo hijinks and Jackie faking her death.

Whatever you say.

Here's what I say, Ev. I want you to do the right thing. I want you to
sign an affidavit attesting to the fact she's alive.

I can't do that.

Top, there's an innocent kid in a prison in Haiti indicted for her murder.
He'll rot away if we don't do anything about it.

I didn't put him there, said Burnette with cold fury. You did.

Tom slumped and bowed his head in remorse and looked up with
plaintive eyes. You're right, he said. I did. What the fuck, Ev. I don't know
what this is all about but help me out here.

Burnette said he had to get back and Tom said he had something to pass
along to the undersecretary and Burnette snapped out of his numb drift

toward wherever this news about Dottie's grave was taking him, remembering his purpose here, the original deflection, was to confront Tom. Tom began to unlock the clasps on his briefcase and Eville asked him to stop and told him why.

What are you talking about? said Harrington, his lips tightening into a smile and when Burnette finished explaining his understanding of the situation, Harrington released an involuntary snort of laughter for which he quickly apologized, calling the notion of entrapping Steven Chambers a judicial fantasy. The tribunal doesn't have the authority to subpoena an American diplomat, said Harrington. Man, I'd love to depose Chambers, the guy was like an enabler, a facilitator, the empire's designated winker. He knows every bloody thing that happened here, he was a witness to the decision-making process responsible for serious violations of international humanitarian law. In other words, war crimes. He can talk with us if he wants, but I don't see that happening, do you? Anyway, Top, Harrington said as he opened the briefcase and removed a manila envelope, will you pass this along to Chambers, Kovacevic, whatever name he uses. I imagine he'll appreciate it.

He attempted to hand the envelope to Burnette, who wouldn't accept it so readily. What's in it? Burnette said.

Something of Jackie's. Here, take it, come on. Look inside if you don't trust me, he said shrewdly while Burnette's suspicious fingers worked to unseal the flap. If you would give that to her father. Or, you know, return it to Jackie if you happen to bump into her.

What Burnette intended as a cursory glance into the envelope's mouth became a hopeless stare at the triple strands of Dottie's Turkish bracelet, its blue-eyed insistence against evil, and he stood riveted and speechless, finally nudging his sunglasses down over his eyes to leave only the quiver of his jaw exposed, his emotions contorted by knife-stabs of gratitude penetrating a sense of powerlessness and defeat, the fresh tearing away of the unexpected chance with Dottie, the entire affair the most provisional, unreliable arrangement but the chance had been there nevertheless, tangible and true and lost, and telling himself he had been wrong to want it hadn't gotten him very far. Here was her bracelet; for him, that was its message.

God, I'm sorry, Ev, but—Tom said, unable to complete the thought. She's really dead, isn't she?

He paused to collect himself in the narthex, cajole and kick himself into the psychic transition away from the sudden great weariness he felt, leaning back against a wall and closing his eyes for a moment, walking down the storm-swept beach hand in hand with Dottie, his hands about their own quick business here in Zagreb, transferring the bracelet to his trouser pocket, holding it as his palm turned sweaty around its glass beads, tossing the envelope into a waste basket. He heard the voice, faraway but amplified, of eulogy. Then the ear voice of Crow saying Burn, where are you? Steve-o on the move. Where's he going? Burnette asked. Where are you? The whatchacallit, the pulpit, said Crow. It's like halftime. Looks like he's going to speak. Roger that, said Burnette. Where are you? and Scarecrow told him he was in the aisle on the right side of the altar and Eville said he was coming.

Vasich's security men fixed him with hard looks as he stepped into the pillared cavern of the nave. He removed his sunglasses while his clearance was double-checked and he noticed the woman from behind the press cordon who had stood with her clipboard between Tom and the cameraman, arguing in hushed tones with one of Vasich's people. He couldn't see the undersecretary but his voice began to echo from within the slanted light at the far end of the nave, and he went over and requisitioned the woman, whispering to the guard, She's with me. Why? she whispered back, recoiling nervously. He asked her if she spoke English and she said yes. Croatian? Yes. She looked at him more closely, with suspicion, and said, Where is Tom? and he told her Tom was outside, Tom was fine, and he asked her to do him a favor. Will you translate for me? Translate what? The man who's speaking. Kovacevic? she said. Please, said Burnette, I want to know what he's saying. Ah, said the woman, I see. Yes, I will help you if you will help me. I'll try, said Burnette. That's all I can promise.

They moved quietly to the right, to the top of the side aisle, slowly making their way toward the front of the hall, the woman whispering in his ear, *He is talking about when he was a child, meeting Starevica when he was a boy, how Starevica was a second father. He says his own father was killed in the world war.* Burnette's eyes wandered over the congregation packed into the rows of pews, his vision floating upward into the cold vastness of sacred space, feeling an uneasy awe. *Now Kovacevic is talking about our war. He says our divine struggle, on heaven's behalf. He is saying some good things about our army and our leaders and about Starevica. Patriotic things.* The thin scent of frankincense began to mix with the pungency of garlic on the woman's breath and the stony breath of the cathedral, itself a source of an unfathomable oppression bearing down on him, an intersection of vanities and ingenuity and aspirations meant, he understood this, to signify mankind's relationship with the cosmos, but the cathedral's power was immodest, its inspiration a wash between faith and fear, more fissure than connection, more arrogance than humility, or so he felt. Halfway down the aisle, she paused, her brow wrinkling as she listened, and he waited for her to proceed and she was whispering again as they tiptoed ahead. *Now he is saying strong things. Kovacevic says history will never forgive us if we stop now. God Almighty will never forgive us.* He had stood on glacial moraines before, staring at ice fields cracking with a deep interior fracturing sound, hearing the stress of the planet, and he had staggered to the top of inhospitable wind-blasted summits only to experience this same sense of human insignificance. *He is making recrimination against the Muslims. We must not allow the Turks to pass through this door, a door of atrocity that has been thrown open by Satan. Like you, Kovacevic says, I want peace in the world and I will fight for it and for Christ.* He had not lived the type of life that offered a familiarity with cathedrals, the soaring majesty that was not barrenness but the abstract made amazingly concrete and the sacred made sarcophagal, a bell jar containing a millennium's worth of anguished spirits. *He is making provocations. He says when the mujos tell us they will drink our blood we will sew their mouths closed with barbed wire.* Burnette thought maybe it was his upbringing, a boy from a ranch in Montana unaccustomed to the monumental grandeur of mankind's achievements, his unworldliness never a liability on any mission but here he felt it as a flaw, a complication to his sense of reverence.

Oh, she gasped, stunned, *my God,* clasping a hand over her mouth in horror. Burnette already felt something tipping out of balance, the increasing volume of troubled noise jumping through the congregation, divided into camps of approval and disapproval, eddies of mortification, spouts of wanton encouragement.

What's he saying?

He is speaking improperly, she said.

What did he say?

It's not proper, she said. His language is bad. He is using a word that for you is fack? Fuck? Kovacevic says the Turks killed his father and chopped his head and killed his aunt and fucked his mother and fucked his daughter and, oh, my God—

There was Scarecrow and Bill and he could see Chambers in the pulpit and he told the woman to wait here and Crow asked, What's happening? and Burnette walked out onto the tiles between the front pews and the altar steps. I'm getting him down, he said, but Vasich seemed to have the same idea, rising from the first pew on the far side of the center aisle and calmly mounting the altar toward the undersecretary's perch, murmuring sympathetically, words Burnette could not hear or understand, the honest sound of respect itself the meaning. A tense hush spread through the cathedral. Chambers fell silent and his face lit up with angelic benevolence as he observed the general's approach, each man beckoning the other to come, and then Vasich was beside him in the pulpit, gently taking Chambers's arm.

Then Steven Chambers was singing most gloriously and Vasich seemed taken aback for a moment but he turned to stand with his hand over his heart and sing, too, joined a few notes later by the choir, and then it seemed everyone in the archbishop's cathedral was singing, Burnette slowly retreating toward the woman, staggered by the transcendent vibrations of so many lungs exhaling such a rumble of harmony, this newborn nation of voices, the spectacular power of humanity's chorus not so much rising up toward the heavens as inducing heaven to lose altitude, shimmer on the roof beams, transforming the cathedral for Burnette into a space he saw and felt for the first time as a place of earthbound beauty.

My God, the woman whispered into his ear, your Kovacevic saved himself. He is singing the anthem. The name is called "Our Beautiful Homeland."

Then the song was finished, Vasich again took the undersecretary's arm and escorted him back to his pew, the priests rose from their thrones at the rear of the chancel, the altar boys rang their bells, and the Mass for the Dead resumed.

At the burial of Davor Starevica in Zagreb's Mirogoj cemetery, the ghosts out and about, Eville Burnette walked at Steven Chambers's side past the Wall of Pain to gather with the crowd at the foot of the open grave, the crush of mourners obscuring the adjacent plots. Since leaving the cathedral Chambers had seemed enervated, his eyes clotted with confusion, then glittering with unspent tears. At the arcaded entryway into Mirogoj, Burnette had summoned whatever courage or stupidity it took to remind Chambers of what the undersecretary had mentioned earlier in the day, something he wanted Ev to see, but the reminder mystified Chambers.

I'm not sure what you're talking about, he said, and Burnette didn't press the matter because he could hardly believe himself Tom Harrington's claim, wondering if he would find Dottie here or not, if he wanted to, or if he could survive not finding her, or survive that moment of discovery if in fact he found her. And hadn't she, after all, made a habit out of dying, forfeiting her credibility as a mortal? She had.

Who died in Landstuhl? He had held her hand.

Who died in Haiti? He had lifted her up.

The president of the republic stepped forward, digging his right hand into the black pyramid of his native soil to pitch its crumbs into the hole, the arm of an attendant poking through the encirclement offering a white handkerchief, which the president used and passed along to Steven Kovacevic to clean the dirt from his own hands. Stepping away, Eville confided into his mic. Two minutes, he whispered, listening to Scarecrow and Bill affirm the transmission.

He went to find her grave and it was right there and it demolished him. There too her grandmother's, people standing on them, the turf muddied by their shoes, and he said to himself, *Are you here?* thinking what use was memory when everything about the journey ahead was unknown, and death bestowed as a homecoming, the end of homelessness, and a family restored to a thing it had lost when it was no longer young, which was togetherness. *Hey,* he said and squatted before the stone and traced her name with trembling fingers and kissed the stone, reading the inscription, The soul is a field in the heart of man.

Hey, I found you, but I have to go.

Scarecrow was talking in his ear, reporting the ceremony's conclusion, asking him how he wanted to handle this and he found Vasich and let him know the change in plans and Vasich said he understood. It's for the best, I think, he said, and went to arrange an escort to the airport and Eville hooked back up with the undersecretary and his detail and there was the woman with her clipboard and her cameraman and Tom hovering in the background. You promised, she said and Eville said I know, but I can't let you ask him about politics, is it a deal?

What can I ask?

Ask about his childhood or something, he said, and stepped around her to speak to Harrington who once again beat him to the draw.

You saw the grave?

Yeah. Thanks.

How did she die?

I thought you were an investigator, Tom. I expect you'll get to the bottom of it.

Help me get that kid out of jail.

I don't know if I can but I'll check it out, he said and looked back over his shoulder at the ITN crew and the undersecretary and told Tom they had to cut the interview short and leave and walked back over to the visibly frustrated woman and said, Okay?

He's not well, she said. He only wants to know when he's going to lunch. He says he's hungry.

BurnOne, he heard Crow say into his earpiece, our boy's walking.

Copy that, said Burnette, his eyes following the undersecretary into the crowd, Chambers headed toward a smoky kiosk out by the entrance selling kebabs. He's not going anywhere, he told Crow, and he slowly followed Dottie's father, who was trying to pay for a skewer of meat with a hundred dollar bill.

Then Chambers seemed possessed, his mouth full of lamb, chewing and talking maniacally about the embassy, the embassy wasn't an intelligence failure, you know, we warned them again and again, he had no information she was going through Nairobi to spend a few days with Mary Beth before the wedding in Zimbabwe, go out to Mombasa, you know, lay on the beach, I suppose, she never told me a fucking thing about that, said Chambers, the tears finally coming. They dug out the two of them side by side in Mary Beth's office, did you know that? She wasn't there a minute before the bombs went off and the blast, the glass, the glass flying into her eyes. Did you know that, Ev? Did you see the reports?

He wanted to return to Mirogoj, he said, to the cemetery, there was something there Ev should see, he wanted them to see it together and say the requiescat and be at peace with all of this and then they were walking to the vehicle, his hand on Chambers's shoulder, opening the door for him, and it struck Eville Burnette as merciless, an existential blow, a man condemned forever to chase the imperiled verities, that this is what we forget about our hearts, that they are with us, that they are there.

ACKNOWLEDGMENTS

First Readers, First Responders:
Barbara Petersen, Bruce Weber, Ed Tarkington, Peter Ives, Mace Fleeger, Susan Moke, Maruta Kalins, Guinotte Wise, John Domini, Keith Jardim, Gail Hochman, Kevin Fedarko, Mark Mustian, Barbara A. Jones

Editorial Savants:
Brando Skyhorse, Josh McCall, Elisabeth Schmitz, Morgan Entrekin

Consultants:
Lieutenant Colonel Tony Schwalm (ret.), U.S. Army Special Forces; Special Agent Robert Dwyer (ret.), Federal Bureau of Investigation; Liesl Schwabe, Istanbul; Devon Pendleton, Arabic; Sarah Todd, Kenya.

Hats Off:
Poet and actor Michael O'Keefe, for the inspiration of *How Peace Begins*; Deb Seager, Catherine Parnell, Jeff Hillard, force multipliers; the Bennington Vortex

From Mr. Shakespeare's pen, this: "There are no more perfect words than these— thanks and thanks and ever thanks."